MW01247037

WHEN FIRST WE

PRACTICE

TO DECEIVE

HEATHER O'BRIEN

WHEN FIRST WE PRACTICE TO DECEIVE

Copyright © 2018 Heather O'Brien

All rights reserved.

This is a work of fiction. All characters, names, incidents, organizations, and dialogue contained in this novel are either the product of the author's imagination or are used fictitiously. Similarities to real persons, living and dead, are unintended.

Eurydice
Poem by Willa Cather (1903)
Public Domain

First edition 2018

Published in the USA by *thewordverve inc.* (**www.thewordverve.com**)

eBook ISBN:	978-1-948225-49-6
Paperback ISBN:	978-1-948225-50-2
Hardback ISBN:	978-1-948225-51-9

Library of Congress Control Number: 2018956602

~~~

WHEN FIRST WE PRACTICE TO DECEIVE

A Book with Verve by *thewordverve inc.*

Cover Design by Artist For Hire
www.artforhire.com

Edited by Megan Harris
www.mharriseditor.com

The Ties That Bind saga

To learn more, visit www.tiesthatbindsaga.com.

ACKNOWLEDGMENTS

I would like to thank family and friends who were with me during the long journey to completing this novel. They know who they are, and if you've read the first two books' acknowledgements, you do too. They're the same cast of characters who have been a consistent source of support and strength.

Continued gratitude to my tireless Beta readers:

Erin Adams, Emily Conner, Cherie Lawrence, Ryan Rayston, and Kim Timperio.

SPECIAL THANK YOU:

My graphics and cover designer, Scott Perry, a true artist who has hung in with me for nearly two decades.

My editor, Megan Harris, who felt almost as bittersweet as I did to realize book three had finally reached an end.

My publisher, Janet Fix, who is a champion for writers and a consistent "voice in my ear" telling me not to stress out – that this is supposed to be fun.

Lastly, thank you to my husband, who makes it possible for me to do what I love most.

When First We Practice to Deceive

A bitter doom they did upon her place:
She might not touch his hand nor see his face
The while he led her up from death and dreams
Into his world of bright Arcadian streams.
For all of him she yearned to touch and see,
Only the sweet ghost of his melody;
For all of him she yearned to have and hold,
Only the wraith of song, sweet, sweet and cold.
With only song to stop her ears by day
And hold above her frozen heart alway,
And strain within her arms and glad her sight,
With only song to feed her lips by night,
To lay within her bosom only song—
Sweetheart! The way from Hell's so long, so long!

Eurydice
by Willa Cather

For Ryan, Charlie, Jama, and Emily

CHAPTER 1

BEN GRANT PEERED OUT AT the dark thunderheads gathered along the southern horizon. The uneasiness that had pilfered his appetite earlier magnified his regret. He regretted their day had so quickly ebbed away. More than anything, he regretted he would soon have to face Cheryl and tell her what he had done.

He cursed under his breath, then called over his shoulder, "Bring 'er about, son. Storm's brewing and it's nearly dusk."

"Aw, Dad," Kyle protested, "just a little longer? I can get us back, I promise. Or even better—we could head back tomorrow! The storm can't be that bad. Hurricane season's months off. Besides, it'd keep us guys out of Mom's hair."

Ben grinned at his youngest. Fourteen years old, smart as a whip, and an impressive negotiator. For a moment, he considered the proposal—mostly because it would buy him some time. Eventually, he resigned himself to his fate. "Another day."

Disappointed, Kyle gathered his various charts and used his prized sextant—more a novelty item than a practical instrument these days—as a paperweight, then made his way to the wheelhouse. "Up anchor!" he commanded his brother in dramatic fashion.

Derek rolled his eyes and mocked "aye aye" as he engaged the windlass.

Kyle started the engine and navigated the Hatteras 74 Cockpit Motor Yacht around 180 degrees until the gauges indicated their proper course.

A steady wind gradually replaced the familiar atmospheric calm before a storm, texturing the Atlantic into little chops as they motored northward at 19 knots.

Derek stood and stretched. "How long ya think before we'll be home?"

"Within the hour, I'd say. We're nearing the cut. We've got ourselves a nice tailwind."

Derek checked his watch and smiled.

"You sure we can't stay just a little while longer, Dad?" Kyle attempted once more.

Derek pointed toward the horizon. "You heard him. We don't wanna get caught in the storm, dufus."

"*You're* the dufus," Kyle shot back. "Besides, you just wanna get home so you can call Summer."

Derek huffed and gave his younger brother a you-don't-know-anything look.

Satisfied with the subtle embarrassment he saw register on his sibling's face, Kyle returned to his navigational duties. He increased their speed just enough to start the boat planing. Derek immediately lost his footing and pitched forward.

"You know he hates that," Ben admonished, grinning despite himself.

"He knows," Derek snapped, righting himself.

With a smirk, Kyle eased back the throttle control, reducing speed.

"I'm going below to clean up," Ben told them. "Try not to throw each other overboard."

Kyle giggled.

Derek checked his watch again, flopped into a seat behind his brother, and folded his arms. "Geek," he spat at his brother's back.

"I'm not a geek."

"Are too."

"Am not."

"You're always burying your head in those stupid maps."

"They're not stupid," Kyle snapped. "And they're not maps. They're 'charts' when you're at sea. You're just jealous 'cause I can navigate and you can't. We could stay out here until midnight with no lights from shore and I could still get us back. What could you do? Call your girlfriend?"

Ben hushed his boys good-naturedly, then headed for the galley.

With their father out of earshot, Derek added, "I'm not jealous of you. *I'm* the one with the car, remember?"

Kyle rolled his eyes. "Big deal. Does Dad know what you and Summer do in that car?"

"Zip it," Derek warned.

"I don't have to do what you say," Kyle told him. "You're not the captain."

Ben tidied up the galley and salon as they made their way back to the Key Biscayne Yacht Club. He cleared paper plates, cups, napkins, and utensils, then sealed their leftovers in storage containers. Guilt besieged him as he thought of the time his wife had spent preparing the sandwiches and potato salad for their boys' day out.

He had rehearsed the speech in his mind a dozen times. Cheryl would understand, he told himself. She would agree. It was the only thing to do.

He cursed again. No matter how many times he envisioned the conversation, he could not escape the inevitable look of betrayal he would see in his wife's eyes. He should have consulted her first.

For months now, the recollection of his only nephew's memorial had tormented him. He and his brothers had congregated on Jordan's sofa after the mourners had all gone home. They nursed their drinks, which politely explained the absence of conversation—at least for that moment. As he had endeavored to process the sadness of the day, it occurred to him he and his siblings had not shared the same space for years. Worse, their distance from one another spanned more than the miles separating them. It had troubled him enough to wage a campaign to rekindle the closeness they had shared as children. And he had failed utterly.

While both Chris and Jordan had eventually moved to Florida, the gulf between them had only widened, eventually shredding their family bonds as they came to death blows for Farin's heart. It had transcended sibling rivalry. It impacted the lives of everyone around them.

And what had Ben done about the situation? He had stood by without judgment—of anyone but Chris. His long-held bias had sabotaged any chance to heal their fractured family. He had convinced himself his place as the first born obligated him to bear certain responsibilities. Be fair. Be strong. Be the one everyone else counts on. Be neutral. But in that neutrality, he had let everyone down.

Ben had never grieved Jordan's death. He had behaved like any good, stiff-upper-lip British expat would by focusing on the matter at hand. He had helped Chris avoid a murder charge, made Jordan's funeral arrangements, comforted their parents, and protected his wife and sons from the media. All sorted, all handled. Now, move on.

Not one person had asked how he felt. Probably for the best, though. Keeping himself busy had its benefits. Still, no one had felt closer to Jordan than he, and he had never felt closer to anyone than he had Jordan. On days like today, sailing out into the bay for a sun-filled retreat with his boys, he missed his youngest brother more than ever.

Once, there had been three brothers to reunite. Now, two remained. Not only was Chase's memorial service the closest they had been in years, it was the closest they would ever be again. Sometimes, Ben found himself longing for that miserable afternoon in Malibu. Given the choice, he would gratefully accept awkward silence over eternal separation.

Since Farin's return, a sorrow he could not shake had unraveled his brave exterior. Guilt choked him over breaking Chris' nose. His brother had carried the weight of a hundred men on him that day. Somewhere along the line, Ben had given up hope Chris would someday find his own integrity. Yet in fairness, Chris had become the man people believed Ben to be. And the worst was yet to come, for never in his life had he kept secrets from his wife.

He cursed again.

"Dad!" Kyle bounded downstairs, bypassing the last four steps with an energetic leap. "Derek said he's gonna throw my stuff overboard."

Ben exhaled through his nose and smiled patiently at his son. "I'll be right up."

"Thanks! Hey, Derek!" he called as he scampered back up to his duty station. "Dad says he's gonna pound you if you don't put those down *right now!*"

The quarrel had subsided by the time Ben returned to the pilothouse. No surprise there. Kyle had resumed his place at the helm. Derek lounged starboard, distracted as he checked and rechecked his cell phone for reception.

"The wind's picking up," Kyle told him. "I'm monitoring the sea state. We'll make land in plenty of time."

Ben eased over and stood behind his youngest. He patted his back as he took in the Miami skyline not too far in the distance. "Good job, son. You'll make a fine sailor someday."

Kyle beamed and squared his shoulders.

Sometimes, Ben regarded his boys with the wonderment and disbelief of a fledgling. Handsome, strong, and as different from one another as a waltz and a conga, they had grown up fast—too fast. In a few short years, they would each have lives of their own.

Derek had already formed a band with some boys from school. This worried Ben, though he acknowledged the hypocrisy of such an admission. Every year, the music business grew more complicated and dangerous, but Derek's devotion to and admiration of his Uncle Chris had all but guaranteed the pursuit. Ben and Cheryl had long predicted Derek would eventually seek to emulate Chris' life path.

Considering their inexperience, the band was good. Good enough he had agreed to write some material for them as soon as they seasoned up a bit. Once they played Miami's local club circuit and started paying their dues on the road, Chris would likely pitch them to Minor 6th Records.

"*Yes!*" Derek exclaimed. He punched the keypad on his cell phone, then held it to his ear. A moment later, he said, "Hi, Mrs. Reece. Is Summer there?"

Ben assessed the contused clouds undulating northward as if racing them to shore. To the west, the sun waned like a fair-weather friend, casting orange and pink hues against the horizon.

Kyle shook his head as Derek's voice fell to a whisper. "They're disgusting."

Ben chuckled. "You won't feel that way much longer."

"*Ew!* No way! Girls are a pain."

"Not all girls. What about your mum?"

"Mom's cool," Kyle conceded.

"And Summer's a nice girl."

"I guess. But if she's so nice, what's she doing with Derek?"

From his seat, Derek called, "I heard that, you geek!"

In many ways, the boys reminded him of the relationship he had had with Chris. They had always fought as children, though they loved each other deeply. Derek favored Chris with his unbridled spirit, where Kyle possessed a more thoughtful, less boisterous temperament. But for all their differences and squabbles, both boys demonstrated an unflinching family loyalty.

"Hold on, babe. I got a call on the other line. Don't hang up." Derek eyed his father and brother in turn, as if embarrassed they had heard his end of the conversation. He stood and headed downstairs. "Hey, Peter, what's up? I've got Summer on the other line."

Ben smirked as his youngest son rolled his eyes.

Kyle had proven himself the more levelheaded, kinder sibling. Cheryl often described him as an old soul, an observation with which Ben agreed. Unlike his brother, Kyle made good marks in school. His passion lay in a more technical direction centered on science rather than entertainment. The first Grant child in generations not bitten by the music bug, Ben often joked Kyle was the only normal member of their family. He preferred studying marine biology, computer science, and astronomy at the MAST Academy and maintained a GPA of 3.9.

Though still three years from graduating, he had already chosen a college. Cheryl had made it clear she would require every bit of that time to acclimate herself to the idea of her baby studying at the world renowned Hawai'i Institute of Marine Biology, over 4850 miles west of Florida. She knew. She had calculated the distance. Every so often, she would remind him that continuing on to the Rosenstiel School of Marine and Atmospheric Science, where he had already applied for an internship as part of his school's requirements, made infinite more sense. It had a wider area of study and better suited his interests. She did not need to add it also suited hers. It was four miles from their house.

Kyle's soft chuckle drew Ben's attention. "What's so funny?"

He turned around, his green eyes sparkling with mischief as he pointed out their coordinates. "Remember?"

Ben dipped his head at the bittersweet memory. "Yeah."

"Chase was so funny that day! You should have seen the look on your face, Dad! You jumped in after him without even taking your shoes off!"

Ben stared into the gray sea as the memory washed over him. Chase's last visit to Florida. Perhaps if he had been firmer with Jordan's only son over the incident, Chase would be alive today. Just another of his many mistakes.

"Sorry," Kyle said, his expression remorseful.

Ben gave him a reassuring pat on the back. "Don't be. You're right. He was quite the water bug, wasn't he?"

"You know he's okay, right? He's with Grandpa. Grandpa's taking care of him."

Ben nodded. "Grandpa's probably taking care of both Chase and Uncle Jordan."

Kyle stared off into the middle distance and considered his father's words, then shook his head. "No, not Uncle Jordan."

"What do you mean?"

"Uncle Jordan's coming back. You know that."

The statement caught him off guard. "You don't believe that, do you?"

"Well, sure...don't you?"

"Son, Uncle Jordan's dead. You know that."

"No he's not."

"You're so stupid," Derek spat as he joined them, his conversation concluded. "Uncle Jordan's dead, Kyle. We went to the funeral, remember? Don't upset Dad by talking bull—"

"Watch your mouth," Ben warned, pointing at his eldest. "Don't speak to your brother that way."

Kyle stood his ground, impervious to the ridicule. "We went to Aunt Farin's funeral, too."

The boys bickered the rest of the way back. For the most part, Ben remained quiet. Try as he might, he could not get out of his head.

Kyle was right. They had gone to Farin's funeral. Exactly how to make Kyle understand Jordan would not also return eluded him. The situations were different, though undoubtedly connected.

They arrived at the marina as the first fat raindrops began to fall. Ben took the wheel and maneuvered the motor yacht into its slip. Derek jumped onto the dock and secured the forward and stern lines while Kyle did the same on deck, using extra line as a precaution against the incoming storm.

In the parking lot, Ben loaded their cooler and beach towels into his SUV.

"I'm outta here," Derek told him. "I've got practice."

"No dinner?"

He shook his head. "Summer's bringin' some stuff over to the studio."

"Don't be home too late, then. Mum'll worry."

Derek headed for his Blazer, hesitated, then doubled back. "Hey," he called to his brother.

"What?" Kyle asked, opening the passenger's door.

"C'mere a sec."

Kyle eyed him suspiciously but complied. They walked a few yards away, out of their father's earshot, as the rain slowly intensified.

Derek looked at his brother. "Don't sweat it, okay?"

Kyle plunged his hands into the pockets of his cargo shorts and dipped his head.

"What's wrong?"

"I think I hurt Dad's feelings."

Derek exhaled and laid a hand on his brother's shoulder. "Don't sweat it. Wouldn't you miss me if I were gone?"

Kyle squinted up at him. "Yeah."

"Well, it's the same for Dad. He misses Uncle Jordan."

"Exactly. I shouldn't have brought it up."

"Like I said...don't sweat it." Derek tousled Kyle's damp blond hair and turned to leave.

Kyle caught his arm and spun him around. "He's really not coming back, is he?"

Derek shook his head.

"Then how did Aunt Farin come back?"

"She wasn't really dead. It was a lie."

"Why would someone lie about someone being dead?"

Derek shrugged. "Dunno. But hey—I gotta bounce. You okay?"

Kyle nodded, then headed back to the Land Rover.

"Hey," Derek called once more.

He turned around.

"Wanna go to the movies tomorrow with me and Summer?"

His face brightened. "Sure!"

The short drive back to the house found Ben and Kyle each absorbed in private thoughts. Ben dreaded the pitch—and the apology—he would soon give his wife.

Cheryl met them at the garage door, all smiles as she welcomed them home. She kissed Kyle first, then Ben. "Looks like you came back just in time to avoid a downpour. How was your day?"

"Brilliant," Ben replied, projecting enthusiasm he did not feel. "And lunch was perfect."

Cheryl regarded her youngest. "How about you, Captain Cousteau? You didn't fill up on chips and soda, did you?"

"I had an apple with lunch," Kyle assured her. "Derek's the one who filled up on junk."

Cheryl giggled at Kyle's unsubtle habit of propping himself up at his sibling's expense. "Oh really? And where is he?"

"Practice," Kyle told her.

"I see," she said. They headed inside. "Well, supper's ready, so why don't you both go and wash up?"

Kyle sprinted off for the stairs.

Cheryl's tone softened as she searched her husband's troubled features. "You look like you're a million miles away."

Ben took her into his arms. "I smell."

"I think I can take it." They embraced a moment, then she backed away, scrunching her nose and fanning her face with a graceful hand. "Okay, maybe not. You're boggin for sure."

"Come upstairs with me while I wash?"

"Ooh." She grinned and flashed her left eyebrow. "Sounds promising. I'd love to."

Her smile scythed through his heart. Once he told her what he had to say, she would feel anything but romantic.

They climbed the stairs, hand in hand. As they reached the second floor, a thunderclap exploded outside.

"Sounds like we're in for quite a storm," she remarked.

He pursed his lips. "We sure are."

***

It felt as if Ross had just presented the Rebellion with plans to destroy the Death Star.

The more Samantha Drake listened to his proposal, the more conflicted she felt. She seesawed between utter dread and morbid fascination. The man was a genius. Everything he said made absolute sense. Still, the plan presented risk—for everyone involved.

"It'll take a few months to organize," he said, his voice devoid of emotion.

Persistent background racket made it nearly impossible to hear him. Twice she had him repeat himself. The annoyance underscoring his tone when he restated his words did not escape her notice.

"You think we can pull it off?" she asked, stunned as the details unfolded.

"What do we have to lose?"

On one hand, the change in her friend and former colleague saddened her. The weariness of a dissipated spirit saturated his speech. His long association with LSI—more specifically, its owner—had beaten him down.

On the other hand, the idea justice might finally find Jameson Lockhardt was intoxicating.

The Ross Alexander she knew would have never suggested something so devious, so underhanded, and so deceptively clever. But as he outlined his strategy, it became clear he had synthesized the pain and grief over his wife's death into a determination that would impress even the old man himself.

His voice strained with impatience. "You still with me, Sam?"

"Yes." She shifted in her office chair and realized she had not moved in nearly thirty minutes. Her leg had fallen asleep.

"Did you get my fax?"

She picked up and scanned the document her assistant had placed on her desk. "I recognize almost everyone on the list. It's amazing. I had no idea so many people still—"

A loud crash assaulted her left ear as the raucous on Ross' end escalated. She heard a muffled plea for quiet as he covered the transmitting end of the telephone's handset.

"Sorry," he said upon his return. "Yes, you're right. You'd think they'd have all bailed out a long time ago."

"Ross, where *are* you?"

"Doesn't matter. It's best you don't know. I want you to be safe."

"So you still think he's tapping your line?"

He huffed. "I think he's capable of anything. In fact, I know he is."

"Should I be concerned?" Her eyes darted around her office.

"He doesn't suspect you. You'd know if he did."

She shifted again, this time uneasily. Ross spoke the truth. If Jameson suspected her of anything, she would know. Proof of this had played itself out last week. The thought made her tremble. She forced her attention back to the document in her hand. "'Jade Larken Trongly?' That's a mouthful. Who's she?"

The noise on Ross' end of the telephone abruptly subsided. He had to have heard her, but said nothing.

"Do I know her?" she pressed. "Is she new with LSI?"

"I'll handle Jade myself when the time's right."

She wrinkled her forehead, her lips scrunched sideways. "Okay. Well, it looks like we have ourselves a plan. What do you want me to do? How can I help?"

"I need you to contact everyone on that list. Everyone but Jade, that is. I can't do it myself."

"You said it would take a while to organize. Should I start now?"

A brief silence filled the line. "Wait until I give you the go-ahead."

"No problem. So...what about you? You holding up okay? Anything you need?"

His voice thickened with undiluted loathing. "You mean anything besides revenge?"

"I guess so," she whispered softly.

"How's Farin?"

"Physically? Much better, or so Ethan tells me."

"Have you spoken to her yet?"

"I'm visiting her tomorrow. I think she's ready."

"Think she'll agree?"

She closed her eyes and shook her head. "I don't know. She has every reason to."

"Don't mention anything we've discussed today. I need time to get it all in place."

"I won't say a word."

"Did you get the package I sent for her?"

"Yes. I'll give it to her when I see her."

He exhaled heavily into the receiver, a mournful sound she could scarcely describe. She wished she could say something—anything—that might matter more than the fact that, when he returned home tonight from wherever it was he had called her, Josephine would not be there.

"When are you going back to work?"

"May first. I'd planned on another month or so, but what's the point?"

"I don't know how you'll face him. He must realize you know the truth."

Ross did not reply.

"I'm sorry. I don't know what to say."

"It's just a race against time at this point."

Lockhardt's ability to ruin lives did not shock her, but she had never considered his manipulations might someday lead to the dangerous situation in which they now found themselves. "Okay, well, let me know when you want me to start making calls."

"It shouldn't be long now."

"Let's hope not. After what happened in Malibu last week, Ethan nearly walked out on me."

"Thank God no one was hurt."

"They hadn't left five minutes before the house exploded."

"I'm sorry, Sam. The last thing I want is to cause you two problems."

"We're okay. He's just worried about me—and Farin. He told Marci to go home and not come to the new place at all. He doesn't want to take any more chances than necessary."

"He's right. It's no place for a pregnant woman. Hopefully Farin'll relocate soon. You have to convince her."

"I'll do my best."

"I'm heading home now. I'll check back soon."

As she replaced the handset, she dropped her head onto her hands and filled her lungs to capacity. Things had gotten out of hand. No matter what they did, Jameson seemed only a step or two behind them—even on their best days.

Now, they had hope. Ross' plan would work. It had to. The tables had finally turned.

***

Miles Macy rehearsed his pitch all morning before calling Alicia Alvarez in Miami. Since his return from Florida back in January, he had left countless messages for the sultry homicide detective—all of them unreturned. As much as he appreciated the ability to hear her hard-edged Cuban accent any time he wanted and consider himself in a semiserious relationship with her answering machine, it seemed she did not spend much time at home or her office. Either that, or she had intentionally avoided him.

Nah.

Maybe she had started seeing someone else. Or maybe she had been involved before they hooked up. She did not strike him as the cheating type, but perhaps she had stepped out on someone and now felt guilty. He hoped not.

His desk phone rang before he summoned the courage to make his call. Noting the internal extension, he rolled his eyes and grinned.

Frank Harper barked into the line without greeting. "I'm missing next week's column. It was due on my desk yesterday!"

Miles leaned back in his chair and propped his feet up on his desk. "I ran it downstairs myself Friday morning. Saved you a trip."

Frank's tone intensified. "You know I have to approve everything you put out, so cut the shit and bring it to me."

"C'mon, Frank. Lighten up. What's the big deal? It's just a piece on that explosion over in Southern California. "

Harper's voice rose to the point Miles imagined the walls of his office shaking despite the fact his managing editor worked two floors above him. He fought the urge to laugh out loud.

It probably should have offended a seasoned reporter such as himself that, after two and a half years of dedicated service, his boss had decided to babysit him. Under normal circumstances, it would have. It sure did offend his assistant, who now spent most of her downtime scouting prospective employment opportunities "just in case." However, Miles took it in stride.

In his tenure with the *Trib*, he had won more awards than he could name—a nationally syndicated journalist with a stellar reputation and an impressive readership base. But as of last week, everything he wrote, every column he created, required Frank Harper's personal approval. He had considered asking why, but he knew the answer.

"What's the matter, Frank? Afraid I'm gonna tick someone off?"

"I'm warning you, Macy. If you don't wise up—and soon—there's gonna be trouble. You're supposed to report on entertainment news, not on the dangers of faulty wiring!"

"Jordan Grant *was* entertainment until his as of yet unsolved murder. Then last week, his house gets blown to bits? How dead does this guy need to be?"

"You got one thing right, Macy. Jordan Grant *is* dead. *Dead*! Dead singers' homes don't sell papers, Macy! Just like dead singers' ghosts don't contact you through computer screens!"

Miles beamed and nodded proudly as he reclined in his chair and crossed his legs. "Ya liked that one, didn't ya?"

"Why the hell aren't you covering the O.J. Simpson trial like every other journalist in America?"

"You've got three other divisions covering that story, including sports! The last thing our readers need is another op-ed on The Juice."

"Then find something else—quick. I need a rewrite and I need it *this afternoon!* Now get downstairs and kill that article!" Frank slammed down the telephone.

"Always a pleasure." Miles chuckled. He sat forward and stabbed the button for his second line, then punched in Alicia's number. To his astonishment, she answered on the first ring.

"Homicide, Alvarez."

"Well, well, well. If it isn't Detective Alvarez," he charmed, defying his concern she might sever the connection once she recognized his voice. "How are you? I was beginning to wonder whether or not you were still alive."

An exaggerated sigh filled the line. "What do you want, Macy?"

"Oh, I don't know. Maybe a returned call once in a while. Is this the way you treat all your boyfriends?"

She whisper-shouted into the line, "You are not my boyfriend! Did it ever occur to you I didn't call you back because I didn't wanna talk to you? Give it up, cowboy. Find yourself some Windy City woman and forget about me."

"I see." He chuckled. "It's a distance thing, then?"

"I'm hanging up this phone now. So don't call back, understand? If you call me again, I'll slap a restraining order on your a—"

"Now, c'mon." He dropped the playful banter and deflated in his chair. "What did I do to deserve that?"

She sighed once more. "I'm flattered, okay? Is that what you wanna hear? Okay, I'm flattered. But it was one night...*one night.* I can't have you stalking my house and office just because we got drunk and lost our heads."

"I wanted to see you more than just 'one night.' I've tried to reach you for months. Ask your machine. Your machine loves me!"

"Great! Why don't I just hang up and let you continue talking to it?"

"Don't be that way. It'll understand. Now, why don't you want to see me again?"

"You want a reason?" she challenged.

"Don't I deserve one?"

Her Cuban accent grew clipped with frustration. "Okay, let's see. Where should I start? How about the fact we don't know each other?"

"That didn't seem to matter when you took me home with you. Besides, we could get to know each other."

"I don't have time to get to know each other. I work all the time. That's reason two."

Miles chewed on the inside of his cheek, wondering how much time she had spent practicing her excuses. "You're still human, Alicia. Why do you have to make this so hard?"

"And here's a third reason. Where do you live?"

"You know I'm in Chicago."

"And where do I live?"

"Want the street address?"

"Hanging up now!"

"All right, all right. I'll downplay the sarcasm." He found himself unable to counter her logic. "So it is a distance thing."

"Partly, yes."

Miles carefully considered his next words. He could not blame her. Few long distance relationships succeeded. Still, something spurred him to pursue the fiery Cuban detective. After thirty-one years of bachelorhood, maybe the time had come to consider a long-range plan. Before he realized the impact of his next words, he heard himself say, "What if I lived in Miami?"

The line fell silent. He wondered if she had made good on her threat to hang up.

"You're crazy." But the subtle change in her voice betrayed her. She sounded softer, almost feminine.

"I could see about getting my old job back at the *Herald*." He heard her sigh into the line for the third time, but she broached no objection. Maybe that was a good sign. "Look. Anything it takes, okay?"

"I'm busy right now. I can't talk."

"Think about it. I'll call you back later. And Detective...I *will* call back. If you don't answer, I'll call again. You can't hide forever."

"Don't flatter yourself, Macy. I'm not running from you. I don't think about you at all."

He smiled at the obviously lie. "Well, then, let's change the subject. Anything new on the Grant case?"

"Hang on a sec." Hold music filled the line. Moments later, she picked up again. "I switched phones. Billy and I're still flyin' solo on this."

"Did you get the results back from his trip to Michigan?"

"Yep. Definitely an incendiary device. Simple and sophisticated."

"Can you prove it?"

"Billy thinks so, but we need more than what we have if we're gonna go to the captain."

"What about Stark's phone records?"

"All that proves is Stark called Lockhardt a few days before he died."

"And faxed him. Doesn't that tie him to the case?"

"Not necessarily. So what if Stark called Lockhardt? That doesn't make Lockhardt a murderer. It could prove the opposite—portray the man as a concerned party who lost his meal ticket."

Miles exhaled in frustration.

"We need motive, means, method. You know the drill. We need proof Lockhardt was responsible for the car bomb that killed Farin Grant—*if* he was. Until then, we can't move forward. So basically, we got nothing."

"Did you hear the most recent news?"

"What?"

"Five days ago, Jordan Grant's Malibu beach house exploded."

"And?"

"And I don't believe for one minute it's just a coincidence."

"Anybody injured?"

"An old man walking along the beach got hurt. His dog died. But no one was inside the house."

"You're getting paranoid, Macy."

"It fits together. I know it does."

"California's out of our jurisdiction, cowboy."

"I'll get you more evidence somehow."

"The circumstantial stuff we have won't cut it."

Miles rocked in his chair, rubbing his chin with his free hand. The bizarre events raced through his mind like blurry headlines. Three years ago: "Singer Silenced at Record Label's Residence." Days later: "Farin Grant Felled by Flames." Two years ago, mere days after Miles discussed the Grant cases with Stark: "Homicide Detective Eats Bullet." And then last week: "Malibu Mansion Mysteriously Explodes."

Two guns, two bombs. Coincidence? No way.

Someone or another had explained away each circumstance. Jordan? Botched burglary. Farin? Accident. Stark? Flubbed drug deal. The beach house? Faulty wiring.

"You done harassing me?" Alvarez asked, breaking into his thoughts.

"For now. Thanks for the update. And I meant what I said, Alicia. I'm not giving up. Not on this case and not on you. So if I need to move to Miami to make a believer out of you, it's already done."

She ignored the personal references but softened again as they said goodbye. "And hey."

"Yeah?"

"Don't think we're just letting it go. We're still looking. Something's obviously going on. We just need to figure out what it is."

"Lockhardt's involved. I know it."

"Well, unless we get proof..."

Proof. Miles could not for the life of him imagine how they would get proof. Whatever Lockhardt's reasons, he had tied up loose ends like a master knotter. They were about as likely to get proof as they were to find a witness.

CHAPTER 2

CHRIS GRANT MET SAMANTHA IN the parking lot just before noon. He had visited only briefly once before five days ago—the evening his brother's former home had burst into flames. He had pressured Ethan into giving him the address after word reached him of the startling events in Malibu. Upon his arrival, Farin had refused to see him.

"You ready?" Sam asked, smoothing down her skirt and squaring her shoulders with a confidence Chris doubted she felt.

He nodded once. "Let's do it."

Uneasy certainty existed between them as they followed the meandering cement pathway through the complex. No accident had caused that explosion. It was a warning. Had it occurred any earlier, it would have killed Farin, Ethan, Marci, and perhaps him as well.

"It feels creepy being here." Samantha suspiciously eyeballed the apartment grounds.

He scratched his neck at the base of his wig. "At least you don't have to wear a disguise. I look ridiculous."

"You're alive. Hopefully this'll all be over soon."

"If she'd tell us what she knows, we could get that bastard. We'd be safe."

"She's stronger now. Maybe she's ready."

Chris shrugged, omitting the details of his last conversation with Farin. Yes, she was ready—for something. What, she would not tell him.

Her guilty confession taunted him as they approached the door. Years too late, she had uttered the three words he had longed to hear. His forced rejection had hurt her nearly as much as it hurt him. But how could she think he would respond differently? Julie deserved better than for him to run away with another woman.

The duplicitousness of the situation mocked him. When had he ever given a moment's consideration for her marriage, or his own? Back then, nothing had mattered. Only her. Only a life together. But it had not happened. Now, it never would.

He willed the confusion from his mind and focused on his vow to avenge his brother's murder. Farin had to help him. They owed it to Jordan, and the stakes had risen significantly in the last week.

"You think she's holding out because of you," Samantha guessed as they reached the door.

"She says no. She says she needs to work some things out. I don't know."

She rang the doorbell and inhaled a deep breath.

Ethan answered with a nervous smile. He shook Chris' hand, waved them inside, then kissed Samantha. "And how's my favorite fiancé today?"

She wore her business smile like a shield. "So far, so good. How about you?"

"I'll be better as soon as this whole thing's over."

"Is she expecting us?"

He nodded. "She asked what you wanted to talk about. I didn't say anything."

"How's she doing?" Chris asked.

"Still building her strength, but that's to be expected. She's put on a brave face, but I think last week really shook her up. The mood swings are less extreme than they were, though. Hopefully she'll listen to what you have to say."

Chris nodded and pulled off his disguise. Before he had left Malibu last week, he pleaded for help putting an end to the mystery keeping everyone's lives at risk. She had refused. Given recent events, maybe today's discussion would end more productively.

Samantha went to the kitchen to procure drinks. Ethan excused himself to get Farin. Chris shook out his brown mane and sat down on the small couch occupying the small living room. His leg bounced absently as he stole glances at the hallway.

Samantha rummaged through the freezer for some ice. "How's practice?"

"Coming along."

"You excited? Nervous?"

"Both, I suppose. It'll be strange."

"You'll be great."

"Don't get me wrong. My back-up band's top-notch, but without Faith there to get everyone in trouble, I don't know what I'll do with my free time."

She laughed as she placed four iced teas atop the coasters on the coffee table. "That's one part I won't miss. I bailed that girl out of jail so many times."

"Never a dull moment with that one."

"You weren't much better," she teased. "I seem to remember Ross having to respond to a handful of paternity suits."

"But none of them were mine. Remember that." The sound of his own words beset him as he fought to banish another unpleasant memory. *None of them were mine.*

She lifted her glass. "To survival."

Chris nodded, touched her glass with his own, then took a sip.

"Any decision on whether you're gonna include that McCartney cover in the set list?"

"I don't know."

She tilted her head and frowned thoughtfully. "Too close to home?"

He shrugged. "It's complicated."

"I understand. But I have to say I was impressed when I heard it on your tapes. It was a good call to omit it from the album, but it'd be a great add for the tour. I'd wager you know the song's history? It's fitting. Paul was going through some similar stuff. Think about it."

Silence settled upon the room as Farin and Ethan entered.

She appeared strangely taller than usual, jaw clamped, chin raised in defiance, shoulders back, arms forced to her sides instead of crossed. It did not fool Chris in the slightest. The events of last week had rattled her. They had rattled them all. Yet there she stood, just daring anyone to try and comfort her.

Ethan looked at Samantha and gave her a doubtful shrug, then sat down on the recliner and crossed his legs. Samantha glanced at Farin, who fixed her eyes mercilessly on Chris. He cleared his throat and dropped his chin.

"How are you feeling?" Sam asked at last.

"Fine."

She patted the couch. "Have a seat."

Farin flopped down and folded her arms. "Ethan said you wanted to talk."

Chris bit the inside of his cheek, tense at the vibe of the room. He had tried to get out of accompanying Sam today, arguing his presence might upset Farin. From all indications, it did.

Samantha soldiered on. "Obviously, things are a little uneasy right now. Perhaps we should discuss what's going on."

Farin set her jaw and stared at Chris. "I said I'm fine."

"Okay, then. I'll say it. We're concerned about you, Farin. You're doing terrific physically, but mentally...*emotionally*. It's no surprise to any of us, what with everything you've gone through. We'd like to help."

Farin shifted to tuck her leg beneath her and looked challengingly at Samantha. "Is that so?"

"Yes."

She shot Chris a hurtful glance. "Well, like I told Chris last week, it's not necessary. You remember me as this sensitive, fragile...*thing*. But that's not me. Not anymore. So I'll say it again: I'm fine."

Samantha stretched her thin, pursed lips into a patient smile. "Fantastic. In that case, let's discuss your plans."

"My plans?"

"What happened last week was no accident."

"You're right. It was another attempt to kill me. Let's call it what it is."

"Agreed. Let's say what needs to be said." She stood and smoothed her skirt, immediately kicking into executive mode. Farin was an adult. They all were. No need to tap-dance around things. "Jameson knows or suspects you're still alive. He obviously knows Chris had something to do with your escape from...from..." With a squint of her eyes, she raised an empty palm and looked at Chris. "What was the name of that place?"

He cleared his throat. "D-Dorothea Dix."

"Dorothea Dix," Samantha echoed with a snap of her fingers. "That's it. Thank you."

He nodded.

She paced the small area like she would the Minor 6th board room. "My understanding is you've chosen not to discuss the details of your...seclusion...with anyone. I can accept that. I don't agree with it, but I won't attempt to pry the story out of you. Suffice to say, you know something that scares the hell out of the old man. He'd have never turned on you otherwise. But now, everyone involved with you has put themselves in harm's way. If you hadn't left when you did last week, I'd be a widow before I had the chance to be a bride."

Farin scooted forward and reached for her iced tea. Chris noticed her hand shaking when she took a sip.

Samantha continued. "Ethan's spent a lot of time making sure you're okay. And now you are. It's done. So I guess what everyone wants to know is, what's next?"

The phone rang. Ethan excused himself and disappeared into the kitchen. He returned carrying the phone base, pulling on the long cord until he could set the bulky apparatus in the middle of the coffee table.

Farin shuddered almost imperceptibly, then massaged her left wrist with her right hand.

Ethan depressed the speakerphone button, then sat back down. "You there?"

"Sure am," came the voice from the other end. "Hey, everyone."

Chris leaned forward and spoke into the machine. "How are you feeling?"

"Great, thanks. Farin? You there?"

"Hey, Marce. No one told me you'd be in on this little intervention."

"Oh, stop. Just hear Sam out."

"Hello, Marci," Samantha greeted.

"Hi, Sam. Sorry I'm late."

"It's okay. I was just asking Farin about her plans."

"Oh, good. This I've gotta hear."

Farin's eyes narrowed at the phone. "What's that supposed to mean?"

"I was joking. Lighten up."

She crossed her arms and flounced back into the sofa.

Despite herself, Samantha hesitated before asking her next question. "Have you thought any more about resuming your career? You'd said no before. Perhaps you've reconsidered?"

Farin rolled her eyes and groaned. "So that's what this is about."

"I was just—"

"You were gonna ask me to sign with Minor 6th."

Unable to spin it any better, Samantha nodded.

Farin wished she could dismiss the idea outright. Truth told, she felt its ungentle tug at the edge of each memory she had recovered. It haunted her like a dirge. Music was everything by which she had defined herself. Had she fantasized about a glorious comeback to her successful career? Of course she had. But she could not separate the threads of her lifelong dreams from the realities she had endured.

Those realities bound the warp and weft of her career, indeed her life, like a blunt needle, binding every person and every experience into an enormous tapestry. They fashioned images of her parents, Jordan, Jameson, Melody, her baby—even Chris—meticulously in place. Attempts to unravel their various strings had proven a fruitless task.

"You okay?" Chris asked softly.

She peered at him, then looked down to find he had placed a comforting hand on her forearm. Moving it away, she regarded Samantha. "No."

A dramatic sigh came from the speakerphone. "Farin, pick up."

"You're not gonna change my mind, Marce."

"Pick up *now*."

She eyeballed the group, decidedly less sullen as she picked up the handset. Samantha and Ethan rose and disappeared down the hallway.

Chris stayed. He lifted his bowed head and held her eyes. Where she had minutes ago stared unmercifully in his direction, she now leaned into the receiver and lowered her chin in a futile attempt to establish some privacy.

"Don't do this," Marci admonished. "It's a great opportunity for you."

Farin fused her eyes shut. "I don't think I can."

"It'll be different this time."

"Not different enough."

"Is it because Chris is with Minor?"

She stole an awkward glance his way. "He has nothing to do with it." She shielded the side of her face with her free hand and turned her back to him, grateful he pretended not to hear.

"No one on this planet knows you—or *loves* you—better than me."

"I know." She damned the hint of moisture welling in her eyes.

"Good. Now hear me when I tell you this: music's all there is for you. Think about it. What do you wanna do? Wait tables? Dig ditches? Work in an office? You skipped almost every day of typing class. Never learned a trade. And you've never held a regular job in your life. What other options *are* there?"

Farin pondered the dismal truth in Marci's words. She had barely graduated high school and never considered college. Instead, she had driven herself along a singular path, in a singular pursuit.

"You have no money," Marci added. "After your...death or whatever, Ben and I asked Ross to and handle your will. You'd left everything to Jordan, and he'd left everything to you. With you both gone, well—"

"So I really am broke."

"Flat broke. Ben took the Key Biscayne home. Chris kept the beach house. But that's all there is—was. Everything else we told Ross to donate to charity. I kept your family Bible, your pictures, and some of your papers, but that's all, Farin. All you've got is what's in that file box in your room. So now you have to decide how you're gonna play out the rest of your life."

The facts riddled Farin like bullets. She had no backup plan. She might as well have been erased.

Someday, old man. Someday very soon. If it's the last thing I do, I'll bring you down.

Farin called Samantha and Ethan back into the living room, hit the speakerphone button, and replaced the handset on its base. When she attempted to speak, words failed her.

"Are you okay?" Samantha asked.

Marci's voice echoed into the room. "She's fine. Where does she sign?"

Samantha turned to Chris, who appeared far less enthusiastic than she thought he should given the news.

Farin lifted her hands, then let them drop to her sides. "How am I supposed to record? I don't want anyone knowing I'm back yet. Seriously, Sam. Not until I say. That's my first condition. If we can't agree on that, the deal's off."

She grabbed her briefcase, balanced it on her lap, and shuffled through paperwork. "Agreed. In fact, I've already thought of that."

Chris' cell phone rang. He excused himself and wandered down the hallway to talk.

Farin watched him leave, all too sure of the caller's identity. "So you have people you can trust? In the studio, I mean."

Samantha smiled. "Even better. I have someone *you* trust."

Farin's forehead creased as Chris slipped back into the room and took his seat. "What do you mean?"

"Taking everything into consideration, it'd be best if you record in Florida, with Ben."

Farin stared at Sam, slack-jawed.

"That way you can record in privacy and at your own pace. We've already discussed it. He loved the idea. In fact, he offered to write the material."

Time and space seemed to fold in on themselves. Key Biscayne. Ben's house walking distance from her and Jordan's home on Matheson. Chris' place a few blocks further down on Harbor Drive. Who could have possibly come up with such a plan?

Then, it dawned on her. *Of course.*

Chris would not rest until she left. His marriage would suffer if she stayed. It was not Samantha's fault. Chris wanted her to go. He had meant what he said. He could never go back.

She glared at him as she gathered her thoughts. He sat to her left, shoulders slumped, head down, and utterly deflated. "This is your doing."

His head shot up. "What? No! Farin, this has *nothing* to do with me."

Marci piped in. "Chris wasn't part of the planning committee here, Farin."

A doubtful bark of laughter escaped her lips.

He met and held her eyes. "Farin, I—"

"—*save it.*" She jutted her chin at Samantha as she swiped her fingers beneath her eyes and cleared her throat. "So when do we do this thing? Is the private jet all gassed up, too?"

"I was waiting until I got your approval before putting anything into action. I need to draw up the paperwork, have you sign, et cetera. You know the drill. I'm thinking you can leave in a few days." She extracted a bulky manila envelope from her briefcase and handed it to her. "Here. This is from Ross."

Farin stood, snatched the package, and tucked it under her arm. "Oh, yes. Ross. When does he plan on seeing me?"

Samantha frowned. "Sorry?"

"If you want me to sign with Minor 6th, and if you both—" She eyed Chris, then turned back to Samantha. "—want me to move back to Florida, I have a couple of other conditions."

"Of course. You have my word. Nothing gets released without your approval. Your timeframe. No problem."

"That's fine, but that's not all I want."

Samantha regarded her with a blank expression.

"I want to see Ross Alexander—in person. No negotiation. You set it up. Not one note gets recorded before I see him."

"O-okay. I'll talk to him about it before you leave."

"Good. And I need a car. I need to take care of some personal business before I go."

The room fell silent.

Farin looked at each of them in turn. "What? Is my license expired? How long have I been dead?"

"If you need to go somewhere, one of us should accompany you," Ethan explained. "You've only been back on your feet a short time. The first six months are important as you build your systems back up. Can this wait?"

"No, Dr. Maxwell, it can't. Jameson wants me dead. Samantha wants me in Miami. And apparently, I'm a pauper now with no means with which to travel the country once you do decide I'm healthy enough. So correction—I want a car with a full tank of gas and twenty bucks to grab a sandwich or something."

"I'll drive her," Marci interjected. "We won't be gone long."

"I'm going alone." Farin crossed her arms.

"Not a chance."

Ethan shook his head. "I don't think it's safe, Marci. This is a volatile situation. I'm certain Elliot wouldn't want you taking chances in your condition."

"I'll—" Chris cleared his throat into the side of his fist. "I'll take her."

Farin shot him a bitter look. "You will *not*."

"Calm down, Farin," Marci scolded. "I'll go. Don't worry, Ethan. We'll take someone with us. Someone Jameson wouldn't know or suspect."

"No." Farin shook her head and barked at the phone. "I don't want anyone else involved."

"You tried to involve him before. Besides, you said it yourself. You don't know when you'll be back. Don't you think you should say hello in person?"

She considered the proposal. "Fine. Samantha'll set up the meeting with Ross. Marci and I'll be gone for about a day. After that, I'll leave for Miami whenever you say. I guess we all get what we want, don't we?"

Chris stood. "Can I talk to you for a minute, Farin?"

"Chris—" Marci warned.

"It's okay. I'll call you later. Thanks for jumping on the phone and helping us sort this out. Take care. My best to Elliot." He punched the speakerphone button with his index finger, severing the connection, then grabbed Farin's arm and marched her down the hall and into the bedroom.

He closed the door behind them and faced her. Banished emotions taunted him. Betrayals. Remorse. His insides ached. He had never wished her a minute's pain—though he had caused her nothing but. She needed to know he would never abandon her. They needed each other.

Last week, they had said all the words, but something about their goodbye had left him empty. "We can't leave it this way."

She arched a defiant brow. "What way is that?"

"It wasn't my idea for you to go. And this new marble pillar persona you've got going on isn't fooling anyone."

With a flare of her nostrils, she pushed her lips out and looked away.

The memory of holding her in that motel room in Yucca clouded his mind. Her bitterness helped him cope with the conflict building inside him. Better not to tell her how he felt. Better to ignore the familiar scent of her hair. Better she leave within the week. "In time, you'll see this was for the best."

"Best for you?"

"Best for everyone. If Jameson tracked you to Malibu, you think he won't track you to an apartment in Beverly Grove? Nobody's safe here. Not Ethan, and not you."

Her eyes blazed into his. "So you'd rather put Ben in jeopardy? And Cheryl? The boys? Are you *crazy*?"

"Ben says it'll be all right. He'll hire some security if he has to. Besides, Jameson probably already checked Ben out. You'll be okay there. Trust me. At the end of the day—"

"At the end of the day, it's dark," she spat, arms folded across her chest.

They had become strangers. At one time, he believed he knew her better than she knew herself. Now, he could not read her. She was right...she had changed. Immeasurable change. "Who killed my brother, Farin?" he asked, his voice little more than a whisper.

She blinked twice and swallowed. The fire in her eyes quelled.

"*Please.*"

She squared her shoulders and straightened her stance. "My father died twenty-two years ago today. Did you know that?"

He frowned.

She opened the door and gestured he should leave. "I guess it's you who has to trust me."

***

Julie Swanson Grant could not remember the last public meal she had eaten in peace. Today was no exception. They had elected a table on the outdoor terrace to enjoy the spring weather, but talking business would prove challenging as usual. The raised brick patio topped with a white picket fence separating patrons from sidewalk traffic at the Beverly Hills establishment was no more than a courtesy. A steady, if polite, stream of tourists gawked as they passed, the braver or less tactful ones hoping to solicit an autograph or quick photo snapped with various cameras ranging from digital to disposable. It never failed.

The restaurant studiously shooed away fans and relegated paparazzi to the opposite side of the street. But no matter. The Ivy was a place to be seen. Julie did not frequent the eatery for its lobster pizza and flowery decor. Nonetheless, when her presence drew marked attention, their waiter offered to reseat her somewhere less accessible to the sidewalk.

"Are you kidding?" argued Gloria Monroe. "This is perfect. Isn't it, Jules?"

"Julie!" one fan waved furiously from across Robertson Boulevard. "Over here!"

Julie shrugged and flashed the waiter a winning smile. She did not mind the hassle of a sporadically interrupted lunch if it strengthened her popularity. As usual, they would allow ten minutes. Then, Gloria would excuse herself to use the restroom, heading instead to seek a private chat with the manager, who would redouble his efforts to avert the crowd. They would catch up for the remainder of their lunch, the bystanders close enough to stare enviously in Julie's direction without the ability to eavesdrop.

Gloria Monroe was a master career builder. She knew all the right people, played all the right cards, and kept all the right secrets. For seventeen years, she had groomed and represented some of the industry's best talent—damn Ford *and* Elite. As if channeling destiny, she sifted through the portfolios of those begging for her services until she discovered a diamond in the rough. Once under the Monroe Agency's tutelage, the lucky unknown could rest assured fame would come knocking on the heels of opportunity. The names and faces differed but the story was always the same. Such was the case for Julie Swanson.

Gloria picked at her crab salad. "I talked to Dharvey. They re-upped. Long term. Big money."

"Great." Julie sipped her sparkling water but scowled at her lunch.

Gloria froze mid-forkful, brows furrowed suspiciously below her creaseless forehead as her client pushed away her plate. "What's the matter?"

Julie shook her head, then massaged her temples with her fingertips.

"You okay? You don't look too good."

The statement sounded in Julie's head like a death knell. Gloria was right. She did not look good at all. And unless she did something soon, she might never look good again.

"You're not coming down with something, are you?"

"I'll be fine." She wished she could feel angry, but the alien in her womb had zapped all her strength.

"Good. This deal with Dharvey's a gimme." Confident no impending crisis would waylay her biggest client's success, Gloria returned her attention to her meal.

Julie nodded. "Like you said, it's a good thing it came along when it did."

"You're not getting any younger. I hate to say it. We both knew this time would come."

She thought she might vomit.

"You've had a terrific run, though. Magazines, billboards, calendars, runways—and now, cosmetics." Gloria retrieved the napkin from her lap and dabbed the side of her mouth. She cocked her head to one side, as if remembering something, then laughed. "And oh! Can't forget music videos, can we, babe? In any case, Dharvey's the jewel, Jules. It'll buy you another two years easy. Then we can reassess."

Unsure where to begin, she said nothing. She had called this meeting to discuss her options, so she had better start talking. The clock was ticking. Her career's expiration date hovered frightfully close. More than ever, she did not regret her decision. "You haven't mentioned the audition. Have you talked to the director yet? I thought he was supposed to call you back yesterday."

As the waiter refilled their glasses and asked after their meal, Gloria gushed at him in that way of hers. "It's *wonderful*, darling. Best I ever had! My compliments to the chef."

With a smile and a nod, the man retreated to attend his other tables.

"It's a salad." Julie frowned at the display, painfully aware of Gloria's attempt to sidestep the question. "Tell me what he said."

Gloria stabbed at her baby lettuce like a fervid spearfisherman. "What was that, dear?"

"The audition." A knot unrelated to the unwelcome barnacle affixed to her womb twisted inside her stomach. "Cut the act, Gloria. You're not a very good actress."

Gloria dropped the utensil atop her bowl, sighed, and sat back in her chair. "Well, Jules, I'm sorry. Apparently, neither are you."

Julie's eyes widened. Her cheeks flushed at the blunt remark from the one person she paid to champion her career. She glanced about, fearful someone may have overheard. "Excuse me?"

Gloria raised her eyes and shot her an unconcerned half-frown, then reached for her bag to grab a cigarette. "Look. You can't be all things to all people. You're a pretty woman. You're a pretty woman with a great career, a great husband, and a great life. You've made a lot of money doing what you do best. So what if you can't act? You don't want to be an actress. Actresses are prostitutes. You don't want to be a *prostitute*, do you?"

"It was just a commercial." Julie's shoulders slumped as her public facade melted away, revealing a vulnerable industry veteran who felt she had just received her pink slip—and not from Victoria Secret. "I only had a couple of lines."

Gloria scoffed, ignoring her client's dejection with a wave of her hand. "In all these years, have I ever steered you wrong? Don't answer. We both know I haven't. Did it not register in your brain that Dharvey wants to keep you? That's fantastic news for a model your age!"

The sound of Gloria's semi-gravelly voice faded to background noise as

Julie pondered her future. Two years from now, she would run out of choices and out of offers. By then, Chris would have left her to reunite with his recently resurrected lover. She would become completely unremarkable, save the seedy stories relayed in the tabloids. No career. No husband. She would be old. Eventually, she would turn into her mother. In the end, she would disappear— again.

Growing up, Julie's entire world existed within a six mile radius of her house on West 4th Street. Adams Middle School. North Platte High School. The Platte River Mall. The Bailey Yard where her father worked. Her first job at the visitors' center in Buffalo Bill Ranch State Historic Park. The Centennial Park Retirement Village where her grandmother had lived her last years. The North Platte Cemetery where they had buried her younger brother. Even with rush hour traffic, her life commute did not exceed eleven minutes in any direction. The North Platte Regional Airport that finally carried her away sat a mere four miles from her front door.

Very early on, Gloria Monroe had rewritten Julie Swanson's public biography to convey a beautiful swan instead of the ugly duckling reality of having grown up in impoverished Middle America. Gloria had painted Earl and Angie Swanson as attentive, loving, even doting parents to a blossoming beauty who shone as the pride of Nebraska Days every June throughout Julie's high school years.

The Monroe Agency's version of Julie Swanson's life omitted the accident at the Bailey Yard that claimed her eleven year old brother's life while he was playing with a friend in an empty railcar. It left out that, to this day, Angie Swanson would not allow another living soul into young Eric's perfectly preserved bedroom. The biography Gloria wrote intimated no reason Julie would not want to return home once her days in the limelight sunsetted.

"I need to know what my options are," Julie asked, composing herself. "You've shot straight with me so far. Okay, so I'm not an actress. My modeling days are coming to an end, but there has to be something else, *something* I can prepare to do after the gig with Dharvey."

Gloria caught their waiter's eye as he approached their table and shook her head slightly, signaling he should give them a couple more minutes before removing their plates. She sat back in her seat and lit her cigarette, taking a long drag and holding the toxic smoke inside her lungs a few seconds before exhaling. "Just enjoy the ride, Jules. Don't roll over and play dead while you're still breathing. You start worrying about this now and it'll start showing. You know I'm right. Look—you have a couple weeks before your next appointment. Why not take some time? Go to the spa. Take Chris and go somewhere exotic. Who knows? By the time the Dharvey deal's up, you may decide to retire completely...maybe push out a few kids, launch a clothing line.

Who knows?"

Julie's eyes narrowed. She leaned in and whispered through clenched teeth, "I'm *never* going back to Nebraska."

"Whoa, whoa!" Gloria chuckled unsympathetically at the display of paranoia. "See what I mean? You're getting yourself all worked up over nothing. Do you have any Valium? Xanax?" She snatched up her handbag again and retrieved a prescription bottle. "Here, have one of mine. Take something, Jules, for Pete's sake!"

"Gloria, we have to talk."

She sucked the butt of her cigarette and inhaled deeply, then checked her thick gold link watch. Exhaling through one side of her mouth, she leveled her eyes at her client. "Shoot. I've got about fifteen minutes. I've gotta be in Bel Air by three."

"I'm pregnant." Julie's face twisted in disgust and desperation as the words spilled out.

Without missing a beat, Gloria procured her cell phone and dialed her assistant. After instructing her to reschedule her Bel Air appointment for the following afternoon, she waved their waiter over to remove their lunch dishes. "And bring me a Manhattan!" she called after him as he left.

Once the server had strode out of earshot, she rummaged through her bag until locating a business card. "How far along are we talking?" she asked, not sparing her client so much as a glance.

"I'm due at the end of September." Julie lowered her head onto her hands. "And Chris is leaving me for a corpse. I may not be an actress, Gloria, but please don't let me become a statistic."

Gloria Monroe neither registered nor cared about her client's melodramatic rantings. Two more years of income from the top model in the industry made their common course a clear one. She squinted and held the business card away from her to make out the number, then punched some digits on the keypad and brought the cell to her ear. A moment later, she greeted the party on the other line. "Courtney, darling! How *are* you?"

Julie watched Gloria laugh at whatever comment "Courtney" had made. She felt numb and nauseated. Too tired to fight, too miserable to protest the obvious dismissal by the only other living soul she had revealed her news to besides Cheryl.

Gloria laughed uproariously. "That's fabulous, darling, just fabulous!"

Then, at last, a spark of hope.

"Put that man on the phone this instant!" Gloria laughed again, this time a hint of mischief in her voice. "I don't care if he's in with a patient! Tell him it's me, darling. Of *course* I'll hold—but not too long, now!"

Once again, Gloria leveled her eyes at Julie. This time, she grinned confidently and winked. Moments later, her voice dropped conspiratorially as the party on the other end picked up. "Clarence, it's Gloria. I'm calling in that favor you owe me."

CHAPTER 3

CHERYL GRANT SAT AT THE foot of their bed, speechless. Unkind thoughts assaulted her machine gun fashion. Two children. Nearly seventeen years of marriage. And not once had Ben cheated on her, disrespected her, or failed to provide for their family. Their marriage had operated on a foundation of commitment that laid waste the fact they had arrived at their nuptials under less than ideal circumstances—with Cheryl eight months pregnant at the time.

Despite the nontraditional beginning to their life journey, Ben had built a career for himself deserving of the acclaim he had received and ensured security for his family. He only drank socially, did not smoke, and did not do heavy drugs. A virtual homebody, he loved his family with a protective loyalty that had weathered every storm they faced, and they had always faced them together, in solidarity of purpose.

Until today.

She restrained her tongue as she replayed her husband's good qualities in her mind in an attempt to dispel her growing anger. "So what you're telling me is you and Samantha Drake have already affirmed these plans."

He stood before her, hands resting on his small waist. "I should have discussed it with you first. I'm sorry."

She shook her head and pursed her lips. Kyle was in his room, studying. Derek was at practice. If she raised her voice, Kyle would hear her. The boys had never heard their parents fight. In fact, aside from a few minor quarrels, Ben and Cheryl Grant had experienced few bumps along their marital highway. "This was a big decision, Ben."

"Yes."

She stared blankly at the floor. "And where will she stay?"

Ben looked down at the floor, then back up at her. His shoulders stooped with regret. A minor acknowledgment given the gravity of their circumstances.

"You want her to stay here." It was not a question.

"Yes."

"In our home."

He folded his arms and nodded.

She tapped her lips with her fingertips as she considered the situation.

Even in the tension of the moment, Cheryl Grant was an elegant woman worthy of every ounce of respect Ben had for her. An aura of class and reason permeated her soft beauty as she drummed finely manicured nails against a hint of tinted lip stain. She understandably resented his springing such serious plans on her. A sense of betrayal emanated from her smooth features and exquisitely understated attire. Her feelings for Farin had not changed.

"And you feel bringing her here to live with us—with our *children*—sounds like a reasonable plan."

He tilted his head back and stared at the ceiling. Had he told her the news last night as planned, the hard part would be over by now. "I can't tell you how sorry I am for not talking to you about this first."

"Our *children*, Ben."

"I know."

Her voice deepened as unchecked resentment crept into her tone. "After all she's done."

He bristled at the jab but thought better of leaping to Farin's defense. Too late, he saw his thoughts register in his wife's eyes.

"Don't even," she warned.

"What was I supposed to do? Yes, we should have made this decision together. You're one hundred percent right about that. But without brushing that fact aside, what else was there to do, love? She's in danger and needs our help."

"Last week, Jorie's house *blew up*, Ben."

"I know...I know. It's not good."

"And what about our sons? What about Kyle? Did you know your son thinks Jorie's coming back to us? Are you really willing to make such a gamble with our family?"

"Farin *is* our family," he dared to say.

Cheryl stood and walked to their bedroom window, swiping a panel of sheer curtain aside to stare out at the day.

He followed behind her and slid his arms around her waist, grateful she did not pull away. "I love you. I'm sorry. This is the only way I know to help. She's been through so much for so long. How long does she have to suffer your judgment too? You're not going to betray your bond with Julie or dishonor Jordan's memory by helping the woman he loved. In fact, it may finally give him peace. Let's do this for him, if not for her."

Her eyes fused shut at the sting of her husband calling her on her bias. But she had been there. She had witnessed Jordan's agony over the affair. She had lamented with Julie over Chris' behavior for the first two years of their marriage, and then again after Farin's rescue. More than anything, she feared bringing Farin here would endanger them all. "And if I say no?"

Nuzzling her neck, he gave her waist a loving squeeze. "I shall never again make a decision that impacts our family without your input. I give you my word. And if you're adamant about Farin not coming here, I'll call Sam right now and tell her we've reconsidered. But I'm asking you. Will you help me? Can we open our home to a family member who needs us? It's time to make things right—for all of us."

Cheryl maneuvered herself around into her husband's embrace and rested her head against his chest. She understood better than he realized his desperation to feel he had atoned for what he considered his failures. Though his and Farin's bond had outlived her short tenure as a member of their family, he asked this as much for himself as he did for her. In the end, Cheryl's loyalty would always belong with her husband.

She lifted her head and planted a kiss on his lips. "We need to prepare the boys."

He held her closer. "Thank you."

"You're the most honorable man I've ever known, Ben Grant." Her eyes glistened with love and admiration. "I'm proud to be your wife."

He buried his head in her shoulder and softly squeezed. Not a man in need of much praise, Cheryl seeing him as he strove to be—imperfections and all— meant the world to him.

"And of course you'll be making it up to me for a very long time," she added.

***

Derek grinned as he parked at the warehouse and recognized the other cars littered in the driveway. The guys were all inside. A good sign. They had pushed hard the last few weeks. With Sawyer Jacobs' recent interest in managing them, Derek no longer worried his bandmates might abandon their efforts as some flight of fancy or fleeting desire to play with a Grant legacy.

He proudly carried his family's name and place in the world, but sometimes it felt more like a burden than an advantage having people judge him by his uncles' success. Some people treated him more like a freak show exhibit than a serious musician. All that would change with Sawyer's involvement.

As he killed the engine and exited his vehicle, his smile widened. A custom, powder blue Golf III Cabrio convertible drove up and parked beside his Blazer. In it sat the most beautiful girl Derek had ever known. Beautiful inside, beautiful outside. And she was all his.

"You know, good Catholic girls shouldn't drive around in sports cars with the top down." He opened her door and offered his hand.

Summer Reece fluttered out of her car with a giggle and wrapped her arms around him. She kissed his cheek. "Or ditch their homework and cheerleading practice to meet their boyfriend's new manager."

"That too."

She fussed with her silky blonde hair, a portion of which had escaped the clip she had employed in an effort to lessen the tangles, an inevitability when cruising around in convertibles on picture perfect days. "Do I look all wind-blown?"

"You look perfect."

"Biased much?"

"You know it."

She leaned in and kissed him again, this time on the lips. "You need to stay focused."

"Oh, I'm focused."

"Not on me, silly. So tell me again. Levoy's sister hooked you up with this guy?"

He nodded and took her hand as they walked toward the warehouse entrance. "Cécile and Sawyer go to U of M together. I get the feeling they've got something goin' on."

She blushed at the implication. "I thought Sawyer was older. He's still in school?"

"College," he corrected. "And he's a lot older than we are. Mid-twenties, I think. But old enough to get us into all the places we need to play."

She shrugged. "Makes sense."

"He's pretty popular around South Florida. Dad knows him a little. Says he thinks he's all right. He's gonna meet with him to make sure it's all good."

The owner of the Virginia Key warehouse had converted the building into a private studio some years back, offering a high-end alternative and more desirable location to that of North Miami's Criteria Recording Studios or Standards. His dad used it from time to time when he needed something bigger than his home studio. The place boasted state-of-the-art equipment and made the perfect place for the band to practice.

Of course, as with anything, it had pros and cons. On the pro side, it was free. As a favor to his dad, the owner let them use it as often as they wanted unless a paying customer reserved it. Since most of the paying musicians preferred night sessions, it worked out well. On the con side, it was bare bones. Studio time did not include an engineer, a producer, or recordings. Basically, they could practice. Fortunately, that was exactly what they needed.

Summer's face reddened as Derek's bandmates welcomed them with whistles of approval. As usual, he warned them to back off. Same scenario every time. Secretly, it made him feel taller, invincible. He had the band. He had the girl. Now, he would have the break he needed without having to trade on his family's name.

Sawyer jogged casually up to the couple and extended his hand. "You must be Summer. Derek talks about you all the time."

She tucked a blonde tress behind her ear and shook his hand. "He talks about you, too."

Derek grinned confidently at Sawyer's wink of approval. Summer made him proud. He enjoyed the respect and envy the others gave him when she was by his side.

Sawyer clapped his hands together and positioned himself in the center of the live room. "Okay, let's get started. First off, I wanted to let you know I've secured a gig for you bozos. It's not 'til the first weekend of June, but it *is* a South Beach club."

The boys erupted with cheers and whistles.

He waved his arms, hands palm down, and chuckled. "Not finished! There's more."

"More?" Brian Keller asked, all smiles. "What more could there be? A tour?"

Sawyer shook his head with a doubtful half-smile. "A tour? You don't even have a name yet!"

The boys talked over one another, laughing as they argued over who had suggested the worst band names since coming together their freshmen year of high school. They had long since forsaken their original name, Rebel Sea, as sounding too mid-'80s.

"Also," Sawyer continued over the din. "*Also!*" He whistled through his top teeth and lower lip to get their attention. "C'mon, guys. I gotta take off soon and you need to practice. No really—you *need* the practice. I need you to focus."

Summer sniggered as Derek peeked her way and lifted his eyebrows.

"If this gig goes well, we'll be able to get more of those club owners to take a chance on you. So if you're serious about this, and Derek says you are," Sawyer glanced over his shoulder at Derek, who nodded affirmatively. "Then don't make me look like the idiot who was stupid enough to get involved with a bunch of high school kids. Let's show 'em what you're made of. You guys really blew me away that night Cécile brought me to hear you. And you know Cécile by now—*nothing* impresses her."

The guys laughed again.

"You got dat wight, mahn," Levoy Laroche said. "She say you da wost she evah 'ad." He played a quick joke roll with his snare.

Sawyer laughed. "Oh, really? That's not what she told me last night."

The boys ooh'd and guffawed at the sexual allusion. Derek cleared his throat to get Sawyer's attention, then inclined his head in Summer's direction.

"Ah." Sawyer tightened the corners of his mouth. "Sorry little lady."

Summer shook her head and shyly smiled.

"Okay. Well, with that, I'm outta here." He fished his car keys out of his jeans pocket and walked backwards toward the door. "You guys practice hard and I'll see you in a week. And get yourselves a name!"

When he left, Peter Neill asked, "You think we can get good enough to play South Beach in basically a *month*?"

"I think we do what we have to do," Derek told him. "I think it's our shot. Anyone who's not serious, let me know now so I can get someone who is." He surveyed the group, weighing their reactions. "Okay then." He pulled his guitar strap over his head and winked at Summer, who had settled in to watch. "Let's do this thing. And just so you know, Summer and I are taking off in a couple of hours to see a movie."

The boys whooped and whistled again, causing Summer's face to flush once more.

"You take 'uh to see dat new Bwando film, eh Dah'eek?" Levoy teased. "Dat *Don Juan DeMahco*?"

Derek rolled his eyes. "We're taking Kyle to see *Bad Boys*."

Brian Keller, Peter Neill, and Levoy Laroche broke into the *COPS* theme song. Summer laughed and applauded as they played. Levoy sang lead with his thick Haitian accent.

Derek smiled and shook his head, then joined in with a screaming guitar lick.

***

Perhaps because they had only married a little over three years ago, he had not yet experienced the mundane ritual of everyday life about which so many couples complained. Or maybe it was her stomach's almost imperceptible pooch, promising to make him a father in five and a half months. Or her smile. Her laugh. The way she cuddled into him in bed. Any, none, or a combination of these things might account for the simplest fact in his life.

Elliot Lawrence loved his wife.

He loved everything about her—even the annoying things. Beautiful, understanding, loyal, smart, independent. He loved to watch her walk with that slight sway of her hips. The way her eyes danced when she laughed. The way her right eyebrow raised as she read her tabloids. When they talked, he felt like the only person in the room. He found her guilt over preferring Led Zeppelin to Mirage almost as adorable as her acceptance of the pet name "Zoso" despite its negative connotations in popular culture. But more than anything, he loved her selfless mercy.

All these things and more caused Elliot to wake up each morning thankful for the life he lived. Further, though he had not told her, it had made his decision about regrouping with Mirage a no-brainer.

Elliot had lived the rock-and-roll life for most his adult life. He had played mediator to Todd and Chris. He had taken his turn as Faith's unwitting bodyguard. He had toured and recorded and performed in hundreds of venues around the world. Pulling sound checks. Sleeping on buses. Spending little to no time at home. The girls, the autographs. Haggling over contracts and concert riders. He had loved it all at the time. And now? Now, he enjoyed a slower pace. A more comfortable existence. He would raise his child, grow old with his wife, and make music on his own terms.

So he had relayed the news to Sam. All in all, she had taken it well. Apparently, he was not the only member of the group who had developed a fatal case of wanna-be-a-has-been-itis.

Marci exited their den. She kissed him on the cheek on her way to the kitchen for a bottled water. "We're leaving soon. Ethan's meeting me near the hospital."

Elliot followed her into the kitchen and sat at the counter. "You sure you're okay to do this? I don't need to worry? I mean, you're my two favorite people right now."

She set the bottled water on the counter, then made her way over and wrapped her arms around his neck. "We'll be fine. Think of it as a girls' day out."

"But I thought you were bringing—"

She cut eyes at her husband. "Your point?"

He chuckled. "Got it. But what if we're having a boy?"

She shook her head and ignored the bad joke. "I have my cell and you have my parents' number. They don't know about Farin yet, so don't mention her if you call. We should be back by late afternoon. I'll call if plans change."

Elliot watched her rummage through and inventory her purse to ensure she had her keys, wallet, cash, bank card, and compact. He loved her hands, her long fingers, and perfectly trimmed nails. "Have you ever played piano?"

She paused and looked up. "Huh?"

"Nothing." He smiled and took her in his arms. "Be careful, Zoso. I miss you already. Give the girls my love."

She giggled, kissed him goodbye, let him kiss her belly and whisper "bye-bye, baby," then headed out the door.

Her first stop was a few of blocks from Cedars in the opposite direction of Ethan's apartment. She snaked down Laurel Canyon Boulevard, made her way over to Santa Monica Boulevard, then found the parking garage off West 3rd Street where she parked in the agreed-upon area on the top level, backing into her space in case she needed to make a quick exit. She had checked her mirrors as she drove, mindful of any suspicious vehicles. It appeared no one had followed her.

Five minutes later, she spotted Ethan's blue Lexus and unlocked her passenger door. He parked nose-first into the space beside hers and lowered his window. Marci lowered hers as Farin dashed from Ethan's car into hers.

He checked his mirrors for unusual activity. "You sure I can't talk you out of this?"

"Afraid not. We'll be fine. I've got my phone on me if you want to check up on us."

Farin wore a disguise similar to the one she had employed during the more popular times of her career—a nondescript, sandy blonde wig with short, straight hair; oversized tortoiseshell sunglasses to obscure her face; and a baggy beige T-shirt to bulk up her frame. She looked in all ways unremarkable.

They made arrangements to regroup in an alternate location several hours later, then Ethan said his goodbyes and headed to the hospital to start his day.

As Marci shifted her vehicle into drive, Farin placed a hand on top of hers. "Wait."

She shifted back into park and looked at her. "What's the matter?"

"Nothing. I...I just want to take a minute."

Marci surveyed the parking lot, then turned back. "You okay?"

Farin nodded. "I just wanted to thank you."

She dipped her head slightly. "You don't have to thank me, Farin."

"But I do."

Marci studied her friend. They communicated for several moments in that unspoken language they had shared since their childhood. Farin smiled. Marci nodded her understanding.

"You're gonna be a momma." Farin placed a hand on Marci's small belly. "I'm happy for you."

Marci noted the faraway sound of her voice and feared Farin might feel conflicted over her condition. She had tried to balance her happiness with empathy during their time together, not wanting to stir up misery over Melody's death so long ago. "Elliot and I want you to be as much a part of the baby's life as you're willing. I just didn't want to push."

Farin smiled through flattened lips as she ran the tips of her fingers beneath her sunglasses. "Push? Are you kidding? I'm gonna be the cool aunt. If it's a girl, I'll teach her she can actually wear clothes that aren't pink."

She laughed at the familiar ribbing. "And if it's a boy?"

"I owe you my life," Farin blurted out, her voice breaking with emotion.

Marci's eyes brimmed with tears as the happy reality she had her best friend back overcame her. "I missed you. I think a part of me was gone these last few years."

"And probably even before that." Farin stared out the window while fidgeting with her fingers. "I treated you terribly while I was in Miami. You put up with so much. Too much. I just want you to know I realize how bad my behavior was. How sorry I am. How...how much I love you."

They embraced, then pulled away and cleared their throats. Farin grabbed Marci's purse off the floorboard, correctly guessing she would find a travel pack of tissues inside. She grabbed two and handed Marci one. Once they composed themselves, Marci shifted back into drive and headed for their next stop.

***

Dale Eastland made good use of the fifteen minutes he had to spare before meeting Marci for their northward trek. Although Colline would not open for hours, he checked the restaurant to ensure things ran according to his schedule and his standards. The new prep cook labored in the kitchen, slicing and dicing fresh vegetables at an impressive pace and level of expertise, while his sous chef inventoried and ensured proper food rotation. Staff bustled about the establishment mixing, cooking, cleaning, and performing the varied tasks that had made Colline a Beverly Hills "it" spot from practically the day their doors opened a year ago.

He harbored no doubt that things would run smoothly on this, his first full day away from the restaurant. He air-kissed a goodbye to his general manager-boyfriend and restaurant namesake, David Colline, then slipped out the back door to await Marci's arrival.

She had missed their annual memorial in January. As usual, he had come home early to ready the apartment. He had prepared Farin's favorite chili, popped her debut CD into the player, and waited until 6 PM. Worried when he did not hear from her, he had left a message on her cell phone. She had not returned the call until the next day. While apologetic, she never explained the reason she stood him up.

A couple of months ago, she had called him again, her voice strained and confused. She relayed the news of the baby, which in his mind accounted for her recent odd behavior. But she had also asked the strangest question. Something about a package. Something about Farin. Even now, he could not weave the conversational thread together.

Yesterday, another call, asking him to accompany her to Santa Barbara.

Dale had never visited Farin's grave. He had not thought himself ready to confront this last stage of grief. Farin remained with him in so many ways. She had had few close friends in her life—she had ensured that—but he was as close to Farin as anyone, save Marci. At the time of her death, that had been enough for him.

He reasoned Marci had finally worked out her feelings and felt the time had come to let go. Maybe she had organized this sojourn north to put the past in its place. Perhaps she wanted them to do it together. No more annual memorials. It made sense after all this time.

He wished he had thought to cook up a pot of chili.

When Marci picked him up, Dale thought it odd she drove Elliot's new Mercedes instead of her Chrysler—a personal preference of hers he had never understood. Odder still was her disposition. She repeatedly checked the rearview and side mirrors, as if auditioning for a part of a paranoid would-be victim on *Murder, She Wrote*.

He approached the vehicle and noticed a figure in the back seat but could not get a clear look at the passenger's face.

"Hello." He slid into the front seat and gave Marci a hug, then fastened his seat belt. "Taking the hubby-mobile out for a spin, are we? You and Iacocca have a fight? I hear he's engaged in some hostile takeover situation—it was on the news today. Looks like your hero may yet return."

Marci chuckled as she backed up, then navigated onto Wilshire and headed west toward the 405. "That's enough now. How are you doing?"

"Wonderful!" Dale singsonged. He glanced over his left shoulder and beheld the form of a woman lying down in the back seat but could see nothing but her jeans and shoes. He looked at Marci expectantly.

"What?"

He motioned behind him. "You appear to have picked up a stowaway. Anyone I know?"

Marci eyed her mirrors. "Just let me get out of the city a bit. Elliot told me to tell you hi, by the way."

Dale settled into his seat. "Okay. Hi back to Elliot."

"How's the restaurant doing?"

For nearly an hour, Marci engaged Dale in banal chitchat about Colline, his health, and his family. She had him recap how and where he and David had met, how long they had been together, and what their long term plans entailed. She spoke as if they had not talked in years, as if she needed a reminder of every significant moment of his existence, all the while checking and rechecking her mirrors.

She evaded discussing the fact she not only had another person in her car, but that she had yet to introduce them. Further, whoever occupied the back seat had either fallen asleep or had died of boredom. He had not heard a peep or seen her move an inch.

A few miles outside Camarillo, Dale finally confronted Marci, using his most understanding tone. "Is it the hormones, doll? Is that it?"

Marci glanced at him, confused. "What?"

"The hormones," he urged gently. "You know. The *baby*?"

The tension in her shoulders eased with each mile separating them from

Los Angeles. The charade must have looked ridiculous to Dale, but she could not risk a scene until she ensured Farin's safety. Bringing him into their confidence compounded their chances of making a fatal mistake.

"It's not the baby, Dale. The baby's fine. And I'm fine."

"Well then?" Dale pressed. "Let's talk about the big fat white elephant in the room, shall we? I think I know why you wanted me to come with you today."

"You do?"

"Yes. I realize you and I have been coming together over the years, supporting each other and whatnot. We really were the two people closest to her. But enough time has passed. Better to jump this last hurdle. We're both adults. In life, we inevitably face death. And we move on. It's not always easy, but we do it. So let's just *do* it." He took Marci's right hand in his left and gave it a tender squeeze. "We'll move on from here. You and Elliot will raise that baby. Life goes on, and we need to move with it."

Marci squeezed Dale's hand, too, then let it go as she engaged her turn signal.

"I thought about it too late," he continued. "I should have brought a pot of chili with us today. Just symbolic, I know, but we did miss our last get-together in January and chili was her favorite."

Marci exited Highway 101 at Camarillo Springs Road, then looped around the off ramp and drove past the golf course, heading west along the tree-lined street.

"But if it's not the hormones, or the baby..."

She located a parking area beyond an apartment complex.

"...and you're not upset or sad..."

She searched for and found an inconspicuous place to park near the back of the sparsely populated area and breathed a sigh of relief that no cars had exited after them. It looked as though they had escaped LA without any unwanted company.

"...can you *please* explain to me why you haven't introduced me to your friend here?" Dale gestured behind him, struggling to get a better view of the person resting in the back as he removed his seat belt.

Marci faced him and put her hand on his shoulder. "Dale? I've got something to tell you. It'll be confusing to hear. I need you to promise you won't make a scene."

"A scene? Why would I make a scene?"

From behind him, Farin sat up and scooted behind Marci's back seat. "Because," she said softly, "you were mistaken." She pulled her wig off and drew her dark glasses down the bridge of her nose. "It wasn't the chili. It was the lemon chicken I loved so much. Remember?"

A deafening shriek erupted from the passenger's seat, startling the women as they watched their friend's eyes grow wide, then roll back in his head as his body went limp.

Farin visually surveyed the area as Marci jumped out of the car and ran around to open the passenger side door. She eased his seat back as far as it would go, bent down, and took Dale's hand in hers. She looked at Farin.

"I guess that didn't go as well as I'd hoped."

"Ya think?" Marci reached for the bottled water she had taken with her from the house but never finished.

It took several minutes for Dale to regain his faculties, and several more to accept the reality presented him before he fainted. He laughed, then cried, then accused Farin of faking her own death before calming down long enough for her to respond. He sat in back with her as they resumed their trek to Santa Barbara. She and Marci relayed what details they could regarding the ordeal she had faced during her captivity. They swore him to secrecy until such time as she made her return public. When Dale asked about the mysterious package Marci had called him about, Farin refused to discuss it.

He procured lunch when they reached the Camarillo city limits. They ate while they drove the final hour to Santa Barbara. When they arrived, Marci dropped Dale and Farin off at the cemetery, then went on to visit her parents. She would return within the hour so they could head home.

"I'm still in shock," Dale told Farin as they walked arm-in-arm up the winding road toward the O'Conner gravesite.

Farin rested her head on Dale's shoulder. "Me too."

The view from the cemetery looked anything but lifeless in the early afternoon. To the west, varying shades of blue fused seamlessly where the cloudless April sky met the calm, dark sea at the horizon. Monuments and mausoleums rose boldly from beneath the manicured earth, their surfaces pristine white marble or hewn stone gray. Cypress and palm trees dotted the property, their healthy green leaves and fronds swaying in the cool ocean breeze. From the narrow paved road meandering throughout the property, rows of flat white grave markers resembled a short, grassy four-lane highway, the larger headstones on either side acting as signposts along a traveler's final destination.

"I barely remember this," she told him as they neared the O'Conner gravesite. "I didn't visit my dad here more than a couple of times. And I never visited my mother."

Dale put his arm around her. "You okay?"

"I wish I'd brought flowers," she mused.

The O'Conner gravestone arched into three fused sections connected by their family name. Two-thirds of those sections, the two belonging to her parents, affected her differently than she had anticipated. No more fear, sadness, or regret. No eerie aftereffects from the nightmares that had haunted her most her life. Seeing their names together coupled with the information she had learned shortly before her captivity caused a peace she could not describe to settle upon her.

Beth O'Conner had done all she could. Farin took comfort in the belief the two of them were whole at last. She imagined they knew she would do what needed to be done. She had a higher calling now and finally possessed the strength to answer it.

As for the final name engraved into the smooth, dark granite before them, Farin felt nothing. She saw the graffiti and inexpertly painted epitaphs left by fans and remembered from somewhere outside herself she had once been someone the world found talented or interesting. And though an unwilling impostor now slumbered beside her parents, the date carved into the stone belonged to her. The person named had indeed died that December morning.

"And good riddance to you!" she hissed bitterly.

"What was that, dear?" Dale returned to her side, having wandered away to give her privacy.

Farin approached the stone and kissed both her mother and her father's names, then righted herself and motioned for him to follow. "Nothing. Let's go. Marci'll be back soon."

On their way out of town, Farin asked if they could drive by her old house over on Mason Boulevard, but Marci said it might not be a good idea.

"I didn't want to tell you this, but the house was torn down along with the two houses next to yours. They built a small apartment complex there last year."

"Did they?" Farin's voice sounded far away. "I suppose life goes on, doesn't it?"

Marci glanced at Dale, then looked at her through the rearview mirror. "I'm sorry."

"No worries."

She navigated the Mercedes down East Cabrillo Boulevard and onto the southbound ramp of Highway 101.

Marci and Dale exchanged knowing looks, wordlessly voicing their shared concern over their uncharacteristically stoic friend.

"You sure you're okay?" he called back over his shoulder.

"I'm fine." She fixed her eyes on the exquisite ocean view to the west. "But I would like some lemon chicken."

CHAPTER 4

B OBBY LOCKHARDT ARRIVED AT THE Music Mill on West 42nd Street late Friday afternoon. The session had started half an hour ago. Not that she expected him. She had spent the entire week recording, her first ever experience in a professional studio. Producer Jim Wilson had called him that morning, urging him to drop by as soon as possible.

"You never told me Bob Dylan and Linda Ronstadt had themselves a secret love child. This little chanteuse of yours? She's gonna own the rest of the decade!"

Yeah—she was *that* good.

Bobby greeted the staff with smiles and handshakes, wishing everyone a relaxing weekend and reminding them of tomorrow's tax filing deadline. Light conversation. Nothing to draw him into detailed discussion. In his mind, he already occupied a seat in the control room, sitting close enough to observe the session without disturbing its producers. He could almost see her angelic face.

As he exited the elevator on the sixth floor, he heard the soft sound of a lone piano fill the air. A good sign—only promising sessions prompted the engineers to broadcast works in progress. A vulnerable, haunting melody floated languidly through the corridor, hovering like mist as a gentle string trio joined in. The sad beauty of the piece made him hesitate when he reached for the doorknob, as if he was about to interrupt a private moment. He glanced above the door frame at the glowing red light that signaled an in-progress recording. Once extinguished, he slipped inside.

A group of engineers, producers, and studio musicians had gathered to watch the session. They welcomed Bobby with friendly slaps on the back, admiring grins, and chin lifts.

Jim Wilson shook his hand, then gestured to an empty seat before reclining in his chair. "Glad you could make it. You really hit the bull's eye with this one."

Bobby smiled. "Yeah? That's good news." He set down his briefcase, unbuttoned his suit jacket, and flattened his tie against his chest as he took a seat in one of several rolling studio chairs. Then, he saw her.

The three times Bobby had met Joni Leighton in person she had either been performing or on her way to a gig. Flawless makeup, perfectly coifed hair, stage clothes. Her striking features and lilting voice had rapt him, so much so he found himself nearly speechless when the manager of the coffee house at which she played introduced them between sets. He had never seen eyes that shade of blue. And though he knew it was only in his head, he would have sworn a golden glow outlined and followed her wherever she went.

Today, he saw no trace of makeup as Joni exited the isolation booth. Never before had he beheld such perfection. She wore a powder blue jogging suit with a white midriff tank. A pink scrunchie held her golden tresses up and out of her face. In her hand, she carried a crinkled piece of used tissue. Upon closer inspection, it appeared she had been crying.

"Is she okay?" he asked no one in particular as his adoration gave way to concern.

Her manager answered, "I'm telling you, man. She's the real deal."

"She's fine," an engineer added. "It's just the song. You gotta hear it. Not as poetic or deep as the rest of her stuff. On the simple side, but still. One take. Amazing."

Joni spotted Bobby and waved, her smile radiant as she dabbed her eyes and made her way into the control room. He stood when she entered. She hugged his neck, which took him by surprise.

"Hey!" she greeted, her southern drawl welcoming and lyrical to his ear. "I didn't know you were comin' by today." She scrutinized her attire with mild discomfort. "I guess I should'a thrown on somethin'...somethin'...oh, I don't know."

"N-no. You look great. Um, I hear things are progressing well. The guys here tell me you just finished something?"

Joni's lips parted in surprise. She turned to the men and smiled. "Did y'all like it, really? You think it's done already? Oh my gosh. I just got so lost in that song. I was afraid I'd messed it up. My voice kept breaking."

"In all the right places, kid," Jim Wilson assured her. "You wanna hear it?"

"I'd love to! Gimme just a second, fellas." Her cheeks flushed as she glanced Bobby's way. "I'm sorry, Mr. Lockhardt. Did you need to talk to me about anything?"

Bobby realized he had not stopped grinning since he had laid eyes on her. "Oh—no, no. I just wanted to stop by and check in. Make sure you have everything you need. You have my card, right? I mean, if you want—need...um, if you need anything."

She nodded. "I do. It's so sweet of you to check in on me. Did you have time to take a listen? I don't want to keep you if you're busy, but I'd love you to stay if you're free."

The eyes of every other man in the room settled upon him. If he did not know better, he would have sworn they were mocking his feeble attempts at conversation. Usually, he found excuses to leave when feeling socially challenged, but today felt different. He could not tear himself away from those eyes. He extended his left hand to the chair beside his and took his seat. "My time is yours."

Jim Wilson nodded at the engineer, who slid on a pair of headphones and cued the playback. As the music started, he adjusted various knobs on the mixing board and slid faders up or down to coax the optimal blend of sound.

The song began with the same music box piano Bobby had heard from the hallway—a short, sixteen-count intro followed by Joni's tender, breathy vocals.

... *What do you see*
... *When you see me*
... *A fragile heart*
... *You'll never see the tears I cry*

Halfway through the first verse, a single string joined the piano.
... *Is love enough*
... *Or do you even realize*

At the chorus, they built further upon the piano's foundation with more string as the vocals slowly strengthened.
... *That every time we touch I fall again*
... *I lose my breath, I can't hold on*
... *Because I love you, baby*

... *And every time you leave*
... *You always take a piece of me and then you're gone*
... *Just when I need you, baby*

A synthesizer's solitary note appeared from nothing and sustained through the second verse.
... *I make believe*
... *And dream my dreams*
... *I wonder if*
... *Together they might come true*
... *What can I do*
... *To make you dream of me too*

Then, fuller synthesizer. A hint of percussion. Stronger vocals.
... *'Cause every time we touch I fall again*
... *I lose my breath, I can't hold on*

... Because I love you, baby

... And every time you leave
... You always take a piece of me, and then you're gone
... Just when I need you, baby

They doubled the vocals for the bridge, preparing the listener for the vocal climax.
... You hold me at arm's length
... But say you want me only
... My weakness fuels your strength
... Then you leave me lonely

A single voice again. Another sustained note accompanied the piano.
... What will it be
... Is there hope for you and me

Finally, the crescendo with synthesizer, percussion, and full voice.
... When every time we touch I fall again
... I lose my breath, I can't hold on
... Because I want you, baby

... And every time you leave
... You always take a piece of me and then you're gone
... I really need you, baby

No dramatic finish. Just the honest plea of the singer for her lover as the additional instruments disappeared one by one in a short musical interlude.
... Because I love you, baby

Finally, a return to the simplicity of the lone piano for the outro.

Bobby did not realize he held his breath until Joni's manager slapped him on the back. "Pretty good, eh? You should hear some of the edgier stuff she did earlier this week!"

His heart pounded beneath his suit like an unmuffled bass drum. Before he could respond, he glanced to his left. Joni had grabbed another tissue at some point and sat dabbing her eyes again.

He touched her forearm. "Are you okay?"

She manifested her embarrassment with a soft giggle and cleared her throat. "I'm sorry, y'all. Ugh! I don't know what it is about that song. Gets me every time." Then, to Bobby, "I guess there's never a second chance to make a first impression, is there?"

Bobby shook his head. "It was amazing."

Joni's eyes met his.

"The song!" he corrected awkwardly. "Not the impression. I mean, the impression was fine. Good—it was good. But the song. Joni, the song was fantastic."

"You really think so?"

"Oh, yeah. I can only think of one problem."

Her smile faded slightly. "What's that?"

"You're gonna have to learn to sing it without crying pretty soon, because it's going to be your first big hit."

***

Samantha had never been particularly fond of parties. Not giving them, not attending them. In her eyes, parties were synonymous with stress. She had enough tension in her daily life. But parties were part and parcel of the industry, so the anxiety increased after hours. The math made sense, if you thought about it: business plus party, times a twenty hour day, divided by equal and opposite reactions depending on celebrity status, equaled the square root of pressure. Top that, Einstein.

When she attended parties hosted by others, she felt swallowed whole by the crowd. The polite conversation, the milling about, the unspoken expectation to turn a blind eye when observing tawdry and often illegal activities by fellow guests. Drugs here, affairs there. The clashing of egos between those so new to the business they had yet to learn the subtle art of one-upmanship without burning bridges. The drunken performances by current chart-toppers failing to eclipse the even drunker performances fueled by loyalty to more veteran entertainers. Samantha felt a complete absence of control when attending parties in foreign surroundings.

The sole advantage to them was the ability to escape after a respectable amount of time, claiming an early day, a conflicting obligation, or the tried-and-true standby: illness.

Hosting such events compounded the pressure, for the angst occurred within her home. That meant no escape. A risky proposition when one considered the tabloid and potential legal ramifications. It seemed she always ordered too much food, though somehow never enough alcohol. She had learned the hard way to temporarily relocate and secure any treasured decor or furnishings that might not survive collision, misuse, or the occasional cigarette burn. And then there was the burden of restoring her surroundings once the last guest grudgingly staggered out into the late night or early morning.

Ridding her house of the lingering smell of smoke, residual white powder, and carelessly discarded drug paraphernalia was both a challenge and her first course of action. She generously tipped the staff she hired to assist, particularly when cleanup included anything resembling body fluids.

The upside was she felt more comfortable within her own four walls.

At first, Sam had felt guilty for scheduling the party for the day after Farin left for Miami. It seemed poor form. She hated for her to leave with the impression they intended to celebrate the fact she had left—even if partly true. Reasoning she could not have attended anyway, Sam gave in and decided to brave the mess, the inconvenience, and the knowledge that tomorrow would find her nursing one hell of a hangover. Deborah had done an impressive job arranging the little soiree, then subsequently begged off for the night. Smart girl. Sam admired her style.

"You made it!" she cheered, martini in hand as she hugged Julie Swanson Grant with her free arm. "Chris said you'd been under the weather lately. I was afraid you wouldn't come!"

The embodiment of feigned enthusiasm, Julie returned Sam's quick embrace. "I'm much better now." She stepped inside, Chris following behind her. "I have a doctor's appointment in a couple of weeks. I'm sure things'll be fine."

"A couple of weeks?"

Julie shrugged. "It was his first available appointment. But it's okay. I feel fantastic. I guess that's what happens though, right? You always feel better once you know the doctor's going to fix you up."

"Did you want Ethan to take a look at you? I'm sure he'd be happy to—"

"Oh no, I'm fine!" she assured, a fleeting glimmer of panic in her eyes at the suggestion. "I'm sure it was just some bug I picked up. Probably don't need the appointment now anyway!" She eyeballed the room for a reasonable distraction, then excused herself, claiming someone had called her name.

Chris offered Sam a weary smile and kissed her cheek. "I imagine you've seen me more than you bargained for lately."

She linked her arm in his and marched toward the patio. "Come on. Let's get a drink."

A DJ setup inhabited the far corner of the smoky living room, blasting the latest chart-topping hits. The house teemed with the Hollywood elite, from actors, musicians, and writers to popular sports figures, powerful executives, and glad-handing politicians. Entourages on their heels, they milled about the place, congregating into various micro-groups. They bragged over their newest successes and upcoming releases, complained about being passed over for coveted roles, and gossiped about last month's Grammy and Oscar winners. As the pumping beat of 69 Boyz's "Tootsee Roll" ended, the DJ followed artfully with TLC's "Creep."

On their way to the patio, Chris spotted Ginny Stevens out of the corner of his eye. She stood amongst a small group of industry heavy hitters and actors whose careers had steadily declined over the previous decade. It surprised him she had come. He had heard her career nosedived after her breakup with Jordan so long ago. The last thing he had seen her in was a laundry soap commercial. With parted lips and an arch of her brows, she waved his way and motioned him over. He pretended not to notice.

They found Ethan, Marci, and Elliot sitting on cushioned lounge chairs organized into a circle around a screened fire pit. The small group huddled together to the exclusion of the crowd trampling the home and grounds of the Hollywood Hills property.

"I'm trying to avoid the secondhand 'smoke as much as possible," Marci explained, sitting forward and extending her cheek into Chris' kiss before he took his seat.

Sam held her drink in one hand while she straightened and smoothed out the smock of her white linen pantsuit with the other. "I'm thrilled you showed up at all, to be honest. I guess this is baby Lawrence's first industry shindig, huh?"

She patted her belly. "It is. But her momma and daddy can't stay out too late."

Elliot laced his fingers across his abdomen and grinned. "We're a couple of old married folks now."

Marci play-slapped his shoulder.

Sam chuckled knowingly. "Not like you were ever much of a partier."

He closed his eyes, projecting complete relaxation. "I left that to the rest of the lot."

Chris straddled his chaise and rested his elbows on his thighs. "Faith and Todd and I had enough for all of us. I think I'm still hungover from those days."

When Julie finally joined them on the patio forty-five minutes later, Samantha nodded to the server headed their way. He carried a tray of six fluted glasses, three bottles of special edition Dom Perignon, and a bottle of sparkling apple cider. When he had popped the tops, poured the bubbly libations, and distributed them to the private party, he retreated to the house. The sound of Tom Petty's "You Don't Know How it Feels" filled the air via hidden landscape speakers.

Samantha sat forward and held her glass aloft. "Tonight, we celebrate. It's been a hell of a year so far, but many positive things have happened or are on the brink of happening. After all we've come through, it's important to remember the good things, the hopeful things, the things to come. As you know, my very handsome husband-to-be finished his residency last week.

He'll join his uncle in private practice June first."

The group toasted and congratulated Ethan on his accomplishment.

"Plastics would have been a more lucrative career path than general practice, mate," Elliot ribbed him. "You could have distributed your business cards to tonight's guest list!"

Ethan raised his glass with a sideways nod and chuckled at the barb.

"And then there's Elliot and Marci," Samantha continued. "Just a few months from now, you'll be perfecting the art of diaper changes and 3 AM feedings."

They laughed and toasted the couple.

"And Julie, I hear you just re-upped with Dharvey," Samantha said, clinking her glass against Julie's. "We love you...and we hate you, of course, because you're a constant reminder of what we don't look like."

Chris tugged Julie's arm for her to sit closer, then encircled her waist with his arm as the others congratulated her with whoops and whistles.

Lastly, Samantha turned to Chris and gave him a wistful smile. "And then there's Chris. The man of the hour. Your tour's starting in a few weeks, you have a beautiful wife, and..." She stopped momentarily, tilted her head upward and blinked several times before continuing. "You have an honor I know your family admires. You're a hero to at least two people who couldn't be with us tonight. And because I've known you as long as I have, you'll overlook any unintended condescension when I say I'm proud of how you've grown. Here's to a long and successful solo career."

"Hear, hear!" the others echoed as they toasted a final time.

Julie smiled and touched her husband's flute to hers, then kissed him as their friends cheered. She could not wait to get to her appointment. It infuriated her that Gloria's associate could not fit her in any sooner.

She drained her glass with a mighty gulp, then set the empty vessel on a side table and grabbed the scotch on the rocks she had temporarily abandoned to participate in Sam's ridiculous recap of everyone's happy news. She spurned the unwelcome tenant in her womb, unconcerned with any ill effects the alcohol might have on the fetus. *Drink up*, she thought. *Eviction day's coming, and you've been served.*

"So what about you, Sam?" Marci asked. "Have you and Ethan discussed having kids?"

"We're going to leave the reproduction to you and Julie." Samantha laughed, cutting eyes at Chris. "How about it? Any pitter-pattering of little feet in your future?"

Chris chuckled as Julie excused herself once more to freshen her drink and make the conversational rounds with other guests. "I'm thinking soon. Julie's committed to Dharvey for now, but yeah...I'm ready. I'd love to."

"You always loved practicing," Elliot added good-naturedly.

A sense of calm settled upon the group as they chatted, the party in full swing inside and all around them. The stars sparkled with a brilliance one could not observe from the gritty LA streets. From their vantage point above the city, the air felt fresher somehow. Cleaner.

Samantha rose intermittently to fulfill her hostess duties but returned as soon as she could break away. While making the rounds to smile and exchange quick "it's good to see yous," "do you really have to gos," or "I just talked to so-and-so the other day ands," she stole glimpses of her house, relieved it remained reasonably intact. For the most part, her guests contented themselves with each other and did not seem to notice her lack of participation.

On nights like these, she found herself appreciating Ethan more than ever. An upper-class gentleman from a prominent New England family, he surely struggled with the company she had to keep. Vagabonds-turned-millionaires, seedy perverts who considered their casting couches little more than carnival rides for desperate unknowns, emotionally stunted musical geniuses who inevitably mismanaged megastardom. The entertainment business had become little more than a hodgepodge of spoon-fed egos dressed up like nouveau-riche hooligans off to visit the Queen. Maybe it had always been that way to some degree. In any case, Ethan bore it like a champ.

If she were honest, she would admit she had considered him little more than eye candy when they first saw each other four years ago during the Will Rogers Memorial Tournament—tall, athletic, with a confident air she remembered possessing in spades in her mid-twenties. They had casually flirted throughout the tournament as they passed each other getting a drink or mingling in separate groups. At the end of the match, she had eyeballed the crowd trying to locate him, curious whether he would introduce himself. When she did not find him, she figured she had her answer. Hours later at a what turned out to be a mutual friend's intimate dinner party, she saw him again. It took him three weeks to call her—two more until they moved in together.

"I see Megan made it," Elliot observed sometime close to midnight. "She's looking well."

"She's doing great," Samantha agreed as she finished her fifth martini of the evening. "It's fantastic to have her."

He cut eyes at her. "Quite the coupe."

"Indeed." Samantha laughed, leaned forward, and touched her glass to his.

"We should have toasted you. You've pulled off your fair share of those this year."

She smirked and gave him a mischievous eyebrow flash.

"So what's this meeting you have us all going to?" Chris asked, picking up on their verbal shorthand. "I take it we've all discussed it with you by now."

Samantha nodded, then leaned back in her chair and stretched luxuriously. "Oh, bother the meeting. Don't let's discuss that tonight. It's been such a wonderful evening. I just want to drink and laugh and pray my house is still standing after everyone leaves."

Ethan retired just before 1 AM. He kissed Samantha and bid their friends good night.

She turned her head to see if the crowd had thinned at all, but the house looked packed. She took Ethan's hand in hers and smiled. "Sorry about the noise. Unavoidable."

He shook his head and gazed into his fiancé's eyes. "Marry me."

She grinned at their familiar exchange. "Name the day."

"November 18th."

In all the time they had danced this conversational tango, Ethan had never countered with an actual date. They had discussed it off and on since he had proposed last Christmas, but events surrounding them always seemed to take precedence over their personal lives.

Her eyes widened. She blinked several times. "That was sudden."

He kissed her hand, then turned to their friends. "And you're all invited," he added before heading off to bed.

They exchanged stunned smiles as he ambled toward the house.

"Was he serious?" Marci asked.

"I think he was," Samantha told her, grinning as she looked over her shoulder and watched his retreating figure. She turned back around, the last vestige of her business demeanor gone. "Huh. Does anyone know a good wedding planner?"

***

Over the last couple weeks, Derek had come home later and later. Cheryl understood and supported his commitment to his band, but a mother's intuition was seldom wrong.

She checked the bedside clock. He had promised to return before curfew, but eleven o'clock had come and gone a half hour ago. She had not received so much as a call to let her know he was safe. In fifteen minutes, she would have to embarrass him by trying his cell phone, which he might very well lose if this pattern continued.

Ben slumbered beside her, unaware his oldest son had pushed the envelope again. Not wanting to wake him, she rose, threw on her robe, and headed downstairs to wait. No use having them both gang up on him the moment he returned. Better she handle it herself—and then let Ben deal with it in the morning as well.

As she descended the staircase, she heard voices downstairs and noticed lights on in the living room. Maybe Derek had returned already. Maybe he had slipped in without her hearing the door chime.

"Hi, Mom," Kyle greeted around a mouthful of grapes.

"Hello, son." Cheryl looked first at him and then their new house guest. "What are you doing up?"

"I was just talking to Aunt Farin."

"Oh?" She sat beside him. "And what were you two talking about at such an hour, and on a school night?"

Kyle finished his snack and set his bowl on the coffee table, wiped his hands with his napkin, then tossed the napkin into the bowl. "She was explaining the way life works."

Cheryl's eyes widened as she turned expectantly toward Farin. The woman looked worn and in need of rest. Why her former sister-in-law had decided to stay up and discuss philosophy with her son escaped her. This was no way to repay them for their hospitality.

"Actually," Farin corrected, leering playfully at Kyle, "we were discussing Jordan."

"Is that so?" She leaned back and crossed her legs.

"Yeah, Mom. Aunt Farin was telling me I shouldn't keeping saying Uncle Jordan's coming back."

"Pretty deep conversation before bed, don't you think?" Her tone grew icy as her left eyebrow rose in disapproval.

Farin flattened her lips, her expression tinged with remorse. "I didn't mean to overstep. He asked if I'd seen Jordan while I was away, and when he'd be coming home."

Kyle bobbed his head. "And Aunt Farin said Uncle Jordan's in Heaven."

Farin nodded warmly. "That's right."

He turned to his mother. "I thought Aunt Farin had gone to Heaven, too. But that's where I got it wrong. Aunt Farin didn't go to Heaven. She went to North Carolina."

Cheryl chuckled at the simplicity of the explanation. "Aye. She's right there."

"I guess I mixed it up because I've never been to Heaven, so I don't know what it's like."

Cheryl frowned at her youngest. "You've never been to North Carolina, either."

"But I *have* heard of the University of North Carolina. They have an awesome physics and astronomy department!"

"I was pretty close to the University of North Carolina," Farin told him.

"Cool! Did you ever visit the campus?"

She shook her head. "No, honey. I never made it there."

When Cheryl heard the garage door creak open, she checked the time. "Kyle, it's late, darling. You need to get some sleep. You have testing this week, if memory serves."

Disappointed, Kyle stood and hugged his mother. "Love you."

She kissed his neck and tousled his hair. "Sleep well."

To Farin's surprise, he hugged her, too. "Love you, Aunt Farin. I'm glad you didn't go to Heaven. And I'm real glad you're here."

"I love you too, Kyle," she said, a catch in her throat. "There's nowhere I'd rather be."

Cheryl watched Farin look away and blink several times as Kyle headed upstairs, then heard the back door open and close. One down, one to go.

She could tell by the look on Derek's face he knew his crime. He walked into the living room on his way to the staircase, but stopped when he saw his mother and aunt seated on the sectional. She extended her open hand. "Keys."

"Aw, Mom. Not the car, please?"

"Another word and I'll have your phone as well."

Derek deflated as he dropped his keyring into her hand.

"Now come here and say goodnight to your aunt."

He sulked over and hugged Farin halfheartedly. "Hey."

Farin shook her head. "I still can't get over how much you've grown. Look at you. You're a man now."

Derek straightened a bit at the adoration.

She smiled. "And I hear your band's pretty good."

"You should come listen to us," Derek told her. Then nonchalantly, "You know, if you want."

"I'd love to. And I'd like to meet Summer. Is she a nice girl?"

His face grew warm. "She's cool."

Cheryl rose from the sofa and put her hand on Derek's shoulder, then spun him around and pointed him toward the staircase. "You can tell her all about Summer and your upcoming gig after school tomorrow. You'll have plenty of time over the next week."

His shoulders slumped as his mother's words registered, but further protest would cost him more time. Dejected, he climbed the stairs as if walking to his doom.

Cheryl stifled a laugh and looked at Farin. She whispered conspiratorially, "You know, you just can't stay mad at them forever. That's why you have to punish them right away."

Farin smiled, grateful for any crumb of inclusion. She wished she could convince herself her sister-in-law's opinion of her did not matter. As she sat back down on the sofa, Cheryl asked if she wanted some tea. She declined.

"You look tired. Maybe you should get some sleep."

"I guess I'm not used to the time difference yet."

Cheryl studied her features. "You sure that's all it is?"

She took a deep breath, then exhaled heavily as she tucked her feet beneath her on the sofa. "Probably not."

"Ben told me he's taking you to visit Jorie's grave tomorrow."

"Is that all he told you?" Farin asked shyly, unsure how much she needed to explain.

Cheryl's brow furrowed. "I'm not sure I understand."

"I hate to keep you up. I'm sorry."

"It's okay. If you need to talk, I'll listen."

For everyone else, three long years had passed since the incidents that hobbled their family. To Farin, it was fresh. She owned the lion's share of the blame for the destruction they had endured. One of the chief casualties sat before her—for if Ben was the head of the Grant clan, surely Cheryl was its heart.

Farin tilted her head. "All right, let's start here. I owe you an apology. It goes beyond the fact I've been inserted back into your home, obviously against your will. But you're too kind and too good a wife and mother to admit it."

Cheryl dipped her head and stared at her nails.

"Most the time you knew me, my behavior was unforgivable. I've got no right to ask your forgiveness or think for one minute you have any reason to believe me when I say I've changed."

"This might be a conversation to have after you're rested."

"You're probably right, but since I'm living under your roof, I'd like us to clear the air."

Without further protest, Cheryl repositioned herself on the couch and gestured for Farin to continue.

"Even though I lost everything except my life, I had no one but myself to blame. But you lost someone through no fault of your own—or his. So do I need to talk? Yes, I do. I need to say the things that need to be said to the people who deserve to hear them. That's why I asked Ben to take me to the cemetery tomorrow. I need to ask Jordan's forgiveness. It's probably more for me than it is him, but I need to do it just the same."

Cheryl rose and gathered the folds of her robe to her. "Perhaps you were right before. Eleven forty-five on a Monday evening is no time to mend broken fences. But thank you. If I've been harsh or misjudged, I'm sorry. This has to be painful for you. Are you certain you're ready to go to the cemetery?"

Farin paused, then nodded. "It doesn't matter now. As a condition to signing with Samantha's label, I told her I wanted to see Ross Alexander. He'll be there tomorrow as well. He's meeting us at the cemetery."

Cheryl cocked her head. "Seems a rather odd place for such a meeting, doesn't it?"

"Oh no," Farin told her. "It's perfect."

***

Each day that passed without word from Moreau brought Jameson Lockhardt to the brink of losing what little patience he had left. He wanted to call the man, complain the investigators found no bodies in the rubble that was once Jordan Grant's Malibu beach house. No body meant Farin Grant was still alive out there somewhere. It also meant that, for the first time in their long association, Moreau had failed to deliver.

It surprised Jameson that such a thorough and reliable professional had not called with plans to rectify the matter, if for no other reason than having received a king's ransom for the successful, complete extermination of the last known member of Kelley O'Conner's ill-fated family.

Three weeks ago, Moreau had told Jameson never to contact him again on the threat of his life. Given the failed turn of events, Jameson decided their deal had been rendered invalid. Besides, as long as Farin lived, his life was threatened anyway.

He would call tomorrow and ready himself for Moreau's response. He knew exactly what precautions to take.

CHAPTER 5

"I CALLED AHEAD," BEN TOLD Farin as they turned onto the property. "I told them the family was visiting today and needed some privacy. They'll keep it locked up while we're here." He acknowledged the security guard with a nod as he drove through the entrance. The gates closed behind them.

Farin crouched in the back seat, her heart thumping inside her chest. The strong reaction bothered her. It made her feel weak. She could not afford weak. Not now. "If you don't mind, I'd like to talk to him alone. Well, both of them."

"No problem, but I'm staying close by. I don't trust him."

Ross Alexander would not arrive for another ten minutes or so. Farin had requested they get to the cemetery early. She needed time to acclimate to her surroundings. More importantly, she needed a moment with her husband.

Ben drove up to and pointed out the plot, dropped Farin off, then drove his Land Rover back to the entrance and parked near the front gate. Farin waved, indicating she could still see him. He gave her a thumbs up.

She double-checked her surroundings despite the cemetery's assurances no one milled around the vicinity—well-tended grounds, mostly green with an occasional patch of yellowed grass. Nothing like the lush, rich landscaping of the Santa Barbara cemetery where her parents rested. But such things probably mattered little in the end. Certainly, the visual impression was more for visitors than those who occupied its space. Nonetheless, it saddened her as she inched forward and whispered a feeble, "Hi."

For the second time in days, she stared at a stone marker that bore her name beside those of the people she loved. This time, in proximity to her late husband. This time, as Farin Grant.

Seeing Jordan's name engraved in granite tested the fault lines of her newly adopted tough exterior. It felt as if decades had passed since she had seen him—since she had heard his sweet voice. Conversely, it seemed only moments ago he had stood in Bobby Lockhardt's living room, trading his life for hers.

She sat down at the foot of the grave. "I, uh...I got here as soon as I could. Ben's here. He brought me."

Memories streamed through her mind like a ghost train. She plucked several blades of grass and glanced up at the sky, unsure where to start.

The day was overcast, warm, and humid. Billowy white clouds contrasted the azure sky, playing peek-a-boo with the late morning sun as intermittent shadows fell across their grave. A steady breeze blew the ends of her wig, periodically whipping synthetic tendrils into her lip gloss. All in all, a perfect day for sailing.

Over breakfast, Ben had proposed an afternoon excursion when the boys returned from school. Even now, Cheryl was home preparing the picnic dinner they would share onboard the *Lyric*. Jordan would have loved a day like this. How unfair he could not join them.

She cleared her throat and spoke awkwardly. "I'm sure you already know this, but I'll tell you anyway. Well, first, an update. Since we died, Jordan, you wouldn't believe how many other people have died, too. Zappa's gone—prostate cancer, you know. Seems everybody had cancer: Roger Miller, Dizzy, Eddie Kendricks. He and Mel Franklin are both gone now. I remember you mentioning after Ruff's overdose how much you loved the Temptations. But Mel didn't have cancer. Oh—and Mick Ronson had liver cancer."

Farin figured she sounded crazy running off a list of the musically departed, but it took the edge off, as if doing so might break the ice. She maneuvered herself around to lie belly down and propped her head up on her elbows. "Nilsson's gone. Donald Pleasence—we lost him back in February. And Kurt Cobain committed suici—" She winced at the thought. The details hit too close to home. "I was so sad when Marci told me. He was so young."

She began to weep.

"I did everything wrong, and I'm sorry. But I survived and I'm going to make it right. For everyone—for you, Jordan, Ben, my mom and dad..."

At last, she regained her composure and rose to her feet. "Please forgive me for hurting you. Thank you for all the love and kindness you gave me, even though I didn't deserve much of it. I love you. I always will."

She leaned down and kissed the top of the grave, then stepped back. The shadow from the clouds receded. The stone drank in bright sunlight.

Ben's car door opened and shut. Using her hand to shield her eyes from the sun's glare, she squinted in his direction. He stood next to his vehicle, signaling the guard to open the gates.

A gray sedan had arrived. Farin watched the vehicle pull in and stop. Ben bent down to address the driver. He pointed in her direction as the cemetery gates closed once more.

Today, the chain reaction would begin.

She regarded the figure of Ross Alexander as he walked her way, having abandoned his vehicle near Ben's—probably at Ben's request. He was still an attractive man. Older, yes. A little worse for the wear, but he had aged well. Farin decided this fact disappointed her.

Samantha had insisted they had Ross to thank for her freedom, that he had given Chris and Marci information that had facilitated her rescue. Looking at the smooth-skinned, perfectly appointed gentleman who approached, Farin doubted he had lost sleep over the circumstances that brought them here today.

When he reached the gravesite, he extended his hand. "Hello, Farin." She might have detected a hint of remorse in his voice, but resented the lack of worry lines on his tan face. He held his hand out for several seconds, but she rejected his greeting.

She folded her arms across her chest and jutted her chin toward the granite monument to her right. "We always did make a pretty couple, Jordan and I. Dontcha think?"

He lowered his head and stared at the ground.

"Who's sleeping with my husband here, huh? Who did my parents adopt back in Santa Barbara? Who took my place?"

Head still bowed, Ross regarded his attire. He had no good reason for having put on a suit today. This was no business meeting. At least in less formal attire there would be no tie around his neck, choking him like a hangman's noose.

"*Well*? Who needed to be silenced that day besides me? Besides poor Charles? I mean, I figure Jameson knew Charles was the one who drove me from Bobby's the night he raped me. He had to go, right? Leave no witness behind? But who else?"

Ross cleared his throat as if to speak, then stopped and removed his jacket. He draped it over his left arm and faced her. "I'll listen as long as you want to vent. I imagine you deserve at least that much."

She scoffed. "That's all you got?"

"It's your meeting, dear. You called it, remember? I didn't come here with an agenda."

"Well *I* did, and I think we both know what it is."

Ross nodded. He knew all too well. "Did you get the package I sent you?"

"It was a lot lighter than I remembered it."

He wrinkled his forehead. "I don't think I follow."

"The one I had with me was bulkier. What? Did you think Childs erased my memory with all that crap he pumped into my system? Or when he ripped out my insides?"

He stood silent and accepted the punishment on behalf of all those who had hurt her.

"Jordan and I were planning to have more children," she spat, a sorrowful break in her voice. "You and the old man took everyone I ever loved, everything I ever had, from me. And you ask me about a *package*?"

He glanced down and to his left. "You must not have opened it."

"Why? Is it rigged? One last-ditch effort to finish me off?"

"I think you know that's not true."

"Then what are you talking about?"

"There were two larger envelopes. You had one on you when you were taken. It was meant for the press conference. The other you'd left with housekeeping."

A chill ran the length of her spine.

"If those are the packages you're referring to, I'm afraid they were destroyed."

She leveled an accusing stare at him. "By who?"

He plunged his right hand into his trouser pocket and lowered his eyes.

Farin clenched her jaw and looked away. She caught a glimpse of Ben in the distance, leaning against his car, watching for any sign of danger.

"I apologize for my part in this," Ross said. "I'm doing everything I can to put things in order."

"And by 'putting things in order,' of course, you mean destroying all the evidence against Jameson. Against Bobby."

"You know he was in a psychotic state that day, Farin."

"I know he raped me two weeks before he blew my husband's head off."

"He has no memory of killing Jordan. Or about…about what he did to you that night."

Farin's eyes narrowed. "How convenient for him. I remember every second."

"And you haven't opened the package? Did you bring it with you?"

"Why? What's in it?"

"A down payment on your future." He shifted his stance. His legs had begun to ache.

"You're not going to buy me off, Ross. Is that what's going on here?"

"What's going on here is when I sent you that package, I signed my own death warrant. Now, you can do what you want. Open it or don't. I understand your bitterness. I'm a member of the same club, in case Sam didn't tell you. Jameson had my wife killed three months ago."

Farin stood stunned as Ross relayed the events that had occurred in February. No one had told her. She checked her feelings as the pieces fell into place. In the end, she felt no pity for the man before her. He had drawn the map to this destination with the blood of her family, even if by Jameson's command. His wife's death made Farin feel sorry for no one but Josephine Alexander.

"I do have a couple of things, though." He fished through his trousers pocket.

Farin saw Ben stand and lift his chin, as if preparing to head over. She shook her head.

Ross' skin felt warm and soft as he set the items in her hand. When she looked down, she saw two items. The first was her wedding ring. The second was a key with a long leather string threaded through its hole and attached like a necklace.

"These were on you when you arrived in Raleigh. Jameson gave them to me to destroy along with the two packages you'd put together. I don't know why I didn't get rid of them. The key was around your neck instead of in your purse. It seemed significant. Look here." He turned the key over in Farin's hand. "The initials 'KBBT' are etched on the back here. Maybe that means something to you. I hope I'm right. I hope it helps."

Farin's stomach flipped as she slipped the ring on. The gold and diamond jewelry felt awkward yet familiar on her finger. The fused engagement and wedding bands fit loosely, a reminder of her struggle to regain the weight she had lost.

Despite her resolve to maintain her anger at Jameson's right-hand man, a feeling came over her she had not anticipated. It felt as if she had regained a piece of herself, as if she might one day be whole again.

She beheld the key. For the first time since Ross' arrival, Farin entertained the possibility his promised assistance might prove genuine. And if the lock that fit this key was still intact and still in place, things had just taken a turn for the better. She had not felt this hopeful since her memories returned.

In fact, only one thing could make her feel better.

"In that case, I guess we're done here," she said. "I have only one more question, and you're the only one who can answer it."

Ross squared his shoulders and inhaled deeply through his nose as if bracing for impact, as if he knew the question before she asked.

She drew closer and searched his eyes, wondering whether he would tell her the truth. Wondering if he could remember what it felt like to do the right thing. She slapped him squarely across the face, then stabbed her finger into his chest and demanded through a clenched jaw, "Tell me, Ross. Where is Jordan right now?"

***

When unsavory rumors about their clandestine meetings began circulating throughout the department, Alicia Alvarez and William Bridgeman decided the time had come for a change of venue. Penny Bridgeman would never believe her husband would cheat on her, but he and Alicia agreed keeping things above board could not hurt. In the end, they decided to meet at his house. This thrilled Penny and the Bridgeman progeny, for not only would their patriarch spend more time at home, they would also have more regular visits with Aunt Alicia, as they now called her.

About the same time, their investigation slammed headfirst into a brick wall.

"What we have here is a whole lot of nothing," Bridgeman complained late Wednesday evening as he and Alvarez sifted through their meager files. "We know the limo was rigged. We know an accelerant was used."

"And we know money had to have changed hands," Alvarez reminded him. "That's something. A professional job like that, to kill one of the biggest superstars of the time? Big money."

He stared at the Forensic Services Bureau's report, which outlined the results of the evidence he had collected from the limousine carcass back in February.

"You're not gonna find anything there you haven't seen before, Billy." Doubting anything new would come of it, she picked up and scanned the photographs Bridgeman had taken of the vehicle.

Penny entered the den with a pot of fresh coffee. She sat it down on an end table and asked how things were going. When her husband did not answer, she looked at Alicia and raised her eyebrows. Alicia shook her head and rolled her eyes. Penny nearly laughed out loud, instantly understanding the nonverbal shorthand. She knew how her husband got when involved in a case. Better not to interrupt. She motioned to the coffee service, winked at Alicia, then left them to their work.

When he finished reviewing the report, Bridgeman turned his attention to the copies he had made of the official Grant files. "If I didn't know better, I'd think this was the worst investigation ever conducted. Makes it look like the Coral Gables scene was half-processed and the limo was almost completely ignored."

Alicia dropped the stack of photos on the desk and leaned back. She yawned and stretched. "I gotta go soon. It's almost midnight. I'm beat."

"Either someone didn't do their job—"

"Hey!"

He frowned and glanced her way. "Not you, Al." Frustrated, he shoved the files away and slumped back into his chair. "Between the murder and the limo bombing, we have a total of 15 reports, nearly half of which are related to the three decedents' autopsies. Nothing from Fire Rescue? We've got little by way of physical evidence, a shockingly limited number of crime scene photos, and no interviews except the family and a handful of neighbors or passersby. It's like half the file is missing. How could the captain sign off on this?"

"Stark had me buried in paperwork after the Chris Grant interview, so I'm not much help. But I distinctly remember Fire Rescue investigating the limo. It's protocol. Since there were bodies, our arson investigators should have been involved. We'll just have to try to reconstruct what we can and go from there."

"Easier said than done. Every report under Metro's umbrella that has anything to do with either case has been reclassified. And now your buddy's too spooked to help us."

"Can you blame him? Even the physical files have either been removed or relocated. He can't find anything in the hard file—including his own reports and the evidence you sent him. I have a feeling whatever this is might be bigger than Stark."

Bridgeman twisted his lips to one side, bit his cheek, and snatched up the folder of copies he had assembled. "Yeah," he grumbled. "Me too."

"You'd said you were gonna reach out to someone. What was that all about?"

He shook his head. "Doesn't matter. The guy never returned my call which, honestly, is as strange as the rest of this mess."

"We need to follow the money. Someone was paying Stark. When we find out who, we find out why. So, question: who did Farin Grant know with a lot of cash? Answer: basically everyone."

Bridgeman poured them each some coffee. He added cream for Alvarez, then sat both mugs down at the desk and grinned. "Your boyfriend's convinced Lockhardt's behind all three deaths. He had the means to pay off Stark and everyone else."

Alvarez narrowed her eyes at him. She blew on the hot liquid before taking a sip. "He's not my boyfriend, and I think he's wrong."

Bridgeman cocked his head. "You sure about that?"

"Lockhardt's got no motive. The Grants buttered LSI's bread. Nuh-uh. If Lockhardt did it, he was attempting financial suicide. All you have to do is pick up a paper and read about it. The company's on its last leg."

Bridgeman considered the assessment. "I can't argue your logic, Al. But who else—" He recognized the look on her face and shook his head. "Don't start that again. Chris Grant had an alibi."

"He also had the money to pay someone to do his dirty work for him. I'm telling you, Billy. The affair between Chris and Farin Grant was well documented. She lived with him while her husband was filing for divorce!"

He listened patiently as he did every time she pushed her theory.

"Then, the happy couple reunite. Chris gets mad, offs his brother, makes a last plea for Farin's heart, then takes her out when she won't come back to him. He has motive. He has means. I agreed for a while he couldn't be our guy but, I'm telling you, he's the only one who makes sense. Plus, I know firsthand he has a temper."

Bridgeman shook his head. "The guy's got no priors, no complaints against him…nothing. And a car bomb to avenge a broken heart? Doesn't sound much like a crime of passion to me. Not to mention the savvy required to pull off a cover-up. That's big money, big secrets, not some jilted lover. What about the son? Doesn't it strike you as odd the murder happened at the kid's place and he wasn't even there?"

It was the same merry-go-round discussion they had had for weeks.

When William and Penny finally walked Alicia to the door that night, the detectives agreed to suspend future meetings until they had a new lead. Their investigation might have triggered some interest. Best to lay low for a while.

William watched Alvarez head down the walkway to her car. He lifted his chin and called after her, "I never asked if you were excited about the news."

She turned around. "What news?"

"Didn't he tell you?"

"*Who*?" Her Cuban accent thickened with exhaustion as she raised her hands.

Bridgeman could not wipe the smile from his face. "Macy."

She perched her hands on her hips. "Not tonight, Billy. I don't have the energy to kick your butt right now."

"So he didn't tell you?"

"Tell me what?"

"The *Trib* canned him. He's transferring back to Miami."

***

Ben understood the embarrassment that accompanied having to rely on a third party for a ride to band practice. Having your parents fill that role would heap humiliation upon humiliation, so when Derek told him he had asked Sawyer Jacobs to play chauffeur for the week, Ben used it as an opportunity to have a chat with the yet-unnamed-band's unofficial manager.

The periodic visits required extra caution. No matter how impressive Sawyer's musical resume was, Ben did not know him well enough to gauge his ability to keep the presence of his formerly deceased ex-sister-in-law a secret should it prove necessary. Therefore, Ben suggested Farin lay low during Sawyer's pickups and drop-offs.

As the week progressed, Ben grew comfortable having him around. Age difference notwithstanding, they shared a lot of common ground. Thursday afternoon, he took advantage of the fact Derek was running late and invited Sawyer back to his studio. The young man jumped at the chance.

Ben offered Sawyer a seat at the board, but he opted to stand. He wandered about the studio, admiring the various mics and instruments before finally making his way back to the control room and sitting in one of the plush leather console chairs.

"Man," he said with an envious chuckle. "What I wouldn't do to live in your studio."

Ben offered a humble grin as he leaned back, crossed his legs, and laced his fingers behind his head. "She'll do, I suppose."

He leaned back casually, crossed his legs, and rested his arm across the console. "You an analog or digital man?"

"I prefer the warmer sounds of analog, but I can see the advantages of digital." He paused and grinned. "Oh, who am I kidding? Death to Pro Tools!"

"Old school." Sawyer chuckled. "I hear ya. I guess the bluesman in me likes the analog sound, but the producer in me likes to experiment."

"Who're your influences?"

The question made Sawyer spring to life. "Dude, where do I start?" He ticked off the names on his fingers. "Son House, Blind Lemon, Patton...all the way to Dylan and Clapton. Too many to count. I busked around the UK a couple of years before moving to Miami. Big Blues following in England, Germany, the Netherlands—but you know that."

Ben nodded. "I've heard you're good. Very good. I'd wager you weren't sleeping in the doss-house while you were there."

Sawyer chuckled again. "I did okay. Made enough to put myself through school."

"Not bad. U of M has a fine program. What made you want to stop performing?"

Sawyer blew air through his lips. "Performing's okay. I sit in from time to time when I'm asked, but I wanted something more at the end of the day than a group of chicks waiting back stage. I wanna get my hands dirty—create something that lasts. I wanna work with guys who're better than me. Help develop their styles and maybe find some success, you know?"

Ben flattened his lips into a frown and nodded. "I sure do."

"That's what I like about Derek and his guys. They're more talented than they realize. They just need some direction. A little discipline. They could be really good."

He smirked. "They ever decide on a name?"

Sawyer grinned and shook his head, then adopted a businesslike affect. "They'll find their name once they find their sound. They're not sure who they are yet. You've got Brian and Derek wanting straight up rock-and-roll. But then you've got Laroche with that Haitian rhythm. That dude can *play*. His sound could really influence their direction."

Ben listened intently, impressed that Sawyer had given the matter so much thought.

"And of course Peter's basically in Switzerland. He'll go with anything Derek wants to do. Best buds syndrome, you know? So, I see one of two things happening. Either Derek and Brian learn to work with Levoy and let him help define their style, or Levoy bounces to form his own band or join one that'll appreciate what he's got to offer."

Derek had slipped in some time during their discussion. He sat quietly and absorbed the conversation, eventually interrupting to remind his ride they were already late for practice.

Sawyer checked his watch and made a face. "Yeah, we'd better hit it." He stood and gave Ben's hand a hearty shake. "Thanks for letting me check out the studio."

Ben walked them to the door. "You'll have to come by again sometime. We'll lay down some tracks."

"You'll rue the day you said that, my man." He laughed as he opened the door and squinted against the brightness of the day. He slid on his Wayfarers and stepped outside.

All at once, a woman emerged from the pool. She lifted herself gracefully out of the water and turned her body in one fluid motion to sit on the edge, using both hands to wipe the water from her face. When she noticed the men, she froze in place, her eyes fixed on the stranger.

Sawyer's initial admiration of the hottie in the black one-piece immediately transformed into stunned disbelief.

Ben looked first at Derek, who stood open-mouth before him, and then Sawyer, who stood still and silent. Farin did not move. She looked at Ben with pleading eyes, as if wishing she could reverse the last thirty seconds.

"Wha—? Wh—" Sawyer attempted, but the sound died in his throat.

Ben nudged his son. "I think you'd better call the guys and cancel for the day."

***

Miles Macy had participated in scavenger hunts before, but never with such high stakes.

The e-mail had unnerved him. He could not know for sure if it was real or a trick, but his intuition had told him to pay attention. So when the moving company had arrived to pick up his belongings and head for Miami, Macy boarded a plane for Santa Barbara.

An attempt to ascertain the sender's identity had netted him zilch.

He had printed two copies of the e-mail, which he then stored in his protected electronic files. The first copy he kept as reference. The second he used to scribble notes. In the last three days, he had reread the mysterious riddle so many times, he had nearly memorized it.

> *A fuller picture won't be drawn*
> *You'll start with those beneath the lawn*
> *A fund for trade, determined will*
> *Across the pond—Himself? Or killed?*

The motivation, his own life
He sacrificed his son and wife
And what is it about a name
A substitute; the price of fame

Too soon to go, too important to fail
Despite the crime, no time in jail
A silenced victim gone no more
Has someone still worth dying for

Without your help she may be lost
That's why you've left your former boss
So start today with what you know
Time's running out; you've got to go

To point you in the right direction
Review the entertainment section
Lest history repeat itself
Don't leave these hints upon the shelf:

Sarah Wellingham
The signing party
Oh what a night (1967)
The Firm
Jade Larken Trongly
Jordan Grant
Nancy Chambers
Hopeful Heart, Fayetteville, NC

The inclusion of Jordan's name had convinced Miles to take a closer look. He had grown even more intrigued when he reviewed his past notes and recalled Farin had both rented a car and checked into a Key Biscayne hotel using the name "Shae Wellingham" just before her death.

"Can I help you, sir?" The cheery teen behind the tall counter could not have been a day over sixteen. Bright, blonde, blue eyes, braces. Perky enough to have never known a broken heart. Probably still waiting for a first date.

Miles presented his card. "I'm with the *Chicago Tribune*. I've got an appointment with a Mr. Barker this afternoon."

The teen asked him to sign in, then excused herself as she sought out a more senior representative. It was probably a Teacher's Assistant period. His request required an actual staff member to verify.

When she returned, an older woman accompanied her—drab, silver hair, aging skin, no bounce to her step. They made a comical pair.

"Mr. Barker's running late," the woman informed Miles. "He's asked if you'd mind waiting a few minutes. The last bell will ring soon."

Miles thanked them and stepped into the hallway. On his way in, he had noticed a large glass cabinet and trophy display. He had heard Kathy Ireland had attended San Marcos High and that the school had produced many notable alumni from Olympian Terry Schroeder, golfers Sam Randolph and Steve Pate, and composer Bruce Babcock, to a host of actors.

Who knew Bobby Lockhardt had spent so many years on the West Coast?

The e-mail had told him to start "with what you know." Aside from the fact Jordan and Farin Grant were dead, he knew little. The reference to "across the pond" was a no-brainer—obviously a UK reference. The Grants hailed from England, as did Lockhardt, so it seemed reasonable to start there. In fact, he had nearly booked a flight to London instead of Santa Barbara.

A gruff voice belonging to a gruff man approached from behind him. "Sorry to keep you waiting." He eyeballed Miles suspiciously, clearly unimpressed by his credentials. "You'll pardon the rush, Mr. Macy. We're finalizing the yearbook. I don't have a lot of time for chitchat. You understand—deadlines and all."

Macy followed Barker down a series of corridors bustling with activity. The man's gait was heavy and his disposition decidedly impatient. He wore gray corduroy pants, a short sleeve dress shirt, and a colorless vest that seemed more an attempt to conceal his rotund middle than anything else. His full beard and mustache had more salt than pepper to it. His thick hair had grown past his ears and collar. He looked disheveled, as if someone had removed him from their luggage after a two week vacation and had no access to an iron.

Students congregated in clusters near rows of royal blue lockers or rushed past them, eager to leave campus for home or various activities. Laughter and chatter filled the air, their voices sounding like the hopeful anticipation of youth only appreciated by those whose youth had long passed.

As they entered Barker's classroom, a group of startled students scampered back to their desks and resumed previously neglected projects.

"You working or playing? We need to get those layouts to print! Two days! Just two days!"

Miles grinned, recollecting his first job during college. These kids could not realize it yet, but they had it easy. Barker was doing them a favor toughening them up and pushing them to the brink.

The man grabbed a yearbook from his desk with one hand and used the other to hike up drooping pants. "You said you wanted information on Bobby

Lockhardt? I checked the date you gave me but didn't see him, so I checked the previous year. Here you go." He handed Miles the annual for the '72-'73 school year and pointed out the juniors section.

As Miles scanned the book, it felt like he had obtained a bonus item for this unnamed game originated by its unknown author. He recognized the clean-cut image staring back at him. That face, though older now, had graced the cover of more trade and business publications than Miles could count.

"I asked around a bit after you called," Barker said as he slumped heavily into his desk chair. He paused to shout at his students to stay on task, then sniffed and continued. "I've only been here a few years, but one of the Phys Ed teachers remembered Lockhardt being in a class of his back in the day."

"Any chance I could talk to him?"

Barker reclined in his chair and fidgeted with the tips of his fingers. "Afraid not. He said he's familiar with your work."

Miles closed and returned the annual. He chuckled at the ribbing, though he suspected he had already overstayed his welcome. "Oh yeah? It's always nice to meet a fan."

"I don't know if I'd go that far," Barker said. "But Arty said Lockhardt was a pretty weird guy."

"Did 'Arty' say why Bobby never graduated?"

"Oh yeah. It was quite the scene from what Arty said. The mother went nuts. And then there was the accident."

"The accident?"

Barker spied several students neglecting their work to eavesdrop on their conversation. He barked a warning at them, then stood and motioned to Miles. "Lemme walk you out. I gotta get back to work."

Years of practice helped Miles appear calmer than he felt. The day had turned out to be the most productive in his fledgling investigation. Too bad he still did not know how the pieces fit together.

With no clear direction where to start, he had decided to begin with the first hint on the e-mail's list: Sarah Wellingham. From there, unexpected doors had opened.

As it turned out, the carefully constructed privacy walls surrounding Jameson Lockhardt's personal life had a weak spot. An archive search and two phone calls had revealed not only that Sarah Wellingham was Jameson's ex-wife and Bobby's mother, but that she had moved to Santa Barbara after Bobby turned five. The search yielded little else. When Miles finally located the former Mrs. Lockhardt, he understood why.

Sarah Wellingham had spent the last twenty-two years in a mental institution. Through less than legal channels, Miles had learned the name of the facility. He had subsequently charmed his way past the staff, who appeared grateful at his arrival. Miles got the distinct impression the woman received few visitors.

The brief encounter had netted little. Sadly, her schizophrenia was uncontrolled. Through her rambling, she mentioned her son and his school, which led Miles to his next stop.

Barker continued as they made their way back to the office. "Apparently Lockhardt was involved in some sort of car accident. He was sixteen, seventeen at the time, according to Arty. I guess his old man came up from LA to bail him out—or was he already here?" He paused, then shook his head. "Anyway, according to Arty, next thing you know, the mother goes crazy and chases the dad with a knife."

Miles wanted to pull out the pad of paper from his inside jacket pocket but did not want to risk interrupting the conversational flow. Better to let the guy finish. Instead, he committed as much as he could to memory. He would write out his notes in the rental car before he left.

"So the mother gets put away. Lockhardt gets pulled out of school. And that's all he said."

"Nothing more about this accident?" Miles pressed.

Barker stopped when they reached the front office. He scratched his head. "Nope, not much more detail. He might have mentioned a fatality, I dunno. Maybe check the local paper."

Miles stuck out his hand and thanked the man for his time. "That's my next stop."

Barker indicated the trophy cabinet as Miles prepared to leave. "Anyone else you want to know about?" He chuckled. "This here's our hall of fame."

Miles nodded his head and politely scanned the trophies, articles, and pictures a second time. "I looked at this earlier. Quite a few notables, huh?"

"We get our fair share." He pointed to a photograph at the far right. "I'm sure you recognize her."

"Who?" Miles asked, his eyes following where the man indicated.

The picture in question revealed a young woman with long, straight auburn hair. She held a microphone, posing as if in mid-performance. Miles froze. He could not believe his eyes.

CHAPTER 6

MAY FIRST SAW THE RETURN of Ross Alexander to the place he now considered a dungeon. To the uninitiated, LSI's walls looked pristine and in good repair. Its lobby and reception areas were replete with smiling portraits of its artists, as well as gold and platinum reminders that Lockhardt Sound had once stood out as a beacon of success in a sea of aspiring talent.

To Ross, these walls might as well have been blocks of worn stone. Echoing throughout its hollow enclosures he heard the haunting moans of the many casualties he had helped Jameson Lockhardt silence over the last twenty-eight years.

Only six and a half months to go. Then, it would be over. Over for Jameson. Over for the victims of Lockhardt Sound's oppressive machinations.

Ross had accepted the fact that when LSI fell, he would fall with it. Its ruination would spare no one. None who did Jameson's bidding would escape. And with Josephine gone, it no longer mattered to Ross whether he lived or died. No prison could feel less comfortable than the empty house in which he lived. That house was no longer a home.

For this reason only, Ross bore the agony of walking through his office door. As he crossed its threshold, he envisioned a large stopwatch set for six months, sixteen days, and ten hours. It would mark the countdown to LSI's final alarm...starting...*now.*

Tick, tick, tick, he thought.

His office had changed little during his leave. Even in the worst of times, it had felt ancient, yet familiar and welcoming. Today, something about it seemed different. Colder, perhaps. Devoid of anticipation for the end of the day.

While the average music executive's office might look more sterile than inviting in this progressive culture, acting as an extension of its boastful lobby with its awards, triumphs, and displays of technical advancement, Jameson had insisted on a different approach. The offices of Lockhardt Sound's upper echelon exuded elegance, intelligence, power. Impeccable at all times, they appeared reminiscent of a bygone era. Their many notable accomplishments remained deceptively encased in underlit mahogany and beveled-glass cabinets.

Ross laid his briefcase on his desk, then plopped into his seat. For long moments, he stared at the far wall, a sprawling ceiling-to-floor bookshelf pregnant with tomes and journals on entertainment law. He wondered how many of them he had utilized over the decades. A scandal here, a favor there. How many loopholes and precedents had he exploited to save his friend's neck during their long association?

Jameson Lockhardt's corporate biography would never divulge the most sinister, indeed the most interesting, facts behind his rise to power. It would never disclose his real name. No one knew the future entertainment mogul had grown up an impoverished, orphaned hoodlum from Canning Town. Or that he had met his legal counsel while driving a minicab for a front business operated by one of the East End's most notorious organized crime groups. Most importantly, the world would never know the legend who would dominate the industry had single-handedly altered its course before giving one thought to working within it.

On some level, Ross understood the old man's arrogance. They had experienced far worse, kept darker secrets, and survived more ominous threats than those posed by Farin Grant.

He had worked exhaustedly for weeks, gathering the information he needed to expose those secrets. In that time, he had finally pulled back the curtain and confronted the ugly truth Jameson never expected him to figure out.

A single moment had sealed their fate—a moment that had ushered in an irreversible change for the music business as the world knew it. A moment that revealed the depths to which the old man would go to secure his future. For decades, Ross had thought it coincidence he had been there that night. Now, he realized Jameson had tapped him as an unwitting alibi, banking on Ross' naive loyalty. And had that loyalty been tested and proven faulty, Jameson would have simply used him as a scapegoat.

This fact was a bitter pill to swallow. It had become a catalyst for every decision Ross had made since his wife's funeral. Now, it was a race against time. And the countdown continued.

Tick, tick, tick.

A picture of Josephine sat in its prominent position on his desk. There she stood, a vision in the cream evening dress she had worn to some benefit dinner. She beamed for the camera, her smile more resplendent than the sparkling emeralds completing her elegant ensemble. He stared at her image, the memories so overpowering they nearly stole his breath just as Josephine had done every moment since they had met.

He picked up the photograph and brought it closer, adjusting the newly prescribed pair of glasses perched upon his nose. The frame, as well as his office, had collected a thin coating of dust. He grabbed some tissue from the box on his desk and tended to the picture with great gentleness and care. Once clean, he again regarded the image smiling back at him.

A familiar set of footsteps made their way down the hall toward his office. Ross kissed his index finger, touched it to Josephine's image, then redressed the frame on his blotter. As the footsteps drew near, Ross rubbed his eyes and sat straighter in his chair.

"Good morning!" came the cheerful greeting of Lockhardt Sound's anointed king. "Mind if I come in?"

He cleared his throat and waved the young man inside. "Please."

Bobby smiled congenially and began to sit, then paused. "You sure it's okay? I know you just got back. This an okay time for ya?"

"As good a time as any," Ross assured in his most businesslike manner. "What can I do for you?"

Bobby began to sit once more, but again stopped short. He backtracked to Ross' door and shut it quietly before returning, then settled into the high back leather chair facing the desk. "How're you feeling? You holding up okay?"

Curiously, Ross found it easy to fall into the deceptive pattern he had long practiced within this building. "I'm fine. Soldiering on. Thank you for asking."

"We were worried for a while," Bobby confided, his smile nervous and warm. "I wanted to drive up to the house a few times but Dad said you'd probably rather be alone."

Ross nodded. "I appreciate the consideration."

Bobby appeared relieved to have bypassed a potentially awkward reunion. For a moment, a disquieting silence settled upon them.

Ross leaned back and unbuttoned his suit jacket, eager to appear calm but longing for some solitude before plunging into what he suspected would be a long day. He watched Bobby fidget with the file he had carried in with him, then pick random pieces of lint from his trousers. "Is there something you wanted to see me about?" he asked at last.

Bobby repositioned himself in his seat. "Um...yeah—I mean, no. I'm sure it can wait. There's plenty of time. Not that I want to wait too long. I'm sure you have a lot to catch up on, not that we let things pile up on your or anything. It's just that—"

Ross sat forward and laced his fingers atop his desk.

"—I didn't want to dump it all on you at once."

How anyone might think Bobby could successfully run a multimillion-dollar corporation, he did not know. Fortunately, that day would never come. He had talked to Samantha last night before turning in. She confirmed she had finished calling everyone on their list. The wheels were finally in motion. Everyone had agreed to come.

"I guess it can wait," Bobby said at last. "I'll get out of your hair for now."

He stood, tucked his folder under his arm, and headed for the door.

Though confident in the weeks prior to Ross' leave of absence, it appeared something had changed. No matter his feelings for the father, he still felt sorry for the son. "Hold up, Bobby."

The young man's shoulders slumped as he returned to his seat. A thin tuft of blond hair slid into his face, causing him to appear younger and more vulnerable. This childlike appearance brought back less painful memories of Bobby's younger years—a friendly lad, eager to please. Sometimes even a touch dashing, however unrefined.

Had Bobby received the proper care, things might have turned out differently. Had he experienced the love a child should have from his parents, Jordan Grant would still be alive. So would Josephine.

Now, no hope remained. Bobby would soon lose his freedom as assuredly as his father would. In Bobby's case, it might not end in prison. Perhaps he would do his time in an institution where he could get the medical attention he required. Either way, he would not end up in the general public. And with the loss of his freedom, he would lose all possibility of having the father he dreamed Jameson might one day become.

"Are you okay?" Ross asked as Bobby fidgeted with the file in his lap.

Bobby nodded sadly.

"And your father?" *Tick, tick, tick.*

"He's okay, I guess. I've been thinking a lot about my mom lately, though. We got a call from the hospital. She had a pretty bad episode a couple of weeks ago. They think they need to change her meds again."

Ross nodded. "I'm sorry to hear that."

"They keep saying it isn't degenerative, but she's getting worse."

"It's been a long time since you saw her. Maybe that's what's bothering you. Have you thought of making a trip out there? I'm sure she'd love to see you."

His body stiffened. He looked far away. "I don't know."

Ross understood the challenges Bobby had experienced with Sarah and how divided his loyalties were. The boy felt an obligation to the woman who reared him but had eluded to some harrowing situations prior to her hospitalization. Ross sat back and scratched his chin. "You don't need to make that decision today. So, what mischief have you gotten me into since I've been gone?"

Bobby's melancholy gave way to a sideways grin. "Actually, I'd wanted to go over an idea I had for the retirement party."

"Okay, shoot."

"A roast."

The thought of roasting Jameson Lockhardt sounded wonderful to Ross, although he guessed Bobby had meant figuratively speaking. "That's a fine idea, son. Would you like some help with it?"

Bobby grew animated as he relayed his ideas. They could have it in the conference hall on the bottom floor of the LSI building. All of Jameson's contemporaries would be there. They would have a banquet with the head table on stage and start the roast after everyone had been served. "And I could be the roastmaster."

Ross nodded his support. "It might work better if you were one of the roasters," he suggested. "I'm sure your father would be pleased to see you up there, taking some parting shots as he stepped down."

Bobby's eyes sparkled with imagination. "That'd be terrific. But that would leave us without a roastmaster. Who do you think that should be?"

Ross considered the question. Then, the final pieces clicked into place like the last metal tooth settling into the notch of a combination lock. What better way to bring down the iron-fisted fear monger of music royalty than to publicly knock the tarnished crown off his head? "I'll take care of it."

"You? I thought you'd want your shot to give the old man a good basting."

He stood and indicated the door. "I think we can make sure he's well done by the end of the night. I'll start working on the details. We'll meet later. I should probably get to work now. Was that all you needed to discuss?"

Bobby's cheeks flushed as he dropped his head. "Not exactly."

"What else is on your mind, son?"

He peered up at him with sad eyes. "I think I'm having girl trouble."

***

Todd Dalton shut his suitcase with an angry snap, then grabbed his tumbler and drained the bourbon until only melting ice remained. He carried the suitcase downstairs, then chucked it across the foyer. It slid along the marble entryway and slammed into the others like a bowling ball crashing through pins.

The car would not arrive for another hour—plenty of time for a few more drinks. Maybe a couple of final toots to keep things balanced. He hoped he would still be able to contact his guy in Cali but would improvise if necessary.

The fact Samantha had talked him into it did not change the way he felt about flying back to America. For years he had nestled happily in the British countryside, far from the flag-waving, gun-toting, overeating, over-tipping, over-sharing, humourless, stuck-up Yanks. He had believed he would never visit America again. But he had to give Sam credit. She had intrigued him. He wondered why they needed to be so secretive about their mystery meeting, apparently enough to make the trip.

He wondered how Lockhardt would react when he found out.

Anymore, Todd did not much care where he was as long as he had enough

Peruvian flake and booze to keep him—with a nod to Roger Waters—comfortably numb. The combination kept him buzzed but alert, enabling him to spend entire nights playing in his studio. It sharpened his focus, helped him avoid darker thoughts.

He wanted to forget it all—the loneliness and isolation, Chris' betrayal, his declining health, and his dwindling financial status. And, let's face it, the real reason he had agreed was he needed the money. Samantha had promised a pot of gold waiting at the end of the tarmac.

Which reminded him. He ran back upstairs and smoked a bowl to increase the likelihood of having a bit of a kip on his flight. Staying awake the entire journey would make Todd Dalton an unpleasant boy. He had not slept in two days—or was it three?

By the time his chariot arrived, Todd's vision blurred and his heart rate had hit a steady rhythm. Perfect for the long flight, which he would supplement with complimentary first-class access to all the whiskey he could drink.

The driver informed him the flight was on time. When he went to grab his charge's bags, he hesitated and peeked back over his shoulder. "Taking everything here, then? Looks like you'll be gone a donkey's."

"All of it," Todd confirmed. He crawled inside the limo and cozied up to the wet bar.

As far as he was concerned, he might never be back.

***

Derek hated keeping secrets from Summer, especially now. Besides, Sawyer knew. Would Summer be any less willing to keep the Grants' family secret during whatever mess his aunt was cleaning up? Truthfully, he did not understand it all. Not that he had given it much thought. He had observed occasional tension in the house, but nothing too bad. Nothing that concerned him, anyway. He was just glad to have his Blazer back.

"We've gotta do better about curfew," he told Summer as they lounged peacefully under their rented umbrella near the Bill Baggs lighthouse. The sand felt warm beneath their blanket. They lay side by side, the tips of their fingers barely touching.

"I know. My mom and dad were totally upset. Especially Dad. I thought he was gonna take my car, too." For a moment, she looked lost in thought. She turned to him with soft eyes. "Do you regret it?"

He frowned and rolled over to face her. "Regret it?"

She nodded, a gentle smile spreading across her face.

"Do you?"

She glanced down at their blanket and pulled at a loose string. "I don't know. I mean, you think we were ready?"

He rolled back and stared at the underside of their umbrella. "I think it doesn't matter whether we were ready or not. It's done. And no, I don't regret it. How could I? I love you."

"But we were supposed to wait. Maybe we should have."

On some level, he admired her faith—and shared it. But sometimes, it frustrated him. "You gonna go to confession?"

She reached for his hand and their fingers intertwined. "I already did. And I think you should, too."

"So you *do* regret it."

"I regret not waiting, I guess. It would have been nice to have something special to give you if we get married someday."

"It will be special, and we *will* get married someday."

Summer smiled and Derek squeezed his hand. "I love you," she whispered sweetly.

Something about the sound of her voice aroused him. Unfortunately, it sounded like their physical relationship had ended as quickly as it had begun. At least for now. He understood, but it disappointed him. He had waited for what felt like forever.

The Grants and the Reeces had known each other many years, though not well. Both families lived in the Village of Key Biscayne and attended St. Agnes Church—the Reeces far more regularly than the Grants. Summer and Derek had attended school together from kindergarten at St. Agnes Academy up to Coral Gables High School, where they would finish their junior year in a few short weeks.

Their families had been friendly since the teens started dating as freshmen, but Derek had once overheard his dad tell his mom he suspected Mr. and Mrs. Reece might have concerns about their family. Between their careers and the tabloid accounts of the various goings-on in their lives, it surprised no one when people made assumptions.

Maybe it was better to leave the details about his aunt alone. The last thing he needed to do was jeopardize his relationship with Summer by adding crazy to the mix.

He propped himself up on his elbows and gazed into her crystal eyes. "I'll never pressure you to do anything you're not comfortable with. You know that."

Her brows arched with hopeful relief. "You're not mad?"

"I could never be mad at you."

"And we're not weird or anything?"

"Well...we may be weird." He bathed in her perfection, mesmerized by the tips of her golden hair curling in the sea breeze. "A musician and a cheerleader? That's weird. But nah, we're cool." He moved in and kissed her, inhaling her scent, a mixture of citrus and ocean air. Nothing too heavy. Just natural. Just beautiful—like her.

Summer sat up and stretched, peering out at the water and then to her right. "It's gotta be close to nine thirty, right? The first tour's gonna start soon. Let's get out of here before people start lining up."

"Where do you want to go?"

"I don't know. I don't want to waste a day out of school on a beach overrun by tourists."

"You wanna take the boat out? I can call my dad. I'm sure he won't mind. We could go down to Elliott Key."

"Too bad Kyle's in school. We could bring him with."

Derek cut eyes at her as they folded their blanket and broke down the umbrella. "Think we need a chaperone?"

She flashed that shy smile that drove him wild. "Maybe."

***

Chris left practice early that afternoon. Fact was, they were ready. The musicians accompanying him were pro. Back-up singers knew the routine. They had finalized the set list and submitted the riders.

He had decided to go ahead and cover "Maybe I'm Amazed" after all. Sam was right. It was fitting. Might as well go all out and send the past where it belonged.

Little remained undone. One of the easiest tours he had prepared for, which conflicted him on some level. It felt almost too perfect.

He called the house on the way home, hoping Julie would be up for a late lunch. When the call went to voicemail, he hung up and tried her cell. No answer.

He popped a copy of the recorded rehearsal into his CD player and audibly inspected every nuance of the performance. By now, he figured he should be more comfortable singing lead. That's what solo acts did—they sang lead.

In the nearly two weeks since Farin had relocated to Miami, he had not heard a word from Ben or Cheryl. It did not surprise him. Not really.

Even though they had mended fences, there obviously remained a shred of doubt that things between him and Farin had ended for good. It would take time for his family to believe his interest in her had shifted. Hopefully her accounts of his rejection would alleviate their concerns. He had made it clear his only residual feeling for her was concern. And even if it was the most convincing lie he had ever told, every fiber of his being intended to make it true.

He wondered if Ben had extracted any additional information about Jordan's murder. Without another thought, he dialed their house.

Cheryl answered on the second ring, a distinct giddiness to her tone as she greeted him. "How are things going? Everything still on schedule?"

"You're talking to a musical amputee. It's like getting ready to go on stage without my arms or legs."

"Did you ever ring Faith?"

"Psh. I'm the last one any of the lot of 'em wanna hear from. I'm truly the solo act."

"It won't feel like that for long. You'll see. In time, you'll get used to it."

Chris asked how things were going on her end, and Cheryl relayed news of the boys, how Kyle was thinking about volunteering at the marina this summer and Derek had recently had his car taken away. Cheryl shared her growing concern about his relationship with Summer. Between that and his band, Derek expressed interested in little else.

"Maybe he needs to talk to someone who's not his mum or dad. Let me see what I can do." He hesitated a moment. "How are things otherwise?" When she did not respond right away, he feared the worst.

"Please tell me she's not the reason you called, love."

"I just want to make sure she's okay. You don't even need to tell her I called."

Cheryl sighed. "She's well. Handled her business with Ross Alexander, though she hasn't given us any details. She's not started in the studio yet although Ben's giving her the nudge. It'll take some time, I think."

Chris fell silent as he drove, barely registering the street signs and traffic lights as he listened to his sister-in-law. He pulled into his driveway and sat with the engine running.

"Now don't you think on it," she scolded. "She's fine here with us. Much better than I thought. The boys like having her around. And Kyle's stopped talking rubbish about Jorie coming back. I have to admit, Farin's had a positive effect on them both."

He nodded but said nothing.

"Listen to me go on like I was your mum. And speaking of mums, how's our girl doing? Is she showing yet?"

"I haven't seen her in a couple of weeks, but I'm sure she's fine. She and Elliot are getting excited. Still a few months to go yet. I didn't notice if she's showing or not."

Cheryl paused a moment. "Are you talking about Marci?"

"Who else do we know who's pregnant?"

Cheryl chuckled. "Don't tease now, ya prat! I mean *our* girl, Julie! I haven't talked to her since she flew home. I've been waiting so you could tell your brother yourself, but I don't know how much longer I can resist! Are you excited? Ridiculous question—of course you're excited!"

"Julie's *pregnant*?"

"Aye! Sh-she didn't tell you? A'm sairy, Chris! I thought you knew! She'd sworn she'd tell you the minute she returned."

He ended the call, killed his engine, and bolted inside. Julie's car was gone. He dialed her cell a second time, but it did not even ring before rolling over to voicemail. He searched their room, the den, then the kitchen for anything that might convey her whereabouts. On the table beneath the wall phone, he saw the voicemail indicator on their answering machine blinking. He punched the button to retrieve the message.

"...yes, this is Dr. English's office calling to confirm Julie Swanson Grant's appointment this afternoon at one. Please arrive at least a half hour early to start your paperwork. The doctor can give you something to relax you if you like. If you've reconsidered having the procedure, please call us back to cancel the appointment. Our number is..."

Reality beset him in waves, but he could not fully process the implications. He dialed the number the receptionist had left on the machine and asked for directions to the office but neglected to ask if his wife had arrived. Without a clear thought, he bounded back into his Porsche and raced to the Beverly Hills address. The time on his dash display read 1:34 PM.

***

Jameson remained in his office late, awaiting his secret visitor. All things considered, he preferred risking their privacy to having Moreau invade his personal space again. No one entered his home without invitation. In fact, the last stranger to come to the house had been the man who had updated the security system the day after Moreau's unexpected appearance—if one could actually call it an appearance at all. Besides, better to have this conversation in the City.

In his lap, he firmly gripped the pistol he kept in his right-hand drawer. He wanted to avoid a scene if at all possible. Knowing the man's demands for anonymity, Jameson had extinguished every light except his desk lamp and had employed the floor-to-ceiling electronic shades to limit undue illumination from the surrounding buildings.

Jameson sensed an ominous presence the moment Moreau arrived. He cocked his pistol.

"I figure it's one of two things," Moreau told him, his voice thin and deadly. "You either can't follow direction, or you're getting forgetful in your old age. The last time we spoke, I warned you to never contact me again."

Jameson set his jaw and projected more confidence in his voice than he felt as his finger trembled near the trigger. "The last time we spoke, you told me Farin Grant would be dead the next day."

Moreau chuckled. "Yes, that. Slippery little vixen, isn't she? She must have moved on. I'm sure she knows your intentions."

"I paid you to do a job, Moreau. That job isn't finished."

The man laughed, still amused by the pet name the old man had assigned him. "We've been over this before, Lockhardt. I don't run a private detective agency."

"Are you suggesting you'd rather refund the money?"

"I think you know the answer to that."

"Then what do you propose?" Jameson noted a sliver of light reflecting off metal near the back of the room. Obviously, they were both armed.

"I've given you the name of a reliable PI. I suggest you make use of that name and let him contact me himself once he locates the little minx."

"You know as well as I do complications arise when too many people get involved."

Moreau sounded wholly unsympathetic. "Oh yes, I know. And you know I told you I'd kill you if you ever called me again. Now, given the status of the job, I'll leave you tonight with your life. But make no mistake, Lockhardt. Someone's going to pay for your indiscretion."

Jameson's heartbeat quickened. The only one he had who mattered was his son.

"Oh," Moreau added before leaving. "And one more thing. Never bring a gun to a meeting unless you intend to use it."

A deafening pop resonated through the LSI corridors.

CHAPTER 7

WHEN JULIE RETURNED HOME, SHE felt sore and groggy, but not as bad as she had feared. Gloria had confirmed the post-care instructions with Dr. English's office. She relayed them as she drove. Her assistant followed them in Julie's car.

"You're on bed rest for a couple of days. Make sure you take the full course of antibiotics. No heavy lifting, no tub baths, and *no sex* for four weeks, Jules. Got it?"

Julie would have to think of an excuse to tell her husband but did not foresee a problem. She nodded. "We should probably push the Dahrvey shoot back. Can you call them?"

"Already done. Nothing to worry about. Just get better and let's move on from this."

Despite the initial cramping and numbness from the mild sedation, Julie felt better than she had in months. No more morning sickness, no parasite aggrandizing in her womb, no stretch marks. In a month, her life would be hers again. Maybe she and Chris would take a vacation when the *Aftermath* tour ended. A few days lounging on a beach in Koh Kood sounded heavenly.

When they pulled into her driveway, Julie spotted Chris' car parked outside the garage. She had hoped she would have some time to get situated before he got back. Disappointed and a little nervous, she gathered her paperwork and stuffed it into the brown paper bag with the antibiotics and feminine pads Gloria's assistant had procured from the pharmacy next door to Dr. English's office. "Thanks for getting me home."

Gloria leaned across the seat, dipped her chin, and eyeballed Julie over the rim of her sunglasses. "We'll talk later. Two days. Bed rest. Call me the first of next week."

Gloria's assistant joined them, handed over Julie's keys, then slid in the front seat of the Mercedes. They drove off, leaving her alone in the driveway.

A surge of pain in her lower abdomen seized her as she crossed the concrete pavers, but she straightened her stance and walked as normally, and casually, as she could. She dropped her keys and purse onto the entryway table and eyed the staircase. Her bed had never seemed so far away. She did not relish the climb to the second floor.

As she lifted her foot to brave the first step, Chris appeared from the kitchen.

Her smile belied her disposition. "You're home early."

He moved forward and embraced her, kissing her forcefully as he held her tight—too tight. "I cut out early. I fancied a little play time. How about you?"

She wriggled out of his arms with an unconvincing chuckle, defying the pain. A hint of something she could not name flashed in his dark eyes.

"What's the matter? We could use some extra time together. I'll be leaving in a few weeks. Won't you miss me?" He grabbed her again and kissed her hard on the mouth. His hands moved up beneath the back of her shirt to unhook her bra.

She winced as she broke free. "Chris, stop. I...I'm not feeling well. It's been a long day."

"Again? Sorry, love. Care to talk about it? Why don't we sit down and have a chat. You had that doctor's appointment you'd scheduled. That was today, right? Everything okay?"

Julie narrowed her eyes, confused by her husband's uncharacteristic aggression and agitation. She held the bag up. "Yes, I saw him. Got some antibiotics. No biggie. I just wanna go lie down for a while. We can talk later. I need a nap."

"Now come on, you should definitely talk it out. I mean, I came all the way home to be with you." He took her hand and led her into the kitchen with a certain degree of force. "You hungry? I could fix us a bite. What do you want to drink?"

Curious now, Julie eased into a kitchen chair, set the bag down on the table, and studied Chris as he grabbed a bottle of whiskey and two glasses off the counter. He sat down opposite her, poured them each a shot, then toasted her glass before downing his in a single gulp.

"What's gotten into you?"

"Me? Why, I'm bloody brilliant." He poured himself another shot, which quickly disappeared, then filled his glass a third time. "The band's great, practice is coming along as planned. All in all, a good morning. What about you? You mentioned it being a long day. Care to share?"

He did not wait for her to answer. Instead, he stood and walked over to the answering machine, rewound the message, set the player for repeat, and pressed "play." He returned to his seat and swallowed another shot. His eyes narrowed hatefully as the message from Dr. English's office began to play. "Drink up...and tell me all about it."

Then, she knew.

His voice sounded lethal. "You haven't touched your whiskey."

"I—" But the words died in her throat. She could not think of a single thing he would want to hear.

"*Drink.*"

Each time Dr. English's message looped, he swallowed another shot. The more he drank, the angrier he looked. "What's the matter? You didn't have trouble drinking at Sam's the other night."

She hung her head and wrestled over the best course of action. Finally, she stood. "I'm going to bed. We can talk about this later, when you're sober."

He bounded up and blocked her path. "It's not that easy." As an afterthought, he grabbed the whiskey bottle from the table.

She jutted her chin defiantly. "You don't scare me. You think this is something *new*? You think this is anything different than the first six months of our marriage?"

He closed the gap between them and peered into her eyes. "Oh, this is very different. And I want you to say it." He gulped greedily from the bottle. Droplets of liquor dribbled down his chin.

She shook her head in disgust and sneered. "And you wonder why I did it. Let me by. I need to lie down."

He grabbed her arm with his free hand. "Tell me what you did! I need you to *say* it!"

Julie stood eye to eye with her husband. "I will if you will," she spat. "You go first."

He flung her arm down and pushed her back toward the table. "You're bloody mental," he slurred. "I never did anything but love you!"

She laughed bitterly. Her lower abdomen protested with pain. "Love me? '*Love*' me? You loved a corpse until four months ago! And now that she's back, you're right back where you were the day we met!" She sat back down, drained her glass, and buried her head in hands.

Chris set his jaw, drew closer, and leaned down, his mouth inches from her ear. "Toys in the attic."

She jerked her head angrily and fixed her eyes upon him. "You think *I'm* crazy? Look at you! For a while you became the man you promised me you'd be. But now? All you ever wanted was her. Well? She's back now, Chris—and she's free. All you need to do is figure out how you two can be together."

He stumbled back two steps and swallowed another drink, then lifted the bottle, his index finger waggling as he pointed at her. "I was faithful to you."

Julie realized she had touched a nerve. She stood, jerked the bottle from him, and gulped at the amber liquid, hoping to ease the pain. "And how long was that gonna last?"

He snatched the bottle out of her hand and cast down the half-empty vessel. It shattered with great force, crashing to the floor as liquid and thick shards of glass sprayed across the tile. "*I was faithful to you!*" he shouted, inches from his wife's face. "How could you do this?"

"How could I not?" she spat in a low, guttural snarl of disgust. "You think

I want to have some little brat clinging to my leg for the next eighteen years while you're off screwing your one great love? You think I'm gonna end my career, ruin my body, and then lose you, too?"

He slapped her hard across the face, then grabbed her shoulders before she could lose her footing. He slammed her against the kitchen wall, pinning her so she could not move.

The act caught her by surprise and left her mildly disoriented. She tasted iron from the blood in her mouth. "Let me go," she warned.

"I told her it was *over*," he spat through a clenched jaw. "I told her I loved *you*. *You*! You knew I wanted children." His voice grew raspy as he shouted. Tears welled in his eyes, blurring his vision. "I lost my brother. I lost my band. I'm going it alone here. I lost...h-her...but I thought I'd found you. I thought we'd be a family. I thought this was it! How could you murder my child, you heartless bitch?" He let up slightly, then shoved her into the wall again, harder this time.

Julie struggled in vain. "You're hurting me, you bastard. Let me go."

Chris eased up again then shoved her a third time, moving one arm across her chest and grabbing her throat with his free hand. "I could kill you right now!"

She attempted to knee him in the groin, but he shifted to his right. The maneuver weakened his hold on her. She shouldered him back, then sprinted toward the stairs. Her left cheek and lower abdomen throbbed as she ran.

Chris followed closely. As she reached the stairway, he lunged forward, clutched a fistful of her hair, and yanked. She flew up and back, then fell on top of him. In an instant, he rolled over on the marble floor and straddled her midsection, pinning her arms with his knees.

The feminine pad the office provided breached, too full to keep up with the flow. Warm blood leaked between her legs. Instinct told her if their altercation did not end soon, she would end up in the hospital, or worse.

Arguing with her husband had yielded nothing, save a few bruises and a missing handful of hair. She considered her options and realized she had best try a different approach.

She looked into his eyes, her face swollen and red. "What are you gonna do, Chris? Kill me? Will that make it all better?"

"*Yes!*" he shouted in a blind rage. He put his hands around her neck and applied pressure.

Julie's eyes widened in panic as she grappled and tried to inhale, but her arms were immobile. She could not get a breath.

He watched as her face grew dark red. Her struggling ceased. Soon, she appeared ready to pass out. As the full impact of the situation registered, he released his grip. His hands shook as he removed them from around her neck.

She immediately coughed and gasped for air.

Chris said nothing at first. He watched her with unfiltered hatred as she lay pinned securely beneath him.

Every cell in his body longed to take her throat in his hands again and finish the job. He wanted to draw back and pummel her million-dollar face until she became unrecognizable. Until his knuckles were so sore and bloodied he could no longer feel them. He did not want her to live. He did not want to feel. He wanted her to regret her actions, yet suspected she was incapable.

She stopped gasping as her breathing normalized and lay trembling beneath him.

Gradually, his eyes lost their deadly glare. He unstraddled her, slid several feet away, and sat on the hard, cold foyer. Devoid of all emotion, he said, "I want a divorce."

Julie brought one hand up to her throat and rested the other atop her pelvis. She lay frozen in place as he uttered the four words she had tried so hard to avoid.

"You can have this house. I'll keep the one in Key Biscayne. We'll each keep what we brought into the marriage, as well as everything we've earned individually. Anything we had together, you can keep. I want nothing from you."

"I'm not giving you a divorce," she countered hoarsely, almost ambivalently. "You'll be lucky if you don't go to prison after what you've done to me today."

"Oh yes, love. You'll not only give me a divorce, but you'll file the papers. Tomorrow."

"I'll do no such thing. Even if I wanted to, I can't go anywhere for two weeks. I'm supposed to be on bed rest."

He scooted across the tile and sat close to his wife. She flinched as he approached. "We can be divorced in Haiti in one day. I've already done the research."

Julie turned her head on the marble floor to look at him. "Divorce me and I'll tell the world she's back. I'll lead Lockhardt to Ben's front door."

He chuckled doubtfully, studying her with a clarity he had not possessed in the three and a half years he had known her. "Mention one word about my family or my business and I'll make sure everyone knows what you've done. We both know you can't afford the bad press—what with your age and all."

He went upstairs and packed a bag. When he returned, she was still lying on the floor, her skirt spotted with blood. He felt nothing. "I'll be back tomorrow to pick you up. I've changed my mind. I don't trust you to do this alone. I'll book the flight."

***

At twenty-three weeks, Ivy Spencer had what Lance Turner considered a perfect baby bump. Given Ivy's small frame, she looked like someone had stuck a red rubber playground ball beneath her shirt. Her face had not plumped up yet. Not an extra ounce of weight. Ivy was all baby.

She and Colin had moved into Lance's townhouse last month, which had resulted in fewer changes to their lives than he expected. In fact, the changes made were generally positive. Ivy looked after the place, which was nice. She did not hassle him about his laziness or his schedule, which was very nice. Every night, while he showered between his rugby game and his gigs, she made them all dinner—which was brilliant.

Had Lance realized what a positive effect the move would have on them all, he would have suggested it long ago. Their two year romance had never felt so right. Colin thrived in the environment, which made sense. The townhouse was much larger than Ivy's council flat in Chatham.

"I don't want you to go." Ivy pouted over dinner that evening. "Things are nice now, and I want you here for the baby."

Lance finished off his second helping of cottage pie and washed it down with the last of his stout. He sopped his plate with a piece of bread. "I told you to come with me."

"You know I don't have a passport."

"I'm sure we could get you fast-tracked, sweetheart."

"And what about our son? Colin's barely over a year old. He'll not be keen to sit still for such a long flight." Ivy cleared their dishes and waddled into the kitchen.

Lance smiled every time he watched her walk. Pregnancy became her. "What about your mum and dad?" he suggested. "Or we could hire a nanny to come with us. She could take Colin and help you, too. Besides, I'll only be gone a little while. Not long at all."

She served the afters and sat at the table. "I'll bet you have some gorgeous Yankee tart waiting for you in Los Angeles."

Lance coaxed. "You should come keep an eye on me to make sure."

"It's too late now. You leave tomorrow."

He shared his apple crumble with Colin, who had played with, more than ate, his meal. He hoped Ivy would change her mind. As usual, she expected him to convince her. He did not mind going through the motions, but time was running short. "I sure will miss you both if you don't come with me. You'll cost me a fortune in long distance if you stay. How can I spoil you and our son if you make me spend every last pound calling home?"

She turned her head and caught a glimpse of herself in the large mirror above the sideboard. "I'll have nothing to wear. I've gotten fat and my clothes are all too small."

"America has plenty of shops. I'll buy you a pretty maternity frock. You'll look lovely."

Ivy smiled at the notion despite herself. A bark of laughter escaped her mouth. "A big, fat pregnant cow with spiked hair. Your American friends'll think you're barmy."

They bickered throughout the evening while they put Colin to bed, when they retired for the night, the entire time they made love, and then again the next morning. Surprisingly, Lance could not convince her to go. Before he departed, he made sure he left plenty of money in their joint account.

The car came round at noon to pick him up. An hour later, he boarded the plane alone. He wondered what it would be like to see Samantha again and about the purpose of this big mystery meeting she had called. As the flight attendant made the announcement that passengers needed to shut off and stow all electronic devices, his cell phone rang.

Ivy sounded happy and irritated, her favorite combination. "You left your drumsticks, you wanker. You can't go off to America without your favorite drumsticks, now, can you?"

A smile stretched across his face. "I guess you'll have to bring them to me."

An exaggerated sigh filled the line. "Well, I suppose so. But I'm going to bring that nanny you went on about, so give me her number and I'll ring her."

"It's in the bedroom on my nightstand, sweetheart."

"And what about tickets?"

"They're in the drawer, next to your passport applications."

***

Miles pushed aside the empty containers of Chinese take-out he had grabbed for dinner, pulled out his writing pad, and reviewed notes while his desktop booted up. He had constructed a temporary workspace by stacking several boxes on top of each other. It was anyone's guess when he would have the time and energy to start unpacking. He had barely managed to get his furniture situated. The phone and cable companies had connected his services only hours ago.

He liked his new digs in Coconut Grove. Great space. Sufficient sized manicured back yard. The familiar tropical surroundings felt like home. It energized him to work the story where it had originated.

His optimism had waned only slightly when he spoke to Alicia the day after his return from California. She did not appreciate him telling her partner about his impending move. She said it felt coercive, as if he had attempted to intercept her rejection with William's favor. Miles could not help but admire her perception. When he had asked her to dinner, she declined.

"You think you can just come down here and sweep me off my feet like some fairy tale princess. You think you're Prince Charming. Maybe you should have moved to Orlando instead of back to Miami."

He had countered her thrust with his best parry. "I'm not asking you to come live in my castle. Well, at least not until my fairy god-cleaner comes and tidies up the place. But why not a cup of coffee or something?"

"Do you have anything new on the cases?"

Miles had not told her about his trip. He needed to put things together before offering any speculation. "Not yet, but I'm working on it."

"Call me back when you have something more than a glass slipper."

"Alicia?"

"What?"

"It's not a distance thing anymore. I'm here. See me."

Opting to keep his mind focused on more productive thoughts, he transferred the handwritten notes from his trip onto his CPU. He had solved some of the riddle, but most of the e-mail still made no sense. He knew he could connect the dots if he could just get a break.

He had lucked out that day at the high school. Had Barker not pointed out Farin's picture in the lobby, he might have never known she had grown up in Santa Barbara. Her professional biography had rewritten most of her history. But while she and Bobby had both attended San Marcos High School, they had not attended at the same time. It fit together somehow, or maybe not.

The local paper had added more to his curiosity than to his ability to solve the e-mail riddle. The article regarding Sarah Wellingham's commitment hearing omitted any association with Lockhardt or her son. No additional articles bore her name—not even Arty's alleged incident with a knife. No hits on the Lockhardt name.

Farin's high school picture had listed her last name as O'Conner, but the archives yielded little with that surname. Just a 1969 advertisement for a law firm, which Miles now knew her father had owned with his partner, Joseph Williams, and a death notice for a Bethany O'Conner five years back.

Sitting in his hotel room that night, he had focused on the second line of the riddle: *you'll start with those beneath the lawn.* No giant leap there—obviously a death or a cemetery. But that could mean any cemetery in the world. "Those" indicated more than one person. Not wanting to squander an opportunity, he had decided to check out the cemeteries the next day. He had also decided to pay Joseph Williams a visit.

There, he had hit pay dirt.

The visit to the office had lasted less than fifteen minutes. He had spent most of that time waiting to speak to the attorney, who happened to be with a client when Miles arrived. When they met at last, the gentleman had immediately refused to speak to a member of the press and insisted Miles leave before he called the police. Fortunately, the walls of Williams O'Conner & Associates had not been so tight-lipped.

The story had played itself out in 5x7 frames in the waiting area. Kelley O'Conner and Joseph Williams opening their law firm back in 1968—a successful pair with perfect wives and lovely daughters. They had worked together, vacationed together. Their children had been best friends.

Until something had happened. What, Miles did not know.

A plaque on the wall had indicated a memorial date for Kelley O'Conner. From there, the tone of the pictures on the wall had played a different tune. Where older photographs had captured smiles and laughter, future frames revealed a marked change. It had appeared that whatever sad fate Joseph Williams' partner suffered also claimed Mrs. O'Conner. Eventually, the Williams had taken in the orphaned O'Conner daughter, who no longer smiled and no longer laughed. She had stayed with them through high school. After graduation, she had vanished from their lives.

At the Santa Barbara Cemetery later that same day, he had located the O'Conner marker. And while he might not have known the name Farin St. John was in fact a stage name, assumedly borrowed from her mother's maiden name, it had become apparent many did. A crew of two men had labored to remove graffiti from her grave as Miles stood nearby, taking notes.

The date of death on Kelley O'Conner's stone was April 11, 1973, less than a month after the man's thirty-seventh birthday. Farin would have been ten at the time, which coincided with the Williams' photos. Miles had wondered how he died. The newspaper had nothing on him. Strange. The man had obviously been a prominent Santa Barbaran. Would his death not rate any mention in the local paper?

More curious had been the date of his wife's death: December 18, 1989. Given her absence in the post-Kelley O'Conner pictures and Farin's shift in countenance, Miles had assumed she died with the husband.

Receiving no help from microfiche at the local paper, he had decided to refocus his energy on his primary target: Bobby Lockhardt. Arty, the faceless Phys Ed teacher, had relayed something about an accident, possibly a fatality. Barker had said Bobby was around sixteen or seventeen at the time. If true, that might have explained why Miles found no mention in the archives. Bobby would have been a minor at the time. Regardless, no way would a man like Jameson Lockhardt have allowed bad press to sully his then-young reputation.

It had taken the Santa Barbara Police Department less than five minutes to throw Miles out of their building. "No comment," they had said. Even if Bobby Lockhardt had been involved in an accident—which they would not confirm—California had strict policies about sealed cases for juvenile offenders.

As Miles had left the station, he mentally constructed the facts he knew about the younger Lockhardt and did the calculation in his head. Bobby's supposed accident would have been around 1972 or 1973. 1973...the same year Sarah Wellingham was committed.

The same year Kelley O'Conner died.

Clearly, 1973 was a significant year for Santa Barbara, California. But what little Miles had learned, he could not piece together. With no local stories and no one willing to talk, the only tie-in he had was his cryptic e-mail and the fact that Farin Grant had adopted the Wellingham name when she checked into the hotel before she had died.

Once home and able to study the riddle more closely at his makeshift desk, Miles became convinced he needed to solve the meaning of the seven hints listed at the bottom of the e-mail before the rest would make sense.

So far, he could only make a check next to the first: *Sarah Wellingham*.

The signing party was a complete mystery to Miles. He wondered whose signing party. Was the reference that followed connected? And if so, might it point to a signing party from 1967? Miles checked the date on LSI's articles of incorporation. They were dated much later...in 1973.

The hair on the back of Miles' neck stood on end.

Adding to his frustration was the reference to *The Firm*. Did it mean the music group? Was it their signing party? Probably not. They had formed in the mid-'80s. Maybe the clue related to the John Grisham novel or the film adaptation that followed a couple of years ago. He made a note to rent the film and start digging up everything he could on the group as soon as he returned to the *Herald*.

One part of the riddle made perfect sense. Whoever had sent him the e-mail orchestrated not only his termination at the *Trib*, but also his return to his former position in Miami. For this, Miles was thankful. The only thing that bothered him was the implication his return might be connected to another victim. The riddle said time was running out.

Jade Larken Trongly, Miles thought. Who was she? Was she the one who might be lost?

Miles pushed his notes away, then grabbed the empty Chinese food containers and dumped them in the kitchen trash. He knew enough to step away when things started frustrating him. That time had come and gone hours ago.

He thought about taking a walk but could not muster the necessary enthusiasm. Maybe a little television, a shower, then bed. This plan made him smile, ironically. Thirty-one years old and smiling at the thought of an uneventful night at home. Hopefully his vocation would not age him too soon.

He grabbed a long neck from the fridge and eased comfortably into his recliner. He channel surfed for several minutes, caught tomorrow's weather forecast, and then switched over to ESPN to get the Cubs score until he could watch the evening news. He missed Wrigley Field already.

His phone rang shortly after 10 PM. The Macy family notoriously ignored the difference between time zones—probably his mother's passive aggressive attempt to punish him for packing up and leaving again. At first, Miles decided to let the machine get it. Then, a spark of hope. Maybe Alicia had reconsidered her position.

He answered on the second ring.

"Okay...the answer's yes."

He tucked his chin and frowned. "Jeanne?"

"How many assistants did you ask to follow you to Miami?"

The sarcastic query made him chuckle. "You're coming? That's great! What did Harper say when you turned in your notice?"

"Not one damn word."

"You must have given him that look of yours, didn't you?"

She scoffed innocently. "Miles Macy, I don't know what you're talking about."

He leaned back to extend his recliner and sipped his beer. "How soon will you be here?"

"I can't start until the end of May, but I'm flying down Sunday. I've got an appointment Monday with a realtor to start looking at houses."

"Need a place to stay? I've got an extra bedroom."

"Thanks, but that's the creepiest idea you've ever had, no offense. Besides, the *Herald* graciously offered me three months' corporate housing while I find a place. Not too shabby for an executive assistant. Who'd you have to sleep with to make that happen?"

He laughed. "Miami's not that bad."

"We'll see. Either way, it'll be nice to be somewhere warm."

"Let me know when your flight arrives. I'll pick you up and show you around."

Before they hung up, she stopped him. "Hey."

"Yeah?"

"Thanks, bossman."

"It wouldn't be the same without you. See you Sunday."

Miles stretched in the fully reclined chair, took another sip of his beer, then set the bottle on his end table. It pleased him Jeanne had taken him up on his offer to come work for him. After her divorce, she had seemed depressed. Now, she could start over. Maybe she would even help him get his place in order.

When the phone rang a second time, he eyed the apparatus with a mixture of annoyance and curiosity. He was certainly popular this evening. Once again, he considered letting his machine take the call but ended up answering in the hopes he would hear Metro-Dade's finest on the other end.

"Hello, Miles."

The female voice sounded familiar, but he did not want to blurt out the wrong name. Definitely no Cuban accent. Definitely not Alicia. Hopefully not Sandra. "Who's this?"

"I'd have thought you'd remember me. I guess I'm disappointed."

He grew inexplicably uneasy. "It's a little late for guessing games, so either tell me who this is or I'll have to hang up."

"I'll tell you but you have to promise you won't hang up."

Miles checked his caller ID. Blocked. "Listen, sweetie, I don't know what sort of game this is, but you obviously know my name. So how about cutting to the chase, huh? It's late. Miles needs his beauty sleep."

"It's...it's Farin," she said, following quickly with, "and don't hang up because I can prove it."

Nothing could have shocked Miles Macy more than the sound of Farin Grant's voice, which he recognized the instant she said her name.

... A silenced victim gone no more

"I know this sounds crazy," she added with a nervous chuckle. "I called because I heard you tried to summon me by having some séance on your computer. I wondered if you still want to talk. No Ouija boards or psychics necessary, promise."

His heart pounded so hard, his head throbbed. "I'm listening. You say you can prove it?"

"I can. But you'd think I wouldn't have to. After all, you're always the one I call when I'm in trouble."

"You'll have to do better than that." It occurred to him he had not moved a muscle since picking up the phone.

"The first time I met you, I denied Chris and I were having an affair. You said we might not be having an affair, but we were 'certainly having something' because he was convinced my baby was his. The last thing I ever said to you was I didn't trust you, but that you were all I had. That's still true. And what I have to trade is big. You know you believe me, and you know you want the story."

"How did your father die?"

A long pause filled the line. "He was killed in a drunk driving accident."

Bingo. "Hang on a minute." He dropped the phone on the couch as he sprinted to the bathroom, where he promptly threw up his entire dinner.

***

Alicia's phone rang at 11 PM. She picked up and barked an automatic,

"Detective Alvarez," before she realized she was awake.

"I've got more than the glass slipper," Miles said. "Will you meet me now?"

CHAPTER 8

AS FAR AS MARCI WAS concerned, October first could not arrive soon enough. Nothing out of the ordinary in terms of the pregnancy so far. The morning sickness had not lasted too long. But without Farin to take care of, she needed something to occupy her time and thoughts.

Since Farin's departure to Miami, she had fallen into a sort of routine. She awoke each morning, went downstairs, prepared a bowl of oatmeal and some fruit, and grabbed the calendar off the kitchen wall. While she ate, she counted. How many weeks today? And that meant how many months? So they had probably conceived on...? Every day, the same thing.

Elliot had a started some new project a week ago. She kept forgetting to ask him about it. He left early almost every day and did not return until early evening. She counterbalanced the solitude with rest, yoga, housework, and reading. Lately she had added baby magazines to her reading list. They needed to start redecorating soon if they wanted the baby's room ready in the next five months—or, more precisely, twenty-one weeks and four days.

But not today. Today, a house guest occupied what would become their baby's nursery.

"Good morning," Marci greeted as she entered the kitchen. "You get any sleep last night?"

Chris looked abysmal. His bathrobe hung wrinkled and loose about him. His long dark hair lay matted and stringy. He answered with a grateful half-smile Marci imagined must have taken every ounce of energy to produce. "You want some breakfast?" he asked sadly. "I made scrambled eggs and potatoes."

She made a face and shook her head. "Sorry. I'm sorta off eggs right now."

Chris nodded. "Sorry about that. I didn't realize. I'll clean up before I leave so you won't be left with the smell." He plated his food and ate near the stove.

"What time's your flight?"

"I'll leave in an hour or so."

"How long do you think you'll be gone?"

He chased a mouthful of food with his tea. "No idea. We won't get in till late this evening. I'd like to get to court as soon as it's open, but it could last a whole day. I'll take the first available flight home when it's finished."

Marci did not ask if he and Julie would return together.

"Thanks for letting me crash here."

"No reason to go to a hotel when you have friends nearby."

He lowered his head a moment, then turned and rinsed his plate.

She felt like she should say something but figured nothing would help. He looked small and inconsolable. It had broken her heart when she got up last night to check on him and heard him weeping through the closed door.

"What can I do, Chris?" she asked as he finished rinsing his breakfast dishes.

He took a seat opposite her at the table. They sat in silence at first, then he answered, "I guess there is something you could do, if you have time."

"Anything. I've got nothing but time on my hands."

His voice strengthened as anger diluted the pain. "I need to get my things out of her house. I've got clothes, personal papers. I'd like to get my equipment and my awards."

"Leave me your keys and the details. I'll make sure you're all set."

"It shouldn't be much, but you'll need some help. Take El with you if you can. He'll know what's what, and he can do the heavy lifting. Don't want to put any strain...on the baby." His demeanor shifted again. His chin trembled as if the dam was ready to burst.

She laid her hand atop his. "I'm sorry. I don't know what else to say."

He nodded and looked away. She tenderly squeezed his hand. He squeezed back, blinked several times, then scooted his chair away from the table. "I should have a shower."

"Of course. I'll get you some towels."

As they left the kitchen, Marci turned back and put her arms around his neck.

He returned the friendly embrace.

She patted his back, then pulled away. "I'll help you pack."

***

Jameson hated his new chair. It had taken him months to break in the last one, to get it to adequately conform to his body. His assistant had procured an exact replica, but it would take time to loosen its cellular structure.

Stacy had acted less than convinced when he explained the pistol had accidentally discharged during a thorough cleaning. No matter, though. She would have been a sight less convinced had he told her the truth—that he had angered a deadly, anonymous man who had, with frightening precision, fired a bullet into the chair some three inches from his head.

It seemed pointless to replace the wounded furniture so close to his retirement, but not replacing it might lead to questions he did not care to answer.

His spirits had lightened since his meeting with Moreau. Setbacks notwithstanding, he was back on course. Why he had used Moreau as a tracker in the first place was beyond him. He had tried to cut corners in his desire for immediate results. Sloppy.

LSI's steady decline over the last couple of years had compounded the angst he felt over Farin's escape. Stepping down a failure was not an option. Bobby could succeed or not once he left. Either way was fine with him. His primary goal was that LSI remained the powerhouse he had created—or that it recaptured its former glory. This quarter's financials hinted they were on track.

Joni Leighton had impressed Jameson after all, as had the fact Bobby had discovered her. They had released her first single practically the moment she had completed the track. The buzz was encouraging.

For all the changes the industry had experienced in the last twenty years, the concept of releasing a single without having to press it to vinyl, disc, or other physical means of distribution would soon become a reality. A whole world had opened up with the advent of the MP3. This singularly amazed Jameson.

Of course, the "B" side to all that progress meant certain death for recording companies as they existed today. In his heyday, Jameson had owned the artist—song, voice, and rendition. Material had essentially belonged to LSI. Recordings of said material had been the property of LSI. Royalties earned from the airing of those recordings had been managed and distributed by LSI. Live performances of the material had required LSI's approval. From the inception of recorded sound, labels had ruled supreme.

However, the combination of music executives taking their greed one step too far and technological advancements had ushered in a paradigm shift. With the advent of the personal computer, artists now had an increasingly sophisticated alternative to traditional recording studios. This gave them more control over their own work. Jameson could read the writing on the track board. Soon, recording companies would either have to play to their base strengths—publishing, marketing, and mass distribution—or they would face virtual extinction. Smaller labels would fail, and even the "Big Six" would further consolidate.

Between its original financing and legendary success, Lockhardt Sound had avoided destruction. But where LSI had historically played the role of the acquiring party to smaller labels, they had narrowly escaped acquisition months ago. A longtime benefactor had made a deathbed endowment to Lockhardt Sound, Jameson's final reward for decades-old loyalty.

He would have liked to have been able to personally attend the funeral last month but figured the Yard would be there, forever compiling their list of potential associates. Even had he not found himself occupied with urgent matters, he would never again take that risk—especially at his age. Reg would understand.

Stacy buzzed his office, announcing his last appointment had arrived. When she ushered him into the office, she asked the gentleman if he wanted anything to drink. He declined.

Jameson's first impression of the man was that he looked as if he had walked out of a Mickey Spillane novel. Too rarely anymore did men wear dress hats with business suits. The man's complexion was ruddy, his eyes shifty and untrusting. Stocky frame, possibly a former boxer. His '50s style flattop haircut, wide face, and strong jaw made his head look square. A no-nonsense type yet not overtly threatening—unlike his more nefarious visitor the other night. At least this guy did not hide in shadows.

It occurred to Jameson he should bill Moreau for his new chair.

Jameson stood and nodded once at Stacy. She closed the door behind her.

"Mr. Radford," he greeted, shaking the man's hand. "It's good to meet you."

"I'm an admirer of your work." Radford removed his hat and they both took their seats.

The comment struck Jameson as odd. "I didn't know you were in the business."

Radford gave him a sideways grin. "I wasn't referring to your current endeavors."

Jameson's amiable exterior melted away. Eyes narrowed, he studied the man with a degree of suspicion, wondering if Radford had intended the veiled threat. "Have we met before?"

Radford shook his head and crossed his thick legs. He brushed off his hat with his palm, then balanced it on his knee. "Not directly, no."

"I see."

Radford pulled out a small spiral notebook and began taking notes as he visually surveyed the office. "Any bugs you know of?" he asked, his voice low. "Have you had the place swept?"

Jameson's eyes darted about his office. He rested his arms on the top of his desk and leaned forward, emulating his guest's tone. "Uh, no. No I haven't."

He slid the notebook back into his breast pocket, then spent several minutes inspecting the office.

Jameson asked bluntly, "Are you a policeman, Mr. Radford? In law enforcement of any kind?"

The man held one hand in the air and pressed the index finger of his other hand to his lips. He checked the windows, lamps, bookcase, framed artwork, ornamental mini-statues and figurines, and every inch of office furniture. Once satisfied their conversation would remain private, he emitted a bark of laughter. "This isn't a sting operation, Lockhardt. Given the party who referred me, I'd have thought that was clear."

It had not occurred to Jameson he might be under investigation for any one of his many crimes. For a moment, he wondered.

Radford sat again, this time settling more comfortably into the tufted high back. He retrieved his notepad, then leveled steely eyes at the man before him. "How can I help you this evening?"

"I need you to find someone. A woman."

Radford nodded attentively as Jameson relayed the pertinent details of Farin's escape, her suspected accomplices, and the failed attempt to dispose of her.

"LA's enormous. If she wasn't in the explosion, it could take some time to find her. I'd bet she isn't with friends or family. Not if she suspects the explosion was no accident—which of course she does. And so does everyone around her. A hot target with good resources is an elusive proposition."

Jameson grew frustrated. "That's why I need a skilled PI. My source tells me you are."

"Oh, I am," Radford said, no hint of arrogance. He tilted his head and thought a moment. "I'll need a list of all known associates. Anyone who might be helping her. We'll set up some surveillance, maybe tap the phones...the usual deal."

Jameson nodded. "Sounds good."

"But I have to ask you a question before we start investing a lot of time and energy here. Did our friend confirm a visual at this beach house?"

Jameson frowned. "I'm not following."

"Are you sure she survived her escape? From what you've told me, no one's positively ID'd her. I'd hate to spend a lot of time locating nobody. You mentioned her condition when you last saw her, but that was months ago."

Jameson disliked the course of the conversation. "And?"

Radford rolled his eyes. "If she escaped and lived, it seems to me you and I wouldn't be having this conversation. You'd probably be in jail by now. I mean, if someone did to me what you did to her, I'd have contacted the cops by now. Wouldn't you?"

In the last four months, this thought had barely skimmed the outskirts of Jameson's mind. He had focused all his energy on finding her, finishing her off at last. A part of him realized he was in a race against time, that he could lose his freedom any day. But it had not occurred to him to ask why that day had not yet arrived. "You make a good point, Mr. Radford. However, if she's dead, why hasn't anyone gone to the police anyway?"

Radford grinned and shook his head. "You appear to be a thorough man, Lockhardt. A thorough man would have ensured someone cleaned up that room at Dorothea Dix to make sure no evidence remained."

"Of course."

"If her friends or family went to the police with her body, they'd be the ones under suspicion, not you." Radford laughed. "After all, possession is nine-tenths of the law."

Jameson eased back into his uncomfortable new chair and laced his fingers as the possibility played through his mind. Was it possible? Had he worried for nothing? "Our friend located some medical waste in a vehicle used by the two who helped the girl escape. I have every reason to believe she's alive."

"Okay. Let's assume she survived the trip back and has been regaining her health for the last four months. I guess the next question we have to ask ourselves is why someone would trade one form of captivity for another. I mean, what would be the motivation for that?"

Jameson's hands dropped to his side. He stared at and past his new associate. A feeling of dread enveloped him as he admonished himself for not considering the possibility earlier.

"Tell you what I'll do. Get me the list and I'll check it out. If my surveillance points to anything interesting, I'll tap the phones. I'll check back in a month—sooner if we get any hits."

It had been a good day, Jameson decided. His spirit always lightened when he knew he had taken another step ahead of his adversaries.

Motivation indeed. What better motivation could she have than finding Jordan Grant?

Jameson smiled grandly. They stood and shook hands again. Radford secured his hat and nodded a curt goodbye.

"I'll get that list for you today, Mr. Radford," Jameson promised as he opened his office door. "I hope you don't mind humidity, because the first place I need you to check is in Fayetteville, North Carolina."

***

The evening breeze acted like a tonic on Farin's nerves. Wine glass in hand, she smiled as she listened to the lilting laughter wafting out to the stone patio from inside the house. It commingled with the rustling palm trees and the bay water intermittently lapping the shore, producing a chorus that defied description. Ben, Cheryl, and the boys had asked her to join them for family game night, but she had begged off.

She watched them through the sheer curtains covering the enormous living room windows. They played Pictionary. Ben and Kyle teamed up against Cheryl and Derek. Their words were muffled but she understood the resonance. The song of family.

"Ahh!" they exclaimed in spontaneous unison before dissolving into laughter.

She studied their interaction with one another as she lounged on a patio chair. Ben occasionally tousled Kyle's hair or encouraged Derek with a pat on the back. The boys traded good-natured jabs as they endeavored to one-up each other. Cheryl freshened drinks and cuddled into her husband. And Farin remained forever on the outside, close enough to feel their familial bond and far enough away to maintain a comfortable distance.

Five felt like an awkward number anyway.

Something about being back in Florida unsettled her. On one hand, she felt relaxed for the first time since she could remember. This was her home in ways California had never been. Key Biscayne was a cocoon into which she could escape, protected from the chaos surrounding her. On the other hand, the relative comfort had begun tearing down the stone wall she had spent years constructing. Her tough exterior challenged her daily to buck up. The fight had yet to begin. Too much was at stake.

Nearly seven years had passed since the Grants had first welcomed her into their fold. It had been a rocky journey—with no end in sight. And to this day, she continued to let them down. Even tonight as she opted for isolation over inclusion.

Whether genuine or merely for appearance sake, Cheryl appeared to have warmed up to her. It could not be easy for Ben's wife to stand by and allow someone into their home who might bring danger to them. The woman was right to be concerned. Adding Farin's history to the mix, Cheryl Grant was a saint. If put in the same situation, Farin doubted she could muster the same humankindness.

As for Ben, he had practiced the patience of Job. She had relocated to Florida with the aim to start recording, but had yet to step foot in the studio. Worse, she fooled no one when she avoided all discussion of material. She had not even tested her voice to see how out of shape her vocal chords were. Behind Ben's enduring smile, she sensed his frustration.

But the biggest letdown the Grants suffered was her seeming unwillingness to ease their pain. Their greatest desire remained learning the details of what happened in Coral Gables. Farin had remained silent on the matter. She had to. Someday, she would tell them the truth. Jameson would pay.

Maybe then Chris would remember he loved her.

Farin finished her wine, then refilled her glass from the bottle sitting on the table. She rubbed moisture from her eyes, annoyed she still possessed the ability to produce tears. The time had come to let him go. To let everything go. Jordan's safe return was all that mattered now.

She sighed and closed her eyes. With a mournful crack of her voice, she whispered, "Where *are* you?" Admittedly, calling Miles Macy was risky, but he was her only hope. She could not do it on her own. For better or worse, he possessed resources she lacked.

The sounds emanating from inside had shifted from familiar to formal. Ben's voice deepened, but she could not discern his words. Cheryl's voice adopted the same tone it did when she welcomed a guest into their house. Farin sat forward, her heart racing as she debated whether to hide.

The patio door slid open. When she realized who it was, she frowned and peered inside the house. Ben stood smiling at her through parted curtains. He gave her a thumbs up and a quick nod, then returned to his family.

"Hey there." came the awkwardly greeting.

She stared at Sawyer, clearly confused. "Derek's inside."

He smiled as he reached the table, then gestured toward a chair. "Mind if I sit down?"

Farin shrugged. "I guess."

"I was in the neighborhood and thought I'd drop by."

She drew her chin back and looked doubtfully at him. "It's Friday night and Cinco de Mayo to boot. You're what, twenty-two?"

"Twenty-four."

"Twenty-four," she echoed. "Why aren't you partying down on South Beach?"

He smiled again—a smile that looked like trouble. "Because I was in the neighborhood. Thought I'd drop by."

In fairness, Sawyer had done a fairly decent job processing the reality of her emergence from Ben's swimming pool that day. Though shocked at first, Ben had explained with zero detail the grave circumstances leading to her would-be resurrection. Sawyer had sworn to tell no one what he knew. If Ben trusted him, she figured she should at least try.

"Nice night." He glanced around the grounds and up at the sky.

"It is." She regarded her glass. "Did you want a glass of wine or something?"

"Sure, that'd be great."

She excused herself and went inside. Atop the kitchen island she found a fresh bottle of wine—already opened. An empty glass sat beside it.

Cheryl peeked her head in. "Did you want me to bring you two something to snack on?"

"Wh-?"

Ben appeared beside his wife. "Everything okay?"

Farin looked at them and shook her head. "He's eight years younger than I am."

"He still might fancy a snack," Cheryl reasoned.

"He came all the way over from the Grove," Ben added.

Farin scoffed. "He's Derek's manager."

They looked at her and smiled, then headed back to the living room.

She shook her head, grabbed the glass and bottle, and headed back outside. Once at the table, she poured a glass for her apparent guest and took her seat.

"Thanks." He lifted the delicate vessel to hers.

When they toasted, Farin downed half the contents of her glass.

It was not that Sawyer was bad looking. Just the opposite. He had the great hair, the dreamy eyes, the five o'clock shadow, the perfect smile, and the lanky musician body. It had not escaped her he looked good in jeans. Tall, but not too tall. Thin, but not skinny. Nice arms. All the things that might have turned her head at one time. But that time had come and gone.

"So how's the recording going?"

"Honestly? It's not." She realized she sounded closed off, but only because she was.

"Ben says it may take some time. That's how these things go. Once you start up again, you'll see. Just like riding a bike."

She decided she disliked the familiarity with which he spoke about her family. As if he had known them for years. Like they were old friends. She stared at the pool.

Sawyer topped off her glass and eased back into his chair. He hummed softly, drumming his thumb and middle finger against his left leg as he checked out the soft illumination and lush landscaping.

"I don't ride bikes," she said brusquely.

"You've never ridden a bike?"

"Of course I've ridden a bike. But I'm a grown woman. I don't ride them now."

His eyes sparkled with a mixture of mischief and amusement. "If you did, you'd know what I mean."

"My point is, it's probably been a lot longer since I've ridden a bike than you."

"I ride my bike all the time. It's about twenty minutes from my place to U of M. Great exercise."

Farin rolled her eyes and scoffed. "You get that I'm trying to point out how young you are, right?"

Sawyer leaned forward as if to whisper a secret. "And you get my reference to 'riding a bike' is just an expression, right?"

She sat back in her chair and exhaled loudly.

They sat and sipped their wine. The more at ease Sawyer appeared, the more agitated she felt. Who was this guy to come over to Ben's unannounced and act like he belonged there? Why had Derek not come out to steal him away? And how long was she supposed to babysit?

"Yeah," he said at last. "It's not exactly going like I'd planned."

"What do you mean 'planned?'"

"You. Us. This conversation."

"I thought you were just in the neighborhood and wanted to say hi."

"Do you blame me? This is some news. And since I'm not at liberty to discuss it with anyone else, I figured I'd hang out somewhere my big mouth can't get me in trouble."

"So what? You want to talk about my tragic predicament?"

"If you want. What I'd rather do is get you in that building over there." He tipped his glass toward Ben's studio.

Farin narrowed unfriendly eyes at him.

"No? Not ready to ride that—"

"—enough about bikes!"

"Okay! Forget the bikes!" He matched her tone, though he remained calm. "Look, you're here. You have access to one of the finest home studios I've seen on two continents. You had a successful career you're able to build on. And, more importantly, you finally have the chance to sing something more inspiring than 'Woman/Child.' That's reason enough to pick up where you left off. If it were me, I'd have been in there from day one."

She folded her arms. "What's wrong with 'Woman/Child?'"

Sawyer wrinkled his nose and sipped his wine.

"What?"

"It's dull, no offense. Pop. Trite. Beneath you."

"The charts disagreed."

Sawyer parted his lips and rolled his eyes.

She scooted to the edge of her chair and rested her elbow on the table. "And you just met me. What could you possibly know about what's 'beneath me?'"

"I know 'Down Deep in Love' was a superior track. Snappy tune. Awesome high hat sixteen count beat. It made you. Awesome late-'80s tune. And yeah, you had a few hits—*big* hits. But just because a song charts or puts some cash in your bank account doesn't mean it's quality."

"You're an infant. What would you know about quality?"

"I produced a few artists over in the UK. Had the honor of recording at Abbey Road *and* Electric Lady studios. Sat in on a couple of Sun sessions. Fell asleep on the couch at the Music Lair after pulling an all-nighter. Laid some killer tracks using the echo chambers at Capital. Worked the Neve console at Sound City. And before you label me a smug name dropper, know this: I not only have a good ear, but I'm smart as hell...with a master's degree from University of Miami's School of Music in my crosshairs."

With exaggerated disinterest, Farin leaned back and crossed her ankles as he continued.

"I've sat in with and studied under the best there is—both in and out of school—without having to pander to the Jameson Lockhardts of the industry. So when I give you a compliment, you can take it to the bank I know what I'm talking about. And when I say you played it safe with some of your freshman tracks, it's a good bet I'm right."

She opened her mouth to protest, but he cut her off.

"I love everything from African soul to Mississippi blues to grunge to mainstream alternative. And where there's a place for pop music, it's mostly like settling for prefab IKEA, do-it-yourself furniture. It may look trendy but it comes apart in two years as opposed to rich, handcrafted mahogany pieces you hand down for generations."

Farin poured herself another drink and leveled her eyes at him.

"So I guess the question is whether you want your legacy to be a four-count ditty that may chart well but is easily forgotten, or whether you want to create something that punches people in the gut and makes them remember more than your pretty smile."

Perhaps it was the alcohol. Perhaps not. Sawyer's arrogance reminded her of Chris several years ago. She wondered if Sawyer swaggered when trying to impress a woman. She set her glass down and clapped her hands in slow motion. "Bravo! Did you rehearse that speech or ad-lib it?"

Sawyer shook his head and downed the rest of his wine. He set the empty vessel on the table and reclined into his chair. "I think you're scared. I think if you don't get back in the studio soon, you're gonna bug out."

"I think you're a musical elitist whose youth and experience have given him an inflated ego."

"Is that so?"

"Hell yeah, it's so. C'mon. You can insult other people's work all day long, but let's be honest. The songs that make the charts, sell a trillion copies, get overplayed and hated, but then end up being beloved tunes on the oldies' stations? They're usually the pop tunes. And they're usually the best tunes. They're chosen by the fans for a reason. To insult a pop artist who sells well is to insult music fans everywhere!"

"I'm not insulting the fans. I respect the fact we all have our individual tastes. I've even been known to sit in on a gig or two with Top 40 bands."

"Then why are you on such a high-horse, criticizing *my* work? And why would you sit in on a gig playing music you think is beneath you?"

"For the same reason you laid that track in the first place. I dig music. I dig it when it's good, and I dig it when it's bad. I just like it better when I can create something I'm proud of."

"I'm proud of the work I create," she snapped.

Sawyer tilted his head and smiled, suddenly the congenial gentleman again. He gave her a sideways grin. "Then get back in the studio."

CHAPTER 9

FAITH PETERSON CHECKED HER LEATHER bags to make sure she had everything. She tended to forget incidentals like deodorant and toothpaste. Somehow she had never grown accustomed to taking care of herself on trips. Her years with Mirage had spoiled her. She had relied on assistants to handle mundane tasks such as packing her things and coordinating her schedule to ensure she arrived where she needed to be on time. A good thing considering that, in those days, she was usually too wasted to do any of those things herself.

Henri hovered near the back of the room, detached from his regular place behind his easel. "How long will you be gone?" he asked with a forlorn pout as he exhaled a stream of smoke.

Faith zipped her overnight case. "I guess it depends. Sure you don't wanna come with?"

Henri helped move her luggage to the front door. He pressed the elevator button. "This really isn't my thing, you know."

"I know." She smiled at the false French accent he had adopted so long ago, he could not shake it. "I'll call every night."

Henri shrugged. "You will or you won't. I'll be here if you do."

"Don't be like that."

"You'll find another man who doesn't make you live in a home with no walls. You'll go with him. And I'll be here. I'll dust your piano."

She stifled a laugh.

The elevator door chimed its arrival. Faith grabbed two of her five bags to start loading them inside, but Henri took her arm. "Wait."

She set down the luggage and checked her watch.

"You have time. Come here a moment. Say a proper goodbye, no?"

Henri had shed his rough exterior over the last few weeks. For longer than Faith could remember, their living arrangement had included none of the outward displays of affection they shared. Each tended to their own business—his painting, her fashion designing. They lived quietly, predictably, and Faith had become the settled individual none of her former fans would recognize without her notorious leather wardrobe. But lately, Henri had focused more attention on her than his art.

At first, she had attributed the shift to a possible painter's block, if those even existed. In the entire time they had known each other, Henri had never stopped creating. He had worked every waking hour of every day, and often into the night. She had posed for him much of that time and had occasionally wondered if he would ever stop. In all likelihood, he would not.

Then, the night of his most recent show, she had come home early to find their bedroom filled with portraits of the two of them. These resembled none of his typical nude paintings of her. Instead, they portrayed a closeness that had previously gone undeclared by either of them. That was the night Faith Peterson knew for sure Melvin Theodore Leberwitz—a.k.a. Henri—loved her.

Since then, he had acted like someone she barely knew. To say she disliked the change would be a lie. He doted on her, told her every day she was beautiful, opened doors for her, asked about her day. These were good things, however foreign. It was not as if he smothered her. He was just...different. It would take a while to get used to this new side of him.

Henri walked Faith to their living room and sat beside her on the couch. "I love you. You know this."

Faith nodded.

"I don't know if I can paint without you here."

"I won't be gone that long. Should I not go? Are you asking me to stay?"

He sifted his fingers through his dark hair, then patted his shirt pocket to find his pack of cigarettes. Faith noticed his hands shake as he lit one, inhaled deeply, then exhaled through his nostrils. "No, that would be wrong of me."

"It's business, Henri. Just business."

"We both have *crap* for business. Too many people. Always the beautiful people. Always parties. Always glamour. And you in your leather. Do you think I don't see the way men look at you?"

She cocked her head. "You're not really that insecure?"

He stood and paced the floor, occasional puffs of smoke trailing behind him like a steam locomotive.

"I'm not leaving you."

He turned around and stubbed out his cigarette in a nearby ashtray, then rushed forward and dropped to his knees before her. "You're the air that I breathe!"

Before she could stop herself, she emitted a bark of laughter. He hated when she laughed at his melodrama, but she could not stop herself.

His eyes held her with dark intensity as he fished through his tattered, paint-stained jeans pockets. He pulled out a two-carat, princess-cut diamond set in platinum, held it up to her, and said, "Marry me."

Faith's mouth opened. A beat later, she felt something in her throat. She swallowed hard.

"Be my wife," he begged.

She regarded him with wide eyes. "Henri, I—"

"You don't like the ring," he blurted out, suddenly panicked. "Not nearly good enough. How could I be so ridiculous? Stupid fucking ring."

She dared to look down at the exquisite piece of jewelry, willing away the sudden feeling of nausea and lightheadedness. "The ring's fine. It's...*beautiful*."

"I should've showered first. How could you marry a man who stinks?"

"That's not it—"

"I should have bought you roses and taken you somewhere special. I should have asked you better. I'm shit. I don't deserve you."

"Henri, *stop*."

"I'm Jewish! That's what it is. You can never love me because of my family. How could a Catholic ever marry a Jew? Your family will disown you!"

"*Stop*! Can I say something?"

When his rant subsided, he dropped his head onto her lap. His words were barely audible. "Do not break my heart, *mon trésor*. I need my heart."

She ran slender fingers through his hair. "I'd never break your heart. But I don't know if I can marry you." He looked up at her. She noticed the red in his eyes and cupped his face with her hands. "I love you. I do. But this is pretty sudden, you know? I mean...*marriage*? Am I ready for it? Are you?"

Henri shook his head emphatically. "I am ready. I'm ready to marry you."

She smiled gently. "I can't give you an answer today. I'm sorry. Why did you ask me two minutes before I have to walk out the door?"

He sniffed mournfully. "Because I do not think. All I do is feel. And right now, I feel you will never come home. I've scared you away."

She pressed her lips against his, noting the pungent stench of tobacco mixed with the faint smell of aftershave. "I'm not scared. I just wanna be sure. I'll have an answer by the time I come back. Not on the phone—so don't think I'm putting you off when we talk."

Henri stood and helped Faith to her feet. Quietly, they walked to the door. He pressed the elevator button once more. When it arrived, he assisted with her bags and eventually helped her get a taxi.

She held him tight before she climbed inside. "I want you to paint while I'm gone," she whispered lovingly.

Hours later, Henri sat at his easel, chain smoking. Tears streamed down his face until he could barely see the enormous canvas upon which he worked. It bore a beautiful portrait of the woman he loved, bathed in white light, suspended in the sky with outstretched hands. Below her was an image of an agonized Henri, unable to escape the fiery pit of hell. He called his painting *Faith*.

***

For all the success, respect, and wealth amassed in his short thirty-eight years, Bobby Lockhardt was no stranger to fear. He knew it intimately. At his lowest points, fear rendered him immobile. When on his game, fear crouched in shadows, ever near, desperate for any possible point of entry.

Juggling his daily responsibilities at LSI while confronting the reality the company would soon live or die under his leadership gave fear superlative access to Bobby's fragile psyche. But for weeks now, fear's primary offensive came not from his business dealings, but from the uncharted recesses of his heart. And it finally hit the bull's eye.

Dr. Stumpf scribbled on a notepad, his thick hands and plump fingers almost completely concealing his ballpoint pen. "You look anxious. Care to discuss it?"

Bobby repositioned himself on the couch. He had felt uncomfortable with the idea of lying down—especially in his suit—and had opted instead to sit. Every couple of minutes he would uncross and recross his legs, straighten or loosen his tie, purposefully extend his arms to adjust them into a seemingly more casual pose.

"I'm not sure why I can't relax," he confessed.

The doctor nodded. He adjusted his spectacles as he flipped through the new patient paperwork Bobby had filled out in the reception area, pausing here or there to make notes. "Why don't we start with what brings you in today. You say you were diagnosed with schizophrenia at the age of seventeen."

Bobby nodded. "Yes, sir."

"And that your family physician prescribed your medication from that time up until his death a few months ago."

"That's right."

"Tell me what was going on at the time of your diagnosis. I see here in your paperwork your mother was diagnosed around the same time as you. Is that correct?"

"It is." Bobby shifted uneasily. He had foreknown coming here would mean answering questions and had tried to prepare himself accordingly, but he disliked discussing his childhood. "It was getting harder to take care of her. For years, I'd noticed her sort of drifting in and out. I don't know how to describe it. It was like she'd just sit around, emotionless. And sometimes I'd hear her talking in her room. A couple of times I picked up the kitchen extension to see who she was talking to, but I got a dial tone, so I knew she wasn't on the phone. I tried talking to her about it, but she made me swear I wouldn't tell anyone. Things got bad, then worse. She had no friends—neither of us did."

"You spent all your time caring for her."

Bobby nodded. "I got teased a lot."

"Any drug use?"

"Me? Or Mom?"

"Yes."

"Mom used to drink a good bit, but no drugs that I know of. Sometimes I'd sneak into her liquor cabinet. Probably a little too much. Yeah, definitely too much. I just wanted to escape, you know? Or fit in or something. But I never really did street drugs. I tried pot a couple of times before my diagnosis. Nothing since then."

"And your father. He wasn't in the home?"

"They divorced when I was young."

"All right. So what happened to cause this family physician to diagnosis you? Do you have hallucinations?"

Bobby creased his brow and shook his head.

"Never saw things that weren't there?"

"No."

"Heard voices?"

"No."

"Any history of distorted or jumbled speech?"

"Nothing like that. Nothing at all."

The more questions the psychiatrist asked, the more nervous Bobby became. He had to confess the whole story. He had never spoken to anyone about the events of that night.

He lowered his head. His voice sounded small and frightened. "I'd drink until I blacked out. One night in particular. I don't remember much. There was an accident."

Dr. Stumpf set his pen down on top of the notebook, laced his pudgy fingers, and looked patiently at Bobby.

Dr. Childs had forbade Bobby to speak of the accident to anyone. His father had echoed those sentiments. Until this moment, he had remained a dutiful son. He wondered what his father would think if he knew Bobby had made this appointment on his own—a Saturday appointment so he would not be missed at the office. What would he think if he knew his son had decided to take charge of his own life, that he had thrown out the number given him for Dr. Childs' temporary replacement in favor of seeking out someone unconnected to their family name?

"A man was killed. It was my fault." As the words left his lips, decades of guilt and shame assaulted him. Then, it felt as if they evaporated.

The doctor frowned, protruded his lips as he considered Bobby's confession, then resumed taking notes. "I'm not connecting the events you describe to your diagnosis. How long had you been a patient of this doctor?"

"My mother was hospitalized a couple of days after the accident, and I went to New York with my dad. I met him a little while after that."

"How long did he observe you before diagnosing you and prescribing the medication?"

Bobby looked down at the floor and shook his head. "He started me on the Haldol right away. He said the blackouts were caused by the schizophrenia, that it was hereditary and I'd gotten it from my mom. He said I needed to get it under control before someone else got hurt."

Dr. Stumpf set his pen down again, moved his notepad to his left, and leaned his large body on his elbows atop his desk. "So you blacked out one night while you were drunk. There was an accident. And now you've been on this medication, unchecked and unmonitored by a psychiatric specialist, for over twenty years?"

Bobby swallowed hard. "I went off it once."

"What does that mean? You discontinued it on your own, or this physician took you off?"

"I took myself off."

"Tell me about that."

Bobby exhaled. No going back now. "I fell..."

The physician waited patiently for him to finish.

"I fell in love with a woman. O-or I thought I was in love. And the meds, well. They made me. I mean, I couldn't—"

"You were impotent," Dr. Stumpf said plainly.

Bobby nodded. His face felt hot. "I didn't think she'd want anything to do with me if I couldn't...you know...*perform*."

"And so you stopped abruptly. No tapering down?"

Bobby hung is head sadly. "I had another blackout. But no alcohol this time. At least none that I remember. From what I was told, I guess I talked to my dad and he could tell something wasn't right. So he came down to my place in Florida and got me. I was inpatient at Dorothea Dix down in North Carolina while Dr. Childs got me back and stable on the meds."

Stumpf rubbed his bearded chin, as if alarmed by all the players and details. "How much time?"

"I don't know. I wanna say I lost a couple of months. I can't remember a thing."

Wide-eyed, Dr. Stumpf released a heavy sigh and picked up his notepad to make some final notes. When he finished, he looked at Bobby and shook his head. "So you've come here today to establish with a new doctor and ensure you don't have another blackout."

Bobby nodded. "And I think I'm in love again."

For the first time since stepping into the psychiatrist's office, Bobby saw the rotund older man break into an almost friendly smile. A sympathetic undertone bridged their professional distance. "Sounds like you deserve a little happiness in your life, Bobby. Is she in love with you, too?"

Bobby shrugged and fidgeted in his seat. "I don't know. We've spent a lot of time together lately, but I'm afraid she'll stop seeing me when she finds out about my problem."

Dr. Stumpf cocked his head and feigned confusion. "What problem?"

"The schizophrenia."

"Well," he said, "I don't know about that. Let's just take this one step at a time. First things first. Let's look at tapering off this medication the right way and see what we come up with."

"What do you mean?"

"I want you to schedule some follow-up appointments. Three times a week to start. Son, I don't know what's gone on with your father or this quack you've been mercifully freed from, but you and I have a good bit of work ahead of us."

***

Miles had arranged dinner with Alicia at a restaurant on Miami Beach. Remembering their first encounter a few months back, he chose Nemo's for its palette-neutral menu and less frenetic location. It sat at the southernmost tip of Collins, away from the rumpus of Ocean Drive.

Although history often illustrated the dangers of declaring victory before an enemy rose their white flag, Miles felt like celebrating. He was back in Miami. He would soon be restored to his position at the *Herald*. And, if Wednesday's mystery caller was who she claimed to be, they were about to bring down one of the most notorious men in show business.

If that did not get Alicia's approval, he did not know what else to do.

Still, Miles would not yet lay all his cards on the table. Despite the woman's convincing words, he had verified nothing that night but a nervous stomach. She had promised to call soon with a time and place to meet. Until then, he would keep most of their conversation to himself.

He arrived early and procured their table, then ordered appetizers and a club soda with lime. No alcohol would cloud his perception this evening.

Beside him sat the bouquet of white tiger lilies he had custom ordered from a florist down in the Grove. He checked his watch periodically, hoping she would not keep him waiting too long.

When she arrived with Bridgeman in tow, his anticipation dissolved into disappointment.

She slid into the seat opposite him at the table "Okay. Whaddya got?"

He stood and shook Bridgeman's hand. "I didn't realize you'd be joining us. It's good to see you."

Bridgeman smirked and inclined his head at his partner. He nearly sat on the flowers, but stopped short. "Why Macy, you shouldn't have."

Miles' cheeks flushed. He took the flowers from Bridgeman and handed them to Alicia. "These are for you."

He thought he caught a trace of a smile before she snapped, "Why are you buying me flowers? This is a business meeting, not a date. You said you had information, so we're here. Spill it."

The waiter arrived with appetizers and then retreated with their drink orders, giving them ample time to review the dinner menu.

Bridgeman helped himself to the sourdough bread and hummus. "Great choice, Macy. I brought Penny here last month. The food's fantastic. Did you know this building was used as a crack house before they restored it?"

The men discussed the FSB report while Alicia browsed the menu. Every so often, Miles caught her glancing his way.

After the group had ordered, Bridgeman summarized. "Our files are shoddy, and we have reason to believe someone higher up has gotten involved. Not sure how far up. But we know the limo was no accident, and we know Stark did one hell of a job containing the information."

Miles nodded. "Lockhardt paid him to. I'm sure of it."

"Unless we can link them together with anything specific, we have no case. The phone records you got us were great, but I dug a little deeper. Records between the time Jordan Grant was killed and six months after his wife's accident don't show a single call between them—at least not on any of the obvious numbers."

"That just proves they were more careful in the beginning," Miles reasoned.

Bridgeman nodded. "And if that's the case, it raises additional questions." He looked at his partner. "Maybe Stark's death is related."

"I'd like to take a look at the photos of the limousine," Miles said.

Alicia sprang to life. "Oh no! Those are part of an official investigation."

Miles looked wounded. "What's 'official' about any of this? Bridgeman says you two are meeting at his house."

Alicia shot her partner an icy stare.

"What?" Bridgeman held his hands up innocently. "We're all in this together, Al." He removed an envelope from his suit pocket and handed it to Miles. "I got you copies."

"Thanks." Miles eyed their fellow patrons to ensure no one had taken an interest in their conversation, then went through the photos.

Bridgeman pointed to one in particular. "There. See that charred lump?"

Miles squinted. "I think so. Where is that, the front seat?"

Bridgeman nodded. "The floor of the front passenger's seat. At first I didn't thinking anything about it. But right before I left, I bagged it."

Miles held the picture closer, then further away. "What is it?"

"A cell phone," Bridgeman said.

"Oh yeah?"

"It's charred and mostly slag, but the circuit board's still intact."

Miles studied the rest of the photos, then tucked them away for later consideration. "Was it the driver's?"

"I have no idea. I've got someone checking that out."

"And you mentioned something about finding some casing in the fuel cell?"

Bridgeman nodded his head and spoke with a mouthful of hummus. "Housed the trigger. Clever guy."

Throughout dinner, Alicia added little to their conversation, which confused Miles. Normally she was outgoing and passionate when discussing her job.

"You have an okay day at work?" he asked her, hoping to spark an interest.

She shrugged and picked at her salad. "It was okay. Paperwork mostly. Billy and I solved a case from a couple months ago. Gang related. At least the family has some closure now."

"So how does it feel to be back?" Bridgeman asked him. "You miss Chicago?"

Miles bobbed his head as he swallowed a bite of salmon, then sipped his club soda. "I miss parts of it. The Cubs, of course. The lake. But it's great to be back. It's home now, you know?" He looked across the table, pleased to find Alicia looking at him.

"I know what you mean," Bridgeman agreed. "The place really grows on you. Penny and the girls and I love it here. People tell me this is no city to raise kids, but Detroit's no better."

"The humidity nearly did them all in at first," Alicia corrected, eyebrow raised. "I didn't think they'd make it. Penny only recently started wearing makeup again."

"She's got great skin. She doesn't need makeup." Bridgeman smirked and waggled his eyebrows at his partner.

They finished their dinner, then ordered coffee for dessert. Bridgeman excused himself to call and see if his wife needed anything before he came home.

"I didn't know what flowers you liked," Miles told Alicia once they were alone. "I wasn't trying to embarrass you. I thought it'd be just the two of us."

"You thought this was going to be a date," she countered bluntly. "I told you, it's not going to be that easy."

Miles put his hand down on the table. "How about a real date, then? Say, next Saturday night?"

She looked at his hand, then at him, then in the direction of the bathroom. "What are you doing?"

"C'mon, Alicia. What's it gonna take?"

"'Take?'"

"Yeah, *take*. I've proven I'm serious. I've moved. I'm here. And now I'm asking you—again. Will you go out with me?"

"You want to take me out to dinner?"

"*Yes.*"

"Maybe come home with me and meet my family?"

He caught her sarcasm. "Sure. I'd love to meet your folks."

"Yeah, Macy. You could come to Sunday Mass and then home for lunch. Mama could whip up some Habañero chili. I know how you like your spicy food."

Sarcasm turned to mockery, which he chose not to take personally. He let her continue until her harsh words were spent. On the upside, he could tell she had derived no pleasure ridiculing him.

Something about her spoke to him on a level so deep, he did not fully understand it. She wore her beautiful, hard exterior like an impenetrable shell that could defy pain, deflect emotion, and dissuade would-be suitors. Had he not seen her out of that shell, for however short a time, she might have succeeded in crushing his hopes to know her better.

But he had glimpsed the woman beneath that shell—loving, vulnerable, passionate. He remembered every moment of that night. The fact she fought so hard to keep people at bay made him feel all the more special for having been granted temporary access to her sacred world.

"One date," he pressed.

She tucked a tendril of dark hair behind her ear and sat forward in her chair, resting her chin on her hand. With a less acerbic edge, she said, "I told you. We're too different."

Miles expelled a heavy breath and looked absently about the bustling restaurant, its staff scurrying to serve their trendy patrons. The sounds of the murmuring crowd mingled with clinking glasses and utensils against plates seemed far away from the island of frustration upon which he sat.

"It was one night," she added. "You know nothing about me."

"I know you like me," he told her, flouting the seed of insecurity planted by her earlier comments. "And I know enough to keep trying. You put on this tough act, but you're not fooling me. So it has to be something else. Did someone hurt you? Lie to you? Cheat on you? Are you seeing someone else?"

"Why can't you just let this go?"

He felt as if someone had punched him in the stomach. "Is that it, then?"

"I'm not seeing anyone. I'm just a busy woman."

"Your partner's married with a family, Detective. That doesn't impede his ability to do his job."

She narrowed her eyes at him. "I didn't say it can't be done, did I?"

"I'm doing everything I can here despite the fact you haven't even said thank you for the flowers. I've moved. I've asked you out. I've tried to discuss your objections. You've given me nothing. But you also haven't said you're uninterested. I think we both know you're not chasing me off."

She looked at him but said nothing.

"C'mon."

Bridgeman returned and apologized for taking so long. "Penny wants me to bring home dessert." When he sat down, he looked to his left and then his right. Neither of his dinner companions responded, which amused him. "So what did I miss?"

"Nothing." She crossed her arms and sat back in her chair, her eyes challenging her would-be suitor. "Just waiting for the big unveiling."

"Outstanding." He scooted his chair forward and turned to Miles. "Al said you have a lead?"

Miles realized he would lose tonight's battle. But if Alicia thought their conversation had finished, she had another think coming. He shook his head, disappointed as he forced his eyes away from hers. "Yes," he said, "I believe I do. I received an interesting phone call earlier this week. If this person's for real, you'll have Lockhardt on the bombing case."

Bridgeman and Alvarez looked at one another and then back at Miles.

"A witness?" he asked, confused. "We've been sitting here an hour and a half discussing flowers and photographs when you have a *witness*? Who is it?"

Miles rubbed his collarbone. "I can't say."

"What?" Alvarez demanded through clenched teeth.

Bridgeman held his hand out in front of her, then looked at Miles. "Do you know this person? Are they reliable?"

"I have no idea," Miles confessed. "I'm suspicious. But if I'm right, it'll not only give you what you want for the car bomb, it could solve Jordan Grant's murder as well."

Bridgeman's eyes grew large. He whispered low as he considered the possibilities. "When are you meeting this person?"

Miles' lips flattened into a downward grin. "I can't give you details right now."

Alvarez threw her head back and sucked in her cheeks.

"Okay," Bridgeman said. "Let me ask you this—"

"Cuff 'em, Billy!" she snapped, pointing a finger at Miles. "He's obstructing justice."

Bridgeman laughed. "Al—"

"I'm not kidding! Protecting a witness in a murder case?"

He held up his hands. "Hold on."

"You won't tell us the name of the witness, Macy. You're obstructing justice."

"Now c'mon, detective," Miles chided. "I don't have to reveal my sources."

"You're not writing a story," she snapped.

"And you're not officially working this case," he countered.

She did not utter another word. She did not need to. Her expression spoke volumes.

"Let's calm down," Bridgeman said. "This is too important to start fighting amongst ourselves."

"Excuse me." She snatched up her purse and stomped off toward the ladies' room.

Miles looked at Bridgeman, then nodded once and ran after her. He grabbed her arm and spun her around. "Wait."

She glared daggers at him.

"Alicia," he began softly.

"You want to date me, but you want to keep your little secrets."

"It's not like that and you know it," he whispered urgently, ignoring the disapproving glares from the unsteady stream of diners entering and exiting the lavatories.

"Who're you meeting?" she asked again as if daring him not to answer.

His eyes pleaded for understanding. At this point, he knew too little. Had Farin faked her own death? Where had she been all these years? How was Lockhardt involved? Why had she not come forward with information about Jordan's murder?

Somehow, these things tied together. But if Farin had gone to such lengths to keep hidden, Miles had to believe adding his would-be cop girlfriend to the equation would be like bringing a torch to a TNT plant. The entire investigation depended on Farin's story. He could not risk spooking her.

"I'm too good a reporter to let my feelings for you influence my judgment," he told her sadly. "And you're too good a cop to ignore the truth if I could tell you."

Her eyes grew wide. "So you do know something you're not telling us!"

"No. But I'm close. And if you'll just trust me a little while longer, I think I can blow this whole thing wide open."

Fury emanated from her body. Miles fought the urge to kiss her.

"Are you meeting with Chris Grant? Is that why you're not telling me?"

"No, and that's as much as I can say."

"Then you've said nothing." She yanked away from his grasp and stomped into the ladies' room without a backwards glance.

Miles returned to their table and dropped into his seat. "Your partner's quite a woman," he said, unclear whether or not he meant it as a compliment.

Bridgeman slapped Miles on the back. "I feel for ya. It wasn't easy for me to gain her trust either. But hang in there. That icy exterior melts eventually."

"You think so?" Miles shook his head. "I think I like her better drunk."

Bridgeman laughed. "Yeah, I guess sometimes there just isn't enough tequila."

Miles scoffed and grabbed his club soda, then toasted Bridgeman's iced tea. "Truer words, brother."

When Alicia returned, she looked angrier than when she had marched off. "I'm ready to go," she told her partner.

Bridgeman ran his fingers through his short hair and exhaled. He looked at Miles and shrugged. "I think we're ready for the check."

"Don't worry about it," Miles said. "I've got it."

Alicia signaled for their waiter. When he brought their bill, she grabbed it before either of the men had a chance. She slid her card into the black leather bill folder without so much as peeking inside, then shoved it at the server with a quick, "Thanks."

Bridgeman looked at her, unamused.

"What? When you've got six older brothers, you learn to move fast."

"I wanted to buy you dinner," Miles dared to say.

"Yeah, well, I wanted to know who you're meeting with, so I guess nobody wins."

Bridgeman closed his eyes and shook his head.

The waiter returned for Alicia's signature, which she hastily scribbled on the receipt before standing and snatching her flowers. She looked expectantly at Bridgeman.

"Wait," Miles said, his interior dialogue cursing his weakness. "Hold on a minute."

Alicia paused and turned his way.

Miles looked at Bridgeman. "I might have a name for you to check on."

Bridgeman motioned for his partner to sit down.

"I was hoping to do some further research before I said anything..."

"What's the name?" Bridgeman asked.

Miles hesitated. He hated giving up information he had not investigated, which accounted for the fact he had not disclosed the e-mail or his trip to California.

"C'mon, cowboy," Alicia challenged, leveling her eyes upon him. "We've shown you ours, now show us yours."

"Nancy Chambers," Miles blurted out at last. "Out of New York. I didn't have much time to look, but I think there may be a missing persons out on her."

Alicia groaned angrily, beckoning Bridgeman to leave with her. "We don't handle missing persons, and we certainly don't handle New York."

"She was Jameson Lockhardt's personal assistant," Miles added before she turned to go.

Bridgeman's eyes darted back and forth across the table as his mind processed the information. Alvarez sat down and covered her mouth with her hand. They looked at each other and shook their heads.

"We need to get to the office," Alvarez said to Bridgeman.

"Hold on." Bridgeman turned to Miles. "What would this have to do with Miami? Was this Nancy Chambers here? Did your witness say something?"

"I haven't talked to her about it yet," Miles told Bridgeman, both men missing the brief flash of jealousy in Alicia's eyes. "She's pretty skittish for reasons I can only guess. I need some time. I'll let you both know the minute I have anything concrete. I was the one who originally came to you, remember? In any case, it would make sense if she came down here with Lockhardt to attend Jordan Grant's funeral. It'll be interesting to find out if you can identify who the cell phone belongs to."

Bridgeman nodded, his thoughts racing ahead of him as the implications hit him. "This is quickly turning into a jurisdiction issue."

CHAPTER 10

WHEN THE PROMISE TO CALL and set up a meeting "soon" turned into nearly a month, Miles all but gave up. Whoever had called pretending to be Farin Grant had obviously duped him. He wondered who had set him up, and why. Was it an attempt to throw him off Lockhardt's trail—or worse, cost him any hope of winning Alicia's heart?

One thing he knew for sure: if Farin were alive, she would contact Chris. Married or not, she would not race to Chris' place after fleeing Coral Gables but fail to contact him when she resurfaced. There was something inevitable about the two of them. Even Miles saw it. Or maybe he was just starting to view things like that through a softer lens.

Chris also owned the beach house at the time of the explosion but had not yet commented on it. Not even through his handlers. Miles found that curious. Unfortunately, he no longer had a direct number for him. Last week, he had left a message for him through Minor 6th Records.

"Just tell him Miles Macy needs to fact check some new developments on that personal appearance over at the Sonesta on Key Biscayne back in '91," he had told Samantha Drake's assistant. "And tell him I'm still waiting on that suit he owes me."

Chris had not returned the call.

Miles had settled back in at the *Herald* with ease, accepting the now congenial attitude of his superiors without lauding over them what everybody knew. He had returned at the request of someone powerful and therefore could not be touched. They had even tried promoting him to assistant managing editor, but he declined. With an increased salary and an assurance his editor would not unduly hardline his work, he saw no reason to step back from doing what he did best: chasing the story.

With his career on a steady track, Miles concentrate on his two top priorities: connecting the dots between Jameson Lockhardt and Farin's murder, and convincing Alicia to have dinner with him. Both matters left him frustrated.

Alicia accused him of lying to her about his potential witness, convinced he had either fabricated the story or was keeping the discussion private. Neither prospect won him any points despite Bridgeman running interference on his behalf.

At night, Miles waited by the phone. He waited for a lead, or an update, or for Alicia to call and say she had reconsidered. And while he waited, he tried to fit the pieces of his peculiar e-mail into a completed puzzle. He used his hard copy to make notes and track what he knew, what he suspected, and what remained a mystery.

~~A fuller picture won't be drawn~~	No further clues coming.
~~You'll start with those beneath the~~ lawn	SB Cemetery. O'Conners. Others?
A fund for trade, determined will	Trade = "in exchange" or "labor?"
~~Across the pond~~—Himself? Or killed?	Europe. Male. Murdered? Suicide?
The motivation, his own life	W/lines above = murder? Self-defense?
He sacrificed his son and wife	Bobby/Sarah. Someone after JL Sr.?
And what is it about a name	O'Conner/Wellingham. Connected?
A substitute; the price of fame	Substitute for what? What price was paid?
~~Too soon to go;~~ too important to fail	Grants. Who can't fail? LSI?
~~Despite the crime, no time in jail~~	Crime = murder. Jordan's? Farin's?
A silenced victim gone no more	~~Farin alive??~~ HOAX
Has someone still worth dying for	
Without your help she may be lost	Someone else in trouble. A woman.
~~That's why you've left your former boss~~	Back to the Herald—YES
~~So start today with what you know~~	Not much, but thanks.
Time's running out; you've got to go	Trip to SB. Maybe one to England?
~~To point you in the right direction~~	
Review the entertainment section	I read it and write it. Point?
Lest history repeat itself	Another explosion?
Don't leave these hints upon the shelf:	
~~Sarah Wellingham~~	SB—mental ward.
The signing party	What party? I'd like to take Alicia to party.
Oh what a night (1967)	Check notable 1967 events; Frankie Avalon?
The Firm	Book? Movie? Band? Tom Cruise?
Jade Larken Trongly	Is she the one in danger? Possible witness?
Jordan Grant	
~~Nancy Chambers~~	Missing persons/NYC? JL's secretary.
Hopeful Heart, Fayetteville, NC	

Combining the clues into a single cohesive story proved more than Miles could handle. It would lead him in a direction—Farin's stage name, for example—then leave him with more questions than answers. If Farin and Bobby had attended San Marcos at different times, how did she come to adopt the Wellingham name when she hid out?

Many people adopted stage names. Many artists started in England. Phone impostor Farin had stated her father was killed in a drunk driving accident but would not elaborate on the phone. How might that tie into Jordan's murder? Or Lockhardt? There had to be more.

The elder Lockhardt had to be the common thread in these events, but Miles could not visualize a pattern. Might the person who sent him the e-mail be in danger? Could the woman who called him a month ago asking to meet be the author of this confusion? And if so, why had she not called him back? Had *she* run out of time? Was the caller actually Nancy Chambers? Maybe she knew too much and was in hiding.

Yet, he had heard and recognized Farin Grant's voice.

Miles left the office before noon on Thursday. He had turned in a story on the sudden departure of Alan Wilder from Depeche Mode—a speculative piece hypothesizing the move might mark the end of the band. Between Gahan's heroin habit and Fletcher's alleged "mental instability," coupled with their chief songwriter's seizures, the group stood little chance. Not his best work, but good enough. Now, he needed some time to unwind and regroup.

On his way home, Jeanne called and said a woman had phoned, insisting she speak with him.

"Who was it?"

"She didn't leave her name, but she acted like it was pretty important."

"Did you get a number?"

"I tried."

"Did she have an accent?" Miles pressed, hopeful. The pause at the other end confirmed he could rule out Alicia. "What did you tell her?"

"That you'd left for the day. She asked if I knew whether or not you were headed home. Odd girl. Sorta pushy. Op! Hold on. That might be her again. No caller ID."

He pulled into the post office at the intersection of South Dixie Highway and Bird Road. His breathing and heart rate quickened in hopeful anticipation. Maybe the woman who called him last month had not run out of time after all.

"It's her," Jeanne confirmed. "I'm telling ya—pushy broad. I told her you were on the other line and she asked me to transfer her to your cell. You wanna talk to her? She still won't give me a name."

Miles gripped his steering wheel with his free hand and squeezed hard. "Absolutely. Do I need to hang up first?"

Seconds later, his cell phone chirped again. Miles stabbed the talk button.

"Hello?"

"It's me."

Skeptical, he asked, "Is this the same person who called me a month ago?"

"Yes."

"The one who said she'd meet me 'soon' and then never called back?"

An irritated sigh filled the line. "Are you free now?"

"I am if you'll show. Where are you?"

"You know I can't tell you that."

"Then where do you want to meet?"

She paused. "Is anyone following you?"

"Is anyone—" He checked his mirrors and scanned his surroundings. "I don't think so."

"I can't take any chances."

"One of us is gonna have to make a move unless you wanna do this over the phone."

Another pause. "I'm in the general vicinity of my old place."

Miles mentally constructed a map of Key Biscayne and it came to him. "St. Agnes Church. Twenty minutes." When she confirmed, he asked, "Are you at Chris' old place?"

The line went dead.

St. Agnes Church nestled off Harbor Drive in Key Biscayne, a modest two-story stucco structure with a covered wrap-around walkway. Rectangular stained-glass windows sat high along the sides of the long building above connecting archways. Deceptively inornate on the outside, it favored a modern-day chapel rather than the old-world grandeur one imagined when envisioning a Catholic parish.

Noon Mass had just ended when Miles pulled into the parking lot. A small crowd of parishioners casually exited the building, some falling back to chat in small groups. Miles hoped he had not chosen too public a place. If it was Farin, her face would be easily recognizable. He hoped she would not realize this, reconsider, and stand him up.

The question of whether or not he was being followed had unnerved him. On his way over he had exited the Rickenbacker Causeway at Virginia Key, looped around and doubled back to Hobie Island, then proceeded to Crandon Boulevard before parking at the church. He thought about waiting in his car, but the heat won out. He went inside, uncomfortable for reasons he did not understand.

His family did not attend church, Catholic or otherwise. The Macys were worldly people, bordering on materialistic—accomplished but uninspired father, beautiful mother, upper-middle class house in a nice Chicago suburb.

White picket fence, older sister, the expectation that one keep silent about private family matters—such as dad's drinking. No time for God. If anything, the Macys worshipped at the altar of mediocrity.

He entered the sanctuary and sized up the thinning crowd, then grabbed a seat in a pew halfway down on the left. The hard wood surprised him. He wondered if Alicia's church had such uncomfortable seating and, if so, how she managed to sit still during a service.

Aging, hardback hymnals and Bibles rested in the pockets behind the pews. He picked up a hymnal, leafed through it, then replaced it and focused on the large stained-glass depiction of a crucified Christ against the far wall past the lectern.

The most famous man who had ever lived was a complete stranger to Miles. He knew nothing about Jesus or the Bible, save the cliché stories shared over time. He counted himself as neither believer nor unbeliever.

But Alicia believed. In fact, despite their few brief conversations and encounters, he could tell her faith meant more to her than anything had ever meant to him. In his gut, Miles knew if he ever expected to win her heart, he would need to get acquainted with his spirituality. Or at least hers.

After several minutes, the sanctuary lay empty except for Miles and a teenage boy praying in the front right pew. Miles watched him bow his head and lean forward. A humble stance, Miles thought. He had never considered the idea of humility and surrender to a Supreme Being. The concept intrigued him.

There had to be a certain amount of comfort in believing in an all-powerful entity with whom you could share your problems and ask for help in times of trouble. To wipe out all the things you had ever done wrong—your "sins." For a moment, Miles considered trying it himself. He could use some help at this point. Clearly, he was in over his head with both his investigation and Alicia. But before he could close his eyes and take the obligatory position, the teenager stood and headed up the aisle.

Miles straightened and nodded politely at the kid as he walked, hands plunged into his jeans pockets, a look of sadness shrouding his face. The boy lifted his chin in response. Then, to Miles' amazement, he sat beside him.

Confused, Miles remained silent as the young man leaned forward, resting his forearms on the pew in front of them. He hoped he would not strike up a conversation. He had never even prayed before—he was not ready to consider conversion.

"You here for Mass?" the kid asked, staring straight ahead.

Miles shook his head. "I must be late."

"You have a cell phone on you?"

He frowned. "Excuse me?"

"A cell phone. A camera? Anything?"

Miles wondered if the church had hidden cameras or a security guard. What sort of area had Key Biscayne become while he was gone?

"You're Macy, right?" he asked.

Miles nodded.

"I can't tell you where to go until I make sure you don't have any recording devices."

It slowly became clear. Miles felt like a fool.

He studied the young man's profile and realized how much he resembled Chris Grant. Miles had heard Ben's oldest boy had formed a band. They were playing a gig on South Beach Saturday night, and Miles had thought it would be a kick to cover them. He had wanted to take Alicia but was now relieved she had declined. If Farin was living with her former brother-in-law, the last place Miles needed Detective Alvarez to accompany him to was a concert where Farin might show up in disguise. Had she been here this whole time?

Maybe God answered prayers after all—even for those who did not know how to pray.

"Derek Grant, right?" Miles held out his hand. "Miles. Miles Macy. *Miami Herald*."

Derek turned and eyeballed the reporter. "You know me?"

"Anyone ever tell you how much you look like your uncle?"

A subtle grin cracked the young man's somber exterior.

"Where is she?" Miles stood up and looked around.

Derek hesitated. "I just need to know—"

"Nothing," Miles said. He emptied the contents of his pockets, then lifted his arms. "Phone's in the car. Nothing here but pit stains from the humidity, which I'm obviously not used to yet."

Derek inclined his head toward the back of the church.

Miles' eyes followed the gesture, then widened in surprise. "You serious?"

"Everyone needs someone to talk to," Derek said. He got up and headed outside, his face once more adopting a look of deep sorrow or regret.

Miles crept toward the large confessional in the back of the room. It was constructed of finely crafted walnut, ornately carved and in two parts. A cross rose from the top of the booth, a small light shining on one side, perhaps to indicate an occupied status. The left side had a door into which he could enter. A thick velvet purple curtain ran top to bottom on the right. He did not know which side to enter. Derek was no longer in sight.

Figuring she would opt for the most secure entrance, Miles drew back the curtain and stepped inside to encounter a tiny, dimly lit booth with what appeared to be half a wooden seat protruding from one side—even less comfortable than the pew. He nearly tripped over a velvet cushioned stool as he endeavored to make himself comfortable in his compact surroundings. Opposite the bench he saw a window with wire mesh separating the two sections of the booth. It appeared to have a wooden panel just beyond the mesh, which he assumed was under the priest's control.

At first, he did not know what to do next. He drew the curtain closed and waited for what felt like hours. For some reason, he felt both exposed and claustrophobic. If there was a God, He surely had Miles in a captive position. And it must have worked, because every bad thing he had ever done slammed into his brain, nearly knocking him off his present course. When he realized he had begun to sweat, he loosened his tie and unfastened the top two buttons of his shirt.

Finally, he heard the door on the other side of the booth open, then close. He detected movement and what sounded like a rustling of papers. For a second, he feared an actual priest might have wandered in.

"H-Hello?" he dared to whisper. "Anyone there?"

"Do you believe in life after death, Miles?" came a familiar female voice. "Is that why you wanted to meet here?"

Despite himself, Miles lifted his head and mouthed "thank you" to the booth's ceiling. "Let's just say I've developed a recent interest in Catholicism."

"I didn't know Catholics held séances."

Miles grinned. "Whatever I did, it worked. You're here."

"I wouldn't give myself too much credit for that if I were you."

"Enlighten me, then. But before you do, I believe we've skipped a step."

"Oh?"

"I don't even know if it's really you. Slide that panel over and let me see your face."

Slowly, the wood panel sealing off the wire mesh between the two sections slid open. Like his, the other side of the booth was dimly lit. But as his eyes adjusted, he recognized the face staring back at him, however obstructed. Beautiful, though surprisingly thin. Dark, almond shaped eyes. Wide mouth. Obviously sporting a wig. And obviously Farin Grant.

"It's you," he whispered.

Farin nodded. "And I need your help."

"I'm here, aren't I?"

"It has to be handled my way, Miles. My life depends on it. And I'm not the only one."

... A silent victim, gone no more

... Has someone still worth dying for

"Does this have anything to do with Jameson Lockhardt?"

She paused. "What do you mean?"

"Your limousine. Clearly no accident. It was a bomb—"

"Who told you that?"

"I've been working with the police and—"

"*The police?*"

"It's okay. All you gotta do is go in and talk to them. I promise."

The wood panel slammed shut. Miles heard more rustling. He rushed out of the confessional just in time to catch Farin making a run for the door. He reached out, arm-hooked her waist, and held her still.

"Let me go," she warned, struggling against his grasp. "I'll scream."

"Just hold on. If you say no cops, it's no cops."

"You're in on it, too," she accused as she squirmed in his arms. "He got to you. Admit it, you coward."

Miles looked around, shocked they had not attracted any attention. He half-carried, half-dragged Farin over to a pew. "Relax. I'm not on Lockhardt's payroll. I'm the one trying to nail his smarmy posterior to the wall. I need you as much as you need me."

She jerked away and slid a couple of feet away, her eyes darting around the sanctuary as if considering whether to hear him out, make a run for it, or scream for a priest.

"The detective originally working the case was dirty," Miles said. "I think Lockhardt had him killed, too. Right after that article I did on you. His partner's investigating that and the car bomb. She's nothing like him. She's on your side."

Farin's brows knitted. "Why? Why would Jameson kill a cop who was on his payroll?"

Miles shrugged, then sat down, hopeful she would not bolt again. "I don't know. Maybe it was a coincidence. Knowing the guy, I'd guess he got greedy. Either way, my hunch is you're the only one who can stop Lockhardt."

"He's been paying off cops since I was ten years old. Maybe longer. You can't trust them, Miles. Any of them. I don't even want to trust you."

"You said yourself I'm all you got. You may think I'm scum, but you have to know by now you can trust me."

Farin weighed his words. "No cops," she finally said. "Not until I say. In fact, nothing happens without my okay."

"No problem. I'm sorry. I didn't mean to freak you out. I remember how easily you freak out."

She shot him a dirty look. "You asked about my father. Where did that come from?"

Miles leaned back into the impossibly uncomfortable wooden pew. "We should probably start at the beginning. But first, we should get you out of here. This seating arrangement is a pain in the—"

"Back?" Farin arched an eyebrow.

"Something like that," Miles said, a guilty smile on his face.

"This cop," she said as they got up and headed for the door. "You're in love with her."

"Something like that." He stretched and massaged his lower spine.

***

It was a pilgrimage. An attempt to forgive and be forgiven. A way to push through the fear, each step replete with meaning, internal struggle, and a fight for independence. He would face the past. He would face himself. And despite the fact Ross had accompanied him, Bobby would face his mother on his own.

At least that was what Dr. Stumpf had told him.

As their private jet landed at the Santa Barbara Airport, Bobby caught a glimpse of the chaparral-covered Santa Ynez Mountains and took in the vast Pacific Ocean. The sea breeze accosted his senses as they deplaned and the crew assembled luggage. It smelled like sixteen. Like the past. He had not been back for over twenty years.

"Should we grab a bite or head to the hotel?" Ross asked as they got in their car.

"I'd like to rest a while, if it's okay," Bobby said.

Ross instructed the driver to take them to the Four Seasons, then sat back and unbuttoned his suit jacket. Bobby was thankful his companion did not fill the silence with conversation. He needed time to adjust and prepare for tomorrow's visit.

Their commute took less than twenty minutes. Bobby stared out the window as they drove, lost in thought. Ross leafed through paperwork. Bobby's stomach flipped when he saw the exit sign for Las Palmas Drive.

"Did Dad ever sell the house?" he asked in a small voice as they passed the off-ramp.

Ross drew his reading glasses down the bridge of his nose. He peered out the window as if orienting himself. "You know your father, Bobby. He doesn't like to liquidate assets."

Bobby nodded. They fell back into their own thoughts for the remainder of the drive.

He ordered dinner from room service and ate alone. Ross left the hotel to have dinner with an associate. They agreed to meet for breakfast in the morning.

In ten days, Bobby would turn thirty-nine years old. He could not reconcile that fact while near his childhood home. Soon, he would take over LSI. He had a girlfriend who seemed as taken with him as he was with her—a miracle as far as he could see. Technically, he was still young. In fact, *GQ* said he was the most eligible bachelor in the United States. Yet being in Santa Barbara confused his thoughts. He felt like his younger self again, disguised as his father.

Such a beautiful city, with such ugly memories.

He considered walking down to the beach after he finished his meal, but could not muster the energy. The sunset was no doubt spectacular. He would prefer to stroll on the sand and think about Joni than hole up in his room and brood about his past. But a heaviness of heart prevented him from leaving the room. Instead, he set his dishes outside his door, turned on the news, and tried to sleep.

He woke up close to midnight, startled out of a nightmare about the last time he saw his mother. His parents had been fighting. He had come out to intervene. He entered the living room in time to see his mother fly across the room toward his father, a kitchen knife in her hands.

Bobby tossed and turned the rest of the evening.

Ross was dressed and looked rested when Bobby met him in the hotel restaurant the next morning. He signaled the waiter to bring another cup of coffee as Bobby sat down. "You want some juice?"

Bobby shook his head. "Coffee's fine. I'm just gonna get something light."

Ross nodded and folded up the *Santa Barbara News-Press*. "I spoke to the hospital. They know you're coming. They'll arrange some privacy for the two of you."

"Doesn't she have a private room?"

Ross shook his head. "There aren't enough beds, son."

The thought saddened Bobby. "Does she know I'm coming?"

"I'm not sure."

The waiter brought Bobby his coffee, then took their orders. Bobby stared at the man as he walked away.

"Are you sure you want to do this?" Ross asked.

He nodded. "Can I tell you something? Just between us?"

"Of course you can."

"I don't want to get Dad all riled up."

"More girl trouble?" Ross asked, as if attempting to dissipate the dark cloud over their table.

A small grin peeked through his somber expression. "It's not that. But I guess it has a little to do with it."

"I'm all ears."

Bobby confided he had gone on his own to see a new physician. He told Ross about the first session with Dr. Stumpf and how the psychiatrist had been slowly weaning him off his Haldol for nearly a month. How things were going well. No untoward side effects. No lapses in memory. No more facial tic. Nothing that resembled the circumstances that followed the last time he quit taking the anti-psychotic medicine Lionel Childs prescribed him.

"Dr. Stumpf hasn't said it outright, but I get the idea he doesn't think I have schizophrenia after all."

Ross' expression flattened as he listened to Bobby's would-be confession.

"I think he thinks something was going on with Childs and Dad," Bobby confided.

Ross said nothing.

"And I get the feeling you know something about it."

The arrival of their meal interrupted their discussion. Ross seemed grateful for the reprieve.

Bobby made no move to doctor up his bagel. Instead, he watched Ross salt and pepper his eggs, then flip his tie over his left shoulder. He ate in silence.

"I know you're the only person on this planet who knows my father's business—*all* his business. And I know you're loyal to him."

Ross washed down a mouthful of hash browns with orange juice, then wiped his mouth with his cloth napkin.

"Did Childs lie to my father about my diagnosis?" Bobby pressed.

Ross set his fork down and eased back in his chair. *Tick, tick, tick.*

"Tell me," Bobby urged. "And what about my mother? Is she sick or was that a lie, too?"

Ross studied Bobby. "At this point, nothing I say will change anything."

"So it's true."

"Yes, your mother's sick. In fact, she's one in a small percentage of schizophrenics who are what they call 'treatment-resistant.' She hasn't responded to the medications they've had her on over the years. New options come out periodically, but they've all failed."

"And me?"

Ross swallowed and squared his shoulders. "Bobby—"

"—don't you lie to me, too," he pleaded.

Ross cleared his throat. "I can only tell you what Childs told me, son. He's the one who diagnosed you. I couldn't tell you why someone would want to lie about something like that."

Bobby stared down at the colorful carpet of the restaurant floor. "So maybe he was just mistaken? Maybe I've spent my entire adult life being drugged because some quack made a hasty diagnosis based on my genes. Who does that?"

"I'm afraid I can't help you there," Ross said.

"Do you think Dad knows? Should I tell him?"

Ross did not answer right away. "Your father's spent the last two decades providing for an ex-wife he never stopped loving and a son he never really got to know until the bottom fell out for the both of them. Now, I know you've never gotten the father you wanted, but you got everything he's capable of giving."

Ross' words lanced Bobby's raw heart. He wanted to leave Santa Barbara and his past once and for all. Maybe this visit was a mistake.

"Here's my two cents worth," Ross continued. "Jameson's going to be seventy years old in a few months. He's heading off into his sunset years. What good would it do now to dredge up the past and give him something to regret the rest of his days? I'm proud of you for going out and getting the help you need. And I'm proud of you for wanting to make this trip. You're finding yourself, living a full life for the first time. You'll be fine. Childs is dead. Nothing he may or may not have done changes your current course."

As the logic of Ross' words found him, Bobby felt an estrangement from his life he had not anticipated when Dr. Stumpf first suggested this sojourn west. The enormity of his future lay before him far less glorious than he envisioned on his better days.

What if his father knew after all? Dare he find out? What if more unpleasantries surfaced as he confronted his past? Might any of it have to do with LSI? Was it possible that, in the end, all his father would leave him was a tarnished legacy filled with secrets and unanswered questions?

Shoulders slumped, he stayed long enough to choke down half of his bagel, then mumbled goodbye as he headed for the hospital, leaving Ross to get ready for his next appointment.

Ross watched Bobby's retreating form as he exited the restaurant. He hated having to lie to him about what he knew. Then again, he could not risk the possibility Bobby would confront his father with these new developments—especially when Ross had lied to the old man about the purpose of their trip in the first place.

Jameson had expressed doubts about Bobby going back to the area. He feared a tinge of guilt or nostalgia might lead his son to the very place he now ventured. Ross had reassured him, pointing to the young Lockhardt's success in scouting Joni Leighton. If the son was anything like the father, Ross had reasoned, this jaunt out west might cause lightning to strike a second time. As a good faith measure, Ross had volunteered to accompany Bobby to ensure he made no trips down memory lane.

Ross stood and buttoned his suit, then checked his watch. His cell phone rang and he checked the number. "Sergeant," he greeted. "I was just on my way out to meet you."

"I got the documents you wanted," the cop told him.

"Wonderful!" Ross smiled for the first time that morning.

***

The facility Sarah Wellingham had called home for the last twenty-two years was different than Bobby had anticipated. Hidden in the middle of ten wooded acres near Old Mission Santa Barbara, the Los Olivos Garden Psychiatric Hospital had manicured grounds, a walking path, fountains, benches, and even a small lake. The two-story building was in good repair. It resembled the Spanish colonial architecture of the nearby mission with its high arched windows and doorways and its red tile roof.

Bobby's car deposited him at the front door. He chided himself for the anxiety that had plagued him from the time they had left New York. He had to give his father credit. He had feared the place would look like a state hospital.

A security guard stood between two sets of glass doors. Bobby identified himself as a visitor. The man nodded his approval and Bobby went inside.

He found a clipboard at the front desk and signed in while the friendly receptionist checked his identification and then contacted the floor nurse assigned to his mother's section.

"Someone will be down to escort you shortly." She replaced the receiver and indicated the room behind him. "If you'd like to take a seat in the lobby, I'll send them your way."

Bobby thanked her, entered the lobby, and sat upon one of several comfortable chairs. Soft rock music was piped through ceiling speakers. Occasional tables brimmed with the latest issues of the most popular magazines. A fully stocked coffee cart stood to the side of the entrance. Overall, a welcoming place.

"Hello, Mr. Lockhardt," came the voice of a middle aged woman in a white physician's coat. "I'm Dr. Jackson, the facility administrator." She extended her hand as Bobby stood to greet her, then gestured to the chair he had just vacated and sat beside him. "I'm so glad to finally meet you. I received a call yesterday from your attorney letting us know you'd be by for a visit."

"I suppose I could have given you more notice," he said.

She smiled warmly. "Not at all. I just want to take a minute to let you know how Mom's doing so you don't have any surprises. I understand how stressful these situations can be. Before I start, did you have any questions for me?"

He thought a moment, then shrugged. "As you're probably aware, this is the first time I've visited. It's been...I mean...I was..."

Dr. Jackson shook her head. "I understand."

Bobby smiled, thankful he did not have to explain. "How is she? I was told she hasn't responded to the medications."

"You know what?" Dr. Jackson stood. "I had the staff put Mom in a family room so you two could visit privately. Why don't I fill you in on the way?"

They talked as they made their way to the far end of the facility, through a back door, and outside to what looked like a small cottage. About fifty yards from the front door, they stopped.

"We built this mother-in-law type outbuilding so our patients could spend time with loved ones in a private setting. We're getting your mom comfortable before I take you in. Before you see her, I wanted to fill you in on a brief history and let you know how she's doing today."

His stomach started doing flips. He concentrated as best he could while Dr. Jackson ran down the "positive" and "negative" symptoms displayed by his mother in association with her diagnosis. In his mind, they read like a laundry list: auditory hallucinations; visual hallucinations such as the belief ants were crawling on her arms; garbled speech they referred to as "word salad"; suicidal tendencies, including one or two previous attempts at jumping out her second-story window; and burning herself with lit cigarettes.

"And for about three weeks now," Dr. Jackson concluded, "Mom hasn't spoken much at all. I don't want you to get your hopes up. She might not talk. Or she may be fine. Of course, should she become agitated, I'm afraid we'll have to take her back to her room."

Sarah Wellingham had been a stunning woman with golden-blonde hair and hazel eyes. Average build, average height, and abnormally beautiful features. There was a lyrical quality to her laugh Bobby could still hear if he concentrated hard enough. It had always brought a smile to his face.

She was charming and eccentric, choosing his company above all others'—at least that was what she had claimed. In hindsight, he now knew she likely had symptoms long before they outwardly manifested themselves. She may have been too scared to go out in public. Maybe the attention she showed him, which had caused him such discomfort, was a symptom of the disease.

He chose to keep those darker days a secret. Just like Ross had said: what good would it do now to make things worse?

When Bobby walked through the door of the cottage, he feared his legs would fail him.

It was her. His mother. Yet it was not her at all. The sad, shriveled figure who sat in one of the two recliners in the vibrantly decorated would-be living room looked flat, vacant...old. Much older than his sixty year old mother should look.

She wore a faded pink robe and matching slippers that had seen better days. In her left hand she held a barrette she must have removed from her hair, which hung thin and lifeless atop her head. Her right hand rubbed compulsively up and down her left arm. Periodically, her head twitched as if she were agreeing or disagreeing with some private conversation.

A dozen memories rushed him like paparazzi on Grammy night. Sarah playing catch with him before he tried out for Little League. Sarah pulling a tray of cookies from the oven as he returned home from school. Sarah screaming into the phone during one of her rare conversations with his father. Sarah climbing into his bed when he was fifteen and telling him not to tell anyone else.

Dr. Jackson placed a hand on his forearm. "You okay?"

He nodded and, with great determination, drew close to the small creature in the chair. He knelt down on one knee and tried to move into her line of sight. "Mom?"

She started at his voice, as if he had snuck up on her from out of nowhere. She looked at him, her expression flat and expressionless.

"Hi, Mom. I-It's Bobby"

She watched him as she rubbed at her arm. "Yeah."

Bobby looked at Dr. Jackson, who nodded encouragement. She looked at Sarah. "Your son has come to see you, Sarah. Do you know Bobby?"

"Yeah. Run up her blanket certainly fell for it at the time. Clever."

Bobby recoiled slightly. He frowned and looked at the doctor again.

She shook her head and moved to a nearby sofa, sitting down and crossing her legs. "Sarah," she said. "It's nice to have your son come by to see you."

Sarah looked at the doctor and nodded. "I think he's gonna tell."

"Is that what they're telling you?" she asked as if it were the most normal conversation she had ever participated in.

"Yeah. They're not real. They're here." Sarah looked at Bobby. "You're old."

Bobby smiled. "It's been a long time."

"I need a cigarette," she said. "I smoke cigarettes. Dr. Jackson? Where're my cigarettes?"

The physician nodded at a nearby orderly, who moved to the woman and gave her a single cigarette, then lit it for her. Sarah inhaled deeply, then exhaled. She made a giggling sound, yet her facial expression remained fixed. "Bobby," she said, looking at her son again.

"Yes, Mom," he said.

"Bobby," she repeated. "Bobby. Bobby. Bobby."

"Yes, Mom. I'm here." He moved forward to tuck a stray tendril of hair behind her ear.

Sarah let out an agonized scream as he approached, her facial expression unaffected. "Dr. Jackson! Help! *Help*! He's gonna do it!" She flailed her arms in terror until Bobby fell backwards. The orderly rushed between them to help calm her down.

Bobby stood on trembling legs and sat next to Dr. Jackson. "I'm not going to hurt you, Mom."

"I crow the flu jar," she said as she took a long drag from her cigarette and resumed rubbing her left arm. "I'm *not* a clock!"

Two hours later, a frazzled, uneasy, sad, and clear-headed Bobby left the Los Olivos Garden Psychiatric Hospital. His visit had convinced him of two facts. First, he would never again visit this forsaken place. Second, his father had some explaining to do.

CHAPTER 11

S ATURDAY MORNING FOUND SAMANTHA ENJOYING the indulgence of a rare day sleeping in with her fiancé. Their schedules had finally started settling into a chaos-free routine. Ethan had transitioned to private practice. Fewer late nights. More dinners together. And today, the chance to be lazy and playful, lying in bed and soaking in the morning sun streaming through their windows.

"What am I going to do with this mess?" She yawned and stretched her lazy limbs, then cuddled into his arms.

Ethan lifted his head off the pillow and smiled at the many fabric samples and miscellaneous wedding couture taking over their bedroom. "It's sort of nice, dontcha think? Has that lived-in feel. And it's all white and pure. Maybe we're in Heaven." He kissed the top of her head and pulled her closer.

She smiled against the warmth of his chest and inhaled to fill herself with his scent. "Maybe we are."

"You busy today, or are you all mine?"

"Not too busy. Just need to check e-mail, answer a few calls."

"Nothing going on tonight?"

"There's always something going on, Ethan. You know that. It's the first Saturday in June. Everyone has summer fever."

"I thought it was 'spring fever.'"

"*Every* season has a fever in LA"

With a downturned smile, he bobbed his head.

She checked the clock. "I should probably get in the shower."

"Want to go to breakfast?"

"Let's stay in." She sat up and stretched again. "We can go out for brunch or something. Let me just answer some calls. And—oh!—I need to get with the promoter. Make sure everyone's set for the kick off. Only a week left. Don't want any kinks in the chain."

"Okay." He chuckled and removed the covers. "You're up now. I know that tone in your voice. Go on. I'll be down in a minute."

She kissed his cheek, sheered on her robe, and trotted downstairs to her office. She checked her messages and responded to e-mails. No drama, no fires to put out.

Chris' tour manager who, by way of being an old friend, had endured Samantha's calls despite the fact she represented the label, assured her they had everything under control. The venues had sold out the week they released the tickets. Riders had been accepted and were in place. Requisite privacy considerations had been arranged.

"I know you're tired of my calls, Lou."

"You know I think you're nuts," the man said.

"It's going to be the tour of the summer."

"We'll know the first night," he said. "One way or another, it'll have people talking."

As a courtesy, Lou promised to keep in touch. When Sam hung up, she made a note to have Deborah send him a bottle of Glenmorangie.

She struck the first item off her list, then decided to confront the second. It would be less successful, but she had to give it a go. She picked up her phone and dialed the number from memory.

"Your ears must be ringing," the friendly voice greeted. "I was going to ring you today."

"Great minds," she said. "How are you?"

"We're good, thanks. How about you? Wedding plans coming along?"

They made small talk briefly before she dared ask after Farin.

"Ah, yes. Farin"

She heard the frustration in his tone. "That bad?"

"Afraid so."

"I take it, then, she still hasn't gotten in the studio."

"Not yet."

Samantha exhaled.

"We're working on it."

"It's been almost two months."

"I know."

"Is it because of this thing with Chris?"

Ben paused, confused. "What thing?"

"He didn't tell you," she said, almost to herself.

"What has he done now?" he asked, suspicious out of habit.

Samantha relayed what little she knew about the quickie divorce in Haiti and the circumstances that led them there. She could not discern if Ben sounded angry over the situation or put off Chris had not told him directly.

"He didn't tell me anything. Julie was pregnant?"

"Probably didn't want to burden you, what with everything else going on."

"How did he manage to keep news like that away from the press?"

"It hasn't been easy. Their publicists started strategizing before they left the country. For some reason, Julie's been very cooperative. Chris wanted to get out of LA for a while, so he's off promoting the tour. He'll be back midweek."

"That's cutting it short considering the tour starts Friday."

"He swears he's ready."

"So you've been dealing with my brother, and I've been dealing with Farin."

"We're quite a pair, you and I." She chuckled. "Tell me what to do, Ben. You think she's ever going back into the studio? I'm sitting here with a contract I can't enforce for a dead woman. I want to help her. I want her with Minor 6th. But I can't reach her."

"Let's be fair. Six months ago, she was still in a hospital bed in Raleigh, drugged out of her mind. She's adjusting—maybe not at the pace we'd all like. She's started spending time with Derek. His band's playing their first gig tonight down on South Beach. I think she's gonna go. It'll be good for her. Maybe spark an interest."

"Is it safe?"

"I think so, yeah. She's got all these ridiculous disguises. Cheryl got her a couple of new wigs. And the band's manager seems to fancy her a bit."

"He knows about her?"

"Long story. Pure accident. But he won't let anything happen to her."

"Let's hope not," she said, whispering a "thank you" to Ethan as he popped in momentarily to set a cup of coffee on her desk. "A public appearance while the old man's still looking for her. It's awfully risky."

"No worries. She's got Derek. And Sawyer."

"So she has a disguise and an entourage, but she refuses to record. I guess you're right, Ben. Maybe she is becoming her old self again."

He laughed. "We'll hope for just south of a full recovery."

Samantha thanked him again for taking Farin in and helping her, for helping them all. He promised to let her know when he had more news.

When they hung up, she lingered momentarily at her desk to consider the potential scenarios once Farin got in the studio and decided to go public. Once the news hit, the calm of the last month would turn into a hurricane, with Farin in the eye of the storm. Coupled with the impending changes to LSI in the near future, Samantha needed to take advantage of the tranquility while she could.

She picked up the phone and made a reservation for two at the Cal-a-Vie Health Spa down in Vista.

***

Herb Radford had thoroughly inspected the remains of the Malibu property. He had spent two weeks sifting through sparse remnants left after the original cleanup, looking for any indication a woman had stayed there in the days or weeks prior to the explosion.

The ocean breeze was not his friend. It required he expand his search hundreds of yards down the beach in either direction, as well as a long stretch of the Pacific Coast Highway. An impossible task when one not only had to identify potential objects but separate them from any unrelated debris along the same path. But he was a professional. He did a thorough job, no matter how long or tedious. In the end, he found no physical trace of his subject.

Posing as an insurance adjuster, he had interviewed neighbors in the general vicinity, asking if they had seen or heard any cars or people coming in or out of the home. Any lights on in the evenings. Any trash cans out on garbage day. Nothing.

Each Friday evening, he called Lockhardt with an update. Normally, he did not spend so much time checking in with clients. Too much communication presented risk. Anonymity was key. However, in this case, it seemed the prudent approach.

His client had a tendency to shift his priorities, which Herb worried would impede his progress. This target, if alive, was mobile. The more the old man called him off one task in deference to another, the more potential of overlooking something significant.

The prime example? His North Carolina trip over Memorial Day weekend. Correction—his *attempted* North Carolina trip. Supposedly Lockhardt's number one priority. After their initial meeting in New York, Herb had received the list of names and places to check out. As they had discussed before he left, Hopeful Heart was there at the top.

"I just need confirmation she's still there," Jameson had instructed.

"And if she's moved?"

"Get me a copy of her file and include the new address."

"'Jade Larken Trongly.' Doesn't exactly roll off the tongue, does it? Is this a matter you'll want me to have our friend clean up?"

"I haven't decided yet."

Herb had checked his messages before boarding the plane. Nothing of note, save the call from the ex complaining she had received her alimony check a day late. It was not like he had neglected to make the unavoidable delay worth her wait. He had sent an extra five hundred bucks for the inconvenience. The soul-sucking bitch had nothing to say about that.

In the time it took him to fly from New York to DC, then hop an airbus into Fayetteville, he had received a message from Lockhardt telling him his services were no longer required at the Hopeful Heart. The matter had been resolved. How, he did not say. But the bonus he received for his trouble more than made up for the extra bills he had sent the ex. Fine with him.

Since then, the old man had remained in a constant state of frustration over the lack of results, but that was not Herb's problem. "You pay me to do a comprehensive job. That's what I'm doing."

"How could there be no sign at all? Everyone leaves traces."

"The scene's a month old. *If* she was ever there at all—"

"She was there. Our mutual acquaintance said he saw her."

"He also said he's not a tracker. From what I heard, there was never definitive ID. In any case, sifting through an already-processed crime scene—especially one so old and subject to the elements—takes time and patience."

"Two weeks' time?" Lockhardt had challenged.

"More. A greedier, less experienced guy would draw it out. It's your dime. But the odds of finding something useful in Malibu are tantamount to winning the lottery. I never expected to find anything there, and I was right."

Not the answer Lockhardt had wanted to hear.

After Herb had done everything but till the Malibu sea strand, he turned his attention to the next item on his agenda. This would take more than time. More than patience. It required precision and finesse. He would have to assume everyone on the list of known or suspected associates would be hypervigilant of their surroundings.

The top name on this list was Farin's former paramour, Chris Grant.

***

Farin was determined not to ruin Derek's big debut with her flashbacks and anxiety. How long had it been since she had played a live set or watched crowds of people lined up in front of nightclubs, pleading with a doorman to grant them entrance as he scrutinized each one, heeding instructions to admit only the most beautiful and trendy?

She had heard Miami Beach blossomed during her absence, but she would have never imagined the explosion of glitterati and celebrities teeming Ocean Boulevard via car, taxi, limousine, boat, and even by foot.

"Thanks for letting me tag along," she shouted to Derek over the din as they climbed a narrow staircase to a private room on the second floor of the Talkhouse.

"Are you kidding?" Derek called back over his shoulder. He smiled as he caught sight of Summer waiting at the end of the long hallway. "I think it's cool you came. Besides, you seemed like you needed a night out."

"Right?" She laughed as she fidgeted with her wig. "I just hope it's worth it. These contacts are driving me nuts."

"If you can get through tonight with no one recognizing you, you're golden."

"You haven't told anyone, right? Not Summer? Or your boys?"

Derek assured her with a squeeze of her elbow as they entered the room reserved for the venue's live performers and their entourage—big enough to accommodate the band, their girlfriends, a handful of friends, and their manager. Sawyer had come through for them in a big way. Derek was sure he recognized Willy Chirino, producer Del, and Ricky Martin mingling with the crowd downstairs.

He greeted Summer with a kiss, then whispered into Farin's ear, "Think Miles Macy'll really show up?"

Farin smiled and patted his back. "I'd bet on it."

"You gon' eentwoduce us to you fwiend dere, eh Dah'eek?" Levoy asked as he approached. Brian and Peter sat on a sofa in the back of the room, craning their necks to check out the hot older blonde Derek had in tow.

He cleared his throat and glanced at Sawyer, who leaned against a side wall, beer in hand. "This is my friend...well, a friend of the family's—"

"—Lisa," Farin finished her nephew's flimsy lie. "Nice to meet you."

Sawyer made his way toward her, a knowing smirk stretched across his face. "'Lisa,'" he mocked, extending his hand. "It's good to see you again."

"You know 'uh, eh Sawyah?" Levoy asked.

Sawyer smiled and gazed into her artificially blue eyes. "Yeah, we met at Derek's a few times when he lost his wheels."

Summer shook Farin's hand and introduced herself. "I didn't know anyone was staying with them," she said sweetly. "It must be nice for Mrs. Grant to have another woman around with all the guys."

"It's refreshing to infuse a little more estrogen into the place," Farin agreed. "I'm glad to finally meet you, Summer. I've heard so much about you. You've made quite an impression on the family."

"I just love them," Summer said, then to Derek, "Is your dad coming? I know he'd talked about it."

Derek shook his head. "He wanted to."

"Then why isn't he coming?"

He straightened his stance. "I told him I wanted to do this myself."

Summer shook her head. "Stubborn."

"Like a rock," Derek said, smiling at her as if they shared a private joke.

They had pulled a sound check earlier in the day, left to grab a bite, and then returned in time to relax and socialize before their gig. The owner had agreed to let them invite a few of their school friends, but insisted anyone under twenty-one would need to stay upstairs during the show. He would not risk his liquor license. Not for Sawyer Jacobs, or even Ben Grant. As the time drew near for their show, the room filled to capacity.

A cacophony of laughter, loud discussion, and indiscernible music filled the room. Farin watched as Derek and his bandmates talked with their friends, a heady mixture of youthful laughter, anticipation, and even envy creating a celebratory vibe throughout the room. She did her best to play the role of a friend and not an aunt. She turned a blind eye to the alcohol and marijuana some of the kids had smuggled in, content that Derek and Summer did not partake. She wondered if their restraint was for her benefit. At least she would not have to lie or betray a confidence later when Cheryl would undoubtedly ply her with questions.

"Here," Sawyer said, handing her a beer. He stood beside her and peered out at the group. "I figured you'd want some non-kid-friendly libation."

She took a sip. "Thanks for getting them this gig. It's a great shot in the arm. I'm sure it'll help build their confidence."

"How old *are* you?" He laughed. "Grow down, will ya? I haven't done them any favors. This is gonna be hard for them. You and I both know they might tank. In fact, they probably will. They don't even have a name yet."

Farin pursed her lips and nodded. "Still—"

"Look, 'Lisa.'" He grinned, again fixing his eyes on her. "You're too young to act like some kind of guardian here. Just chill out and have some fun. Trust me. You need it."

"What are you talking about?" Suddenly aware of how close he stood, she stepped back a foot or two and sipped her beer.

"I'm talking about the fact there're probably four dozen people here and you're standing against this wall like a chaperone at a high school dance."

"Newsflash, Sawyer: they *are* high school students."

"Not all of 'em. Not me."

She scoffed. "You need more chaperoning than any of them."

"Ooo." His voice dropped an octave as he inched closer. "Sounds promising."

She smiled despite herself. Her cheeks felt warm. "Don't get any ideas."

He finished his beer in a mighty gulp, then looked away. "Not a chance. I don't date school marms."

Farin rolled her eyes. A moment later, an overwhelming wave of nausea mixed with a sense of disorientation caused her to shoot her hand out and touch the wall for support.

Sawyer touched her shoulder. "You all right?"

"It's nothing. Just feels a little weird being here. Brings up—"

"—memories, I know." He fished into his pocket, then pressed something into her hand. "Here. Take this."

She looked down and saw a small blue pill. "What is this?"

"Ten milligrams of relaxation."

Her lips parted, then shut. She closed her hand and tried to give it back. "I can't. Thanks anyway."

"Take it. I'll look out for you."

"I had a problem with these, Sawyer."

"I know you did. But you're only getting one, so you'll be okay. Besides, you're dead. You can't be addicted to something after you're dead."

"'Oo day'd?" a female voice asked from out of nowhere. A beautiful bohemian-looking woman with radiant dark skin slinked up from behind Sawyer and stood close to him. Slipping her arm around his neck, she drew him in for a kiss, then jutted her chin and looked at Farin, awaiting an introduction.

"Always fashionably late." He disengaged to stand between the two women. "Cécile, this is Lisa. She's a friend of Derek's family."

"'Allow." Cécile's features exuded strength and pride as she looked Farin up and down.

She extended her hand. "You must be Levoy's sister."

Cécile nodded and briefly clasped her forearm, then moved back into Sawyer's space. "You know mah bwudder, eh? Dat 'ow you know mah mahn?"

Derek shouted for the group to quiet down, then announced they needed to get downstairs. The band headed out amidst a chorus of well-wishing from friends, followed closely by Cécile, then Sawyer, who grabbed Farin's hand as he passed. They descended the steps, but he turned back momentarily and motioned for her to lean down.

"Take it," he said into her ear. "And loosen up. I'm going to kiss you tonight and I don't want to picture an old school marm in my head when I close my eyes."

Shocked by the abrupt declaration, Farin struggled to respond. But Sawyer was already several steps ahead of her. She looked down and regarded the pill in her hand.

Chris was never far from her thoughts. He haunted her like an old song. Like so many memories. His rejection still hurt. But he was married. He had moved on. He had told her so.

For just one night, Farin wanted to feel something other than longing. Longing for Chris. Longing to find Jordan. Longing for the courage to open Ross' package. Longing for the day she would exact her revenge. Longing to know whether she would ever sing again.

She popped the pill in her mouth and chased it down with the last of her beer.

The turnout was amazing. She knew Ben and Sawyer had talked up the gig to people in the area, urging them to support Derek's band, but even she had not envisioned a standing room only crowd. Sawyer led her to a previously reserved table up front and sat next to her. Cécile followed the band backstage.

"You're presumptuous," Farin told him as she signaled a nearby waiter for another beer.

"Am I?"

"And a cheat, too."

"Really?" He chuckled,

Farin nodded and scratched at her blonde wig. She could not wait to get home and remove her disguise, including the ton of makeup she and Cheryl had applied. Anything to make the anonymous "Lisa" look like anyone but Farin Grant. "I may be an old school marm, but I'm not deaf or blind. Cécile made it very clear you're with her."

"Psh. Cécile likes to mark territory. We're not exclusive."

A bark of laughter escaped Farin's lips. "'Exclusive?' And you ask me how old *I* am?"

The room erupted with cheers and applause as Cécile Laroche stepped out onto the small stage. She waved and blew kisses at the audience, exquisite in her trendy white gauze ensemble and sandals. Periodically she swept back dozens of her waist-length, beaded braids that spilled forward in response to her almost feline movements.

"You wedday tah gayt dis pahtay stahted?" she shouted, flirting with her sexy Haitian accent.

The crowd whistled and whooped back enthusiastically.

"For da fust time evah in Mee-uh-mee Beash—or ahnywhay else, for dat maddah! You make mah boys feel welcoom, eh?" She covered her microphone and looked down at Sawyer. "What dey call demselves?"

Sawyer shrugged and shook his head, laughing. "Make something up!"

Cécile rolled her eyes in exaggerated fashion. The crowd laughed and applauded.

"Okay, den!" she shouted to the audience. "You nice peopall geev dem sooggestions for a name, eh? For now, please welcoom...uh...F-L-A!"

Farin stood and cheered as Cécile made her way to the table and scooted her chair close to Sawyer under the guise of getting a better view. The boys emerged, waving awkwardly and smiling as they took their places. They began their set with an authoritative percussion intro from Levoy. The crowd whistled and clapped, then settled in to enjoy the music.

Using less tact than he should have, Sawyer increased the distance between himself and Cécile while simultaneously reducing the space between him and Farin. Cécile glanced over her shoulder and noted the positioning. She shot Sawyer a dirty look, then narrowed her eyes at Farin as if warning her to back off.

The unsubtle game made Farin uncomfortable. She wondered what Sawyer was trying to accomplish by essentially pitting two women against each other. The juvenile overtones of the situation disappointed her. If something had happened between him and Cécile, she wanted no part of it.

Their server returned with a round of drinks. Sawyer palmed the guy some cash, then slid the sleeves of his long T-shirt up past his elbows and leaned forward, resting his arms on the table top and bobbing his head to the music.

When one of the programmed stage lights flashed their way, Farin caught a glimpse of a long scar running the length of his left wrist. He noticed her staring and repositioned, letting his arm fall to his side. She turned her attention back to the stage.

The set list included two original pieces written by Derek and Brian, a Miami Sound Machine cover, and an instrumental percussion duet featuring Levoy on kettle drum. He called his sister up to join him on congas, her thin, dark braids whipping wildly as she moved in time with the piece.

Farin watched with amazement as Cécile performed, alive and uninhibited. She moved her perfect sepia-brown body with strength and fluidity, interacting with the band and the audience while careful to keep their primary focus on Derek and the boys. Cécile Laroche was born for the stage.

Slowly, Farin grew jealous of the woman—less so over Sawyer, though she realized a part of her had reacted to Cécile's possessiveness. But it was more than that.

She missed being on stage.

"Nice hair."

Farin looked up and discovered Miles Macy standing beside her. "You made it!" She stood and greeted him warmly, an unplanned reaction she credited more to his being a rare familiar face than anyone she might consider a friend.

He smiled. "And blue eyes!"

They hugged awkwardly, as if that was the thing to do. Farin had never hugged a member of the press before. Then again, tonight in this place, she was just Lisa. She whispered her alias to Miles before introducing him to Sawyer, then offered him the seat to her left.

"I've been here a while," Miles said, projecting his voice loud enough for her to hear. "I didn't recognize you at first."

Farin asked what Miles was drinking, then flagged down their server for another round. When it came, she touched the neck of her beer to Miles', then Sawyer's. Lifting her chin toward the stage, she asked the reporter, "What do you think of them?"

"Looks like the Grant name lives on," he said.

Sawyer casually leaned to his left, crossing in front of Farin. He regarded Miles with a wink and a smile. "Then I'm sure you'll do a bang-up job on the review."

Miles chuckled and lifted his chin, then leaned toward Farin. "Remember that piece of correspondence I told you about?"

She nodded, visually scanning the room as if by habit. "Did you get something else?"

He shook his head. "I'm stuck. I was hoping you could come by and take a look at it. If you can get out of the house for a concert on South Beach without being recognized, I'm sure you can slip off to my place for a bit."

"I'll do my best. I think I may have something for you to look at as well."

"What is it?"

She shook her head. "Not here."

Miles held up his hands in defeat, then eased back in his chair. He moved his head in time with the music, as if neither of them carried the weight of the world on their shoulders.

Sawyer looked at both of them in turn. "Tense table." He took another drink, then leaned into Farin. "Did you take it?"

"Yes," she said, somewhat embarrassed. "But I never said I'd kiss you."

"Oh, you'll kiss me."

She studied his features, unable to decide if his sexy confidence annoyed or intrigued her.

The crowd whooped and whistled as the instrumental ended. Cécile took a deep bow and stretched her arms out to the group. She applauded them along with the crowd, then approached the microphone. "You 'aving foon? You like mah boys oop 'e-ya?"

The audience roared their approval.

"We all 'ave de same pahson to tank for bwinging us togedder tonight. Geev eet oop fah Sawyah Jacoobs!" She pointed to their table. A spotlight shone on Sawyer. He nodded and waved graciously, then pointed back to the boys.

"C'mon oop 'e-ya, beeg mahn," she challenged as the audience laughed and applauded the idea. "'Ep de boys bwing 'uh 'ome."

Sawyer shook his head and mouthed a string of "nos" as the band, the crowd, and Cécile beckoned him.

"Eet wood be ah shame to pees off de ownah aftah 'e been so nice tah layt dese boys play," she chided with a flirty sing-song.

Farin pushed on his arm. "Go on. Get up there. Show me what you got."

"Really?" He stood slowly and looked challengingly at her. "Why don't we go together?"

"'Lisa' doesn't sing," she countered playfully.

He straightened up and put a hand on his chest, gave a slight bow, then jogged up to the stage. Cécile handed him an electric guitar as the crowd raved with enthusiasm.

"Well, okay," he said into the center mic. "Cécile, you play dirty, but we all know you like it like that."

The room erupted in laughter, whoops, and whistles.

Cécile nodded. "You know it, bah-bay!" she shouted.

Sawyer strummed the guitar and played a quick riff to loosen up his fingers. "You boys gonna follow me?"

"Sure," Derek said.

"Okay, then," Sawyer said. "But we're gonna do things a little different now. You all know I'm a blues man through and through."

The audience cheered louder. People whoo-hoo'd and shouted their approval.

"All right," he said. "Boy's? Gimme a 'D blues' and follow me from there."

The vibe in the room transformed as the band began a juicy, 12-bar blues progression. Sexy and slow. The type of music that could make a woman's thighs ache. Sawyer moved as if his guitar were an extension of his body, swaying and grinding to the music as if making love to the moment.

Farin watched in awe as he crossed back and forth across the stage, working the crowd who clearly loved him. The pill she had taken finally kicked in. A measure of relief she had not known in ages flooded her senses. It was more than the mixture of alcohol and medication. It was the whole evening. She made a mental note to thank Sawyer for pressuring her to attend. Had she not come, she might not have realized Jameson Lockhardt had succeeded for too long in robbing her of the joy music brought her. Maybe she would let him kiss her after all.

"Are you with him?" Miles asked incredulously as he moved his head from side to side.

"Sawyer?"

He nodded. "He hasn't taken his eyes off you the entire time I've been here."

"Maybe he likes blondes."

He chuckled and turned his attention back to the performance. "He's good."

"He *is*." She hated to admit it. As it turned out, he had not merely boasted that night they sat together poolside. He really was that good.

"You look happy," Miles observed, a hint of surprise in his tone. "Good for you."

"Not yet, but I can see it from here."

"I want to dedicate a song to a new friend of mine," Sawyer announced between tunes. His guitar fell into a steady rhythm. "Let's write it together, shall we...? We're gonna call it...'Young Man Blues.'"

He fell into a slow I-IV-V chord progression, nodding at the band at each change and encouraging them to follow. Once they hit a solid follow, he walked to the mic.

My woman is a mystery; no one knows that she's alive
Said my lady, she's a mystery; and nobody knows that she's alive

But, oh, if she ever disappeared, well you know I couldn't survive

Ever since the day we met she's had me on my knees
Don't you know that since the day we met,
I been beggin' please, baby, please
Won't you give this young boy just one chance
'Cause this old heart won't never be free

But she keeps me at a distance
Said she's heard the lines before
Says she knows about my women
And she shows me to the door

Well, I ain't got no other woman, though I've had my shady past
No, baby, I ain't got no other woman and I'm done with livin' fast
So if you say you'll be my baby, oh I swear you'll be the last

Farin's cheeks warmed as she listened. Sawyer and the crowd became as one, in tune with one another, enjoying the improvisation as they swayed to the sultry beat. She stole a glance at Cécile, who stood just offstage. The woman's nostrils flared angrily as she set her jaw and folded her arms, swaying to and fro despite herself. In no time, she turned and stomped away, returning to the table and jerking her chair out to take a seat.

When the song ended, the audience response was frenetic, the crowd cheering and whistling at impossible levels. Sawyer stepped to the side and gestured to the band, who bowed awkwardly and smiled at the praise.

The venue's manager caught Sawyer's attention from behind the bar and held up a finger, indicating they had time for one more song despite the fact the set had already run long.

Sawyer stepped over to Derek. "They want you to do one more."

Derek frowned and turned his head away from the audience. "We only planned the songs we did for the set."

"I guess you'd better improvise then," he said, lifting the guitar strap over his head.

"But—"

"—hey, buddy. That's the business. You're here tonight to cut your teeth. So take a bite." Sawyer waved at the crowd, bowed, then hopped offstage and swaggered confidently back to sit between Cécile and Farin. This time, Cécile scooted away.

Derek huddled with the boys at the drum set. They nodded in agreement and Derek went to the mic.

"We, uh, wanna thank everyone for coming out tonight," he said. "You guys have been really cool. Before we play our last song, I want to introduce the members of the band." He looked to his left. "On bass, we have Brian Heller."

Brian dipped his head and played a riff on his instrument, plucking, slapping, and popping the strings as the crowd cheered him on.

Derek turned to his right. "On rhythm and lead guitar, Peter Neill."

Peter smiled at the applause and launched into a jazzy solo, fingering his axe like a pro twice his age.

"You all know crazy Cécile Laroche, who was nice enough to sit in with us tonight."

The crowd went wild, whistling, cheering, and catcalling for Cécile, who stood up at the table and waved her arms, then danced a quick salsa.

"Her baby brother's on drums," Derek continued. "Give it up for Levoy Laroche!"

Levoy opened his mouth and opened his eyes wide as he launched into an animated Latin rhythm on his drum set.

"And I'm on vocals and lead guitar—like my Uncle Chris. I'm Derek Grant."

The crowd rose to their feet and cheered louder than at any other time that night, taking Derek by surprise. He thanked them, then played a gritty, rock-infused guitar riff.

"It's only appropriate to close tonight's show with a dedication to my uncle," he said. "We could never do it like he did, but we hope you like it. This is for you, Uncle Jordan."

The group launched into a medley of Jordan's music, a retrospective of his most famous songs, brought to life with a fresh arrangement of Levoy's percussion stylings and a less pop-oriented, Latin feel.

Farin grew quiet. She watched her nephew and his friends pay tribute to her husband, unable to react. She felt...everything. With each note, their life played itself out in her mind. She remembered the night they met. Their wedding. Dancing with him at Lorelei's on Islamorada.

"You okay?" Sawyer asked, his face serious. "I didn't know they were gonna do this."

Farin cleared her throat, then grabbed her beer and took a long drink. "No. It's okay. It's a beautiful tribute."

"You wanna take off?"

Farin looked at Miles, who nodded. "You go," he said. "I'm gonna interview the band when they're done. Give 'em a nice write up."

"Thank you." She stood and hugged him, meaning it this time. When she broke away, she grabbed something out of her handbag and pressed it into his hand.

His forehead wrinkled in confusion as he eyeballed the key. He looked at her, then leaned in close to her ear. "What is this?"

"I need you to go and get something for me. I can't risk being seen."

He listened to her instructions, nodded, and pocketed the object.

Farin caught Derek's attention, winked, and blew him a kiss. Without missing a beat, he nodded his understanding.

Cécile ignored Sawyer's attempt to say goodnight and shot Farin a wicked look as they left the table.

"You didn't ride your bike here, did you?" Farin asked as they headed for the door.

Sawyer chuckled. He stopped, grabbed her arm, and drew her to him. "I'm gonna kiss you now, Lisa."

A sudden roar erupted from the crowd toward the front of the club, pulling their attention before their lips met. They looked toward the commotion.

Farin gasped in disbelief.

Chris.

CHAPTER 12

CHERYL HAD NOT SPOKEN TO Julie since late January—the day Julie had lied to her face as they drove to the airport. She had promised to tell Chris about her pregnancy the next time she saw him. And where Cheryl had reasoned at first that Farin's reemergence into their lives might explain or even justify Julie's temporary hesitation, she now knew the truth.

Their once close relationship had ended abruptly after that day. It made sense now that Julie had not contacted her since. Not to give her the okay to share the happy news with their family. Not to ask for support and advice.

A couple of weeks ago, the phone had started blowing up with calls. Messages laced with tearful pleas for understanding and the chance to tell "her side" of the story clogged their machine. The idea that Julie believed she could warrant her actions sickened Cheryl. She had not answered one call or returned a single message.

Today, however, as she labored in the kitchen unloading the dishwasher and cooking breakfast, she decided she had had enough. When the phone rang at 7 AM, she rinsed her hands off in the sink, dried them on her waist apron, and picked up the handset.

"Can you talk?" Julie asked, clearing her throat. Her voice sounded hoarse and mournful—or maybe hungover.

"I can." Cheryl switched off the burner and covered a pan of home fries, then took a seat at the kitchen table.

"Are you alone?"

"Am I alone? Aye, Julie, there's no one here but me."

A huge sigh filled the line. "I don't know what to do."

"About?"

"He left me!" she cried. "I told him about the baby and he went nuts."

Cheryl could barely hold her tongue as Julie relayed her fantastical account of the event. "I can't imagine Chris having such a reaction." She did not try to mask her disgust.

"He *hit* me, Cheryl! Nearly killed me, then threatened to end my career if I told anyone."

Summoning all the patience she could muster, Cheryl set her jaw. "Are you all right?"

Her sobbing intensified. She spoke in short, semi-comprehensible bursts. "I-I...didn't know what else to do. He...still loves h-her."

"It was never a question of his loving her. It was a question of his integrity. You can't help who you love. But you can make choices about your life. Which you've obviously done."

The line fell silent. Occasional, pitiful sniffs were the only evidence the call had not ended.

"This family stood by you. We accepted you. We agonized with you over your battle to make your husband commit to your marriage. But he did that. He chose you. Even after Farin's return, he chose you. And he would have continued to choose you, particularly if he had known you were about to fulfill his deepest wish."

When Cheryl received no response, she continued, stabbing the table with her index finger as she spoke. "If he physically assaulted you as you say, I'll offer no excuses for his behavior. But over the last four years, I've watched him become the man everyone always hoped he'd be. You rewarded this change you campaigned for by killing his unborn child. So congratulations. You win. I backed the wrong horse. But know this: it won't happen again."

"Cheryl, please—"

"Lose our numbers, Julie. It's not a request." She hung up the phone, then returned to finish preparing their meal.

She missed her youngest son, who had just left for astronomy camp. Anymore, Kyle was the only member of their family not anchored with burdensome thoughts. After the success of their triumphant debut gig last night, there would be no living with the lead singer of "F-L-A." Ben still struggled to coax Farin into the studio. Farin still refused to give them the closure they longed for regarding Jordan's murder and the subsequent bizarre series of events that had landed her as a temporary member of their household. And Chris' sudden appearance last night would surely set back any progress she had made.

So this morning, Cheryl did what she knew to do. She cooked.

One by one, they assembled in the kitchen for coffee and juice. The telephone had acted as an unwitting alarm. It did not surprise her everyone found it impossible to get back to sleep. These days, the restlessness of the Grant household was worth its weight in gold.

"Can I help with breakfast?" Farin asked through a yawn as she doctored her coffee.

"Don't be ridiculous, hen," she said, smiling as she handed her a glass of cranberry juice. "Go sit down."

Farin leaned to the side and whispered in Cheryl's direction, "Is he still here?"

She nodded. After a moment's hesitation, she turned and gave her a hug. Farin's forehead wrinkled in confusion as she returned the gentle embrace.

"You're going to be okay," Cheryl whispered.

"Thank you," Farin whispered back.

Cheryl pulled away, checked to see if anyone else was in earshot, then sucked her teeth as she considered her next words. "I have something to tell you. It's not my place to do it, but I'm going to anyway."

"Is it about Chris? What's he doing here?"

She lowered her head and lifted an eyebrow, clutching both of Farin's forearms as if to brace her for impact. "He's moving back."

Farin's eyes widened. "What?"

The echo of footsteps descending the staircase put an abrupt end to their discussion. Farin took her juice and coffee and sat zombie-like at the table, processing the news.

Ben and Derek entered the kitchen together, laughing and chatting cheerfully about last night's success and the overwhelming response F-L-A had received. Ben beamed with pride as Derek relayed the details. He ribbed his son over the fact Cécile Laroche had finally given them their name. They each greeted Cheryl with a cheek kiss before taking their beverages and joining Farin at the table.

"And where's your brother this morning?" Cheryl asked, her attention on perfecting the last omelet so she could serve.

"Camp," Derek said, as Ben simultaneously announced, "The studio."

Cheryl eyed them with a sideways grin, then regarded her son. "Go tell your Uncle Chris breakfast's ready."

Farin shot out of her seat. "I'll go." In one fluid movement, she pivoted and stalked out the patio door.

Not one clear thought passed through her head as she stomped past the pool and across the yard. He had mentioned nothing about moving back to Florida last night during their brief encounter at the club. Only that he had come to talk to Ben and support Derek's debut—an odd visit considering his tour kicked off on the other end of the country in just five days.

The good news was the pill Sawyer gave her had helped her sleep. The bad news was she had not merely dreamt Chris had shown up at the club as she and Sawyer were leaving. Further, his presence had robbed her of that kiss, which she decided disappointed her.

She found him in the control room hunched uncomfortably over the sound board, snoring. When she shut the door behind her with a fair amount of force, the sound sent him up and back with a start. "Cheryl wants you to come eat."

He rubbed his eyes and stretched. "What's wrong?"

"Were you ever gonna tell me you're moving back? Or were you just gonna start showing up to visit the 'fam?'"

He stood, stretched, and strode past her toward the door. "I don't know, Farin. It seems our new relationship is all about keeping things from each other."

"Don't start this again."

He turned back and pointed an accusing finger at her. "So you came down here to start rebuilding your—"

"—I was forced to move here so you didn't have to see me."

He drew his chin back. "You know that's not true."

"Do I?"

"And you still haven't recorded a note."

She crossed her arms. "You've made it clear you're no longer interested in me, so what's it to you?"

"When I get a call from Sam relaying some cryptic message from Miles Macy, who *clearly* knows you're alive—"

"What are you talking about?"

"You won't tell my family what happened to our brother, but you'll tell a *reporter*?"

"I haven't told him anything yet."

He threw his hands in the air. "*Yet*? What does that mean?"

Her arms shot down to her sides, her fists clenched. "Why are you moving back here?"

His frustration ebbed. He took in and then exhaled a deep breath, his shoulders slumping as he raised his hands up to his hips. "Let's just say it's time to get out of LA."

She noticed the red in his eyes and fought the instinctive urge to comfort him. He looked tired, or something deeper than tired. But he was not hers to fix. Let Julie take care of him. "How long are you staying?"

"I have a flight back this afternoon. Who was that guy you were with last night?"

She shifted her weight from one leg to the other and averted her eyes. "Derek's manager."

He leveled accusing eyes at her but said nothing as he shook his head. "I see. Young guy. Obviously into you. Are the two of you seeing each other now? Are you confiding in him as well, or just Macy for now? Is it just this family you don't trust with the truth?"

"Don't worry. I've learned my lesson about trusting *anyone*."

"Why did Miles Macy contact me?"

She shrugged. "I don't know, Chris. Maybe you should ask him yourself."

"I don't cozy up to the press."

"Ha! If that were true, neither of us would know him."

"I guess we all make mistakes."

"I guess we do."

"I just hope none of them lead Jameson to Ben's front door."

"What's that supposed to mean? Are you saying it's a mistake for me to be here? I came here because this was where you needed me to be. I thought you needed to stay away from me or keep me away from you. So why are you here?"

"Sam wanted—we *all* wanted you here because we thought it would help you get back to the world of living. We thought you'd do something with all that new strength of character you keep trying to convince everyone you have. But so far, looks like all you've managed to do is find some young guy to start up with."

"Why, Chris Grant, is that a hint of jealousy I hear?"

He stared at her with sad eyes, his jaw clenched in weariness and irritation. "How long are you going to have to hate me in order to be around me, Farin?"

She closed her eyes, then turned and yanked the door open. "Breakfast's ready. Cheryl's waiting. You should probably come in and eat so you can get home to your wife."

***

Bobby had intended to confront his father immediately upon his return from Santa Barbara but was sidelined by the message he received from Joni upon his return to New York. She had missed him while he was away in California. This prompted him to push his planned confrontation to Monday morning.

He spent the weekend at her place. They stayed in the first night, eating takeout and discussing the progress of her album, which was coming along ahead of schedule. She was quickly earning the label "one-take Leighton." The studio was impressed and the news had traveled to LSI.

"I'm going to buy you a crown," he told her as he lay in her arms on the sofa that night. "You're now the queen of LSI. You'll be the biggest solo artist in history."

"You stop that right this minute, Bobby Lockhardt," she said with her sweet southern drawl. "You know I get nervous when y'all talk like that." She leaned down and kissed him.

He drank in the taste of her lips, savoring it like fine wine. The ensuing arousal that tented his trousers was the greatest feeling he had ever had, and one he thought he had been robbed of forever.

Somehow, when he was with her, every tragic moment in his life faded away, replaced by plans for a future the likes of which he had never dared to dream. He saw children. A home in the suburbs or out in the country. Grooming an apprentice to whom he could delegate responsibilities at LSI in order to spend quality time with his family. With Joni, he believed he could put those plans in motion.

Still, a long road stretched out ahead for them. Only recently had they come out and officially declared their relationship. She was as shy as he was uncertain. And even though they now regularly spent evenings together cuddling in the luxurious Manhattan apartment LSI had kept for years, they had yet to take things to the next level. He had not disclosed his condition to her. Then again, given recent events, he no longer knew exactly what his condition was, or if he had one at all.

"Do you think we might should go into the other room?" she asked shyly as their kisses intensified.

Bobby gazed into her eyes. "I don't know. I don't want to rush this. It's too important to me. You're too important to me. I don't want you to think it's—"

"—shhh." She kissed him deeply. "You don't have to explain anything to me. You're a gentleman. I love you for it."

"You do?" His heart skipped a beat. Had he heard her correctly?

She nodded. Several strands of silky blonde hair spilled forward and brushed his cheeks as she leaned into him. "I think I'm falling in love with you, Bobby."

Monday morning saw a newly confident Bobby Lockhardt stroll purposefully into the LSI corporate building and into his father's office without announcement.

Jameson started as his son burst through the office door. "What are you doing here so early?"

"I'm here to keep an eye on business," he told him matter-of-factly, unbuttoning his suit jacket as he took a seat. "In case you didn't notice, I've been working my tail off righting this ship."

Jameson half-smiled and nodded his head, then straightened in his seat. "I've noticed, and I have to say I like what I'm seeing from you lately."

Bobby gave him a curt nod. "I appreciate that, Dad." He handed him a thick folder with several documents, which Jameson reviewed in detail.

"You've kept yourself quite busy scouting and developing these new acts, haven't you? Excellent." He read through the documents one by one until coming across the last few pages. Instead of artist summary sheets, they looked like physician progress notes that might come from a medical file. "What are these?"

Bobby nodded toward the file. "They're from my doctor."

Alarmed by the unfamiliar name at the top of each page, Jameson looked up at him with cautious yet curious eyes. "I thought I gave you the name and number for—"

Bobby shook his head. "I don't need Childs' recommendations or LSI's new physician, thanks. I found someone who specializes in schizophrenia."

Jameson slowly closed the folder, laid it on his desk, then sat back and beheld his son. Despite all attempts to appear casual and aloof, the pigment faded from his face.

Bobby gave him a curt nod. He regarded his father expectantly, as if he had finally excavated a long-buried truth. "I'm ready to listen if you're ready to talk."

***

Farin stepped into the studio for only the second time in the six weeks she had been back in Florida. The first time she had come in fueled by determination to confront Chris about his impending relocation. Today, something deeper beckoned her.

Ben sat in the live booth, strumming his guitar. He looked up when he noticed the sun stream in from the open door as she slipped inside. Shocked and hopeful, he grabbed the neck of his guitar and met her in the control room.

"You busy?" she asked in a small voice.

"Not at all." He propped his instrument against the console, sat down, and indicated a chair. "Have a seat."

She swallowed hard, pain and longing covering her features like a memorial shroud. She eased herself into the soft leather and stared at the console as if it were a lost love.

Ben lifted his brows and pursed his lips. "What's up?"

She shook her head, her eyes fixed on his console.

He considered filling the dead air with conversation but thought better of it. They sat in silence for several moments.

"I always wanted to learn to play an instrument," she said at last.

He nodded casually, encouraged by her interest. He leaned back and laced his fingers behind his head. "What did you want to play?"

"I like the sound of the acoustic guitar. When I was five, my dad told me he'd get me lessons if I'd promise to get good and play for him someday."

"What happened?"

She shrugged. "Someday never came."

Ben dipped his head. "It's a funny thing about 'someday,' isn't it?"

Farin nodded.

He gestured toward the shelves of masters lining two of the four walls in the control room. "My brothers pestered me for years about doing something together. I've probably got hundreds of songs we played around with over the years. Pop songs, rock anthems, little ditties we came up with. Some aren't too bad, actually. I've considered talking to Chris about maybe releasing a couple. Maybe limited editions for B tracks."

"I didn't know you sang." Farin shifted in her seat, seemingly more at ease.

Ben shook his head. "I don't. Not really. But I flirted with the idea of making a record with them...someday."

Farin nodded sadly and looked back at the sound board.

"So maybe you should do it."

"What?"

"Learn to play. You're welcome to use one of my guitars. Or Sawyer and I can help you pick one out for yourself."

She shook her head. "It's too late for that now. I'm too old."

"You think so? You're what, thirty-two?"

"I feel like an old woman."

Ben smiled thoughtfully. "You sound like a John Prine song."

She raised her right shoulder, unamused. "That's the way I feel."

"We're not our feelings, Farin," he dared to say.

"What am I doing here, Ben? I don't know what I'm doing."

He exhaled and rubbed at his beard but did not answer. He recognized the conflict inside her. Maybe it was a good thing. Maybe she was coming around. "I know you've got Minor 6th pushing on you pretty hard, and Sawyer's been beating you up pretty good. But let me ask you: do you even *want* to sing anymore?"

Farin's left thumb fidgeted with her wedding ring as she beheld the studio. Ben could not detect if she was happy there or if the mere sight of a vocal booth tortured her.

"You know, you've got a clean slate now," he told her. "You can choose."

She nestled into the chair and peered at him. "I don't even know if I can do it. It might not matter what I want. What if my voice is gone?"

He sucked his teeth as he thought. "Have you tried at all? In the shower? Anything?"

She shook her head.

"Well, remember the vocal chords are muscles. You probably need to start exercising them, at the very least—I mean, if you want to."

She stared at the carpet and nodded.

"You know, those masters from your duets with Jordan never got released. Think you might want to finish them up? Let Minor put them out as previously unreleased material? That could start you out easy, work up a bit. Give the fans some closure. Generate a bit of money?" He looked at her and tried to gauge her interest.

She raised her head. Moisture brimmed her eyes. Normally he would have made a move to comfort her. He had done it countless times before. But this time, something told him to remain still. This time, he did not so much as offer her a Kleenex.

"I'll have to think about it," she said.

Ben smiled softly. "Maybe 'someday?'" Her hint of a smile encouraged him.

"How would it work anyway? Even if you provide the material, are you really prepared to do all the music tracks?"

Ben sat forward and leaned on his left forearm as he flipped some switches on the console. A moment later, background tracks filled the air. "I've thought about that, actually. Sawyer and I thought about maybe getting Derek's guys to play."

Farin tilted her head and scratched behind her ear. "I can't trust a bunch of high school kids to keep me a secret!"

He chuckled. "That's true. But they don't need to keep a secret. They don't even need to know who they're working for. They're green, Farin, and they need the practice. After the gig last night, they'll be dying for the work. Pay them peanuts. Give them back-up credit."

She nodded absently as she considered his proposal.

"But for now, let's get you started on your basics." He switched off the controls, grabbed his guitar, and placed it in her lap.

"What are you doing?"

"Channeling John Prine," he said. "Mostly a simple three-chord progression. I expect you to practice until your fingers bleed. Don't worry, they'll callous up in no time."

With gentle instruction, Ben helped position her left index finger on the fifth string of the second fret and her middle and ring fingers on the sixth and first strings of the third, respectively. "Now strum."

She moved the top of her right thumb down across the strings with an elegant motion. The muffled fret buzz made them both laugh.

"You need to push down harder on the strings," he encouraged. "Be sure to use the tips of your fingers. It'll hurt for a bit, but it'll be worth it."

She winced as she applied more pressure. When she strummed a second time, she smiled with delight at her near-perfect G note.

"Teach me a song," she asked, suddenly energized.

For the next two hours, they practiced the four chords she needed to play John Prine's "Angel from Montgomery" from beginning to end. He even convinced her to let him record her singing with the music—just for her to use for practice or harmonies, of course.

When her fingers were too numb and tingly to continue, she asked Ben to lay a music track. When they had the track they liked, he decided to take a chance.

"Lay down a vocal," he suggested, his eyes focused on the board.

Farin's smile dimmed. "I don't know."

"It's just us, kid. Let's see what we've got to work with."

She sucked in her top lip.

"You think about it. I'll be right back. Can I get you anything to drink? I've got a fully stocked fridge."

She agreed to a water, then watched him disappear into a back room. Her eyes darted from the insulated walls to the dozens of knobs on the sound board. She could not decide how she felt about being there. The studio's silence enveloped her, tying her in place with the strings of her memories. They lived in the equipment, the instruments, the acoustic tiles. She believed if she closed her eyes and concentrated hard enough, she might hear them.

There remained so many things to do. How dare she even consider the idea of recording? Such things took time—time she did not have. Jordan was out there somewhere. She needed to reconvene with Miles to go over the e-mail he had mentioned. The waiting killed her. They could not get together again until he returned from his assignment in Anaheim—ironically enough, covering the kickoff for the *Aftermath* tour. Hopefully the key she had given him would open some doors.

Ben returned with two bottled waters in one hand and clasping something in the closed fist of his other. She thanked him and took one of the two bottles. The other he placed on the console desk. He sat in his chair and rolled it close to face her, then motioned with his fingers to give him her hand.

"I've had this for a long time," he said, placing an item in her hand. "It's rightfully yours. And maybe you need it now. Maybe more than ever. Maybe it'll help you remember who you are."

Farin covered her mouth with her hand as she recognized the piece of jewelry. She stared at it through sad, blurry eyes.

Jordan's record necklace. The one she had given him after his *Umbra* tour. She had put it on his neck that night. They had made love in the back yard. He swore he would never take it off, and he had kept that promise through every bump in their rocky road—even while he had planned to divorce her.

"Where did you..."

"It was returned with his things from the coroner's office."

With trembling hands, she undid the clasp. She stood, turned around, and held her hair up so Ben could fasten the chain around her neck.

"Thank you," she whispered as she took her seat and stroked the pendant. Then, more clearly, "Ben, are you gonna ask me what happened?"

"Not today, kid," he assured her. "Not today."

CHAPTER 13

CHRIS' CELL PHONE RANG AS he arrived at the LA Forum for the *Aftermath* tour's three-night kickoff. Julie. He let it go to voicemail, then promptly deleted the message without listening. He would not indulge a rant from an ex-wife. Not tonight. Especially not tonight.

The next three months loomed before him as though he were about to jettison into space. Some might argue the distance put between him and the chaos of the last several months would give him time to think. Put things into perspective. And maybe they were right. Had he known his life would experience a complete derailment before his first show, he would have committed to the original request to take the tour worldwide.

Inside, the celebratory atmosphere crackled like a faulty electrical current. Lively banter and laughter mixed with piped in background music. Photographers milled around the premises digitally cataloging and preserving the moment. Long-haired roadies in worn jeans and faded rock-n-roll T-shirts wore lanyards displaying laminated event badges. They hauled and hefted amps, instruments, and miscellaneous equipment. Lighting and sound engineers, stagehands, and facility managers oversaw the production's finalization. Groupies who had done "whatever it takes" to acquire coveted backstage passes bustled about the facility. Security guards wandered unobtrusively to ensure order.

He was no stranger to the venue. Decent sound. Good size. And when the vibe was right, the seventeen-thousand capacity seating felt more like twenty-five. Mirage had played there many times during their career.

Tonight, he would play alone.

No one had to stress the importance of camaraderie over the next few weeks. Chris knew the expectations of those who supported him. It would not bode well to kick things off by giving the impression he felt above the opening act. Nonetheless, he sequestered himself in his dressing room after pulling sound check, leaving Samantha and his handlers to mingle in the green room.

He considered having a drink to take the edge off, but felt oddly frozen in place as he waited to head to the stage. By sheer will, he performed a series of vocal warm-ups.

Every song on *Aftermath* had been an homage to his lost love. He had recorded his pain and longing with morbid pride, each track a step along his path of rebirth, in full view of those who had condemned him for his past. On some level, Farin's death had legitimized his feelings. It had shut the mouths of those who judged him—even Ben's.

Now that she was back, the tunes haunted him. They mocked his self-assurance, reminding him with every note what he dared not speak aloud: he would never stop loving her. Not in death, not in life.

The stage manager rapped on his door. "Five minutes. Let's go."

Once on the darkened stage, he positioned himself like a statue at its center—head down, guitar over his shoulder, left hand gripping the mic stand. A rumble of anticipation reverberated through the arena. The audience sent up periodic whistles and shouts as they began to perceive movement despite the absence of light. His opening act's forty-five minute set had revved them up. Standing there with his racing heart, he could not remember their name. He could barely remember his own.

At last, a single blue spot pierced the darkness and shone down upon him, bringing the capacity crowd to their feet. The band played the haunting intro to "Obsession." He opened his eyes, raised his head, and stared with great intensity in the direction of the audience.

The hungry eyes of a man
A silhouette, just watching
Just waiting, just hoping

The throng nearly quelled his amplified voice. Their screams sounded like the first twenty years of his career. A distant memory streaming like sunlight through the fog of his addled mind.

The musky trace of love
Insane desire, just touching
Just holding, just her

Bathed in the blue spot, he pulled his guitar over his head and played softly as the piano continued with a nearly imperceptible crescendo.

Living for a memory, burning in the fire
Making love like it was forever, afraid I'd disappear

He fingered artful guitar riffs as the roar intensified. Then, between the first and second verses came an epic drum break and earsplitting guitar with a simultaneous eruption of lights. It looked like a hydrogen bomb had detonated. The blast drew the crowd into a frenzy.

And Chris realized he was home at last.

The hungry arms of a man
A pirouette, just reaching
Just dancing, just spinning

The cruel reality of love
On the ledge, just jumping
Just crashing, just her

Existing in a memory, consumed by the fire
Making love like it was forever, I watched her disappear

The hungry heart of a man
With no regret, just falling
Just pleading, just knowing

The price is paid for love
Water rushing, just wanting
Just needing, just her

Drowning in a memory, no putting out the fire
Making love like she was never, I want to disappear

Fans fist-pumped, raised their arms high, threw up peace signs and hand horns, and jumped in time with the beat and the light show. Girls sat atop the shoulders of their boyfriends and swayed their heads. As the song ended, the cacophony of their applause, shouts, whistles, and cheers resonated throughout his body.

He played another song from *Aftermath*, which received equal praise. When he finished, he gestured dramatically back to his audience. The roar of the crowd was deafening.

"*LA!*" he shouted. "How you doing tonight?" He continued to play softly as he spoke, keeping his fingers limber. "It's great to be back! It's been too long, hasn't it?"

Girls cat-called and cried out his name. He lifted his hand to shield his eyes from the spotlights. "Thank you, darling," he said, flashing his trademark grin. "Can't quite make everyone out with these lights, but I'm sure you're beautiful. Come meet me after the show."

Several girls "whoo hoo'd" loudly. The crowd laughed at the exchange.

"Joking. I'm a reformed man, you know."

Good-natured "boo's" followed, along with more laughter.

"I know, I know. Sounds like a lot of Mirage fans in here tonight."

The cheering escalated.

"Yeah," he said in mock jealousy. "You ladies must be looking for Todd Dalton. I hear he's still making the rounds somewhere across the pond."

More whistles, cheers, and laughter as Chris launched into his next song.

He had scheduled two sets. The first included highlights from the *Aftermath* album, an obligatory tribute to each his brother and Farin, and ended with a medley of cover material he had painstakingly arranged himself. The second set would include his McCartney cover and several Mirage fan favorites. He would encore with his recent single, the title track from his album.

Before the first set ended, he introduced the members of his back-up band, then played an unlikely excerpt of Ravel's "Bolero." He had arranged it with a hard rock edge, an erotically charged piece reminiscent of his younger, more carefree days. Days when an array of different women were so plentiful in his life they might as well have not been there at all.

The song ebbed and flowed with a marching band cadence, an insistent guitar undulating from sweet agony to sated afterglow. As the melody softened, it bled seamlessly into a sampling of Led Zeppelin's "Kashmir." His thoughts turned to Farin and all the danger of loving her. How we wanted her. How he took her. And how he had lived to regret his actions.

The piece rose unwaveringly upon its ascending chromatic ostinato over a pedal drone, his axe oozing sensuality in its 3/8 time signature. Then, in an ingenious and almost imperceptible transformation, he heeded his electric guitar as "Kashmir" gave way into his sideman's acoustic stylings of "Silver Wheels."

The crowd roared its approval of the temporary lull until acoustic paired with electric. The concert hall surged with white light as a single flash transformed the venue in synchronism with the iconic first electric note of Heart's "Crazy on You."

Sweat poured down Chris' face as he performed. The pulsing tempo had the audience on their feet, grooving to the fresh rendition of the classic tune. He fused his eyes closed as he sang the second verse. His mind fixated inexplicably on Farin standing on the balcony of his home in Key Biscayne. Torrential wind whipped her auburn tresses. Her damp nightgown clung to her body. She had dared the storm to take her that night. She had called for it. Begged for it.

Chris stirred the crowd to near mania, encouraging them to sing along with the bridge.

As the anthem came to an end, the band took turns soloing on their various instruments. Minutes later, they downtempoed the beat until it hit a steady four-count rhythm, morphing at last into the final number in the medley. In a fluid movement, Chris traded his electric guitar for acoustic and brought down the house with Blind Faith's "Can't Find My Way Home."

A montage of memories fluttered around him like a charm of hummingbirds. Each suckled at the nectar of his psyche, some barely registering fully in his mind before flitting away. Years of touring with his band. Laughter and carefree nights lost in the music, the women, and endless afterparties. Simpler times. Happier times. Had it been that long since he had felt whole? Since his soul longed for nothing more than the feel of his instrument or a warm and willing body?

His heart rate stabilized as he and the audience relaxed to the slower, bluesy piece. Fans who had rocked out now swayed trance-like to the acoustic rhythm. Boyfriends wrapped their arms around their girlfriends' waists and sang in their ears. Whoops and whistles continued sporadically. And when the 25-minute medley ended in an apex of guitars, high hats, and the final sustained bang of the drum, Chris hoisted his guitar triumphantly into the air in a cathartic declaration of freedom.

The arena echoed with delight. Slowly, the light crew killed the illumination until they circled back to the single blue spot, and then extinguished it, leaving the facility in darkness just long enough to get the band off stage before bringing up the house lights for the break.

As Chris followed the marked path to exit the stage, he caught a glimpse of Miles Macy watching him from the media section. He did a double take, then nodded and pointed his way.

An enthusiastic Samantha Drake waited by his dressing room. She handed him two water bottles. "That was fantastic, Chris."

"Thanks." With a nod, he accepted a towel from a nearby attendant, then opened his door and gestured her inside.

"How are you feeling? You okay?"

He guzzled the water, discarded the towel, and shook out his hair. He smiled at her through the mirror as he scrutinized himself to see if he needed a clothing change.

She smiled back. "I take it that's a yes. I didn't know how you'd be, so I made sure no one else was here to bother you between sets."

He turned and kissed her cheek, then disappeared briefly to relieve his bladder. "You should be a manager, Sam."

She called after him, "Your manager was all too happy to let me handle you tonight."

He laughed. "I'll bet. Is Ethan here?"

She shook her head. "Sorry. He's on call. Couldn't make it."

"No worries." He returned and grabbed a fresh shirt, rubbing on some stick antiperspirant before throwing the crisp button-up around him like a cape and plunging his arms inside the sleeves. "How about the opening act—what's their name again?"

"Shame on you," she chided.

"I know. My mind's spaghetti tonight. I'll be better. Humor me."

"Nylon Fred."

His hands froze mid-button. "Shut up."

"Serious."

He shook his head.

"Think 'Steely Dan.' They're pretty good, actually."

Chris tucked in the shirt, then headed for the door. "You can introduce me before the second set."

"Where are you going?"

He frowned again and gestured with his thumb. "Green room."

"You don't have time for the green room."

"What are you talking about? It's on the way back to the stage."

She moved in front of him before he reached the door. "It's closed."

His brow wrinkled. "What?"

She shook her head innocently and rolled her eyes. "Accident. They're cleaning up. I don't know what happened."

"Well, I need to see 'Nylon Fred' and apologize. My head was all nuttered up before. Don't want them to get the wrong idea."

"They won't. We talked to them earlier. Told them you'd see them tonight at the hotel after the press conference."

"All right. As long as they don't think I'm Johnny Ego."

"I said I *talked* to them, Chris. I didn't say I could fix your reputation."

He tilted his head to the side and grinned. "Well, I should at least talk to my band. Where're they congregating?"

Samantha lifted her shoulders innocently. "I imagine they're resting before they have to go back on stage."

"C'mon, Sam. Is this a rock tour or a retirement home? What gives?"

She sat on a leather love seat and tried to appear nonchalant. "First night, Chris. Trust me. If you're looking to party, I'm sure you'll have ample time."

His smile dissolved. He leaned back against the counter and folded his arms. "Is there something wrong? It sounds like you're making excuses. Is it that no one wants to see me? Is there some problem?"

Samantha attempted to speak but he cut her off.

"I know I haven't been very social lately, but I don't want to spend the entire tour alone in my trailer."

"It's not that at all," Sam assured him. "Like I said, first night. Don't worry. We'll get all the bugs out tonight after the press conference."

When Samantha walked him back to the stage after the break, Chris tried to maintain the buzz he had felt from the first set. The intensity of the music and the crowd had infused him with living energy, a vibe reminiscent of Mirage's heyday. He wanted that vibe to sustain through the night, and indeed throughout the tour. But the conspicuous emptiness of hallways and the absence of crew baffled him.

"Where *is* everyone? What's going on?"

Samantha turned and faced him, fixing his eyes with hers. "Listen, Chris. Tonight is your night. There's nothing going on. That first set was the most alive I've seen you in years. And I want this second set to show the world you're back. For you. For me. For every demon you exorcised from your psyche tonight. You hear me? Things are *fine*. It's just new, not having Mirage out there. But you'll get through this. You already have. Now get out there and give your fans what they came for."

Chris nodded.

"I'll be waiting in the wings."

He reached out, gave her hand a squeeze, then trotted back onto the darkened stage and grabbed his guitar.

The silhouettes of his band members looked like life-size trophies, tall and motionless as he took his place center stage. He wished he had time to talk to them, apologize for any slight they may have perceived. But Samantha was right. They would sort things after the show.

A lone piano played the opening bars of Paul McCartney's "Maybe I'm Amazed." He grabbed the mic just as a warm spot showered him in amber.

He spoke softly to the audience. "Is everyone having a good time?"

Fans cheered, whooped, and shouted. Several items whizzed by him on either side. Single roses, rolled joints, phone numbers, and women's underwear littered the stage as a tribute to their musical hero. Chris flung several guitar picks back, playing a note before tossing each to a lucky recipient.

"I'm, uh...I'm sorry it's taken so long to get back to you."

The piano looped back to the beginning amid the din of the audience shouting, cheering, and crying out. Chris batted a beach ball that had been tossed toward him back into the masses.

"But I have to say. I can't imagine a finer group to kick off my solo tour. Thank you all for being here tonight."

The amber gel remained the only light in the auditorium as he sang the first verse of the song. He had always loved the simplicity and depth of feeling McCartney captured in its melody and lyrics. The tension he felt over his isolation evaporated with every note. The essence of the pianist's style reminded him of a crazy Brooklyn redhead he had played with for decades. He smiled at the memory as he sang.

At the halfway point of the first verse, the rest of the band joined in, accompanied by background vocals. And as the lights grew brighter, the audience exploded into a tumult that seemed oddly out of place, given their place in the piece. Fans rushed at and pressed against the stage, straining security in their zeal. When he turned around to offer the band an appreciative smile, he understood why.

His voice cut out mid-verse.

Walking toward him, playing rhythm guitar, he saw Todd Dalton. His smile looked resplendent as he approached, nodding gracious thank-yous at the audience. When he reached center stage, he embraced Chris with his strumming arm. The clamor grew louder as the music looped back through the first verse.

"What're you doing here, man?" Chris asked into his ear, overjoyed and confused.

"Are you barmy? Look around! I'm here to pick up those joints off the stage."

Chris laughed heartily, then caught sight of Lance Turner sitting in the middle of the drum kit, hitting the skins. Lance twirled a drumstick then struck a cymbal. He smiled at Chris who stood open mouth, shaking his head.

Todd shouted at him, "Gonna play that guitar, you tosser? You're tanking the song."

Chris turned to the audience and raised his arms. He leaned into his mic and said, "This was *not* on the program!"

Laughter mixed with whistles and cheers. Chris engaged his guitar and fell in with the other instruments but searched the stage, curious now. He looked to his right just as Elliot Lawrence sidled up to him, working his bass as he sang-shouted into his ear, changing the song's lyrics. "Maybe you're amazed at the way Sam planned this all along, made us learn your songs...Maybe you're amazed that you never saw this coming..."

Chris bent over, belly laughing. He repeated the rhythmic riff, then stood back up. He rushed to the drum kit to squeeze Lance's neck. He shouted, "How you doin', mate?"

Lance did not miss a beat as he leaned in and told Chris, "I've got one son and another on the way...and I'm getting married!"

Chris pulled back, smiling his congratulations.

A piano adlib drew his attention as he played. He looked over, and there she was. His eyes grew moist despite himself.

"*Sing!*" she shouted. "I don't want to play this fucking song all night!"

He winked, then broke into a guitar lick. The band followed him with ease, and they stepped in unison back into the cover. Faith laughed and shook her head. Her fingers danced masterfully across the keys.

As the song continued, Chris skipped over to each of his friends, thanking them in turn. The irony of the lyrics beset him as he sang. When the number finally ended, the fans applauded, screamed, whistled, and catcalled. The band stood and took a bow, then resumed their places.

For the next hour and a half, they played together as if no time had passed since their last gig, that hateful night in Miami. Their sound remained tight, their harmonies sharp. Their solos followed one another with the kind of instinct that came with two decades of familiarity.

They played the old songs. Their best songs. And when they played the encore, Chris was amazed at how well they knew his work.

The hotel banquet room hosted the post-show press conference. When the members of the band arrived, cameras flashed like strobe lights. Reporters spoke over and interrupted each other as they shot questions machine-gun style at Chris, who sat at the center of the long table, his sidemen to his right and his former bandmates to his left.

"Chris! Was this a scheduled reunion or a media stunt?"

"Is Mirage reuniting, Chris?"

"Chris! Will you be together for the remainder of the tour?"

He could barely answer one question before the next hit him.

"This was definitely *not* scheduled. I was as surprised as you were."

"I don't know what this means yet. I haven't talked to anyone. Not sure what our plans are. I just know I'm happy they're here. Can't wait to catch up."

Discussion centered more on the impromptu appearance of his mates than the overall show. Some artists' egos might have bristled over sharing the attention, but Chris did not mind. In fact, he welcomed it. He had confidence the first set blew the audience away. No one needed to reassure him he would see favorable reviews.

More than anything, he wanted to thank Samantha. She knew he had struggled with the prospect of playing solo. Even more than that, she knew he did not relish the idea of sitting in a room of reporters who might wax nostalgic and ask questions about his family. The hype created by the would-be Mirage reunion had overshadowed any discourse of the past. What a brilliant move.

But Sam had taken off before the encore. She left a congratulatory note in his dressing room that said, in part, "Best show ever. Go celebrate. And remember: it's *Nylon Fred*."

***

Bridgeman wiped his mouth, dropped the soiled napkin on his plate, then sat back and patted his full stomach. "I'll have to bring Penny here sometime.

She's developed quite a taste for Cuban food."

Hubbell folded his long arms on the table and casually sucked his teeth. "I try to come in whenever I get down here. The *tostones rellenos con langosta* appetizer's worth the trip. Plus, it's only minutes from the office."

"I had no idea you came down here."

"That's probably because we haven't seen each other since, what...? '88?"

"'89, I think," Bridgeman corrected. "Penny and I went to see you graduate from the FBI Academy."

"That's right! Wow, almost seven years." He chuckled as he shook his head, his naturally loud *basso profundo* voice unwittingly drawing harsh looks from nearby restaurant patrons. "You'd gone back to Detroit to be a cop. I'd headed over to Quantico—"

"And never left."

He smirked. "If you'd grown up in my neighborhood, you'd get as far away as you could, too."

If Bridgeman had heard the story once, he had heard it a dozen times. Hubbell Quarles had grown up in one of the poorest neighborhoods in Cleveland, Ohio. His father, a Korean War veteran, had died during the Hough Riots of '66, leaving his wife to care for Hubbell and his two older sisters. The area further declined after the riots as a result of population loss and an economic downturn. Life in Hough was not for the weak of will.

Desperate to break out of an impoverished existence, he had enlisted his mother's help to construct a life plan that would help them all—a road map of sorts to lead him out of Hough and provide him not only a successful life, but a way to move his momma out of the ghetto. He had a keen mind, a large frame, and intimidating height, which helped him excel not only in academics but athletics, playing both football and basketball during his years at East High School.

Major universities had recruited him, including the Naval Academy. This presented him an obvious solution to the problem he faced deciding whether he would follow his father's footsteps into military service or go to college. In the end, Hubbell had become a Marine officer.

Fifteen years in, he had finished his masters in criminal justice, graduated from EOD training, reached the rank of captain, and expressed interest in and an aptitude for criminology. Before he could consider a second eight-year re-enlistment, the FBI recruited him.

His roadmap had ultimately taken him to his prized destination. Now, Special Agent Hubbell Quarles lived in Occoquan, Virginia, with his wife and three sons. His mother occupied the spacious mother-in-law house on his property. Goodbye, Hough. Hub had earned everything he had and made apologies to no one for it.

Their waitress delivered their after-dinner *cafecito* and two flans. She cleared their plates and asked if they needed cream. Both men declined.

Hubbell stirred the sweet crema floating atop the strong espresso. "But look at us, both successful family men now. A long ways from EOD, that's for sure."

Bridgeman lifted his mug and waggled his brows, a mischievous glint in his eyes. "Initial success..."

"...or total failure." Hubbell hunched his shoulders, immediately adopting a threatening stance as he smiled and touched his mug to Bridgeman's. They followed with a synchronous "Yut!" that met with some clipped, under-the-breath Spanish complaints from the women at the booth behind Bridgeman.

They chuckled at the shared memory, then finished their desserts in silence. Bridgeman was happy for the opportunity to catch up with his friend and fellow Jarhead. However, Hub had yet to explain why he had taken nearly two months to return his call and what business had brought him to Miami. Something told him the unexpected visit had not come about by accident.

He nodded his gratitude when the waitress refilled their water glasses, then leaned back and stretched his arm to rest it along the top of the vinyl booth. "You still see any of the guys?"

Hubbell wrinkled his nose and shook his head. "Not much. I hear Scott, Benny, and Victor are all over at Lockheed now. Some of the others are working weapons ordinance overseas."

He watched Hub scrape his plate for the last bit of caramel and custard, then push his plate away. "Thanks for calling me back. I was beginning to wonder if you'd gotten my message."

Hubbell nodded without looking his way. "I got it."

"Been busy, huh?"

"Always. You know how it is."

"That I do. So what brings you to Miami? Think you'll be here long enough to come to the house for dinner? Penny'll kill me if she finds out you were here and didn't stop by."

Hubbell cocked his head and stretched his thick lips into a straight line. "I think we both know why I'm here."

Bridgeman's pulse quickened with anticipation. "Do we?"

He narrowed his eyes. "Don't we?"

"Are you here to ask me what I know? Or are you here to tell me what you know?"

"Are we on or off the record here, buddy?"

Bridgeman exhaled through his nose, then leaned forward and rested his crossed arms on the table. "For now? Off."

Hubbell nodded.

Confidentiality established, Bridgeman leaned in and whispered, "So why did the Feds freeze the files on the Grant cases?"

***

Faith rarely questioned her decisions. Strong and outspoken, she had made deliberate moves in her music career and in her new fashion gig. She had stood out as the unpredictable firestorm within Mirage, the only woman among a group of crazy male rock musicians.

That feat had taken dedication. Intent. Energy. Vigor. It took a gimmick— a gimmick that had enabled her to launch her equally successful post-rock-n-roll career when the time had come. Leather had become her signature attribute. It enswathed her in mystery and scandal. She had savored it, cultivated it to perfection.

But tonight, she only wanted to slip into something comfortable. Strip off the long gloves. Free herself from the restrictive corset that inhibited the full expansion of her lungs. Peel off the thigh-high, five-inch-heel boots whose laces painfully crisscrossed her legs. Tonight, she hated the thought, sight, feel, and smell of leather.

Or maybe it was something else, something that ate away at her psyche like a rodent gnawing wood. Tonight, she questioned everything. She questioned the decision to fly to LA. To be part of Chris' big night. To let herself near him.

"Fool," she spat at the reflected image in the mirror as she prepped to join the others. "Why now?"

The phone rang and Faith did not have to guess the caller's identity. His timing could not have been more perfect had it been scripted.

"How was the show?" he asked.

"Honestly? Amazing." She plopped down onto her bed, still clothed, and crossed her fully sheathed legs. She winced at a slight pinch of leather into her flesh.

"I see."

She heard him exhale on the other end of the line and imagined a cloud of smoke escape his nose and lips. "Don't sound so disappointed. It's a good thing. Would you rather it tanked?"

"Of course not," he told her, a hint of annoyance in his faux accent.

"Did you dust the piano again today?"

"Of course."

"Did you paint?"

Silence filled the line.

"I'm not gonna be responsible for this. It's been a month, Henri. Whatever's gotten into you, cut it out."

"Have you made up your mind yet?"

She sighed audibly, then snapped. "About which thing?"

After a short pause, he pressed on. "How long are you staying? Are you coming home or staying with the tour?"

She set her jaw and fixed her eyes on the ceiling's scalloped molding. He deserved an answer. "I haven't talked to the guys yet. I just came back to the room to freshen up. I'm getting ready to head out again. Can't snub everyone, you know?"

"Parties..."

"People..." She grinned despite herself.

"...what a farce."

"I love you, Henri. I'll talk to you tomorrow." She hung the phone up, hoisted herself off the bed, and returned to the bathroom to fix her hair and makeup. No point in changing. No one would recognize her in jeans and a T-shirt.

Chris invaded her thoughts, a common occurrence since she had left New York last month to prepare for tonight's surprise performance. She had known seeing him again, playing with him again, would stir up memories. But she had not anticipated the butterflies she felt when those lights came up and she saw him center stage.

Best friend. She had donned that moniker for years. The one to whom he had conveyed the details of his conquests. The one he felt driven to make amends with when Lockhardt canned them. The one he took care of when she overdosed. The one who effectively deserted him after his marriage. The one who did not so much as call after he lost Jordan, or Farin.

"...and so I'm sorry, Chris," she explained at her mirrored image as she scrunched and sprayed her red curls. "I came to apologize. But that's not why I'm here."

The day Henri proposed, she realized she needed to make peace with a part of her no one else even knew existed. She needed to know: had Chris ever felt that spark between them?

A strong and painful realization overcame her. As if on autopilot, her brain screamed within her: November 8, 1991! Her sobriety date.

As she smashed tubes of mascara and lip balm into her purse, she considered calling her sponsor. Truth told, she had not spoken to Gale since the night before she left New York.

She flung her makeup bag onto the marble countertop. "You need to buck up and stop feeling sorry for yourself, Faith Annelisa Peterson."

Or, she could go see Todd and chase away the anxiety with one quick toot. He always had something.

CHAPTER 14

ELLIOT GRINNED AS HE STEPPED out of the shower and found Marci waiting for him with a towel. "Wow...remind me to send a note to management for the incredible service."

"I figured we were in a hurry."

He wiped down, then wrapped the towel around his waist. "No hurry, love. It's kickoff night. They'll be at it until dawn."

Marci grinned at her husband through the mirror. "You're loving this."

He raised his shoulders and widened his eyes in mock innocence. "I don't know what you're on about. I'm just helping Chris...*acclimate*."

She chuckled and shook her head, then left him to finish his routine while she dressed. She chose a pair of maternity jeans and a long pink tank top with frilled shoulder straps. Not formal. No need for formal. For this, she was thankful.

The irony that Elliot had kept this hole-and-corner reunion from her until almost the last minute because of her unlikely friendship with her former nemesis did not escape her. He had correctly guessed she would support his decision but feared her sympathy for Chris' situation might tempt her to ruin the surprise in an effort to lift his spirits.

She eyed her husband and smiled knowingly as he emerged from the bathroom to dress. "So how long are we 'acclimating,' you think?"

He grinned but did not look her in the eye. Instead, he stepped into his jeans, skinned on a T-shirt, then sat beside her on the bed.

Something about the way his damp brown hair fell forward as he bent over to tie his sneakers stirred her. She could not recall the last time he had gone for a haircut. This longer look suited him. Maybe an homage to his younger days. Maybe a protest against next year's milestone 40th birthday.

She elbowed him playfully. "You gonna keep me in the dark about this, too?"

He slid from the bed onto his knees, then crawled between her legs and rested his hands to either side of her thighs. "I'll tell you anything you want to know."

"Have you made a decision yet?"

"I have made no decision yet."

"Will we talk about it—either way—before you do?"

He nodded. "Promise."

She leveled her eyes at him, more serious. "Are you hesitating because of me and the baby?"

"Yes."

She drew her head back at the brute honesty.

He pulled her closer and wrapped his arms around her waist, kissed her growing baby bump, then drew her down for a kiss. "I love tonight. The buzz, the music, the guys. I love it. All of it. But it wouldn't be such a high without you. Or without our little one here. I don't want to lose anything I have right now—including that high. So if we decide to play a few more nights together and nothing comes of it, I'm out. I'm not looking for anything, Zoso. I have what I want."

She felt his damp hair through her tank top when he embraced her. The last eight years of her life flickered in her memory. Maybe she should have called Farin tonight before leaving for the concert. Eight years ago tonight they had sat together at Le Dome celebrating what they believed would be the turning point in her journey to stardom. Eight years to the day since she had met Jordan and all their lives had changed.

Perhaps such a memory did not warrant a stroll down Recollection Boulevard after all.

Elliot pulled back and frowned at her somber expression. "You okay?"

She gave him a bittersweet, far-off smile.

"We can stay here if you don't feel like going, but I haven't been to a decent afterparty since the Bark at the Moon tour in '84."

"You call that 'decent?'"

He laughed. "Zoso, Ozzy snorted *ants*. Up his *nose!*"

She shook her head in mock disgust. "I can't believe I'm having a child with you."

"Too late to change your mind now. You're stuck with me."

"True. And with this weight gain, I probably couldn't get my wedding ring off anyway."

"But seriously. If you don't want to go, we'll stay here. Your call."

"We have to go. And be honest—you want to go."

He nodded enthusiastically. "I do. Do you?"

She smiled. "Can't wait."

"Then let's do it!"

"Pregnant wife and all?"

He stood and took her hand. "And *all*."

***

The hour-long wait for a table at Colline gave Herb Radford plenty of time to size up the swanky LA establishment. Trendy. Colorful. Maybe a tad garish for his taste. He waited at the bar, polishing off his second overpriced martini while he studied the wait staff. Twenty minutes in, he wondered if his visit was for naught. No sign of anyone who looked like a manager, much less an owner.

Then again, who cared? The various aromas wafting off expertly plated entrees as servers wove through the tables had started his stomach growling. Tonight would end a success or a bust. Either way, Lockhardt would foot the bill.

He held out his hand at the waitress passing by with a tray of cocktails. "Is the owner in tonight?"

She smiled, bright-eyed and patient. "Which one?"

"There's more than one?"

"Mr. Eastland and Mr. Colline are co-owners."

Radford nodded, his upside down smile pulled to one side. "Eastland. He around?"

The waitress lifted her chin and scanned the room. "I don't see him on the floor. Is everything okay? I'd be happy to assist you, or I can get Mr. Eastland for you in a moment."

He shook his head and straightened on his stool. "That won't be necessary. I just wanted to know if he'd be in tonight."

"Mr. Eastland's here most nights, sir."

He nodded again and waved his hand. "That's fine. I'll catch up with him later. Thanks."

"As soon as I deliver these drinks, I'll let him know you'd like to see him, Mr....?"

He leaned to his right, then plunged his hand into the front pocket of his slacks, pulled out a money clip fat with bills, and peeled off a twenty. "Don't trouble yourself."

She nodded appreciatively as she pocketed the cash, then continued on her way.

Once seated at his table with his third martini, Herb relaxed and perused the menu. Nights like these were rare in his line of work. Most the time he found himself in a cheap motel room poring over records and reports, or sitting in vehicles for long hours hoping to spot his target. Tonight, he intended to take his leisure and enjoy the upscale digs. He had had enough take-out in the last month to choke a pig.

A fresh-faced twenty-something metrosexual in pristine white and black wait attire approached him, hands clasped behind his back. "I'm Skylar, and I'll be your server this evening."

Herb resisted a chuckle at the effeminate mannerisms as Skylar told him the evening's specials. LA was some town. Of course, New York was scarcely different anymore. The whole damn country had gone crazy. Nobody knew who they were anymore.

"Can I get something started for you? An appetizer, perhaps?"

He ordered the spring rolls and chose the rib-eye for his entree. Skylar assured him he had made an excellent choice, told him he would return with his starter and a fresh martini in no time, then left to put in the order.

A gentle hand on his shoulder made him simultaneously cringe and jerk to the side.

"Forgive me!" came the sing-songy trill of the hand's owner. "I didn't mean to startle you!"

Apparently Colline's staff was better trained than Herb had guessed. The waitress had obviously mistaken his generosity for a bribe. Standing beside him in an impressively tailored black pinstripe double-breasted suit and a head full of hair gel was Dale Eastland.

Herb shifted in his seat and extended his hand. "Not at all. You caught me with my head elsewhere. Nice place you have here."

Dale stepped aside as a server passed them holding a tray high above his head. He repositioned himself beside the chair opposite his patron, then leaned in and shook Radford's hand. "Thank you. One of my girls told me you'd asked to see me. Is everything okay, Mr....?"

"Smith. Herb Smith. Actually, I'd just asked if you'd be in tonight. Hate to interrupt you on such a busy night—especially for something so frivolous."

"Nonsense!" Dale waved a dismissive hand. "I love meeting my guests."

"It's not for me, exactly...well, hell, I'm sorry, Mr. Eastland. It was a foolish whim."

Dale squinted, seemingly intrigued. He pointed at the empty chair. "Do you mind?"

Herb half-rose from his seat, held his tie to his chest with one hand, and gestured with the other. "Not at all. Please."

"So...tell me about this whim of yours. I detect an accent, Mr. Smith. New York, isn't it?"

Herb laughed jovially, in fact downright innocently. "Guilty. You see, I'm out here on business for the first time and I promised my daughter I'd stop by and try to get your autograph."

Flattered and curious, Dale's chest rose as he tucked his chin. He chuckled graciously. "My autograph? Whatever for?"

He twisted around to grab his blazer and procured from the inside pocket the cassette tape he had happened upon at a used record store in Hollywood two days ago while constructing his plan. With a careful swipe of the plastic cover, he handed it across the table. "My girl's a big fan of Plectra."

Dale leaned forward with a get-outta-here wave of his hand and laughed uproariously. "*Plectra?* My heavens, that was a decade ago! You're kidding!"

"Afraid not," Herb told him, the epitome of embarrassment mixed with fatherly pride. "She graduated from UCLA back in '86. Used to spend more time partying on the Strip than studying, I suspect. She's a good kid, though. Made a decent life for herself. Anyway, she recorded this from a show you did at a club down here one night and made me promise to come by and see if you'd sign it."

Dale looked over the bootlegged cassette. It appeared in all ways unremarkable. Just a Maxell cassette with a gold label and red text in a black and clear plastic holder. He smiled at the memory, as Radford had figured he would. Nostalgia—the key to deciding his next move.

Herb had gotten Dale's name from the list of associates he had received from Lockhardt. For all her notoriety, it turned out Farin Grant had few friends. Since his time in LA, Herb had found nothing in the Malibu remains, nothing at the best friend's place, and zilch at Chris Grant's seemingly abandoned home. It had begun to look like Farin had moved on, if she had ever been here in the first place.

Then, as he perused the used records store a couple of days ago, he got to talking with the store employee. The kid was probably in his late twenties, he guessed. A stereotypical laid-back LA beach bum, probably still living at home with his parents and working a part-time, dead-end job to avoid the responsibilities of adulthood.

The kid started boasting about all the bands he had seen at local clubs before they became famous. Notably, he mentioned Farin Grant's former band, Plectra. When Herb pressed him for information, he mentioned her former keyboard player had left the business and became a successful restaurateur. When the kid subsequently dug through some old tapes and found the bootleg, Herb had paid him twice the asking price, then suggested he get a haircut and a real job before walking out with his prize.

This was Herb's last shot in LA. If he got nothing from this flamer, he would move on to the next possible hiding place a couple of hours north.

Herb had come on a good night. The restaurant seemed to run smoothly without the need to interrupt its owner as he reminisced with the stranger from New York about his days under the spotlight.

Dale stopped one of the servers and asked him to bring him an indelible marker, then stayed and chatted while they waited. "So what line of work are you in, Mr. Smith? Will you be in LA long?"

"I'm in pharmaceutical sales. I just finished a weeklong conference. I'll be heading back to New York tomorrow morning."

When his appetizer arrived, Herb asked if Dale would join him, knowing he would decline. He did, but instructed Skylar to bring a bottle of their finest red wine for his guest. Herb insisted Dale join him.

The marker and the wine arrived at the same time. Dale signed the cassette and slid it across the table so Radford could pocket his treasure, then nodded as Skylar uncorked a bottle of Bryant Family Cabernet Sauvignon.

Herb complimented the spring rolls and sipped the California red. He was nobody's wine connoisseur, but could tell it must be expensive. Once he had washed down his appetizer, he asked, "What made you give up the music business? My Sandy says some famous gal singer—what's her name, Grant something or other?—was in Plectra with you."

A misty smile stretched the corners of Dale's lips. "Yes. Farin. Farin Grant. She was our lead singer."

Herb snapped his fingers. "That's it. Farin. Pretty name."

He looked down and away. "She was a pretty girl."

Herb froze, feigning surprise. "'Was?'"

Dale's disposition shifted. He lifted his shoulder and fidgeted uncomfortably in his seat as he reached for his glass and sipped at his wine. "She died a few years back."

"Oh, gosh. I didn't know. I'm sorry. I'm afraid my Sandy's the music lover in the family. I haven't listened to anything more recent than Engelbert Humperdinck since the mid-seventies."

You know, Eastland. You've seen her. Looks like I'll be staying in LA a while longer after all.

***

Lance returned to his room after the press conference on a high he could achieve from no drug. Their surprise reunion had set LA abuzz. Before heading down to the afterparty, he would ensure the limo he had arranged at LAX had safely brought his young family to the hotel. Only one thing left to make the night complete.

His natural high gave way to concern when he found Ivy sobbing at Colin's bedside. Obviously still in her travel clothes, her luggage remained just inside the door of their three-room suite.

He went to her and put an arm around her. "What's the matter, love?" When he tried to coax her into the living room, her sobbing intensified. "Now, now sweetheart. Come into the other room. The time difference'll be an adjustment for him. You don't want to wake him up, do you?"

"No chance of *that*." Ivy sniffed bitterly through her tears as Lance led her out of the room. She wiped her face with the cuff of her long-sleeve T-shirt before collapsing beside him on the sofa and burying her head in his lap. "He hasn't slept since we boarded the plane. It was all screaming and the occasional, 'Where's Daddy?' 'Mummy, fat feet,' 'Don't cry, Mummy.' I shouldn't have come at all. He didn't stop talking or crying the entire trip! That's a whole ocean, Lance! *And* the entire United States!"

He stroked her heavily gelled and sprayed hair. "But you're here now. And

I heard the nanny in the other room. She's probably freshening up. As soon as she returns, we can go. We'll get you some time away. That'll sort things for you."

"*Oh, no!*" She shot up and pointed past their master suite into their private bath. "I'm not going anywhere but that rather large tub in the loo. Then it's off to bed for me. I'll not have my son telling everyone in America his mum has fat feet!"

His brow furrowed with disappointment. "You look brilliant, Ivy. You always do. Besides, I just told Chris I'm a father. I want you to meet my band, show you off a bit."

Her disposition stiffened as her features turned harsh. "Your band? Your band's home in London. This is your past, Lance. You promised. The reunion ends tomorrow night after the show. Then it's off to Disneyland and a bit of sightseeing, then home. Our children are going to have a quiet life in England. They'll not be raised on airplanes and tour buses."

He inhaled deeply, then exhaled through his nose and held her to him, thinking as he bit the inside of his cheek. When the nanny returned and announced she would stay with Colin in case he woke during the night, he felt Ivy's tense body relax in his embrace. "Are you sure you won't come out just for a bit, love? I want you to be a part of this with me, especially if it's going to be the last time. Who knows when you'll have the chance to meet the others if we don't do it now."

Her head and one hand rested on his chest. "Maybe at breakfast tomorrow, then, after I've had a shower. I've been in these clothes for donkey's years."

They sat in silence. Ivy tucked her swollen feet beneath her on the sofa as she rested, eyes closed, inside Lance's embrace. Every once in a while, he would peek at his watch. Half an hour passed before he decided he might as well put it in the mixer.

He moved out from beneath her and stood before her as she maneuvered herself into the warmth of his abandoned space on the sofa.

She cooed softly, "You off, then? Don't be late."

"Please come with me. I need you with me tonight. Especially tonight."

With a scoff and a frustrated slap at the sofa, she flounced into a sitting position and rubbed her enlarging baby bump. "I'm knackered, pregnant, and too irritated to deal with a party tonight. And even if I weren't, I look a mess."

"You're nearly perfect, sweetheart."

She raised a single brow.

Before either of them knew what he was doing, he pushed the coffee table far enough away to get down on one knee before her. "Change your shirt, Ivy. You need to meet my mates. They'll want to see."

Her eyes widened as she watched him fish something out of his jeans pocket. "What are you doing?"

He reached for her left hand and produced the contents of his pocket, sliding it onto her finger. "It fits fine, you love it, and you'll say yes without argument—just this once. Marry me, Ivy Spencer."

She brought her free hand to her opened mouth and studied the audacious diamond setting fit for a princess. "Lance—"

"*Now* you're perfect. Let's go."

***

Todd prepared four lines of powder on the mirror he had yanked off the bedroom wall and laid atop the table in front of the couch. It had not taken long to find someone holding enough product to get him through this three-night stand in LA. No matter how he did not want to think about the inevitable, he knew he would have to huddle up with the others tonight and start talking about their future. On one hand, he needed the money. On the other, he wanted to paste Chris Grant in the face.

"Been here a month and I already played our stuff—and yours—better than you bloody did," he mumbled as he tapped the powder residue from the razor, then scraped and dragged it into perfect formation.

At least the road manager had agreed to give him the suite on the floor above Chris'. Of course it was part of the rider he had submitted. For however long the members of Mirage ended up accompanying Mr. Solo on his tour, Todd would not travel on the same plane or bus and would not stay on the same floor. He had demanded accommodations as good as or slightly better than Chris Grant at all times. That or no deal. It was his fucking due. After all Chris had done, he should be grateful Todd showed at all. He had made this night the success it was.

Tonight, he would party himself into oblivion. Sod the rest.

Sweaty from the gig, he stood and stripped off his T-shirt, used it to wipe his face and armpits, then tossed it on the sofa and reached for the near-empty bottle of Jack. He killed the pint with a hefty gulp, capped it, then tossed it on top of his shirt before kneeling beside the table.

"Come to daddy, you beautiful bastards," he said, gazing down at the generous lines he had created.

When he reached to his right, he realized he had neglected to procure something to snort the coke with. He patted his back jeans pockets but he had left his wallet in the bedroom, so he could not use a pound note or dollar. Eyeballing a hotel pen on top of a scratchpad by the phone, he rose and snatched it up, then disassembled the apparatus and snapped the plastic shell just before the tip. It broke in a jagged pattern, but it would work.

On his way back to the table, a knock came at the door. He frowned and hesitated. Should he stash the mirror? It had taken a lot of effort to get everything in place. As a compromise, he dragged the table out of the obvious line of sight.

As soon as he opened the door, his slight paranoia dissolved. He stepped back, opened the door wide, and extended his arm, welcoming her in. "I knew you'd show up. You always did have a nose for the good stuff."

***

To Sawyer's credit, she had needed to say nothing more than "Come get me." He had arrived twenty minutes later. She left a note for Ben and Cheryl on the fridge, then slipped quietly out of the house, hoping not to wake up the family.

They drove back to his apartment with the windows down. 2 AM and still 80 degrees. Wind generated from the moving vehicle cooled her cheeks even as the humidity caused tiny condensation beads to form on her skin. At least they would mask any tears that successfully fought their way out.

He glanced her way. "You okay?"

She could not bear to answer. Instead, she turned her body toward the passenger door and rested her head on its frame. No. Nothing was okay. Maybe it never would be again. In the past twenty-four hours she had received two jolts to her system. She did not know how much more she could take.

Upon arriving in LA, Miles had called her at Ben's. The key she had given him for the Key Biscayne Bank & Trust had indeed worked, but the box had long since been reassigned to another customer. When he had inquired about the contents of the safe deposit box belonging to its former owner, Farin Grant, the manager informed him the Metro-Dade PD had confiscated it back in January of '92 after showing up with a warrant. The manager could not recall the name of the detective who had taken it.

"You said you were working with the cops," Farin had urged, desperate the items she had preserved be located. "Can you find out if they have it?"

"What's in it?"

"I—"

"Don't hold out on me now, Farin. What's the point? I would have seen it if it had been there anyway."

"It's evidence incriminating the Lockhardts."

"I can promise you Metro doesn't have it, then. They've got nothing on the Lockhardts. Stark must have destroyed it."

Before they had hung up, they made plans to get together and review the mysterious e-mail/riddle he had received, and still struggled to solve, as soon as he returned from covering Chris' concert.

Chris. When she had seen him last weekend, he had conveniently omitted the fact he had gotten a divorce. No wonder he had decided to move back. He wanted to be near family. Yet he did not want her—not even now that he was free. Worse, her attempts to find Jordan had met a sad and disappointing end. With the evidence no longer available to use as a bargaining chip, she had no idea where to look. She felt more alone tonight than ever in her life.

In the absence of conversation, Sawyer engaged his CD player. Dave Matthews Band's "Typical Situation" cut through the silence. Thankfully, he did not make a second attempt at conversation.

They parked in his assigned spot at the off-campus apartment complex in Coral Gables. A shiver ran the length of her spine at the close proximity of the complex to Bobby's former home. With the exception of the trip from the airport to Ben's place a few weeks ago, she had left the confines of Key Biscayne only once—to attend Derek's Miami Beach gig. A mixture of fear and rage filled her as she followed Sawyer to his door. Her wig sat askew on her head. She did not care.

He unlocked, opened, and held the door for her. Once inside, he dropped his keys in the basket on the kitchen counter, then walked to the living room to move some of the accumulated clutter from the couch so she could sit down. He made no apologies for the mess. She broached no complaints. When he turned around, she was behind him. A moment later, she dissolved into his arms, burying her face in his neck and sobbing as if her world had come to an end.

"Shhh," he whispered, peeling the wig off her head and dropping it atop the clothes he had just scooped into a pile. She wept on his shoulder while he stroked her long curls.

From where they stood, his foot could just reach his stereo. He stepped on the back of his heels to slide out of his leather sandals, then hit the "play" button with his big toe to activate his system. A moment later, Tab Benoit's *Standing on the Bank* overrode her mournful cries.

They lingered through the first three songs. When the CD's title track began, her tears had softened. He broke away from their embrace, interweaving his fingers with hers and leading her into his bedroom as she wiped the moisture from her eyes with the back of her free hand.

Wordlessly, she crawled into his unmade bed and lay down on her left side, her back to the far edge. He stripped off his shirt and tossed it aside as he made his way to the bed, then doubled back to his closet. He pulled a worn, frayed Stevie Ray Vaughan tee from its hanger and returned, beckoning her to him with his index finger.

She rose to her knees and crossed the bed, then lifted her arms so he could remove her midriff tank. His nostrils flared slightly and he drew a deep breath. When he arched his eyebrows, questioning if he dare remove her bra, she nodded. He did not so much as graze her bare skin with the back of his hand as he unhooked the item and skimmed it down her arms. This astonished and curiously aroused her. He slid the tattered T-shirt over her head and guided her arms through its openings.

"Lay down," he whispered.

She complied with the request without question and positioned her body in the center of the mattress. Cupping his hands beneath her knees, he dragged her to the foot of the bed, then unzipped her jeans. Carefully, he peeled them down past her hips. A flicker of surprise or concern registered in his eyes when he noticed the angry jagged scars along her abdomen.

A brief wave of insecurity washed over her, but she defied it as he slipped off her pants one leg at a time. She wished he would turn out the lights but found herself uncharacteristically uninhibited. When he lifted his chin toward the headboard, she scooted back using her elbows and rested her head on his pillow.

Still in his khaki cargo shorts, he climbed atop the bed, took her left foot in his hands, and kissed her toes. As he ran the palm of his hand up her thighs, she watched his similar reaction to the scars on the top of her foot and shins. Instinct prompted her to explain. But not tonight. She had no energy to make excuses for her imperfections.

The feel of his lips at the side of her hips elicited a sharp, indrawn breath. His tongue made a moist, silky line from one hipbone to her naval. He looked up at her as if to gauge her response. She swallowed hard, closed her eyes, and tilted her head back.

Inexplicably, he pulled the T-shirt down to cover her abdomen, then crawled up beside her to encircle her in his arms. She turned to face the bedroom window and nestled into him, enjoying the feel of his arms around her as they spooned. He made her feel safe, though she could not guess why. They barely knew one another. And although she had no preconceived agenda when she had called him tonight, she realized she felt disappointed he had halted his would-be seduction as quickly as it had started.

She dared to whisper, "It's the scars, isn't it?"

He nuzzled her neck, his body moving against hers in time to the sultry blues on the stereo. Slowly. Rhythmically. He caressed her hips and abdomen. "Hmm?"

"I know. They're...a little shocking."

He brushed her hair off her shoulder, then rested his chin near her ear. "You think so?" His voice sounded breathy and sensual.

For the first time since they had arrived, she became aware of her rapid heartbeat.

He reached around her and held up his wrist so she could see it. She beheld the scar she had first noticed at the Talkhouse last weekend. When he moved against her from behind, she could feel the evidence of his arousal. "Does it shock you?"

Her inner thighs began to ache—so much so she nearly forgot the conversational thread. She arched her back enough to push her hips back against his. "Nothing shocks me anymore."

"Really?" He lifted his left leg and intertwined it with hers, pinning her limb as he traced the scars on her abdomen and teased his fingers across the middle of her hips. "Because you seem like you're still afraid. I can tell. Either you don't know what you want or you're afraid to have it."

She shook her head, unable to speak. Unable to reconcile the sexual tension with her normal, contrary replies. Her lips parted as he slid his fingertips beneath the elastic waistband of her panties. An audible intake of breath escaped her when his index and middle fingers moved lower and then inside her.

"No? You think I'm wrong?" Gauging the moisture, he brought his fingers back up and tasted them, then grabbed her left wrist and drew it up to her shoulder. "I came for you tonight. Remember? You called and said 'come get me,' and I came."

"Yes."

"But you don't want me, Farin."

Her mind grew confused. Worse, she feared he might be mistaken. Chris' unflinching rejection, coupled with Sawyer's skillful game of catch-and-release, left her wondering why she had called him in the first place. She felt so lonely. So hopeless.

"Or do you?" He kissed her wrist, then her palm, then her fingers one by one. When he got to her ring finger, he took the entire digit in his mouth. Gently, he moistened her finger, then removed her wedding ring with his teeth. He deposited the jewelry into the center of her palm with his lips, then traced his fingers down her arm and underneath the borrowed shirt.

"Sawyer—"

"Farin." He spun her around and lay on top of her. "Tell me to stop. Tell me I'm too young, that you're too fucked up in the head right now. Tell me you want to leave and I'll take you home. Do it now...or kiss me. Come for me like I came for you."

Knowing she could not wake up tomorrow and blame alcohol, forbidden desire, or a lack of good judgment, she threaded her fingers through his shaggy blond hair and pulled him to her. Chris had moved on. She knew what she needed to do.

CHAPTER 15

PERFORMERS, HANDLERS, ROADIES, AND CREW occupied every room of the Hyatt on Sunset's top three floors. By the time Chris finished the press conference, stopped by his room to change, and deleted another message from Julie, the afterparty was raging. He had tried unsuccessfully to reach Samantha on her cell, but left her an uncharacteristically humble message.

"Thanks for giving me back my arms and legs. Please join us tonight. If not, let's touch base tomorrow. Oh—and I promise to make nice with 'Rayon Joe.'"

Groupies and guests cavorted up and down hallways, mingling with members of the crew and periodically disappearing into private quarters. Most congregated in the large suite at the end of the top floor. Inside, they lounged on couches, hovered around the stocked bar, or sat on the floor strumming guitars. Lance stood at the far end of the room, drumsticks in hand, talking to one of Chris' sidemen. When Chris caught his eye, Lance raised his chin and held up his index finger.

Chris looked for but did not see Faith, the only person he had yet to greet personally. He had even spent time with the members of his opening act—whose name he did not insult. Nylon Fred's members were an easy-going bunch of guys who embraced their gimmicky niche in the concert circuit, content to open for bigger acts whose audiences appreciated their high energy and classic rock style.

"You killed tonight, bro!" lead singer Dickey Marks told him. He indicated the seat beside him on the couch. "I've always been a fan, but tonight you made me a true believer!"

Chris thanked him, then accepted the bottle of whiskey one of the road crew offered as he passed by. He noticed several young women throughout the room eyeing him suggestively as he scanned the crowd for Faith. A few gulps later, he decided some of them looked promising.

Dickey lit a joint, inhaled deeply, and passed it his way as he asked through his held breath, "You glad to be back at it?"

Chris tucked the bottle between his legs, toked the joint, held the smoke in his lungs, and nodded. When he exhaled, he coughed. "Last time I felt this good was probably our last tour back in '88. World tour, in fact. Man, Amsterdam was wild." He scanned the room. "And the party started off something like this, with me trying to figure out where Faith had run off to. You seen her?" He passed the joint to his left, not unhappy to see one of the young women he had noticed sitting beside him. "Why hello, darling. Fancy a bit of the good stuff, then?"

"No flirting," came a jovial reprimand from his other side. "You need to come meet my fiancé."

He turned and saw Lance, then smiled and stood for a quick hug, nearly stumbling over the whiskey bottle as it tumbled to the floor. "I guess old age gets the best of us, eh? Finally tying the knot!"

"Tying something." Lance laughed as he slapped his back with both hands.

"Eh, you need someone to toss you about a bit."

"That she does!"

Chris visually surveyed the room. "Where is she?"

Lance nodded toward the balcony. "We're keeping her away from all the smoke—and the noise. She just got in a couple of hours ago. She's done in."

They wove their way through the crowded suite. Before they reached the balcony, a round of congratulatory cheers erupted behind them.

Chris turned and saw Elliot with Marci. He nudged Lance with the back of his hand. "Hold up, mate. I think we've got another one for the nonsmoking section."

They returned to the living room where Lance shook hands with Elliot and gave Marci a congenial embrace. Chris hugged her as well, lingering just long enough to pat her shoulders as he broke away.

"It was an amazing show, Chris," Marci told him, her eyes sparkling with an exhilarating mix of excitement and pregnancy hormones.

He thanked her and leaned in toward her ear. "This your first afterparty?"

A bark of laughter escaped her glossed lips. "Aside from Farin's, yes. I guess I've finally 'arrived,' huh?"

He lifted his brows at Elliot and pointed at the balcony, then touched Marci's shoulder and inclined his head toward the sliding glass door. "Farin never knew how to party. Whatever you've read about them in your favorite 'journals,' it's ten times worse. Let's get you out of all this smoke."

"Can't have your godchild getting a contact high, can we?"

He stopped and spun around. "What did you say?"

She glanced back at Elliot and motioned for him to join them. "I was supposed to wait until we could tell you together."

He swallowed the lump in his throat as Elliot arrived.

"That is, of course, if it's okay with you."

Elliot wrapped his arm around his wife. "You told him, didn't you?"

Chris looked from Marci to Elliot. "You sure about this, mate?"

"On one condition."

He cocked his head.

"Let's get her some of that bloody fresh air."

Lance had arrived ahead of them to see about Ivy. When Chris and Marci stepped out onto the balcony, Chris bee-lined for the only other pregnant woman there. She stood to greet them, either a smile or a sneer on her lips. He could not tell which.

Visibly uncomfortable, Ivy apologized to the group as she insisted on sitting back down. "Our son has decided his mum has fat feet. Humiliated me in front of the entire bloody flight crew."

Marci giggled sympathetically and took the seat beside her. "Don't you move, then. We'll have the men wait on us like we're the queens of the afterparty."

Ivy looked at Lance and gestured at Marci with her thumb. "I quite like this one. You heard her. Get me some ice water, love."

Elliot winked at his wife as he, Lance, and Chris headed inside.

Ivy twisted her body toward Marci and leaned in conspiratorially. "They're not really getting back together for good, are they?"

Marci shrugged and whispered back, "I have no idea. But we should definitely talk about it over lunch tomorrow while our men are suffering with their hangovers."

Ivy's eyes widened. "I've a nanny for Colin, if you're serious."

"Really? Well, you know what that means, don't you?"

Ivy shook her head with wondrous anticipation.

"It means we arrange a car for your son and your nanny to spend the day at the beach while you and I go for a spa day. Hair, nails, massage...the works! We'll show them whose feet are fat. You'll come back feeling and looking like a million bucks. We'll charge it to the tour!"

Ivy clasped Marci's hand, squeezed, and leaned back in her chair, exhaling blissfully as she stared up at the LA stars. America was not so bad after all.

Inside the suite, Chris waited for Faith to show. He sat on the couch between Elliot and Lance, who periodically went outside to check on the ladies. "Was she feeling okay?"

"Who?" Elliot stared past him with dull eyes, unable to decide if he had missed part of a conversation. It had been ages since he had smoked. If they continued on the tour beyond LA, this night would have to be an exception, not a rule.

"Faith. I haven't seen her since the presser."

Elliot frowned and scanned the room. "Me neither." He leaned forward and asked Lance, "How 'bout you?"

Lance shrugged. "I haven't seen Faith or Todd."

Chris looked at Elliot. "You don't think..."

Elliot closed his eyes and shook his head. "Let's hope not."

"Maybe I should check on her. What room's she in?"

"I forget the number. She's down one floor, last door to the right off the elevator."

Chris stood and headed out, then turned back. "One of you should check on Todd, too. Is it just me or is he looking a bit rough?"

A burst of disgust escaped Lance's lips as he lifted his beer for a sip. "You've no idea."

When Chris opened the door, he nearly collided with Miles Macy. He quickly slipped into the hall and shut the door behind him. After a second thought, he dashed back inside to grab his bottle of whiskey and a six-pack of beer. He handed the six-pack to Miles. "You got my message, then?"

Miles extended his free hand and smiled. "The message, the backstage pass, *and* the new suit. Gotta hand it to you, Grant. You've got good taste."

Chris scanned the busy hallway one last time for Faith, then decided to forego his search long enough to have a little chat with the pesky reporter. "Never let it be said I welsh on an agreement."

"C'mon now," Miles joked. "We say a lot worse than that."

"That's what I'm afraid of." He marched toward his room with Miles following behind.

They set the alcohol on the wet bar inside Chris' suite. Miles helped himself to one of the imports, leaving the harder stuff for Chris, who grabbed a glass and the bottle and then sat down in one of the two upholstered chairs in the living area. Miles sat on the plush sofa and crossed his legs.

Chris gave himself a generous three-finger pour and set the bottle on the table beside him. He rested his elbows on his knees and leaned forward. "What do you know?"

Miles chuckled. "That's a loaded question. You'll have to be more specific."

He peered at him, jaw set, eyes narrowed in agitation. "Do you know who killed my brother?"

The smile ran away from his face. He shook his head. "Not yet, no."

"Did Farin tell you what she's hiding?"

"I'm working on it."

"What's that supposed to mean?"

Miles balanced the longneck atop his crossed knee. "It means what it means. I can't force her to talk. You know how she is."

"She's scared."

A burst of air escaped his lips. "I don't know about that. She seems a helluva lot more determined than scared at this point."

Chris took a hearty gulp from his glass.

"She did get a bit of bad news the day I flew in from Miami, I'm afraid."

He hung his head. "I know. I should have told her myself. I wasn't ready."

"Ready for what?" Miles asked.

Chris tucked his chin and squinted. "What news are you talking about?"

"What news are *you* talking about?"

"My divorce."

Miles uncrossed his legs and sat forward. "*Divorce*? How the hell did I miss that one?"

Chris casually leaned back in his chair and shot the reporter a self-satisfied grin. "I paid handsomely to ensure it, mate. And since this isn't an interview, I'll assume nothing we discuss here will find its way to print."

Miles held his hands up, holding his beer with two fingers. "I've brought no pens, paper, or recording devices. Ask your nephew. I've learned not to carry them when I meet with your family."

Chris looked him over, more confused with each exchange. Miles shook him off and told him not to worry about it. He finished his glass, then poured himself a second as Miles nursed his beer. "So what other bad news did she get? And why did she contact you in the first place?"

"I suspect she needs access to my resources. Besides, it's not like she can get around freely. Given what happened in Malibu, I'd say it's a safe bet you're all being watched. In fact, I take it back—maybe you don't have such good taste after all. How the hell did you ever get hooked up with that maniac Lockhardt, anyway?"

He tensed his jaw. "Did Jameson kill Jordan? Is that what Farin told you?"

"Like I said, Farin hasn't told me much at this point. All I know is that Lockhardt's responsible for what happened to her and he's paid off a lot of people to cover it up. In fact, I've learned enough to see a pattern with him. I'm almost positive he killed the cop who investigated Jordan's murder."

Chris raised his brows. "You mean that pint-sized tart who tried to charge me with Jordan's murder?"

Miles stifled a laugh. "Alvarez?"

"That's the one."

He shook his head. "No, not her. The other one—Stark."

Chris eyeballed him. "You're kidding."

"Nope. The official story's a failed drug bust, but I have reason to believe your man's behind it."

"I've known Jameson my entire adult life. None of this makes any bloody sense."

Miles sighed and set his beer down on an end table, then dug into his slacks pocket to retrieve a folded piece of paper. "You went to Raleigh to get Farin back, right?"

Chris nodded.

"Did you see anyone when you were up at that nut house they had her in?"

"Jameson was there."

"Anyone else?"

"A woman—a nurse, I think. It looked like she was the one giving Farin the drugs they used to keep her knocked out."

Miles unfolded the paper and handed it to him. "Is this the nurse?"

The color drained from Chris' face as he read the newspaper account of Tami Evans' fatal overdose. Her picture was unmistakable. "That's her."

"I showed this to Farin but she couldn't make an ID. She says she never saw the faces of those who came and went. The name of the place was this Dorothea Dix, right?"

Chris nodded again as he scanned the article in amazement.

"Do you realize that's where Bobby Lockhardt was at the time of Jordan's murder?"

His jaw slacked. "Have you given this information to the police?"

Miles leaned back and gave him a sideways frown. "Unless Farin agrees to come forward, what good will it do? Why would they care? Besides, Raleigh's out of their jurisdiction."

Chris went to the bar for a handful of ice. "Jameson must have someone cleaning up his mess for him. Maybe he didn't kill Jordan himself. Maybe he had someone else do it. Maybe Jordan found out something that threatened the old man. You know, he'd flown up to New York a couple of days before he died. Maybe he confronted Jameson about something?"

"Well, it seems this isn't the first pickle Lockhardt's gotten himself into. He might have been involved in a cover-up here in California back in '73 as well."

Chris frowned at the thought. "Unlikely, mate. He was in England with us in '73."

"Not for the whole year he wasn't."

He dropped the mini ice cubes in his glass, then sat down and poured another shot of whiskey. "I guess you're right. He started LSI that spring and brought us to America. Crazy days. We didn't know what was going on."

"Mirage was in LA the spring of '73?"

Chris nodded. "We flew to New York first. Ross Alexander was rushing around to file the company paperwork so we could sign the bloody contracts." He shook his head at the memory. "I remember thinking it seemed hurried or backward or something. Then, no sooner had we landed in New York than he announced we were off to LA."

"To start recording?"

He shook his head. "We signed the papers out here. The old man couldn't decide if he wanted to be based in LA or New York. I don't understand all of it, but he'd said we'd be LA-based right up to the morning we signed. Had the signing party here and everything."

Something resembling recognition flickered in the reporter's eyes.

"But the next day he said he'd changed his mind and LSI would be based in New York after all," Chris continued. "Had us all fly back ahead of him while he and Ross handled some last minute business with Bobby, I think. I don't remember everything. I was pretty much drunk the whole week we were here."

Miles quieted as Chris finished his jaunt down Memory Lane. He looked confused or in the middle of some deep thought. Whatever the case, Chris had grown both tired and frustrated trying to fill in the gaps between what Farin had told him and what she had relayed to the reporter. If the old man had indeed orchestrated some cover-up all those years ago, it had nothing to do with him or Jordan's murder.

He excused himself to hit the loo. When he came back, he found Miles depositing his empty beer bottle in the trash beside the bar.

"I've taken up enough of your time. I think I'm gonna head back to my hotel now and get to bed. I can't compete with the company you keep."

Chris walked him to the door. "If Farin needs anything...or if she says anything that might help us identify Jordan's..."

Miles slapped him on the back and nodded. Before he left, he turned around. "Off the record, now?"

"It better be."

"You still love her?"

Chris dipped his head and grabbed the doorknob. "No comment." As he opened the door and Miles stepped into the hallway, Chris saw Faith leaning against the wall opposite the door.

She smirked. "Should I take a number, or is it my turn?"

***

Bobby lay fully clothed atop his comforter, his hands folded behind his head. Unable to sleep, he wished Joni was beside him. Her parents' surprise visit had put a wrench in their plans to celebrate his birthday alone. Ah well, the more the merrier, he supposed. His real birthday was not until Sunday anyway. Maybe they could sneak in a quiet celebration after her folks flew out Sunday afternoon.

His answering machine engaged at half past nine, and he did not pick up. He had turned off his phone's ringer when he returned from dinner and was not up for another heated debate. At this point, he did not know what to think.

"Listen, son," his father's voice boomed awkwardly into the recorder. "I'll not continue operating in such a manner. I've told you all I know. I never went to medical school. You can't blame me, and Childs is gone now. Let's focus on more important matters, such as the state of LSI and the fact you're finally free of this nightmare. I'd like to take you to the Met tomorrow to celebrate your birthday. Joni's welcome to accompany us. Call me back at your leisure."

He had pondered his father's claims of ignorance for days, unsure what to believe. How could such an intelligent, successful man control and choreograph the illustrious careers of so many, yet be blind to his personal physician's egregious misdiagnosis of his only son? Did demigod Jameson Lockhardt care so little for his own flesh and blood that he would fail to get a second opinion to confirm such a life-altering diagnosis? It was inconceivable. Heartbreaking.

All his life, Bobby had yearned for his father's love. Now, he knew definitively he not only never had it, but he never would.

Dr. Stumpf had worked closely with him over the last month. Though Bobby had done his best while around others to mask his fear and pain, the Haldol withdrawals made him feel like a prisoner inside his own body. Shakiness. Dry mouth. Fleeting feelings of aggression. But no lapse in memory. No hallucinations. No missing days or weeks. Dr. Stumpf said he had made amazing strides overall. Soon he would be medication free. And while a certain measure of anxiety had manifested itself in the process, they had reason to hope for the best. Even Bobby's telltale facial twitching had abated.

Last week, he had started counseling sessions at Dr. Stumpf's recommendation. It made sense. The more Bobby suffered, the angrier he felt. Feelings of betrayal consumed him. He did not want to risk these negativities spilling over into his relationship with Joni. She was all that mattered to him now—that and assuming his rightful place as President & CEO of Lockhardt Sound, Inc. He had earned his birthright. In spades.

"Baby, pick up the phone. Are you there and just screenin'? You're not mad, are you? I'm sorry. I didn't know they were comin' until they called up from the lobby."

He swung his legs off the side of the bed and grabbed the phone off his nightstand before she could hang up. "No-no. I'm here. How are you?"

"I'm okay. Just had to call 'cause I missed you. It feels weird not havin' you here. Never imagined New York could feel so cold in June."

Her sweet Southern drawl comforted him amidst the hurt and loneliness. He leaned back in his bed and smiled. "That sounds like a line from one of your songs." The lilting sound of her soft laughter stirred him.

"I mean it, silly. Momma and Daddy just turned in and I'm here all alone in this huge bed. I wish you were here with me."

"I do, too."

"So you're not mad?"

"How could I be? It was nice having dinner with your family. Of course,

I'm not used to eating so early. I can't remember the last time I had dinner and got home before eight at night."

She sighed into the line. "It's just their way. Farmers—early to rise, early in the sack. You know that old John Sommers song, right?"

"John Denver?"

"That's right! Anyway, that's my momma and daddy to a T. Thanks for bein' so nice to them. They said they really like you." She giggled quietly. "They said they want me to bring you on home for a visit when I get the chance. Daddy's never said that about anyone. Momma said she thought you were handsome and a complete gentleman."

Despite his prone position, the compliment made him square his shoulders. "I arranged for a car to take them to the airport Sunday. Let them know they're welcome back anytime, but tell us in advance so we can bring them out. No need for them to spend time booking flights or transportation just to see their daughter. I'll handle that for them anytime they want."

"I love you, Bobby."

"I love you, too, Joni. With all my heart."

They talked for an hour before she fell asleep. Not as good as being there, but even her voice over the phone lifted his spirits. Joni would ride with her parents to the airport Sunday, then have the car drop her at his place so they could spend his birthday together.

He chose not to mention the invitation to go the Met tomorrow. Why bother? He did not intend to go—with or without her.

***

"*Arsehole!*"

Before Faith could step one foot into Chris' room, Todd Dalton appeared from nowhere and decked him so hard, it sent him back and onto the floor. Faith immediately rushed forward to help him, but Todd pushed her aside and staggered across the threshold. The door nearly slammed shut, but Faith wedged her high-heeled leather boot in its path before it closed.

"What the hell are you doing, Todd?" she shouted as a small group of onlookers immediately crowded the entrance to observe the scuffle.

Todd reached down and grabbed Chris by his upper arm, yanked him into a standing position, then drew back his fist, prepared to punch him a second time as he yelled, "You selfish, swaggering, silver-spoon piece of shit!"

Though temporarily disoriented from the initial impact, Chris ducked before Todd landed a second blow. He rushed head-first into the lead singer's midsection, pushing him out the door, through the gawking bystanders, and into the wall across the hallway. Chris connected with three solid hits before Todd swept his arms up and pushed him back. He windmilled all the way down to the carpet. Todd maneuvered himself to straddle Chris' waist.

The witnesses parted like the Red Sea in time to avoid getting toppled by the wrestling rockers. A handful took off toward the afterparty's central suite while Faith continued to shout for Todd to back off.

Dickey Marks found Lance and Elliot out on the balcony. "Dude, I think you better go see about your band. A couple of guys just ran in and said there's a fight near Chris' suite."

Elliot turned wide eyes to Lance, then Marci. She shrugged, closed her eyes, and shook her head. "Go get him. I'll be right behind you."

Ivy hefted herself out of her seat with some effort as Lance rushed off with Elliot. "Oh, bugger me sideways. I knew I didn't want to leave my room tonight."

Marci stayed behind to help Ivy. "I'll walk you back."

"No chance, petal. My Lance is a bit of a curtain twitcher. Last time he tried to bust up a fight, we were both detained at her Majesty's pleasure trying to sort it out. My son already thinks his mum has fat feet. I'll not have him thinking his dad's a bloody brawler as well."

By the time the ladies reached the scene, the crowd had clogged the hallway beyond security's ability to break through. Elliot had wrapped his arms around Faith's waist in a futile attempt to peel her off Todd's back while Lance sandwiched himself between the two men and endeavored to separate them. In the end, it took Lance, Elliot, Nylon Fred's keyboardist, three security guards, and a can of mace to separate them.

Marci attempted to wade through the crowd but decided it best to back off given her condition. She caught the attention of a fourth security guard and verified the few people who should be allowed to remain near Chris' suite versus those they should disperse. It took another ten minutes to redirect those who had no part in the situation back to the party.

When the women finally managed to enter Chris' room, they found him seated on his sofa with Faith holding a cold compress to the left side of his face. His bloodied hands rested on his knees.

Todd glared at him from his place opposite the sofa, sitting on one of the two upholstered chairs. His nostrils flared, his eyes filled with contempt.

One of the security guards stood nearby. "You sure you don't want me to call an ambulance?" he asked the room in general.

Faith removed the compress and studied Chris' face. "He doesn't need stitches. I think he'll be okay."

"Tell me there were no reporters," Chris said, his head resting on the back of the sofa.

Todd shook his head and huffed, "Unbelievable."

Lance knelt down on one knee beside the chair and asked Todd, "What about you, mate? Should we get you looked at? You may have a broken rib or two."

"Nothing I can't handle," he spat, his eyes focused hatefully in Chris' direction.

Ivy moved toward Lance with the full intention of pulling him away. Enough mischief for one night. But as she stepped forward, she caught a full glimpse of the man seated to his left. She gasped at the sight.

Marci placed a hand on her shoulder. "You okay?"

She turned her back to the men and faced the door. "I'm fine. Just knackered. I think I'll head out. Can you tell Lance for me?"

Marci frowned. "Of course. You sure you're all right?"

Ivy nodded and hastened to the door. "I'll need to check on Colin anyway."

"Okay, well, call my room tomorrow morning and we'll go for that spa day."

"Sounds lovely," Ivy told her as she stepped into the hall and closed the door behind her.

Faith got up to rinse and refresh Chris' compress. On her way to the mini bar's small sink, she slapped the back of Todd's head. "What the hell's wrong with you?"

He swatted her away, his eyes still fixed on Chris. "Why don't you ask the plonker who started this whole mess?"

Chris sat forward. "*Me*? What did I do?"

"You got us sacked, mate!"

Elliot and Lance exchanged tired glances and disbelieving shakes of their heads.

Chris threw up his hands and sank back into the sofa. "Not this again."

Marci kissed Elliot and explained she had had enough excitement for one night and needed to turn in. He promised to meet her back at the room as soon as he could.

Faith slapped Todd's head again on her way back with the fresh compress.

"Would you cut it out?" Todd shouted, covering his head with his hands and ducking an intended third slap.

When the phone rang, Chris rolled his head back and forth against the sofa. "Anyone care to get rid of my ex?"

Faith tucked her chin and frowned. "Ex?"

Elliot moved forward and answered the phone. When he recognized the caller, he grinned despite the situation. "Oh hi, Sam."

Lance's eyes darted toward Elliot.

"Oh you heard, huh?" Elliot chuckled. "Yes, it was a bit intense, but I think we're getting it sorted." He paused as he listened, then turned to group. "Samantha would like to know if we're still on for the rest of the tour."

Chris lifted his head and peered at Todd, then glanced around at the others. For a moment, the room fell completely silent. "Well, I'm bloody in," he snapped.

Faith looked down and fidgeted with the ends of the compress that lay on her lap. Todd continued to stare at Chris with lethal intensity. Lance folded his arms and sighed.

"Looks like we're presently undecided," Elliot chirped into the phone. "What-say we get back to you tomorrow morning?"

They debated for an hour after the call but did not come to a decision whether or not to continue as a group for the remainder of the tour. They agreed to sleep on it and meet the next morning for breakfast.

At 3 AM, Lance dismissed the security guard and convinced Todd to let him take him back to his room before turning in. Elliot shook Chris' hand and kissed Faith's cheek before heading back to his room.

"You didn't tell me you and Julie broke up," Faith said once she and Chris were alone.

He accepted another replacement compress with a thank you. When she sat beside him, he turned his body to face her. "I've been looking for you all night. I'd started to think you were avoiding me. Wait—is there a geriatrics' convention this weekend?"

"Ha ha," she said with no hint of laughter as she brushed her hair off her shoulders. "I gave up the mature crowd when I started dating a Jewish painter impersonating a Frenchman."

Chris shook his head. "The princess and the frog."

"Stop that."

"Can't do it, love. God save the Queen."

"Well, it's a little ironic if you think about it. Jews don't eat frogs."

He winked at her with his right, less painful eye. "Guess he's a faux frog, then. In any case, it's good to see you've come to appreciate a firmer—if less mature—type."

She rested her right elbow on the back of the couch and gave him a wry grin. "You're in rare form for a man on the mend. How hard did Todd hit you, anyway?"

He took the compress away from his face and touched his skin with his fingers. The pain made him wince. "I guess some things are inevitable, eh?"

Faith hooked the top of her foot under her thigh. "I guess so."

"How 'bout a proper greeting? You've kept me waiting all night. I've missed you." He held his arms wide and lifted his chin.

She scooted forward into his embrace and rested her head on his shoulder. "It's been a long time."

He nodded and squeezed her tight. "You're my best mate, Faith. You always have been."

She shut her eyes and held him closer. "I know."

They lingered in silence for a while, then ended their embrace. Chris shook his head as Faith scooted back a foot or two and snagged the heel lift of her boot on the carpet. "Tell me you're as uncomfortable as you look. Or do you still strap yourself into the leather bikini you used to sleep in on tour?"

She laughed at the memory. "I was just thinking tonight before I left my room how much I wished I could get out of this ensemble for one night and wear sweats and a T-shirt. You realize I only wore that bikini on tour to get a rise out of you and Todd."

He lifted a mischievous brow and grinned. "I knew. And believe me, it worked."

"Did it?"

"Of course! Back when we had civil conversations, Todd and I traded our fair share of stories about what each of us might try if we had the chance."

Faith's heart sped up as they spoke. She inched forward and jutted her chin as if daring him to continue. "You had plenty of chances."

"Really? And here we thought you only had eyes for the coffin-dodgers."

She pulled the sides of her mouth into a frown and huffed, then sat back and adjusted her confining attire. "At least they know how to take a hint," she muttered under her breath.

Chris looked at the table and realized someone had either consumed or relocated his whiskey bottle. When he spotted it on the bar, he stood and gestured to her. "Nightcap?"

She nodded. "A quick one. I really do need to get back and unstrap."

He filled two tumblers with ice, then poured both glasses half full. Returning to his seat, he handed her one of the two. The other he sipped then held against his left cheekbone. "I have an extra pair of sweatpants and a spare T-shirt."

"Yeah?"

"Sure, why not?"

Before he had a chance to change his mind or tell her he was only kidding, she stood and headed for the bedroom. He directed her where to look and waited. When she reappeared, she wore his Humble Pie tee and some denim blue sweats with the drawstring pulled snug and the waistband rolled down three times to keep them from slipping off her tiny frame.

She raised her hands and spun around to show off the ensemble. "There you have it, folks. The Faith Peterson you'd never thought you'd live to see."

Chris chuckled and clapped his hands. "And me without a camera. Where're the reporters when you need one?"

She flounced down on the couch, slightly closer than before. "Hopefully back in their holes until tomorrow night." She ran her slim fingers through her hair. "I'm beat. I'd forgotten how exhausting this life is."

He glanced at his watch. "It's late."

"Should I go?"

Chris held his glass with both hands. He stared at the melting ice cubes as he considered her question. "You know what? If you're up for it, I'd really rather have you stay. To be honest, the last few months have been a rollercoaster ride I can't seem to get off of."

She dared to reach out and brush his hair away from his wounded face. "For what it's worth, I'm sorry about you and Julie. I didn't know. The irony is, I came here to apologize for a lot of other things."

He looked at her with sad eyes. "You don't owe me an amends, Faith, if that's what you mean."

She shrugged. "Maybe I do. I basically dropped out of your life after our last concert. I never called after Jordan died. Skipped the funeral. Trust me, I've done my fair share of things in need of amends."

He nodded, then took another drink.

"Should I ask what happened with Julie, or...?"

"That's something I'd rather not discuss. Not yet."

She studied him for a long moment, aching for the hurt she saw—most of which Todd had not inflicted. "Want to hear some news?"

He shook his head like a dog shaking off bath water. "I'd bloody *love* to hear some news that has nothing to do with me. Yes. Tell me your news...please."

"Henri asked me to marry him."

His jaw slacked. "No."

She nodded.

He glanced down at her finger and frowned. "But he didn't spring for a proper ring?"

"Oh, he got the ring, all right. It's huge."

"So why isn't it on your finger, then?"

She lifted her shoulders.

"You didn't break his heart, did you? Poor sod. He should have called one of us before he proposed. We'd have told him how to handle the situation."

She stuck her lips out and to the side. "I, uh...I haven't given him my answer yet."

"Do you love him?"

"I do. I love him with all my heart. It's just..."

Chris ran the back of his fingers down the side of her face. "Don't put him off, love. If I've learned anything, it's that those ridiculous clichés everyone quotes are true. We're not promised tomorrow, you know."

"I know. But I can't give him an answer until I settle another relationship

I've had...well, pretty much in my head for more years than I can remember."

He wrinkled his brow and tilted his head. "Anyone I know?"

She looked into his eyes, her heart racing until she felt it might burst as she inched closer. "Don't make me say it, Chris. I'm sitting in your room wearing clothes four sizes too big for me. I'm completely out of my element here."

His eyes widened with understanding. "You mean—"

"Is it just me? Is it just this addict monkey brain of mine?" When he did not immediately reject her with a laugh or insist he had never shared her feelings, she grew bolder. She touched his lips with the tips of her trembling fingers. Still no resistance. "You don't have to be alone tonight. I'll stay with you. If you want me, I'll stay."

She pressed her lips to his. When he kissed her back and wrapped her in a passionate embrace, every nerve ending in her body came alive.

CHAPTER 16

THE POUNDING AT THE DOOR startled Sawyer awake and into a sitting position. He noted with immediate disappointment the unoccupied space beside him in bed.

"I know you in dere, beeg boy!" came the demanding, broken English originating from outside. "Opeen oop now."

He exhaled through parted lips as he rose and skinned on the cargo shorts he had abandoned the night before. Probably better Farin had taken off when she did. The last thing he needed on a Saturday morning was a cat fight. For a fleeting moment, the mental image of Farin and Cécile in a hair-grabbing, nail-scratching, shirt-ripping altercation titillated him. Then again, if Cécile ever pulled the wig off "Lisa's" head, his hot Haitian sometimes-lover might do some irrecoverable damage.

"C'mon now, Sawyah! Don't keep Cécile waiting."

If he had any chance of getting together with Farin for anything more than what they had shared the night before, he would have to break things off with his semi-regular fling. No way around it. She did not strike him as someone who liked to share. Plus, she spooked easily.

"School marm," he chuckled quietly to himself as he approached the front door. Gauging by her performance last night, Farin Grant was anything but a repressed spinster.

The pounding intensified as he reached his entryway. "Saw-yah!"

He yanked the door open and squinted out against the sudden assault of Miami sunshine. "Geeze, baby, what's your problem? It's not even noon yet. Most my neighbors didn't even get to bed until a few hours ago. You wake them up and they're gonna hate me."

Cécile pushed past him and into the apartment, dropping her purse on the coffee table and plunking down on the couch. "Don't pees me off, bahbay. I might not buy you bweakfast."

"Breakfast?" He whistled. "Nice. What's the occasion?"

She yawned and patted her mouth, then inspected her long, painted nails. "Mahbay I want to be weef you, eh? Spend de day?"

He grabbed his sandals, then sat in the armchair opposite the couch and slipped them on. "I can't do the whole day, but I could definitely use a bite."

"You 'oongry, den?"

"Not starving, but I could eat."

She stood and walked toward him, the rich glow of her sepia skin smooth and tempting in her flowing salmon sundress. Eyes like midnight and twice as mysterious, she held his stare as she kicked off her shoes and eased her long legs through each arm of the chair to straddle his lap. "Not stahving? Mahbay we need to wahk oop yah appeteet fust."

Her lips were warm and moist, her breath minty with a hint of coffee. She moaned and moved into him as they kissed, threading her slim fingers through his shaggy, uncombed mop of hair.

The sensual familiarity of their embrace aroused him at first, then he drew back and cupped her face. "Cécile, we need to talk."

She slid the wide straps of her sundress down and lowered her top, then took one of his hands and placed it on a supple breast, squeezing seductively. "We talk laytah. Now, we make love."

His nostrils flared despite himself as he massaged her hardened nipple with his fingers. Slowly, she began to gyrate her hips atop him, her sighs of pleasure urging him on. Through the sexual fog, he slid his hands inside the back of her dress and cupped her buttocks, not the least bit surprised to find no panties.

They kissed and petted for some time, then Cécile moved her hands beneath her to unzip Sawyer's shorts. He thrust his pelvis forward to meet her fingers, then suddenly lurched forward and dug the tips of his fingers into her fleshy, firm bottom.

"Ki sa ki lanfè a?" she exclaimed as she pitched forward and arched her back. "Bay easy weef Cécile, now."

Pressing his lips to hers, he inched to the edge of the chair, scooped her up, and stood. She wrapped her legs around his waist as he walked, nibbling and suckling his lips, then tracing his mouth with the tip of her tongue.

Without a word, he disengaged and dropped her onto the couch. "Seriously. We need to talk."

She wriggled into a sitting position with a certain amount of indignation, then set her jaw and eyed him suspiciously. "Eets dat woomahn, eesn't eet? I could smell huh scent the moment I walked een."

He grabbed a shirt from the laundry pile he had relocated to the floor last night, gave it the sniff test, then skinned it on. "It's not like this thing between us was serious anyway. We've both dated other people. Don't get all *Fatal Attraction* on me."

She sat forward and pierced him with a dark, lethal stare. "What deed you say to me?"

"It's nothing personal."

"Pahsoonal?"

"We always said it was casual. Like friends with benefits. You're phenomenally talented, beautiful, amazing in bed. Don't pretend you're hurt. Don't be that girl."

She thought a moment, then jutted her chin up and to the side. "What dis woomahn 'ave, ahnyway? Gold een 'uh pahnts?"

He chuckled as he walked into the kitchen. "Still want to go to breakfast? I'll buy. I owe you that at least. Or I can make you something here."

She stood up and fixed her dress, slipping her toned arms through the straps and then wiggling into her shoes. "I tink I'd wadder maintain mah deegnuddy and leave weef mah 'ay'd 'eld 'igh. Mahbay slahp yah face oon de way oot. Baysides, you a te'ibble cook."

"Ah, now that's just mean." He disassembled his coffee pot, then engaged the faucet as he grabbed the coffee and a filter. Digging in his jeans pocket, he found a labeless prescription bottle. Only three more Xanax. He would need to call his guy before heading over to Key Biscayne later. In fact, he had gotten low on most his supplies. Time to stock up. "But seriously, we're still friends. Nothing's changed with that. We just can't sleep together anymore."

"What you gonna do? Mahray dis woomahn?"

He peeked his head out from kitchen door. "Marry her? Where did that come from? We just met!"

She sucked air through her teeth and pursed lips. "Den why ahll de sooden you need to make a bweak, eh? She say she wan' you for 'uhself?"

He shrugged, pressed the button on the coffee maker, popped one of the three pills in his mouth, and then returned to the living room, this time opting to sit next to her on the couch. "It's new. We haven't exactly laid out the rules yet."

"Mahbay she won' feel de same, eh? What you do den? Come bahk to Cécile?"

He rested a hand on her shoulder. "Would you still have me?"

She snorted doubtfully and rolled her shoulder to shrug him off, then looked down at her hands as she fidgeted with her handbag. "I mah bay yah casual piece oof ahss, Sawyah, boot ahm noo one's toy."

"Maybe I should have thought twice before dropping you on the couch, huh?"

"Mahbay so."

He lifted her chin to catch her eyes. "You're not just a piece of ass, Cécile. Trust me."

She brushed several thin braids off her shoulder and flattened her lips.

"You sure you don't want that breakfast?"

"I nevah wanted dat bweakfast, Sawyah. Don't pwetend you don't know why I came."

He waggled his brows.

She gave him an understanding smile, but her eyes widened when he scooted closer and pulled her to him. "What you tink you doing now?"

He maneuvered himself around to a prone position on the couch and pulled her down on top of him, enjoying the feel of dozens of braids falling atop and around him as he took her mouth with his.

Once again, she slipped her arms out of her dress and bared her perfect bosom.

"Take it off," he whispered in her ear.

"You shuwah dees time?"

He took her hand and placed it between his legs. "What do you think?" She stood up beside the couch long enough to step out of her dress. Before she climbed back on top of him, he held up a hand. "Wait."

She raised a single eyebrow.

He unzipped his shorts, slid them down his legs, kicked them toward the dirty pile of laundry, then laid back down, his arousal clear. "You are one good looking woman, Cécile. Did I ever tell you that?"

She motioned with her hand for him to sit up, then lowered herself on top of him. "I don't need ahny mahn to tell Cécile she's good looking. I own a mi-wah."

***

"Thanks for picking me up," Farin said. "I hate to keep asking."

"It's okay," Derek told her as they crested the William Powell Bridge on their way back home.

"Did you let your mom and dad know you were coming to get me?"

He nodded. "I left them a note. Mom hadn't gotten up to make breakfast yet."

She stretched her neck to the left, then to the right. "I hope they're not upset."

"They understand, I'm sure. It must suck not having a way to get around."

"Like you don't know."

"Still, you should have waited at Sawyer's. Why'd you go and sit at that coffee shop?"

She shrugged. "I didn't want to wake him up. Or have to explain why I was leaving."

He nodded. "I get it. The morning after. Do you stay? Do you go?"

She gave him the side eye. "How do you know about all this?"

"C'mon, Aunt Farin. I'm almost seventeen."

Unable to argue with the logic and unsure she wanted to know how he had come to know so much about the awkwardness of a one-night stand, she looked out over the bay. South Florida mornings had always enthralled her. Even at her lowest she had found it difficult to avoid the almost automatic lightening of her mood when she beheld the majesty of a sunny day.

Okay, maybe it was just the sex. And not just good. Really good.

Last night, she had felt as if despair would eat her alive. Calling Sawyer had been an act of sheer desperation. Her life exhausted her. She was tired of worrying. Tired of living in fear. Done with the victimhood of hiding in shadows and waiting to move forward with her plan. But where the stranglehold of depression had threatened to consume her the night before, she now found herself rested. Peaceful. Determined.

Somehow, she would convince Ross Alexander to give up whatever information he had on Jordan. She would find a way. He owed her. They all did. And the time had come to stop feeling sorry for herself and get moving.

"Your dad's trying to teach me guitar," she told Derek, holding up her left hand to show him the blisters on the tips of her fingers. "I guess this is what he'd call progress. I don't know. What do you think?"

Derek glanced down and expelled a bark of laughter. "Looks about right. I was eight when I got mine." He crossed his left arm over to her and splayed his fingers. "See?"

She pressed his fingertips and felt the hard calluses beneath his skin. "If you've been playing for nine years, I guess it must be worth it."

"It will be. Someday."

Someday. She nodded and looked back out at the water as they veered southeast on the causeway.

"So do you know anything about this gig my dad offered the guys and me?"

She turned back and frowned. "What gig?"

"He asked me to talk to the guys about doing some back-up work. Recording. It's weird. He says we'll get album credit and that it's a big name, but he won't say who it's for."

She gave him an innocent shrug. "What's the material?"

"I dunno yet. I'm gonna talk to the guys today at practice and ask them about it. I think Dad already mentioned it to Sawyer."

"Could be good practice."

"If we get album credit, I'm all in."

"Any more local gigs? I had fun last weekend. It was nice to get out."

He shook his head. "I think there've been some calls from some clubs. Sawyer's working all that out. Until we're all twenty-one, it'll be hard to do the regular rounds here."

"Well, for what it's worth, you sounded great. I was really impressed. And you saw Miles Macy's article. You owned Miami Beach. I could tell Summer was impressed."

Derek sat straighter in his seat and gave a sideways grin. "Yeah, it was cool. What about you? Am I allowed to ask how it's going? You get in the studio yet?"

"Soon, I think."

"Good."

She adjusted her wig, flipped down the passenger sun visor, and checked her look in the mirror. Out of the corner of her eye, she saw Derek glance at her, then look away. "What's the matter?"

He shook his head. "I just feel bad."

"Why, honey?"

"I wish you didn't have to hide."

She snapped the visor closed and looked out the front windshield. "Me too."

"Everyone in the family's afraid to talk about what happened. And they've told me and Kyle not to talk about it either."

"I know. I'm sorry. It's a terrible burden for everyone to have to tiptoe around me, isn't it?"

"It's not that."

"No?"

He followed the southwestern curve of the causeway as they passed the Crandon Park Arena exit on Key Biscayne. "You know...if you ever need someone to talk to, you can talk to me."

She gave him a warm smile and patted his shoulder. "Thanks, Derek. That means a lot to me."

He nodded.

"But I've decided today's a good day. Today, I'm focusing on the possibilities."

"Yeah?"

"Yeah."

"Cool. In that case, mind if I play our CD from last weekend?"

"Of course not! I'd love to hear an encore!"

Derek pressed a series of buttons on his CD player. A moment later, Sawyer's improvised blues song came through the speakers. He smiled. "That dude's wicked talented."

When she felt her cheeks flush, she turned and stared out at the sign for the Crandon Golf turn off. "You think so?"

"Oh yeah."

Oh yeah, indeed.

"So are you two gonna get together now?"

She shrugged. "I don't know."

"I know he likes you a lot."

"Really? How do you know?"

"Doesn't take a brain surgeon. He stares at you all the time he's around.

And when you're not around, he asks about you during practice."

She wrinkled her nose. "There's a bit of an age difference."

Derek snorted. "Like that matters."

As they made the turn onto Harbor and passed Chris' house, she wondered how his first night had gone. For a moment, her bright and shiny outlook dimmed. Did he think about her? Or did the chaos and tumult of the tour steal his thoughts away just as being with Sawyer had given her mind a temporary respite from missing him?

It seemed every time she thought she knew the answers, the questions changed. In LA, she told herself he had moved on because there was nothing else he could do. But he had come to Ben's last weekend and never mentioned his divorce. Freedom had not resurrected his feelings after all. Whether time had made him whole or he simply resented her unwillingness to come forward with what she knew about that day in Coral Gables, it was becoming increasingly clear she fooled only herself if she believed they might somehow have a future together.

Derek's cell phone rang as they pulled into the driveway. He killed the engine, answered, then handed her the handset. "It's for you."

She tucked her chin in curiosity.

He grinned as she took the phone. "I'll see you inside."

She held the cell awkwardly to her ear. "Hello?"

"You really know how to bruise a guy's ego," Sawyer admonished. "I never took you for the love 'em and leave 'em type."

Her cheeks and thighs warmed the instant she heard his voice. "I've told you a million times. You don't know me as well as you pretend."

"No? Well, give me time. I'm getting there. What's on the agenda for the day?"

"Um...probably practicing my guitar and staying out of the way of any visitors that come by the house, as usual. Why?"

"Because there's a horse in Ben's back yard with your name on it. Time to saddle up."

"What do you mean?"

"I mean you didn't like my bike metaphors, so I'm moving on to another form of transportation. Time to get back on the horse."

She knitted her brows.

He sighed into the line. "Okay, lemme spell it out more clearly. I just got off the phone with Ben. If you'd have waited a half hour before sneaking out of my bed, I'd have driven you back home myself. Why, you ask? Because today's the day we start planning your new album."

"Sawyer, I—"

"Give it up, Grant. Time to start your new life."

***

By the time Chris woke up, it was nearly time to head back to the Forum. Not only had he missed the big breakfast meeting to discuss whether the others would agree to continue through the rest of the tour, but he had not eaten all day.

"I'll see you at breakfast?" Faith had asked as she left earlier that morning.

"Give me fifteen minutes. I'll meet you downstairs," he had promised. But the moment she left, he had passed out on the sofa.

Opportunities to sleep would come and go over the next few months. Like last night when he stayed up to play, only to fall out before breakfast and sleep all day. It would get worse once he began traveling. He hoped he would not have to do it alone, but asking his former bandmates to effectively be his back-up group was a selfish request. And after the row last night, Todd had probably booked the first plane back to England.

He shaved and showered, hoping to revive his numbed brain before calling room service for a meal. The water soothed him, washing away the drama of the night before. Focusing on the capacity crowd at the arena gave him the shot of adrenaline he needed. He could not remember ever feeling so tired—the kind of tired people feel after fighting a great, extensive battle.

The message indicator on the hotel phone blinked red as he left the bathroom to slip on some clothes. He had not heard the phone ring all day, though he might have slept too hard to register a ring. Sam had probably called to check up on him. Maybe she had talked to the others.

The robotic female voice announced three calls. As he had anticipated, the first was Sam calling to congratulate him again on the successful night. Unfortunately, she would be unable to attend tonight's show but she knew he would be okay from here on out. She wished him well, told him to keep in touch, and assured him how excited Minor was about starting his next album when he returned. As he marked the message for deletion, an intense feeling of loneliness enveloped him.

"Fifteen minutes, my ass!" came the good-natured but agitated rant of the second call. "If it were Todd we'd all be worrying he'd overdosed! So what gives? Did last night wear you out that bad? Get down here and eat! You need your strength!"

He smiled as he marked the second message for deletion.

The third message started with a long, dramatic sigh. "Okay. So no breakfast for you then. But I thought you might want to know I knocked some sense into Todd and we're all done with our little pity parties. Looks like you're stuck with us through September. After that, we're out. We're all meeting for dinner at five but I'm not sure where, so I'll call back. I think I'm gonna go take a nap. Maybe you're the one who wore me out last night. Anyway, catch you later."

Faith. He could always count on her.

He checked the time. Two thirty. Good thing he had already showered.

He called the front desk to ensure they would send someone up to clean his room while he was out, then raided the mini bar for a snack to tide him over until dinner. A bag of chips, a granola bar, and a small can of almonds would have to suffice.

In no time, the protein in the nuts revived him. He downed two bottled waters and turned on the bedside radio, hoping to hear some feedback from the local station about last night's show or a teaser about tonight's performance while he brushed his teeth and readied himself to leave.

Apparently, the last person to employ the radio was a country and western fan. They had left the dial set on 105.1 KKGO. That would not do. He turned the knob left toward KCAL at 96.7. Passing KIIS FM, he stopped as he recognized the outro of the current song.

"...and that was a flashback from 1989. 'Woman/Child' by Farin St. John. Coming up after the break, we've got some more great music for you, including Blessed Union of Souls, Brian Adams, and the brand new single by TLC debuting at number thirty-nine on the Top 40 charts this week. The song's called 'Waterfalls,' and you won't want to miss it. So stay tuned..."

He jerked the dial to 96.7, then went in to brush his teeth.

At this point, he counted on the *Aftermath* tour to help him forget everything. Julie. Farin. Jordan. Every detail of every agonizing minute he had spent dealing with the complications of his life outside music.

The last seven years had taken everything he loved from him. Worse, they had stolen his ability to pretend he did not care about anything but playing his guitar, bedding dozens of adoring women, and keeping his family so distant he did not have to feel. Not guilt. Not hurt. Not responsibility. Nothing.

The phone rang as he finished prepping. He rushed to pick up, thankful Faith had decided to stick with him. Plus, he was starving—probably why he had yet again descended into morbid reflection over things he could not change.

"So I guess you couldn't stay away after all," he chirped into the phone. "Don't know if we'll be able to recapture the bombshell you lot dropped on the crowd last night, but I say we give it a go."

"Chris?"

He fused his eyes shut and cursed under his breath.

"Are you there?"

"What do you want?"

"Well, I left about a million messages on your cell over the last twenty-four hours and you never called back, so I thought I'd try the hotel. I was hoping to reach you before the show."

"Did it not occur to you the reason I didn't return any one of those million messages was because I didn't want to talk to you?"

She sniffed and swallowed. "We can't just leave things like this, you know? I mean, I know we both said and did some horrible things—"

He stabbed an accusing finger in the air as he spoke. "No, Julie. *You* did an unforgivable thing. The only horrible thing I did was letting you live."

"You don't mean that."

"I most certainly do."

"No, you don't. You're hurt and you're angry. I understand."

"Why are you calling my hotel room? How did you manage to get the front desk to put you through?"

"I remembered you always register using the name 'Mallanaga Vatsyayana.'"

He smirked despite himself, then sat down on his bed. "Good memory."

"Yeah."

"What do you want, Julie?"

"I—I really just hoped we could talk."

"Talk? I'm on tour."

"Well, you're still in town through tomorrow night. Maybe we could meet up for a late dinner...or I could come by the hotel."

"You're out of your bloody mind."

"We were married, Chris. I was your wife. You can't just expect me to go away without settling our life together."

He pursed his lips, closed his eyes, and shook his head. More struggle. More things to work out. Talk about. Settle. Did it never end? "You got the house, right?"

"Yes," she said softly.

"And our bank accounts and finances are all sorted. The money's been adjudicated and whatnot?"

She did not respond.

"If the property's all been transferred into our individual names and the money's divvied up, it sounds like we've settled our life together."

"Don't you miss me? Even a little?"

He searched his feelings like a stock clerk conducting inventory. Checking the shelves and the reserves. Did he miss her? "No, Julie. I don't miss you. Not *you*. Do I miss the beautiful creature who I lived with, and loved, and laughed with, and fucked...? Yes, I miss that woman. But she's not you. You're nothing but a myth. I'm not even sure if you ever existed at all."

"You don't mean that."

"Oh, but I do! I *really*, really do! But okay, if you insist. Let's look at it again. You want to talk? Want to 'settle our lives together?' Okay, brilliant. Let's do that. Let's see, then. You told me you'd consider having children once your career ratcheted down. That was a lie. You got pregnant and never told me. You lied to Cheryl and said you'd tell me. You made me sick with worry thinking you were ill, and I was running about fixing you bloody chicken soup and begging you to see a doctor when all the time it was morning sickness. You drank alcohol—and quite a bit of it at that—at Samantha's party while you were pregnant. And then you went out and got an abortion. Does that sound like the beautiful, loving, sexy woman I thought I'd married? *No!*"

Several sniffs on the other end of the line told him she had not yet had enough to hang up.

"And you weren't even going to tell me about the abortion, were you? I'd have never known if I hadn't come home early that day to spend time with you."

"You know, there are two sides to this story. I know it seems like I'm the villain here when you see it from your end, but what about what I went through?"

"Oh, I'm sorry, love. Did I kill a human being who belonged to you?"

Crying now, she pleaded into the phone. "Please, Chris. Can't we just meet and discuss this in person?"

"Why? Is that other woman—the one I thought I married—going to be there?" Frustrated, he ran his fingers through his hair, then rubbed his forehead. "I have a show to do, and you call me and want to do this now? Does it ever stop, Julie? The selfishness? Does it ever bloody end?"

A knock on the door pulled his attention. He told her to hold on if she had anything left to say. When he answered, Faith stood before him, arms crossed, an expectant and disapproving frown on her face. "Are you fasting or something?"

He stepped aside and gestured for her to come in. "Where are we eating?"

"Elliot and Marci called some local restaurant. They're bringing a bunch of food in so we don't get mobbed going out before the show. Why didn't you answer the phone?"

He closed his fist, then held his thumb and pinkie up to his mouth and ear.

She nodded. "You ready to go or should I head over with the guys?"

"Let me meet you there," he said.

With a curious glint in her eyes, she asked, "Who're you talking to?"

He lifted his brows and cocked his head.

"Oh my gosh, you've gotta let me stay." Her voice lowered until she nearly mouthed, "What does she want?"

Chris rolled his eyes and made an air gesture like someone had strung him up with a hangman's noose. "I'll tell you about it later. You go on ahead and I'll catch up."

"All right, if you're sure."

He nodded, then opened the door for her. "Maybe I'll get lucky and she'll have hung up by the time I get back."

She squeezed his shoulder. "Don't be long. Elliot and Marci said the food this guy makes is incredible, and I'm not saving you any if you're not there."

"I can always count on you," he said with a chuckle.

She winked and headed down the hallway.

Chris hoped against hope he would return to a dial tone. Unfortunately, when he picked up the receiver, he heard sobbing and sniffing instead. "I'm back."

"Who was that?"

"Faith."

She huffed an indignant, "Oh."

"Are you jealous of *all* the women in my life, Julie? I thought it was just Farin."

"You don't have to say things just to hurt me."

"Oh, why not? It feels so good."

"That's horrible."

"Isn't it? I guess that's what we've been reduced to—trading below-the-belt punches in a worn down boxing ring."

She cleared her throat, then put the phone down long enough to blow her nose. He made a face and turned his head away from the noise. When she came back on the line, he asked, "What more is there to say? What more can we do tonight to bloody each other up?"

"I just wanted to come by the hotel tonight after the show. Maybe we can talk."

"Or maybe you can try to manipulate me into taking you back."

She said nothing.

"Well, as much as I hate to be the burr in your paw, kitten, I have plans later tonight."

Her voice sounded clipped and deflated. "You do?"

"Yes."

"With who?"

"Does it matter?"

"It matters to me."

"It shouldn't."

"But it does."

He exhaled with frustration.

"Is Farin back? Is that it?"

"Farin?"

"Mm-hmm."

"Why would you say that?"

"Because, Chris. You may be genuinely unaware of this, but you're still in love with that woman. You may always be in love with her."

"Then why would you want to try and reconcile with me knowing I'll always love her?"

She paused. "Because the two of you will never make it work."

His eyes narrowed in hatred of the voice on the other end of the phone. "What would you know about it?"

"Oh," she scoffed, "I know plenty. I know she only wants you when she can't have you. In fact, isn't that how you both play that little game of yours?"

"You're bloody insane."

"Am I? Are you two back together now? I mean, you and I got divorced over a month ago and she's not by your side? What's the matter? You're free."

His face grew hot and he ground his teeth. Somewhere in the conversation, he realized a part of him had wanted her to convince him she had changed, that there still existed within her some semblance of the girl he had eventually believed he had grown to love. He wanted her to make him regret the split, to evoke a desire to apologize for his part in their broken marriage, for loving another woman he could never have. Instead, she baited and mocked him.

She was exactly the person he exposed the day she murdered his child.

"Since you're so worried about my relationship with Farin, let me assure you of two things. The first is, I love her. Happy now? Do you feel superior knowing you were right? Well, there it is. I *love* her with something inside me I never thought possible. I never loved anyone before her, and I'll never truly love anyone but her. And maybe someday after everything's put right, we'll find a way to make it work. That may be the only thing I want in this life. Because when I look at her, I see forever. And all I see when I look at you is the child you stole from me. Is that what you want to hear? Congratulations! There it is!"

Julie's pitiful cries on the other end did not move him. In fact, he realized that for some time now, he had had the emotions of a stone. He felt dead most the time. The only time he got anything resembling relief was on stage. Last night, he had felt alive for the first time in years.

"I still love you." She sniffed.

"Is that all, then?" he asked unsympathetically.

"You said two things. You said you could assure me of two things. What's the other?"

His nostrils flared with a hatred reserved solely for her. "The other is this:

I will never in my life talk to you again."

He slammed the phone down, grabbed his wallet, and headed out the door, eager to meet up with his mates and looking forward to the feast Elliot and Marci had arranged.

CHAPTER 17

MILES KNEW THE MINUTE HE opened his front door it would be a long evening. In fact, he had known an hour before when she called to confirm she would be there by seven. The irritated edge to her voice sounded all too familiar. Did all women have that tone when men failed to deliver whatever expectations they built up in their minds? He suspected this was the case. He had grown accustomed to hearing that same frustrated sigh of agitation in every woman in his life—his mother, his sister, his assistant, his would-be girlfriend, and now, Farin.

"You'd said we'd meet up as soon as you got back from LA," she complained as she stomped into his house and shed her wig and dark glasses. "That was two weeks ago."

He told her to make herself at home and offered her something to drink. "I can explain. I promise," he called over his shoulder as he went to fetch her iced tea and a cold beer for himself. In fairness, she had some explaining of her own to do.

He returned in time to catch her making a face as she beheld the living room, which he had still not unpacked to any degree. Stacked boxes, mostly still taped shut, occupied much of the house. Better than it was before she got there, though. At least he had cleared out enough space so they could sit on the couch and talk.

"You didn't tell Jeanne who I am, did you?" she accused as she plunked her purse on top of the boxes stacked beside the end table and took a seat. "She doesn't even ask who I am anymore when I call you at work. It's like she already knows or something."

He placed her iced tea on the coffee table, then dropped down on the opposite end of the couch and drank his beer. "Jeanne's the best assistant I've ever had. She's sharp, and she's smart. She probably stopped asking because she knows whoever you are, you're the only one who calls and refuses to identify herself. Besides, Chris is the only person I've talked to about you."

The mention of his name elicited a subtle change in her demeanor. Less aggressively, she asked, "How is he?"

"You didn't read my review? I'm wounded."

She sighed, emitting that special female tone of irritation. "The shows were good. Mirage made a surprise appearance. They're backing him for the rest of tour. Blah, blah, blah. I'm more interested in what you *didn't* write.

How's he doing?"

Miles squinted and scrunched his lips as he looked up and off to the side. "I'd say he's doing as well as can be expected given the fact he's recently divorced, doesn't know who killed his brother, and can't resolve his feelings for you."

Farin shifted uncomfortably in her seat. "Anyway, where have you been for the last two weeks? I thought you wanted to go over that mail you'd gotten."

He sat his beer down on the table, then locked eyes with hers. "If I'm going to help you, Farin, I need you to help me."

"What's that supposed to mean?"

"It means let's talk about your dad."

The confused expression on her face transformed into something resembling a combination of fear and sorrow. "What about him?"

He leaned back casually and rested his left arm along the back of the couch. "When I asked you on the phone that night how he died, you said it was a drunk driver. But you didn't tell me who that driver was. From what I've gathered in my research, I'm thinking you could have made both our lives easier."

"What research?"

"Well, let's see. I told you about the weird anonymous e-mail with all these cryptic phrases and hints. That led me to Bobby Lockhardt's hometown of Santa Barbara where, lo and behold, I discovered you two attended the same high school."

Her eyes widened in shock, then narrowed. "I didn't know Bobby went to San Marcos."

He shrugged. "Long story short, I spent the next day getting kicked out of your dad's old law firm and brushed off by the local cops, then finally ended up at the O'Conner gravesite. The date on your dad's gravestone coincides with a certain incident semi-relayed to me the day before by a colleague of your old Phys Ed teacher. I thought to myself, 'Hmm, coincidence?' And then, when I got back to Miami, you called from the great beyond. But you left out more than you told me, didn't you?"

Her body went rigid. "We're wasting time I don't have. I need your help. That's why I called. But if all you're trying to do is uncover the big mystery behind my father's death, you can forget it."

"Why did Jordan fly to New York two days before he was killed? Was it to confront Jameson Lockhardt about something?"

Farin's face paled at the question.

Miles rose and grabbed his working copy of the e-mail off his makeshift computer desk, then returned to the couch and read it aloud. "'A fuller picture won't be drawn. You'll start with those beneath the lawn. A fund for trade, determined will. Across the pond—himself, or killed?'"

He glanced up to see the startled confusion on her face, then continued. "'The motivation his own life, he sacrificed his son and wife. And what is it about a name? A substitute, the price of fame.' Any of this ringing a bell, Farin O'Conner?" He lowered the e-mail and looked at her expectantly.

She reached out to snatch the paper, but he jerked it away. "There's more. But before I read it to you, you have to promise you'll help me fill in the gaps. I've figured out some of it already, especially after talking to Chris in LA, but there's still a whole lot more that makes no sense at all. I'm willing to help you, but you've got to help me."

He waited for a response before continuing. At first she sat frozen in place, as if weighing the pros and cons of breaking her silence. She sipped her tea, then sat back and fidgeted with her fingers. He noticed the absence of her wedding ring, which she had worn the day he saw her at the church.

"Okay, deal. But if I trust you and I tell you these things, and then you go and tell your girlfriend or your 'sharp and smart' assistant or anyone else, you'll ruin things in a way you could never imagine."

"Why won't you go to the police, Farin? Tell me. I'm pretty sure I know now, anyway."

She wrinkled her brow. Her lips parted. "You do?"

He continued reading the e-mail. "'Too soon to go, too important to fail. Despite the crime, no time in jail. A silenced victim gone no more has something still worth dying for.'" When he glanced her way, he saw a single tear slide down her cheek. "'Without your help, she may be lost. That's why you've left your former boss. So start today with what you know. Time's running out. You've got to go.'"

When she reached for the paper a second time, he let her take it. Her expressions ranged from bafflement to horror as she read the rest of the riddle. "I..."

He nodded with urgent encouragement. "Go on. Say it. Did Jordan go to New York to confront Lockhardt about the fact his son was the drunk driver who killed your father?"

Sadly, she nodded her head.

"Did Jameson Lockhardt kill Jordan?"

"No." She looked down. "It was Bobby."

As she relayed the horrific details surrounding that fateful day, Miles vacillated between shock and relief. Dozens of previously unanswered questions finally made sense.

"So Jordan had made a trip to Santa Barbara as well?"

She nodded. "He'd said he was in LA on business, but he told me later that he went to Santa Barbara to figure out what happened with my dad. I guess when Jameson paid off the cops after the accident the name James Wellingham came into existence—probably another layer of distance to protect Bobby. Growing up, all I ever knew was that some guy by the name of 'James Wellingham' had killed my dad. Jordan eventually discovered James Wellingham was really Bobby Lockhardt."

"But after all those years, why would Jordan be involved? Why go looking for this guy if it was an accident? I mean, unless you have more information than I do, it seems to have been an accident. A terrible accident, but an accident nonetheless. What was Jordan hoping to find?"

She gazed mournfully down at the floor. "He was trying to help me."

He nodded with understanding as Farin explained about the nightmares, supplementing the account with his own observations of her behavior during the few times they had interacted. As she spoke, he found himself moved by Jordan's selflessness. "He obviously loved you very much."

"He did."

They sat in silence. "This isn't your fault, Farin," he finally said.

She cleared her throat, shook off the memories, and strengthened her stance. "Not all of it. Anyway, now you know."

Miles picked up and studied the paper she had set aside. "There's still a lot I don't get. So far, I've connected Sarah Wellingham to Santa Barbara and between you and Chris, it's obvious the author of this note wanted me to know Jameson and Bobby's part in your past. The mention of the signing party, got that. But these references to 1967, 'The Firm'…'Jade Larken Trongly.' Do those things make any sense to you?"

She leaned forward and scanned the list of hints, then shook her head. "I don't know what any of that means. But…" She drew closer and pointed at the bottom of the page. "Nancy Chambers. She's Jameson's secretary."

He shook his head. "Not anymore."

"What?" Her eyes widened.

"I did some digging. Turns out Nancy Chambers was reported missing back in December of '91. My hunch is she's the woman they subbed out for you that day. That would make her the one who died in the limousine. In order to take you, they needed to make sure there was a body inside to be found once the crew put out the fire. Do you remember seeing anyone when they pulled you out of the car? Or anything else going on around you when you were taken?"

Farin stood and paced the cramped space. She looked like a pinball bouncing from one stack of boxes to another. "I'd left the hotel and got in the car. Charles drove to the gas station on Cranston and Harbor because the tank was low. When he went inside to pay, my door suddenly opened. Before I could react, someone put a cloth or something over my nose and mouth. I was out after that. The next thing I remember is waking up in that room they kept me in."

"Do you think there's any chance the driver was in on it at some point?"

"Not in a million years." She gave him an emphatic shake of her head. "Charles Russell was a good man. He's the real victim in this. He's the one who helped me after..."

"After what?" He noticed her hands shaking as she nibbled the nail on her ring finger. "Tell me."

She crossed her arms and shifted her weight, jutting her chin to portray an impassive air of aloofness Miles saw right through. "Bobby raped me the night of Mirage's farewell concert."

"He *what*?"

She nodded.

Miles looked away. He pulled at his upper lip with his thumb and index finger as she spoke. The more she told him, the more questions he had. As a journalist, it conflicted him on some level. Maybe his colleagues were right. Maybe somewhere along the line he had lost his objectivity. This was no longer just a story...it was a mission.

"Tell me about the contents of the safe deposit box. What evidence was there to implicate the Lockhardts?"

She sniffed and sat back down, then sipped her iced tea. "Look. I've given you a lot to work with. You read that letter. I'm running out of time. I'll tell you the rest as soon as you help me. "

He sighed and flattened his lips. "I already have."

She stared at him, unable to speak.

He pointed to the last clue on the paper. "You see this? This is what you're looking for."

Her eyes widened. "But you don't know—"

"I do."

"You can't possibly. Are...are you serious?"

"As a heart attack. You wanted to know where I've been? I spent the last two weeks in Fayetteville, North Carolina nosing around. I just wish you'd told me about this sooner."

"Why? What's wrong?"

"The Hopeful Heart burned to the ground Memorial Day weekend."

"Jordan!" she gasped, covering her mouth with her hand.

***

Few people in Jameson's sixty-nine years had managed to cause him pain—Adolf Hitler, Sarah Wellingham, and now, his only son. Many angered him. Most irritated him on one level or another. But actual, heartfelt pain? No.

"Maybe it's a good thing," Ross reasoned as they wrapped up their standing pre-weekend meeting, which had included an increasingly confident young Lockhardt spewing facts pertaining to LSI's impressive second quarter numbers, updating them on the results of their most recent PR campaign, and committing to completely revamp their A&R department before leaving with little more than a "have a good weekend."

Jameson rose from his desk and peered out his window, his hands clasped behind his back. "Ross Alexander, the eternal optimist."

Ross bit the inside of his cheek and stared spears into the center of Jameson's back. "I don't know about that."

"Then what, pray tell, could possibly be good about Bobby's matter-of-fact departure this evening? Stacy's going to return any moment from picking up the tea-smoked duck I'd had her order from Aquavit. It was meant to be a surprise. After the comeback we've made, I thought we should celebrate."

"Did you want me to call him and ask him to come back?"

He spat a doubtful huff. "He's made it clear he has no further interest in after-hour socializing. He's probably with that girl. That Joni."

Ross gathered some papers into a folder, then leaned into the high back chair he had occupied for the last hour and a half. He looked past Jameson out the window to the artificially illuminated buildings. "I'm sure you're right."

"Has he told you anything about that psychiatrist he's been seeing?"

"He's told me he thinks he might not have schizophrenia after all. And yes, he feels betrayed. By you and by Childs. He hasn't said it outright, but I'm pretty sure he blames me, too, on some level because I never told him the truth."

Jameson unclasped his hands and let his arms fall to his sides as he paced back to his chair. He regarded the furniture with disdain, resentful he had not yet managed to break it in the way he wanted it.

Today's announcement that LSI had crawled from the brink of insolvency back to the land of prosperity should have satisfied him more than it did. The anxiety he had lived with for the last six months should have decreased. Instead, he felt restless. He had hoped a celebratory dinner with the company's notable players would lift his spirits.

Alas, he had only fooled himself. Until he received definitive word on his special project from his special colleague, he would not know comfort.

Nearly two months of detecting had netted no positive reports. Herb Radford had urged him to exercise patience and insisted he was a thorough man. Thorough indeed. Over a month in Los Angeles and nothing to show for it but hotel bills, food bills, rental car bills, petrol bills, and the ultimately unconfirmed suspicion that Farin's former keyboardist knew she was alive.

"She's not in LA," Herb had assured him last Friday. "I've done everything here but take a jackhammer to the sidewalks."

"You're headed to Florida, then?"

"Not yet. I think I'll drive up to Santa Barbara and see what I can find there. I'd hate to leave the west coast and find out later she was hiding out in her old stomping ground. It'd be a waste of time and resources."

Grudgingly, Jameson had agreed.

Ross stood and stretched his arms, then collected his folders and readied himself to take off. "In any case, I'd say give him some time. Let him adjust to his new lease on life. Like I said, maybe it's a good thing. He's becoming exactly who you groomed him to be. Strong, confident, business savvy. Maybe you'll end up with a couple of grandkids to boot."

Jameson grumbled at the thought, then watched with disappointment as Ross headed for the door. "No duck for you, then?"

"I'm afraid I'll have to decline. Betty asked me to come by for dinner at her place. With Josephine gone, I'm just about all she has left."

A spark of understanding passed between the two men. Jameson could no more pretend he did not notice than Ross. Neither openly acknowledged the other.

Ross strode toward his office. He turned back long enough to ask, "Would you like your door open or closed?"

When Stacy returned with the celebratory dinner, Jameson sent her home with two of the three orders of tea-smoked duck. A thank you from the company for her and her husband, he told her. She thanked him and left soon after.

Jameson ate alone in his office.

***

"Two weeks?" Alvarez complained. "How can you think of taking two weeks off with so much going on?"

Bridgeman rose from the table, handed Penny his plate, and gave his stomach a satisfied pat. "Lunch was great, hon. Anything you need me to do?"

"Not a thing. All our stuff is ready and the girls are packing their bags as we speak." She smiled and gave him a quick kiss, then set his plate to the side as she busied herself putting the leftovers in plastic containers and rinsing off dirty dishes.

William grinned at his partner. "I still don't understand why you didn't take some time off, too."

"Because there's too much to do." She shoved the last forkful of marinated skirt steak in her mouth.

"If it makes you feel any better, I'll probably come back with a ton of helpful information. I figure I can finagle a heck of a lot more Intel out of Hub over a relaxing family vacation at the beach than I can interrogating him like some police detective."

She swallowed hard, then spat, "You *are* a police detective."

"But he's a federal agent. A Special Agent."

She scoffed. "If he's so special, he'd understand we need to solve this case yesterday."

"I hate to sound insensitive, Al, but the bodies aren't going anywhere. Yes, it's urgent, but there's nothing we can do about it today. Besides, I haven't taken a real vacation in over two and a half years. Penny'll divorce me soon if I don't take her and the kids somewhere for a change of scenery."

Penny raised her eyebrows and nodded her agreement as she rinsed glasses and dropped a handful of utensils into the dishwasher's silverware basket.

"That's not exactly comforting when you figure whoever the hell killed our vics is still running around out there doing who knows what to who knows who. And, for the record, look around, Billy—there's sand everywhere. You're actually leaving Miami and paying good money to go visit...the *beach*? What kind of change of scenery is that? Do you realize how crazy that sounds?"

He laughed, then opened his arms wide in time to scoop up his middle child as she rushed in full speed from the hall.

"Daddy, Daddy!" Aubrey squealed as he lifted and curled her like a barbell in his arms. "I packed my suitcase all by myself!"

"You did? All by yourself?" He rooted his nose into her middle and growled like a monster. She screamed and giggled with delight. "And what about your sisters?"

"Annie's still on the phone."

He glanced at Penny, who rolled her eyes with a she's-gonna-get-it shake of her head, then righted his five year old onto the kitchen floor and glanced up at the wall clock. "How about Abby?"

"Abby's sitting in her suitcase playing with her Barbies." Aubrey looked at her mother. "I tried dragging her out but she tried to bite me. She says she wants you, Mommy."

With a slightly impatient smirk, Penny shut off the faucet, dried her hands on a kitchen towel, and beckoned Aubrey to follow her. She winked at her husband. "We'll be right back."

Alvarez crumbled then tossed her napkin onto her plate. She thanked Penny for the meal as the woman disappeared down the hall. She had to admit, though only to herself, that Penny Bridgeman's *vaca fritas* recipe tasted even better than her aunt's.

William refilled their ice water glasses from the Brita pitcher on the counter, then sat back down. "Hub'll be more relaxed on vacation. On the job, he's all business. This way, we can brainstorm. In fact, we could use a third brain. You sure you don't wanna come? I'd love to introduce you."

She made a face. "Two weeks touristing along the Gulf Coast is not my idea of rest."

"Maybe you'll come up next week for the fourth, at least? You could meet us in Biloxi. The view of the fireworks from Lighthouse Pier near Treasure Bay is beautiful. The lights reflect off the water. You can see the Gulfport show from there as well. Two for one. You'd love it."

She shook her head. "No thanks, partner. I'd rather stick close to home."

"You've gotta take some time off, Al. It's good to step back and regroup every once in a while."

Her brows knit in deep thought as she drew on the kitchen table with her index finger. "So Hubbell says they've been after some guy for the last five years and they still don't know who it is."

Bridgeman inhaled deeply and leaned back in his chair. "I think at this point it's as much identifying the right suspect as it is linking someone to the various crimes. Apparently they have a nickname for him. They call him 'the ghost.'"

"And they think the Grant cases might be related...?"

"Maybe. They started building their initial profile after some big-shot hedge fund manager up north was accused of hiring a hitman to blow up his competitor's business—with the competitor inside. Local law enforcement investigated, but they couldn't find sufficient evidence to tie the accused to the crime. Because whoever did it used a homemade bomb, the Feds got involved. Over time, other cases with a similar MO sprung up. They began noticing a pattern of unrelated 'accidents' and 'suicides' surrounding those they suspected might have done the hiring."

"What type of 'accidents?'"

William shrugged. "Falls in showers. Electrocutions from faulty wiring. Drownings. That sort of stuff. Incidents most local cops wouldn't think twice about, let alone connect to the bigger crimes the Feds were investigating. Anyway, they started realizing all those accident victims and even the suicides had something in common. They all seemed to pose some threat or another to the person they originally suspected had the most to gain by hiring someone to commit the crime. The Feds started seeing certain commonalities. Rich men. Dead associates—even victims related to associates. Custom incendiary devices."

"So your friend believes all these cases trace back to one killer?"

"Could be. The working theory is, the ghost's earned quite a rep in high circles and has become a sort of go-to for the wealthy to help make their problems go away. The bad news is, the homemade bombs are the only definite common denominator. The good news is, the ghost may not be as smart as he thinks he is. All these suicides and accidents are similar. Like the ghost has a limited menu of options to do away with the peripheral targets. And since the bombs all fit the same materials and the basic pattern, the Feds think the guy might be getting sloppy."

"So they seized the Grant files because of the limo explosion?"

He clicked his tongue and nodded. "That report your source at FSB did for us triggered something in their database. Notice we didn't even get a report on the cell phone analysis or a trace on the glasses."

She frowned. "But Jordan Grant's death wasn't a suicide or an accident. It was murder."

"I don't know, Al. Like I said, I think I'll be able to get more information over a few beers on the beach than I can meeting him for a lunch or dinner while at least one of us is on duty."

"So what about Macy? Does Hubbell know he's got a potential witness?"

William waggled his eyebrows and gave her a sideways grin. "Not on your life."

A cough of laughter escaped her lips. "You want him to show his cards first."

"Absolutely."

"He's your friend."

"Probably my best friend. And believe me, he'd do the same. Based on what Macy told us over dinner that night, I'd hate to start rattling cages and spook an eyewitness, whoever she is."

Alvarez continued to draw on the table. "You hear from him lately?"

"Macy?"

She nodded.

"Not since before he left for that LA assignment. I figured you had, though."

"He's left a couple messages, but they didn't seem to relate to the case."

He bit his upper lip to stop from grinning. "Personal, huh?"

She leveled dark eyes his way. "Don't start with me, Billy."

He raised innocent hands. "Hey. I'm just thinking if you're gonna refuse to take vacation time because you're so worried about the case, you might want to return the guy's call and find out if he's met with that witness he said he had. You keep rejecting the guy and he might decide to give up and take his sources with him. I mean, c'mon, Al...sometimes you gotta take one for the team."

She ignored her partner's attempt to get a rise out of her. "Did we ever get a call back from the driver's next of kin?"

He shook his head. "I called a second time yesterday afternoon and spoke with one of his nieces, I think she said. She promised to leave another message but said not to count on anyone calling me back. I guess the Russell family's unhappy with Metro's lack of results. That report I found hidden away in my desk? They'd hired an attorney to conduct an independent investigation into the crash after the limo company refused to pay out some accidental death policy because our official determination declared the driver negligent."

"That report confirms there was a bomb. If the family was looking to pressure Metro into changing their official stance, you'd think they'd have pushed the issue even if Stark tried to hide that report you found. Basically, that report proves the family right."

"I guess the family dropped the lawsuit."

"But why would they do that?"

"Who knows? Anyway, I asked the niece if her uncle had talked to any of them in the days or weeks prior to the accident. She says she doesn't remember but asked if we'd talked to his old girlfriend."

Alvarez lowered her eyes, trying to recall the witness statements she had taken so long ago. "I don't remember interviewing a girlfriend. There's no report in the file. No surprise there, though."

"The niece gave me her name and number. I left the information on my desk. If you want, give her a call while I'm gone and we'll talk to her when I get back."

Penny marched into the kitchen and bee-lined for the corner cupboard. "You're taking all these leftovers, Alicia, right?"

"You couldn't stop me," she confirmed as she watched Penny tap out two tablets from an ibuprofen bottle. "I've gotta stop eating here. You're gonna make me fat."

"Don't be silly." Penny came around the corner and grabbed William's water glass to swallow her pills. "You seem to have the metabolism of a fifteen year old marathoner."

"Psh. I noticed when I hit thirty my metabolism started to slow. I work out five times a week now just to fit in my slacks."

"Well, you look great."

"You know, Al, you should think about varying that workout routine of yours. Maybe add some regular couples' cardio or something," William said.

Penny slapped her husband's shoulder. "Pay no attention to him."

"I make it a point not to," Alvarez confirmed.

CHAPTER 18

FARIN PEERED DOWN FROM HER third-floor window at the goings-on below. Dozens of water-logged teens lounged by the pool, swam, or tried to one-up each other in shoulder war challenges while others chatted in groups around large round tables or made a pass through the outdoor buffet of hot dogs, burgers, and barbecued chicken. Shoes, towels, and beach balls littered the lawn.

Never in her teens had she enjoyed the kind of festive birthday celebration Ben and Cheryl had provided Derek. She had always admired the intense love and unflinching dedication with which they raised their boys.

They had nearly relocated the party to a local park. "We wouldn't dream of asking you to stay upstairs for the day," Cheryl had told her.

"It'll give me time to practice my guitar," she had countered. "I wouldn't feel right about having you change your plans for me."

She had played for the first two hours until her fingers started cramping. Persistence had paid off, though. The blisters had finally given way to calluses. She had made a fair amount of progress in the few weeks since she had picked up the instrument. If nothing else, it distracted her as she waited for Miles to return her call—again.

Maybe no news was good news. At least that was what she told herself in her feeble attempts to remain calm. If they did not make some inroads soon, she would lose her mind. After hearing the Hopeful Heart's fate, she had almost given up.

She glanced down at the handset she had borrowed from Ben and Cheryl's bedroom. The blinking light told her it needed a charge. When her bedside clock read 6 PM, she knew she would not get an update until next week. She was tired of waiting. Months of waiting.

"You need anything?" Ben called from her bedroom door.

She spun around, then exhaled as she clasped her free hand to her chest.

"Sorry. Thought I'd pop up and check on you. Hungry yet? We can bring you something."

"I'm fine, thanks. Looks like everyone's having a good time down there."

He crossed the room and swiped the sheer curtains to peer out the window. "For the most part, yes. Something's off with Derek and Summer, though."

"I hope they're not having trouble. Especially on his birthday."

He shook his head. "I don't know."

"Maybe you can ask him about it tonight after everyone goes home."

"Hmphf."

"You never know. Maybe he needs someone to talk to, especially his father."

Ben turned and walked back to the bedroom door. "I'm not counting on that, I'm afraid. Seventeen's a hard age. I'd wager he'd talk to Chris before me. I'm not cool enough. Speaking of Chris, I didn't even think to check the machine. Has the phone rung at all?"

She gazed at the dying handset. "Not once. I think this one needs a charge, though."

"Kyle?" he called down the hall. "Can I get you to do me a favor, son?"

"Sure. What is it?" he answered as he made his way toward his father's voice. "Where are you?"

Ben peeked his head out and waved his youngest inside. "Can you go find a phone with a full charge, then put this one back on my side of the bed?"

In no time, the boy returned with a charged replacement and handed it to Farin. "Here you go."

"Why aren't you downstairs swimming?" she asked.

Kyle shrugged. "It's my birthday present to Derek."

"What is? Staying away?"

He nodded and gave her a cheesy smile. "Exactly."

The simplicity of his answer warmed her. "Not much fun for you, though."

"It works out okay. Mom's letting me play online during the party. Usually I only get an hour here or there. So, happy birthday Derek."

She frowned. "What's 'online?' A video game or something?"

Ben palm-slapped his forehead. "That's right. No wonder the phone hasn't rung all day. Sorry. This whole online world of his is new to the rest of us."

Farin watched them, disheartened she might have missed Miles' call over a video game. "I don't understand."

"C'mon, Aunt Farin. I'll show you. We'll stay away together."

She looked at Ben, who shrugged. "You two go ahead. I'm on chip detail anyway."

Curious and desperate for something to occupy her mind, she nodded.

Ben called after them. "I'll check back in a bit. Sawyer'll be here soon, by the way. Maybe after everyone else leaves, we can go over the latest tracks the boys laid down. I think you'll be pleased."

Maps of constellations and charts of scientific formulas covered every visible inch of Kyle's bedroom, giving the false illusion he kept it messier than he did. Aside from the habit of leaving his bed unmade, it looked as tidy as his parents'—and smelled ten times better than his brother's.

He pulled out the chair beside his desk and positioned it next to his. "Have a seat."

She could not make out the rapid activity at the center of his computer screen. In the center of the soft blue screen she saw a box with up-scrolling type. New writing continuously appeared at the bottom, pushing up the words preceding it. Along the left side of the screen's top border running its length was a bunch of writing that made no sense. A mailbox with the word "mail" beneath it, a picture of a card with a pencil had the word "write" beneath it, a thick stick figure to the right of that had the intials "IM" below it, and so on.

Her cheeks flushed with frustration and embarrassment over her ignorance of all things related to technology. Kyle Grant was less than half her age, yet clearly twice as smart. "So is this 'online' something you play on your computer?"

The boy chuckled, then quickly apologized. "Not exactly, no." He explained, "'Online' refers to the Internet. You 'go online' to 'get to' the Internet."

Still clueless, she shook her head. She knew exactly two things about personal computers: first, she knew what they looked like; and second, she knew an increasing number of people used them. "And what is 'the Internet?'"

"The Internet is a way to connect with people and places without doing it in person. You don't even have to leave your room."

The simple explanation set her heart pounding like a wrecking ball in her chest. Connecting with people without doing it in person or having to leave your room. In other words, completely anonymous. No wigs, no fake colored lenses. No disguises. Invisible.

Intrigued, she focused her full attention as Kyle clicked a series of buttons that made the images on his screen disappear. Once gone, the computer screen had an image of the solar system on it.

"So how does this 'connection' with people work? Was that the screen with the scrolling type on it?"

He nodded. "Yep. That's one way, at least."

"How do you know who you're talking to? How do you find them? Where are they?"

"How about I walk you through it?"

"I'd love it. Thank you."

"No problem, but I'm gonna explain it to you like you're a five year old 'cause I don't know what you know."

"Perfect. I know nothing."

He laughed and bobbed his head. "It's okay. I've explained it to Mom twice so far and she still doesn't get it. Anyway, let's start with the basics. This is a 'monitor,'" he told her as he ran his flexed hand in a circular motion around the area of the screen. He then proceeded to go through each component of the overall machine and explain its functions. When he finished, he showed her how to change the background desktop picture, access the system menu, and where to find files. He offered to explain how to change the screen saver but she declined.

She fidgeted impatiently in her seat. "Okay, so…you said something about being able to connect with people and places on this Internet. How does that work?"

"It's a cinch. Watch this." Kyle double-clicked the America Online icon on his desktop. Farin watched and listened intently as he explained the drop-down box on the startup page, the function of a screen name, and how to sign on to the program.

When he initiated the program, the picture of three large boxes with the America Online logo on top appeared. The first had a larger version of the same thick stick figure man she had seen earlier above the initials "IM." The second two boxes remained blank.

At the bottom of the first box came a series of flashing lines of text. The last read, "Dialing…" Immediately, the sound of a telephone speed-dialing a phone number came through Kyle's speakers, followed quickly by several beeps and a scratchy static sound.

In less than a minute, an identical stick figure man filled box two, this time with three straight lines behind him, as if he were running. The caption below the box read, "Connecting." Finally, the third box filled with a picture of a small group of stick figures waving with the word "Connected!" beneath it.

"You've got mail," came a greeting through Kyle's speakers. Keeping his eyes on the screen, he tilted his head her way. "That just means someone sent me an e-mail—a message through the Internet. The greeting gets old after a while, believe me."

She nodded, her mind and heart racing at the possibilities of this new technology. "What sort of 'places' can you see on the Internet?"

A burst of air escaped the boy's lips as he navigated his mouse. "A lot of places. MTV, Nine Planets, Encyclopedia Britannica, the White House. I've visited a bunch of websites—"

"'Websites?'"

"It's like a virtual location that visually represents the business with pictures and stuff. You 'go' there to look around. Like if you were to 'go' to Encyclopedia Britannica, you could look up and read pages of information. Or if you visit a museum online, you could look at pictures of the cool junk they have there instead of having to purchase a ticket and be on your feet all day."

She nodded and bit her top lip. "I hope I can remember all these terms."

"They grow on ya. So…ready to learn about chat rooms?"

***

The contractions began around one that afternoon. In Cleveland. Over Eggs Benedict.

Amidst the lively chatter of the hotel restaurant, and their four-tables-pushed-together party of fourteen in particular, it appeared only Colin Spencer noticed his mother drop her fork on top of her plate and grab her belly.

He wriggled his small body in a futile attempt to extricate himself from his high chair. "Mummy?"

She kissed his shoulder to calm him. "Mummy's fine, Colin. Now sit down and finish your breakfast or you'll not go to the zoo today." She looked past him to the nanny seated at his right. "Jayne, I think you'll be taking Colin on your own today if that's okay."

Jayne's eyes widened with understanding. Ivy shrugged.

When Colin started to fuss for his mother to hold him, it caught Lance's attention. "Need me to take him?" But when he glanced down and noticed Ivy holding her abdomen, his eyes grew larger. He looked her over quizzically. "You all right, then?"

"Finish your breakfast. We have plenty of time."

He stood and scooted his chair back with his calves, then reached into the back pocket of his jeans for his wallet.

"Really, Lance. Eat up. It could just be false contractions. Those Braxton Hicks deals."

The word "contraction" made Marci look up from her meal. Soon, all conversation at their table ceased.

Ivy blushed from the attention. "Bloody hell, don't you lot have a sound check to pull or something? Off with you then. I'll be fine." When no one responded—or moved from their seemingly frozen positions—she turned around to kiss Colin's cheek, then hefted herself into a standing position and waddled off toward the elevator. "If it'll make you all feel better, I'll go upstairs and have a kip. Anyway, I'm not due for a week. If this baby's to be born in America, it'll happen in New York City."

Todd bolted up in his chair and addressed Lance. "You're goin' after her, then, aren't you?"

"You're the last person to tell me what I should do with my family, mate," he snapped. "You lost that right when you knocked her up and never contacted her again."

"I've told you a dozen times! *I didn't know!*"

Faith clenched her teeth and exhaled through her nose. "I thought we'd decided to put all the drama aside and be friends again. I'm warning all of you: if I have to deal with one more fight this tour, I'm out after the Garden."

232 | HEATHER O'BRIEN

Marci dabbed the corners of her mouth with her napkin, dropped it on her plate, then gave Elliot's arm a gentle squeeze before rushing off to assist Ivy.

Chris asked Lance, "Anything you want us to do? I'll ask the front desk for directions to the hospital."

Lance craned his neck to see out past the busy restaurant to the elevator doors where he glimpsed Marci reaching out to Ivy, who stood bracing herself against the wall with one hand. The other still clutched her abdomen. He looked back and faced his bandmates with an enormous smile. "We're having a baby—near the Rock and Roll Hall of Fame! Beat *that!*"

The observation drew a chuckle from the table.

"Lance!" The sudden shriek echoed from the bank of elevators, followed immediately by a guttural, "My water just broke! Get your arse over here!"

***

Imani Vaughn lit a cigarette, took a long drag, then blew a thick stream of smoke out the side of her lips. She folded one arm across her chest and perched her other elbow atop it. "The reason they dint tell you 'bout me's 'cause they hated me. I never was good enough for Charles far as they's concerned." Despite her better judgment, she creaked open the battered screen door of her home near Dorsey Park and held it for the detectives. When they entered, she peered up and down the street before shutting and locking the door. "You want somethin' to drink? I don't have much. Just milk and water."

"No thanks." Alvarez eyeballed the room. "We won't take much of your time. Like I said, we just wanted to ask you a few questions about Charles."

Imani waved them in the direction of a tattered couch with earth tone upholstery. "This have somethin' to do with that defaming lawsuit his momma tried to file a few years back?"

"Uh, no ma'am." Bridgeman unbuttoned his suit jacket, then held his tie against his chest as he sat down. "I'm curious about that, though. The whole thing seems to have just...stopped. I'm not even sure there was a lawsuit filed."

Imani snorted with disdain. "Naw, Detective. They done shut they mouth real fast. Only thing the Russell family loves mo' than they baby boy is money."

Alvarez fought the instinct to steal a sideways glance at her partner. Instead, she focused on the disposition of their surroundings. Clean if a bit musty. Window unit for the A/C in both the living room and the kitchen. Low ceilings. Old furnishings, probably either handed down or purchased over time from various yard sales or swap meets. The carpet probably should have been replaced a couple of years ago. But by no means the worst residence Alvarez had visited in her career. Imani Vaughn was probably a hardworking woman doing the best she could with what little she had especially after losing the second income of her live-in boyfriend.

Bridgeman leaned forward and handed Imani his business card. "Forgive me, ma'am. I wasn't around here back then so I'm a touch unfamiliar with the specifics of the case. I don't recall hearing Metro paid out any money to the victim's family."

"Shoot," Imani said through a cloud of exhaled smoke. She sat at the edge of her recliner, knees locked, and tossed the business card onto her coffee table. "They dint get no money from no *po*lice. They'd-a said somethin' if that was the case. They'd-a loved that."

"Maybe we should start at the beginning," Alvarez suggested. "How long were you and Charles involved?"

The detectives listened to a half hour rundown of Charles Russell's and Imani Vaughn's courtship. Sweet. Simple. Steady. But completely unrelated to their purposed visit.

"And do you remember when Charles first started driving primarily for Farin Grant?"

Imani nodded. "It was right after she moved here. That Lockhardt fella arranged with Charles' boss to do all their company's driving. Mrs. Grant liked my Charles, and he liked her back. She could be a bit demanding there for a while, but she was a good woman. I dint care too much fo' that Jameson fella, tho'."

Bridgeman cocked his head. "Did you meet Mrs. Grant at any point?"

Imani laughed and tapped the tip of her second cigarette into a thick glass ashtray. She leaned back into her recliner and crossed her legs. "Not me. I 'spect she would-a been shocked to see her fay'rit driver outside that shiny limo, just sittin' at home wit' his skinny ol' lady in her house coat and Charles in 'is old blue jeans. Naw, Charles dint mix bid'ness with home. But he talked 'bout her a good bit. To be honest, he felt sorry fo' the lady. 'Specially on account-a that boy rapin' her an' all."

At the end of the interview, the detectives thanked Imani for her help as they walked back to their car. With a nod and a two-finger wave, they drove off toward the station.

Their smiles disappeared the moment they were out of sight. Faces forward, neither spoke the entire twenty minute drive back to the station. When Bridgeman parked the car in the Metro lot and killed the engine, they made no attempt to exit the vehicle.

"Bobby Lockhardt raped Farin Grant," Alvarez said at last, her voice grave as she stared out the windshield.

Bridgeman's tone mirrored his partner's. "Jameson Lockhardt, Bobby Lockhardt, and Ross Alexander were all at the Coral Gables scene the morning of Jordan Grant's murder."

"...and Charles Russell planned to go the police with what he knew as soon as he safely delivered Farin to the funeral."

"We need to call Macy. We need to know if he's talked to that witness."

Alvarez nodded, too stunned to argue.

They noticed the questioning eyes of passersby as they made their way to their desks and realized their faces likely gave them away. The stunning revelations Imani Vaughn had given them today had surpassed anything they had imagined. Now, all they needed to do was find proof to back up Ms. Vaughn's account.

Once inside the elevator, Bridgeman stared at their reflection on the shiny steel doors. "If Macy wants to meet, when are you free?"

"As soon as possible."

The atmosphere in the office was curiously casual for a Thursday afternoon. Several of their colleagues sat or stood around in a circle laughing and chatting. Some held Styrofoam coffee cups while others held bottled water or cans of soda. As they drew closer, they realized their desks were at the epicenter of the informal gathering.

Bridgeman did not notice when Alvarez abruptly stopped following him. He painted a congenial smile on his face and pushed through the others with as much patience as he could muster. A friendly chorus of "Hey, here they are!" came from a few of the men as they stood and stepped aside so the detective could get through.

"Looks like someone forgot to invite us to the party!" He studied their faces in turn, until his eyes settled upon the woman seated in the chair beside his desk. Should he know her? He tried and failed to place her face. She was a handsome, stocky woman, though well put together in her skirt and blouse. Maybe a little older than he. Fully gray. Wholly unfamiliar.

Captain Ward seemed to appear out of nowhere to make the introductions. He smiled and gave Bridgeman a hearty slap on the back as he addressed the woman. "And this is the man endeavoring to fill your husband's shoes. He's doing a great job so far—not that it's an easy task. Irene Stark, I'd like you to meet Detective William Bridgeman. Detective Bridgeman came to us all the way from Detroit!"

By sheer force of will, Bridgeman remained smiling as he extended his hand. "Mrs. Stark. It's nice to meet you."

At that moment, he realized his partner had lagged behind. He turned around to find her standing slackjawed at the rear of the crowd of cops. Irene Stark gasped and rose from her chair. With outstretched arms, she caused the small group of men to step aside as she headed straight for Alvarez. Bridgeman thought it amazing no one seemed to take note of the stunned look blanketing her features.

"Alicia!" Irene wrapped her up in her arms and rocked her side to side. "Oh, darling it's so good to see you." She pulled away and grasped Alvarez's upper arms, then looked her up and down. "Still so young and beautiful. How have you been, dear?"

Alvarez stammered periodically as Mrs. Stark walked her to her desk, her arm around her shoulders as if the detective were unable to make it on her own. "I...I-I'm doing well. Work still t-takes up the majority of my time."

"No boyfriend? Oh, Alicia, we talked about that a dozen times."

She glanced at Bridgeman and shot him a warning look. "W-What about you? I thought you'd moved out west."

Mrs. Stark waved in disgust as she took her seat. "Why my husband wanted to live on a cattle ranch in Alpine, Arizona I'll never know. In fact, until he died, I didn't even know his plans. Honestly...funneling all that money into two hundred acres in the middle of nowhere. You call that a dream? It *snows* in Alpine, Arizona!"

Bridgeman pulled his chair out and dropped down, exhausted from the day yet eager to call Macy and schedule a time to talk.

"So you're back now?" Alvarez asked patiently.

"You bet I am. I guess the good news is I managed to get myself a nice little profit. I'd never managed to sell our place here, so with the sale of the ranch and Chucky's pension, it looks like I'm free and clear."

Captain Ward nodded his approval. "That's wonderful, Irene. I'm happy you'll have some security."

Over the next few minutes, Irene Stark detailed the inconvenience of moving all their belongings to and back from her temporary home. One by one, the officers waved or mouthed their goodbyes and returned to their work. Even Captain Ward seemed to want to avoid listening a second time to the same story he had heard before Bridgeman and Alvarez's arrival.

"Anyway," Mrs. Stark concluded as she stood and grabbed her purse. "I was hoping I could get you to help bring some boxes up from my car." She nodded at Bridgeman. "You look healthy enough to assist a couple of ladies. Whaddya say?"

Alvarez rose from her seat and followed Irene out of the office, shrugging at Bridgeman as she passed. He brought up the lead and remained quiet as the woman continued her never-ending diatribe on the woes of being a widow living slap in the middle of eastern Arizona. The lack of humidity had given her dry mouth. The cold winter kept her inside for nearly three solid months and left her depressed to the point her doctor wanted to prescribe her pills.

"And of course I'd lugged all Chucky's things with me. I should have gone through them before I left, but I just couldn't bring myself to do it."

When they reached her car, Alvarez dared to interrupt the stream-of-consciousness rant. "What exactly did you need us to carry upstairs, Irene?"

Irene Stark pressed the trunk button on the fob of her new BMW. Inside were three large boxes. "Why these, of course. I certainly don't need them, and when I peeked inside and saw they were extras from that old case of his, I thought you might want them."

Bridgeman moved forward and lifted the lid on one of the boxes. Glancing at the name on the top of several labeled evidence bags, he nodded at his partner, then addressed Mrs. Stark. "Of course we'll take these off your hands. No use having you carry them around. Right, partner?"

Alvarez moved in and lifted the lid of the box Bridgeman had viewed while he pulled out the other two from the Bimmer's trunk. She caught sight of a lipstick tube in a sealed evidence bag.

The label on the front read "Grant."

***

Faith was impressed. Not even the clank of the elevator door interrupted Henri's sleep. It did not even pause the loud snoring. Either he had finally found himself a way to sleep during her nearly four-month absence, or he had drunk himself into a stupor. He had never been much of a drinker, but either scenario worked. She had half-expected to find him passed out at his easel.

As she moved through the loft, she noted the juxtaposition of the disorganization of his studio space and their living area. He had kept it clean. Cleaner than she did. Even the several ashtrays placed throughout the space were emptied and wiped down. She grinned as she glanced at her piano. Not a speck of dust in sight.

She crept over to the bed, careful not to disturb him. For all the cleaning and sleeping he had done, he had somehow not found the time to shave. Maybe it was a guy thing, like a sports player who wears the same socks for weeks on end for good luck. Henri had never been a fan of facial hair. Maybe he had decided to grow it until she returned. Judging by the length of it, she assumed that was the case.

A burst of sunlight crested the bottom of the skylight's frame. Faith often joked she could set her watch by that skylight. She watched the stream of light cut a path across the floorboards no faster than a snail's pace. If she did not make her move soon, Henri would wake up and spoil the surprise.

She returned to the living room and unlaced her boots, then slid them off and set them on the floor beside her. It had been a short flight in from Boston, but she felt like she had been flying for days. Months, maybe. Thankfully, only three more weeks remained in the tour. After that, she would be done. Done with life on the road. Done with eating unhealthy crap and traveling at odd hours. Done living with a bunch of men who had sadly failed to find a way to reconnect after a lifetime of sharing a bond closer than family. In fairness,

Todd was the primary problem. But they all felt it. Mirage had run its course. At least this time, most of them would part as friends.

The overarching triumph in their reunion, however temporary, was that it had taken the last word on Mirage's fate out of the mouth of the monster. This time, they had chosen for themselves to split up.

She unfastened the series of hook-and-eye closures on her leather corset and felt huge relief as the cool loft air hit her moist skin. Peeling off the restricting garment, she caught sight of a stack of boxes that had been delivered while she was gone. Juggling the heavy demands of the road with the even heavier demands of running her company had left her mentally exhausted, her decision making iffy at best. She wished she could chalk up her lapse in judgment that first night with Chris to temporary insanity.

No dice.

At least nothing had happened that they could not take back. They had no sooner started kissing than they heard the crash. It had startled them, sending them out onto the balcony to identify the source of the commotion. They had peered down to find what appeared to be a smashed television set on the cement ground near the pool. Glancing upward at the balcony above his, they had witnessed Todd leaning over the edge, giving them the middle finger.

By the time they returned inside, they both knew the moment had passed. Whatever sadness had enveloped Chris to the point he felt vulnerable had eased. He no longer needed someone there to chase away whatever demons haunted him. Knowing he did not need a shoulder to lean on left her with mixed feelings. Relief that his anguish had passed. Curious what had him so sad, or lonely. Mostly, it had saddened her, even though she did not feel the sting of rejection.

"You don't have to go," he had assured her. "It'd be nice to have someone nearby."

He had slept on the couch that night, giving her the bed. The next morning, she had woken to the sound of him strumming a dirge on his acoustic guitar. As he played, she had surveyed the space. She realized she missed the skylight in the loft waking her with its harsh rays each morning. Even the absence of stale cigarette smoke and paint thinner unsettled her. What the hell was she doing in LA? She missed New York. She missed Henri.

Lying in bed as Chris played Cat Stevens' "The Wind" and then Marshall Tucker Band's "Can't You See," she had inventoried her selfish behavior over the months since leaving New York. She did not regret her decision to join the tour. It had healed them as a band—even with Todd's lingering bitterness over their ultimate fate. She did, however, regret throwing herself at her best friend. No matter how they defined their bond, crossing the line into the physical would have damaged them both.

Her mind finally settled, she had gathered her clothes together and padded into the bathroom. Chris had transitioned into a bluesy rendition of "So Very Hard to Go" by Tower of Power that made her sad and wonder how she might help him get through the obvious pain he felt over his divorce. As she had pulled on her binding leather pants, something fell out of the small pocket just beneath its waistband. It was the bindle of cocaine Todd had supplied her with on their way to join the rest of the band at the afterparty.

Before exiting the bathroom, she had unfolded the paper and sprinkled its contents into the commode, then promised herself she would call Gale as soon as she returned to her room. She had called her twice each day since then. Hopefully, they could attend a meeting together before she had to get to the Garden later this afternoon.

For now, she needed to tie up a final loose end.

She left her clothes piled on top of her boots and crossed back to the bed. Sitting on his nightstand near the lamp she saw a velvet box. Inside, she found the ring, which she slipped on her finger before easing the lid shut to avoid the inevitable "snap."

The ring felt heavy on her finger. Its weight made her smile. She would relish each minute of getting accustomed to it.

Quietly, she padded to her side of the bed and slipped beneath the covers. She moved in beside and then on top of Henri, who encircled her completely naked body in his arms before fully realizing he had woken up.

He tucked his chin and beheld her with sleepy eyes. *"Mon trésor?"* he asked in a groggy voice.

She nodded and kissed him.

"But how...? I thought I would not see you until the show tonight."

"I flew down early. I missed you."

His arms drew her closer. "Tell me you're home for good."

"Just a few more weeks," she promised.

"You look tired."

"I am tired."

"Do you want to sleep or do you want me to make the coffee?"

She shook her head. "Neither."

He frowned, then broke their embrace long enough to bring one hand up to scratch his growth of beard. "No coffee? No sleep? What shall we do then?"

She lifted her left hand out from under the covers and wiggled her fingers so he could see the ring. "I say we stay in bed and celebrate."

CHAPTER 19

"**D**ID YOU BRING IT?

"Did *you*?"

"I asked you first."

With a groan of frustration, Farin plunged her hand inside her overlarge handbag, pulled out the opened manila envelope, and shook it at him. "There. Now you."

Miles reached into his back pocket for his wallet. He opened the billfold, extracted a plastic ID card, and handed it to her. "There you go, 'Lisa.' You're legit."

"Thank you so much." She studied the card with wide eyes, then scowled up at him. "It took you long enough."

"You realize I have a regular job, right?"

She rolled her eyes.

"Are you seriously not following the OJ Simpson trial on television?"

She tucked the fake ID into the inside pocket of her purse, then flounced down on his sofa. "It's hard to miss, but I've been a little busy lately. Between trying to stay off Jameson's radar and being nagged to resurrect my career, there isn't a lot of time to sit around and watch TV."

"Yeah well, as soon as those gloves didn't fit, my boss wanted me back in LA pronto. I'd stalled them as long as I could in order to check things out in Fayetteville—burned up my PTO to do it—but I couldn't put them off forever. I spent all of July and the first couple weeks of August stuck in a room with a bunch of other news hounds. It was like being trapped in a kennel with a bunch of rabid dogs. If I hadn't gotten a reprieve to cover Jerry Garcia's memorial up in Frisco, I'm pretty sure I'd have gone nuts."

She nodded sadly. "It was a shame about Jerry."

"It was." He grabbed two bottles of water from the fridge, handed her one, then sat beside her. "So, are we done beating me up for two minutes so we can discuss that package?"

She looked around the room. "Are you ever gonna get this place in order? It looks like you can't decide if you're coming or going."

He broke the seal on his bottle and gulped the clear liquid, then sighed as he surveyed the mostly unopened boxes still cluttering his space. "Not exactly the lived-in look, I'll give you that much. Now stop stalling. What did he give you?"

She gestured toward the manila envelope, which she had dropped onto the coffee table before sitting down. "Not exactly huge revelations. Go ahead and look."

Miles snatched it up and eagerly dumped the contents onto the table. Several stacks of money spilled out, along with a black velvet ring box. A thick, stapled document landed atop the pile. "This is it?"

She leaned forward and snatched up the velvet box and stowed it in her purse. "Like I said. But it's a start."

"So, basically, he's paying you off."

"If you call thirty thousand dollars a payoff."

He rummaged through the bills and arranged them into a tidy stack. "There's a bit more than that."

"The rest is what I had on me when they took me."

He nodded as he lifted the document to take a look. "So you're not broke anymore. That's good."

"Hopefully it'll get me where I need to go. And now that 'Lisa's' finally mobile, maybe I can finally finish this thing."

Miles studied the paperwork in his hand, flipping the pages back and forth. "Why do you have a copy of Jameson Lockhardt's will?"

"Ross sent it along with the cash."

"But...why?" He skimmed the first few pages. As he read, his eyes widened. "Have you gone through this?"

The sides of her lips stretched into a satisfied smirk. "I have. I wish I had sooner."

Miles flipped to the end to check the signature page. "Why would he have signed this?"

"I don't know. I don't care."

His lips parted in shock as the implications hit him. "You own this guy."

"I will soon enough."

"Lockhardt's son's gonna be pissed."

"Bobby Lockhardt's gonna be in jail where he belongs."

Miles dropped the document on the table, then turned to face her. "Listen, I need to talk to you, and I need you to not be angry when I do."

"What is it?"

"I've sort of hit a wall as far as finding Jordan...but I think I've found a way to get the cops to help. That way, everyone stays safe."

"I knew it." She stiffened in her seat. "You've been talking to your girlfriend about this, haven't you?"

"No. Well, not exactly. But there have been some developments."

A suspicious frown shrouded her features. "What developments?"

"Metro found your box."

Her lips parted. "They did?"

Miles nodded. "They know, Farin. Almost everything. They know about the rape, they know who was at Bobby's the day Jordan was shot..."

"How? You'd said that murdered cop destroyed the evidence."

"They thought he had. Turns out the guy'd been keeping it at his house. I'm guessing as an insurance policy while he continued to blackmail Lockhardt."

She rose from the couch, snatched up her water bottle, and took a drink. She began pacing, then stopped. "They don't have enough to make an arrest, do they?"

"Right now they're still determining what of the evidence they can use. Some of the samples from Bobby's house may have degraded over time. Depends on how well Stark stored it. In the meantime—"

"If I don't find Jordan before the cops get to Jameson, he might do something drastic."

Miles leaned forward and rested his elbows on his knees. "It's time to come in, Farin. You need their help. If you go to them first, they can help find Jordan before the old man has a chance to hurt anyone else."

She folded her arms. "Or they can bring me in, detain me for questioning, and the whole world will know I'm alive in about thirty seconds. Jameson will know where I am. I'll be safe, and Jordan..."

He let her mull it over a bit more before adding, "It may be the only way to finish this once and for all. Last thing I found was an address outside Fort Bragg linking the Hopeful Heart and that Jade Trongly mentioned in the e-mail. I've been so busy I haven't been able to check it out. I don't think I can without making someone at the *Herald* suspicious. They want me back in LA on Monday. We can't do this alone anymore."

With a jerk of her hand, she accepted the piece of paper with the address scribbled upon it, then squared her shoulders and tilted her head, one eyebrow arched in defiance. "Good thing I've found someone else who can help me, then."

"What? Who?"

"I met someone online."

"Online?"

She nodded. "What? You think I've been sitting around while I've been waiting to hear back from you? No, I've been taking this situation into my own hands."

He scrunched his forehead in apprehension. "I hope you're being careful."

She propped a hand on her hip. "As a matter of fact, I've never felt more empowered. Not only did I finally find the courage to open that stupid envelope Ross sent me, I actually started recording again. And you know what?

I'm *good*."

"So who's this person you found online? You haven't told him who you are, have you?"

"Of course not," she snapped. She stooped down and gathered the paperwork and money back into the envelope, then stuffed them into her bag.

"How's this person supposed to help you, then? Who is it?"

"His name's Herb Smith. He's a private detective."

***

Labor Day weekend seemed the appropriate time to close the deal. He had honed his line of BS for six long weeks. Skittish broad, but no dummy. It had taken a subtle approach. He dared not rush things lest he give her reason to suspect him—or worse, give her the impression he had some ulterior motive like trying to get into her pants.

He knew enough about her to recognize the daddy issues. No matter how much trauma she had suffered at Lockhardt's hands, it was clear she subconsciously still sought the emotional protection and heroic assistance with her life from any man she considered older, stronger, or more stable than she. Even a total stranger she had never before laid eyes on. Poor kid. Under different circumstances, he might have helped her out.

Before settling in for their nightly chat, he grilled up a thick New York strip, which he topped with a sautéed mushroom and onion mixture. Steak fries and a sensible green salad—a nod to his doctor's recent admonition to include more roughage in his diet—rounded out the meal.

The late summer day's temperature had climbed no higher than 81 degrees, allowing him to eat his supper out back on the large deck of his Colonial home off Grand Avenue. Three times bigger than anything he needed, but he would not dream of giving up the place. It had been in his family for over seventy-five years. Besides, there were worse things than having the Mighty Mississippi just beyond your backyard.

Usually he followed the strict rule of not celebrating until he had completed a job, but tonight he fudged a bit with two bottles of Cabernet, the first of which he polished off while he prepped his food. What the hey? If things went as planned tonight, and he had reason to believe they would, he would soon begin a nice long vacation. Cash money. Unknown and untouchable by the ex.

The vibrating buzz of his burner phone drew him inside. He swallowed a mouthful of romaine tossed with Thousand Island dressing, set down his plate on the kitchen counter, then picked up. "You beat me to it. I was gonna call you in a few. I'm just finishing up dinner."

"Mr. Radford, I'm growing impatient with this 'new approach' you've explored. In fact, I'm beginning to question the veracity of the recommendations that convinced me to hire you in the first place."

Herb smirked and nodded. Just as he had suspected.

"Unless you find that girl by our call next week, I'll be forced to discontinue our arrangement."

"You're one impatient SOB, Lockhardt. That's for sure."

"Indeed."

Herb sucked his teeth and used his tongue to help dislodge a small remnant of beef caught between a canine and a premolar. "Like I told you the first time we met, I'm as thorough as you are impatient. If you want to call it quits, it's your prerogative. But I'm not one to make promises before I can guarantee results. I can tell you this, though: I'm close."

The angry sigh on the other end nearly caused him to chuckle aloud.

At first Lockhardt had labeled this new approach "silly." It quickly changed to "lazy." Who knew? Maybe it was a little of both. Still, it netted him more progress than anything else he had tried.

"How close is 'close?'"

"*Very* close."

After leaving LA for Santa Barbara and still coming up empty-handed, Herb had grudgingly resigned himself to moving on to south Florida with all those damned bugs. It had been a long two months with depressing, even embarrassing results. He had ended his weekly state-of-the-investigation call with Lockhardt feeling frustrated and defeated.

In an effort to avoid dwelling on his failure and clear his mind long enough to start planning his next course of action, he had taken a walk to a local liquor store down on State Street, picked up a six-pack of Heineken, and returned to his room to lose himself in a little television.

By the time he had returned from the store, he had missed *Jeff Foxworthy* by forty-five minutes. Disappointed, he channel-surfed past *Touched by an Angel* and *COPS*, then finally settled for the last half of the *John Larroquette Show*. The mixture of import brew and the live studio audience's laughter soon lightened his spirit. When the sitcom ended, he switched over to *America's Most Wanted* to see if he might recognize anyone or perhaps figure a way to drum up some business.

During a commercial break, he saw an advertisement touting the timesaving, mind-easing merits of using America Online, an Internet online service that enabled one to locate information without a library, book travel arrangements without calling an agent, and "talk" to people through their computer. Initially the concept had made him laugh. In fact, the commercial zipped by with such a frenetic pace, he had dismissed it as the newest in a long list of passing fads.

Later that night, long after six empty beer bottles had been deposited into the wastebasket beside the desk, he had switched over to find an HBO movie he could use for background noise while he tried to sleep. Lo and behold, before the opening credits of *Blown Away* started, up came another advertisement for America Online—this one a full two minutes long.

Two preppy thirtysomethings commiserated over the unlikelihood of getting to the game on time due to an insurmountable number of errands to which they were committed. But oh no. American Online to the rescue. Not only did they complete their honey-dos and make the game, they managed to take a minute or two to "chat" with some new "online friends."

By the time the advertisement ended, Herb had formulated his next move.

Over the following twenty-four hours, he had purchased an IBM ThinkPad, convinced the hotel desk clerk to part with one of several America Online trial disks they "received in the mail every day," and created an account: screen name PIHerb4108. Sure enough, the time it took to change the destination of his plane ticket from Miami International to Southwest Iowa Regional by way of Des Moines blew the alternative away.

"The way I see it," Herb told Jameson, "she's understandably skittish, yet to be searching for help online, she's also desperate. You know her a lot better than I do, but based on what I've learned, I'd say she's resistant to the idea of talking to the cops. I wouldn't worry about that at this point."

"I don't pay you to do my thinking," Jameson snapped. "And I have no interested in throwing an endless amount of money at a problem that shows no sign of resolution. You spent the first two months running up expenses with no results and the last two doing the same thing from the comfort of your living room."

Herb frowned at his half-eaten, lukewarm New York strip. The sautéed mushroom-onion mixture no longer steamed with warmth and goodness, but rather congealed amid the frigid red blood from his steak. The barely-touched baker looked cold and unappetizing, the salad wilted beneath a coating of the now deep orange Thousand Island dressing. The possibility of reviving the meat and potato in his microwave was an unappealing option.

He resented having his dinner interrupted. Assuming he would submit his final invoice tomorrow morning, he made a mental note to add the cost of the spoiled meal *and* its eventual replacement. "I'll agree with you on one thing, Lockhardt. LA and Santa Barbara were a bust. No sign of her anywhere. In fact, for all the money you're so worried about wasting, you might want to factor in the expense of that bonfire you commissioned over in Malibu. But hey, none of my business. That was before my time. All I know is that since I started thinking *in*side the box, specifically a computer box, it's been anything but 'no results.'"

"Is that so? Then why haven't you located her yet?"

"Who says I haven't?" When Herb heard nothing but breathing on the other end of the line, he knew he had piqued the old man's attention. "And if I have, do we really want to chance blazing in—*pun intended*—without better confirmation than a distant shadow in a window from a beach at sunset?"

It took little else to convince Lockhardt to back off. His sole concern was the ability to contact their mutual acquaintance to finish the job once and for all. On that point, they agreed.

Herb scraped his ruined dinner into the garbage can, then rinsed his dishes and corked his second bottle of Cabernet. His celebration would have to wait. Back to the matter at hand.

He fixed a ham sandwich and grabbed a Bud from the fridge, then deposited both onto the end table beside his overstuffed La-Z-Boy before closing up his doors and windows for the night. Once he secured the house, he settled into his recliner and booted up his laptop. She usually popped up between 9 and 10 PM. Better to be there when she logged on. It made her come to him and felt infinitely less stalker-ish.

He logged on and checked his Buddy List, then switched on his set to watch a little TV while he ate and waited. Every so often, the screen saver engaged and he would wiggle the TrackPoint pointer with his middle finger to get back to the main screen.

Just after 9 PM, her screen name appeared on his otherwise empty Buddy List. Almost immediately, an Instant Message popped up at the top left of his screen.

RedMayden: Hi.

He greeted her and asked after her day.

RedMayden: I've had better.
PIHerb4108: Sorry to hear that. Wanna talk about it?
RedMayden: Not really. It's complicated.
PIHerb4108: Okay.

The conversation lagged. He did not push for fear of seeming too eager. He set his laptop aside and gathered up his dishes to walk them back in the kitchen and grab another beer. When he returned, he smiled to find his patience had paid off.

RedMayden: You still there?
PIHerb4108: Sure am. Thought you didn't want to talk.
RedMayden: I'm okay to talk. I just don't want to talk about my day.

PIHerb4108: Okay. What would you like to talk about?
RedMayden: I don't know. Just feeling isolated.
PIHerb4108: Why's that? Boyfriend out of town or something?
RedMayden: I don't have a boyfriend. Well, sort of. It's complicated.
PIHerb4108: You say that a lot, Red.
RedMayden: I know.

It took every bit of self-control he had to let her lead the conversation. Unlike previous nights, she seemed hesitant to open up. He decided to sign off and try again tomorrow. Maybe something had happened to spook her. But before he could send his goodnight salutation, another message popped up on the screen.

RedMayden: Are you really a PI?
PIHerb4108: Why? Hit a dead end with that search you were doing?
RedMayden: Yes.

His brows rose above curious eyes.

RedMayden: I think I need to hire a professional.
PIHerb4108: Good choice.
RedMayden: But I don't know where to start. I need someone discreet.
PIHerb4108: I'm discreet, but I don't know if you could afford me. lol
RedMayden: What is "lol?"
PIHerb4108: lol = laugh out loud
RedMayden: Oh.
PIHerb4108: Anyway, find a local guy. I'm all the way in Miami.

He grabbed his beer and gulped half its contents, then stared intently at his screen, wondering if she would take the bait.

RedMayden: I'm near Miami.
PIHerb4108: Really? And here I thought I'd used my computer to escape.
RedMayden: So do you think we can schedule a consultation?
PIHerb4108: Like I said, I don't know if you can afford me.
RedMayden: I imagine we could work something out. lol
PIHerb4108: Tempting.
RedMayden: Yeah?
PIHerb4108: Kidding. Cash only. I don't mix business with pleasure.
RedMayden: Good. That was a test.

He rolled his eyes and shook his head.

PIHerb4108: How soon you looking to hire?
RedMayden: Yesterday.
PIHerb4108: Sorry, I was booked solid then.
RedMayden: You sound like a busy guy. Maybe that's a good sign, huh?
PIHerb4108: I pay my bills.
RedMayden: So how do we do this?
PIHerb4108: I need to know what you want, then I'll give you a quote.
RedMayden: Okay.
PIHerb4108: But to be honest, I don't go online to troll up business.
RedMayden: What does that mean?
PIHerb4108: I'm legit, Red. Real people, not phantom screen names.

This was it. The moment of truth. He did not flinch at the pause in the conversation. He figured she would need a minute.

RedMayden: Makes sense. Sorry.

He started to type, then stopped and let her mull it over a bit more.

RedMayden: You still there?
PIHerb4108: Yep.
RedMayden: What are you doing Sunday?
PIHerb4108: Church. Family. Sunday's out.
RedMayden: Monday?
PIHerb4108: Let me check my schedule. brb (brb = be right back)

Herb took his time relieving his bladder and grabbing another beer. Steady and breezy—that was the key. She needed to believe she wanted it more than he did.

PIHerb4108: Wednesday's better. That too late? You seem rushed.
RedMayden: Nothing sooner?
PIHerb4108: Afraid not.
RedMayden: I guess Wednesday's okay then.
PIHerb4108: Afternoon? My 2's open.
RedMayden: That's fine. How much for the consultation?
PIHerb4108: No charge. Maybe a cup of Joe.
RedMayden: You got it. Thanks, Herb.
PIHerb4108: Don't thank me yet. I haven't taken the case.

RedMayden: Understood. Where's your office?

PIHerb4108: I meet new clients on neutral ground. Keeps things light.

RedMayden: I'd prefer someplace as low-key as possible.

PIHerb4108: You running from the cops or something, Red?

RedMayden: lol

PIHerb4108: A non-answer. Interesting. Someone's got some secrets.

***

Derek had arranged for Summer to join them for lunch after church Sunday. Ben and Cheryl had welcomed the idea, though they did not know why Derek had asked so formally. Summer was welcome anytime.

During the service, the teens had opted to remain near their parents instead of sitting in the back pew as usual, close enough to brush shoulders and write notes on the day's bulletin. Even more curious, Derek had elected to carpool with his family instead of driving on his own.

"You sure you're all right, son?" Ben asked on the short drive home.

Derek nodded dismally but said nothing.

"You and Summer having a bit of a row, then?" Cheryl asked over her shoulder.

"We're okay."

Kyle sat beside his brother, uncharacteristically quiet.

Ben and Cheryl exchanged worried glances but refrained from further interrogation.

By the time they arrived home, Farin had already made herself scarce in anticipation of the arrival of their lunch guest. Cheryl removed from the refrigerator trays of deli meats, cheeses, and the fresh sandwich fixings she had pre-arranged that morning, then scooped spoonfuls of fruit salad into a serving bowl. Ben helped with dishes, utensils, and serving tongs while the boys prepared the patio table. The doorbell rang the moment they finished laying out the feast.

When Derek disappeared to answer the door, Cheryl leaned up and over to whisper in her husband's ear, "This is eerily familiar."

He nodded. "I was thinking the same thing."

"Do you think they've told her parents yet?"

"I doubt it. You know the Reeces."

"Aye. They'll be wanting us on their side first, I imagine."

"I'm not sure what to say about this."

"It's not ideal, Ben, but things rarely are."

Out of the corner of his eye, Ben watched Kyle fold his placemat and stack it with his utensils on top of his plate. When he grabbed the place setting and his glass before sneaking back inside, Ben called out, "What're you doing, son?"

The boy shrugged. "I thought I might eat up in my room. Let you guys talk."

Cheryl dipped her head down and to the side. "No computer on Sunday."

"Then what about TV?"

"It's a beautiful day. Why don't you want to eat with the family?"

The sides of his mouth arched downward. "I don't wanna be here when you start yelling."

Ben lifted his hands to his waist and nodded toward the table. "We'll eat as a family. No one's going to yell."

Kyle hunched slightly as he returned to the table and reconfigured his place. He sat down, head on his hand, and waited for the others.

When Derek and Summer joined them out back, Cheryl greeted her with a smile and open arms. "I didn't get a chance to talk to you at church. I meant to compliment your sundress. Is it new?"

Summer attempted a weak smile. She nodded and held out the sides of the garment. "Yes, ma'am. My mom brought it home from their trip."

"I didn't know your parents were on holiday. Where'd they go?"

Ben clasped Derek's shoulder and flattened his lips. "Why don't you go on and get the pitcher of lemonade from the fridge? Help your mum out."

Derek nodded and headed for the kitchen.

They made small talk throughout lunch. Summer wished Ben a happy belated birthday and apologized for not joining them Friday evening for his celebration dinner as planned. "What with my mom and dad getting back so late Friday afternoon, I couldn't get away."

"You were missed, but I certainly understand."

"So it was business, then?" Cheryl asked. "That's too bad. I've always wanted to visit Ecuador—go see the Galapagos Islands during hatching season." She lifted her chin toward Ben. "We should go there some time. See the hatching before Kyle's off to Hawaii."

Kyle piped in with an impish, "The hatchings are in December."

Ben shot his youngest an appreciative smirk and winked.

She shrugged and lifted her brows. "A Christmas trip then, maybe."

Derek and Summer sat huddled near each other like a couple of beaten puppies. Every once in a while, Summer would peer at Derek with pleading eyes and he would offer a placating nod, as if swearing an unspoken oath to make it all better.

"You've not touched your sandwich, Summer," Cheryl observed, concerned. "Is everything okay?"

Summer nodded sadly. "I'm sorry. I had a big breakfast earlier and I guess I'm not as hungry as I thought." She looked at Derek with big eyes, her lips stretched tight across her teeth as if urging him to talk.

Cheryl caught the surreptitious exchange, swallowed a bite of melon, then casually reached for her glass. "You'll need to keep your strength up. It may be a struggle for a couple of months, but you'll find your appetite again. For now, keep a sleeve of saltines near your bed with a glass of water. That'll help first thing in the morning."

Derek's jaw slacked. He peered at his mother with wide eyes. "Mom, I—"

"*Dinnae!*" she snapped and shot up the index finger of her free hand. Calmly, she drank her lemonade.

He looked at his father. "Dad?"

Ben nodded as if acknowledging some inner dialogue. He looked at each of them. "How long have you known?"

Derek slumped in his chair. Summer looked down and away.

"They found out on his birthday," Cheryl asserted, her eyes darting between the two.

Summer fidgeted with the cloth napkin on her lap as she faced them. "Mr. and Mrs. Grant, I'm sorry we've waited so long to tell you. I...I wanted to see a doctor first. Until last week, we'd only done a box test from the drug store."

"What about your parents, then?" Cheryl asked. "Have you told them yet?"

"No, ma'am. Not yet."

Ben shot Derek a stern look. "You'll be at Summer's side when she tells them. She stayed by you when you told us."

Derek nodded, but Summer shook her head. "Oh no, sir. I-I couldn't have Derek do that."

"He's the father, hen," Cheryl said. "That's the only way. He'll not leave you to face this alone."

Derek dared to take Summer's hand in his. "She won't be alone."

Summer tucked a strand of blonde hair behind her ear and smiled softly. "I know my parents. Trust me, it'll be better coming from me alone. But maybe we can all sit down together once I've told them?"

Ben nodded. "We'll do all we can. I can't say I'm happy with this turn of events, though. You're both still so young. There's a lot to consider here."

Cheryl added, "But we're all adults. We don't need to figure everything out today. Now Summer, eat your sandwich. I'll go in and fix you a cup of tea with ginger. That ought to set you right. Ginger always helped me when I was pregnant with Derek."

By the time Summer left later that afternoon, the tension in the house had eased. Summer thanked Ben and Cheryl for their understanding and promised to call them soon to schedule a time they could all sit down together, discuss their situation, and decide on some short-term—and perhaps even some long-term—plans. Cheryl assured her things would work out. Ben hugged her goodbye. Derek walked her out to her car, his stance straighter and more confident than his parents had seen in weeks.

"See?" Cheryl said, turning to her youngest as they stored their leftovers. "No one yelled."

"You and Dad were pretty cool," Kyle admitted as he burped a container of sliced ham. "Maybe this is the time to tell you about this girl I met at school. Her name's—"

"Not funny."

The boy chuckled. "You're right. Especially since I really met her online."

Cheryl's expression shifted momentarily. "You're not serious, then?"

"Nah," Kyle said. "I sorta had a crush on this one girl at school, Libby, but she's with an older guy. He's sixteen."

Cheryl stacked the containers and organized them in the fridge. "And what's Libby like?"

Kyle shrugged. "She's on the volleyball team."

Cheryl smirked. "Aye, my boys. Cheerleaders and volleyball players. Don't go turning your nose up at the rest, now. You'll never be satisfied with a pretty face. Find someone who makes you laugh and thinks like you. You'll never go wrong with a lass like that."

"I know. You've told me a million times." He set the emptied bowl of fruit salad in the sink and handed his mother the secured plastic receptacle.

Cheryl snapped her fingers as she shut the refrigerator door. "Can you run upstairs and let Farin know everyone's gone, please? She's probably starving by now."

Kyle scampered off, taking the stairs two at a time, while Cheryl settled in the living room with Ben. She snuggled into his embrace and released a huge sigh. "I thought we handled that well."

"Our son's going to finish high school," he said, rubbing her shoulder. "Summer's going to as well."

She rubbed his chest. "They'll find their way. It's not like we're abandoning them."

"I guess it's hypocritical to say it, but it feels wrong."

"I know, but what are we to do about it now? Insist on an abortion? Scream and yell as if there's a way to undo it? That's not us, Ben. Especially us."

"Think they'll get married?"

"If she'll have me," Derek said as he entered the living room. "I'm gonna ask her."

Ben and Cheryl unlocked their embrace and regarded the young man. "Marriage is a big step, son," Ben said.

Derek plunged his hands into his slacks pocket. "I was gonna ask her anyway once we graduated. I love her, Dad."

Cheryl's features softened with admiration at the sincerity of his expression.

Ben nodded. "It's a big responsibility."

"So's being a father," Cheryl added.

"I know," Derek said as he moved into the living room and dropped onto the sofa. He slid his shoes off and placed them off to the side. "I'm not saying it'll be easy, but I'm letting you know I've given this a lot of thought."

Cheryl eased herself back into her husband's arms. "We'll sort it, Derek. First things first, though. Summer needs to tell her parents. Are we sure you can't go with her?"

He shook his head. "She's afraid of them. I think she doesn't want me there in case her dad explodes."

Ben frowned. "You don't think he'd hurt her."

The sound of Kyle running downstairs brought his parents upright on the sofa. He bounded into the room clutching a piece of paper.

"What's the matter?" Ben asked.

Kyle moved forward and handed them the paper. Breathlessly, he announced, "Aunt Farin's gone!"

CHAPTER 20

NOT THE HOMECOMING HE HAD envisioned. Not by a long shot. Chris had intended to come home and sleep for two solid days before making any decision more complicated than what to eat or when to bathe. Months on the road had left him mentally and physically spent.

Though he had severed the relationship for good, the details leading up to his divorce still hurt. He would be lying if he said he did not miss Julie on some level. But each time he thought of that message from the doctor's office on his answering machine, what little regret he harbored turned to rage. Nearing forty as a divorced man, with little chance of freeing his heart to the point he could invest in another monogamous relationship, stung like belly flopping into the icy waters of the North Atlantic. He had finally given up the notion he would ever have a child of his own. Julie did that. He would never forgive her.

And then there was Farin. What to do about her? Not even the deafening noise of sold-out venues could drown out her unanticipated declaration of love that day in Malibu. Yet despite her heartfelt profession, she did not trust him. Not even after all they had been through. Apparently she saw him less trustworthy than a smarmy reporter when it came to divulging the details about what Jameson had put her through and what had happened to Jordan. Anymore, he resented her as much as he still loved her.

Maybe Julie was right after all. Technically, he and Farin could brave his family's scorn and be together openly. No more secrets. No more hiding. They were both free now.

Or maybe not. Maybe they never would be.

The residual ringing in his ears from months of deafening performances still echoed in the stillness of his home as he rose and prepared his tea. Normally, he would have engaged his whole house audio system by now. Bach would surely set him right. But today, he relished the silence and solitude. He needed a break before returning calls, regrouping with his manager, touching base with Samantha about planning the next album, and re-engaging with his family. Just a couple of days to get his feet beneath him.

Instead, he found himself heading to Ben's as soon as he finished showering. Word had reached him the moment he left the Miami stadium where they had played the final night of the tour. Another family crisis. No surprise, it revolved around Farin.

"She couldn't have gone far," he reasoned as he studied her note with bleary eyes. "She has no resources and no way to move about."

"That's what I thought as well...before I spoke with my sons." Cheryl stood nearby, arms crossed, glaring at Derek and Kyle. "Might as well spill it," she scolded. "What have you two been up to?"

Derek stood sullen in the center of the room, hands plunged into his cargo shorts. "I've been helping her out is all. She's got no wheels. It didn't seem fair."

Ben stood by the floor-to-ceiling windows along the back of the room and peered out at his studio. "You said you took her to the church to meet some reporter a few months back?"

"I know about him," Chris interjected. "It's the same guy who's kept doing all those newspaper articles on Lockhardt. I talked to him after the first show back in LA."

Ben frowned at him. "The séance guy?"

Chris nodded. "He knows about her. In fact, I get the impression she's been confiding in him."

Cheryl's eyes widened with something between dread and hope. "Do you think she told him what happened with Jorie?"

Ben turned and studied his sons. "Maybe it's best if the boys go upstairs and let us talk this through."

"We're not babies anymore," Derek snapped. He nodded toward his brother. "Right?"

Kyle shrugged, then nodded uncomfortably.

"We've had to get over Uncle Jordan's death and all this mess with Aunt Farin just like you guys have. You think if you send us off to a friend's house for a night or a boating weekend we won't know something's going on? We're part of this family, too!"

Chris placed the note beside him, then leaned forward and lowered his weary head onto his hands. "You're right, mate. Ben, they should stay."

Ben said nothing. He sat down at the far end of the sectional opposite his brother and crossed his legs. "What else, then? Where else have you taken her?"

Derek shifted his weight, his eyes darting toward Chris then back to his father. "I've taken her to the reporter's house a few times and I dropped her off at Sawyer's once or twice."

Cheryl added, "And you picked her up from there that morning as well."

Chris felt like someone had shoveled gravel into his stomach. He lifted his head. "She's been seeing Sawyer?"

Ben cleared his throat. "Yeah. They're, uh...they've grown rather close."

"He's helping her with her new album," Derek added. "Me and the guys are doing the music."

Ben's forehead wrinkled above narrowed eyes. "You know about that, then?"

"Dad, you said we'd be getting album credit for playing back-up for some big name artist you didn't wanna name. I'm not stupid."

"And the rest of the boys? Do they know?"

"Not a chance. There's way too much crazy going on in this family right now. They probably wouldn't believe me if I told them."

"Wait," Chris said, shaking his head. "Farin's dating Derek's manager. And...now he's helping her with her album?"

Ben flattened his lips and nodded. "The guy's bloody brilliant."

"He is," Derek agreed almost apologetically.

"Does Sam know about this?"

"There's more, Ben," Cheryl interrupted. She gestured toward their youngest. "Kyle? Care to tell your father the rest?"

Kyle swallowed hard, then looked down at the floor and toed the carpet with his sneaker. "I think Aunt Farin might have gone to meet someone."

Simultaneously, Chris and Ben asked, "Who?"

He lifted his shoulders. "I don't know who he is. She met him online."

"*What?*" Chris exclaimed.

Ben cocked his head to the side and touched his hand to his mouth.

"Aunt Farin's been waiting until everyone's in bed and then coming in and using the computer in my room. I set her up with a screen name on AOL back on Derek's birthday. She was bored. I felt bad and wanted to give her something to do."

Cheryl pressed, "How did she meet this person? Is it a male or a female?"

"I don't know for sure, Mom. Farin didn't say, and there's no way to tell online. Heck, I could create a screen name that said I was a forty year old business woman. Who'd know the difference?"

Chris' eyes darted around the room as he processed the disturbing news.

"This was in one of those chat rooms you spoke about?"

He nodded. "But I also noticed her in IMs every once in a while."

"What are 'IMs'?"

"They're instant messages. Private conversations outside the chat rooms."

Cheryl let her arms fall to her sides. "Did you ever see what she and this person were talking about?"

"No. I wasn't gonna sneak up behind her and read over her shoulder."

"Might there be some sort of record of their communication?"

Kyle shook his head. "Chats aren't automatically saved. You have to create a log if you want to keep them. I never showed her how to do that."

"Can you get on under her screen name?" Ben suggested.

"Uh-uh. She's got her own password."

"Do we at least know if this was a local person she was talking to?"

"I dunno, Dad. I caught a glimpse of the screen name once when I woke up to get a drink of water, but I can't remember it."

Chris leaned back and stared up at the vaulted ceiling. "So basically, she could be anywhere—with anyone. For all we know, the old man could have set her up." He closed his eyes and tried to recall anything that might give them a clue to her whereabouts, then picked up the note and read through it again.

> *Ben and Cheryl,*
>
>   *Thank you for all you've done, but I need to take care of things once and for all. I wish I could explain, but I promise—it's almost over. I'll be in LA in time for the meeting. See you there.*
>
>   *Farin*

Derek's shoulders stooped as he edged closer to his father. "I need to get to practice. Did you need anything else before I go?"

Ben gave his son a disappointed frown. "I suppose not."

Cheryl brushed his arm as passed her on his way to the door. "Isn't Summer telling her folks today?"

He nodded sadly. "We're meeting at Sir Pizza after practice. I won't be home for dinner."

"It'll be fine," she soothed. "You'll see."

Derek doubled back to Chris and handed him a folded envelope he had retrieved from his back pocket. "Here. Aunt Farin left another note. It was on my dresser. She asked me to give this to Miles Macy if anything happened to her. I guess I should have said something before. I didn't want to rat her out, but maybe you should have this."

Chris stared at his nephew in openmouthed shock and nodded as he accepted the sealed envelope.

The minute Derek left, Chris tore through the seal. Ben scooted forward. "What does it say?"

Chris' face paled as he read. "'Miles, I took your advice, but I can't wait any longer. If anything happens to me, tell my family everything.'" He swallowed hard, then cursed under his breath. "This still doesn't explain how she's getting around. Did you two give her any money?"

Ben and Cheryl shook their heads.

"We would have," Cheryl said, "but she hasn't needed anything substantial since she's been here." Out of the corner of her eye, she saw Kyle dip his head and bite his upper lip. "What do you know, then?"

Kyle buried his hands in his jeans pockets, his face sheathed in guilt and regret. "She's got plenty of money."

"How do you know?" Ben asked.

"That big manila envelope she had in her room. It had tons of cash inside."

Chris' head jerked angrily as he uttered a voiceless curse. He bolted up from the sofa. "Kyle, come show me where you found the note."

Farin had left her room in pristine condition. Bed made. Dresser cleared off. Closet in order. Chris opened the night-stand drawers but found nothing but empty space. The small writing desk was bare, its drawers empty as well.

"She left most her clothes," Cheryl said as she leaned against the door frame. "That's a good sign. Seems she plans to come back."

Ben slipped his arm around his wife's waist. "She'd better come back. We just started making progress in the studio."

After finding nothing in the room that might provide a clue to her whereabouts, Ben and Cheryl followed Kyle to his room to see if they might be able to figure out Farin's password so they could go in and poke around. Chris stayed behind.

He sat at the desk and visually swept the room. Propped up in the far corner, he spied an old acoustic guitar and wondered if she had started learning to play. Ben had not mentioned it if she had. Besides her clothing, all she had left behind was the faint aroma of her perfume clinging to the curtains and bedding. Once again, she had disappeared from his life. Yet again, he had returned only to find her gone.

Ben popped his head in. "We couldn't figure out her password. Any suggestions?"

Chris shook his head, then shrugged. "There's nothing here."

"The meeting's in two weeks. She said she'd see us there. I don't know what else we can do. It's not like she wasn't free to leave."

"But there's no one to protect her out there."

Ben gave a thoughtful shake of his head. "She's a smart girl."

Chris scoffed. "Smart and stubborn. But Jameson's smarter. What if he concocted this ruse to get her out and alone?"

"We could call the police, but that would make for a complicated conversation, wouldn't it?"

"So, what, we just sit here for two weeks and hope she makes it to LA? How is it she can travel, anyway? Money's one thing, but she can't even buy a ticket anywhere. She's got no ID. I bet she's still local. Did you check her and Jordan's place?"

"We did that first thing. No trace of her."

Cheryl peeked her head in. "I'm fixing brunch. You'll join us, yeah?"

He nodded. "I'll be down straightaway."

Unsure what he thought he might find, he gave the room another once-over before heading downstairs. He checked under the bed, between the mattress and box springs, and beneath pillows, ran his hand along the underside of drawers, and searched the bathroom. Nothing.

As a last ditch effort, Chris knelt at the desk and ran his hand along the underside of its drawer and all around the bottom. He looked aside as he felt around, until he glanced inside the waste basket. Inside, there appeared to be several shredded pieces of paper.

He grabbed the basket and dumped its meager contents on top of the desk. A dozen or so bits of paper and one larger crumpled ball fell onto its surface. He checked to ensure he had them all, then returned the small can to its place beside the desk.

Each tiny section of paper had a single letter written on it. Carefully, he spread the pieces about the desk top. Es, As, Ls, Ns...all in Farin's handwriting, all seemingly torn to shreds after having been written on a pad of lined paper. Unfortunately, he had not found the pad anywhere in the room.

He uncrumbled and smoothed out the larger intact piece and peered at the writing, confused as he read. The name "Jade Larken Trongly" was written near the center but had been scratched out with a single line. Beneath it, she had written the name "Jordan Kelley Grant."

"What the—?"

The Trongly name did not ring a bell. Worse, Jordan's name made no sense as written. His middle name had been Andrew.

Frustrated at his inability to figure out the significance of the names, he began pushing the torn bits of paper around. On a hunch, he arranged them to spell out the "Jordan" name. But no. It was missing an R and the Y. Perhaps the bits spelled something different.

He inspected the waste can again and discovered one of the pieces had lodged within the folds of the liner. It was an R. Despite a more careful search, he did not find a Y.

When he again returned the can to its place, he glimpsed another piece of paper on the floor, partially hidden by one of the desk legs. He leaned down to pick it up. When he turned it over, he hitched his breath. Y.

Cheryl called up from the bottom of the stairs. "You coming, then? We're about ready to eat."

"Sorry! I'll be right down," he shouted back. Hurrying now, he slid the last two letters in place. Together, they spelled out "Jordan Kelley Grant." He studied the crinkled paper again. All at once, a wave of nausea assaulted him.

It could not be.

Hands shaking with fearful anticipation, he rearranged the letters. When he finished, the name "Jade Larken Trongly" lay before him.

Chris' shoulders slumped as the implications hit him. He brushed the bits of paper into a single pile, then scooped them up along with the crumbled paper and headed downstairs, shoving them into his pocket as his pace increased. He called ahead, "Someone get me a phone!"

***

"The car's here," Bobby called from the living room. "Ready to go get yourself a couple of moonmen?"

Through the closed bedroom door, he heard the toilet flush for the third time in forty-five minutes. Poor thing. She had battled frayed nerves since hearing about her nominations.

He moved aside when she opened the door and stepped out in her glistening silver and crystal ensemble. "Wow. You look...*amazing.*"

Joni's perfectly stained lips lifted into a nervous smile as she gave her coiffed updo several self-conscious pats. "Does my hair still look all right? Baby, I'm so embarrassed for you to see me like this. I guess the good news is there's no more lunch to lose. I think I've gone through an entire bottle of mouthwash, though."

"It'll be fine. And your hair looks beautiful."

"I don't know if I'm ready for this. Six months ago, I was milkin' cows in Cedarcreek, Missouri. Now, I'm wearin' a Gucci dress on my way to the MTV VMAs. I think Momma and Daddy have the whole town meetin' together in their living room to watch."

"They're proud of you. We all are." He grabbed her matching handbag off the dresser. "Here."

She thanked him, then paused and cupped his cheek with a trembling hand. "You've been so wonderful. How did God know you were the perfect man for me? Every night, I thank Him for you—well, for you and everything you've done. You've changed my life, Bobby."

Gazing into her violet eyes, his heart swelled. "You've done more for me than I've done for you, Joni. That, I promise."

She kissed him, careful not to smudge her face or stain his. "Okay, then. I'm ready if you are."

"No more nerves?"

"Hold my hand and I can face anything."

Between the usual Manhattan commuter traffic and the influx of limousines lined up for curbside delivery of the music industry's elite, the three mile trip from LSI's Upper West Side luxury apartment to Radio City Music Hall took over an hour.

"You'd mentioned earlier you had somethin' to tell me," Joni said as their car inched into the queue for drop off.

He kissed her hand. "We've got all night."

"Is it good news?"

"It sure is, but I'll tell you after we get back. Tonight's your night."

"There's no way I'll win, but I'm sure excited about the nominations."

"You don't know. You could surprise them all."

Her eyes sparkled as they reflected the neon lights of the buildings outside their car. "I'm serious. This is enough for me. Enough for tonight."

Bobby laughed as the limo pulled up to the red carpet and an attendant immediately opened their door. "You mean you're not one of those ego-centric, award-seeking, hair-pulling, hate-you-behind-your-back types?"

She brushed by him as she extended a graceful hand to the attendant and exited the vehicle. "Oh, I am. Just not the first time. You'll see."

Joni Leighton had racked up two MTV Video Award nominations: Best New Artist in a Video and Viewer's Choice. The debut video for her chart-conquering single, "I Fall Again," had been released a mere three months before the nomination deadline and had received instant critical and fan acclaim.

Despite the glitz and grandeur of attending her first awards show alongside artists she had only ever seen on TV, Bobby doubted she could possibly feel more nervous excitement than he. Whether Joni won or lost, he was the real winner tonight. He had the girl. He had the reputation as the man who had resurrected a dying company. And, as of eleven o'clock this morning, he had a clean bill of mental health.

"While I'd recommend you continue on with your therapist while you adjust to this life change and find a way to work through your issues with your father," Dr. Stumpf had said, "I see no reason at this time to continue seeing you for medication management."

Bobby had peered at his psychiatrist with saucer-like eyes. "So you were right?"

The doctor had nodded. "I've ruled out schizophrenia. Over the last few months, we've tapered you down and then completely off the Haldol. Other than the anticipated side effects of coming off the drug itself, you've demonstrated no symptoms of the disorder."

The details of how Childs had reached his irresponsible diagnosis still left him confused, but the freedom of no longer living like a slave to injected drugs for fear of losing his mind made him nearly giddy. All day, his thoughts had exploded with dreams and plans for his future. In every one of them Charlene Johnson, a.k.a. Joni Leighton, stood center stage.

Arm in arm, they strode down the red carpet leading from the curb to the entrance. The cheers and clamoring for Joni's attention periodically drew him back a step or two in deference to the paparazzi and photo journalists endeavoring to capture a perfect shot of the budding young singer. She smiled and waved to fans held at bay by temporary barriers amid exploding camera lenses. The press competed for her attention for quick interviews. She stopped for *E!*, *Entertainment Tonight*, and a host of cable and network news reporters. They fawned over her dress, raved over her song and video, asked about her thoughts on her meteoric rise on the charts, and wished her a successful night.

For the most part, Bobby fell back and watched, mesmerized by her charm, her sweet smile, and her seemingly natural repartee with the interviewers. A few reporters pulled him forward and asked questions about their relationship. They relayed little, but the way they looked at one another said it all.

Some asked for an update on his father's imminent retirement. Bobby either changed the subject or, if pressed, declined to comment. He would not allow discussion of his father to ruin this perfect evening.

"You all right?" Joni whispered as they finally took their seats before the show began. "You've been actin' a little funny about your dad. Anything I can do to help?"

He adjusted himself in his seat and unbuttoned his jacket, then took her hand and kissed the tips of her fingers. "You've already helped."

She searched his eyes as she beamed up at him. A moment later, she barely contained a squeal of delight. "Oh my gosh, I think I just saw Michael Jackson! And isn't that Ed Kowalczyk from Live? And over there, there's Alanis Morissette!"

Watching Joni enjoy the event and the performers made it feel new to him as well. He had attended so many awards shows, the thrill had long since ebbed away. But tonight, though she had accurately predicted her ultimate loss of both awards for which they had nominated her, he felt star-struck...for her alone.

At the end of the evening, she nuzzled into him as the limo drove them back to her apartment.

"You sure you don't want to make the afterparty rounds?"

She smiled contentedly and shook her head. "I want to be right here with you."

He hoped she would still feel the same once he told her his news. Something assured him she would.

***

The guest bedroom in Alicia's home had transformed over the last couple of weeks. She had given the unused full size mattress and matching bed set that had occupied its space to her oldest niece, who had complained for weeks to her father about needing to graduate out of her twin. A futon now filled the space. It gave her the flexibility to sit and stare at the once bare wall opposite the furniture, which she had turned into a crime wall, or take a cat nap when all the facts and photos connected with sometimes intersecting lengths of string secured with push pins made her head swim.

Once she had considered her home her private space, a refuge where she could let her hair down and decompress. Now, Bridgeman practically lived there with her. And as if that were not bad enough, they would soon add a federal agent to the mix.

Bridgeman came in carrying two cups of coffee and handed her one. "I just got off the phone with Hub. His plane landed about fifteen minutes ago. We ready?"

She blew on her mug, then took a careful sip. "As ready as we can be. I still wish we didn't have to turn over our files. We've got a pretty solid story now, what with the information in those boxes."

He shrugged as he studied the wall. "Let's just see what he has to say."

"From what you told me, Billy, he's not saying much. He's happy to take what we give him, but he doesn't seem to grasp the 'quid pro quo' concept."

"We still have Macy in our back pocket."

She scoffed. "What good is he? He's been in LA for weeks."

"But he's got the witness."

"No, partner, he *says* he's got the witness."

"The guy can't help it if he has an assignment, Al."

She harrumphed. "Convenient excuse. Just another reason I don't trust men."

"Ouch!"

"Romantically," she clarified.

"So if this witness pans out in the end, you gonna take it all back and cut the guy some slack?"

She walked her coffee to the futon and set the mug down on a coaster atop the end table before taking her seat. "If Miles Macy presents an actual witness to the Grant shooting *or* the rigging of the limousine, I'll even agree to go out on an official date with him."

Bridgeman whistled. "Wow. You must be warming up to the guy. I guess absence really does make the heart grow fonder."

She flashed him a cynical side eye. "No. That just shows you how sure I am he's nothing but another windbag."

Hubbell arrived on her front doorstep with his suitcase in one hand and a leather portfolio in the other. "I decided to come straight over instead of checking in to my hotel first. Traffic's a nightmare. I didn't want to waste any time."

Alvarez showed him inside and shook his hand, which by comparison made hers feel like a toddler's. "The wall's in the back bedroom. Help yourself to something to drink." She pointed at the kitchen. "And Penny sent some snacks over with Billy. I don't cook. She's the designated chef of the family."

He chuckled and gave her a curt nod. "I just need to visit the little boy's room first. I'll be there shortly."

A few minutes later, he joined them in the room balancing a plate of finger sandwiches, macaroni salad, and a Mango Madness Snapple. He had tucked the leather portfolio under one arm. His height and full frame made for close quarters. It had never occurred to Alicia how low her ceilings were until Hubbell had to dip his head slightly to get through the bedroom door.

He bobbed his head in approval as he assessed the space and scrutinized the wall. Alicia watched his eyes linger a beat longer on the three boxes of evidence they had received from Irene Stark. Intuition, she figured. Impressive.

Bridgeman gestured to a table so Hubbell could set down his plate, then shook his hand. "Al's done a great job getting things in order. Hopefully we can put our heads together and figure out our next steps, including any coordination of resources."

He swallowed a mouthful of salad and pointed to the wall. "Just so we're all on the same page, let's recap. According to the reports, on December 13, 1991, Jordan Grant was murdered in Coral Gables at the home of one of the top executives of his record label. The only witness to the shooting was his wife. Purportedly, the property owner-slash-resident was inpatient at a mental facility in Raleigh, North Carolina at the time of the incident."

Bridgeman and Alvarez interrupted, talking over one another in their attempt to relay the new details they had learned from their recent interview with Imani Vaughn.

Hubbell held up a finger and continued. "Metro only interrogated one suspect—the vic's brother—who was on the scene when the local police arrived. The witness had fled the scene and was not apprehended despite an extensive manhunt ranging from Miami to Orlando. Three days later, there was a vehicle explosion on a Miami bridge that later turned out to be the witness' limousine. A local newspaper reporter claimed to have received word from her asking for a press conference after the vic's funeral. He'd tracked her down to a Key Biscayne hotel and was on his way to interview her when he saw the explosion. The hotel later verified she'd stayed there under an assumed name. Dental records later confirmed the identity of our witness and the driver."

Bridgeman added, "And then the lead detective on the case hid evidence, falsified reports, and pushed the 'failed robbery' theory for the murder while circumventing fire investigators' requests for further investigation on the burned limo, which he later deemed an accident. Despite our initial suspicions, we don't think anyone higher up in our department was involved in a cover-up."

Hubbell nodded. "The additional information you collected from the limo flagged our system as a match to the homemade incendiary devices used in several cases the Bureau's been looking at for the last few years."

Alvarez piped in, "And for your guy—the ghost—to be the one who rigged our explosion, there would have to be something bigger at stake than one homicide."

"We've received some further information and can confidently rule out the failed robbery angle." Bridgeman added. "In fact, we think we've just about figured out a motive."

Hubbell gestured toward the board. "You two mentioned having some phone records linking Stark to the record label."

"Yes," Alvarez told him. "Jameson Lockhardt. His son owns the Coral Gables house."

Hubbell grabbed the portfolio and retrieved a glossy photo amongst several newspaper articles, then approached the crime wall. Several unused push pins stuck to the bottom right of the enormous cork board covering the wall. He grabbed one and stabbed it through the top of the photo, securing it above Lockhardt's picture.

"Who's that?" Alvarez asked.

"I did a little digging into the illustrious Mr. Lockhardt," Hubbell said. "Clever man. Originally came to the States from London back in late 1967. I'm still checking with the Yard, but so far, they've found no priors. Not from a Jameson Lockhardt, anyway."

"You think he changed his name?" Bridgeman asked.

"I'd bet my career on it."

Alvarez studied the picture of the smileless face Hubbell had stuck to the wall. The man was not altogether unattractive for an older man. Close-cut gray hair, well-groomed beard and mustache, slightly blotchy skin, and blue eyes that looked as if he had seen a thing or two in his day. Experienced eyes. Eyes that warned you not to get too close.

Hubbell continued, "The first mention of Jameson Lockhardt appears to be his British passport, issued mid-November of 1967. It was put to almost immediate use. Lockhardt arrived in America in mid-January 1968."

Alvarez pointed to the wall. "So who's this guy? What's he got to do with any of this?"

"This is the man who brought him to America. I'm still looking into the specifics of their association. I don't see they had any verifiable interaction after the immigration, but that doesn't necessarily mean anything."

Bridgeman shrugged. "You're losing me here, Hub."

Hubbell stabbed his finger at the picture. "This man is one of only two Brits ever to be accepted by the American mob. Not a *made* man, but a close 'friend' of several of the most notorious New York crime families in the country. Back in the UK this guy was a henchman for one of the most infamous music men around. Agented a lot of the big rock artists of the era and on into the '70s. Notably, he also had close ties with the Firm."

"'Firm.' That doesn't ring a bell."

"Arguably the most notorious East End gang of the '50s and '60s. Mostly gambling and protection rackets. Its two leaders were arrested in the spring of '68 and eventually convicted of murder."

Alvarez sat down on the futon and folded her arms. Rock stars and gangsters. Where was he going with all of this? "I still don't see what that has to do with our case."

Hubbell shrugged and returned to his plate, then shoved an entire finger sandwich in his mouth. He chased it down with half his drink. "Maybe nothing. But it does establish Jameson Lockhardt as having some pretty interesting connections that precede establishing his label. At least enough to know how to hire someone to take care of any problems he might have. Maybe Lockhardt hired the ghost we're trying to find to handle a loose end."

Bridgeman cleared his throat and indicated the boxes on the floor. "I think you may be right. These boxes contain the missing evidence we couldn't locate. Turns out Detective Stark had them at his place—a nice piece of real estate in the Southwest he could have never afforded on a cop's salary. Anyway, we also interviewed the driver's former girlfriend. She says he was planning on coming in to give a statement on the Grant murder. Seems Bobby Lockhardt wasn't in North Carolina at the time of the murder after all."

Hubbell casually munched his food. "He wasn't. They admitted him the day after the murder."

Alvarez's lips parted. "When did you find out?"

He held the back of his hand up to his mouth as he chuckled, nearly choking on a bite of salad. "Last week. Did you know Lockhardt's son's a schizophrenic?"

Bridgeman and Alvarez exchanged looks as more pieces of the puzzle locked into place. With what they had learned from the contents of the safe deposit box about Bobby's part in Farin's father's death, coupled with the rape, it made sense.

"His doctor died a few months back. Quack of a physician. Seems he worked exclusively for Lockhardt like some corporate physician. Who the hell has one of those?"

Bridgeman thought a moment. "We're almost certain Bobby Lockhardt's our man for the murder. At the very least, he was there. We need to bring him in for questioning. But before we do that, we need to officially reopen the case. I understand the limo explosion's part of the FBI's ongoing investigation into this ghost assassin, but the Grant murder's still local. There're other crimes we're looking at him for as well, but there are jurisdictional issues."

Hubbell's eyes flitted across the board as if mentally connecting the dots. He scratched his bald chin, then turned back to the detectives. "I can't have you officially reopen this case yet," he said. "If you do, the press'll jump all over it. If Lockhardt *is* involved, it could spook him and probably alert the ghost. Let's go through the evidence you have here and we'll figure out who needs what."

"Some of this stuff dates back to 1973," Bridgeman said. "There's a lot more than just an exploding limousine and a dead celebrity."

Hubbell snatched up his portfolio and removed several newspaper clippings, which he tacked onto the board. "Hell yes, there's more. I haven't even begun to tell you about the trail of bodies we've found all around Lockhardt's associates. His lawyer's wife, some FSB employees, potentially even one of the Raleigh nurses who took care of the son during his stay in that nut house. Oh, and those glasses you bagged from the limo? They belonged to his former secretary, Nancy Chambers."

Bridgeman nodded gravely. "We heard about her. Missing person report on her around the time of the explosion."

He nodded. "Right. And you find her glasses in the limo? Strange coincidence, dontcha think?"

"What about the cell phone?"

Hubbell shook his head. "Couldn't trace it. Anyway, there're plenty of other leads and people to interview, but until we assess the rest of *this* evidence, I don't want to risk pulling the son in."

"We can't continue our investigation without interviewing more people," Alvarez protested.

"I realize that, but before we go for the big players, we need to chip away at their wall of silence. The son's not going to say anything, especially if he's the one who dropped the hammer on the vic. We have to assume Daddy's helping him cover it up."

Bridgeman's nostrils flared as his eyes darted across the board. "That's our working theory at this point."

"I've been watching someone lately who may be willing to shed some light on this. I'm hoping I can convince him to talk."

"Who?" Bridgeman asked.

"The lawyer. His extremely fit wife took an unfortunate, and fatal, fall in her shower back in February."

CHAPTER 21

T HE THIRD TIME CHRIS CALLED Miles Macy's office, he lost most the civility he had originally employed. He needed to get to Ben and Cheryl's soon so they could leave for the airport. At least that was the plan. If Macy had any reason for him to stay behind, Chris needed to know now.

His voice strained with frustration. "You told him it's urgent we speak?"

"Yes. I told him when he called in earlier this week."

"Did he give you any hint if or when he'd call me back?"

"Maybe I could help you better if you told me what's so important."

He opened his mouth to speak, then stopped short. Rubbing the tips of his fingers against his forehead, he tried a calmer tone. "Jeanne—it is Jeanne, right?"

"That's correct."

"Jeanne, I'd love to sit here and explain all the whys, but I'm about ready to catch a flight to LA. Now, I know Macy's there covering the Simpson trial, but I need to speak to him in the next three hours. How about you give me the name of his hotel, or another number I can reach him at? Does he have a cell phone?"

"I really wish I could help. The best I can do is tell him you called again. Since you'll be in LA, maybe he'll call you and arrange a time to talk. There really isn't anything else I can do. I'm sorry."

He stared out his kitchen window into the bright, sunny morning. A fleeting image of Farin sunbathing poolside stole into his thoughts. It had never occurred to him when she lived with him that life could get any more challenging. Now, he longed for its lesser complications. "All right. But this time, tell him I want to know what he's got on Jade Trongly." He spelled the name at Jeanne's request.

"Did you want to leave the name of your hotel or just the cell?"

"Just the cell. That way I'll get his call no matter where I am."

"You got it. Anything else?"

"Yeah. One more thing. Tell the bloody bastard he should give you a raise. You make one hell of a bulldog."

When he ended the call, he ran upstairs to grab his bags, then placed them in the foyer. The big mystery meeting would take place day after tomorrow. Hopefully, Macy would contact him by the time he arrived in LA later tonight and they could meet sometime tomorrow.

He had driven himself batty trying to figure out the contents of Farin's waste basket. He had a hunch, but could not fully accept the implications. If right, he had more questions than answers. It would, however, explain why she had left. He opted to keep his theory to himself.

The top of his desk looked like an unassembled ransom note, its littered bits of paper arranged to spell out the names listed on the letter. Given Farin's cryptic instructions to Macy, Chris had no doubt the reporter could shed some light on their significance. After the recent urgent pleas to discuss the situation with Farin, it seemed odd the reporter would avoid talking to him now. Odd and ironic. Chris had never tried so hard to speak to a member of the press.

His phone rang, sending him rushing back to his kitchen where he had left his handset. He stabbed the call button and answered before checking his caller ID.

"Wow. You sound out of breath. Everything okay?"

"Marci, hiyah. Yes, sorry. I'm expecting a call."

"Have you heard anything?"

He walked over and sank into one of his kitchen chairs. "Not a thing. How about on your end?"

"Afraid not. I'm half expecting her to show up on our doorstep. She always did that before."

"Makes you miss her more dependent days, doesn't it?"

"Right?"

"Ben says we shouldn't worry unless she doesn't show up for the meeting."

"You don't think she'd go up to New York and confront Lockhardt, do you?"

"I think she's still local. I think she has to be."

They discussed various theories about where she might have gone and why she left. All stabs in the dark. Chris asked if Marci had ever heard the name Jade Trongly. She had not.

"Sam says she's on the invite list for the meeting."

"I've never heard that name in my life. Did Sam say whether she'd heard from Farin?"

He snorted and dropped his head in his hand. "She's only finished half an album. The last person she'll call is Sam." Less cynically, he said, "I hope she's all right."

"She's been through a lot, Chris. More than that, she's survived a lot. Something tells me she's okay. Just stubborn. You know her. As for me, it's two weeks before my due date and I'm big as a house. I have to keep myself as upbeat as possible, so I refuse to consider the worst."

"You and El excited, then? Everything going as planned?"

"The doctor says I'm fine. I'm drinking tons of water and keeping my feet up when I can. Been having some Braxton Hicks the last couple days. Other than that, I feel great. In fact, I've had this incredible burst of energy over the last few days. You should see the house—it's spotless!"

He leaned back more casually in the chair and crossed his ankles. "Yeah? Well, take it easy. Ivy thought her contractions were false alarms and look what happened to her."

"I can only hope my labor goes as smoothly. From contractions over a late breakfast to a baby by six that night. Technically, Lance could have played the show."

"I still tease him about making me replace him last minute."

"Ivy's going to be so happy to fly back home Saturday. She says she's tired of living in hotels. Can't say I blame her. It'd be rough trying to settle in with a newborn knowing anything you purchase will have to be either shipped back to England or abandoned and replaced once you're home. I offered to have them stay with us. I told her you, Ben, and Cheryl wouldn't mind roughing it in a hotel, but I think she and Lance like the privacy. She says little Hugh's got a big appetite but isn't too fussy. That's good."

"I've never seen so much hair on a baby. Derek had a decent amount, but nothing like that kid."

"Are the boys staying on their own while you're here or with friends?"

"They were campaigning pretty hard to stay at home, but Cheryl made arrangements for them to stay with friends."

"I can't believe the news about Summer."

Chris exhaled a deep breath and drummed his fingers on his kitchen table. "Yeah. Quite the shocker, that one. I guess Derek hasn't seen her since the day before she told her parents. He keeps calling but they say she's either unavailable or not home. She hasn't even been in school. Derek's torn up about it. Won't even talk to me. "

"I hate to hear that. He's a good kid."

"He is. Anyway, I need to get over to Ben's. Call me if you hear anything from Farin. Our plane leaves at two."

"Elliot's got the itinerary. He'll be there to pick everyone up. Your rooms are all ready."

"Brilliant, thanks. See you tonight."

On the way over to Ben's, Chris stopped at the house on Matheson to check for any sign of Farin. He searched each room, inspected the locks on the doors and windows, and peeked inside the trash cans. Not so much as a strand of hair or a fast food wrapper.

When he arrived at Ben's, he pulled into one of the open garage bays and parked, then carried his bags inside through the kitchen. At first, the house seemed abandoned. Then, he found Cheryl on her way in from the patio.

She kissed his cheek, then busied herself emptying the dishwasher. "You can set your bags in the entryway with ours. Your brother's out in the studio. I'm just making sure everything's handled before we go."

He peered through the back curtains, then craned his head to glimpse the family room as he headed to deposit his things. "Kids at school?"

"Aye, at least physically. Can't say they're there mentally. Probably trying to devise some manipulation to stay home on their own. I wouldn't mind so much under normal circumstances. But between Summer's pregnancy and all the mess with Farin, we just didn't feel right about it. Derek's suffering something terrible over Summer."

He arranged his bags, then returned to the kitchen. "Still no word?"

She shook her head sadly. "I worry. The Reeces are a respectable family, but the father's a harsh man. Stern business type. You know what I mean. Enviable career, perfect wife, perfect home. Strict man. Hope his daughter's worth more than his pride. I guess we'll see."

"Anything I can do? I tried to take Derek out on the boat last weekend, but he said he had practice."

"He's burying himself in his music, for sure."

Chris rested his elbows on the kitchen island. "I understand that."

"Of course you do," she chirped knowingly, giving him a side eye and a wry grin. "Hero worship and all. The lad's more like you every day. Now go get my husband and tell him we're ready to go. We're stopping on the way to the airport for lunch."

Chris stood and knocked on the counter, then headed out to the studio. As he drew near, he cocked his head and narrowed his eyes in concentration, trying to discern what sounded like two voices coming from inside. When he opened the door and stepped in, his demeanor visibly shifted.

Ben welcomed him with a smile and indicated a seat. "Sawyer and I were just discussing Farin's album."

He nodded, jaw set, lips pushed to one side as he sat down and pivoted his chair to face Ben. "Hopefully, she'll come back to finish it."

Sawyer leaned against the wall by the door, thumbs hooked into his jeans pockets, one foot hiked up behind him. "She'll be back. If there's one thing I've learned about her, it's that she always comes around. Maybe she just needed to get out and clear her head."

Chris' face contorted into a barely contained sneer of rage, his nostrils flared as he slowly turned his chair to address the stranger who had wedged his foot into the door of his family. "Oh really? You've 'learned' that about her in the three minutes you've known her, have you? Good thing you were here.

I'd started worrying."

Sawyer's unaffected chuckled grated on Chris' nerves. "No need to worry, buddy. If she comes back while you're gone, she knows who to call. I promise she'll be in good hands."

Ben dipped his head slightly. He stood up, slid his hand into the back of his jeans to smooth his shirt, then hiked his waistband. "I think we're about finished for now."

Chris jerked out of his seat and yanked the door open. He stepped outside and called back over his shoulder, "Ben, Cheryl told me to tell you we're ready to leave."

***

Samantha could tell by Deborah's stunned expression that she had perplexed her assistant when she had insisted on personally verifying the boardroom setup met her specifications. For a long time she stood inside the double doors, arms crossed, a crooked index finger across her top lip as her eyes surveyed the space. Tomorrow needed to go off without a hitch. Every detail mattered.

A leather portfolio containing a pen, a pad of paper, and a nondisclosure agreement lay atop a desk pad before each of the fifteen assigned seats surrounding the twenty foot boat shaped conference room table. They would not require any audiovisual equipment, so she had stowed the various Ethernet cords and plugs into the data ports.

Since Ross would lead the meeting, she had reserved the seat at the head of the table for him. She would sit opposite him, closest to the door, ensuring Deborah's easy access should she need to pull her away for any unforeseen issue needing her immediate presence. In keeping with the ruse Ross had concocted in his attempt to prevent Jameson from expecting anything, she had convinced Minor 6th's board that a delicate meeting would take place here and it would better serve the company if all nonessential personnel stayed off the seventh floor. Her stellar reputation bought their agreement. And, in fairness, she had not lied—technically.

Seating had challenged her, what with the various egos and entanglements of the group. Word had gotten back to her over the summer. Todd still resented Chris, though the two had managed to declare a sort of truce enabling them to remain intact throughout the tour. Todd's drug habit grew increasingly worrisome. Issues had erupted between him and Lance as well after the discovery that Todd had fathered Ivy's first child. A couple of people had claimed Faith spent the first night in LA in Chris' hotel room. Who knew what that meant? And then there was the intensity between Chris and Farin. Minor 6th's conference room was large, but it was anyone's guess if it was big enough to contain this group for two hours—especially once Farin appeared for the big reveal.

Hopefully, she had found her way to LA. They would know by ten o'clock tomorrow.

Two long credenzas butted up against the long, wall-length privacy windows. The west facing room meant the sun would allow them to leave the blinds open, though they might shut them anyway as an extra precaution. They would use the credenzas as buffet tables. Deborah had ordered a beverage service with an assortment of juices, bottled water, soft drinks, and coffee as well as an assortment of fruit, pastries, muffins, and breakfast breads.

Deborah peeked her head inside as Sam's cell phone rang. The caller ID told her it was the florist. She rejected the call, sending it to voicemail, then gave Deborah a patient smile. "What's up?"

"Is there anything you need me to do or change or...?"

Sam turned back and gave the room a last look. "It's perfect. I love it. Thank you for doing this. I love the personalized place cards. Great touch."

"Thanks. Ross Alexander just called and said he needed to speak to you. He said to call him at home."

Her face paled. "Home? He's not here in LA yet?"

Deborah shrugged. "I guess not."

Sam thanked and dismissed Deborah, then took a seat at one of the extra chairs lining the back wall. Before she could dial Ross' number on her cell, the missed call indicator light blinked. She checked the time and pursed her lips. A half hour late for her final wedding dress fitting. Not good. Not good at all.

She rushed back to her office, grabbed her purse, told Deborah she would return in a couple of hours, then called the designer back and said she would be there in twenty minutes. Her second call went to New York. "Why aren't you here already? Is everything okay?"

"I thought I told you I wouldn't be in until today. Jameson knows I've got business there tomorrow, but I figured it would give him less time to worry if he believed I had little idle time between my flight and my meetings."

She sighed with relief. "So you're okay."

"Yes. I'm sorry to have worried you. I'll leave for the airport within the hour and arrive late tonight."

"And you said Jameson knows. That went as planned?"

"Megan played her part perfectly. Jameson was quite excited when she called and told him she'd like to discuss re-signing with LSI. He didn't hesitate having me fly out to meet with her under your nose."

"Good. And I'll ask even though I'm sure I know the answer. Have you heard from Farin?"

"No."

Sam stopped for a red light at the corner of Wilshire and Doheny and leaned back onto the head rest. After all the months of involving her fiancé in a potentially life-threatening ordeal, surreptitiously organizing a contract for a long-dead singing phenom, and arranging a meeting designed to end one of the most notorious mega-moguls in music history, she had no more fight in her. She had a wedding to finalize.

Her life with Ethan had settled into a nice rhythm. Two months from now they would be honeymooning in Positano, far from the chaos of LA. Just this last hurdle to jump.

"And what about Jade Trongly? Chris mentioned something about her when he called and told me Farin had taken off."

"He did?"

"Mm-hmm. I meant to mention it before but my mind's been preoccupied lately with the wedding plans. Is she coming?"

A paused filled the line. "I'm, uh...I'm not sure now. I lost track of her."

"Is she important? Can we continue on without her?"

"Let's hope we don't have to."

The light turned green and Sam continued on, making a left and heading northward through sparse traffic. "Well, call me when you get in tonight. I hope you have a safe flight." She waited for his reply. When it did not come, she frowned. "You still there, Ross?"

His voice became little more than a whisper. "Oh no."

"What is it?"

"This black sedan with tinted windows just pulled into my driveway."

Her stomach flipped. "Who is it?"

"I'm not sure."

"Are you okay? Should you call the police?"

"Something tells me they're already here."

***

Derek eased into the pickup queue at the MAST Academy. He lifted his chin as Kyle waved and jogged toward the Blazer. When the boy had deposited his backpack in the rear and hopped in the front seat, Derek wove through several cars to exit the school, then headed for home. He glanced at his brother. "Did they buy it?"

"Sure did."

"So they don't expect you back?"

"Nope. What did you say to them anyway?"

"I didn't."

Kyle eyeballed him with a mixture of suspicion and curiosity. "Then who did?"

"Don't worry about it. Let's grab some grub before we go home."

They cruised through the village with the music up and the windows down, despite the fact that the under-90 weather felt a good ten degrees hotter. Derek had played Bush's *Sixteen Stone* so much, his CD should have worn out by now. Instead, he increased the volume when "Little Things" came on and sang-shouted at the top of his voice while Kyle rode patiently in the passenger's seat. When it ended, Derek turned the player down and asked if Kyle wanted burgers, pizza, or Chinese.

He shrugged and looked out the side window. "I don't care. Whatever you want, I guess. I'm not that hungry."

"What's wrong? I thought you wanted to stay at home."

"I do. But you know we're gonna get caught."

"Psh. No way."

"If Mom and Dad call to check up on us and they find out someone called and said they were coming home early…"

Derek gave a cocky, doubtful shake of his head and rested his wrist atop the steering wheel. "No one's gonna call. They're too wrapped up with all that junk going on in LA. I'll take you back over there if you want, though."

Kyle hunched slightly and peered down at the floor mat.

Derek hit his signal to make a U-turn but Kyle stopped him. "No! I wanna stay home with you!"

"Okay, then. Now what'll it be?"

They grabbed four Stromboli blankets from Sir Pizza and drove on to the house. Derek parked next to Chris' porch, shut the garage door, and told Kyle they could grab their gear after dinner. Instead, they ate and played five straight hours of *Air Combat* and *Ridge Racer* on the PlayStation their father had surprised them with earlier in the month.

"Why aren't you going to practice tonight?"

"I canceled. What's it to you?"

"Was Summer at school today?" Kyle asked in a small voice.

Derek stared straight ahead as if entirely engrossed in navigating his F-4 Phantom to drop missiles on enemy targets. "Nope."

"Have you talked to her?"

"Nope."

"What're you gonna do?"

"Just shut up and play, dufus."

By ten o'clock, Kyle had nodded off on the couch. Derek nudged him awake and told him to go upstairs. He secured the house and went to bed, but tossed and turned for a couple of hours, unable to shut his mind down long enough to sleep.

Figuring the physical exertion of a dip in the pool might help, he trudged back downstairs and swam laps. At 2 AM he headed back upstairs, none too convinced it had helped. As he hit the light switch downstairs, there came a knock at the door. Cautiously, he checked the peep hole. When he recognized the face on his doorstep, her hurriedly unlocked the door and yanked it open.

Summer raced into his arms, sobbing incoherently. He fused his eyes shut and held her to him, unable to talk at first. He shushed and petted her hair until he finally uttered the words, "It'll be okay, babe. I promise."

"My..." Her words came through in spasmodic stammers as he ushered her inside and closed the door behind them. "My dad s-says I have to give th-the baby away."

"*What?*" Derek pulled back and searched her red, swollen eyes. "What are you talking about? I thought we'd agreed to have our parents get together with us and talk about this."

She shook her head mournfully as the tears spilled down her cheeks. "They're sending m-me away. I have an au-aunt in New England..."

"No!" Derek cried. "They can't do that! It's my baby, too, and I won't let you go!"

Kyle padded down the staircase, rubbing his sleepy eyes with his fists. "Are you guys okay?"

"Go back upstairs, Kyle!" Derek shouted. "Stay out of this!"

"D-don't yell at h-him," Summer pleaded. "It's not his f-fault."

When Kyle reached the bottom step and dared to approach her with open arms, Summer wept as she moved into the embrace. "H-how you doing, little g-guy?"

He looked at her with big eyes. "You okay, Summer?"

She painted on a brave but unconvincing smile. "I-I'll be f-fine now that I've seen y-you. But Derek's r-right. You sh-should go back up t-to bed, sweet-h-heart."

Kyle studied them both, then grudgingly agreed. Summer watched him disappear up the steps. When she turned back around, Derek was gone, only to return a moment later jingling his keys.

"What are you doing?" she asked, wild-eyed. "Where are you going?"

"I'm going to your place to talk to your dad."

She reached for his arm. "No, Derek, you can't! They'd kill me if they knew I was here!"

Derek pulled away and faced her. "So now you're not allowed to see me?"

"They've kept me at the house since I told them about the baby. After dinner tonight they told me I had to leave for Connecticut tomorrow."

"I won't let you go, Summer. I'll talk to you dad. We can work this out!"

She buried her head in her hands and sobbed. Derek encircled her in his arms. "What am I going to do?"

"You could stay here," he suggested. "My mom and dad'll help."

"They threatened to call the police if I ran away."

"Then we'll run away together, somewhere no one can find us."

"And what? Hide out for the next year until we're eighteen? What about your life here? Your family? Your band?"

"You matter more to me than *any* of that. Don't you understand?"

"Don't say that," she begged. "It only makes it harder. We have to think of the baby. This isn't right."

He bit the side of his cheek as he tried in desperation to come up with a reasonable option. "You could call family services."

She sniffed and shook her head. "I don't have time. I'm leaving this morning."

"Tell them no!" he pleaded.

She placed her hands on either side of his face and drew him in for a kiss. "I couldn't leave without seeing you. Without telling you. I don't regret a minute of last summer. And I don't regret having your baby. I'm sorry. I need to get back before my dad realizes I'm gone."

Derek made several unsuccessful attempts to block her way as she struggled to get to her car. "Don't do this, Summer. I love you. Don't leave me."

"I don't want to go Derek, believe me. I have no choice!"

"You always have a choice! Just refuse to get on the plane!"

"It won't work! You don't know my dad. He said if I stay, he'll make me get an abortion!"

"But you're Catholic!"

"I know! See? He's lost his mind over this. He sees this as a problem, and he wants the problem gone! I have to get on that plane. It's the only way we can make sure the baby lives!"

"Then run away as soon as you land! I'll come get you! There *has* to be a way!"

She hesitated briefly as she opened her car door, then slipped in behind the driver's seat, buckled her seat belt, and buried her face atop the steering wheel. "I love you," she whimpered. "I'm sorry."

As soon as the engine engaged, Derek raced to the passenger's side and reached for the handle but she hit the door lock. "Let me in, Summer! I won't let you go!"

"Derek?" Kyle called from the front door. "What are you guys doing?"

"Get inside!" he shouted. "Don't make me tell you again!"

"Step away, Derek," Summer warned. "I have to go. I don't have a choice."

"Not until you promise you'll stay and fight this! Let me call my parents! Let me call a lawyer—something!"

She shook her head sadly. "Please, Derek. Don't make this harder than it already is."

As she pushed on the gas, he leapt over the door and into the passenger's seat. "If you're going, you'll have to take me with you!"

"You're crazy!" she shouted as she drove, increasing speed as she headed down Harbor Drive. "My dad'll kill us both."

"If that's what it takes, so be it. This baby is ours. It's our decision!"

She shook her head and stared at the road. "This isn't helping. His mind's made up!"

"So's mine!"

"I'm turning around and taking you home."

"You're wasting your time. I'm not getting out of the car. If you take me home, I'll get my wheels and drive to your place. This isn't going away, Summer! And neither are you!"

They argued as she drove past the turnoff for her house, past St. Agnes' Church, over the causeway, and eventually southbound on the turnpike.

"Where are you going?" Derek asked.

"I don't know. You won't get out of the car so I guess I just keep driving!"

"Do you blame me? I can't let you walk out on me with my baby!"

"I'm not walking out on you! It's not *me*!"

The more they fought, the harder she cried. The harder she cried, the worse he felt. Panic had set in, precluding one clear thought as they barreled onto the Overseas Highway toward Key Largo.

"You think I want it this way?" she demanded, her foot pressing further down on the pedal as she watched the road through blurry eyes. "I thought we'd start a family! I realize it's early. I know we're young! But it's *us*, Derek. You and me."

"And it should be *our* choice!" he agreed, a crack in his voice. "That's what I'm saying! I can't let your dad send you away. He needs to know we love each other. That we can make it!"

She shook her head and sniffed as the car neared eighty-five miles per hour, flying past the Manatee Bay Marina beyond the Monroe County road sign. "He doesn't care. It doesn't matter to him. He's just worried about his reputation."

"Well it matters to me and to my family. He doesn't get to decide all by himself. What does your mom think?"

"Mom'll do whatever Dad says. You know that."

"There has to be a way!"

"There's no way—that's what I'm trying to tell you!"

"What if I tell them I want to marry you?"

Out of the corner of her eye, Summer perceived what looked like a cat in the middle of the highway where the two southbound lanes merged into one. She jerked the steering wheel left. The car fishtailed and nearly hit the median. Immediately, she yanked the wheel right but overcorrected and lost control.

Before either of them could react, the Cabrio raced off the road, through the guardrail, and careened across the shoulder and through the fence. The moment the car's front end made high-speed contact with the stone embankment beyond the fence, the front end lifted. It flipped once, ejecting Derek up and out of the convertible and into Long Sound before landing upside down in the water.

CHAPTER 22

EN PACED THE HALLWAY OUTSIDE the Minor 6th conference room while Ross and Samantha welcomed their guests, feigning a smile and nodding his own warm greeting as they disappeared inside to grab refreshments, do some light mingling, and find their seats. He checked his watch repeatedly. No sign of Farin. No word at all.

Megan Price broke away and trotted over to give him a quick hug on her way in. "I haven't seen you in ages. How are you?"

He kissed her cheek as she pulled back. "Brilliant, thanks. You look great. How've you been?" As she gave him the thirty second rundown on her career and the new man in her life, he caught a glimpse of Cheryl inside talking to Marci. They turned his way and gave him an inquisitive look. He flattened his lips and shook his head. They looked away sadly.

"Is everything okay?" Megan asked.

"No worries." Ben hugged her again, thanked her for coming, and said he would see her inside.

He and Cheryl had arrived early, drawn to the hub of the day's activities by something more than the fact that their internal clocks were still set on Eastern Time. A restless air had hung about them over tea with Marci and Elliot that morning and now seemed to hover about the entire floor. Ross had said nothing. Neither had Samantha. Yet he knew they both felt it, too. They all did.

It did not help matters that they had neglected to put their cell phones on their chargers last night before going to bed. Both devices had died sometime during the night. Thankfully, the boys were safe with friends. One less thing in an ocean of problems to worry about.

He felt a hand on his upper arm and spun around to see Samantha's assistant.

"I'm sorry to startle you, Mr. Grant. They'll be starting soon. Is Chris coming up?"

He glanced again at his watch. Ten minutes before ten. "Yes. He popped downstairs for a moment. He should be back straightaway."

"No problem." She nodded and turned on her heel to speak with Samantha.

Ben called after her, "No messages for me or my wife, then?"

Deborah returned long enough to assure him she had dedicated someone to monitor Ms. Drake's line for any incoming calls for the meeting's participants and would pull him out should someone need to reach him.

Downstairs, Chris stared out the frameless glass walls onto the street, waiting for a taxi, a limo, or any vehicle that might stop in front of the building and safely deposit Farin as she had promised in her note. He had heeded his brother's advice. He had waited. Maybe not patiently, but he had waited nonetheless. Now, no more waiting. Something had happened to her. He was sure of it.

"No sign?" a voice asked from behind him.

He glanced over his shoulder, then back to the street. "I thought you were upstairs."

"I just came down to see if she'd made it yet. We're about to start."

Chris pursed his lips. "Where is she, Ross? You must have some idea where she's gone."

"I..."

He turned and narrowed accusing eyes upon him. "You do. Spill it." Ross extended his arm to pat Chris' back but, he shrugged him off and stared him down. "What do you know?"

"Nothing specific. Nothing I can discuss at this time."

The calmness with which Ross spoke evoked a nearly overpowering urge within Chris to lay him out as he had done that evening in Palm Springs. Samantha trusted Ross. That did not mean Chris did. "Is she safe?"

Ross dipped his head down and away. "I think so. I hope so."

They rode the elevator back up to the seventh floor in silence. When they entered the conference room, Chris saw hopeful anticipation on Ben's, Cheryl's, and Marci's faces fade to concern. As he passed along the side of the table on the window side of the room to take his seat next to Cheryl, he gave Marci's shoulder a comforting squeeze.

Cheryl leaned in to whisper, "Did you want me to get you some water? Juice? Tea?"

He shook his head and whispered back, "Any more tea and I'll be spending more time out of the meeting than in."

"Aye, like you've done the last hour? You need to calm down, love."

"She should be here."

Cheryl patted his hand, then turned her attention to Ross as he strode the length of the conference table toward his place at its head. Samantha stood opposite him at the far end, smoothing her skirt down before taking her seat. Deborah backed out of the doors, shutting them in front of her.

"I appreciate the time you've all taken to meet with Samantha and me this morning," he began, eyeing each of the thirteen attendees. "I realize you've been wondering why we asked you to be here today."

Ross' voice fell to background noise as Ben surveyed the group. Opposite his seat and to the right, Faith's fiancé Henri held her hand as he listened intently to Ross' opening comments. Between Faith and Lance, an empty chair with Ivy Spencer's nametag sat atop the portfolio on the table. It would remain unoccupied as Ivy had opted to stay at the hotel with the nanny and the kids to finalize arrangements for their return to England.

Todd sat next to Lance, his hands shaking as he guzzled cups of black coffee, ran the back of his hand up and down his throat, and used multiple napkins to wipe his nose due to what Ben could only guess was a slight cold. Megan occupied the last seat, next to Samantha. Every so often, she would make notes.

"I want to thank Megan personally for making it possible for me to attend today with as little scrutiny as possible. You can all appreciate the effort it took to convince my employer I wasn't flying to LA to interview for another job." The attempted levity fell flat.

She smiled and glanced shyly at the group.

Faith shifted in her seat and folded her arms atop the table. "Can I ask a question?"

Ross lifted his chin. "Of course."

"Who the hell's 'Jade Trongly?' I mean, I've asked every other person in this room and no one has a clue. We all know each other, but no one knows her. You've got us sitting here like a bunch of preschoolers in these assigned seats but whoever she is, she's not here—and there's a place between her name and Chris that just says 'reserved.' What's going on?"

All eyes turned expectantly in Ross' direction.

"I'm afraid I'm unable to discuss Jade at this time. I'd hoped she'd be with us today."

The interface on Chris' phone lit up to indicate an incoming call. He checked the number, then pressed a button to reject it. Macy had had his chance.

The device lit up twice more and was rejected each time. A part of him worried it might be information on Farin's whereabouts. A bigger part had grown irritated after leaving countless unreturned messages for the reporter.

"Before we begin, I need each of you to sign the nondisclosure form you'll find inside your portfolios. We'll be discussing some highly sensitive information over the next hour or so. It's imperative there be no public discussion after you leave here about the contents of this meeting. Anyone who chooses not to sign the agreement will be asked to leave."

"Good thing Ivy's not here," Lance chirped as he south-pawed his copy of the document and slid it toward Sam with a mischievous wink. "My fiancé's capacity for gossip is legendary throughout the whole of Chatham."

Faith let out a bark of laughter and shook her head, sliding the NDA from the sleeve of the leather folder to review. "No wonder she's always kicking your ass. Did you hear what you just said?"

Todd scribbled his signature on the paper without reading it, then slid it to his left and nodded at Megan, who passed it to Samantha.

"You're not gonna read it first, mate?" Lance asked.

He shrugged. "Who'm I gonna talk to?"

"Everyone here except Cheryl, Marci, and I have worked with Lockhardt Sound at some point," Henri piped in, hesitating before he signed. "If this agreement's sensitive to the company, does it even matter if we sign? We're under contract to no one, past or present."

"I appreciate the question," Ross told him. "I'm afraid I need everyone's signature for reasons I'll go over shortly."

Samantha reviewed each copy as she received it. Once she had collected them all, she gave Ross a thumbs up and leaned back in her chair.

Ross nodded, sipped water from the Styrofoam cup next to his desk pad, then picked up the pen—more as a crutch to occupy his hands than anything else. "As Henri pointed out, the one thing everyone in this room has in common is Lockhardt Sound. One way or another, each of you is or has been involved with Jameson Lockhardt's business, even if only through your spouse or fiancé. Though none of you are currently under contract with LSI, you're all in possession of a sizable share of company stock."

"A sizable share of worthless stock, you mean," complained Todd.

"Oh, but it's picked up in value," Megan corrected, eyeing the group. "Over the last couple of quarters, LSI's rebounded quite a bit."

Ross pointed the pen in her direction. "You're absolutely right. But I'm not here to argue about the value of your existing stock per se. What I'm suggesting is something far better."

"Tell me you didn't bring us here today to try to get us to invest!" Faith spat. She looked aghast at Ross, then Henri, then down at Sam. "Did that son-of-a-bitch send you here to talk to us about bailing out the company?"

"Hold on, Faith," Ross said. "I'm afraid it's a great deal more complicated than that."

"C'mon, Henri," she said, jerking out of her chair and standing up.

"Please," Ross called after her as she stomped toward the doors. "You hate him, right?"

She whipped around. "You have no idea. Oh wait—who'm I kidding? You know it all, don't you?"

Ross exhaled a troubled breath. "Then stay here and fight."

She narrowed her eyes quizzically.

He extended his arm and indicated her chair. "Hear me out." When she returned to her seat with a doubtful huff, he continued. "Let's be honest. That's what we're really talking about, right? That's what we really have in common? Because I assure you all here and now I hate him, too. Almost more than the rest of you combined. And together, we can take the only thing that ever really mattered to him. We can end LSI."

Chris' phone continued to light up, silently announcing call after call from Miles Macy. Each notification infuriated him. He wanted to turn off the device completely but worried Farin might try to get through.

"The people represented at this meeting now own controlling stock in Lockhardt Sound."

"What?" Faith's jaw dropped. "Are you sure?"

Ross' confident expression left no doubt. "Quite."

Elliot occupied the last chair along the table to Samantha's left. He quietly absorbed the details as he rocked back and forth, splitting his attention between Ross' explanation and his wife's obviously increasing physical discomfort. "And Lockhardt has no knowledge of this?" he asked as he leaned to his left and rubbed her belly. She glanced his way and gave a slight shrug.

"None," Ross affirmed. "I've spent an enormous amount of time and energy working out the particulars. I assure you neither Jameson nor Bobby know."

"What does this mean?" asked Lance. "Are we going to boot the old SOB out of his own company or what?"

"I'm no financial wizard, but I know our portfolio pretty well," Ben interjected. "I can't imagine the shares we have would put us anywhere near a controlling interest."

The participants' voices mingled over each other in agreement.

Ross held his hands out and down to circle them back. "I realize it may not seem like you would, Ben. And let me clarify. I'd arranged some...shall we say 'creative' accounting while LSI struggled. Basically, I put together a safety net of sorts at Jameson's behest. With the company's recovery, we no longer need that safety net. I'd been charged to dissolve it. Instead, I've been buying up the stock from shareholders such as yourselves and building up a holding company. Essentially, that company owns the lion's share of LSI stock. One party in particular. The remaining shares belong to the folks in this room. You're all that's left."

Chris cut eyes at Ross who seemed to nod a confirmation of his unasked question.

"But if Mr. Lockhardt asked you to set up the company in the first place, how is it he knows nothing about its activities? Doesn't he attend board meetings? What about his stock?"

"Good question, Megan. I'm not at liberty to go into the specifics.

However, I can tell you he has for some time now been preoccupied with other matters, leaving me and his accountants in charge of the day-to-day matters. He knows what I tell him."

"But why would you do this? And why did you want to bring us all here to talk about it?"

Ross took a deep breath and held it a beat. He studied the faces seated around the table one by one, as if trying to decide what, if anything, he should say. "Over the coming months, you're going to hear about the complete destruction of Lockhardt Sound. With it, Jameson, Bobby, and I will be taken into custody to face serious criminal charges. At this time, they're both unaware of the impending actions. The crimes in question are unrelated to LSI's day to day operations. However, it will certainly have a fatal impact on the business. Essentially, the stock you now hold will be useless. And so, I've come here today willing to buy your shares outright or encourage you to trade them in for shares in the holding company. By the time the clock stops ticking, I should be personally divested of all interest and be able to transfer ownership elsewhere."

Samantha gasped. "Ross, it can't have come to this. Not you, too. The last time we spoke, was that—"

He nodded. "I'm afraid so."

"But can't you come to some sort of arrangement? Surely there must be a way to get them to cut a deal."

"I'm supposed to meet someone here after the meeting to discuss my options. I imagine they'll want a statement from you as well."

She held her hand to her mouth.

Ben and Cheryl traded shocked looks with Marci, Elliot, and Chris.

Faith glanced back and forth from one end of the table to the other as Samantha and Ross discussed matters in verbal shorthand. "Wait—what's going on here? Is that pig finally going to jail?"

Elliot grabbed the arm of Marci's chair, pulled it closer to his, and rubbed her shoulder. He leaned in and asked, "You okay?"

She nodded. "I think so. I'm feeling really uncomfortable."

"Like pain?"

"No, nothing like that. Just discomfort."

"Should we call the doctor?"

"I'll be fine. It's probably stress over this whole situation. I'm getting really worried about Farin."

"She'll be fine. Too much has happened for her to be in any kind of danger now. I have to believe that. Otherwise, what's the point of all this?"

"You're right, I'm sure." She peeked under the table to inspect her legs and feet. "No swelling. That's a good thing."

He maneuvered his arm back around and took her hand in his. "You let me know if we need to take off."

She nodded again and turned her attention back to the discussion. Out of the corner of her eye she caught Cheryl looking at her questioningly from several seats to her left. Marci shook her head, indicating there was no emergency. Cheryl winked her understanding, then leaned back.

"How long do we have to consider what we want to do?" Henri asked. "I know I would like to discuss this with Faith before she makes a decision."

She scoffed. "Are you kidding? I say we all keep our stock, call an emergency board meeting, and have his ass out of the building by the end of the day!"

"And then what?" Elliot asked. "Are we prepared to take over? You heard Ross. He's not going to be around much longer. Are we going to march in and start running things like we know what we're doing?"

"Why not?" she snapped. "I've been running my own business for a few years now. We could do it. How about having Sam come back to LSI and run it? Sam?"

Samantha looked at her with parted lips. "Faith, I'm flattered but...but I can't just pack up and move back to New York. As it is, this meeting is much more of a conflict of interest than I'd thought it would be. It'd be unfair to Minor to just...take off."

"Okay, then, whatever. We run it ourselves. What's the worst that could happen? Sony or Warner force an acquisition? So what? Lockhardt gets a little orange jumpsuit, a competitor gets LSI, and we pocket the money. Good riddance, as far as I'm concerned!"

Henri considered the situation as Faith ranted beside him. "No-no-no, *mon trésor*. Let's discuss this first. At home." He turned back to Ross. "How long do we have? How long before these events you speak of?"

"Conservatively, I'd say you have a couple of weeks to make a final decision, but I'd urge you to act quickly. As with every other issue surrounding Jameson Lockhardt, plans are fluid at best. And many of the people at this table know as well as I do that if Jameson gets wind of what I'm proposing, he could...well, let's just say he could throw a wrench in our plans."

Samantha caught Ross' eye and nodded. "Are you sure there's nothing you can do to save yourself? It seems so unfair. After everything you've done to help."

"So are you two gonna tell us what happened?" Lance asked. "If you're going to jail with Bobby and the old man, it must be big."

Chris swore under his breath and stood up. "I'm sorry, Ross. I need to take this call."

Ben, Cheryl, and Marci looked at him with wide eyes. He shook his head and said, "It's not her." As he left the room, the others exchanged curious glances.

"What is it?" he demanded as he stormed out and closed the conference room door behind him. He scrutinized the expansive hallway, relieved to find no one wandering about. "I've called you for days trying to meet and you blew me off, and now you're calling me machine-gun style? I'm in the middle of a meeting!"

"I couldn't get away before now! And even if I could have, I didn't have anything new to report."

"You could have told me where she went. I know she must have let you in on her plans, what with you being her new confidant."

"All I did was get her a fake ID and do a little bit of research."

"Research about what? Did she leave Miami?"

"She headed back up to North Carolina."

His face paled. "And you didn't tell us?"

"I didn't know until this morning! There wasn't anything I could say!"

"What happened this morning?"

"She called. I talked to her."

The elevator chimed as the light near the sliding doors came on, indicating someone had arrived from downstairs.

"Where is she?" Chris demanded.

"She's on her way."

"On her way how? Is she still in North Carolina or is she here in LA? Is she okay?"

When the elevator door opened, a tall, muscular black man in a crisp suit and tie stepped out onto the floor. Farin followed close behind. In her arms she carried a small sleeping child.

***

It irritated Alvarez when witnesses tried to flirt with her during an interview. As if they believed doing so would impress her, put her off her game, or maybe distract her from figuring out exactly who had stabbed the old lady in the back right in the middle of Bayside. As if the attention would make her giddy and prompt her to twirl a strand of hair, abandon her investigation, and tell her partner she would meet up with him later because she felt the sudden urge to take a romp in the sheets with the manager of the GAP. Yeah. So her.

"I already gave my statement to the officers who responded to the 911 call. The whole thing happened so fast. Besides, that was two days ago. I can't really add anything to what I told them, but I'm happy to stand here and try as long as you're willing to stay and pretty the place up. Anybody ever tell you you've got beautiful hair?"

"The suspect ran into your store," she reminded the forty-something male with the gelled hair and clothes an entire generation too young for him. "He didn't say anything? Make any threats? Touch anything we might be able to dust for prints?"

The man folded his arms, frowned, and shook his head. "Nope. Nothing. He ran in through the front entrance, sprinted through to the store, then slipped out the loading door in back. Your people already dusted for prints. Guess they haven't caught him yet, huh? What'd you say your name was again?"

She rolled her eyes, wishing Bridgeman would finish up in back so they could leave. "And you witnessed the stabbing."

"Yeah." His head bounced up and down as he talked, either out of the shock of observing the violence or trying to impress her with his nonchalant response. "Gruesome. It's a good thing you missed it. That's something you don't get out of your head, ya know?"

"Was the suspect alone? Did you see him with anyone prior to the incident?"

"I don't think so. I really didn't notice anyone until he ran at her."

"Was there an altercation between the suspect and the victim? Did they talk or argue...or did she seem like she was trying to get away from him or anything?"

"Nah, nothing like that. The guy just sort of came up on her, stuck the knife in her back, grabbed her purse, and took off. He didn't even seem to be aiming the thing, if you want to know the truth. Just sort of stabbed at her." He grew animated as he tried to reenact his description of the incident.

Alvarez pivoted her stance to ensure she remained firmly positioned between the witness and her holstered pistol.

"I'm not even sure the guy was actually trying to kill her. I think he just wanted her bag."

She consulted her notes. "And you described the suspect as 'medium height, skinny, dark hair, dark skin—'"

"Exactly. A Mexican, for sure. Like you."

She clamped her mouth shut and glared at the witness. "Mexican?"

He bobbed his head. "Oh yeah. Positive. Just not hot like you."

"I see."

"So what do you say? It's Friday. End of the work week. You free for a drink later? We've been busting our humps for the last week finishing up our pre-Fall inventory. But for you, I'd be happy to get my assistant manager to close up tonight. Say, eight-ish?"

"Uh...she'd love to," Bridgeman interrupted as he slid up beside her and stuck his hand out to give Mr. Smooth his business card, "but we're having dinner with my folks tonight. You know how it is, what with it being our engagement dinner, after all. But here's my card. If you can think of anything else that might help us identify the suspect, give us a call." He turned his head and smiled at her. "You about ready, sweetie?"

"'Sweetie?'" she spat with disgust as they returned to their unmarked in the busy parking lot. "Is that what you call Penny? Sweetie?"

Bridgeman adjusted himself behind the wheel and secured his safety belt. "I believe the words you're groping for are 'thank you.' You're welcome."

"Okay, partner. You win. 'Thank you.'"

He tucked his chin, eyes wide. "Wow. That was easy. Too easy. Everything okay?"

"Fine other than the fact we have no leads on the suspect's identity and the knife had no prints. For someone who spontaneously ran up on the vic and stabbed her to get her purse, he sure was prepared. I don't know, Billy. Perps are getting more and more savvy. What are they doing, assembling little kits of vinyl gloves, bleach, and silencers to have on hand in case they come across some unwitting victim?"

"Either that or they're getting paranoid." He checked his mirrors and pulled out into the steady flow of traffic exiting the outdoor marketplace.

"I guess."

"You want to stop for a late lunch on the way back to the office?"

"Sure. Maybe we could get some Mexican—you know, the food of my people."

"Right, right." Bridgeman laughed. "But are you sure? It might intimidate the servers. After all, they're 'just not hot like you.'"

She scoffed and finished writing out some last notes, then stowed her pad and pen. "Now that you mention it, I'm starving."

Bridgeman called in their location and let dispatch know they would be out for lunch. Instead of Mexican, they stopped at a diner off W. Flagler. He ordered the Cobb salad. She had the patty melt.

"Oh to be young again," he mused.

"There's nothing wrong with meat, Billy. You can't survive on lettuce. Besides, you're not that much older than me."

"You'd be surprised what a difference a few years can make. Particularly in your thirties."

Halfway through their meal, Bridgeman's cell phone rang. He lifted his brows as he checked the number. "I think it's Macy."

"Don't you dare answer it!" she demanded through a mouthful of fries.

"Why not?"

"You know why not! Honestly, Billy, you need to stop trying to interfere with my love life."

He shook his head but silenced the ringer and set the device on their table.

"Penny and I just want you to be happy, Al. That's all."

"I am happy," she snapped. She sucked down the remainder of her Pepsi and flagged down their server for a refill.

When the phone rang a second time, he checked the number and frowned at her. "It's him again."

She cocked her head. "He usually doesn't call twice in a row, does he?"

"Not when he calls me. Maybe something's up."

She repositioned herself and grabbed the second half of her sandwich. "Forget it, Billy. Macy hasn't given us squat since that night at Nemo's. I don't know what his angle is, but he's got zilch."

He checked for messages. Nothing. Two minutes later, the phone rang again. This time, it was dispatch. He picked up and answered.

Alvarez watched his face as he mostly nodded and gave a series of "uh-huhs" and "okays." When he signed off, he added, "I'll tell her. Thanks."

"What was that about?"

"You need to call Macy. Well, one of us does."

She dropped her sandwich and wiped the grease from her fingers. "Are you telling me he called the office and...and 'paged' us?"

"I guess so." Bridgeman signaled their server for the check.

Alvarez wrapped what little remained of her patty melt in two napkins, procured a to-go cup for a full soda, then followed Bridgeman outside to return the call from the privacy of their vehicle. "He'd better have something this time. If not, I'll kill him."

Bridgeman started the car and engaged the air conditioning. Once cool air fought the stuffy heat that had turned the inside of their car into an oven, he pulled out and took the long way back to the station.

Alvarez fumbled with the cell phone as she finished her lunch. She dialed the number from the call history and stabbed the speakerphone button, then rested the phone between them on the front seat.

Miles answered on the first ring. "Thanks for calling me back."

"Why are you stalking us at work?" Alvarez snapped.

"Oh, hey! I thought Bridgeman was calling me back. How are you?"

"I'm here, too," William told him. He grinned. "You think she'd call you back without a gun to her head?"

She scowled as they chuckled. "You didn't answer my question, Macy. Why are you blowing up the phone?"

"I had to call during the recess," he explained. "I heard from my witness."

Alvarez rolled her eyes. "Oh yeah? The mythical 'witness' you swore you had four months ago and then we never heard about again?" She swore in Spanish and waved her hand toward William. "You talk to the guy. I've got nothing to say."

"It's not like the trial of the century's going on here in LA or anything," Miles defended. "Not like I have a job. But anyway, she says she's willing to come in and talk to you. I just need you to promise you'll keep things as low-key as possible. She'll give you Lockhardt in a big red bow."

Bridgeman glanced down at the phone when he noticed the indicator for his call waiting. He lifted his chin at Alvarez as he recognized Hubbell's number. Torn, he decided to stick with Macy and return his friend's call after they got back to the station. He tightened his grip on the steering wheel. "How soon can we get her in?"

"Well, she's in LA right now. I'm thinking she'll be back in Miami sometime in the next few days."

"Is she with you?"

Alvarez set her jaw and peered straight ahead.

"Not exactly, but I'm hoping to see her before she leaves. I'm gonna ask her to agree to give me the exclusive rights to write a book about her ordeal."

"You're writing a book?" Alvarez scoffed doubtfully. "Is this why you've been slow-playing us this whole time?"

Bridgeman cut her off. "What 'ordeal?' You said she was a witness. Did Lockhardt do something to her, too?"

"Look," Miles said, "both the prosecution and the defense rested today. As soon as they give closing arguments and release the jury for deliberation, I should be able to fly back to Miami for a few days before they reach a verdict. Unless something unforeseen happens, let's plan on getting together with her a week from today. That should give her some time to get settled."

"Are you going to at least tell us who she is?" Alvarez challenged.

"Not yet. You'll understand when I bring her in, I promise."

"Your promises mean zero to me, cowboy. You've proven that."

Bridgeman shot her a disappointed glance and shook his head.

"Is that so?" Miles pushed back. "I guess we'll see. But when I bring her in, I'm going to make it a point to collect on that date Bridgeman told me you'd agree to if I produced an actual witness."

Alvarez jerked her head and stared at her partner, openmouthed and incredulous.

Bridgeman shrugged, grinned, and turned his attention to the road before him. "Gee, Al. Anybody ever tell you you've got beautiful hair?"

CHAPTER 23

THE GROUNDS OF THE HARBOR Boulevard home appeared uncommonly quiet as Herb Radford lowered his binoculars and studied the street. He had combed over the Matheson place and both Harbor residences Wednesday night after his arrival, then stayed inside Thursday to monitor the chat room so as to avoid any of the Key Biscayne neighbors noticing a stranger lurking around. Maybe tomorrow he would rent a boat and check out the homes from the water's vantage point. A part of him wondered if something had happened. All three places appeared to have been virtually abandoned.

He hated humidity, sand, and those skittering lizards he remembered from the Orlando trip he and the ex had taken with the kids back in 1976. As a result, he had done everything in his power to avoid having to fly down personally. Unfortunately, he had promised Lockhardt—and more importantly, he had promised himself—he would not call their guy in for the final phase until he had made visual confirmation.

The fact she had not found it in herself to remain in Los Angeles in the first place put him off. And who the hell knew now? Maybe she had never come to Miami at all. She had stood him up for their scheduled meeting two weeks ago and he had not heard from her since. Maybe she had known all along it was a set-up. If so, things had taken a complicated turn. Truthfully, he did not know where else to look.

When his stomach got the better of him, he left his stakeout and tooled into the village to procure some lunch. Key Biscayne was busy yet quaint—somewhat more touristy than he would have figured given the notables in area. Not as bad as Miami Beach, but still enough to inconvenience residents who preferred more anonymity.

He grabbed a sandwich and two sodas from a mom-and-pop shop and ate in a shaded area back in Cranston Park. A nice idea, or so he thought until he had to close his windows. Damn bugs almost immediately smelled a free meal. With no way to keep his car cool without cranking up the A/C, he wolfed down half the sandwich and wrapped the other up in the paper for later, then made his way back to Ben Grant's house. For good measure, he checked out the other two houses again before parking.

Sparse traffic drove up and down Harbor over the next hour, but he caught sight of no activity around his target area. He decided to call it a day and head back tomorrow by boat. Maybe bring a couple of six-packs and make a day of it. As he buckled his seat belt and went to turn the key and start the engine, he spied a police car in the rearview mirror. Quickly, he grabbed the clipboard and pen he had brought with him earlier as a ruse should anyone question his business in the area.

The officers inside paid him no mind as they drove just past him and pulled into the very property he had surveilled all morning. This piqued his interest. Maybe something had happened after all.

He set down the clipboard and grabbed his binoculars, but before he could employ them, another vehicle pulled up to the property. This one slowed down long enough to let a passenger get out, then drove away seemingly without noticing the police car parked further in.

A teenage boy around 15 or so, Herb guessed, flung his backpack over his shoulder and meandered up his driveway. The moment he noticed the police car, the pack slid off his shoulders and he hastened toward the vehicle.

Herb used his binoculars to see if he could get some idea why the cops had arrived.

Metro-Dade's finest, a man and a woman, turned around when they noticed the boy. They met him at the bottom of the long cement steps and pointed to the front door. The boy nodded and went past them, unlocking the front door with his key and sliding his pack inside. The officers talked a bit more and the boy nodded his agreement or understanding.

Then, Herb saw the boy's face contort in horror. He lifted his hands to his head and grabbed handfuls of hair as if in distress. The male cop moved forward and patted the boy's shoulder, then lifted his chin and pointed toward the house. A moment later, the boy disappeared inside with the two officers.

Herb checked his rearview and side mirrors. As much as he wondered what had gone down, he decided it best to take off. Maybe tomorrow he would glean more information from the vantage point of the boat. He hoped so. The sooner he figured out what was going on, the sooner he could wrap things up. He wanted to leave Miami as soon as possible.

***

They gave him a choice of the green Cirrus or the white Seville. White seemed more practical. Less conspicuous. It was not as if he would get blood all over it anyway.

"Let's see." The agent chirped as he typed the information from his customer's driver's license into the system. "I've got your insurance info, your waivers. I just need to print out this contract, get your signature, and you're on your way!"

He nodded, slid his license off the counter, and tucked it back into his wallet.

The agent disappeared long enough to grab the contract and make several X's near boxes throughout the multi-page carbon copy document. He went over each provision in detail, getting a signature or initials near each one. Once finished, the employee tore the perforated sides off and separated the company's copy from the customer's. He then folded up the duplicate and slid it into a brochure-shaped sleeve. "Is it business or pleasure for you this trip?"

He smirked at the idea and slid his dark glasses back on. "I suppose it's both. I rather enjoy my work, to be honest."

"What a fantastic attitude!" the agent gushed with a cheery uptick to his voice. "Can I get you anything else before you take off? Any maps?"

"Nope. I think I got it. Just point me in the right direction."

The gentleman handed over the keys and the contract, then pointed out where he needed to go to pick up his vehicle.

He saluted the agent with the contract, made his way to the lot to grab his vehicle, loaded his bag, then headed out. The drive from LAX to Santa Barbara would take upwards of three hours. More if he stopped for lunch, which he would. But not in Malibu—just in case.

Normally, he avoided revisiting areas in which he had recently worked. One never knew when a random encounter might jog the wrong person's memory. He would have preferred to forget about Southern California altogether. Too bad the old blowhard had forced his hand.

After he completed this task, he would do one more job. Unfortunately, he had committed himself long ago. But once Farin Grant was dead once and for all, he would disappear for a nice long vacation. Business had boomed over the last five years. At this point he had more money than he could ever spend. No need to start taking chances. No reason to get greedy. In fact, he probably could have just let this one slide. Revenge was boring anyway.

But no. Lockhardt needed to be taught a lesson once and for all. There was such a thing as respect. At some point in time, he must have forgotten.

He supposed everyone needed a little reminder every once in a while.

***

Chris stood and stared for what seemed like an eternity at Farin, then the child, then the man accompanying them. He had not heard Macy hang up from their unfinished call. In fact, his phone had slid out of his hand as the impact of the situation hit him full force.

Her brows lifted and softened as their eyes met. "See? I told you to trust me."

He nodded, still stunned as his blurry gaze fixed on the bundle of toddler in her arms. At first he hesitated to approach them. As if he had no right. Then, he moved slowly toward her on rubber legs. "Is...is this Jade Trongly?"

She nodded. "Come meet your niece. Her real name's—"

"—Jordan." He nearly choked on the words.

"How'd you know?"

He nodded. "I found the paper scraps in your room."

The large man who had arrived with Farin put a hand on her shoulder. "Are you gonna be all right? I need to get in there and have a chat with Mr. Alexander."

"Thank you for your help, Agent Quarles," she said, rocking the child in her arms.

"I'll be in touch for a more formal interview once you get your daughter back and settled in Miami. If you need anything before then, you have my card and my cell number."

Their conversation did not fully register in Chris' mind. His attention remained focused on the little girl who lay sleeping peacefully in Farin's arms. He wished he could get a better look at her, but could clearly see traces of his brother in the child's soft, round face. Her sandy brown hair fell in long, shiny strands about her shoulders, partially covering her plump cheeks. He wondered if her eyes were green like Jordan's or maybe brown, like Farin's.

"She fell asleep in the car on the way over from the hotel." Farin stepped forward to close the gap between them and let Chris run the back of his fingers against her cheeks. "She's slept a lot in the last few days. I think she's as exhausted as I am."

"Is she okay?"

Farin rested her head gently atop the girl's head. "I'm gonna ask Ethan to take a look at her before we leave, but she seems okay. A little scared, I think, but physically okay."

"How old is she?" He looked off to the side to calculate a guess. "Around three?"

She nodded. "Three last month."

"Where's she been all this time? How'd you find her?"

Farin explained that Jameson had taken the baby away from her some months after the delivery. That he had initially used little Jordan to try to keep her in check. There had been intermittent promises made, with Jameson or Childs insisting she could take the baby and go if she would quit screaming out from her room and stop trying to escape. They had made her believe if she promised to keep her mouth shut about what she knew, they would eventually set her free. She had complied for a couple of weeks here or there only to realize they had lied, at which point she would begin searching again for a way to escape. In the end, Jameson had taken little Jordan from her. Soon after, the drugging had begun.

Only after meeting Ross at the cemetery shortly after returning to Florida did she know definitively that Jameson had not killed little Jordan but had instead taken her to an orphanage. Since that day, she had tried everything she could to locate her daughter.

"I contacted Miles Macy because I figured he could help me find her. He discovered the orphanage had burned down at the end of May. I thought for sure Jordan had been killed. But he managed to locate her under the Jade name a while back. I couldn't risk anyone knowing. If Jameson suspected anything, he'd have surely had her killed."

"So you were pregnant when..."

She nodded.

"I thought it was impossible. After Melody—"

"Jordan and I'd planned on getting a second opinion. Everything went down before we got the chance."

"And that's why Jameson kept you alive?"

She gave the girl a slight squeeze. "I guess so."

His eyes brimmed with tears as he stroked the young girl's hair. "I can't imagine how you've come through all this. I guess I didn't make it any easier for you, did I?"

"I didn't dare say anything until I got her back safely. You understand now, right?"

He shook his head as he processed the details. "What about—"

"I'll tell you everything, Chris, but not here. Please let me get my second wind."

He nodded. "Ross and Samantha have been planning this big meeting for months. As soon as you walk in those doors, it'll pretty much be over. You realize that, right?"

"I know. But he'd said he wanted me here, so here I am."

"With an FBI escort to boot." He grinned. "How'd you manage that?"

"Let's just say I knew I was in over my head and decided it was time."

"Is there anything you need? Anything I can do to help?"

She shifted her stance and lifted the girl to sit higher on her hip. "Actually, I'd like to sit down. I haven't quite built up my baby-carrying arms yet. She's getting a little heavy."

He reached out for the child. "Can I take her?"

"I want you to, but she's still getting used to me at this point. I don't want to overwhelm her any more than she already is. And you know as soon as Cheryl sees her—"

A gasp of disbelief came from the direction of the conference room doors. They looked over and saw Cheryl peek through and then slip out of the room. Her lips parted in shock and joy as she drew nearer.

Farin smiled and Chris stepped to the side. He gave his sister-in-law a weak grin. "Come meet our niece."

With outstretched hands, Cheryl went to them. She brushed the girl's hair back, kissed her forehead, and whisper-gushed, "Look at the wee lass! What an angel!"

Farin lightly bounced and rocked Jordan proudly as Cheryl fawned over her.

"What's her name, then?"

"Jordan. Jordan Kelley."

Her lips flattened and stretched in misty approval. "Aye, of course." She leaned in close. "And if you're not the spitting image of your father, I don't know what."

"What color are her eyes?" Chris asked.

"They're sort of an amber color," Farin said. "Like a golden green almost. They're beautiful."

"Of course they are," Cheryl cooed.

As if it were the most natural thing in the world, Farin did not protest when Cheryl reached in and took the sleeping girl from her. She shrugged at Chris, who relieved her of the bulging diaper bag she had carried over her shoulder. Together, they walked back toward the conference room.

"I guess this is the moment of truth." Farin took a deep breath.

Chris rested his hand on the middle of her back. "You're safe now."

She nodded. "Jordan's safe. That's the only thing I care about."

"So has Jameson been arrested?" Chris asked. "If the FBI knows you're alive—"

"No," Farin told him. "Not yet. But soon."

"Shh," Cheryl hushed as she nodded for Chris to open the door. "No more talk of police and arrests. Let's get this wee one inside to meet her Uncle Ben."

Before they could open the door, Jordan stirred. She rubbed her eyes with her small fist and glanced around the hallway. At first, she panicked and looked like she might scream. When she saw Farin, she squirmed out of Cheryl's embrace and reached out her arms. "Momma?"

Farin lifted her up and regarded Chris and Cheryl. "I think we need a minute. You two go on in. We'll be there soon."

Chris doubled back to pick up his cell phone off the floor. Farin waved for him to give her the diaper bag, then stepped out of sight as they returned inside. When the door closed behind them, she took little Jordan to the ladies' room so they could both freshen up before making an appearance.

"How're you feeling?" she asked as she ran a brush through the girl's baby-fine hair. "Are you hungry yet?"

Jordan shook her head, then sat on the counter and quietly played with the hairbrush as Farin dabbed on some fresh face powder and lip stain. "Is this your meeting?"

Farin smiled. "You have a good memory."

The girl nodded, ran the brush through her hair, bristles side up, then turned to catch her reflection in the mirror.

"You did a fantastic job with that brush, Jordan," Farin told her. "Whaddya say we get you your own when we get home?"

"To Minami?"

"To Miami, that's right."

She watched herself twirl the brush awkwardly in the air. "Jade."

"What, sweetie?"

"I'm Jade, Momma. Bemember?"

"Oh, that's right." Farin frowned sadly and gathered their things back into the bag.

Jordan lifted her arms so Farin could help her down off the counter, then used the facilities before they left. She got through most of the ritual by herself, then let her mother help clean her up and give her a fresh Pull-Up.

"Good job, Momma!" Jordan patted her shoulder.

"Thank you. You did a good job, too."

Jordan took Farin's hand as they walked back to the conference room. Farin fidgeted with and patted her hair with her free hand.

"Momma?"

"Yes, Jord—Jade?"

"You have pretty hair. I don't like your wig."

She smiled and scrunched her nose. "Me neither. Hopefully I won't have to wear it much longer."

They stood before the conference room doors a moment while Farin took and held a deep breath, then exhaled through pursed lips.

Jordan looked up at her with curious eyes. "What's the matter?"

She shook her head and smiled down at her. "Not a thing. You ready to go inside?"

The girl took an energetic leap. "Yep!"

When Farin opened the double doors, the room fell silent. Chris and Cheryl smiled from their seats on the far right. Most of the room's occupants sat slack-jawed in disbelief.

The next few minutes whirred by them in a chaotic flurry of activity as the various parties experienced shock upon shock.

Farin, alive. Farin, a mother. Farin, safe after having disappeared for weeks.

They spoke over each other, clamoring for her attention and pitching questions left and right until Jordan backed away, fearfully overwhelmed and clinging to Farin's leg.

Chris moved behind them and shut the doors to avoid encountering any unforeseen passersby, then knelt down next to his frightened niece. "Hello."

She looked at him with big eyes as she used her index finger to twirl a few strands of hair near her scalp.

He glanced up at Farin, who urged him on with a lift of her chin. "What's your name?"

"Jade," she answered in a small voice.

"Hello, Jade. I'm Chris. It sure is loud in here, isn't it?"

She nodded, her tiny lips protruding in a pout.

"I don't like noise, either. Especially around a bunch of strangers. It's kinda scary, isn't it?"

She nodded sadly.

Marci waddled uncomfortably up to Farin. "Why didn't you tell me? She's beautiful!"

Farin hugged her, then broke away and looked her up and down. "Look at you! You're ready to drop!"

Marci rubbed her belly. "Any minute now, actually."

"Are you serious?"

Elliot came up beside her. "Afraid so. We were just getting ready to take off."

Marci added, "The contractions are about twenty minutes apart, if they're real. I've got plenty of time, but my husband's insisting we go to the hospital." She smiled down at Jordan. "Hello there."

Jordan looked up at Marci, then away, her cheeks crimson from all the sudden attention. Her big eyes darted nervously about the room. She reached up and tugged on her mother's shirt.

Farin bent down and lifted her into her arms. The girl buried her face in the crook of her mother's neck. "Who are these people?" she whimpered.

Farin paused a moment and studied them each in turn. "These people are our family." She introduced Jordan to her aunt and uncle. More shy than frustrated, the girl gave up reminding them her name was Jade.

"Are you thirsty?" Cheryl asked, pointing to the credenza with all the refreshments. "We could get you some yummy juice."

Jordan allowed her Aunt Cheryl to take her by the hand and lead her over to the far end of the room. Farin and Jordan kept a close eye on each other as Cheryl fixed her a plastic glass of orange juice, then pointed out the muffins and fruit on the other side of the room.

"She's beautiful," Chris said.

"She really is," Marci agreed.

"She's got Jordan's nose," Farin observed, her eyes misty as she cleared her throat. "And his lips."

"She looks just like him," Chris said.

"She looks like both of them," Marci corrected. "My mom has some old pictures of us as kids, probably just a couple of years older. She's the spitting image of Farin."

Chris' cell vibrated in his pocket. He checked the caller ID. When he did not recognize the Florida number, he rejected the call.

Farin talked to Marci as Elliot collected their things. "You realize you're going to have to move to Florida."

She scoffed uncomfortably. "My parents would love that, wouldn't they?"

"Bring 'em with," Farin suggested. "They'll want to be around both their grandchildren, right?"

She grinned. All at once, her face transformed into shock.

"What's the matter?" asked Farin.

Elliot made a face and groaned as he joined them.

When Farin looked down, she saw a puddle of moisture on the rug. "Oh no."

"Samantha's gonna kill me."

"Maybe not Sam," Elliot quipped, "but the cleaning staff won't be too fond of you, I'm sure of that."

"You go," Farin said. "I'll tell Sam."

"I think the meeting's been over since the guests of honour arrived anyway," Elliot agreed. He took Marci's hand and helped her over the puddle. "Who's the tall chap talking to Ross, anyway?"

Farin opened the door, then helped Marci and Elliot out into the hallway. "FBI," she said as the three of them walked carefully toward the elevator. "I'll explain later."

Marci hugged Farin as they waited for the elevator. "Any chance you can meet us at the hospital?"

"I wish I could. I don't think I should risk it yet."

"She can be there for the next one." Elliot grinned at Farin.

"*Next one?*" Marci exclaimed.

Farin heard Jordan call for her. "I've got to get back. Please call the minute she has the baby." She rattled off her hotel name and room number.

Inside, Megan Price and the Mirage members corralled Ross as he finished up his sidebar with Agent Quarles. He apologized for the interruptions and promised to speak with each of them personally over the next couple of weeks to discuss their decisions.

Ben, Cheryl, and Chris hovered around little Jordan, who sat contentedly at the table, legs dangling off the chair as she drew on a pad of paper. Chris caught Farin's eye as she made her way toward Quarles. He winked, then turned his attention back to the girl and gave her an encouraging "ahhh!" as if witnessing the second coming of Seurat.

As the participants casually filed out of the room, they awkwardly expressed their shock and delight over the stunning turn of events. They offered her belated condolences over Jordan, asked questions about her ordeal too complex to answer with any brevity, and told her how beautiful her daughter was. Megan Price even hugged her.

Lance lingered a moment with Sam. He tenderly squeezed her arm, then leaned in to kiss her cheeks.

Once they had all gone, Farin explained the issue of the carpet to Samantha, who seemed far more concerned with Marci's impending delivery than anything else. She made a note to have Deborah call about getting the carpet steam-cleaned, get a flower arrangement sent over to Cedar's, and arrange a champagne dinner for Elliot and Marci for the first night after the baby arrived.

"And what about you?" she asked Farin. "How're you holding up?"

She shrugged. "I'm okay."

Sam scrutinized her appearance. "You look exhausted."

"Yeah, that too."

"When's the last time you slept?"

She blew air through her lips. "I try to nap when Jordan sleeps."

Sam peeked over her shoulder at the young girl, then looked back at Farin. "She's gorgeous. I'm sorry Jordan couldn't see his daughter. It must take every bit of restraint you have not to go to New York and deal with that bastard yourself."

Farin nodded, her nostrils flared as she swallowed a catch in her throat. "He'll get what's coming to him if it's the last thing I do."

Samantha nodded. "You're a lot braver than I gave you credit for."

"I'm braver now. Jordan's my motivation."

"You don't think someone's going to tip Jameson off now that you've taken her, do you?"

Farin lifted her chin toward Hubbell Quarles, who nodded and waved her over. "That's all being taken care of, I assure you. Thank you for your help, Sam. And thanks for pushing me."

"Get that album done. Ben says you've really started making progress. In hindsight, I'm surprised you were able to concentrate on it at all."

She promised to update her in a couple of weeks, then excused herself to speak to Agent Quarles. Ross stood at his side. He extended his hand as she approached them. She hesitated, but accepted the gesture.

"I'm about to take off," Quarles explained. "I wanted to see you before I left."

She glanced at them in turn. "What did we decide? Are you going to pick up Jameson and Bobby?"

"I think we've come to an understanding," Ross told her. He looked at the agent, who nodded his agreement.

"What does that mean? I thought we wanted them brought in. Jameson's still trying to kill me!"

"We need him to keep trying," Quarles told her matter-of-factly. "Or at least think he's trying. Just until we can get the last bits of evidence against him."

"I'm going in to give a formal statement," Ross clarified. "It's no use arresting Jameson before they have all they need to put him away indefinitely."

"What about Bobby? How much longer is it going to take?"

Quarles and Ross eyed each other.

"That long? I have my daughter to worry about! And my family!"

"You let us worry about the details," the agent assured her. "Mr. Alexander here has made some interesting suggestions on how to wrap this up. We'll be sure and get some people to look out for your family while we put things in place. In the meantime, some colleagues of mine in Miami need to interview you about your husband's murder. I'll arrange a time when I can sit in on it with you. For now, you concentrate on getting that baby acquainted with her family and finishing up this new album of yours. I'd say you'll be able to come out and promote it in no time. And I hope to get an autographed copy."

When Hubbell left, Ross did not linger for long. Sam gave him the signed nondisclosure agreements, which he tucked into his briefcase. He thanked her for hosting the meeting, such as it was, told her he would check in with her soon, then hurried out, claiming he had a plane to catch.

"Mom-ma," Jordan singsonged as she finished up her masterpiece.

"Yes, Jordan." Farin leaned over to view the picture from the opposite side of the table.

"Jade!"

Farin eyeballed the others, half embarrassed and half frustrated at the correction. "Sorry, Jade."

Jordan tore the sheet of paper off the pad and lifted it up so her mother could see. "Like it? It's a puppy!"

Farin's eyes danced enthusiastically across the page, taking in the stick figure drawing. "It's beautiful! You're a wonderful artist!"

"Uncle Ben's already promised to get her an art set when we get home," Cheryl said, giggling.

"Two!" Jordan corrected. "One for me and one for you!"

"That's right!" Ben nodded proudly. "That way, you can visit any time you want and make lots of pictures for Aunt Cheryl to pin up on the refrigerator."

Jordan smiled up at her mother. "Uncle Ben's got a pool!"

Farin's eyes widened with shared wonderment. "He does?"

"Yeah!" she chirped excitedly.

"You about ready for lunch?" Farin asked. "Or did Aunt Cheryl fill you up on fruit and muffins?"

Jordan shrugged as Cheryl shot Farin a guilty grin.

"We're staying at Marci's," Chris explained. "You want to head back there with us for lunch? No need to stay at a hotel. There's plenty of room. It's probably safer there with the rest of us anyway."

Farin agreed. Cheryl packed up the diaper bag while she and Jordan visited the ladies' room once more.

"How about you, Sam?" Chris asked. "You want to have some lunch with us?"

"I'd love to, but I promised to meet Ethan and go over the menu for the wedding. You're all coming, right? I don't remember whether I received your response cards."

"A fall wedding is so romantic," Cheryl told her. "Ben and I wouldn't miss it. I sent our response out a few days ago. I'm sure you'll have it soon."

Chris' phone rang again. He frowned at the unfamiliar number. "This bloody thing's been ringing all day." He rattled off the number and asked if Ben or Cheryl recognized it. When neither of them did, he rejected the call.

"Someone needs to go over the details of the meeting with Farin," Samantha told them. "Ross reminded me before he left. I guess she has some stock left in the company as well."

Cheryl made a note in her portfolio before packing it up. "Ben or I'll sit down with her when we get back home."

When Farin and Jordan returned, Cheryl gave the room a visual sweep before heading out. Chris' phone rang again. Same number.

"Why not just answer it?" Ben told him. "Maybe it's important."

Chris sighed. "It's probably just a wrong number. Give me a second." He headed out to the hallway.

Cheryl helped Farin straighten her wig, tucking a stray tendril beneath its hair line.

"Jordan hates this thing," Farin told her. "She thinks it's ugly."

"Maybe you can get rid of it soon," Cheryl said.

"Let's hope so."

When Chris stepped back inside the room, all the color had drained from his features.

"What's wrong?" Ben asked, instantly concerned.

Chris extended his hand to give his brother the phone. "You need to take this."

"Why?" he asked, trading a worried glance with his wife.

"It's Kyle," his voice broke with emotion. "T-take the phone, Ben."

Cheryl gasped. "Is he okay?"

Ben rushed forward and grabbed the phone.

"Dad?" came the broken, mournful voice of his youngest.

"Yes, what is it, son? Are you all right?"

Kyle began to weep into the phone.

Ben saw Samantha's assistant rush into the room with a note. She came forward and handed it to him. "What's going on, Kyle?" he asked as he unfolded the paper and read. Scribbled in the middle was a number for the Metro-Dade Police Department. It read simply, "Call ASAP."

"Are you and Mom coming home?"

"Tell me what's going on, son. What happened?" He handed the note to his wife, who accepted it with trembling fingers.

"It's Summer. Summer's de...she's dead, Dad."

Ben swallowed an immediate rush of emotion. "Where's your brother?" he demanded.

"He was with her. There was an accident. A car accident."

It took every ounce of resolve Ben could muster not to drop the phone. "Where is he, Kyle?"

"He's at the hospital."

"Where are you?"

"H-h-home."

"I need to call the police, son. Stay where you are and I'll call you back as soon as I talk to them."

"They're...they're here."

"They are?"

"Uh-huh. Please come home now."

"I'm on my way as soon as I talk to them. Put them on."

Kyle sniffed bravely, then began to sob once more. "I'm sorry, Dad. We should've listened."

Confused, Ben did not want to worsen the situation by asking questions that did not readily matter. "It's okay. We'll sort this out. Is your brother okay?"

"I don't know."

"Is he *alive*?" he shouted more forcefully than he would have preferred.

Cheryl faltered as Chris rushed over to support her. "Ben?" she called out, then shouted, "*Kyle?*"

"Yeah," Kyle's voice creaked him. "But I think he's pretty bad off."

"Put the police on the phone, son." He studied the stunned, saddened faces of Cheryl, Farin, Samantha, and Chris as the sound of the phone shuffling across the line told him Kyle had handed it over to the authorities. A moment later, he addressed Deborah. "Please find a way to book us the first available charter to Miami. We need to leave straightaway."

CHAPTER 24

BECAUSE SHE HAD LIVED IN the LSI apartment since moving to New York, Joni had only a few personal belongings and no furniture to transport to Bobby's penthouse mansion on W. 77th Street. They spent Sunday morning packing her clothes into several pieces of luggage and her toiletries into a couple of boxes, then the rest of the day divvying up closet and bathroom space in the master suite. She used the lion's share of both. He did not mind in the least.

She made him an early dinner late Sunday afternoon—the first homemade meal he had eaten since leaving home at seventeen. A simple meal. Baked chicken, brown rice, broccoli, and boxed cornbread. He ate two plates.

"This is amazing," he said as finished his third sliver of cornbread. "So much better than restaurant food."

She watched him eat, a twinkle of pride in her eyes. "It's nothin' really. If we'd had the ingredients I coulda made Momma's fried chicken. Another time, though. I'm glad you liked it."

He helped her wash and dry the dishes. "I can't remember the last time I ate so much. I'm going to have to get on the treadmill before bed!"

"Or we could go outside and take a walk. You know, under the stars?"

He shrugged but lifted his brows at the idea. "I don't know how many stars we can see, but yeah. That might be nice."

She gave him a sweet, seductive side eye. "I'll let you hold my hand."

"In that case, forget the treadmill. A walk it is!"

The New York evening was cool and dry. Bobby helped Joni skin on the light sweater she had brought just in case. They walked past the Museum of Natural History toward the park. Joni noted the Italian restaurant on the corner of W. 77th and Central Park West and suggested they stop in for an after dinner glass of wine before they returned home. Bobby agreed. He would have agreed to anything.

They meandered along 77th Street into the park. When they had passed beneath the Stone Arch, Joni smiled and closed her eyes, then took and held a deep breath. He watched her in awe as she seemed to sense and feel everything around her. He had never considered his surroundings as anything to stop and appreciate. Joni soaked up life like a sponge.

They held hands and walked a good fifteen minutes in, then turned back. Little conversation passed between them as they enjoyed the waning light of dusk. When they returned to the Stone Arch, they sat down a moment on a nearby bench.

"If you're okay with it, I'd sure like to bring Momma and Daddy out to stay with us some weekend. I know I've got a big push what with my publicity campaign and all, but maybe when my schedule lightens up? What do you think?"

He covered her hand with both of his own, noting the warmth of her touch. "It's your place, too. You can have them as often as you want. They're always welcome."

"I'd like to introduce them to your daddy, too." She looked at him with hopeful violet eyes. "Maybe we can all spend Christmas together."

He exhaled sharply through his nose and leaned back onto the bench. "We can talk about that later. Honestly, my father's never been the Christmas-y type."

"What about Thanksgiving, then? I'll be singing in the Macy's parade this year. It'd be wonderful having our folks all get together afterward. Like a traditional Thanksgiving, you know? Momma's turkey's always been the envy of Cedarcreek."

The last Thanksgiving Bobby had spent with his father had been the year they had flown up to New York from Miami with Farin—the day Childs had prescribed the pills upon which she had subsequently grown addicted.

He stared at the ground, thinking as he bit the side of his cheek. He wanted to reject the idea out of hand. Socially, Bobby had not spent five minutes with his father since before his birthday. In fact, he wanted to circle back with Ross and cancel the retirement party. At least his part in it.

Joni put her arm around him and rubbed his shoulders. "He's still your daddy."

"You don't understand."

"Maybe so. Why don't you explain it to me?"

"He's not who I thought he was."

"None of our parents are who we thought they were. When we're kids, they all seem larger than life. Perfect. Wise. And then when we get older, we see them as…well, just people. I remember the first time I saw my daddy drunk. I never even knew he drank. He'd wait until my brother and I were asleep and the house was quiet, then sit in the kitchen for hours at night and sip his whiskey. Momma used to cry alone into her pillow because he wouldn't come to bed. I never knew that until after I turned twenty-one."

Bobby looked at her. "They seem so happy."

"They are happy. Now. Daddy had too much pride to tell Momma he was worried about making the mortgage and the payment on the farm. He had a lot of worries. But he loved us. I'd always thought he was a brilliant man, confident, my protector. And he was all those things. He still is, but he's also human."

Bobby nodded and stared back at the ground.

"You're daddy's only human too, baby. He wanted to do right by you. True, I may not understand that whole mess about you being schizophrenic and then not schizophrenic, but some things we just have to let go of. That doctor's dead and gone. You'll never know what went on in his fool head. But don't you think your daddy's as upset with the guy as you? You're his son."

He lifted his shoulders and scrunched his lips to one side. "I don't know. My family's a lot different than yours."

She lowered her head onto his shoulder. "I don't know. We're all basically the same inside, I think. God gave us plenty of differences, but we're all made in His image."

"You believe that?"

She nodded. "With my whole heart. I was raised on it."

They stood and strolled back toward the Italian restaurant for their nightcap. She looped her arm in his and snuggled into him as they walked.

Bobby ruminated on Joni's optimistic assessment of his situation. He admired her faith. Even envied it. If only he shared it.

***

Jameson scowled at the bounce in Ross' step when he came in for their Monday morning meeting. Chipper dispositions at the beginning of the work week warned of lackadaisical effort. Or maybe things had gone better in Los Angeles than he had anticipated. "How's Megan doing? Has she made a decision yet?"

Ross dropped down in the seat facing the old man's desk and looked through some files. "She and her manager are going over the Minor 6th contract this week to see about loopholes. All indications are she could come back to LSI before the end of the year."

"Hmm. I'd have liked to have gotten her back on board before my retirement. Any chance you can fast-track the transition? You and Samantha still seem to be on pretty good terms. Maybe throw a bit of cash her way? Make it worth her wile?"

He offered a downturned smirk. "Maybe. Just maybe. Let me start working on it. Can't promise anything, but you never know. It's the end of September already. May be an ambitious goal."

Jameson leaned back, one elbow perched on the arm of his chair. "I've seen the transition reports. Looks like things are well underway. I uh, I heard through the grapevine you've decided to retire as well. Congratulations."

"It seemed like the ideal time to make a clean break."

"Yes. I suppose so. Is that what's got you so cheerful this morning, then?"

"I don't know. It's been a long, painful few months without my bride. Last night was the first decent sleep I've had since I can remember. Maybe it gave me a boost of energy."

He studied him with a measure of suspicion. "You sure that's all it is?"

Ross scoffed, incredulous. "I'd think a lighter disposition would be a good thing. What's the matter? Having second thoughts about giving it all up? I for one relish the day I'll be free of the need to fix my tie every Monday through Friday. I might even take up golf. In fact, maybe we could take lessons together. When was the last time we did anything together that didn't have LSI in the mix?"

He narrowed his eyes like a predator sizing up its prey. "It's been a while, indeed."

"Exactly. Now that we're both going to be retired, we have time to see each other more socially. Correct me if I'm wrong, but after so long in business, we're pretty much the only friend the other has. Not to mention our history."

Jameson nodded but did not respond. He studied his colleague with curiosity and decided it might be prudent to circle back with Megan Price directly—just to double-check things went down the way his "old friend" said.

When Jameson looked past Ross through his open office door and down the hallway, he saw Bobby walk into his own office. Out of habit, he consulted his watch. "If there's any doubt my son's ready to assume my position, I'd appreciate your letting me know sooner rather than later. There's still ample time to push back my retirement."

"To be honest, I had my doubts the last couple of years, but he's made a believer out of me. The numbers are good. New artists are producing—and charting. He's made some positive improvements to the bottom line. And he's clearly got your instincts. Be proud of him. He's finally strong enough to face the road before him."

"Ever since he started seeing that girl, he's changed."

Ross nodded. "That and getting off the medication. They happened around the same time. Who knows which gave him the bigger shot of confidence?"

"Let's hope it's not the girl. Women are...well, they're complicated. I hope he doesn't get in over his head."

"Joni seems like a sweet girl. He could do worse."

Jameson sat forward and arranged some correspondence on his desk. "We'll see."

Ross stood and made ready to leave. "I wanted to apologize about not having the time to put together any type of retirement shindig for you. Bobby had pushed for it but it's been a rough few months, like I said. With LSI's comeback and the transition, I couldn't see my way into it. Perhaps we can plan something intimate. Dinner with the VPs or something. Sound good?"

Jameson waved him off. "I told you before, I don't want a fuss. Just a quick meeting with the employees to say goodbye before I head out. It'll be my birthday anyway. That makes it a little awkward. Besides, Bobby mentioned something about going to dinner and a play. Maybe he'll be talking to me again by then. I guess we'll see."

"Let me know. We want to mark the occasion one way or another. It's the least we can do for you after all you've done for us."

Jameson asked Ross to close the door behind him when he left. He picked up the phone and stabbed line 2, then dialed Herb Radford's cell phone number from heart. He hated knowing the number by heart. Doing so meant they had taken far too long to conclude their business.

The call went straight to voicemail. Jameson hung up before the automated robot instructed him to leave a message at the beep.

Where was Farin? And what was she up to? At first, it made sense she would attempt to find the child. Then, after the fire at Hopeful Heart, he had been assured the complication no longer existed. But things had been too quiet for far too long at this point. Either Moreau had made up Herb Radford's stellar reputation to get him off his back, or Farin had managed to stay one step ahead of them all. The latter seemed unlikely.

Something did not add up.

***

Derek's band huddled around Levoy's drum set in the Virginia Key studio as Sawyer updated them on their friend and lead singer's progress. It was a somber day. They had not even come to practice. Lost over the tragic turn of events, they simply did not know where else to go.

"I've been trying to call him," Peter Neill told the group. "His mom says he's pretty out of it and can't talk."

"They just brought him home yesterday," Sawyer explained. "I haven't even been over to see him yet."

"Is he gonna be okay?" Brian Keller asked.

Sawyer bobbed his head absently. "It's gonna take time, and it's gonna be painful. I'm no doctor, but I've heard shoulder surgery is tough. Plus, he broke a couple of ribs and there's a lot of bruising."

"What about studio wahk, eh, Sawyah?" Levoy asked, repositioning himself awkwardly as the others shot him incredulous looks. "Sowwy, but we 'ave a joob. We'uh getting ahlboom cwedeet. I just want ta know eef dis means de gig ees done. Dah'eek wooe'd ahsk de same."

"You don't worry about that album." He eyed the boys with confident reassurance. "It's almost done anyway. You'll get your due. That's a promise."

Peter looked down and away. "Is he ever gonna be able to play again?"

Sawyer stood up and chuckled at the dejected young musicians. "What're you talking about? Of course he's gonna play again. This is a setback. It'll take him longer to heal his heart than his ribs and shoulder, trust me. What you all need to do is be patient, supportive, and don't give him too much slack. Sure, we'll let him have his space for a month or so. But you're his friends first, right?"

They nodded and grunted their mournful agreements.

"Then that's what we'll be—his *friends*. Call him and let him know you're thinking about him, but don't be pushy...at first. I'll let you know if we need to start kicking his ass back into gear. For now, keep practicing. He'll catch up when he's better. You mark my words."

When he had finished the FLA pep talk, he left the studio and headed for Ben's. As much as he worried over Derek's situation, he wanted to see Farin. It bothered him she had not talked to him before she had taken off. Their relationship would not work this way. He had not broken things off with Cécile only to be casually discarded by Farin.

He wanted to stop and get flowers but decided it too weird. Ultimately, as FLA's acting manager, his support belonged with Derek. Showing up with flowers for his aunt might make it appear he had his priorities skewed.

When Ben opened the door, Sawyer felt the full weight of the situation spill out onto the front porch steps like broken boulders from an avalanche. Usually, he heard chatter or music when he entered the Grant house. Today, there was silence.

He shook Ben's hand. "How's he doing?"

Ben gestured for him to come in. "He's pretty hopped up on pain meds right now."

"I hate to say it, but it's probably best for him to be zoned out for a while. The pain's one thing. But losing Summer?"

Ben nodded and headed for the living room. "Right."

Cheryl wore a forced smile as she offered him a glass of lemonade, which he accepted. He sat on the living room sofa and looked around, disappointed Farin was nowhere to be seen. He wanted to ask, but swallowed his curiosity along with the tangy beverage.

"I'm sorry," he said. "I can't help feeling this is as much my fault as anyone's."

"I'll be honest, Sawyer. I'm not happy about it, but you didn't cause the accident."

"I guess I remember being his age is all. It seemed harmless to help them stay home alone. They're such good kids."

"Aye." Cheryl joined them, taking a seat beside her husband. "But even good boys get into mischief. If we'd wanted them here alone, we'd have said it was okay. It's not a matter of trust, mind you. We had our reasons."

Sawyer pushed his lips out, nodded, and stared at the floor. "I understand. I'd hate this to negatively affect our relationship."

"We're a family that heals," Cheryl assured him, giving her husband's belly a loving rub. "I'll trust this won't happen again. But let's be honest. If Derek had been at Peter's like he was supposed to be, it might have happened anyway. He'd been worried about Summer for weeks. It's not likely Peter's parents would have been able to stop him from slipping out so late at night."

"What about Kyle? How's he doing?"

Cheryl gave a long, mournful sigh. "That's another story. He's quite upset over the ordeal. He was very fond of Summer, and of course he's devastated over his brother."

"Poor kid."

"I have to find a way to put it in perspective," Ben told him. "Maybe this will teach him a lesson as he's learning to drive."

"Have you talked to the Reeces?"

"Cheryl's made a casserole to take over this afternoon. We wanted to give our condolences in person."

A knock at the door sent Ben up and toward the entryway. Sawyer sipped his lemonade, a part of him still guilt-ridden over his part in the tragic set of events. Had it happened with his parents, they would have never extended such grace.

Ben returned with Chris in tow, which immediately set Sawyer on the defensive. He straightened his posture like a settler driving a stake into a piece of land. Chris raised his chin. He returned the tepid greeting.

"Is he awake?" Chris asked his brother.

Ben indicated the stairs. "I'm not sure. You can go on up if you want. Let him know his mother and I can get him some lunch if he's hungry. He hasn't been eating much."

Chris nodded and trotted upstairs.

Sawyer dipped his head and ran his fingers across the back of his head, then glanced sideways to ensure Chris was gone. "So...I hate to sound like a cad, but I was wondering if you'd heard from Farin yet."

Ben drew in his chin and frowned. "She hasn't called you?"

He shook his head.

"She's home," Ben told him, resuming his spot next to his wife and putting his arm around her shoulder. "She made it to LA and flew back with us. I guess I thought you'd have talked to her by now."

"I haven't heard a word from her since before she left. Is she here now?"

"She's in the studio. But before you go out there, there's something you might need to know."

Upstairs, Chris found Derek sleeping on his back, his left arm still in its sling and propped up on a pillow. The boy had scratches on his face and a split lip. On his nightstand was a bottle of pills and a glass of water.

He sat down at the foot of the bed, which caused Derek's drowsy mind to stir. He looked at his uncle with bleary eyes as he struggled to get his body into a sitting position using his right arm. Chris stood and assisted him, propping pillows up behind him. "How're you feeling?"

Derek dipped his head, wiping the sleep from his eyes and then grabbing the glass for a sip of water. "Okay, I guess."

"You look pretty rough."

Derek nodded.

"I just wanted you to know I'll be around. I'm back now and I'm not going anywhere. At least not until you're better."

Derek accepted a quick, gentle hug from his uncle, then leaned back onto the pillows.

Chris watched his unfocused eyes stare into the middle distance and realized there was nothing he could say to ease the type of pain he endured. He knew that pain all too well. "If you need to talk..."

Derek nodded again. He sniffed and swallowed as his eyes began to tear up.

Chris stood and touched the boy's leg, then turned away to give him his privacy. From the doorway, he said, "Your mum and dad wanted me to ask if you're hungry."

Derek glanced up and shot him a look that required no explanation.

He nodded, then took off, calling over his shoulder, "Get some rest. And call me anytime day or night if you need to talk."

"Uncle Chris?"

He stopped and turned around.

"I'm glad you're gonna be around more."

He flattened his lips, gave him a curt nod, and left.

News of the accident had curtailed his intention to speak with Farin. The first few days had gone by in a blur, with them huddled predominantly at the hospital. He wanted to ask her more about little Jordan, gauge her interest in talking about where they stood, and finish their discussion about the details of Jordan's murder. She had promised to tell him everything. The time had come for her to make good on it.

He trotted downstairs, brisked through the house, and headed out back, bypassing the kitchen where he heard Ben and Cheryl's quiet chatter. Fortunately, he did not see Sawyer.

Inside the studio, he found little Jordan sitting near Ben's shelves, a small plastic bin of crayons beside her. She rummaged through them to find the right color, then added to the scribble of her picture. When she noticed him, she greeted him with an enthusiastic smile and jumped up to hug him.

"Uncle Chris!" She wrapped her small arms around his neck.

"How are you doing? I see you're creating another masterpiece for your collection."

"This one's for you!"

"It is?" He set her down, then sat beside her Indian-style and sorted through the crayons. "Make sure you include a lot of green."

"Is that your favorite color?"

He nodded. "It is."

"Okay." She dug through the bin and picked out several variations of green, placed them on the floor beside her, and rubbed the colored wax across the page.

"Where's your mum?"

Her expression changed slightly as she pointed to the kitchen.

He petted her soft hair, then went to look for Farin. When he walked into the small kitchenette, he found her locked in an embrace with Sawyer. His stomach knotted at the sight.

He thought about interrupting them. In fact, he thought about punching Sawyer square in the jaw, but instead he turned away before they noticed him, circled back to give his niece a kiss on the cheek, and told her he would see her soon.

***

The thick pot holders she used to hold the chicken Alfredo casserole warmed her hands just short of too hot. She used her elbow to ring the doorbell, then waited as she heard footsteps approach.

The Reeces' housekeeper answered the door. When Cheryl asked to speak to Mrs. Reece, the woman told her to wait on the steps, closed the door, and called out for her employer.

Cheryl found the lack of warmth odd, but kept a sympathetic expression on her face as she stood on the doorstep holding the thick ceramic baking pan. After a couple of minutes, she wondered if anyone would come to the door. When she heard heavier footsteps—undeniably male—she stepped back and lifted her chin to brace herself for the inevitable.

"What is it you need, Mrs. Grant?" asked Frederick Reece.

"I came to pay my respects, to tell you how sorry we are about Summer."

He stared down the bridge of his nose at the casserole as if it was a bucket of slop.

"Is Ulani available? Is she okay?"

"No, Mrs. Grant. My wife is neither available nor 'okay.' None of us are."

"I understand."

"I doubt it."

The sharp reply stung. She attributed his abrupt tone to the intense pain he doubtless felt over the loss of his only child. Looking at him in his impeccable suit and perfectly combed hair, one might not realize what he was going through. Her heart went out to him. "Derek's home from the hospital now. His surgery went as well as can be expected. He's got a long road ahead of him, but he'll be okay with some physical therapy and hard work."

He snorted with disdain. "Is that your way of notifying us you intend to sue over your son's injuries?"

Her lips parted in surprise. "*Sue* you? Of course not. Fred, this was nothing more than a tragic accident. Ben and I are devastated by your loss. We can't imagine how you and Ulani are coping."

"So you thought you'd bring us food."

She lifted one shoulder and stammered. "I...I really didn't know what t-to do. We're all so sad. We loved Summer very much. We considered her a part of our family."

"Well, she wasn't your family. She would have never been part of your family."

"I figure Ulani's not up for guests and certainly not up to cooking." She extended her arms and offered the dish. "I hope this will help in some small way. We'd like to know when you schedule the funeral. Ben asked me to tell you we're praying for you and Ulani every night. And of course, if there's anything we can do—"

He slammed the door in her face.

***

The Los Olivos Garden psychiatric hospital's security left much to be desired, but it did allow him easy enough entrance. He simply waited for a small group of visitors to engage the guard and slipped in with them. Easy peasy.

Tuesdays were particularly busy in terms of guests visiting loved ones. He knew because he had done a fair amount of research on this job. Far more than usual. Then again, the facility represented a higher than normal risk—particularly with cameras everywhere he looked. He could not feasibly avoid them. Good thing he had opted to park a block down the street just in case.

Still, he detested his disguise. The fat suit impeded his usual agility. Ah well, it did the job. He looked pretty good with dark hair even if he said so himself. But the beard and mustache made his face itch. All the more reason to get in, get the job done, and get out as quickly as possible.

He glanced at the sign-in sheet as the people in front of him chatted with the receptionist. When they left, he stepped forward and signed in using a fake name and jotted down a random guest in the "name of resident" section he noted from further down the list. He nodded at the receptionist as if he knew her, then stepped out of the way to allow the next visitor to sign in. No question. No hesitation.

A framed piece of paper hung on the wall beside each room foolishly listing the name of the resident who lived there. It made his job almost too easy.

Some of the plaques listed two names, indicating a shared residential space. He hoped he would not have to deal with a roommate situation. It seemed a shame to have to take care of someone unrelated to his target. That had never been his style.

None of the rooms in the main building displayed the right name. When he exited through the rear of the building, he worried for a moment he might not gain entrance to the second. A security guard stood watch by the door.

He looped back around and headed for the common room he had spotted during his search so he could take a moment to devise a plan to get inside. Maybe he should have waited until dark and snuck in. He could have avoided the disguise and the chance of someone later recalling the strange man who seemingly just walked the floors.

The common room buzzed with activity. Some residents watched TV, some chatted with their visitors, while others played cards. He strolled the room, smiling when seen, as he considered his next move.

"Sarah? We need you to eat, hon. If you don't eat lunch, we'll have to call the doctor in to take a look at you."

He spun around at the name and saw a nurse kneeling beside an elderly woman seated on the couch. Her hair was clean and held up in a clip, leaving her neck exposed. He smiled as he moved closer to catch the conversation.

"Dr. Jackson," the woman said.

"That's right, Sarah. Dr. Jackson's concerned you're not eating lately."

"Jackson," she said. "Faction. Fraction. Action."

Another nurse joined them, squatting down next to the first. "What can we get you to eat, Ms. Wellingham? Dr. Jackson said if you didn't have some lunch, she'd have to come down and speak to you."

The patient jutted her chin and shook her head as she ran her right hand up and down her left arm.

The nurses stood up and walked away, shaking their heads.

"She's having a bad day," one of them said.

"More like a bad month," corrected the other.

"I don't see why the family doesn't relocate her closer to them. There are so many good facilities in New York. It's not like they come visit here. And they never call...it's a shame."

"It is. It really is."

He scanned the room, gauging the interest of the other residents and their guests. Either they had not heard the conversation or they had politely ignored it. *Good. Very good.*

It took seconds to slip his hand into his pants pocket, pull out the syringe, and administer the lethal dose of succinylcholine into the appropriate vein. Quick, if not perfect. So quick, in fact, Sarah barely made a peep. Sure, the needle mark would be found in an autopsy, but who cared?

He would be gone before they realized she was dead.

CHAPTER 25

"I COULD DRIVE YOU ALL the way to station," Sawyer told Farin as she buckled her seat belt then flipped down the visor to check her wig and makeup.

"I appreciate that, but I made a promise. Macy helped me find my daughter. The least I can do is let him be the one who takes me over to talk to the cops. Besides, we're not meeting at the station."

He frowned. "Why not?"

"It's still too early. Whoever helped the dead cop cover up Jordan's murder and the whole limo 'accident' may still have connections. If Jameson paid off one cop, there are likely to be more. Maybe even the captain. They don't know yet."

Sawyer shook his head, popped in Robert Cray's *Some Rainy Morning*, and rested his forearm atop the steering wheel. "Moan" filled the truck with its upbeat blues lamentation of lost love. "This is some nutty stuff, Farin. Just sayin'."

"Wow, did you just figure that out? I'd have thought it was clear the first day we met. But if this is too much for you..." She shrugged.

"I didn't say that."

"Then what are you saying? I mean, think about it. You're still so young—"

"Oh, come on. Don't start with that again."

"What? It's true. I'm a thirty-two year old widowed mother of a three year old, which you yourself just observed is pretty complicated. And you're a twenty-five year old single college student and band manager whose only wrinkle in life appears to be his choice in women."

"And?"

"And...*that's* some nutty stuff."

They motored along in silence through the village, over the causeway, then down Biscayne Boulevard on their way to Miles' place in Coconut Grove. Dark clouds obscured the morning sun, making their short commute a humid, dreary one.

"I think Ben and I'll be able to finish the album with the tracks the boys already laid down," he said at last, forfeiting his position in their contest of wills. "I can always fill in for Derek on the guitar spots if need be. You should be fine. Have you talked to Minor about a potential release date?"

She carefully threaded her long fingers through her artificial hair, pushing it back and away from her neck. "I haven't really thought about it, to tell you the truth. Right now I just want to get in, give my statement, and push for the Lockhardts' arrest. It's time. In fact, it's past time. With little Jordan safe, there's no reason to put it off any longer."

He bobbed his head almost imperceptibly, acknowledging her despite his frustration. "It'd do a lot more damage to Lockhardt if you succeeded despite him. The minute you release a new piece of work, you're on top again. The album doesn't even have to be good."

Her eyes shot daggers of indignation his way. "What's that supposed to mean? Are we doing that again? You tell me I'm great while insulting my work?"

"What's wrong, Farin? Ever since you got back, you've been one misunderstood comment away from ripping my head off my shoulders."

"'The album doesn't even have to be good,'" she mocked. "What a vote of confidence. Thanks for that."

"I didn't say it *wasn't* good. I said it doesn't matter if it's good or not. The point is, your story's gonna eclipse the record. The sensationalism alone will send shockwaves out across the world. You know that, and you know what I mean. So chill already."

She maneuvered her neck back and forth to relieve the tension from her restless night. Ever since she had found Jordan she had harbored fear the little girl would never fully adjust to the disruption of her young life.

Jordan had lived in an orphanage for her first two and a half years. Nothing but a group of under-invested, rotating caregivers who oversaw dozens of children just like her. No personal bonding. No comfort. No mother. Then, she was temporarily placed with a couple she would not have much chance to get to know before being whisked off by the woman who had appeared out of nowhere and announced she was her mother, and that they needed to leave right away.

Farin had to hand it to her. Jordan was nothing if not resilient. So far she seemed to have adjusted well. The Grant household showered upon her everything she had previously missed out on. Ben and Cheryl adored and interacted with her. The boys had immediately fallen in love with and doted on their cousin—even Derek, who could barely move let alone process the myriad shifts within the household and his own circumstances.

Nonetheless, Farin worried whether Jordan would ever fully accept her. She called her Momma and acted excited every time Farin entered a room to check on or play with her. But the stubborn insistence that everyone call her "Jade" was disheartening. Maybe things would change in time. It had to be confusing at three to be told your name was not the name to which you had answered your entire life.

Farin sighed. "You're right. I'm sorry. It's just that I'm worry about Jordan, the album's nearly finished, I've got a niece in California I've never met, and I really miss Marci. All that and I'm still hiding out and wearing disguises. I just want it to be over. Maybe I do need a chill pill."

Sawyer dug into his jeans pocket and pulled out a small plastic resealable bag with about a dozen small peach-colored tablets. "I just happen to carry a few of those with me."

Her upper lip scrunched up and back. "I was speaking metaphorically. I don't want that."

"Sure you do. You just don't want to say you do."

"Is that what you think of me?"

He scoffed. "Here we go again."

They found Miles waiting outside on his porch when they drove up. Farin jerked her purse up off the floorboard, thanked Sawyer for dropping her off, and told him she would talk to him later.

Before she exited the vehicle, he grabbed her forearm. "Don't leave like this. I don't wanna fight."

"I don't want to fight either, but something about this isn't feeling right."

He nodded. "We'll work it out. Things are just tense right now. Let's not start analyzing the relationship too closely when there's so much going on, okay? I'm going to go back to Ben's and start mixing that new song you did last night. It was good. You're great. The album's gonna be amazing."

She cocked her head to one side. "Yeah. My 'story' will ensure it, right?"

"You're more than your story, Farin. And, for the record, you're more than a thirty-two year old widowed mother of a three year old. You're a beautiful, talented, sexy woman. As a matter of fact, I think I'm gonna ask Cheryl if she'd mind taking care of the kid for the night." He waggled his eyebrows.

"I don't know. It seems awfully early to start being away. Besides, I'm a little tense."

"No, you're a *lot* tense. And I'm gonna dedicate the entire night to loosening you up."

When he tugged on her arm, she leaned in and kissed him, then got out of the car and waved at Miles, who lifted his chin at Sawyer then got in his own vehicle.

"You okay?" Farin asked as she settled in.

Miles yawned as he watched Sawyer back out of the driveway, then shifted his car into reverse. "I'm okay. Exhausted more than anything else. I just got in last night. How about you? Big day, huh?"

She sighed. "I don't know why I'm nervous."

"Don't be. All you're doing is telling them what Lockhardt's done. They already know most of it anyway. You just need to connect the dots. The sooner it's done, the sooner they pick up the bad guys—and you can lose that ridiculous wig."

Farin rolled her eyes and settled into his leather interior. If she heard one more person comment on her disguise, she thought she might scream.

Miles navigated onto Bird, then headed west under the Palmetto Expressway and into Olympia Heights. They chatted as he drove, with Miles giving Farin a snapshot of how the various parties got involved and started comparing notes.

"I can't believe someone bought the limousine," Farin said. "Who does that?"

"Fans'll buy just about anything associated with their icons."

"'Icon.' I don't know how I feel about that."

He chuckled. "You're a lot different than I remember you."

She stared absently out the window. "A lot's changed since then."

"Don't I know it."

"So where's this place you're taking me?"

"To the home of one of the detectives."

"The one you're trying to impress?"

He lifted his lips into a sideways grin. "Something like that."

They arrived at Alvarez's place at ten as scheduled. Farin checked out the area as she exited the vehicle and followed Miles up the cement walk to the door. She noted the unmarked police car parked on the street and a large terracotta flower pot sticking out of the ground at an angle near the front of the house.

A dark-haired woman in a tight yet flattering business suit flung open the door. An instant look of disbelief clouded her pretty features as she stood slack-jawed, glancing back and forth between them.

A satisfied grin stretched across Macy's face as he stood straighter. "See? Told ya!"

The woman scoffed as she opened the screen door and stood aside to let them in. "I still think Billy should have arrested you," she spat.

Miles made the introductions as Alvarez eyeballed Farin with a mixture of suspicion and shock. When Farin extended her hand, the detective gave her a hearty handshake.

"I understand you've been in touch with Special Agent Quarles," she said.

Farin nodded. "I have. He helped me get my daughter back after Miles found her."

Alvarez side-eyed the reporter but said nothing.

A moment later, another detective appeared from the hallway and greeted her with a warmth Farin found curious given the first detective's abrasive first impression. "I'm Detective Bridgeman. You have no idea how glad we are to meet you. Don't mind my partner. To know her is to love her. Just ask Macy."

Farin tucked a strand of synthetic hair behind her ear and smiled as she addressed Alvarez. "Miles talks about you all the time."

"Really?" she snapped as she gestured toward the couch. "I wish he'd talked about you all the time. We've been working our asses off trying to warm up this cold case."

"Anything you want to know, just ask. I want to ensure my husband gets the justice he deserves." She sat down on the sofa next to Miles and stared at the brightly colored Our Lady of Guadalupe wall art above the dark wood credenza.

Bridgeman and Alvarez carried in two chairs from the kitchen table and positioned them to face Farin. Bridgeman picked up a clipboard off the coffee table and slid his hand inside the pocket of his suit jacket for a pen. "I appreciate your agreeing to talk to us. You can imagine how anxious we are to get your statement."

She nodded. "I realize it's been a long time coming."

For the next two hours, Farin chronicled every uncomfortable memory of her life, starting with the loss of her father at the age of ten to her mother's subsequent alcohol abuse to Jordan's discovery of Jameson's cover-up and Farin's death-dealing impulsivity in confronting the men responsible. Though painful, she maintained commendable strength as she described in detail Bobby's sexual assault and Charles Russell's selfless care in the days that followed. Lastly, she told them what happened the day Bobby Lockhardt murdered her husband and explained how she was kidnapped and nearly killed until Jameson learned of her pregnancy.

"I can only assume that, given the rape, he believed the baby might be Bobby's," she concluded. "They tested her right away. I can only assume that once he realized she wasn't his granddaughter, he started making plans to take her away from me."

The sobering series of events left both detectives and Miles shaking their heads. Even Alvarez softened at the ordeal. She regarded Farin as she lifted her chin in Miles' direction. "You know, you owe Macy a lot for helping you out. He's been tweaking Lockhardt's nose for years."

"That's why I went to him first. It's not his fault he couldn't tell you about me, Detective. Until I found my daughter, I couldn't tell anyone. Now, it's time to make the Lockhardts pay for what they've done to me and my family. So whatever we need to do, let's do it."

***

Surprisingly, Ross' hands did not tremble as he navigated his vehicle back to the office from his interview with Agent Quarles. Interesting. He had figured after revealing the truth about Jameson's lifelong crimes he would fear the very idea of going back. Instead, a certain peace settled upon him. Decades too late, he had done the right thing. Josephine would have been proud of him.

Of course, he left out the one event that had started the dominoes falling. He had thought long and hard whether to bring it up before finally deciding to leave the incidents in London alone. Why complicate things at this point by getting Scotland Yard involved? Besides, he needed to have at least one last card to play should things not go according to plan.

When he got back to his office, he filtered through a stack of opened mail Stacy had left on the desk, returned a few phone calls, then sought Jameson out to get his okay on a couple of contract changes requested by one of their new artists. He found him in his usual place at his desk, though he had turned his chair around to face the window.

He knocked lightly on the open door. "Do you have a minute to discuss a couple of contracts? I'm hoping to get them finished and signed before the end of the day." There came no response. Curious, he dared to take a couple of steps inside. "Jameson?"

The man turned around slowly, cleared his throat, and scooted in closer to the desk. He waved Ross inside. "If it's quick. I'll be leaving for the afternoon. I'm taking Bobby up to the house."

Ross studied him with curious eyes. "Can this mean you two have finally started talking again?"

Jameson looked up at him, and Ross noticed the man's red, puffy eyes.

"Is something wrong?"

He motioned for Ross to shut the door. "I haven't told Bobby yet. I don't know how."

Ross eased into a high back chair and set his folders on the desk.

The old man cleared his throat again and sniffed, then swallowed. "You never really, uh...you never knew Sarah."

Ross wrinkled his forehead.

"You met her long after her condition robbed her of her mind. She was the most beautiful woman I've ever seen. Strong. Full of life. Passionate."

He relaxed his body into the seat as Jameson spoke about the only woman he had ever loved. How they had met. How she had changed his life. How she had saved him. As he spoke, his tone carried an undercurrent of raw emotion and regret Ross had never before heard. "Has something happened to Sarah?" he asked at last.

Jameson nodded as he stared sightlessly at his desk, his heavy jowls pulling the corners of his mouth into a mournful, hopeless frown. "She's gone."

Ross' lips parted. "*Wha*—how? What happened?"

"Heart attack."

He rested his elbow on the arm of the chair and covered his mouth with his fingers. For a long moment, he could not think of anything to say or do. Part of him had long separated himself from any ounce of pity or concern for the man who had spent most of the years they had known each other manipulating him. Another part of him beheld the shell of the man before him with deep understanding. *Tick, tick, tick.*

Quietly, he rose and went to the wet bar. He poured two rocks glasses with straight Scotch and placed one on the desk blotter before sitting back down with the other. He touched the vessel with his own, then took a sip.

Jameson regarded the glass with an empty expression, then lifted his eyes to Ross. "How am I going to tell Bobby?"

Ross slowly shook his head.

"I should have taken the time to see her more often. I should have visited."

"Is that what she would have wanted? I guess I was under the impression she preferred you stay away."

Jameson grabbed the glass, downed its contents in a mighty gulp, then sank back into his chair. "She'd have refused to see me. But I should have gone anyway."

Ross considered the man's words. "How can I help? What do you need me to do? Are there arrangements that need to be made?"

"When the hospital contacted me, I gave them some initial instructions. I've picked out her casket. But I told them I'll be arranging to have her body flown to New England and placed in the family plot. You remember the details, I trust."

He nodded. "Certainly. I'll get in touch with the appropriate parties right away."

Jameson lifted a finger at the folders on his desk. "Is there anything significant in those or can I sign them?"

"Nothing major. I've gone through the requests, pushed back on the things we care about. I think they're fine."

He sat forward, gestured for the paperwork, and grabbed a pen. "Did you see Bobby on your way in?"

"I didn't look."

"I asked Stacy to put a lunch meeting on his calendar. I'm taking him to my place for the afternoon."

"Okay. I'll leave word with her before I leave tonight and let you know where we are with the arrangements."

Jameson scribbled his signature on the contracts and handed them back to Ross. "I guess it's a good thing Bobby went to see his mother back in June."

The hair on Ross' neck stood at attention as he tucked the contracts back into their folders and attempted not to respond. "Wasn't that during our trip out west?"

A slight change of disposition temporarily tabled the old man's grief. "Indeed. I'd asked you to look after him and ensure he didn't go to the hospital."

"I did my best. He was adamant. I couldn't physically stop him."

"Apparently not."

Ross peeked up at him. "You never mentioned it when we returned. I didn't realize you knew."

"I knew. After all these years, I'd think it was abundantly clear—I always find out eventually."

He calmly gathered his files, downed the remnant of his drink, then placed the empty glass near the small sink before he left. "I'll get on those arrangements right away. For what it's worth, I'm sorry about Sarah. If you need to talk, give me a call. I know how it feels to lose the only woman you ever loved. Give Bobby my condolences."

***

Alicia's lips curled up and back as she grudgingly approached Miles' passenger door and glanced in the back seat. "A picnic basket? You've got to be kidding."

He did not so much as attempt to suppress his enthusiasm as he rushed in front of her to open the door. "Hey, take it easy on me. I didn't have a lot of time to plan this out. But I didn't want to give you a chance to renege on your promise either."

She rolled her eyes and flounced into the front seat. "You could have planned it further out than a day."

He sprinted back to the driver's side and lowered himself into his seat. "Not a chance. I've waited too long. I'd have taken you out last night after I got Farin back to her place if it'd been up to me. Just sit back and relax. You're here anyway. How bad can it be?"

The doubtful lift of her brows as she clicked her safety belt in place spoke volumes.

He turned the ignition key, then shifted into reverse and began backing out of her driveway. Before the tires reached the road, he tapped the breaks and looked at her. "No work today. Deal?"

She looked at him as if in protest.

"It's a date, not a debriefing."

Exasperated, she sighed. "Okay, okay."

With a curt nod, he continued on. He needed a break from the story as much as he figured she did.

During his time in LA, he had continued to try to make sense of several portions of the e-mail/riddle that still confused him. At this point, there appeared no need to share his mysterious project with the Feds or his girlfriend and her partner. Farin and her daughter were safe. Now that the wheels were in motion to deal with the Lockhardts, maybe those portions still unsolved no longer mattered. It seemed they dealt mostly with people or events "across the pond" anyway. He had no intention of teaming up with Scotland Yard, which seemed the next logical step if he were to pursue it further. Sometimes he had to remind himself he was a reporter, not a cop.

The mostly cloudy sky and resultant humidity discouraged him from putting the windows down. Instead, he kicked on the A/C before backing out of the driveway, stealing a quick glance at the beautiful passenger to his right. The aloof expression on her otherwise perfect features could have taken the wind out of his sails, but he decided to forge ahead. He was happy enough about their date for the both of them. Maybe that was enough for now. Maybe she would come around.

"So where are you taking me?"

"North," he said, a playful smirk tugging at one side of his mouth.

"'North?'"

"Yep."

She shook her head and folded her arms. "North it is."

He asked if she wanted to listen to some music. At first she declined, claiming she had never been much of a music lover. But when he agreed and told her the absence of sound would allow them plenty of time to talk as he drove, she asked him to turn on the radio. He found a light jazz station before they hit I-95, then took the on-ramp, almost immediately settling into the easy Sunday traffic pattern so he could set his cruise control.

"Are you nervous?" he asked. "I know I am."

"Why would I be nervous?"

"I don't know. I've been asking you out for so long, and now we're here. Maybe the hype of getting you to say yes won't live up to the actual date."

She crossed her ankles and perched her elbow on the side window ledge as she stared ahead. "It doesn't matter, does it? It was a bet between Bridgeman and me. I lost. I'm here."

"Is that really all this is to you?"

Her eyes flicked downward.

"You know, we've been through a lot together trying to figure out all the details around the Grant cases. I realize a lot of that time has felt like we're at cross purposes, but it's not like we're strangers."

"Practically."

"No, not practically. But Alicia, if you're honestly only here because you lost a bet, I'll turn around and take you back. I've waited way too long for you to have such low expectations about something that means so much to me."

She dipped her head and moved her lower jaw slightly to the right.

With a scoff of hurtful disbelief, Miles sat up straighter in his seat. He eyeballed his side and rearview mirrors, tapped the brake pedal to disengage the cruise control, then flicked on his turn signal.

Alicia reached out and touched his forearm. "Wait."

Immediately, Miles killed the turn signal. "If you don't want this, Alicia, I don't want to force you. That's not what this is about. Not to me."

"Just drive...north."

"You're sure?"

She settled back into her seat, wiggling her shoulders and back until comfortable, then closed her eyes. "Don't make me say it again, Macy."

He grinned and relaxed in his seat, guiding the steering wheel with his left arm. "I won't ask again."

The sparse but steady end-of-weekend traffic lulled them both into a sort of peaceful truce as Diana Krall's "Only Trust Your Heart" stilled their shared edginess of the last year and a half into a long, overdue rest. Miles exited the freeway near Ft. Lauderdale, navigated east to the A1A, then continued north.

Alvarez tilted her head to the side and watched the waves roll up along the sea strand then recede like an awkward schoolboy who had stolen his first kiss. Periodically, Miles' eyes darted her way as if to reassure himself she truly sat beside him. His whole body swelled with hopeful anticipation mixed with an inexplicable sense he could not manage to take a full breath for the pounding in his chest.

"I'm tired," she told him in a lazy voice.

His forehead wrinkled with concern. "I...uh, okay. I'm sorry. I can turn around—"

"Macy." She rolled her head along the back of the seat and gave him a downward grin. "I was making conversation."

He lifted his chin, exhaled, then nodded.

She rolled her eyes, then stared ahead at the road. "Tired inside, you know? I feel responsible in a way for this whole thing. I know Stark was the one who manipulated files and took money, but my name's on those reports, too. I wasn't a very good detective."

"You were following orders. He outranked you. Not much you could have done different from my estimation."

She shrugged.

"He wasn't a very good partner. You don't need me to tell you that."

"Billy's a better fit for me, that's for sure." She jerked her head toward him and pointed at him. "Don't you dare tell him I said that."

Miles chuckled softly. "I won't say a word."

She relaxed her body and turned back to watch the ocean. "I'm not good at this."

"At what?"

"This. Dating. Being still. Getting to know someone—especially some gringo who's so white he listens to smooth jazz on the radio as he cruises up the coastline."

He reached for the radio to change the station.

Without looking his way, she grabbed his hand in hers. "Don't. It's nice."

His heart felt as if it skipped a beat as he interlaced his fingers with hers.

"Your hand's cold," she observed.

"I think my circulation's still trying to get used to being near you."

Her lips lifted into a smile.

They parked the car at Boynton's Oceanfront Park Beach. Alicia grabbed the picnic basket out of the back seat while Miles pulled out two folding lounge chairs from the trunk. They made their way down to the sand and looked north, then south for an ideal spot close enough to enjoy their surroundings yet far enough away to anticipate the inevitable encroaching tide.

"It's not too crowded," Miles said. "You know, there are portions of this beach that feel like they've never been touched by man."

She tilted her head back and inhaled. "I'll follow. You lead."

"Yeah?"

She raised one eyelid and smirked. "Just this once."

They walked along the strand until Miles decided on a place far enough away from the other visitors littering the beach. He put down the lounge chairs and took the basket from Alicia. A red-and-white-checkered blanket lay folded on top. He shook it out, arranged it on the sand, then situated the chairs close together with just enough room for the picnic basket to sit between them. She sat down, folded her hands in her lap, and looked inside the basket with interest.

"I figured we'd grab something more substantial on the way back if you want," he explained as he unpacked a bottle of wine, two plastic glasses, sealed containers of fruit and cheese, some butter, and a loaf of crusty bread. "Nothing too heavy at first, I thought. Then, if you don't feel up to dinner, well..."

"Stop trying so hard," she said. She helped unseal and arrange the light fare, popping a ripe grape into her mouth as she leaned in to check the basket. "Where's the knife to cut and butter the bread?"

Miles' eyes grew wide. In the fading afternoon light, his cheeks reddened as he palm-slapped his forehead. "I knew I forgot something."

She grabbed the loaf and tore off one end, then gently scraped a piece along the stick of butter and handed it to him. "We'll improvise."

He took it from her and smiled, then stuck the end in his mouth.

They sat on the sides of their lounge chairs, facing each other as they ate and discussed the Grant cases at length. Slowly, the conversation veered to other topics of their families, childhoods, and past relationships.

"I don't know how you managed to survive with so many brothers—being the youngest to boot? No wonder you're so tough."

"Me? What about you? An older sister? Explains a lot, Macy."

His eyes twinkled mischievously. "Why? Because I'm so understanding with women?"

"No, because you never know when to give up. They must have spoiled you rotten."

"Persistence isn't such a bad thing."

"Come on. Give it up, cowboy. They did, didn't they?"

Her relaxed smile undid him. He mirrored her infectious expression and nodded. "Guilty."

A bark of laughter escaped her mouth as she half-lunged toward him. "I knew it!"

"It's served me well, actually. I couldn't have gotten as far in my line of work as I have if I didn't know how to stay the course. Sorta like you, right? I can only guess it's been rough trying to prove yourself in a predominately male profession. Growing up with so much testosterone must have given you some advantage in your career."

"You're smart, Macy. Smarter than I figured."

He swung his legs around to lie back on his chair. Looking up at the sky, he noted darker clouds gathering. "Looks like we're gonna get rain after all."

She swiped some bread crumbs off her hands and followed his gaze upward. "You're right. I think we might need to pack up."

"It's only five," he argued. "What sort of a date am I taking you on, anyway? A Sunday afternoon?"

She stood and waved him up off his chair, then helped him gather the leftovers. "First off, the date isn't finished. You promised me dinner—and I want steak."

He gazed at her affectionately as she swept some sand from an overturned container. "Anything you want."

"Second, it's a long drive back."

"Yes."

"And third, the next time you want to take me out on a Sunday, we're going to church first. My tía will kill me if I miss another Sunday."

He smiled. "I promise."

They trudged back through the sand and managed to pack everything into his trunk before a light rain began to fall. Miles clicked his fob to unlock the car doors, then opened Alvarez's for her.

She brushed his upper arm as she moved past him. As if an afterthought, she turned back, searched his eyes, then grazed his lips with her own. "This is nice."

He leaned forward for a better kiss a moment too late. She had already tilted her head and slid inside as if nothing had happened. Closing the door, he temporarily lifted his chin skyward, allowing the rain to mist his face—the closest thing he could get to splashing himself with a palmful of cool water.

As he wiped the dampness away and moved around the car toward the driver's door, he took a deep breath and wondered how long he should wait before asking her to marry him. Almost immediately, he rethought the spontaneous idea. He had a mother, a father, six brothers, and at least one "tía" to charm before he could even think about popping the question...even if he had already picked out a ring.

CHAPTER 26

ANYMORE, BEN HATED CEMETERIES. HE had found himself sheathed in black and standing mournfully beside his wife and children before a shiny, flower-drenched casket suspended above a deep man-made hole far too many times. Worse, most of those he had come to pay his final respects to were younger than he. Summer had barely reached her seventeenth birthday.

He pulled into the Our Lady of Mercy visitors' lot and parked next to Chris' Porsche, then hastened out to help Derek exit the lower-sitting vehicle.

"I got it, Dad," Derek protested as he struggled to lift himself out. He grabbed the door frame with his right hand and relied on his grip, his hips, and his thigh muscles to put him right.

Ben reached out his hand as Chris circled around from the driver's side to join him. "Just don't want you to be in pain, son. It's only been a couple of weeks. Those ribs and that shoulder are far from healed. Don't let the pain medication fool you."

Derek ignored his father and clasped his uncle's hand. Once standing and with Chris' help, he straightened and tucked his shirt into his slacks, then fixed his thin suit jacket.

Chris caught Ben's eye and shrugged apologetically.

Ben dipped his head as Cheryl touched his back. He took her hand and put his arm around Kyle's shoulder. Chris and Derek in the lead, they crossed the parking lot and followed a group of mourners toward the chapel.

He leaned in to whisper in his wife's ear as they walked. "Are you sure about this?"

She glanced at him, shocked and offended. "The Reeces must expect we'll be here. I'd told Fred we wanted to come."

"Right before he slammed the door in your face?"

"Our son has a right to say goodbye, Ben."

"I agree, but Peter told me he'd heard from someone at their school that the Reeces don't want him here. And I don't want him hurting any more than he already does."

"Aye, but he'd be a sight more hurt if we didn't come, wouldn't he? Ever since the accident he's grown more and more distant. Like he's angry at us. For what, I don't know."

"He is angry, but he's angry at the whole world. We need to be patient. I'd wager he's doing the best he can."

"I'm his mother, Ben. It's not that easy. I'm supposed to be able to comfort him."

He gave her hand a gentle squeeze. "I know, love. But we have to face facts. Our son's a man now. Things have changed."

Dozens of mourners filed inside the beautiful yet tranquil marble and stain glass chapel, stopping briefly at the front door to accept a program from one of the two young ushers stationed at either side of the entrance. Chris and Derek had gone on ahead of them. Ben kept a watchful eye from his place farther back in line.

"Dad, can I go on inside and light a candle for Summer?" Kyle asked.

He nodded. "I'd prefer if you didn't engage her parents, though. We'll see them after the service as a family."

"I understand."

He heard Derek call after his brother as the boy wove his way through the crowd. When Kyle told him what he was doing, Derek looked back and shot his father a hateful glare.

Confused, Ben shrugged and raised his palms, mouthing, "What?"

With a disapproving shake of his head, Derek turned back around.

"We should probably find a place toward the back," Cheryl said as they accepted their programs with a thankful nod. She pointed to an empty pew to their left. "How about over there?"

As they broke off from the crowd and sidestepped from the aisle down to the end of the dark wood pew, they recognized Derek's voice toward the front. Ben looked up to see Fred Reece marching toward his son, pointing an angry finger in his face. Derek stood his ground, willful and unmoving. The mourners who witnessed the scene began whispering in each other's ears as a deacon approached the pair.

Cheryl's eyes narrowed in concern and a measure of instinctive protection for her son as the scene caught her attention. She looked at her husband expectantly.

He nodded. "I'm on it."

By the time Ben reached the altar, Chris and Kyle had joined Derek, flanking either side of him, their chins jutted defiantly as if daring the older man to lay a hand on any of the three of them.

"Fred," he greeted with an outstretched hand. "I'm sorry. I'll have them sit in the back with us."

"Dad!" Kyle and Derek protested in unison.

Fred Reece ignored the friendly gesture. Tight-jawed and surly, his nostrils flared with a mixture of unchecked contempt and grief. "Mr. Grant, I'll ask that you and your family leave this place right away. You have no business here.

Not today."

"He just wants to say goodbye," Ben reasoned. "We're all mourning Summer. It's been a terrible couple of weeks. Please, Fred, show some of that mercy we sing about every Sunday at mass."

Fred snorted. "Hardly every Sunday for you."

Ben cocked his head, struggling to restrain his growing agitation. "Boys, go sit with your mother."

"I'm not going anywhere," Derek spat. He stared at Fred Reece with moist, merciless eyes. "I'd asked Summer to marry me! We were gonna get married! And it was *our* baby! You had no right—"

Ben reached for his right forearm. "This isn't the time or place, son."

The boy jerked his arm away, then winced in response to the pain in his ribs. He pulled a folded piece of paper from his slacks pocket and turned back to Fred Reece. "I'm leaving this on Summer's coffin. You won't stop me."

Chris leaned in. "Derek, maybe we should take a seat like your dad said. I'm sure Mr. Reece will let you leave the note during the burial."

Derek set his jaw and eyeballed his uncle as if betrayed.

The deacon who had stood quietly beside Fred Reece during the altercation interjected with a soft tone. "Perhaps if he gave the note to me I could slip it beneath the flowers atop the coffin. Would that be okay?"

Derek lowered his head and took as deep a breath as he could manage. He repositioned himself with slow movements, clearly as frustrated as uncomfortable with his sling. Grudgingly, he extended his free hand toward the deacon to relinquish the note.

Fred raised his hands and stepped between the man and Derek. "You'll do no such thing." He turned to face the deacon. "I want this boy and his family removed at once. They can go on their own or we can call the authorities."

"Please be reasonable, Fred," Ben attempted once more. "You know they loved each other."

"My daughter's *dead* because of your boy," he seethed. "Reason has nothing to do with any of this."

Before Derek could defend himself, Chris put a quieting hand on his back and shook his head.

Kyle stepped forward and glared at the man. "We loved her, too! It's wasn't Derek's fault! It wasn't anyone's fault! It was an accident!"

Ben quieted Kyle and nodded toward the deacon. "I apologize for the disruption. I'm sure you understand we're trying to make sense of this horrible situation." He looked past Fred to Ulani, who stood several feet away, weeping. Friends and family held and comforted her. They stared at him, shaking their heads as if saying he should be ashamed of himself for allowing such a raucous. "I'm sorry," he told them, and then to Fred, "I'm truly sorry for your loss."

Chris took care as he pulled Derek away, whispering in his ear as they made their way out of the crowded chapel amid accusing stares, craning necks, and even excited recognition of the famous family Fred Reece had publicly humiliated. Derek ignored them all as he angrily swiped the back of his hand across his eyes.

Ben caught Cheryl's attention, shook his head, then inclined his chin toward the door. She nodded sadly, exited the pew, and joined them.

***

One good thing had come of his son moving in with his girlfriend. It freed up the LSI penthouse Joni had occupied for the last several months. Her relocation could not have happened at a more opportune time.

Jameson had not left Manhattan since hearing about the death of his ex-wife, despite his much unrealized plan to fly Bobby back home to Rhode Island to deliver the grim news of his mother's passing. He had tried everything short of begging to get him to agree but the boy had resisted to the near-point of a shouting match. In the end, Jameson had been forced to relay the sad announcement in the hallway between their offices. Not ideal, but Bobby had left him no choice.

While the news had hit Jameson hard, he found himself wrestling with the facts of the situation as much as the rare flood of emotion—something he disliked confronting in the first place. In one short month, he would retire. His role as businessman would end. And while LSI had made a miraculous recovery, it seemed he would leave much unfinished as he set out for the proverbial sunset. He had not yet received a definitive report on Farin's whereabouts. Worse, he had started questioning his ability to handle Moreau.

Virtually no time had passed between hearing the Los Olivos Garden psychiatric hospital director's voice tell him his wife had died and the echo of Moreau's ominous words the last time they had spoken: "...*make no mistake, Lockhardt. Someone's going to pay for your indiscretion.*"

Heart attack, indeed.

Shoulders slumped in sorrow, Bobby slid into the booth beside Joni and held her hand as the host seated them and placed menus at each of their table settings. He ordered himself a water and an iced tea with lemon for Joni, who had long given up trying to understand why most Yankee establishments did not have sweet tea on tap.

Jameson unbuttoned his suit jacket before sitting down, then gave the waiter his drink order and turned his attention to peruse the menu.

"It was a nice service," Bobby said. "She would have loved it, even if the three of us were the only ones there."

"The flowers were breathtaking!" Joni agreed. "Did you pick those out, Mr. Lockhardt?"

His stern expression did not fluctuate in response to the cheery if overtly enthusiastic comment. He nodded. "Sarah had a fondness for all sorts of flowers, sweet peas in particular."

Joni bobbed her head as he spoke, eyes fixed intently upon him as if he were imparting the wisdom of Solomon. "Well, they were beautiful arrangements. The fragrance was incredible. I'll bet she smelled them all the way up in Heaven!"

He did not indulge the girl's lighthearted enthusiasm. Something about her whimsy and irritatingly consistent upbeat mood bothered him. Whether uncomfortable around him or simply eager to ingratiate herself into her boyfriend's father's good graces, the effort would fail. His criteria for judging whether or not she made a good fit for his son did not rest on such frivolous gestures.

With an incongruous glance over the top of his open menu, he asked, "What shall we order in honor of your mother? I hesitate to say it, but she was never much of a cook. She did, however, have impeccable taste."

Bobby brooded over his choices as if not reading them at all. "Was that some sort of family plot we buried Mom in? It seemed like every grave around hers belonged to some family named 'Nock.'"

Decades of practiced nonchalance precluded any outward reaction to the boy's unsettling observation. "I suppose I didn't notice what with all the effort it took to get her out here."

"Do we know anyone named Nock? Are they relatives?"

Their server returned with their drinks, giving Jameson due time to concoct a reasonable response should Bobby push the issue. The waiter rattled off the day's specials from memory, ensured they had the wine list, then nodded his understanding when Bobby explained they would need more time to decide. "Take your time. I'll return shortly."

"How's the publicity campaign coming along, Joni?" Jameson asked as he set his menu to the side and pretended to refocus his attention.

She brightened at the slightest interest, nearly wiggling in her seat. "Hectic, but I'm loving every minute of it. I had no idea it'd be such work! All those photographs and interviews and guest appearances."

"I have it on good authority you're considered quite the up-and-comer." He lifted his glass and held it aloft. "Let's toast to a long and successful career."

Bobby's mouth stretched into a weary yet sincere smile. He touched his glass to hers, then to his father's, much to Jameson's surprise. "To Joni."

She toasted both men, then gave Bobby a coquettish side eye. "If it weren't for you, I'd have never been able to get through these months. I'm just so green and you've been so helpful. I don't know why you're celebrating me. You're the one who deserves the credit."

He leaned over and brushed her lips with his. "You're the one with the magical set of pipes. Besides, everything I've learned, I've learned from my dad."

The public display of affection turned his stomach, but his son's unexpected compliment turned it back. It was the closest thing to a profession of forgiveness Jameson had heard since Bobby had confronted him about his contrived condition. Perhaps Joni was good for his son after all. At least she was good for his own attempts to rally the boy back to his side.

When they placed their orders a few minutes later, Jameson ordered two bottles of wine for the table. Once they arrived, he went through the obligatory smelling of the cork and tasting rituals, then relaxed into his seat and swirled the exceptional red in his glass. "I was thinking about taking the next week off."

Bobby tucked his chin and stared at him, wide-eyed. "You?"

"Why not?"

"I don't remember you taking a day of vacation in your life, let alone a week."

"That may be a slight exaggeration, son."

"No, it's not."

"I think it's a wonderful idea, Mr. Lockhardt!" Joni enthused. She dared to reach out and give his forearm an encouraging squeeze. "Where are you thinkin' of going?"

Bobby rolled his eyes. "*This* I've got to hear."

Jameson exhaled an indignant snort, a hint of something in his tone that almost sounded like congeniality. "Actually, I was going to ask the two of you to join me up at the house. I think we could all use a little time away. Bobby, you and I can strategize and brainstorm the last bits of the transition in a more relaxed atmosphere. And Joni, I imagine you're due for a short break as well. How does that sound?"

Bobby's jaw slacked as he held his wine glass in one hand and propped his free hand on his hip. "You want us to come up to the house? You never have people up there."

He opened his arms in a rare and manufactured flourish. "I'm about to be a retired man. I should think you'd be happy to spend a week alone with just...your family."

Despite the weeks-long resentment directed toward his father and a deep sense of grief over his mother's passing, Jameson watched Bobby's disposition steadily shift to one of renewed hope. "You're serious?"

He sipped his wine, then leveled his gaze upon his son and gave a curt nod. "As a heart attack."

***

Herb Radford readied himself to sign off for the night. In fact, he had nearly come to the conclusion he should delete his account altogether. Farin Grant had not popped up on his screen for over a month and a half. Clearly she had figured out the ruse. Or maybe Lockhardt had found himself a better PI to locate her. Someone willing to take more risks. Who knew? He and Lockhardt had been playing phone tag for weeks as well.

Ultimately, a heavy presence of cops and cars had chased him away from his stake-out at Ben Grant's place and sent him packing—not that it had taken much to convince him to abandon south Florida. Before leaving he had rented the boat as planned and spent a day with a few St. Pauli Girls, surveilling the posh estate with waning interest.

It had initially appeared the teenage boy he had seen talking with the police the previous day had left. No sign of life at all until later in the morning when a limousine had pulled up and dropped off several pieces of luggage—but no people. He had waited until well after his single day rental had expired, then found himself having to hurry back to the marina before incurring exorbitant late fees for the vessel. Great beer, though.

By the time he had returned to Key Biscayne with his rental car, he caught sight of the teenager with a man he had assumed was the kid's father. Together they had walked inside and extinguished the lights. The next day, the house had emptied before he arrived. Another police car had shown up an hour later, only to leave when no one answered the door.

Herb had flown home to Iowa that same evening. More and more, the investigation had lost its appeal. He had intended to wrap up this job, take the money, and start enjoying life long before football season started—accepting zero professional obligations until after the holidays. Maybe even invite his estranged kids over for Christmas if they could tear themselves away from the ex for two damn minutes. It would be nice to finally meet his grandkids. He sure had sent enough presents over the years. What good was this big old house without people to visit once in a while?

But no. Here he sat in front of a computer screen waiting for a phantom to appear. Who knew anymore if Lockhardt's intended target had survived the supposed rescue from North Carolina in the first place? He had made contact with "someone," but that someone had never definitively identified herself. And even if Farin Grant was indeed the woman he had spoken with via AOL's Instant Messenger over those six weeks, it appeared she had somehow gotten spooked before their planned meeting. Either that or something had happened to—

RedMayden: Hi, Herb.

His eyes grew large at the ping and sudden appearance of the chat window on his screen. He checked the time on his laptop tray and mentally added an hour. Should he respond right away or make her wait?

He hit the john, then grabbed a bottle of Jack Daniels and a glass before returning to his den. He poured a shot, threw it back, then poured another before poising his thick, stumpy fingers over the keyboard.

RedMayden: Guess you're not there. Sorry I missed our appointment.
PIHerb4108: Hey Red, how's it going?
RedMayden: Pretty good. Are you mad?
PIHerb4108: What do you think?
RedMayden: Sorry. I had to leave town at the last minute.
PIHerb4108: You don't own a laptop?
RedMayden: I use my nephew's computer. I don't have one of my own.

He wanted to press her for details but chastised himself to back off.

RedMayden: And then my other nephew was in a car accident.

Okay, now that would explain the cops.

RedMayden: So I've been busy for the past few weeks. A lot's happened.
PIHerb4108: Sounds like it. No sweat.
RedMayden: You're not mad?
PIHerb4108: I don't know you well enough to be mad, Red.
RedMayden: Well, how can I make it up to you?
PIHerb4108: Maybe I'll bill you for the missed appointment. LOL
RedMayden: Sure thing. I'd be happy to pay you for your time.
PIHerb4108: I was joking.
RedMayden: Okay. Well, I have good news.
PIHerb4108: What's that?
RedMayden: I found the person I was looking for.
PIHerb4108: You decide to go with another private dick?

He waited for a response, then realized his choice of words might have offended her delicate sensibilities. Instinct told him to apologize. Jack Daniels convinced him otherwise.

He poured another shot and tossed his head back to swallow the strong brown liquid. Eyeballing his desk, he realized he had forgotten to grab a chaser. He hurried to the fridge for a Bud, then sat back down and twisted off the cap.

RedMayden: As it turns out, a friend of mine found her.
PIHerb4108: That's great. Congrats.
RedMayden: Thanks.
PIHerb4108: So you're back in Miami now?
RedMayden: For a while now. But things have been hectic.
PIHerb4108: You said your nephew was in an accident. He okay?
RedMayden: His girlfriend was driving. She died. He's not doing so well.
PIHerb4108: Poor kid.
RedMayden: Kid? I never mentioned how old he was, did I?

Herb grimaced as his fingers momentarily froze in place above the keys.

PIHerb4108: I assumed he was a teenager. You don't seem too old.
RedMayden: Either that or you read the newspaper report.
PIHerb4108: Hmm. Maybe. If so, that would lead to more questions.
RedMayden: I guess it would.

Herb took another shot, then followed it up with a couple of gulps of beer. Between the warmth in his belly, the growing numbness in his lips, and a foggy sensation clouding his head, he wondered if he dared push. Months had passed since he had accepted this job. He had grown as weary with the target as Lockhardt had grown angry with the lack of progress. Maybe it was time for a Hail Mary pass.

PIHerb4108: You're cool with it if I ask?
RedMayden: I suppose so.
PIHerb4108: There was a wreck near Key Largo weeks back. That him?

She hesitated at first, then confirmed.

PIHerb4108: So Derek Grant's your nephew?
RedMayden: Yes.
PIHerb4108: Wow!
RedMayden: I couldn't really say anything until now.
PIHerb4108: Why not?
RedMayden: It's a long story.
PIHerb4108: I won't push.
RedMayden: Thanks.
PIHerb4108: So how's he doing?
RedMayden: He's pretty messed up.

PlHerb4108: I bet.

He made small talk for a few more minutes, hoping to sell an air of indifference. No more doubt in his mind. No more doubt at all.

When he found a casual time to break away from the conversation, claiming he had an early meeting with a new client and needed to turn in for the night, he told her he appreciated her circling back with him about their missed meeting and then signed off as quickly as he could. He then staggered around the den and living room to find the missing burner phone he had last used several days ago. Eventually, he found it tucked down into one side of his couch—dead battery and all.

Without a thought, he grabbed his home phone and dialed Lockhardt's number. He cursed under his breath when it went straight to voicemail. "Lockhardt, it's Radford. I've got her. One hundred percent. She's right where I thought she was. And I'm calling our guy right now."

He hung up and dialed the second number. A series of chirps and beeps and digital tones commenced, then finally gave way to a proper ring. Someone picked up the line. He could hear someone breathing, though he did not talk.

"It's me," he said. "That you?"

"Yes."

"I found the Grant girl."

"You sure this time?"

"Positive. She's in Key Biscayne with her in-laws. You're up."

"Not yet."

Herb's forehead wrinkled in concern. "What?"

"It'll be a couple of weeks. For both our sakes, I won't say when."

"A couple of weeks?"

"What's wrong? You think she's suspicious?"

"Until tonight, I wasn't sure. But nah, she's got nothing."

"Then there's no rush."

"Lockhardt thinks there is."

"I can handle him. And he knows it."

Herb exhaled through his nose and tried to string his muddled thoughts into a coherent plan. "I guess I can maintain contact with her for a while. Monitor the situation."

"Fine. But unless you need to contact me, don't."

"Of course."

"Did you notify the client?"

"Yep."

"Good. I didn't want to have to be the one to call the old bastard."

Herb had no interest in getting involved with whatever falling out had occurred between Lockhardt and their mutual associate. He kept the call short as usual. Only after he hung up did he rethink using his home phone to place the call. Ah well, it was just the one time. Besides, they would soon go their own separate ways once and for all.

He whistled a tuneless melody as he returned to the den, grabbed his shot glass, the bottle of Jack, and his half-full beer, then walked them all out to the living room to catch the local news before retiring. Tonight, he would sleep like a baby.

A knock on his front door drew both concern and curiosity. Ten o'clock. He hoped his neighbor had not had another altercation with that no-good husband of hers. Why she had not kicked out the SOB years ago, he could not understand. But if she thought he was going to get involved or give her a place to stay for the night, she had another think coming.

He flipped on the porch light, then unlocked and opened the door without checking the peephole. Standing on his front porch were two men in a dark suits. A sudden surge of adrenaline slayed the buzz he had worked up during the last couple of hours.

The larger of the two men stepped forward and flashed a badge. "Herb Radford?"

His lips parted. "I...I...yes, that's me."

"My name is Special Agent Hubbell Quarles of the FBI."

***

Eeny, meeny, miny, mo...catch a tiger by the toe...
If he hollers let him go...eeny, meeny, miny, mo...
My mo-ther told me to pick the very best one and you are not it...

Engine, engine number nine...going down Chicago line...
If the train should jump the track...do you want your money back?

He loves me, he loves me not...
He loved me, he loves me not...
She loved him, he loved me not...
He loves me, or maybe not

What to do about Chris?

During her post-trick-or-treat bath to wash away the tribal makeup Cheryl had helped apply to enhance her Pocahontas costume, Jordan announced she wanted black hair—forever.

"But your hair's beautiful the way it is," Farin assured as she toweled her dry and helped her into her little nightie.

"I want black hair, Momma. *Please*?"

"Maybe when you're a little older."

She stuck out her bottom lip and looked down at the floor. "I want my happy ending."

Farin tilted her head and squinted quizzically at her. "What do you mean?"

"Like Pocahontas. She had her family in her happy ending."

"You have your family too. You know that, right?"

She nodded sadly, close to tears. "But what if I don't get my happy ending?"

Farin wrapped her arms around her daughter and squeezed her tight. "No matter what, your family will be here with you, honey. Uncle Ben, Uncle Chris, Aunt Cheryl—"

"What about you, Momma?"

She nodded. "Especially me."

The promise appeared to satisfy her. She looked up at her mother. "But can I still have black hair?"

Farin grinned, "How about if I let you sleep in your costume and we'll talk about it tomorrow over breakfast? Aunt Cheryl's making waffles and bacon."

"Yay!" Jordan wriggled about, joyful again as Farin changed her clothes. She sat still long enough to help her mother brush her hair, then scampered happily into bed.

Farin kissed her forehead, told her she loved her, then switched the light off as she left. "Sleep well, Jordan."

"Jade."

"Good night, Jade," Farin echoed sadly.

She stood outside the door for some time trying to decide whether to retire for the night or return downstairs. Sawyer had left over an hour ago, claiming he needed to run an errand. Chris still lingered with the family. She figured he and Ben would go out to the studio soon to work on some tunes Chris had mentioned he wanted to include on his next album.

For reasons she might never understand, Halloween had a strange way of bringing the Grants together—and pushing them apart. Maybe it was something in the air. Maybe some bad juju, not that she believed in such things. Or maybe because the first time she had slept with Chris had been on Halloween. Who knew?

She grabbed a cordless phone and retreated to her room. When she called Sawyer's cell phone, it went straight to voicemail without ringing. She left a message telling him she was tired and needed to go to bed so he did not need to come back into the village.

Her second call was to California. "I suppose my restlessness is the one good thing about our time difference," she told Marci. "Chances are you're not yet ready for bed even when I can't sleep."

Marci yawned. "I pretty much sleep whenever I can these days. So why are you restless?"

Farin collapsed onto her bed and lay on her side. "I miss you."

"I miss you, too. When are you bringing Jordan out so we can take her to see my folks?"

"As soon as I can travel and your parents are prepared to learn their deceased would-be second daughter is actually alive. When are you and Elliot bringing my niece to Florida? Cheryl asks every day."

"Actually, I was going to call you tomorrow to discuss that. I had to call Sam and tell her Elliot's going to the wedding without me. I hate to miss it, but it's too soon for the baby to travel. We were thinking it might be nice to fly out for a week in early December. How's that sound?"

"Perfect. Not soon enough, though. I wish you were here."

"What's the matter, Farin?"

She lifted her shoulders. "I'm out of sorts."

"What's going on with the Lockhardts? Have the police figured out what they're going to do about all this?"

"They've been coordinating with the FBI. It's almost over. They've made a plan."

"Maybe that's why you're anxious. But this is good. You should be relieved."

"I guess."

Trying to convince Jordan's brothers to do nothing with the information she relayed had proven more difficult than she had imagined. Threats and calls for vigilante justice had erupted as they learned the unfathomable truth about Jordan's death and Bobby's assault. Nonetheless, she had told them. Everything.

Well, not everything.

Lately, the lie she had told about Melody's paternity chiseled at her insides, particularly watching Chris interact with little Jordan. To confess the truth now would only open old wounds.

"How's Chris doing?" Marci asked. "We haven't talked to him in a couple of weeks."

"I think he's getting ready to start recording again. He and Ben are downstairs right now discussing some tracks they want to play with."

"What about Derek?"

"Cheryl's worried about him. We all are. He's healing pretty well physically, but the poor kid's suffering. I feel so helpless. I don't know what to say."

Marci sighed into the line. "I hate that for him."

"Me too. Tell me something happy. How's Miss Vivian doing?"

"Her needs are small at this point. Food, sleep, and diaper changes."

"Are her eyes still blue?"

"Like sapphires."

"I can't wait to see her." Farin sat up and ran her fingers through her hair, then padded over to her purse.

"I wish our girls were closer in age."

"Me too." She reached inside and pulled out the velvet box Ross had included in the package he had sent her. "But I'm sure they'll be close. We just need to make sure we spend more time together. I still think you should move out here."

"Speaking of which, when are you and Jordan moving into your own place?"

Farin scoffed. "You mean 'Jade?'" She tucked the box into the top drawer of her dresser.

A knock came at the door, nearly causing Farin to drop the phone as she hitched her breath and turned with a start.

Marci asked, "You okay?"

Chris stood in the hall as if waiting to be invited in. When he saw the phone in her hands, he waved an apology and started to leave.

"Wait," Farin called after him. Then, to Marci, "Chris is here. Can I call you back?"

"Just call me tomorrow. I'm gonna try to get some sleep before the next feeding."

She promised, then quickly ended the call. Butterflies flitted around inside her stomach as she placed the handset on her writing desk, then turned to find him standing behind her. "What's up?"

"You didn't have to end your call."

"It's fine. I was just catching up with Marci."

He folded his arms and nodded. "How're they doing? The baby okay?"

She sat down on her bed and gestured to the desk chair. "They're good. Hopefully, they'll come for a visit soon."

He made no move to sit. "That's good. It'd be nice to actually meet my goddaughter."

She tilted her head slightly. "You okay?"

"Yeah. You?"

"I'm good. A little tired. I can't seem to turn my mind off long enough to sleep."

"I'll bet."

Her eyes narrowed in curiosity as he stood before her, bobbing his head with her every response as he stared at the floor. "What's going on?"

He lifted his head but did not meet her eyes. "Is Sawyer coming back?"

"I called him a bit ago and told him I was tired. Why?"

"I was hoping we could talk."

She swallowed hard. "About what?"

"About us."

After finally opening up and answering their questions relating to Jordan's murder, life in the Grant household had transformed from one of constant worry and unresolved sorrow to that of hope. Their collective focus had shifted from fear to determination. Derek needed to recover from his physical and emotional injuries. Farin needed to release her album to Samantha Drake, pending her go-ahead for a Minor 6th release. And, somehow, Jade Trongly needed to understand she was Jordan Grant.

The only thing left was to decide what to do about Chris.

She ran the heel of her hand across her forehead. "Is that something we can work through tonight?"

He gave her a halfhearted smirk. "Halloween's always sort of been our night."

"I don't know, Chris."

He unfolded his arms and rested his hands on his hips. "We could go back to my place."

Every part of her yearned to go with him. "I can't leave little Jordan. What if she wakes up? She doesn't sleep very well."

"She's probably in a sugar coma after the night she's had."

"Still..."

He shrugged. "That's okay. I won't push."

She stood and grabbed his forearm as he turned to leave. "It's not that I don't want to."

His eyes locked with hers. Most of the time she had known him, those eyes revealed a forbidden desire. Tonight, they appeared lost and lonely.

She swallowed again. "It feels like things are spiraling out of control again."

He nodded sadly but stepped toward her.

The smell of his cologne made her heart race as a hundred guilty memories played inside her head like an 8 mm film reel.

"Come with me," he urged, his voice little more than a whisper.

"Chris..."

"This bloody mess is almost over. And I'm finally free."

Her lips flattened beneath downward arched brows. "But I'm not."

A bark of indignation or frustration escaped his lips. "Sawyer?"

She nodded.

"You can't be serious about him. He's a boy."

When he moved closer, she lifted her hands to his chest and looked up at him. "We have no right to keep hurting other people. Haven't we learned our lesson by now?"

He covered her hands with his own. "Do you still love me?"

She pulled away and walked to the dresser, fully intending to go into the top drawer and retrieve the box. "We need to stop asking each other that question. We both know the answer never changes, but it never seems to make either of us happy."

"Then something needs to change."

"Everything's changed."

"You're not married."

"No, you're right there."

"He's not the right guy for you."

She ran her fingertips along the dresser drawer handle, then turned back to him. "I don't know if he is or not. All I know is that I'm learning how to be a mother, trying to ensure the men responsible for my husband's death are dealt with once and for all, and working to resurrect my career. To be honest, Chris, loving you is the easy part. Yet it's the hardest thing I've ever done."

A sudden, mournful whimper came from Jordan's room. She raised her hand. "See? Like I said, she doesn't sleep well. I have to go to her."

Chris caught her arm before she walked out the door. "I've done everything in my power to let you go. I can't do it, Farin."

She searched his eyes. "I know." The whimpering from Jordan's room continued. "I need to go to her."

He released his grip, nodded, and left the room. She watched him descend the staircase, then hurried off to check on Jordan.

CHAPTER 27

SAMANTHA BUSTLED AROUND HER ROOM, uncharacteristically unable to decide what to pack. New York was cold, with highs in the 50's. Positano averaged maybe ten degrees warmer. Shorts and short-sleeved shirts, out. Capris, slacks, and layers, in. Lingerie, absolutely. Trendy strappy sandals, a must.

Stop overthinking things, Sam. Pack the entire trousseau.

In hindsight, she should have taken Deborah up on her offer to come over and help her pack for her flight. At least that way she would not end up rushing around at the last minute, invariably forgetting half her toiletries.

Ethan had left for New York a week ago. His parents had graciously agreed to oversee the wedding plans on their end despite voicing their misgivings about his marrying a woman several years his senior. It might have helped had she and Ethan made any effort to arrange introductions before letting them know their plans. Instead, she would arrive late tomorrow night—a mere week before the wedding.

Hello, Mr. and Mrs. Maxwell. So glad we could meet before the rehearsal dinner.

Comically, Ethan would have a similar conversation with her father and siblings. It was anyone's guess if her mother would show up. Samantha had never managed to keep up with the dates for the various tennis tournaments around the globe.

Ah well, it could be worse. In fact it was, because she would not arrive at the Maxwells' place in Old Greenwich until after the retirement party Tuesday night.

That promised to be an interesting evening. If all went according to plan, it would make her honeymoon all the more memorable. Her life would be truly complete.

Ethan had called earlier to touch base and go over her list. The easy tone to his voice had irritated and amused her. "Honestly? Not a single nerve? No cold feet?"

"Get here soon. I can't wait to chastise you as 'Mrs. Maxwell.'"

"I still haven't decided on a last name configuration," she had reminded him.

"Well figure it out. I can't wait forever for you to tell me what to call you."

She inventoried her overnight case to ensure her makeup, face creams, and favorite colognes were accounted for, then switched over to check her purse to triple check she had her travel documents and passport. A brief bout of panic beset her when she could not find the latter. Then, she remembered she had set it on her desk and had not yet put it in her bag. She trotted downstairs to grab it.

The phone rang halfway there. She picked up her pace and managed to grab the handset before it rolled over to voicemail. Slightly winded, she answered.

"Whoa, whoa, whoa..." came a lighthearted titter from the other end. "Enough of that, then. No need to pick up if you're indisposed."

She smiled warmly, sat down behind her desk, and held the passport in her lap. "How are you?"

"Brilliant but not as good as you, from the sound of it. Things on the home front are going well, I take it," Lance said.

"Always that sense of humor."

"You loved it. You just don't remember."

"How are Ivy and the kids?"

"Growing like weeds. Colin loves being a big brother. Ivy's letting him feed Shuggie by himself every now and again. Props them both up on the sofa with a mess of pillows while she cooks dinner."

Samantha shook her head at the mental image. "I never thought I'd see you domesticated. All that's missing is that piece of paper, huh?"

"Nope! Actually, Ivy and I put on the balls and chains last weekend."

"Wow! Congratulations! No wedding planning? What did you guys do?"

"We had a small ceremony with her parents and the kids. Ivy yelled at me the whole time her father walked her down the aisle. I'd forgotten my cummerbund at the flat."

"Oh dear." She laughed despite herself. "That must have been something."

"It was. And Todd was my best man."

"Really? How's he taking the whole thing?"

"Truthfully? With a ton of drugs and plenty of drink to chase it down."

"That bad, huh?"

"Afraid so. Ivy's not happy with him coming 'round to see Colin, but at least he's making the effort."

"I hope it's not too confusing for Colin."

"Nah. Todd tells him he's his uncle."

She rattled her head at the complex dynamics. "Wow. I guess if it works for you."

"Right. Could be worse, though. He could have been a massive prick and just walked away."

"True enough." She checked her watch and sat up straighter. A car would pick her up within the hour. "How about the others? Any word? I've been so busy with the wedding plans, I haven't managed to find a minute to touch base with everyone as a group."

"Ah, Sam, there's no more group. Mirage is through."

Her shoulders slumped. "Oh no, are you sure? I'm having dinner with Faith Sunday night. If I talk to her, maybe she can—"

"Give it up, love. Touring with Chris was a good time and all, but everyone's doing their own things now. Besides, the row between him and Todd isn't going anywhere. Even if the rest of us wanted to have another go, it wouldn't be the same. It's not right without the lot of us."

In her heart, Samantha agreed. "I understand. I'm not happy about it, but I get it."

"So enough business, and enough about me. You knew I couldn't let you go off and tie the knot without saying a proper goodbye. Had to make sure you're happy and all that."

She gazed down at and studied her engagement ring. A warm smile stretched across her lips. "Yeah. I'm happy."

"That's all I ever wanted for you."

"I feel the same. I'm happy for you and Ivy and the kids."

"I guess there's only one thing left to say between us, then, isn't there?"

She cocked her head. "What's that?"

"Whatever you and Ross have cocked up, I hope you nail the son-of-a-bitch to the wall. The old man plucked the soul right out of Mirage. Faith's overdose, Chris and Todd's fallout and Todd's health. Not to mention what all he's done to Farin and who knows how many others. He deserves the worst you can serve up. Give him a double helping for all of us."

***

LSI had never seen a busier Tuesday. Absenteeism sat at zero. Every employee clamored for their chance to send Jameson Lockhardt off with the type of reverence any prominent leader deserved after more than two decades of meteoric success in a company he had built with his own two hands. The company rightfully predicted it would accomplish little by way of work, particularly those on the executive floor. An air of bittersweet celebration permeated the hallways, offices, and conference rooms.

One of the secretaries even claimed she had passed Mr. Lockhardt on the way back from the break room and he had nearly smiled.

Bobby left shortly around 3 PM, after the staff presented his father with a smaller version of the enormous cake he had arranged for later that evening. He stood amongst the LSI VPs as they wished Jameson an emotional farewell, bemoaning in exaggerated fashion the idea they might never see him again except on the occasional golf course should he take up the sport. Not one of them let on they had already checked off and returned the place card with their names and requests for one of the three entree choices the caterer had sent the guests attending tonight's festivities. And no one dared go near the lobby level conference hall where an event coordinator and her staff worked to prepare for the black tie gala dinner.

"Joni?" he called as he bustled inside their apartment. When she did not answer, he called again, then realized he must have beat her home from her appointment. To save time, he jumped in the shower first. By the time he finished, she had returned.

"Sorry. Traffic. But we're fine on time," she promised, rushing past him as she stripped off her clothes and jumped in the shower before he could turn off the water. "How's your dad? Is he suspicious yet?"

"He didn't seem to be, but you never know with him. It's okay if he is. I've got it covered."

As a precaution, he had arranged a phony reservation at Jameson's favorite restaurant. That way, should his father grow suspicious as to whether Bobby really intended to take him out for a quiet birthday dinner, he could always call to confirm.

"I'm so glad you two have found a way to mend fences. It was nice spending time with him up north. His house is amazing. All those bedrooms!"

Bobby grabbed a garment bag from the closet and hung it on the door, then unzipped the bag to remove his tuxedo. "It's too big. If he'd had other kids or remarried, that would have been one thing, but twelve bedrooms? Who needs that?"

Joni hurried into the bedroom wearing her robe and a towel wrapped around her head like a turban. Her face moist with post-shower sweat droplets, she grabbed her favorite body lotion and worked it into her arms, legs, and torso.

Bobby watched her out of the corner of his eye while he tried to focus buttoning his cuff links. He loved her uninhibited style and willingness to walk around their apartment wearing nothing but what she had been born with. It came in decided contrast to her otherwise shy nature. She trusted him. No one had ever trusted him so much.

"What time'll the car be here? Do I have time to do my hair or should I pile in top of my head and call it a day?"

He moved toward her. "We should be ready in an hour. The car will be here at six thirty."

"Perfect!" she chirped. "I have time for the hair dryer after all!"

He snagged her arm before she could scamper back to the bathroom. He needed to do it before he lost his nerve. "Wait a minute."

She turned back and smiled as he led her over to sit on the bed. "What is it?"

"I, uh...I love you. You know that, right? I love you. I love your mom and dad. And I think they like me okay."

Her eyes danced as she chortled happily. "Of course they do. They love you."

"I talked to your dad last weekend."

"I didn't know Daddy called. Is everything okay?"

"I called him."

"You—" Her eyes widened.

Bobby slipped down off the bed onto one knee and dug a small black velvet box out of his trousers pocket. His face paled as he cleared his throat and swallowed. He nearly dropped the box as he fumbled to grip the hinged top.

Joni covered her open mouth with one hand and gathered the folds of her robe with the other. "Bobby..."

"I'm not good at most things, Joni. It feels like I got started late in life and I still have a lot to learn. But in the past several months, you've given me love and support and a willingness to do all those things I'm not good at. I'd like to say you're the first one I'm asking, but I've already asked your dad because I know you'd want his blessing. Well, I have it. And now I'm asking. Charlene Johnson-slash-Joni Leighton...will you marry me?"

The towel around her head gave way and slid off to the side. She let it drop to the floor as Bobby opened the box to reveal an enormous diamond ring. Tears brimmed in her eyes as she nodded and stuck out her left hand. It trembled as he slid the engagement ring onto her finger. "I will. I'd love to be your wife."

He stood and brought her to him, kissed her lips, then enveloped her into his arms.

She laughed as she cuddled into him. "I can't believe you asked me when I was wearing a robe."

"I couldn't wait any longer. I didn't want to leave here tonight until you were officially my fiancée."

"What about your father? This is his night. His birthday. His retirement."

"I know. I couldn't help it. So now it's our night, too."

A permanent smile stretched across his face as he waited for her to do her hair and makeup and sheath herself in a beautiful blue evening dress that brought out the violet in her eyes. At six thirty on the dot, they descended the elevator arm in arm and strode through the lobby to their waiting limousine.

It would be a night none of them would ever forget.

***

The night served as a satisfying end to both his birthday and his career.

Dinner. The Met. And the knowledge that any day now he would get the news Moreau had finally disposed of Farin Grant.

Herb Radford had finally come through for him. And as soon as Moreau crawled out of the shadows to finish the job, all would be well. It felt intoxicating. So much so, the fact it had taken seventy long years to finally establish peace in his life no longer mattered. After tonight all those who had opposed him along the way would either cease to exist or no longer matter. Not even Ross, who had proven an unworthy adversary.

Neither of the men had bothered to bid the other farewell before Jameson left the LSI building for the last time.

Before readying himself for the evening, Jameson had called the restaurant to verify Bobby had indeed made their dinner reservations. The lines of familial communications newly revived, he had wanted to ensure his son had not intended to over-celebrate the day's momentous occasions. Two milestones had been reached on an otherwise unremarkable Manhattan Tuesday in November. Quiet in victory. A relaxing dinner at Rao's with Joni and Bobby, a performance of *Un Ballo in Maschera,* then a triumphant—and permanent—return to Newport.

Jameson approached the limousine with a regal stride as the chauffeur opened the door. He crawled inside and sat opposite his son and the boy's girlfriend.

Joni rose from her seat and hunched over in the small space. She held the folds of her gown up so she would not trip, then moved forward to plant an unexpected kiss on his cheek. "Happy birthday, Mr. Lockhardt. And congratulations on your retirement."

He pulled slightly away and gave her an awkward pat on the upper arm, uncomfortable with the sentiment. "Thank you."

She returned to her seat, snuggled into Bobby, and wrapped her arm in his. "I'm so honored to be here with you to celebrate."

He gave her a curt nod, then stared out at the New York streets as the driver took off. "I'm pleased you could accompany us."

"You'll be proud of me, Dad." Bobby grinned at his father. "I didn't get you a present."

An uncharacteristic bark of laughter escaped his lips, perhaps hinting at a softer side of himself he had not visited in decades. "Not even a gold watch?"

"You have a dozen of those."

"True enough." He turned and inclined his head to the boy. "Thank you for the thought. I appreciate it. Besides, dinner and a show is an ideal gift."

Bobby patted his tuxedo jacket, then frowned and looked at Joni. "Did I give you the tickets?"

She shook her head, then grabbed her clutch to inspect its contents. "I told you to make sure you had them. You didn't grab them before you left?"

"I thought I did." He lifted himself slightly off his seat and swept his hand across the leather beneath him, then checked his pockets. "They're not here."

Joni's shoulders drooped. "They must still be at work."

Jameson lifted his left eyebrow, immediately suspicious.

Bobby pushed a button on the ceiling console, lowering the privacy window between them and the driver. "We need to make a pit stop. Please take us to the office."

The driver nodded and engaged his turn signal.

"What's going on, son?" Jameson dared to ask.

Bobby shrugged innocently. "I just need to run in and grab the tickets."

He slowly shook his head, unamused and certain his quiet evening at the theater had just been canceled.

Joni made several unsuccessful attempts to wipe the gleeful smile from her face as the car wended its way down 6th Avenue. Jameson observed Bobby's moronic efforts to surreptitiously shush her as he squeezed her hand. He also noticed a rather large diamond engagement ring on the girl's finger.

"I'll just run upstairs real quick," Bobby said when the car pulled up outside the building. "I won't be a minute. We're still good on the reservations for Rao. Don't worry."

Jameson set his jaw. "Mm-hmm."

Joni asked, "Baby, do you mind if I go with you? I need to use the ladies room. Sorry."

Bobby checked his watch and feigned a sense of urgency. "Okay, but hurry."

Jameson sat inside the car, wondering how long it would take for someone to come and get him, faking some last-minute complication that required his attention despite the fact that, as of 5 PM that afternoon, he was little more than the majority stockholder.

From inside the lobby, one of the two men stationed at the front desk came trotting out. He opened the door with an apologetic, "I'm sorry to bother you, Mr. Lockhardt, but…"

Jameson held a hand up. "Don't bother." He rolled his eyes and exited the vehicle, then followed the man inside, resigned to his fate—and sick at the idea of more celebratory cake.

He entered the lobby and asked where he needed to go. Deflated, the man gestured toward the conference hall. Jameson inhaled deeply, sighed, and lifted his chin high as he opened the door.

Inside, more than three hundred people rose from chairs which had been arranged cabaret style around banquet tables. They applauded as he walked through the double doors and shouted choruses of "Congratulations!" as he moved forward and acknowledged the crowd with a manufactured half-smile and nods of appreciation he did not feel.

The high walls were filled with massive photo enlargements of Jameson at various stages of his career, as well as pictures of past and present LSI notables. Near the front of the stage, a reproduction of Jordan and Farin Grant laughing and holding each other hung in a prominent place, probably in memoriam. He stared into Farin's smiling eyes and tried not to sneer. To him, the room looked like he had died and now faced cosmic judgment by a vengeful god.

Bobby and Joni stood off to the left against the wall, cheering and clapping along with the crowd welcoming him. Bobby waved him over and pointed to the stage. Jameson noted the large leather high back chair resembling the one at his desk positioned in the middle of the stage toward the front. Head tables ran along the front of the stage on either side of it.

"Surprised?" Bobby asked enthusiastically.

"You've no idea," he answered over the din of the crowd.

Joni approached him and took his arm. "C'mon now. Our table's up front."

He submitted to being led through the crowd that refused to stop cheering as they wove through the maze of tables. Every once in a while, he would nod and acknowledge a familiar face, though if he were honest, he would admit he knew very few of the attendees falling over themselves to congratulate him.

When he noticed Samantha Drake standing beside a chair at a table near the front, he did a double take. Only then did he realize he knew many of the people shouting their well-wishes. The CEOs of LSI's most formidable competitors—including all the heads of the Big Six—each sat at their own tables with their VPs, preening as if eager to confirm the retirement was not merely another one of his publicity stunts. Dozens of entertainers who were or had been on the LSI label scattered about the place, accompanied at all times by their various sized entourages. Jameson noted several local politicians. He even saw a section occupied by select journalists and television reporters, none of whom Jameson would recognize without hearing their names. He hoped Miles Macy had not made the final cut.

Scanning the faces, his eyes settled on man at the front table. Ross stood pointing at the seat next to his. The hair on the back of Jameson's neck stood at attention.

He leaned over to his son and nearly shouted, "What have you done?"

Bobby slapped his father's back as they reached their seats. "It'll be okay. It's just one night. Kick back and have some fun for once in your life! You've earned it."

But when Jameson saw Faith Peterson glaring at him from two tables away, with Elliot Lawrence and Megan Price in tow, something told him his son had oversimplified matters. He felt the sudden urge to slip away, take his private elevator up to his old office, and check his voicemail one last time. Although never a praying man, an inner voice silently pleaded to no one in particular that Moreau had finished the job.

Ross made a show of extending his arm and giving him a hearty handshake. Unsure if his paranoia was justified, Jameson played along. He pulled the man into him amid the cheers of the guests. As they embraced, Jameson accused, "This is your doing, isn't it?"

"It's the least I could do after all you've done to me," Ross countered.

They locked eyes, their public faces melting away as they sat down.

Bobby trotted up the steps and approached the table top lectern set up on the head table to the right of the leather chair. He flicked the microphone switch on and greeted their guests, then peered down at Ross. "Well, we did it. For the first time in my life, my father wasn't three steps ahead of me."

The crowd laughed as they took their seats.

"On behalf of my father, Ross Alexander, and myself, I want to thank everyone here for joining us. It's going to be a great evening." He glanced down at his father. "Lots of surprises in store! But first, let's eat!"

Jameson shot a hateful glare at his longtime colleague.

Ross picked up his highball glass, toasted Jameson's untouched water glass, then took a hearty drink.

Throughout dinner, Jameson asked his son repeatedly what festivities they had planned, arguing he had come into the event ill-prepared and wanted time to set his expectations. Bobby and Joni refused to spill the beans. Ross' only hint was that he might want to have a few drinks.

A full staff bustled around the room, dropping off and picking up plates. Jameson found it impossible to enjoy his meal. Not only did a steady stream of smiling well-wishers come by to personally offer their birthday and retirement wishes, but he had apparently left his appetite back in the limo.

Once the wait staff had collected the dessert plates and began serving after dinner drinks, Ross stood and clasped Jameson's shoulder. "It's show time," he said, his expression threatening instead of jovial as he headed for the stage.

Jameson scowled at the man's back, wishing he and Moreau had not come to an impasse. The carefree attitude he had experienced earlier must have made him delusional. As long as Ross Alexander lived, he would never find peace.

The guests applauded as Ross hopped up the steps like a man half his age and approached the microphone. He waved to them and stepped to the lectern.

"Tonight, we come to honor a man I've known since..." he made a show of looking up and off to the side, then grimaced, "...twenty-eight years. Wow!" He looked down at Jameson for visual confirmation. "Can you believe it's been that long?"

Grudgingly, Jameson shook his head.

"It's amazing. Well, at least one of us has aged gracefully," he quipped.

The crowd laughed.

"In talking to my esteem colleague's only son, we decided it only fitting to celebrate Jameson Lockhardt's birthday, his retirement, and indeed his legacy by organizing a roast."

Jameson peered at his son, who sat smiling openmouthed as he nodded toward the stage, rapt by Ross' every word like a hypnotized cult member.

"Now usually, the guest of honor knows about these types of events in advance. They're planned with plenty of input from the victim—I mean honoree. But anyone who knows my old friend here knows he'd never agree to anything that might resemble fun. Don't believe me?" He gestured toward the table. "Just look at those sagging jowls of his. The man hasn't laughed since August 24, 1967. That's a lot of gravity. If I didn't know better, I'd swear he hides all his money in his neck."

The crowd laughed again. Many winced at the insult.

"But enough about tax evasion. The night's young, and we've got plenty of time to discuss his various crimes against humanity—some of which are actually worse than his bad looks." He shot Jameson a satisfied grin.

Jameson leveled steely eyes at Ross, unamused.

Bobby playfully elbowed his side. "C'mon Dad, it's all in good fun."

He did not turn around. "Indeed."

Ross stepped to his left and indicated the high back chair in the center of the stage as he leaned in to the microphone. "So without further ado, let's kick things off by welcoming to the stage the man of the hour, the birthday boy himself, LSI's dungeon master and my very best friend in the entire executive floor, Mr. Jameson Lockhardt."

Cheers and applause prompted Jameson to stand, take a short bow, then plod toward the stage. He attempted to whisper a warning in Ross' ear, but the man managed to stay clear of him as they shook hands once more. Ross returned to the microphone without sparing him a glance.

"Now, as you can see, our dais is empty tonight. No, it's not just because Jameson's inner circle consists solely of Bobby and me. It's not even because we couldn't find one person with a good word to say about him. We discussed it and decided we probably wouldn't get him up on stage if he walked in and was immediately confronted with a group of people who had agreed to come out of the Jameson Lockhardt Witness Protection program long enough to give him a good basting."

Jameson flattened his lips and nodded with resignation at the laughing audience. Inside, he envisioned himself tearing Ross' head from his shoulders.

Ross performed a mock inspection of Jameson's chair, then pointed over at Bobby. "I thought you said you were bringing the restraints."

Bobby laughed and shook his head, then lifted his arms.

"Well, I guess we'll have to make do. What's the worst that can happen? He's too fat to make a run for it."

Jameson shook his head as the crowd ate up the show.

One at a time, Ross introduced the roasters. After they spoke, they took their place at the dais. Industry executives touted and insulted his business prowess and suspected underhanded dealings. Singers smiled while relaying the harsh conditions under which they worked while LSI kept most the profit. Each speaker spoke the truth about their similar experiences with Jameson Lockhardt and LSI as the unwitting audience belly-laughed at what sounded like absurd tales.

For the most part, Jameson pretended to get into the spirit of the fun. The sooner it was over, the sooner he could leave.

When Megan Price finished her turn, she went to Jameson with outstretched arms, bent down to kiss his forehead, then gave his arm a loving squeeze. Jameson quickly asked if she had made a decision whether or not to come back to the label. As she straightened up, she patted his cheeks with an air of indignant condescension and laughed in his face. "What label?"

He frowned, curious and suddenly alarmed.

Ross waited until Megan took her seat, then returned to the microphone. "We were so glad Megan agreed to come up for this. Isn't she beautiful, folks?"

The crowd cat-called and shouted their agreement. Megan covered her mouth to kiss the inside of her hand, then waved in Ross' direction.

"And speaking of beautiful women smart enough to run fast and far from our guest of honor's grasp, I'd like to call up to the dais a dear, dear friend of mine. We spent many years doctoring each other's wounds while she systematically worked herself down the ladder of success. Since escaping LSI, she's proven herself to be a force to reckon with. She's now the president of one our competitors and has subsequently signed at least two of our biggest money makers in the process. This weekend, she's marrying a doctor, probably because she's concerned that after her appearance tonight her former boss might physically harm her." He addressed Jameson in a conspiratorial tone, pointing down at the stage floor. "Watch your feet, now. We set that trap door up just like you told us to."

Jameson seethed as he waited for Samantha to stand up and take the stage. He caught sight of his son at their table, laughing and having a wonderful time. Clearly, Bobby had no idea what Ross had in store. It was not his fault.

The room erupted with shouts and adulation as Samantha Drake stood, smoothed down her dress, then marched confidently up the steps to the lectern. She shot Jameson a haughty smirk as she approached the microphone.

"Wow," she addressed the crowd. "Thanks! What a warm reception! Are you cheering because you're happy to see me or because I managed to get back in the building without being struck down by lightning? I bet a few of you believed he'd killed me years ago. It's hard to keep the defectors and victims sorted in our heads, I guess."

She paused for dramatic effect, then glanced back at him. "I don't know why Ross made all those comments about your appearance. You look good. Real good." She momentarily turned back to the crowd. "Doesn't he look good for seventy?"

The audience applauded and whistled.

"But I don't know. Something about you looks...*different* than the last time we saw each other. Maybe it's all that work you've been doing digging LSI out of near-bankruptcy after I took Megan Price and Chris Grant off your hands." She rubbed her stomach. "Oh wait a minute. I know what it is. Have you lost money?"

Jameson's nostrils flared as she spoke. All attempts to pretend for the sake of the evening, for the sake of his son, failed him. He could not wait until Ross' parade of fools ended and it was his turn to speak.

"You know, Jameson, I say these things in jest. We've known each other a lot of years. You were my mentor. You taught me everything I know about this business. So don't let all this talk upset you, especially on your birthday and retirement. During Dean Martin's roast of Sammy Davis Jr. back in the '70s, Mr. Davis made the astute observation in his closing remarks that it was an honor to have one's friends come together to make fun of them. That when they stopped making fun of you, it meant they didn't give a damn about you..." She turned to the crowd and waved. "Goodnight!"

The audience guffawed and winced amid various "oooos" as Samantha took her seat at the dais. She winked at Ross, who chuckled as he returned to the podium.

"Inspiring, Sam," he said. "The truth just *sounds* funnier, doesn't it?"

She nodded, her wide smile brilliant as she sat back without as much as a glimpse to her right.

"It would be remiss of me not to call forth tonight the one person who's received the lion's share of Jameson's inattention over the years. For all of Bobby Lockhardt's disadvantages growing up the son of a wealthy entrepreneur with zero parenting skills, he's learned resilience while managing to remain kind and decent—just one of the perks of the lack of direct contact with his father. Ladies and gentleman, LSI's anointed king...Robert Jameson Lockhardt, Jr."

The crowd rose to its feet to honor the incoming president of Lockhardt

Sound. Bobby's cheeks flushed as he took the podium. He doubled back to hug his father's neck. Jameson gave him an awkward pat on the back, then Bobby mouthed "I love you, Dad" and went to the mic.

"First of all, I wanted to thank you all once more for coming to share my father's birthday and celebrate his retirement. I can't help but believe that, somewhere deep inside of him, he feels a sense of gratitude as well...beneath the sour expression, the pursed lips, the disapproving snarl, the unspoken plots of revenge forming in his head, and the whispered threats to those with the courage to go near him."

Jameson tuned out the laughter of the crowd as he listened to his son try and fail to come up with zingers to insult and "honor" him. His thoughts turned to the week he had spent back in Newport with him and Joni. It had been a lovely, easy week despite the residual mourning for the loss of his mother. He decided to indulge his boy, however uncomfortable it made him, for the remainder of the evening.

"It's not that I never saw my dad. Ross has a tendency to exaggerate when it comes to my father's misbehavior. So I'm here to set the record straight. Any time I needed my dad, I knew he would be there for me. How did I know? Because I made each appointment at least two weeks in advance and always reconfirmed with his assistant the night before."

Jameson winced at the jab, playing along as Bobby glanced back and smiled at the effort.

"I always reminded myself it's not easy for him. As a Brit, he was probably raised to have their famous stiff upper lip. I don't know. I never knew his family. In fact, we never really talked about them. But don't judge him too harshly. My dad's a fighter and a winner. Whatever his circumstances, he did what he had to do. That included relocating from London to New York to chase after the American dream...life, liberty, and the pursuit of his ex-wife."

In the end, Bobby received another standing ovation before sitting with his fellow roasters at the dais—probably out of pity, Jameson decided. He joined in with the applause and saw the gesture register in Bobby's proud features. But when Ross introduced the next roaster, Jameson's stomach flipped and the smile ran away from his face.

Faith Peterson stomped angrily up to the podium. As the audience nearly fell out of their chairs laughing at what appeared to be a comical entrance, she narrowed angry eyes Jameson's way. As she spoke, she looked back and forth between him and the audience.

"I'm not very good at this. In fact, I'm not really even sure why I'm here. Look at all you fine people, all dressed to the nines with your tuxedoes and evening gowns. And here I am looking like I got lost on the way to a Hell's Angel's convention."

She did not indulge a pause for the audience's lively reaction.

"I've been listening to the various accounts of other people on this dais, wondering if I should show the SOB seated in the big leather chair a little mercy. He's old. He's finished. And I'd bet he can't get it up anymore. So what's the point, right?"

Jameson ran his tongue along his back molars and closed his eyes briefly, all too certain what would come next.

"I know, I know. I'm the foul-mouthed, classless wild card in this group. The only girl in the biggest act LSI ever had. The only American in Mirage. The shortest. The loudest. The drug addict. I can only imagine how you see me. But I know things about this pig up here. Unlike his son, I had plenty of access to him as a teenager. As a matter of fact, I was only seventeen when I started sleeping with him."

Jameson looked into the crowd in time to see Elliot Lawrence spit his drink onto the floor.

All eyes settled on Jameson as the room filled with the murmurs of the disbelieving crowd who did not know if Faith Peterson's "speech" was a planned gag or an unexpected confession.

"I'm really only here because I didn't want to miss the expression on this asshole's face when he gets his big birthday present." She peered back at him. "And it'll be the gift that keeps on giving."

With that, she stomped over to the dais beside Samantha and fell into a vacant chair.

Bobby studied his father with sad, confused eyes. Jameson started to shake his head in denial, then abandoned the pretense and stared at the stage floor.

CHAPTER 28

ROSS STRUGGLED TO WIN BACK the audience after Faith's shocking personal revelations about their esteemed roastee. He had realized setting the wild redhead loose for such an occasion would inevitably yield a measure of discomfort to the crowd at large. She had not disappointed.

He had been privy to their brief affair but never knew the depth of bitterness Faith still harbored over its demise. It satisfied him greatly to have provided her a platform upon which she could publicly excoriate the man who had tried to appease her broken heart with a gig that would reinvent her life for the better and worse.

The last roaster to make his way up to the stage may have appeared an odd choice to an audience filled predominantly with those inside the business. Those who worked hard to keep a modicum of privacy in an industry of constant exposure might not take kindly to the invasion by a member of the press. Ross thought it perfect.

"Our last roaster this evening has made a career out of dogging our guest of honor..."

Jameson jerked his head to the right side of the room and narrowed his eyes at the young, dark haired man buttoning his tuxedo jacket and grabbing what looked like a small note pad.

"He's boosted his popularity by standing on the back of every tragic occurrence LSI has suffered in the past four years. His columns are abrasive and accusatory. At best, his writing style lacks humanity. At worst, it's libelous. I've even considered filing a suit against him and the newspapers he's worked for. Unfortunately, it's almost impossible to sue someone for libel when you're a public figure—particularly if they're telling the truth. Since it's considered poor form for a journalist to insert himself into his own story, it seemed appropriate to invite him here tonight and rob him of the chance to profit off my sole client's misery. Ladies and gentleman, the most hated man on LSI's long hit list, Mr. Miles Macy of the *Miami Herald*."

Miles smiled and waved as he trotted up to the stage amidst cheers, applause, and a few good-natured boos. He shook Ross' hand and then turned to the microphone as he retrieved notes from inside his breast pocket and laid them on the lectern. "Such flattering sentiments coming from Jameson Lockhardt's distinguished consigliere," he began. "I'm truly touched. You realize I'm dating a cop now, right?"

Ross' eyes grew wide in mock panic. He watched with intense glee as Jameson's eyes darted over to the reporter's table and saw a beautiful Latina seated beside his abandoned chair. She squared her jaw in what looked like a challenging expression as she locked eyes with the old man.

Miles addressed Jameson directly as he spoke into the mic. "It's truly one of the highlights of my life to be standing so close to a man I've systematically tried to unmask. I'll admit, for last few weeks, I was afraid I'd never meet you outside a jail cell."

The audience roared with laughter.

For the first time that night, Jameson fidgeted uncomfortably in his seat. He appeared genuinely concerned. The observation filled Ross with immense joy. He suppressed a sated grin.

"In fact..." The reporter broke away and scurried over to Jameson's chair. He gave the man a toothy grin and stuck his hand out. Jameson's upper lip curled into a deadly snarl, but he submitted to the gesture. Miles pumped the man's hand enthusiastically. "I'm a huge fan," he proclaimed loud enough for the audience to hear his unamplified voice. When they laughed, Miles drew nearer and told him in a lower voice, "Farin says hello. She wanted me to let you know the baby's fine and thanks for asking."

Jameson recoiled. He peered at Ross in disbelief. Ross offered him a contemptuous nod.

Macy returned to his notes and continued. "Seriously, though. I've been sitting here all night listening to everyone poke fun at my primary journalistic obsession—or as I like to call him, the man who's cost me two jobs—and certain thoughts came to me." He waved his notes in the air. "I even wrote down a few stream-of-consciousness observations, if you'll indulge me."

Intrigued by the show, the crowd waited. Miles looked at them with a slight shake of his head and waited. "Well? Do you want to hear them or not?"

When they erupted into encouraging applause, he cleared his throat and perused the handwritten slips of paper. "Let's see here. Ah, yes. Without a doubt, Mr. Lockhardt's a legend in his time. We all know this. He seems to have everything. Things the rest of us could only dream of. Wealth. Power. Notoriety. Airtight alibis."

Several of Jameson's contemporaries from the Big Six shook their heads, unamused.

"What?" Miles asked, waxing defensive. "This is some of my best stuff. You know I'm right. The guy's got it all. Fine clothes. Chauffeurs. Who knew blood traded at such a high rate of currency?"

Many in the audience began to boo him as others laughed.

"Now calm down. Contrary to the way it may sound in my columns, I'm certainly not accusing Jameson Lockhardt of *killing* anyone. That's just silly.

He hires that work out to others. Well...or he relies on his son."

Ross looked over at Bobby, whose smile had disappeared almost as soon as the reporter took the stage. His brows arched downward when he saw Ross as if wondering why he did not put a stop to Miles Macy's unfunny, unappreciated rantings.

"Okay, okay," Miles told the now-grumbling crowd as he gathered up his notes and tucked them back into his breast pocket. "I get it. This was supposed to be a happy occasion. But honestly. Everyone up here tonight has spoken in one way or another about our guest of honor's amazing success and more importantly—certainly more entertaining—his greed. But let's not forget he's so much more than greedy. His legacy shouldn't be overshadowed by so much focus on his greed. Speaking as a journalist, I find that highly unbalanced. There are dozens of worse crimes he's guilty of."

Ross watched the color drain from Jameson's features. Bobby rushed to his feet and shouted, "That's enough! You need to stop this right now."

Miles spun around. "Or what? Gonna shoot me in the head in front of my girlfriend?"

Bobby's eyes grew twice their normal size. His jaw slacked. He looked at his father who sat exposed and, in that moment, appeared quite small in his seat.

Miles turned back and continued without missing a beat, ticking off items on his fingers as he spoke. "Let's see, there's obstruction of justice, fleeing the scene of a crime, kidnapping across state lines, bribery, accessory to murder, conspiracy to commit murder. The list is endless. In fact, I'd hate to get them mixed up, so I'll close tonight by introducing the real guests of honor for tonight's festivities...the Federal Bureau of Investigation."

The double doors on either side of the back of the hall opened. Dozens of uniformed men carrying rifles poured inside the room and shouted for everyone to freeze and remain seated. In immediate response to the sudden shift in the increasingly uncomfortable evening, many guests bolted up out of their chairs in wide-eyed shock and panic. Several people screamed while others inexplicably lifted their hands. The procession proceeded toward the stage en masse, with officers dropping out at regular intervals to guard the room.

Despite the influx of law enforcement barking orders to control the movement and chaos that ensued, a full half of the room attempted to leave, rushing the officers with claims they were not involved, that they wanted to go home, or that they could not afford to be associated with a crime due to their public position. Several managed to slip past in the confusion but were detained in the lobby by even more officers. The more urgent and emphatic the room became with warnings to sit down and maintain order, the louder their protests grew.

When Ross turned around to savor the inevitable expression of horror he anticipated would blanket the old man's face, the chair was empty and Jameson was nowhere to be found.

Bobby rushed toward him, a frightened Joni Leighton in tow. "What's happening?" he demanded.

Ross recognized the almost boyish sense of betrayal peppered with bewilderment as the boy looked to him for answers he could not provide. Deep down, he regretted he could do no more. For years he had tried to be the father Bobby never had. But that ended tonight. For all of them. "There are things you're going to hear," he said awkwardly. "Things that won't make any sense."

"What's he saying?" Joni asked Bobby as she trembled at his side.

His face contorted in pain and near-understanding. "What have you done, Ross?"

He shook his head. "It's too late, Bobby. There's no time to explain."

"What's that supposed to mean?"

"Your father's going to jail tonight. And I'm sorry, son, you're going, too."

Joni's eyes widened. She stared at each of them, openmouthed. "Why? What happened?"

Bobby's chest rose and fell with deep breaths. He bent over and grabbed his thighs as if trying to prevent himself from hyperventilating. "Was that reporter telling the truth? Did I kill Jordan?"

When the question registered in her mind, Joni stifled a scream. "*What*?"

"You need to cooperate with the police," Ross advised. "If you do, you'll be fine."

"What about you? Can you come down to wherever they take us and help us out? You're not part of this, are you?"

Ross nodded sadly. "I've always been a part of it, Bobby, because I'm a part of you and a part of your father. But no, son, I'm not going anywhere. I can't help you anymore."

***

Jameson knew every inch of the Lockhardt Sound building. He knew its hiding places, private entrances, and secret passageways. As armed officers rushed through the halls, searching and securing each room from the bottom up, he procured a stowed copy of the executive elevator key from a hidden wall compartment and slipped up to the top floor unnoticed.

An odd combination of anxiety and relief enveloped him as he entered his office. Using outstretched hands, he felt his way around the vaguely familiar darkened room, unwilling to switch on a light for fear of giving away his position. How odd that despite the fact he still needed to clear out his few personal items—a task he had agreed to put off for a later date at Bobby's suggestion—the office now had the feel of a distant memory. Somehow, in the mere hours since he had last exited the building, he had transformed into a virtual stranger in the space he had historically felt most comfortable.

In truth, he did not know why he had bothered to flee. What had he intended to do? Jump out the window? Snatch a hostage and make empty threats or demands? Retrieve the pistol from his top right-hand drawer and splatter his brains out? Preposterous ideas, every one of them.

Slowly, his eyes adjusted to the low light provided by the east-facing buildings along 6th Avenue. He made his way to the window and peeked down to behold the cars inching their way up and down the busy street, then grabbed his desk chair and swiveled it around so he could sit and stare out at the night as he had done countless times over the decades during moments of contemplative reflection.

It made for a fitting end, he supposed. Having Federal agents descend upon the peace and serenity of his property and seize him from his home would seem too common. But here...no matter how strange it felt to be back so soon after effecting the mental separation needed to come to terms with the concept of retirement, *this* was where he truly belonged. And if this ship had finally breached, this was the helm at which they would go down together. His sole regret was that he had never fully broken in his new chair.

He squinted to read his watch, then mentally estimated the time it might take the Feds to reach and apprehend him. Maybe ten minutes. Maybe fifteen. They had dozens of floors to search. It brought a smile to his face to think of them bustling about with an inflated sense of urgency for fear he might commit suicide before they could find him and drag him away. They did not know him at all.

Jameson Lockhardt valued life—at least his own.

The one person aside from himself he spared a thought for was his son. Bobby must have fallen apart by now, confused and overcome by the startling turn of events. So much for the engagement. Joni would surely find the risk of aligning herself with a family of alleged criminals far greater than any reward she might have anticipated by hitching her wagon to the Lockhardt name. Too bad. It had appeared she genuinely loved him.

He wondered how much the Feds knew, even though he entertained no doubt as to how they had come by their information. *Touché, old friend. Well done on you.*

When he perceived movement behind him, he did not stir. Let them take him. He only hoped that somehow Moreau had finished his final job. That would make all the shame of tomorrow morning's headlines worth it. He might go down, but Farin would finally lose her life.

The glow from the opposing buildings had transformed his window into a dim mirror. From behind him, he glimpsed the shadow of a woman advancing from the shadows. He watched with shock, then anger, then disappointment, and finally resignation as she unfolded her arms and helped herself to one of the chairs facing his desk.

"You know, it occurs to me the last time we met in this room, someone ended up losing their freedom. This time, I'm glad it'll be yours. You've taken enough from me, wouldn't you agree?"

Slowly, he swiveled around to face her. His features remained even and without a hint of outward response. "You're looking rested, my dear. Good for you."

"Thanks. I feel a hell of a lot better than the last time you saw me. There's nothing like a little freedom, a little fresh air, and a steady diet of solid food to cure what ails you. Of course, getting off the Thorazine helped."

He scrutinized her appearance with an arrogant sneer, noting her almost emaciated frame which seemed to swim inside an oversized sweatshirt and a pair of tight blue jeans. But she was clear-eyed. Strong-willed. In many ways, whole. This disappointed him. "A little more of that solid food would serve you well. Besides, you're a touch casual for such an important evening."

She glanced down to assess her attire, then shrugged with indifference. "I wasn't much up for a party, to be honest. Motherhood takes a lot out of a woman."

He smirked. "Ah yes, Jade."

"It's *Jordan!*" she snapped, lunging forward in her chair, a dark glint of malevolence warning him to keep her daughter out of the conversation.

He held up his hands in mock surrender, though her overreaction prompted an upturn to the sides of his mouth. "But aren't you concerned about how you'll be portrayed in the press once they haul me off in proverbial chains? You were once a beautiful young woman, my dear. If you have any chance of reigniting your career, I'd recommend paying closer attention to what you wear out in public. Come now, I can't keep grooming your path to stardom forever."

The feeble insult failed to evoke further reaction. She eased back in the chair and adjusted her shoulders as if shrugging off a confining winter coat, then looked past him to take in the view outside the windows. Her eyes sparkled in the reflected amber glow streaming into the office. "It's funny, you know. I thought I'd kill you with my bare hands if I ever saw you again. It scared me a little because I found myself planning it. All the way up from Miami, I'd fantasized about how I'd do it. And of course when I stepped foot in the building, I thought about it even more. I wanted it to be painful—and drawn out. I've hated you for so long. Years. In fact, my hatred for you was the only thing that got me through the last eleven months."

"Well don't give up so easily," he encouraged dryly, unfazed by her words. "I never do."

She shook her head. "But then I realized I'm not you. I don't want blood on my hands. I don't have a black enough heart or the necessary energy to hate someone who's met such a pathetic end."

"Perhaps you've not yet regained all your strength."

She rested her elbows on the arms of the chair and folded her hands across her belly. "No. You're wrong there. Thanks to you, I'm anything but weak. For all your effort, all you managed to do was turn me into a survivor."

He inclined his head and gave her a condescending nod. "You're welcome."

"So how does it feel to be on the losing end of a war despite winning almost every one of its battles?"

His expression lightened as the sides of his lips pulled upward into an incongruous smile. With a subtle shake of his head, he said, "But I haven't lost yet."

The assertion gave her pause. "You can't possibly think there's anything else you can do to hurt me." She sat forward and stabbed his desk with her index finger. "You're going to *jail* tonight, and you're never getting out. Don't you get that? There's nothing else you can do."

He scooted his chair forward and reclined, crossing his thick legs. "I may still have a trick or two up my sleeve."

She rolled her eyes, sank back in the seat, and chuckled. "I hope you don't mean Herb."

The self-assured air about him evaporated like mist.

"The FBI grabbed him a while back. Didn't you wonder why you haven't heard from him in so long?"

Jameson's thoughts immediately shifted to Moreau.

"It's finished, Jameson. Game over. Despite everything you've done or tried to do to me, I've come through. And I did it for my father, my mother, my husband...and our daughter. We've won. You know, I look back over the time I've known you. How naive I was when we first met. I used to think of you like a father figure—I loved and respected you. Later on, I feared you. And eventually, I hated you. But I don't anymore. I don't feel anything for you. I'm just ready for it to be over."

"Is that so?" He leaned in and perched his left elbow atop his desk, positioning himself with ample cover in order to access his drawer. At this point, he wanted to shut her up as much as he wanted her dead. "Is this the grand climax of some cheap dime-store novel wherein the heroine gives the villain her triumphant soliloquy before the police come storming through the doors to drag him away in humiliating defeat? Don't be so sure of yourself,

Farin. This is far from over. That's a promise."

Her confident disposition visibly withered as his targeted words hit their mark. "What more could there possibly be? Why should I believe you?"

"Because you know despite whatever shortcomings you may ascribe to me, I always keep my promises."

Her dark, angry eyes fixed themselves upon him. "You're the most evil man I've ever known in my life. What happened to you to make you this way?"

He scoffed. "I'll spare you the tragic story of my past. We all have one."

She folded her arms across her chest. "I pity you."

"Psh. Pity's a weaker man's game. I thought you said you're stronger now."

"Looks like I'm stronger than you are. That's why you're here with me right now instead of downstairs facing the inevitable. You deny it, but I can see it in your eyes. You're scared to death. What more is there? What are you hiding?"

"I've hidden plenty from you in your life. I'll admit as much. And contrary to what you think, I did it in an honest effort to protect you and give you back some of what had been taken from you. But the rest of it, my dear, I'll let you find out on your own if you think you can. Maybe that scrawny reporter friend of yours can help you. Maybe not. Maybe this really is the end. It's interesting the way the lives of such different people can intersect, isn't it? How a single moment can pull in complete strangers and tie them together for all time?"

Seeds of doubt blossomed in her mind like daisies at dawn. He could tell by the way she knitted her brows and looked off to the side as if wrestling with confused thoughts, that he had laid waste her smug belief she had finally gained the upper hand—prison or no prison.

"Take heart, child. I'm sure the authorities will be making their way up here any minute to cuff me and haul me off to jail for the world to see."

"Don't forget about your son," she countered. "This isn't only about you. In addition to the Feds, there're two Miami homicide detectives downstairs arresting Bobby even as we speak. He'll get the chair for what he's done. And I'll be in the front row, watching him fry."

He gave her a hearty laugh. "Spoken like someone without the requisite energy to hate another person. Bravo, Farin. But what on Earth has Bobby done?"

She twisted her face in disdain. "What are you talking about? He killed my father. He killed Jordan...and then there's what he did to me."

He waved her off. "Mark my words. Bobby won't spend any meaningful time in prison, and he certainly won't be put to death."

The assertion acted upon her like a physical blow. "You're as crazy as he is."

"As a matter of fact, I'd wager it won't take long before he's released and sitting in this very chair, running LSI without a single concern for the silly accusations against him."

She stood up and jutted her chin. "That will never happen. I promise."

"I guess we'll see, won't we?"

"We already have."

"Ah, my dear. I always did love your Don Quixote view of the world around you. It's made my mission to kill you so much more interesting. Now run along. There's no need to babysit me. I'm not running from anyone."

"Oh, I'm not here to babysit you. I came up to look around a little. I didn't even realize you'd come up here." She turned and studied her surroundings, her lips protruding as if deep in thought. "You know, I think it's time this office had a makeover. I've always hated the dark, oppressing feel to it. It's so dreary and last century. I'll have to find a good interior designer. I'm think maybe Faith or Henri can recommend someone good. To start with, I'm thinking about having the entire executive floor gutted and remodeled. Transform it into something that looks forward instead of back. What do you think? After all, in four years we'll be looking at the start of a whole new millennium! Well, some of us will."

He paid little attention to her ramblings. Taking advantage of her shifted focus, he quietly gripped the drawer handle.

"And of course a name change is one of the highest priorities on my agenda. I've already discussed it with the others and they all agreed. No one wanted to keep it. I'm sure those under contract will be fine with it. And of course, I'm sure *you* understand."

Her words slowly earned his attention. He watched her wander about the office, hands clasped behind her back, assessing the space as best she could given the lack of illumination. "What are you saying?"

"Ross didn't tell you?"

"Tell me what?"

She sucked her teeth in mock sympathy. "I guess we're also gonna need a good assistant. You know, it would have been great if we'd been able to get Nancy Chambers. She was a real pro. But she's no longer available, is she?"

His eyes narrowed.

"I can't decide if I want to tell you flat out or wait until the press conference and let you find out while you're behind bars. A part of me feels like I owe you some gratitude for not killing me after you found out your rapist son didn't gift you with a grandchild."

He cocked his head and stared at her.

She sat back down and bent forward. "I've changed my mind again. I *do* hate you. I hate your son. I hope you live just long enough to hear he's been put down like the rabid dog he is before you take your last miserable breath."

Jameson seethed with rage as he slowly pulled the drawer ajar. Enough toying around. If Herb Radford had been arrested, chances were Moreau had been picked up as well. Maybe that accounted for the unexpected appearance by the Feds. Ross being such a coward, he might not have been the one to talk after all. Particularly since he would have to implicate himself.

Both Radford and Moreau—or whatever the hell his real name was— would doubtless point their fingers at him, especially if promised reduced charges or a get-out-of-jail-free card in exchange. Who knew? Perhaps they had already cut a deal.

Losing his freedom was bad enough. He could not bear to go to jail without knowing he had ended Farin Grant once and for all.

"Lockhardt Sound's gone," she pressed, taunting him. "Or rather, it's no longer yours."

Jameson's eyes widened then narrowed suspiciously. "More daydreams, Farin?"

"Nope. It's done. You can thank Ross the next time you talk to him. Or wait, that's right. He doesn't want to see you either."

As she explained the shift in stock ownership, the buying and selling, and the final board members divesting themselves of all interest in LSI by way of the Double Maguffin takeover and its majority shares, Jameson pieced together the details of Ross' ultimate act of betrayal.

His blood ran cold. It could not be. His inattention to his company while he had single-mindedly pursued his prey from one end of the country to the other and back again had ended in the loss of his legacy. The one thing he had built over a lifetime. The one thing he had to give his son.

Farin's smile was triumphant as she leaned forward, her head low. "You're finished, old man."

Jameson scowled as he recognized the whirring sound of his private elevator. It had taken them long enough to discover it. Simpletons.

He yanked open the drawer and plunged his hand inside to grab his pistol. Farin would be long dead before they reached the top floor.

To his shock and dismay, the drawer was empty.

CHAPTER 29

ELEVEN O'CLOCK FOUND BEN AS restless as he was weary. Ever since Derek's accident and the arrival of little Jordan in their lives, the Grant household had started shutting down earlier and earlier each night. Sometimes as early as nine. Ben could tell Cheryl loved the new routine. She adored waking up with the sun and sending her family off to start their day with a hearty, balanced meal fueling their bellies.

Little Jordan had emerged as quite the assistant chef, often helping her crack eggs, butter toast, or measure flour when they had pancakes. After breakfast, she would carry a big-girl sippy cup filled with juice outside and draw or color while Ben and Cheryl enjoyed their morning cups of tea and read the *Herald*.

It was nice having a young child in the house again. However, Farin had talked more and more about taking their niece and moving back into her Matheson place. Ben predicted such a move would break Cheryl's heart—even if it was less than a ten-minute walk from one house to the other. It would all work out in the end, though. After Minor's upcoming release of Farin's new album and the resultant demands on her time, Aunt Cheryl would doubtless find plenty of opportunities to babysit.

But tonight, thoughts of future living arrangements and Farin resuming the hectic pace of her career lay far back in the recesses of Ben's mind. Unable to sleep, he had dragged himself out of bed to avoid waking Cheryl with his tossing and turning. His mind echoed with the struggle of a dozen cluttered thoughts competing for his attention—none of which he had the power to control.

Had things progressed as planned up in New York? Would the morning news include the shocking account of FBI agents arresting Jameson Lockhardt and his son as the revelation that Farin Grant lived stunned the world? Was Farin safe? Should he have stepped in and encouraged her to exercise caution and agree to let Sawyer go with her? Or even Chris?

No, not Chris. Authorities would never get Jameson or Bobby into custody if Chris were anywhere near them. Still in avenger mode, he would have killed the pair with his bare hands and Ben would have to step up to help him out of potential murder charges for a second time.

"I wish she'd call," Chris had complained during dinner after coming over earlier in the afternoon to check in on Derek and give little Jordan an impromptu swimming lesson. "I should have flown up there on my own no matter how much she complained about it."

"The last thing Farin needed was to have you stalking her up there. Instead of protecting her, you two would have ended up fighting as usual. She was anxious enough about confronting those maniacs. Your heard what she said. She was determined to do it on her own."

"Besides, the party hasn't even started," Cheryl had reasoned. "There couldn't possibly be anything to report yet. Give it time. I'm sure we'll hear from her first thing in the morning. She'll be ringing us to check on the baby anyway."

Chris had listened and eventually agreed. Better for their collective sanity not to borrow trouble.

No matter, though. Ben could see the anxiety that had settled in Chris' lower jaw. Concern had ensnared his brother like a fishing net, and the more he struggled against it, the more it immobilized him.

He wandered downstairs and fixed himself some tea, then went outside to enjoy the clear, cool evening. He plunked down into his lounge chair, sipped the hot beverage, and attempted to banish the tension in his shoulders by concentrating on the comforting sound of the bay softly lapping the breakwater at the end of his property, watching twinkling stars in the evening sky, and practicing controlled breathing.

"After tonight, it'll all be over," he nearly chanted as he defied his racing heart and willed it to a lesser beat. His family was safe at last. Any minute now Jordan's murderer would find himself behind bars. Perhaps it had already taken place.

No more secrets. No more hiding. No more dramatic cross-country rescues or confusion over the horrific details of his brother's death. And no more peeking over their collective shoulders to dwell upon a past none of them could change. The tragic circumstances of their lives amounted to no more than an unfortunate excerpt in a broader tale. Heartbreaking, yes. Dramatic, certainly. Confusing, often. But these things did not tell their entire story.

The Grant legacy would not portray them as a shattered family lost in perpetual mourning. In the end, it would show them victorious through their temporary defeat. They would emerge stronger, unified. Chris had already paved the way as a shining example of how to overcome seemingly insurmountable obstacles. Tomorrow, Farin would return to Florida a free woman and resume her hard-earned place in the world. Derek would recover from his injuries and the grief of losing Summer, and he would move on. As for himself, Ben determined to be a better man, a better husband, a better father, and a better brother. Together, their family would honor Jordan's memory in the only way they could—by vanquishing all that had transpired with their shared love for one another.

And eventually, despite all his and Cheryl's resistance to the idea, they knew Chris and Farin would eventually end up together. Life had to go on. The time had come to put away petty resentments and hurtful judgments. The two of them were inevitable. Deep down, even Sawyer had to know. Ben could sense the young man's frustration in his efforts to replace Chris in her heart. A futile proposition. Poor guy.

Glancing over to the far left end of his property, Ben felt his studio beckoning him like a neglected friend. For a moment he considered going inside to work. It was not as if he could sleep anyway.

Throughout each of their professional careers, he and Chris had never once collaborated. Recently, they had played around with a few ideas, which had resulted with them co-writing seven new tracks for his new album. The songs were so good, they left the pair wondering why they had never before put aside their stubborn differences long enough to explore their creative commonalities.

A spark of inspiration hit him as he relaxed in the lounge chair, tempting him to abandon the worries that had initially drawn him from his bed. He set his teacup down on a tempered glass table and lifted himself halfway out of his chair, then thought better of it and plopped back down again. If he started working now, odds were he would lose track of time and not return inside until dawn. No. He needed to savor this quiet moment in the absence of chaos. Who knew the next time he or his family would be able to enjoy a still, private moment in their own home?

He made a mental note to call first thing in the morning and arrange for security for both his place and the Matheson house. It should have been scheduled days ago.

Starting tomorrow, the press coverage would explode again. He, Chris, Cheryl, and Farin had already discussed it. In fact, Ben could not help but wonder what he might encounter if he opened his front door. It was entirely possible the more motivated reporters had already started pitching camp along Harbor Boulevard, readying themselves to pounce on them at the first sign of movement. More important than anything else, they needed to keep an eye on little Jordan to make sure she did not become frightened or overwhelmed amid the flashing cameras, shouts for their attention, and the sheer number of people watching their every move.

Welcome to the family, little one.

He smiled in spite of the anticipatory intrusion into their lives as he recollected Cheryl and his niece returning from the store yesterday with enough food to feed a small army of men for a week. Always practical. Always thinking ahead to ensure they had what they needed. Something about having a toddler around brought out the best in her—as if there was anything but the best in everything his wife did.

The very thought of her motivated him to finish his tea and head inside to tidy up before slipping back into bed beside her. Maybe she would wake up and help him shut off his restless mind. Maybe she would need him as much as he needed her.

For days now, curiosity had played with the less worrisome thoughts in his brain. Cheryl did not fool him. How long would it take her to start campaigning for them to have another child? They had discussed it semiseriously over the years. She was only thirty-six. Still plenty of childbearing years left. Perhaps it was time—especially with the boys preparing to go off on their own to college or career.

His thoughts ping-ponged back and forth from concern to practicalities, from whimsical fantasy to frustrated grief as he walked across the patio toward the house. He glanced up with sad eyes to Derek's darkened window, wishing his oldest had not shut him out.

It was the age, he had told himself numerous times. That, coupled with the agony of losing Summer. Or even the ill effects of the pain medication from which his mother had helped him slowly taper off over the last couple of weeks.

Teenagers pulled away from their parents. No surprise there. It was a rite of passage. He had done it. Jordan had done it. And Chris had nearly broken their parents with rebellion. Cheryl had made her peace with this season of their son's growth. Why did he find it so difficult?

After closing and locking the sliding glass door behind him, he walked his cup into the kitchen and placed the vessel in the sink, then started upstairs. On a whim, he doubled back across the foyer. Pulling back the sheer curtains with the back of his hand, he peeked out one of the side panel windows on either side of the front door. Their porch and driveway lay still. Lush tropical foliage obstructed a full view of the street despite the dim light of the waning moon and the street lights along Harbor. If reporters had started gathering, at least they had not yet dared to trespass upon their property.

Upstairs, Ben checked on the children one by one. He crept inside little Jordan's room. The stuffed dolphin Kyle had given her shortly after her arrival had fallen on the ground beside her bed. He picked it up and tucked it near her, then pulled up the covers she had kicked away in her sleep. Before he left, he bent down and kissed her forehead, then winced as he stood back up, realizing too late the unfamiliar tickle of his beard on her skin might wake her up. When she did not stir, he moved on.

Kyle lay sprawled atop his unmade bed, mouth open. He wore a pair of drawstring sweats and a faded school T-shirt. A book on the ecology of marine invertebrate larvae lay open-face on his chest. Ben picked up and closed the book, then set it atop a small pile of papers on his son's cluttered desk and exited the room with a smile. At least one of his sons had yet to decide his parents were oppressive, know-nothing enemies of teendom.

He hesitated as he reached Derek's door. Since the accident, the young man's sleep patterns had proven erratic at best. More often than not, he did not sleep at all. Ben had heard him many a night wandering up and down the hallways. Cheryl had gotten up with him once or twice, only to be turned away with reprimands of, "I'm *fine*, mom. Geeze!"

A moment's hesitation notwithstanding, Ben decided to weather the possible storm of his oldest son's temper. Maybe Derek would be awake and in need of someone to whom he could talk. One thing was certain—though his physical therapy had started to bring back a measure of mobility to his shoulder, the counseling he and Cheryl had insisted he attend had thus far netted zero improvement in his attitude.

He tapped the door three times with his knuckles, keeping the noise intentionally low in case his son had finally succumbed to exhaustion. When there came no response, he quietly turned the door handle and entered the room.

Clothes lay strewn across the floor in random, smelly heaps. Dirty plates, used napkins, and various trash littered his desk, his nightstand, and even a disorganized bookcase overstuffed with dusty books, stacks of CDs, and back issues of *Rolling Stone*, *Guitar World*, and *Music Connection*. The olfactory assault on his senses caused his nose and upper lip to scrunch in protest. In general, the room looked like one of south Florida's infamous hurricanes had swept through it.

But no Derek.

He stepped out into the hallway and closed his eyes, listening for any sound. Nothing from the nearby bathroom or downstairs. Though it seemed improbable, Ben checked the spare rooms before widening his search throughout the remainder of the house, then the studio and around the grounds. No sign of him anywhere.

Lastly, he checked the garage. The Blazer was gone.

Ben rushed inside and called Sawyer's cell phone. When the man answered, he sounded out of breath.

"Is everything okay?" he asked, his voice saturated with concern. "Did something happen to her? Did she call?"

"No, not yet. I'm calling about Derek. He hasn't come by tonight or called you, has he?"

"Come by? He's not driving, I hope. Are you saying he's missing?"

"Afraid so."

"Gee, Ben. I haven't talked to him since yesterday. I'm up near Miami Beach right now. Want me to swing by your place? Or better—I could go out and look for him. Would that help?"

"If it's no trouble, I'd appreciate it. I'm going out as well."

"No problem. And I'll call the guys. Maybe he went to Peter's."

Though he regretted having to do it, Ben woke up Cheryl and apprised her of the situation. He knew if she woke up to find him gone, she would worry.

"Where would he go?" She rubbed her sleepy eyes and pulled back the covers. "He didn't seem any worse tonight before he went up to bed. Did you call Peter's?"

As he threw on some jeans and tennis shoes, they heard little Jordan's soft whine from down the hall. He peered at his wife with down-turned brows. "Sorry, love. I didn't mean to wake her."

She bustled out of bed, twirled on her robe, then patted his back as she walked him out their bedroom door. "You didn't. I've got her. You go find our son."

He jogged downstairs and snatched up his keys and wallet. It dawned on him he had not yet called Chris. Grabbing his cell phone, he dialed the number on his way to the garage. Maybe he had overthought the situation. Maybe Derek had snuck off for a visit with his uncle.

Chris answered on the first ring, echoing Sawyer's anxious inquiry over Farin's status. When Ben told him Derek was missing, he insisted Ben pick him up, claiming he had not slept all night anyway. He pulled out of the garage and paused at the end of the driveway to assess the parked cars up and down the street before making a left onto Harbor Boulevard. Thankfully, the press invasion had not begun...yet.

"Any ideas where he'd go?" Chris asked as he climbed into the Land Rover. "Did you call the boys in the band?"

"Sawyer's doing that. I wanted to get going straightaway—and now I don't have a bloody clue where to start looking."

They cruised around the village checking the local teenage hangouts, all of which had closed hours ago.

"Maybe I should call home and ask Cheryl to wake up Kyle. He'd know where his brother hangs out, wouldn't he?"

Chris shook his head, his eyes darting up and down the streets for any sign of his nephew. "It doesn't make sense he'd be hanging out somewhere without telling you he'd gone, does it? If he'd wanted to go out with his friends, all he'd have had to do was say something. He's injured, not grounded. Besides, he hasn't wanted to talk to anyone since the accident. He barely talks to me."

Ben slammed on his brakes, bringing the vehicle to an abrupt stop at the corner of Sunset and Crandon.

Chris' body lurched forward, then back. He reached up instinctively and clutched the roof handle above the window. "What's the matter?"

He faced him with ashen features. "The lighthouse."

Chris shrugged. "What about it?"

"Derek and Summer used to spend a lot of time hanging out down there. They'd have picnics and whatnot."

"That's a state park."

"And a high climb."

"There'd be no access down there so late at night, would there?"

Ben flipped the SUV around and headed south on Crandon. "Let's see."

They drove silently along the two-lane road. Ben bypassed the closed drive-through ticket booth by veering left where the road forked before approaching the building. They motored down the wrong side of the road until an unobstructed side road allowed the Land Rover to pull back onto the correct-facing lane. Thick tropical growth on either side of the paved drive coupled with intermittent turnoffs made for a protracted and increasingly frustrating search.

Chris glanced at Ben, his face sheathed in grave contemplation. "You don't think he'd hurt himself. That's not Derek."

"You tell me. I don't know who my son is lately. You're the only one of the two of us who's experienced anything like this. How did you feel when you thought Farin died?"

He turned back and stared at the road.

Ben parked the car as close as he could get. With no direct access to the lighthouse, they had to hoof it the rest of the way. Once there, they did an initial search to ensure Derek had not gained access to the stairs. They then split up and walked in opposite directions along the beach and the erosion fence, calling his name and checking the dense landscape for any sign of him.

The absence of the Blazer's presence along the road or near where he had left his vehicle comforted Ben on one hand, yet frustrated him on the other. He wished he had thought to grab a couple of flashlights out of his car. The pre-midnight search without a decent source of light proved futile.

Eventually, they met back at the lighthouse. When Ben realized neither of them had found a trace of his son, his apprehension increased until it nearly took on a life of its own.

They returned to the vehicle and headed back out of the park, thankful they had avoided an encounter with any possible park security roaming the grounds or triggered by any monitored video footage of them entering the park outside visiting hours.

Ben clenched his teeth as they returned to the village. He wracked his brain trying to think of where to try next. Maybe he should call home and ask Cheryl if Derek had come home on his own. Probably not. Such a conversation could only make things worse. Besides, if their son had returned, she would have already contacted him.

He called Sawyer again to see how he had fared.

"Peter and Brian were both home asleep, according to their parents. I went by Levoy's personally. Cécile says her brother's been at the house pretty much all day with her and their parents. Sorry I don't have better news."

When they hung up, Ben pursed his lips and cast the phone at the passenger floorboard, barely missing his brother's foot.

"We'll find him," Chris promised. "Why don't we try the school?"

"Why would he go to school? He never much cared about going there *before* the accident. I can't see he'd have any reason to want to go back there now. Maybe I'll drive down to the warehouse."

"Would he go to the warehouse without the rest of the band?"

"Maybe he's ready to try to start playing again."

"Maybe." Chris snorted. "With all this focus on Farin and making sure the Lockhardts are dealt with, I guess none of us realized what was going on with him."

Ben's shoulders slumped in defeat. "Maybe it's time to call the police."

Chris stooped down and picked up the cell phone off the floorboard. "I'm sorry. I should have realized how depressed he is. I've been there. I should have noticed the signs."

"How could any of us have dreamed he'd just up and leave? No note? No nothing?"

"He must plan on coming back, then. I remember Julie used to get so angry when I'd—"

Ben frowned at him. "When you'd what?"

The expression on Chris' face transformed from panic to instant relief. He instructed Ben to head into the city. "Call Cheryl and tell her everything's okay. We don't need the cops. I know exactly where he is."

***

The room fell silent as a tomb at the cocking of the pistol. "Looking for this?"

Jameson spun around. Instead of a small cadre of cops and FBI agents coming to subdue him as he had anticipated, Ross emerged from the hidden doorway separating his office from the private elevator. A sliver of light reflected off the gun's steel barrel as he moved toward the room with cautious steps.

Unable to decide whether to belly laugh at the man's farcical display of bravado or rush him with the loud roar of an impending attack, Jameson let his arms fall casually to his sides and stood still. He raised an indignant brow. "A rather fearsome young man once instructed me to never bring a gun to a meeting unless I intended to use it."

Ross hit the light switch on the wall with his free hand, then crossed the office and planted himself a reasonable distance from the old man. "That's good advice."

"What's the matter, old friend? Run out of insults?"

"Who knows? The night's young and you're still not in handcuffs."

"An oversight I'm sure they'll correct in no time."

"You should hope they hurry up and get here."

Farin stepped forward on trembling legs. "We're done, Ross. It's over. Let's go. He's not going anywhere and he's not worth any more trouble to either of us."

Ross narrowed hateful eyes at his old nemesis. "I'm afraid I know him a bit better than you. At least well enough not to know not to trust him when I can't see him for myself."

Jameson lowered himself into his chair. Ross trained the pistol on him, warning him to keep his hands in full view. The threatening display evoked a sardonic chuckle. "I don't know if you fancy yourself a modern day Pat Garrett or someone more glamorous—say, James Bond. Either way, you look ridiculous. Put down that gun before your hurt yourself."

He lifted his chin. "I mean it. Put your hands on your desk."

Jameson rolled his eyes and flopped his hands down upon his blotter as instructed.

Ross positioned himself where he could more easily address Farin while maintaining a keen eye on Jameson. "Before you leave here tonight, you're going to admit what you did to my wife."

Farin's lips parted. She glowered at Jameson, then peered back at Ross. "Don't. Think of how much better it'll feel to have him admit his crimes on the stand before a jury. He'll die in prison. Isn't that what you want?"

Ross shook his head. "I want to hear him say it. He'd rather die than confess his crimes, especially in a court of law. Tell her, Jameson. It'll all come out sooner or later anyway. Tell her you'd rather have me shoot you than admit the crimes you've committed over the years. Things she'd never believe."

Jameson stared at him, cold and vacant.

"Say it," Ross goaded the man.

"I'm afraid I have no idea what you're talking about."

He puffed a doubtful snort through flared nostrils as he addressed Farin. "See?" In a flash, he turned and fired the pistol into Jameson's mahogany trophy case, shattering the glass door and nicking one of his Grammys.

Startled, Farin covered her ears and stifled a scream.

Jameson leveled steely blue eyes upon him.

"*Say it!*" Ross demanded.

"I've never killed another human being in my life."

He raised an eyebrow and gave him wry grin. "Oh, come now. We *both* know that's not true. If it were, neither of us would be here right now."

Jameson exhaled sharply and dropped his shoulders. "It always goes back to London with you, doesn't it?"

"That's where it all began, right? So why not go back there?"

"I don't know if you want to use London as a bargaining chip. Seems to me you had far more motive than I did. After all, I was just the driver."

He shook his head. "Nice try. You're not going to pin that on me. I'm not afraid of that anymore."

"I suppose time will tell. I wouldn't dismiss your involvement just yet."

"Is that a threat?"

Jameson lifted his shoulders with a nonchalant flare. "You're the one holding the gun. Besides, I don't make threats. You of all people should know that."

Farin lifted her hands and approached Ross. "Maybe you should go and let Special Agent Quarles know we've found Jameson. Don't let him win, Ross. Your wife wouldn't want you to throw away your life like this, would she?"

He studied her with pained eyes as he slowly lowered his arm. "Josephine *was* my life. I have nothing left without her. No family. No future. I'm an old man now, Farin. You wouldn't understand. This is between me and Jameson. It's been a long time coming. You should go."

Bolder now, she inched closer. "If it were that simple, why would you go to the trouble of coordinating this elaborate evening with the Feds? If you'd intended to kill him, why all of this? The best thing we can do is hand him over and wait for the trial."

Jameson sneered challengingly at Ross. "He's not going to kill me. His conscience won't allow him to do it. God doesn't condone murder, does He, Ross?"

Farin jerked her head at Jameson. "Are you trying to get yourself killed?"

He rolled his eyes and reclined in his chair.

They stood quiet for what felt to Farin like an eternity. Ross and Jameson glared at each other as if daring the other to break the silence.

She shuddered with fear as she beheld the gun in Ross' hand. The memory of Bobby producing a less sophisticated version that day in his living room looped in her mind. Over and over, she heard the deafening shot and watched in horror as the life instantly left her husband's eyes. She could not bear to witness another death. Not even Jameson's.

For the second time, she begged for the life of the man who had authored every one of the most agonizing days of her life. "Think about what you're doing, Ross. Don't let him turn you into someone you're not. You're angry and hurt. I get it. I thought I wanted to kill him, too. But this isn't what Josephine would want. It's not what Jordan would want." She held out a trembling hand. "G-g-give me the gun. I'll watch him while you get Quarles."

Instead of talking him down with cool-headed logic, her words seemed to galvanize him. He straightened his arm and pointed the gun at Jameson's chest. "Tell me you killed my wife."

Jameson clutched the arms of his chair and lifted himself up, then buttoned his tuxedo jacket and raised his arms to his sides. Lifting his chin, he taunted, "Shoot me. If you have the courage to pull that trigger, do it. Otherwise, take Farin and leave me be. The last thing I want to do is spend my last few minutes of freedom dealing with a coward and an imbecile."

Ross inclined his head her way but remained focused on his target. "You need to leave, Farin."

Her eyes widened in shock.

"I mean it!" he shouted. "Get out of here!"

"No!" she argued defiantly. She moved closer until she stood mere feet away, dismissing the growing nausea in her belly. "I won't let you do this!"

He fired another warning shot, this time at Jameson's abandoned chair, then turned the gun on her. "Don't make me shoot you, too."

She drew her head back in openmouthed shock.

His voice cracked. "Go home to your little girl, Farin. Your place is with her."

Tears filled her eyes as she watched what little reason Ross possessed fade away like the evening sun. She froze in place. Afraid to move, afraid to leave, afraid to stay.

Out of the corner of her eye, she spotted Jameson creeping toward them. She screamed for Ross, who stepped back as Jameson lunged for the gun.

He fired the pistol, hitting him in the left knee. Jameson cried out in painful fury, then dropped to the floor.

"*Go now!*" Ross ordered her.

Terrified by the unraveling scene before her, she sprinted toward the elevator. As soon as she was out of sight, she heard the commotion as if it played itself out behind muted layers of soundproof padding. Shouting. Threats. The chaotic scuffling of bodies.

Then, another shot.

The elevator chimed and the doors opened. She hurried inside and pressed the lobby floor button with a shaking finger. As the car began its descent, she strained to make out any additional sounds but could hear nothing aside from the distinct ringing in her ears. It felt like a nightmare, or a memory. Momentarily lost in another time and place, she gazed down at her trembling hands, half expecting to find them covered with blood.

Overwhelmed by the events of the night, she turned to the side and bent over, emptying the contents of her stomach onto the platform floor. The perception of falling added to the nausea of her weakened stomach. She grabbed the side rail with one hand to steady herself.

All at once, her body heaved with retching sobs. She howled mournfully, *"Jordan!"*

For all the healing she had assured herself she had done over the many months of trying to find her daughter, stay out of Jameson's grasp, and maintain what little sanity she had left, her strength had finally reached its limits. A montage of her loved ones' faces whizzed through her mind. Little Jordan, Marci, Chris, and Sawyer, then her beloved parents, and at last, Jordan. Somehow, watching Ross shoot Jameson with his own gun had hurled her headfirst back to that fateful day.

She staggered to the rear of the elevator and clutched the side rails with both hands, battling her mind to stay in the present and willing the recovery of her ability to hear.

It's almost over, she told herself. *You're almost free. Just five more floors to go.*

Why had she insisted on coming alone? Stubborn as usual. Sawyer had begged her to let him join her. Yet something about involving him felt wrong. This was not his fight. He did not understand. Besides, she preferred to think of him untouched by the darkness of her long journey. He made her feel she could recapture the youth Jameson had systematically stolen from her. She needed Sawyer to keep her strong and moving toward the future.

Four more floors.

But Chris. Her heart ached for him. She wanted to believe he waited for her downstairs, that he had defied her wishes and followed her to New York— always there, always loving her, always the knight in shining armor. She wanted to fall into his arms and hear him tell her she was safe. That they all were and would be from here on out.

Three more.

How would Jameson leave the LSI building tonight—in handcuffs or a body bag? Had Ross wounded him? Or had he made good on his threat to end the old man once and for all?

The torment in Ross' eyes had flooded her with sadness. She shared his loss and could hardly blame him for wanting to prevent Lockhardt from harming another living soul. But for him to lose his freedom over his thirst for vigilante justice grieved her. She resolved to do whatever necessary to stand by him. She would talk to Special Agent Quarles and explain. Had Ross not shot Jameson, the old man would have certainly overpowered and killed him.

Two floors.

She longed for little Jordan. It had been too soon to leave her. By selfishly insisting on witnessing Jameson's defeat, she had gambled that her daughter might revert back to the initial days of fearful confusion following Farin's arrival at her foster parents' front door. It had been no small feat trying to make a three year old understand she had a mother who loved her and had come to take her home.

One.

But from here on out, things would be different. She and Samantha would need to figure out the details of a fair publicity schedule. One that would satisfy Minor 6th while maintaining ample time for motherhood. Maybe Jordan would join her on the road.

In fairness, Sawyer was right. No matter how good or bad her comeback album was, it would do well. The unbelievable events surrounding the last few years assured it. That coupled with giving Miles Macy the rights to her biography would result in a lifetime of financial security.

While many decisions still lay ahead, Farin now had the career and financial security she needed to make a better life for herself and her daughter. A life that would enable them to not only survive, but *live*.

She closed her eyes as the elevator touched down at the lobby floor. Safe at last. Despite her still-racing heartbeat, she blinked to clear her vision, then rushed forward as the doors slowly slid open.

Before she could alter her momentum, she ran straight into the arms of Bobby Lockhardt.

CHAPTER 30

BEN CRANED HIS NECK AS they pulled in and searched the darkened Our Lady of Guadalupe Catholic Church parking lot. Chris squinted and leaned forward, then pointed off to the right. "I think I see the Blazer. Look. Over there."

Visually confirming the location of his son's car, he inhaled deeply then emitted a slow sigh of relief through puckered lips. "You're bloody brilliant, brother. Have I ever told you that?"

The side of Chris' mouth hitched into a grateful if sarcastic smirk. "Not once."

They parked next to Derek's car, then got out and peered into the darkness toward the cemetery, hoping for an accessible alternative to scaling any iron fences.

"This place is huge," Chris observed.

Ben nodded. "I'll lose my sense of direction if we try to go in through the side. We'll need to head in through the front."

"It's a long walk back."

He grabbed a flashlight from his SUV's emergency kit, tested it to ensure the batteries had not died, then locked up the vehicle.

They walked back to the lot entrance near the street, then cut left onto the cement bike trail running between the church and the cemetery. Several minutes later, they reached the gated entrance.

Chris braced his hands against the stucco wall some feet beyond the higher entrance gate and lifted himself on his tiptoes to get an idea of what they would land on if they climbed over. "At least it's not too tall over here."

"If Derek *is* in there, he would have had to have come this way. Let's hope he didn't re-injure his shoulder."

"Trust me. Here's there."

They hoisted themselves up and over the stucco wall and began their search.

Ben waited until they had walked far away from the compound of buildings and mausoleums clustered near the front before engaging his flashlight. "I don't even know where to look. For all I know, the Reeces have a private family crypt."

Chris shook his head. "They have a family plot. I know where she's at. Derek had me call Peter a couple of weeks ago to find out so he could send her flowers. Peter found out from some of the mutual friends he and Summer went to school with."

"How far is it?"

He pointed off and to the left. "Towards the northwest end of the property."

Ben squinted and looked to his left, then his right, in a futile attempt to get his bearings.

They trudged along, Chris leading the way. No sooner had they walked around a small lake than the sprinkler system came to life, spraying the thirsty grounds with water and drenching the two men to the skin. They picked up the pace and sprinted across the wet grass until coming upon a paved road.

"I think we're almost there," Chris said. He shook out his hair and jerked his arms up and down to dispel drops of water, then stomped his feet atop the asphalt.

Ben combed back his hair with his fingers and flicked the excess water from his hands. "It never occurred to me until just now, but what if we get there and he's already gone?"

Chris clasped his damp shoulder and urged him on with a lift of his chin. "Wild horses, brother. Jagger sang it best."

When they finally reached their intended destination, the fault lines of Ben's hopeful uncertainty nearly breached. He exhaled a breath of relief saturated with compassion as he beheld the form of his grieving son sleeping atop Summer Reece's grave.

Chris shot out a hand as they approached the boy, stopping Ben in his tracks. "He's gonna be pissed off we came after him. You know that."

He nodded. "Not forever, he won't."

"Right that."

"Maybe you should go on ahead. I'll wait here. I don't want to make it any worse for him. He needs to know I'm here, but I think he needs you more right now."

"You sure?"

"I'm not sure of anything at this point. But go on."

Chris jogged over to the grave and crouched down, then put his hand on Derek's shoulder. The boy started at the contact, then looked around to get his bearings. He allowed Chris to help him up and into a sitting position, wincing with pain for having fallen asleep on the hard ground. When he noticed his father standing a few yards off, he hung his head and looked away.

"You all right, then?" Chris asked, sitting down Indian style beside his nephew.

Derek shrugged his good shoulder.

"Wanna talk about it?"

He shook his head.

"Mind if I do?"

Derek looked up at him but did not respond.

"I figure you're a man now. You've learned about life the hard way—not that there aren't scores of lessons left before it's all done. But the way I see it, you've earned the truth. Maybe you'll think less of me when I tell you, but as a man, I'm prepared to risk it."

Curious now, Derek asked, "The truth about what?"

"I've been where you are."

He rolled his eyes.

"It's true. Different girl, different cemetery. Same pain. The pain that gets inside your bones. You know the one. And it hurts more than that bloody shoulder or yours ever will."

Derek wrapped his good arm around his brace and glanced at the gravestone bearing Summer's name.

"You were too young at the time to realize what was going on, but in case you ever wondered why your dad and I fight so often, I'll let you in on a little secret. I'm a bit of a black sheep in this family."

The teen grinned despite himself.

"And before your Uncle Jordan died, I made the mistake of trying to take something that belonged to him."

The grin dissolved into confusion. "Why would you do that?"

Chris dipped his head. "Because like death, love chooses us far more often than we choose it."

His eyes widened in understanding. "Aunt Farin?"

He nodded.

Derek scowled and stared at the ground, as if unsure where his loyalty should lay.

"Like I said—different girl, different cemetery. Same pain."

He looked up. "You used to go to the cemetery to visit her grave?"

"Often. And for years."

"Wow."

"Yeah."

"When did it stop hurting so much?" he asked, a catch in his throat.

Chris sighed through pursed lips. "Ah, mate. Wish I could tell you. I don't know if it ever did, even now that we know she's alive. Death isn't something we get over, it's something we get used to. It's takes as long as it takes."

When Derek swiped hot tears from under his eyes, Ben dared to come forward and sit with them. The boy did not spare his father a glance, but rather stared into the space between his dad and uncle.

"Any words of wisdom for your son, then?" Chris asked Ben.

He slowly shook his head. "This is new territory for me. I've only ever lost a brother, not that it didn't feel impossible to get over at times. But I don't know what I'd do if I lost the love of my life and our child. It'd take a stronger man than me to survive something like that."

Renegade tears trickled down Derek's cheeks faster than he could catch them. He cleared his throat and rubbed his eyes with his thumb and index finger. He straightened his back to try to work out the kinks, then leaned in to his sore shoulder, hoping for some relief.

"You about ready to call it a night?" Chris stood and brushed off his damp jeans, the area around which he had sat thick with mud.

Derek eyeballed his father, then jerked his head away. "I'm not going home. Not yet."

Ben opened his mouth to protest, then clamped his jaw and nodded. "That shoulder okay to drive back later?"

He nodded.

"You haven't taken any pain medication?"

The nod transformed into a sullen shake of his head.

"Need any aspirin or anything? Water?"

"I'm okay."

Ben stood and swiped at his similarly muddy jeans. "Okay then. I'll let your mother know so she doesn't worry. But it's late. If a security guard comes and gives you the boot, don't bother arguing. You can always come back tomorrow."

Tears brimming in his eyes, Derek faced his father at last. "Thanks, Dad."

He nodded and stuck out his hand, which Derek accepted. "You're a good man."

With every grudging step back through the cemetery, Ben fought the urge to turn around for a final glimpse of his boy. Derek would doubtless be watching, waiting cynically for some sign his father regretted his decision to let him stay or perhaps did not trust him.

Until he and Chris had reached the SUV and headed back toward Key Biscayne, he refused to acknowledge even to himself that in the time it took to reach out his hand, he had witnessed the transformation of his first son. For all intents and purposes, Derek was now a man. It had happened without warning or fanfare, but there was no unringing the bell. Ben could no sooner direct his future than he could shelter him from the grieving process. Dragging his son away from the cemetery would have harmed far more than helped.

Maybe Jagger did sing it best.

Ben dropped Chris off at his house, then called Sawyer to assure him they had found Derek safe and well. He omitted the details, for which Sawyer did not ask. When he parked his car and entered his home, he found Cheryl on the phone with the police. He tried to interrupt and call off the search, but she gave him a stern look that told him in no uncertain terms to let her finish.

"But we found him," he explained when she finally ended the call.

"Good. Maybe the police will find the man I just chased out of our front yard."

***

He refused to think he was slipping, though he did believe he had needed more than a few weeks of relaxation to get back on his game. If he were honest, he would admit his enthusiasm for his job had waned. He simply did not enjoy it like he used to.

It was probably the client.

Ever since Lockhardt had hired him, he had found himself taking risks he would have never before imagined. Rush, rush, rush. No thinking. No creativity. The pressure made for some sketchy choices—the most recent one, tonight. And this one had looked mean.

"Checking in, sir?" asked the chipper desk clerk.

It was everything he could do to not make a sarcastic comment. That would not do. Now more than ever he needed to remain as unrememberable as possible. Just another face in a sea of tourists. Check in, check out, and gone. Nothing to see here, folks.

But the earlier encounter needled him. She had seen his face. However obscured by the dark of night, they had locked eyes. No one had ever seen him unless he had intended. At least no one who had lived long enough to report it. Now, he had another potentially sketchy choice to make. Killing her was the obvious answer. And it would no doubt thrill his client. Then again, he had already given the old man a freebie or two.

He wrestled with his options as he collected his room key and luggage, then rolled his carryon to his room. Not the nicest place he had ever stayed, but not the worst either. When he had originally booked it, he had not considered he would have to spend more than one night in Miami before flying back out. Now, he would need to lay low a day or two before proceeding. Let the occupants settle down a little, make them believe some random local hood had attempted to burgle them. In a couple of days, they would forget all about it and lower their guard.

Lifting his suitcase on top of one of the two queen-size beds, he realized the last time he had eaten had been on the layover during his multi-country flight. Lousy food, almost inedible. He detested German cuisine. Sort of ironic, since both his parents had been full blooded. In any case, he fully intended to get a decent meal in his belly before he called it a night. Come to think of it, he was beat.

As usual, his first order of business included situating his toiletries to make sure he would not find himself ready to shower or brush his teeth only to discover he had forgotten to pack his toothpaste or deodorant. Next, he stacked his clothes in the dresser on top of his weapon. Not the most original hiding place, but who cared? It was Miami. Everyone carried a gun.

Though tempted to bypass his routine, he realized he needed to call Lockhardt with an update. Personal feelings aside, he did run a business. That required certain client concessions. Besides, they had not spoken directly for some time. He wondered if the old fool had gotten the message he left in Santa Barbara back in September—namely, do not cross him.

He sat down on the bed and bounced up and down several times to test the mattress. The hard, cheap lump of springs disappointed him. Maybe he would find a better option tomorrow. A man could not possibly expect to function properly sleeping on an uncomfortable mattress.

Digging the burner phone out of his pocket, he depressed the power button, then waited for the device to start. He grabbed the television remote off the nightstand and turned that on as well. Late night HBO. The last bastion of hope for anything semi-entertaining for the insomniacs of the world. Nothing but B-movies and soft porn. What a joke. He switched the TV off.

His mind continued to contemplate his course of action over the witness as he dialed his client's number. Why he wasted such mental energy, he did not know. He had no intention of running a charity organization. Instead of complicating the matter, he would continue on as planned. He would take care of the Grant girl, then head back to Malé. They liked him there. He spent money. Lots of money.

The call rang several times, then went to voicemail. Too bad for Lockhardt. He would not try again. After careful thought, he decided to call Radford and see if he would mind relaying the status of the job on his behalf. Not the preferred route. Not the most professional approach. Too bad his girlfriend had decided to stop acting as the receptionist for his phony Z-Master Imports.

Herb Radford answered on the second ring, his voice uncharacteristically edgy when he recognized the caller.

"Is this a bad time?" he asked without identifying himself.

"Uh, no—not at all. What can I do for you?"

"You sure you're okay?"

Herb cleared his throat. "Of course I'm sure! Why? Who the hell do you think you are, my doctor?"

"I haven't been a doctor in months." The instant memory made him chuckle.

"Did you call to chat or do you have some news? Where are you, anyway?"

His eyes narrowed in suspicion. The PI sounded nervous. Not good.

"Well?" Herb demanded.

Against his better judgment, he continued on. "I tried to call our mutual acquaintance to give him an update. You talk to him lately?"

"Ah, no. No I haven't. I've done my part. I'm not involved anymore."

"So you've severed all contact?"

"With a sharp knife."

"Can't blame you there. I'll be doing the same thing very soon. But did things end amicably?"

"Why do you ask?"

"I was hoping you could relay a message for me. Nothing too detailed."

A pause filled the line.

"Is that a no?"

"Uh...you know what? Sure. I'll give him a call for ya. What's the message?"

He opened his mouth to speak, then stopped short as his suspicion mounted. Something did not seem right. He consulted his watch to check the amount of time they had spent on the phone.

All at once, he heard a faint crackling noise. Not quite the sound of distortion. Not a bad connection.

"Well? Gonna give me the message for Lockhardt or not?" Herb demanded.

He pulled the phone away from his ear and stabbed the end call button.

For the next half hour, he raced to remove any possible trace of evidence the police might find if they searched the motel room. Fingerprints, stray hairs, a random eyelash. They would find nothing to tie him to this room.

He wiped down the key card for the door, then left it in the room before sneaking out the back entrance and shoving his luggage in the back seat of his rental. From there, he drove to the first water access he could find. With steady hands, he removed the battery from the phone and flung the entire contraption into the Miami River.

Fortunately, locating alternative accommodations on a Tuesday night would present no problem.

It took every bit of his resolve not to catch the next flight out of the city. Instead, he found an all-night eatery and ordered a large meal and two desserts. He was starving. Moreover, he was angry. He always ate more when he was angry.

"Where did you put it all?" his waitress asked as she slid his check down and refilled his coffee cup. "You're such a tiny little thing."

He winked as he stood up and pulled his wallet from his back pocket. "High metabolism, I guess." He checked the ticket, then dropped enough cash on the table for the dinner and an ample tip, then headed off to find another hotel.

The woman who had spotted him would have to go after all. Things had gotten hot. He could not risk someone identifying him. It looked like Jameson Lockhardt would get another freebie after all.

***

Several officers piled into the small alcove near the concealed elevator entrance amid the commotion. Farin batted her hands furiously at Bobby as they struggled to move away from each other.

He shrieked at the sight of her. "What the—*Farin*?"

She cried out in fear and panic. "*Help!* Get him away from me!"

"But they said you were—!"

Alvarez ducked and slid in between them to pull Farin away. She snapped at her partner, "Cuff the SOB, Billy! What're you waiting for?"

"I thought you said you wanted to wait until he took us upstairs." Bridgeman stepped forward and subdued Bobby, who stared openmouthed and pale as he beheld Farin.

Joni Leighton backed up against the far wall and covered her mouth with her hands as she shook her head in disbelief. Her hair had become mussed in the pandemonium of the evening as everyone had scattered like dried leaves in a torrential wind to avoid or demand answers from the authorities. Mascara and eye makeup smeared her beautiful features. She called out to Bobby in a small, frightened voice, "What's going on, baby?"

Alvarez slit her eyes expectantly and stared at Bridgeman. "*Well?*"

He held Bobby in place with one hand atop the handcuffs and the other on his shoulder. A knowing grin played at the corners of his mouth. "Go ahead, partner. This is your baby."

Giving him no time to reconsider which of them would count coup in the apprehension of their most sought after suspect, she squared her shoulders, positioned herself between Farin and Bobby, then jutted her chin toward her suspect as she reached inside the plunging neckline of her dress to produce her badge. "My name is Detective Alvarez. I work homicide for the Metro-Dade Police Department in Miami, Florida." She gestured behind him. "This is my partner, Detective Bridgeman. Bobby Lockhardt, we are placing you under arrest for the murder of Jordan Grant, the aggravated rape of Farin Grant, false imprisonment..."

Farin's blood ran cold as Detective Alvarez ran off the long list of crimes for which they had apprehended him. She felt nothing as the woman read him his rights. Once he had been her closest friend—closer than Marci at one point. He had toured with her, kept her going as the demands on her time left her crippled with exhaustion. In so many ways, he had taken care of her. She had trusted him with her life. It seemed forever ago now.

"Is it really you?" His voice broke with emotion as if he had not heard a word Detective Alvarez had said, as if completely unaware he stood before them trussed in restraints and would soon be led away.

Watching him peer at her in utter incomprehension, her senses flooded with the image of him painting Melody's nursery. One moment out of thousands where they had laughed together, him expressing his excitement for her and Jordan as they looked forward to becoming parents, poking fun at Chris' bitter reaction to the news. Him dancing about the nursery and singing that dreadful song. Bobby had defiled that space just as he later defiled her.

The thought enraged her.

Bobby glanced behind him as he became aware of his circumstances, then at Alvarez, and finally back at Farin as Joni hovered nearby pleading for someone, anyone, to explain why they were arresting her fiancé. "What happened? Where have you been all this time? Are...are you okay?"

The feigned innocence shredded her self-control. She stepped toward him, but Alvarez instinctively and immediately shot her hand out and ordered over her shoulder, "Stay back, Mrs. Grant. Let us handle this."

From behind her, she heard Special Agent Quarles ask, "Did you see the father upstairs?"

She spun around. "He's in his office."

With a curt nod, Quarles directed several officers into the elevator.

"There's a gun," she warned. "I heard shots."

Quarles eyed her up and down. "Are you hurt?"

She shook her head. "No, but Jameson was wounded. Maybe worse, I don't know. I ran."

"*Dad?*" Bobby shouted. He struggled perfunctorily against Bridgeman but quickly ceased his resistance when the detective strengthened his grip on his shoulder and yanked him back a step.

Quarles touched his earpiece, then dipped and tilted his head to speak. "We need medical up on forty. And get us an ambulance."

Bobby's brows arched above sorrowed eyes. "Is he okay? Please, Farin! Is my dad all right?"

She started to lunge at him once more. Alvarez turned and spread her arms, then nudged her back. Through gritted teeth, she whispered, "Farin, if you don't back off, I'll have no choice but to have you removed. Do us all a favor, huh? If you can't take it, go find Miles. He's waiting for us in the conference room."

Quarles asked, "Did you get a look at the guy who shot him?"

She swallowed hard and nodded. "But it's not his fault."

"Who was it?"

She lowered her head. "It was Ross Alexander."

"*What?*" Bobby erupted again, this time straining harder against

Bridgeman. "No! That can't be! Ross would *never*—"

"Billy, slap some legcuffs on our suspect, will you?" Alvarez snapped. "He's getting agitated and it's starting to piss me off."

Bridgeman rolled his eyes, but reached behind his back to unsnap the leather case affixed to his belt. "You heard the lady. And trust me, you don't want to piss her off."

Quarles trained his eye on Farin to help her stay focused. "You witnessed the shooting?"

"There were two warning shots, then Ross shot him in the knee. Jameson had rushed him to try to take away the gun. It was the only thing Ross could do. Jameson would've killed us both."

"Okay. And you initially said, 'maybe worse.' What does that mean?"

The memory overwhelmed her. She buried her head in her hands. Miami had never seemed so far away. "He yelled at me to leave."

"Who did?"

"Ross. And when I did, I heard another shot."

Bobby hitched his breath.

Quarles glanced up at Bridgeman, then Alvarez, then shook his head and looked back at Farin. "Did you hear anything else? Someone calling out in pain or maybe asking for help?"

"Nothing."

Bobby collapsed to his knees as Bridgeman secured the leg restraints. Before he could react, Joni Leighton rushed to Bobby's side and threw her arms around him. "It's gonna be okay, baby. Your daddy'll be fine, I know it."

Bridgeman reached down with an open hand. "Miss, I'm afraid you're going to have to step away."

She set her jaw, ignoring the gesture. "Where are you taking my fiancé?"

"He'll be heading to Miami first thing in the morning."

"Miami? But this has to be a misunderstanding! Bobby wouldn't hurt anyone!"

Farin scoffed, then spat, "Are you schizophrenic, too?"

Joni leapt up and stepped toward Farin, her face red and hot. "He is *not* schizophrenic!"

Bobby lifted his head. "Joni, it's okay."

She turned his way but pointed an angry finger in Farin's direction. "Oh no! I will *not* just sit back and let her spread that ugly mess about you!" Calmer, she addressed Bridgeman. "I need to know where you're taking him tonight so I can contact his lawyer."

The elevator door pinged, prompting the group to back up en masse. When the door opened, they saw Jameson seated on a reclining gurney, his knee bandaged and his hands cuffed atop his lap. Law enforcement flanked the apparatus, crowding the paramedics who endeavored to wheel him out.

Joni's expression brightened. She glanced at Bobby, then looked as though she would go to Jameson as she had gone to him before. Alvarez snagged her arm and shook her head.

"Dad!" Bobby exclaimed as he struggled to stand. Bridgeman helped him up but kept him back as the officers wheeled his father through the hall.

Jameson stared straight ahead, chin raised defiantly as medical personnel wheeled him out of the alcove and toward the lobby. He ignored the calls of his son, his future daughter-in-law's promises to meet him at the hospital as soon as possible, and Farin's look of concern as she stared passed him, searching the elevator for any additional passengers.

Special Agent Quarles instructed Alvarez and Bridgeman to collect their suspect and head out so he and his team could wrap things up. Bridgeman led Bobby through the hall with Alvarez taking up the rear amid the protests of Joni Leighton.

Quarles inclined and dipped his head and held his index finger to his ear once more, this time listening intently as someone updated him on the situation upstairs. A moment later, he acknowledged the caller then nodded toward Farin. "I'm going to have someone meet you in the conference room to get your statement about the events in Lockhardt's office. You're free to go after that."

The words echoed through her mind as the procession leading Bobby Lockhardt away disappeared around a corner. She followed Quarles out of the hallway and across the lobby. His footsteps echoed upon the marble floor as his heels punched the large tiles with each step. She had never seen the LSI building so empty.

For the next couple of hours as she gave her statement, the events of the evening took on a surreal quality. She had struggled most her life over the Lockhardts in one way or another. It hardly seemed possible the nightmare had finally ended. She could not wait to get home and see her family.

Before finally leaving the building, Farin found Quarles near the front doors talking to another agent. She approached him and touched his arm.

He lifted a finger to his colleague, then turned to her, his dark eyes patient and kind. "What is it, Farin?"

Something inside her begged her not to ask, but she had to know. "What about...?"

His features softened, then he shook his head and offered her a sympathetic frown.

A ping from the elevator bank captured her attention. When the doors opened, she saw no medical personnel or additional officers file out into the space like before. Instead, several men wearing wind breakers that read

"Coroner" on the back wheeled a second gurney into the lobby. Atop it lay a zipped body bag.

CHAPTER 31

L OCKHARDT SOUND: THE SHOCK HEARD Around the World
-- Miami, FL, Miami Herald (AP), Thursday, November 16th by Miles Macy

Bedlam ensued in the conference hall of Lockhardt Sound, Inc.'s corporate offices Tuesday night when Federal Authorities crashed a birthday/retirement party hosted for its founder, President and CEO Jameson Lockhardt, Sr.

And they came bearing gifts.

Following a months-long investigation into LSI's top three executives, Special Agent Hubbell Quarles of the Federal Bureau of Investigation executed an arrest warrant for the infamous record mogul responsible for the careers of some of the most notable musical acts of the last three decades, including legendary rockers Mirage, country and western phenom Megan Price, up-and-comer Joni Leighton, and Farin Grant, whose musical career had been tragically cut short by a shocking, if suspect, set of circumstances following the December 1991 murder of her husband, pop idol Jordan Grant, another LSI heavy-hitter.

In a stunning twist of fate, we have confirmed that Farin Grant is not only very much alive, but will be the FBI's star witness in a case involving murder, conspiracy, kidnapping, false imprisonment, and child abduction.

You read that right. Farin's back, and she's brought her three year old daughter, Jordan—named after the child's famous father—with her. And you thought last month's not guilty verdict in OJ Simpson's trial of the century was scandalous?

Homicide Detectives William Bridgeman and Alicia Alvarez of Miami's Metro-Dade Police Department accompanied the Feds to apprehend another LSI notable, incoming president and Jameson's only son, Bobby Lockhardt. He has been arrested and charged with the murder of Jordan Grant, rape, and other crimes.

The whirlwind evening had started with a roast by Lockhardt's peers and colleagues, including former Mirage keyboardist-turned-fashion designer Faith Peterson, Minor 6th Records' VP and newlywed Samantha Maxwell, and even yours truly. Roastmaster and LSI attorney Ross Alexander gave this reporter the very great honor of announcing the arrival of the authorities who had come to take him into custody.

Apparently, Mr. Alexander had been cooperating with the FBI for several weeks as part of a plea deal to avoid arrest due to his own involvement in the myriad alleged crimes associated with

Lockhardt and his son. Sources say it was Alexander's statement coupled with Farin Grant's account that gave the Feds enough to obtain a warrant for the man they had investigated for some time in correlation with a separate case. Details of that separate case have not been released, as the investigation is still ongoing.

After storming into the conference room, authorities initially lost track of the elder Mr. Lockhardt, who had fled the scene. A floor-by-floor search ensued, culminating in the man's arrest in his office on the top floor. He was found injured, having suffered a gunshot wound to his knee. It is believed Ross Alexander discovered Lockhardt's whereabouts long before the Feds and shot Lockhardt to prevent his escape. For reasons still unknown, Alexander then turned the gun on himself and subsequently died of a self-inflicted gunshot wound to the head.

Perhaps as an act of contrition before meeting his own end, Alexander worked behind the scenes along with Farin Grant and others with financial ties to the notorious record label to hammer the final nail into Lockhardt Sound's coffin. A new company, Double Maguffin, has apparently obtained ownership of LSI by way of stock acquisition and a new board of directors who have moved to oust the younger Mr. Lockhardt from his anointed position. Lockhardt received this news while being processed into the Dade County Jail this morning.

As if a final blow to the suddenly defunct record label, it turns out Farin Grant has signed a new multi-record deal with LSI competitor Minor 6th Records. According to VP Samantha Maxwell, Farin's fans will be delighted with her upcoming album, aptly named *A Message for the Living*. It is slated for a December 1st release and will include two never-before-heard duets featuring her late husband.

Details are still emerging as this breaking story spans the globe. As an admitted critic of Jameson Lockhardt's for some time now, this reporter will be following this epoch-making riches-to-rags story with delight and provide updates as they become available.

Farin Grant has personally assured me I will no longer require the assistance of a computer séance.

***

Farin woke to the feel of little Jordan playing with her muss of curls. She lay still and kept her eyes shut, enjoying the tingly sensation spreading down her shoulders, calming her more effectively than any sedative she had ever ingested. When she finally turned to face her daughter, the girl's eyes widened with joy as she tucked her head into the covers and softly giggled.

"I like your hair," she said with a shy squeak.

Farin smiled and brushed the child's cheek with the back of her hand. "I know you do. Thank you, Jordan. I like your hair, too."

"Momma, I'm Jade."

"I know, honey," she whispered. "I just like calling you by the name I gave you."

"You gave me?"

Farin nodded.

"Why you gave me Jordan?"

"I named you after your daddy."

She looked at the covers as if in deep thought. "I have a daddy?"

"You did, yes."

"Can I see him?"

Farin managed a misty smile through flattened lips. "I can show you a picture of him."

"Why can't I go see him?"

"Because a long, long time before you were born, he died."

She frowned. "What's died?"

"It means he's not here anymore. But he would have adored you."

Jordan rolled over and lay on her back. She watched herself fidget with her fingers.

Farin pointed to the wall beyond the foot of the bed. "See that?"

The girl peeked over, then smiled as she saw the faint shadow of her hands caused by the early morning sun streaming in through the bedroom window. She wiggled her fingers to make the shadow move.

Farin pulled her arms out of the covers and made finger puppets, pretending to gobble up those made by her daughter, who giggled with delight each time the shadows made contact. They lingered and played until the angle of the sun rose to a point it chased all the shadows away.

Kitchen sounds soon pulled her attention. Then came the smell of bacon. Burnt bacon.

She rolled over on her side and brushed away rebellious strands of sandy brown hair from her daughter's face. "You about ready to get up? I think breakfast's cooking."

The girl scrunched her nose and made a face. "I want to go home. I want to see Aunt Cheryl. She makes the best breakfast."

Farin's eyebrows arched, then softened into a sad frown. "I know. Soon, I promise. But you know, we have our own house we'll be moving into soon."

The girl shook her head and pouted. "You promised my happy ending, Momma. I wanna stay with Aunt Cheryl."

They had had similar exchanges over the last week. It pleased Farin that Jordan had formed such quick attachments to the family. Still, these temporary provisions had illustrated how important it was for them to move out and establish their own lives.

Farin rose and pulled on a pair of sweats, then grabbed two hair clips from the dresser. She banked her mess of curls and secured it with one, then helped Jordan put on a robe and used the other to secure her thick morning 'do.

When they exited the room and passed through the living room into the mini dining area, the smell of overcooked bacon grew stronger. A thin layer smoke filled the air. She coughed, then doubled back to open the living room window for fear the smoke detector would sound off.

"Morning," Sawyer greeted with a smile as he struggled to manage two pans of improperly prepared breakfast foods. "Hope you're hungry."

Farin helped Jordan up onto one of the three barstools along the counter separating the small kitchen from the dining room table. She rested her forearms on the counter and leaned forward to peek at the mess he had made. "Need any help?"

"Ah, no! It's a breeze." He reached up and flipped the switch to engage the range hood above the stove, then returned his attention to the fried eggs that had become a scrambled mess in the pan.

"I think you might have the burner on too high."

He bent down to adjust the knobs. "I think you're right."

"You're sure you don't need any help?"

He smirked and squinted at her. "Are you saying I've ruined breakfast?"

"Yes," Jordan piped in. "It smells yucky."

Farin tried to suppress a grin.

He beheld his culinary train wreck to ascertain if anything had survived, then gave up and moved the pans off the active burners, which he then switched off. Raising his hands in defeat, he asked, "Who wants donuts?"

Jordan brightened with a burst of animation, bouncing excitedly in her chair. "Me!"

Sawyer grabbed a pre-prepared sippy cup of orange juice from the refrigerator and slid it across the counter to Jordan, then handed Farin a cup of coffee. "Your wish is my command, kid. What kind you want? In fact, why don't you just come with me?" His eyes darted to Farin. "That okay, Mom?"

"You can come too, Momma!" Jordan trilled.

Farin scrunched her nose and shook her head. "I don't think it'd be a good idea. I don't have the energy this morning to put on my wig."

Jordan deflated in her chair.

"C'mon, school marm. You've been holed up here since you got back from New York. If you don't start getting up and out a bit, I'm gonna have to start charging you rent."

She inclined her head and pulled back the corners of her mouth. "Stop it."

"I mean it! Thanksgiving's in three days. I'm leaving tomorrow to go see my folks. I hate the idea of you just sitting around here. Call Macy and get that press conference scheduled. Give the damn newshounds the story so they'll leave you alone."

Her eyes widened beneath raised brows. "You think they'll leave me alone after that?"

"I think the novelty will die off if you just give a statement. People need to *see* you. We talked about that. Besides," he said, tilting his head Jordan's way, "the kid's bored here. This is a college-oriented apartment complex. It doesn't even have a playground."

Farin glimpsed Jordan sitting sadly in her seat, nursing her juice. Sawyer might as well have come right out and said she was acting selfish by keeping her daughter cooped up like a hostage while she avoided confronting the press. Worse, he was right.

"C'mon." He left the kitchen and circled around to the counter, then hopped up on the last bar stool. "You've made some progress, right? You got your old publicist back on board. The album's coming out next Friday. Your first single's already at number one—*and* it's a killer track. You can't put it off forever."

Unable to come up with a reasonable argument, she grudgingly agreed to make some calls while he and Jordan procured breakfast. Sawyer swept the girl up and off the bar stool, then waited while Farin helped her change into some clothes and comb her hair into a high ponytail. Before they left, Farin asked if Sawyer would bring back something a little more substantial than donuts. He agreed, kissed her goodbye despite Jordan's groaning protest, then headed out.

Once alone, she grabbed the cordless phone and flopped onto the couch. Her first call was to her publicist. When the call went to voicemail, she sighed with relief. Maybe Thanksgiving week would find most her contacts away. That would suit her fine.

For days after the news broke, the Grant household had transformed into a hub of activity. The phone had rung incessantly. Reporters swarmed the Key Biscayne residence, prompting what Ben had described as renewed complaints from their neighbors reminiscent of the period following the tragic circumstances of '91. He had hired security and bodyguards for the house and family and ensured the Matheson place was monitored at all times while the decorators worked to prepare her former home for her return the day after Thanksgiving.

Black Friday. How fitting.

After leaving a non-urgent message for her publicist, she called Miles at work and spoke with Jeanne.

"It's nice to put a name with a voice," she teased. "How're you holding up? Boss man said it was quite a scene up there."

They chatted a bit before Farin asked to speak with the reporter. Jeanne complained about having to go back to Chicago for the annual obligatory family gathering but said she and Miles had managed to coordinate their flights so at least neither would have to endure the airtime alone. He had even upgraded them both to First Class as an early Christmas present.

She chortled as she added, "I think he's trying to talk that detective girlfriend of his into joining us. And mark my words—if he does, I'll get booted back to coach real quick."

"He'd do that to you?"

"In a heartbeat. With promises to make it up to me, of course. But that's okay. I'm just glad he's happy. Along with your situation finally getting taken care of, he's turning into a pretty cool guy, which makes my job infinitely more enjoyable."

When Jeanne told her Miles was tied up in a staff meeting, Farin left a message asking him to get ahold of her publicist when he had a chance so they could coordinate the press conference he had begged her to let him arrange.

"You're ready, then?"

"No," she said. "But I'm doing it anyway."

The call ended with Jeanne's words of encouragement, which curiously comforted Farin on some level.

There. When Sawyer returned, she could tell him she had done her part. After the holidays she would start a more concerted effort to narrow down an agent. Though Bill Taft had contacted Ben's place as soon as he got the unbelievable news she was alive, she had resolved to discontinue doing business with anyone remotely connected to Jameson or LSI.

LSI. Another item on her increasingly full agenda. The idea of stepping in to confront the myriad tasks associated with their triumphant takeover made her head swim. She was no executive. Had never dreamed of such a role.

Ross' suicide had left her devastated. Though they had not made peace until shortly before his death, she felt his loss. Moreover, she saw the toll it had taken on Samantha who, instead of spending her pre-wedding days greeting out-of-town guests and spending quality time with family she had not seen in years, had assumed the role of pseudo next of kin in the absence of any blood relatives Ross had left. Ever efficient and organized, Sam had arranged his small funeral to take place the day before her and Ethan's wedding. Only Samantha, Ethan, and Ross' ailing former sister-in-law had attended.

Farin hoped she and Ethan were enjoying their Italian honeymoon. If anyone deserved a vacation, Samantha Maxwell did.

For the last week, Farin had endeavored to put the enormity of that night's events out of her mind. Had she not, they would have overtaken her. In reality, her life had started fresh. She had found her freedom and her daughter, relaunched her career, and found someone uncomplicated to spend time with—someone who spurred her on to achieve even greater success. From the looks of things, she should be happy. Mostly, she was.

She ran her fingers across the cordless phone's keypad, wondering if she dare call Chris. He had called several times, but Sawyer had intercepted each one and claimed she was busy. For some reason, she had neither complained nor called him back.

Tossing the phone aside, she rose and turned on the stereo in an attempt to drown out her thoughts. She navigated the radio dial away from Sawyer's favored jazz station over to Y100 and caught the tail end of Natalie Merchant's "Carnival" before Collective Soul's "The World I Know" began to play. Settling back down on the couch, she eyeballed the phone, unable to decide whether to pick it up.

She glanced at the digital time display on the stereo system and wondered when Sawyer and Jordan would return. As she reached for the phone, there came a knock at the door that elicited an automatic start.

For too long now, she had panicked at the sound of unexpected noises. She shook off the sensation and reprimanded herself as she crossed the room to peek through the peephole. The image that met her sent her heart into her throat. She opened the door and stood back. "What are you doing here?"

Chris pulled his sunglasses down the bridge of his nose and stepped inside. He glanced around as if appraising the place. "I was in the neighborhood and thought I'd come check on Jordan. I've been trying to call..."

She lowered her head. "I know. I'm sorry. We've been laying low. Come on in."

"I shouldn't. It'd be awkward."

"I'm the only one here right now. Sawyer took Jordan to go pick up some breakfast."

He moved into the entryway as Farin closed the door but stopped short of the living room. "How's she doing?"

"She's okay. She misses Ben and Cheryl. Well, and you. She adores you."

A faint smile reminiscent of his more egocentric days played at the corners of his mouth. "Yeah?"

"You always did have a way with the ladies."

"We all miss you two."

She folded her arms across her chest and lifted one shoulder. "I thought it would be a good idea to keep her away from the reporters for a while. She's not ready for that."

He nodded. "You're probably right. It's only a matter of time, though."

"I know, you're right. How's Derek?"

"It's still raw. There's a lot of anger in him right now. He's working through it."

She shook her head sadly.

"You coming over for dinner Thursday? Cheryl's already started cooking."

"Of course. Jordan should be with her family on the holidays."

"It'll be your first one with her."

She smiled in earnest.

"You all ready for the move on Friday?" He coughed into his fist. "Is Sawyer helping you two get settled?"

"He's flying out tomorrow to spend Thanksgiving with his family."

"You're coming back to the house, then?"

She nodded. "I was just about to call...Cheryl and let her know."

"They'll be thrilled."

In the background, Take That's "Back for Good" played on the radio.

When their eyes met and locked, every word Farin longed to say got stuck in her throat.

"Mind if I step in and help you get Jordan settled while Sawyer's out of town?"

She nodded. "We'd love it."

"Maybe order a pizza and hang out for a while after?"

"Sounds perfect."

"It's a date, then." He turned back toward the entryway. "I'd better get going. When she gets back, tell her Uncle Chris came by?"

Before she reached the door handle, Sawyer and Jordan came bounding inside. Jordan started right in with bubbly chatter over the pink frosting donut she had picked out but stopped at the sight of her uncle and rushed toward him.

He stooped down to catch her and lifted her into his arms. She wrapped her tiny limbs around his neck and squealed, "Uncle Chris!"

Sawyer peered at Farin as he moved past her into the kitchen, his fixed expression far less enthusiastic.

The negotiations started almost immediately, with Jordan begging her mother to let her go with him to see her Aunt Cheryl. Sawyer was quick to take her side, reasoning she would have a lot more to do there than she would being stuck in a small two bedroom surrounded by the few college students who had not yet left for the week.

"I can bring her back later," Chris said. "Or she can stay. You're coming back tomorrow anyway, right?"

Sawyer nodded, his brows arched upward. "That's true. You'll be back tomorrow anyway."

Chris slit knowing eyes at his would-be competitor.

Farin reached out and touched Jordan's face. "You sure you're okay? There's a big crowd of people around Uncle Ben's house right now."

Jordan cuddled into her uncle's neck. "How come, Momma?"

"Because you're so pretty, everyone wants to see you and take your picture."

"They do?"

She nodded. "They've got cameras and everything. I don't want you to get upset."

Chris tucked his head back to look at her. "I'll take care of it. You don't need to be scared."

"Can I, Momma?"

Farin relented, then walked her back to the spare bedroom to pack her things.

Sawyer winked, then slapped Chris on the back as he passed through on his way to living room. "Thanks for running interference. I was hoping Farin and I would have a little time alone before I take off."

Chris set his jaw and waited in the entryway until Farin returned. Jordan followed behind, rolling her tiny Pocahontas suitcase behind her. When they left the apartment, it did not escape Farin's notice that Chris did not look back.

When they left, Sawyer beckoned her to join him on the couch. He had switched the radio station and turned on Eric Clapton's new CD.

"That was an unexpected surprise." He drew her in and kissed the nape of her neck. When she tilted away, he backed off. "You okay?"

She nodded. "Just not feeling it right now."

"Wanna talk about it?"

"Not really."

"Is it gonna be this way every time you see him?"

She shrugged.

He leaned in and kissed her, then lingered close. "I'm going to make you forget about him, Farin."

"It's not that easy. There's history."

He scoffed and scooted closer. "And?"

She moved her head back to look at him. "*And...it's complicated.*"

"Everything is. I've been around you enough to hear that loud and clear. But have I ever steered you wrong?"

A montage of their short time together played across her brain. He had this way about him. A confidence he had thus far backed up every step of the way. She could not deny the attraction. It had grown while they had worked together on her album. Though his cocky assurances sometimes irritated her, his way of drawing her out and pushing her to strive for more resonated within her. Had it not been for him, Ben, and Derek's band, she would not be ready to embark on this next phase of her career. Bottom line, he was good for her.

She kissed him gently at first, then more passionately as the intensity between them caused her heart to beat in time with "It Hurts Me Too."

"I'm not just gonna step aside. If you want me to compete—if that's what does it for you, I'll play that game." He lay back on the cushions and positioned her on top of him. His breathy declaration in her ear stirred her as he caressed her back and nibbled at her neck. "C'mon, school marm. Stop making it so difficult. You're right where you need to be."

Somewhere deep inside, she knew he was right.

***

The minute the commuter plane landed in Miami, he hastened into the terminal to check the monitors for the next leg of his trip home. The Departing Flights list indicated a forty-minute delay for London. It would be a long couple of days getting back to Malé. That did not bother him. What bothered him was getting out of the United States as soon as possible.

If he had had the choice, he would have never returned to Miami from Nassau, where he had fled the morning the news reached him of the Lockhardts' arrests. Anticipating increased passenger scrutiny by order of the Feds should Lockhardt give him up, he had chartered a helicopter to the Bahamas to ride out the storm.

He had immediately abandoned any intent to complete the job for which the old man had paid him. As far as he was concerned, Farin Grant and the angry woman who had chased him off her lawn could live long and productive lives. Best to them. His freedom remained his sole priority.

Now a week later, his confidence had returned—if only slightly. The buzz surrounding the defamed mogul had fizzled out. Only celebrity news continued to hype the "Farin Grant lives!" angle. No calls for a manhunt. No APBs. Either the old man had kept his mouth shut or he did not know enough to point any fingers. Possibly the former, he supposed, but more likely the latter. He had done yeomen's work to protect his anonymity.

Seeing no point in standing around the gate, he figured he might as well get a drink and try to relax. Passing up trendier "foodie" choices, he settled on the one establishment that did not try to be more than a watering hole. Thankfully, only three other people were inside, including the bartender. He rolled his carryon beside a bar stool, then climbed upon the seat and ordered a bourbon on the rocks.

The female bartender barked at him with a clipped Cuban accent, "I need to see your ID, cowboy."

He pulled his passport out of his breast pocket and flipped it open.

She gave him a curt nod, then wandered off to get his drink.

"Where you headed?" asked the man seated several stools away. He side-eyed him from behind that day's issue of the *Miami Herald*. "Headed home to see the family for turkey day?"

He slumped his shoulders and shook his head slowly. Up until now, he had avoided banal chitchat. "Nope."

"Vacation then?"

"London," he told the guy as he nodded his thanks to the bartender who had set his drink atop a bar napkin.

"London," the guy echoed. "I've never been there." The top half of the newspaper bowed over as he addressed the woman. "You ever been to London, Al?"

"Never wanted to leave Miami, to be honest."

Hoping to convey his lack of interest in exchanging pleasantries with the Docker-clad, polo-shirted man, he nursed his drink and watched the barkeep wipe down the bar. The man must have taken the hint, for he soon returned his attention to his newspaper.

At a table near the entrance, a bear of a man dressed in similarly casual attire sipped a beer as he watched ESPN's recap of last night's Knicks-Grizzlies match-up on a television secured high against the wall.

The commentary on Patrick Ewing's performance in the game caught Mr. Newspaper's attention. He looked over his shoulder at the bigger guy. "You know, the Heat's taking on the Warriors here in town Wednesday night. We should go."

"The night before Thanksgiving? The wives would have our heads."

"Twenty bucks says they'll be thrilled to have us out of their hair. We'd just be watching it on the tube at the house anyway."

The big guy thought it over a bit, then shrugged. "True enough. Whaddya say, Alvarez, wanna come with?"

At first he had paid no attention to the conversational thread. But when his brain registered the name "Alvarez" in his head, his mind snapped to attention. Alvarez. Where had he heard that name? Why did it ring a bell?

"Sure, why not?" the bartender said. "Macy's with his family in Chicago until Thursday afternoon anyway. I could go for a game."

Mr. Newspaper chuckled. "Sure you don't want to stay and bake pies with the ladies?"

She slit eyes at the man. For a second, it looked as if she might fling the dirty bar rag at his face. "What's the matter, Billy? You think I can't hang with you two? You think because I have a boyfriend now that makes me some soft-bellied domesticated cat?"

A mischievous glint flickered in his eyes. "I can't speak to the soft-bellied part, but I seem to recall seeing the evidence of some fairly nasty claw marks."

She jerked her head at him, shooting him a warning look.

He raised his hands in surrender. "Aw, c'mon, Al. Come to the game. We'd love to have you. In fact, the beer's on me."

The man at the table rose and approached the bar, leaning against the counter without taking a seat. "We'll be able to get all this paperwork done beforehand, I'm sure. It'll be a nice way to celebrate the wrap up, dontcha think?"

The pieces of conversation fit together in a way he could not immediately figure out. But despite the lack of clarity, the hairs on the back of his neck stood erect. Something was not right. He felt it. These people knew each other.

He checked his watch. Still a good half hour before he needed to get back to his gate. But something told him he might want to head out anyway.

The bartender jutted her chin his way. "You want another bourbon?"

He sized her up as his suspicions mounted. "No thanks."

"You sure?" she pressed. "I know I'd want another if I were in your shoes."

He narrowed his eyes, then attempted to assess his surroundings without appearing too obvious. The other two patrons now stood no more than a couple of stools away, one on either side of him. Instinct warned him to try to make a run for it. Maybe the big guy to his right carried too much bulk to chase him down. Then again, that bulk looked to be pure muscle.

Wanting to keep things casual, he pulled his wallet from his back pocket and withdrew a ten dollar bill. He tossed the money on the bar, swallowed the remainder of his drink, then stood and grabbed the handle of his roller suitcase.

The man to his left folded his paper and placed it on the bar. An engaging smile stretched across his teeth. "You're not leaving, are you? I was just about to buy the next round! Give you a nice little send-off for London."

"London?" the other man echoed with a manufactured shudder. "Too cold. You should stay here in Miami. The weather's great. Hell, if my job didn't keep me up north, I'd move down here permanently."

His mind raced to form a plan to extricate himself from the bar. They were closing in. But if he could slip outside, he could easily disappear.

"You should see about getting a transfer," the newspaper man suggested.

"Maybe I should," the bigger man concurred.

"I think you should both concentrate on the matter at hand. I'm getting tired of standing behind this stupid bar." The woman grabbed a bottle of Jack Daniels and four shot glasses, which she lined up along the bar before inexpertly sloshing the brown liquid into each. "Have a seat, cowboy. This one's on us. We'll have a toast before you take off."

He did not move. Not to sit down, and not to accept the shot.

The three of them each grabbed one of the whiskeys. They looked at him expectantly. When he remained motionless before them, they shrugged, toasted their shot glasses—including the one she had poured for him—then tossed back the strong liquor with a single gulp.

The big man slammed the empty glass upside down on the bar and emitted a sated *ahh*. "I've never been one to celebrate before finishing a task, but that one felt good."

The other man slid off the barstool and swept his hand along his waistline to freshly tuck his polo into his Dockers. "I'd say we're about done here. Everyone ready?" He eyeballed the bigger man, then the bartender, and then rested his eyes on him.

At last, the pieces clicked into place. He wondered if Lockhardt had added to whatever statement Herb Radford had given the Feds or if Herb had single-handedly ratted him out. And who knew how many former clients had cut similar deals to save their own skins?

His body jerked slightly as if he would attempt to flee. But no. He was a smart guy. At least smart enough to know resisting would only make his bleak situation worse. No reason to goad them into beating the shit out of him on top of everything else.

The big man approached him, pulling out and flashing his badge as he procured a set of handcuffs from a buttoned pouch affixed to the rear of his belt. "Zane Ilgenfritz?"

He tilted his head with a mixture of disappointment and acceptance. "That's me."

"I'm Special Agent Hubbell Quarles with the Federal Bureau of Investigation. You're under arrest."

Before submitting to the Fed, he reached over to the bar, grabbed the shot glass, and downed the whiskey.

CHAPTER 32

THURSDAY BROUGHT WITH IT MANY reasons to give thanks.

In Chicago, Miles gave thanks he could tell his family he not only had a girlfriend but that she had agreed to accompany him to Chicago come spring so she could meet them. It was only fair given he had started getting to know her parents and all six of her older brothers.

While disappointed he would not return until then—not even for Christmas—they were happy he had finally decided to settle down. His father comforted his mother as she shed happy tears. His sister gave him a wink of approval as she passed him the yams. He told no one he intended to propose on Christmas Eve.

Herb Radford found plenty of reasons to be thankful, even though he had overcooked the turkey and undercooked the potatoes. He had dodged a probable charge of conspiracy to commit murder in exchange for information on Lockhardt and their mutual friend. Moreover, for the first time in their adult lives, his children had agreed to spend the day at his place. By the time they had all finished their meals, he was more than ready for them to leave. They fought the entire visit. With him and with each other. Worse, their kids were spoiled brats. After they left, he was thankful for the pint of rum he had stashed in the cupboard.

Sawyer stayed alone in his hotel room just off the Las Vegas Strip, thankful he had scored enough product to help him sleep all day and sit in with a local band all night. The last six months had worn him out. Farin was the coolest, sexiest, most talented chick he had ever been with—except for maybe Cécile. But a kid? He had not bargained for motherhood. Moreover, he had never given thought to the idea of becoming a father. Not even a stand-in father.

He had much to consider. He did not want to be the jerk stupid enough to let the hottest female act in music slip through his fingers because he could not hang with a toddler. That was probably the reason he had agreed to move in with them when he got back to Miami. Why not? It beat living in an apartment.

Dale Eastland and David Colline were so thankful for the continued success of their restaurant, they partnered with a local charity to provide two thousand meals to the LA homeless population. They also decided to make their own partnership stronger by planning a ceremony in Maui after the first of the year. They wanted those friends and family members who supported them present when they exchanged vows of commitment at a beachside do. Though it might not be legal, it promised to be one hell of a celebration.

Desperate for a career comeback, Ginny Stevens spent the afternoon on the casting couch of one of the biggest television producers in Hollywood giving the performance of her lifetime. Harley Nagelschmidt turned ink into Emmys and had recently announced plans for a much anticipated new nighttime drama he intended to pitch to NBC. Ginny intended to do "whatever necessary" to land the lead female role, a forensic psychologist working as a profiler for the FBI.

When their liaison ended, Harley thanked Ginny for her time and promised he would contact her agent after the holidays to let her know if she could come back and read for the pilot. Before Ginny left, he added he might want to have her return for a callback or two—"if" she knew what he meant—before making his final decision. With Marilyn Monroe pouty lips and a naughty giggle, she winked and told him she could hardly wait. She kissed his thick, sweaty cheek before heading out his office door, thankful when she made it back to her car without vomiting.

Faith and Henri stayed in bed all day, thankful to have given her parents another year of successful excuses as to why she would not attend their traditionally stuffy family dinner. As they cuddled in the mid-afternoon, she confessed she had started feeling she should stop having such a potty mouth. He agreed and said he had started feeling he should stop smoking. After all, he was not getting any younger. The last thing he wanted to do was develop lung cancer.

That evening, he threw out two cartons of cigarettes while she fashioned together a "muck mouth" jar. She committed that each time she swore, she would have to slip a dollar into the jar. Henri suggested an interesting incentive to keep her from getting used to dropping in an easy buck: implement a penalty for filling the jar whereby she would have to go down to the bank and open a savings account designated for the children they had recently disagreed on having once they married. His suggestion ticked Faith off so much, she let lose a stream of obscenities. Frustrated, he responded by digging out a pack of cigarettes and chain-smoking the rest of the evening.

Alone and depressed, Julie Swanson Grant had finally agreed to go home to North Platte, Nebraska and spend the day with her parents, who were thankful to see her after so many years. The house was every bit as dreary and lifeless as she remembered. Her brother's room remained unchanged. Angie Swanson yelled at her to get away from his door when she went to peek inside. Earl yelled at Angie and warned her not to give their only daughter any more reason to stay away. When Julie went to put her overnight bag away in her old room, she tried to call Chris but it went directly to voicemail.

Over dinner, Angie nagged Julie about getting rid of her elongated last name, arguing it sounded pretentious and wholly unnecessary—especially given the divorce. Earl argued it was none of Angie's damn business what Julie decided to do with her name. Dinner was scrumptious and soul-crushing. Julie was thankful she would leave in the morning.

Fred and Ulani Reece spent the day in separate rooms, each grieving their daughter in their own way. Ulani cried unceasingly as she filed through pictures of Summer at various cheer meets, school events, and family vacations, thankful for the ability to surround herself with so many good memories. Fred sat alone in his study, drinking heavily and staring out his window at the mostly cloudy day. He had heard about and even witnessed the nightmare of activity over at the Grant house as reporters clamored for their attention. This had created much resentment from their neighbors. Rumor had it that if the insanity did not stop soon there would come pressure for them to move. Fred decided he would be thankful if they left.

Joni Leighton spent much of the day on the phone. Despite Bobby's earnest pleas and the representation by one of the top criminal defense lawyers in the country, the Miami judge who had arraigned him ultimately denied his bail request. Bobby's alleged history of mental illness coupled with the severity of the charges had sealed the deal. Joni had spent two days in Florida and intended to remain there indefinitely if necessary, but Bobby had insisted she return to New York.

Between having to cancel her publicity commitments, keeping in touch with the lawyer, and visiting an almost completely uncommunicative Jameson at the hospital, she had grown exhausted. Her parents had arrived at her and Bobby's Manhattan penthouse the day before Thanksgiving, which had caused her to break down in tears. She had forgotten they had made plans to get their families together for the holiday. When her mother insisted Joni stay in bed late Thursday while she prepped the turkey, Joni was thankful to have two such understanding and uncomplicated parents. At dinner, they said a prayer for guidance and strength to stand firm in the face of whatever lie ahead for Joni, for Bobby, and for Jameson.

Marci and Elliot took baby Vivian for her first car ride the day before Thanksgiving. They braved impossible northbound LA traffic to ensure Papa and Gammy Williams could spend the day with their granddaughter. Having learned of Farin's amazing story of survival a week before, the festivities took on a grander feel, though they wished she and Jordan could have flown out to make the gathering complete. Promises of "next year" sufficed. They were thankful to receive an unexpected phone call from her. She told them she loved them all and said a long overdue thank you for the years of care and love they had given her.

Elliot spent much of the day drinking imported beer with his father-in-law, pretending to like American football. Marci and her mother prepared delicious hors d'oeuvres and cooked traditional Thanksgiving fare while Vivian mostly slept in the portable bassinet they placed atop the dinette set near where they labored. Still suffering from a fair amount of sleep deprivation, Marci was thankful neither of her parents asked when they might have a second grandchild. At dinner, they toasted to all the recent good news and told a hundred stories of Marci and Farin's childhood escapades.

***

By the time Miles recovered his car from long term parking and drove to the Bridgemans' house, he figured their impromptu celebration would have long since died down. According to the voicemail invitation he had received the night before from a jovial if fairly inebriated William, Miles expected it to have been canceled altogether due to an extreme hangover. But as he pulled up to the house, he noted two other vehicles parked on the street near the driveway. One belonged to Alvarez.

"You're here!" Bridgeman cheered as he opened the door. He teetered aside to let him in, then gave his hand a hearty shake. His voice was thick and saturated as much with carefree relief as alcohol. "We were beginning to think you'd decided to stay in Chi Town after all. Come on in and have a drink!"

Inside, oldies music filled the air as children danced and cavorted through the rooms. No sooner had his feet hit the entryway than he spotted Alicia's smiling face. When she approached, she gave him one of the two beers in her hands and kissed him full on the mouth—notably sloppier and far less discreet than usual. Her breath smelled of hops. A thin filmy haze covered her eyes as she smiled and tilted her head back to see him. "Glad you could ma-make it, cowboy."

He grinned and took a swig from the long neck. "If you're here, I'm here."

She gave him an exaggerated wink, then headed into the living room. It did not escape his notice that both detectives swayed when they walked.

Penny wove her way over and greeted Miles with an apologetic smile as she beckoned him with a wave of her hand. "You'll have to excuse them. Alicia didn't get here until a couple of hours ago—"

"Hey!" she protested, falling into her seat on the couch and patting the space next to her. "I had to shop! It's Bla-bla...it's Black Friday, you know. I promised my tía! Ask Mi-Miles. No one stands up my tía."

Penny gave him a sideways grin. "Needless to say, she's already caught up with Hub and my husband."

Amused at the sight, Miles fixed loving eyes on her as he addressed Penny. "She holds her own, that's for sure."

Hubbell's gait was considerably less impaired, though the whites of his eyes were markedly red. He stuck his hand out as Miles moved into the living room to sit next to Alvarez. "The man of the hour!"

Miles squinted doubtfully. "I don't know about that."

"*Oh* yes!" Alvarez broke in as she scrambled back to her feet. "Yes, *yes*! If it hadn't been for you, we'd have never solved this motherfu—"

Miles reached out with his free hand and wrapped his arm around her neck, then pulled her to him and whispered in her ear, "Children, detective. There're children present."

Her eyes widened in regret. She nodded and held her index finger up to her protruded lips, then turned and waved her arms in the general vicinity of the kids. "Sorry. Sorry about that. *Mala mía, nenas. Tía Alicia no lo dijo para ofender sus oíditos.*"

He winked as she grimaced and sat back down. She upended the bottle into her mouth, then frowned when she realized it was empty.

"So Hub, didn't you say you were married with a couple of kids?"

He nodded. "They're up in Virginia. I tried to get them to fly down for the holiday since I'm here working, but my mother wasn't up for the flight. They may fly down next week if things go according to plan."

"How long you staying in Miami?"

"As long as it takes. These cases have had so many moving pieces. I got Lockhardt in a New York hospital recovering from a fairly nasty gunshot wound before they transfer him to jail, and our ghost is still here. Neither of them are talking, so..."

Bridgeman stumbled over to sit in one of the dual recliners. "But we got 'em all dead to rights. All that evidence Stark tried to hide makes a pretty strong case for the son. And thanks to our pal here, we got the witness to the the father." He raised his beer to Miles. The others followed suit.

Hubbell dropped down on the other recliner. "I forgot to tell you. Our guys went through the Alexanders' house and actually found a hair in the bathroom where the wife was found. DNA matches our ghost. Guess he's mortal after all."

"It's poetic justice you guys arrested him so close to Thanksgiving. I hear he won't even have his initial appearance until Monday."

He stuck out his lips and nodded. "A minor victory. Something tells me things will get complicated real fast if he has anything close to a good attorney. I foresee change of venue motions, challenges to the evidence. The usual. Especially with Florida being a death penalty state."

Miles listened intently even as the alcohol on his empty stomach began to warm him. "Think you'll try to get the dad transferred down here instead of trying him in New York?"

Hub shrugged. "We did our part. We arrested him. The lawyers can figure out the rest. I'm just happy I'll be spending Christmas at home instead of chasing some phantom across the country."

The conversational thread died off. Soon, Bridgeman and Quarles started talking sports. They discussed the Heat's 103-93 victory over the Warriors Wednesday night, then argued over who made the best plays during the Thanksgiving day football games. Penny busied herself with refreshing drinks and plates of heavy hors d'oeuvres, then sat down on the arm of her husband's recliner and joined their conversation. Every once in a while she would call out for the girls to be careful or to quiet down.

Sitting there, arm around his sometimes lucid future fiancée, Miles brooded over the details of the case. More specifically, the e-mail riddle he now suspected he had received from Ross Alexander in the man's attempt to settle old scores with his corrupt boss.

Ross' words at the roast echoed on the outskirts of his brain. Supposedly in jest, he had told Samantha, "The truth just sounds funnier, doesn't it?" And before that, some mention of a date in 1967. Miles wished Ross were still around. Clearly there remained many mysteries to solve. What happened in England in 1967? "Oh what a night," he whispered without realizing he had said the words out loud.

Alicia turned and looked at him with heavy lids. "What?"

He shook his head, kissed her forehead, then waited for a good time to interrupt the armchair sportscasters seated facing them. "Anyone ever hear of anything called the Firm?"

"The book?" Penny asked.

"Not the book or the movie. Maybe something to do with England?"

"The rock group?"

He shook his head.

Hubbell's eyes glistened with curiosity. "I've heard of the Firm."

He slid his arm out from behind Alicia's neck, then set his empty bottle on a coaster on the coffee table and leaned forward to rest his elbows on his knees.

"It was a gang in London's East End," Hub continued.

Miles felt his face go numb and knew the single beer he had consumed had not caused the lack of sensation.

"Why do you ask?" Hub pressed.

He shook his head and leaned back. "No reason. Just something I read."

For the rest of the afternoon, Miles felt Hub try to surreptitiously get his attention. A glance. A head tilt. The Special Agent knew something. Worse, he figured Miles knew something. But Miles was not yet ready to give up the e-mail. He needed to figure out what Ross wanted him to know.

Thanks Hub, but I've got it from here.

When he had originally received the riddle, he had nearly flown to London instead of Santa Barbara. In the end, he had made the right choice. California had yielded many secrets. But those secrets had since been revealed by Farin anyway.

Apparently the time had come to dust off his passport. He wondered if Alicia would agree to take some additional vacation. She did not much like taking time off. Her agreement to the upcoming trip to Chicago had astonished him. But who knew? Maybe she would like to take a trip across the pond.

An hour before they left, Alvarez switched from beer to bottled water. Though far from sober, her senses and memory slowly sharpened. She scrutinized Miles as he sat lost in thought. In an effort to pull his attention, she rubbed his upper arm. "Where are you?"

His drawn features transformed into a gentle smile. "You about ready to head out? We'll leave your car here and pick it up in the morning. You shouldn't be driving."

She agreed. "Just let me say goodbye to Penny and the girls first."

He finished up the last of his third beer, which he had nursed most the afternoon in an effort to be social while staying sober.

Alicia started toward the girls' room, then snapped her fingers as if she had forgotten something. She turned back to Miles. "Before I forget, we got the results on all that evidence from Irene Stark."

He shrugged, not following. "Was there something wrong with it?"

"No, nothing like that. But as far as the car accident in seventy-three—"

"—I know. Not your jurisdiction."

"No, there's more. Farin's not gonna wanna hear it, but that case isn't going anywhere. First off, the statute of limitations on manslaughter is long past. But second, I'm no attorney, but from where I sit, the evidence isn't there. Her mother's letter and those pictures she took aren't enough."

"Even with the DNA from the empty liquor bottle?"

"That DNA didn't match Bobby Lockhardt's. In fact, aside from the fact the car belonged to him, there's nothing I saw that put him at the scene." She stood on her tiptoes and kissed his cheek. "I'm gonna go say goodbye to everyone. Be back in a sec."

The thought of relaying the frustrating news to Farin did not thrill Miles. After all this time and effort, she would not find justice for her father. Every sad circumstance that had followed as a result of her struggle to find closure was for naught. The irony beset him. He could not imagine how he would tell her.

And yet, Lockhardt had gone to great lengths to ensure the truth about the accident remained buried. Why do that if his son had not killed Kelley

O'Conner after all? And why would Ross draw Miles into the scene?

His gut told him he would find the answers in London. And his gut was never wrong.

***

Ben rushed out his front door before Farin could crawl into the passenger's seat of the small rental truck. They had parked it at an angle in the circular driveway to avoid the prying eyes of reporters crowded near the entrance to the property in the hopes of getting a coveted shot of any member of the family. He held the guitar he had taught her to play. With a quick lift of his chin, he called out, "Don't forget this. I expect you to practice."

The instrument twanged when she grasped its neck. With a misty smile, she hugged him with her free hand. "You and Cheryl act like we're moving across the country. It's only a few blocks up."

He patted her back. "It's been good having you here."

"Thank you for everything."

He took back the guitar long enough for her to climb inside the cab, then handed it to her once more. "Take your time getting things sorted. We're happy to keep Jordan as long as you want."

Farin glanced over at the driver's side and addressed Chris. "It shouldn't take too long, should it? There's not much here. Mostly just Jordan's bedroom furniture."

He shrugged. "I'd say a couple of hours or so. I can return the truck myself."

"No, I'll go with you. You promised us pizza tonight, remember? Besides, I left my car at your place." She turned back to Ben. "We'll call you as soon as we drop the truck off."

Ben moved forward and shut the door. "She's excited to see her new room."

"That makes two of us! I had her walls done to look like a scene out of Pocahontas, all that green and the river bend. There's even a huge willow tree painted on one side."

He chuckled. "Spoiled already. We'll have to come over so she can show us."

"She'd love that."

"Cheryl says to come for dinner Sunday, by the way. She's making some casserole dish from yesterday's leftovers. Maybe you'll join us for church first?"

She flattened her lips into a noncommittal smile. "We'll see about church. Definitely dinner, though."

Chris navigated the truck through the animated crowd calling their names. Farin waved and nodded several thankful acknowledgments. Some hopped in their vehicles and followed them the half mile to Matheson, but

Chris drove through and systematically activated the tall electronic gate before any of the bolder journalists managed to exit their vehicles and attempt to rush inside.

They transferred the few packed boxes to their proper rooms, then worked together to carry in the pieces of Jordan's bed for assembly.

"I can get the rest of the furniture on my own," he told her. "Go ahead and get settled."

"What I really need is a shower. I didn't take one earlier because I knew we'd be moving."

"Go on, then. I've got this."

"You sure?"

"Positive."

Walking the halls of the house proved easier than she had anticipated. Somehow, she had expected to see her husband's ghost around each corner. She had expected to feel a rush of emotion, mostly loss, at the idea of coming back. So many memories lived in these walls. As much turmoil as happiness. How would she confront the regret, the sadness, the seeming betrayal of their marriage in having Sawyer move in next week?

But instead of guilt, an overwhelming sense of peace settled upon her. Her experiences with mourning had taught her a thing or two in the last few years. The time had come to let go. Jordan was too good a man not to want her to be happy in his absence. He would want her to raise their daughter as best she could, and he would want her to move on. He had always wanted her to move on. In fact, he had given his life to ensure it. So she would honor his sacrifice. More than anything else, she owed it to him to find happiness.

Despite her resolve, flashes of Bobby's assault haunted her as she showered. The memory of bloody water filling the tub floor and slowly disappearing down the drain in stringy pathways filled her head. She closed her eyes and inhaled the smell of her lavender shampoo, forcing her mind to concentrate on the joyful anticipation of Jordan taking her first bath in her own home. The Lockhardts would not steal another minute of her life. Not even in thought.

She finished her shower, then hastened to perform her ritual of hair drying and makeup application. Once she deemed herself presentable, she met Chris in Jordan's room. He had not only assembled the canopy bed, but he had dressed the mattress with the linens she had prepared.

"You didn't need to do that."

He smiled and stepped back, extending his arms to present his finished project. "Looks pretty good, yeah?"

She moved to him, wrapped her arms around his waist, and rested her head on his shoulder. "I couldn't have done it better myself."

They lingered together in the room for some time in the absence of conversation. A first for them. Farin would have never thought it possible. She closed her eyes as he held her, happy for their ability to simply exist together without a lot of tension. For this and so many other things, her heart swelled with gratitude.

After returning the truck, they stopped by Sir Pizza to collect the order Chris had called in ahead of time. Picking up Jordan turned into a bittersweet moment of tears and laughter. The little girl insisted on staying with her aunt and uncle at first despite Cheryl's promise to come over and visit tomorrow. Jordan asked her if she would stay for a sleepover. With a tousle of her hair by Uncle Ben, a kiss on the cheek from Aunt Cheryl, and her focus redirected to the super special surprise bedroom she would find at her new and final home, Jordan finally climbed inside the Porsche and sat on Farin's lap.

"You ready to go have movie night with Uncle Chris?" Farin asked.

Jordan wiggled around, kissed her mother's cheek, and squealed, "Yeah!"

The three of them cuddled together in Chris' darkened viewing room amongst their dinner, sugary drinks, and an assortment of snacks as they watched Jordan's favorite Disney movie on video—twice. Halfway through the second showing, she nodded off. Farin checked the time and whispered to Chris that she should get her daughter home.

When he beckoned her into the kitchen to talk while he wrapped up the leftover pizza, she eased herself out from beneath Jordan's slumbering body and covered her with a blanket. More memories flooded her senses as she entered the kitchen and went toward the pantry to grab a roll of plastic wrap. He made room in the fridge while she transferred the pizza to a plate, then sealed it with the wrap.

"Here you—"

He stood before her, his arms on either side of the counter as he slowly leaned in to kiss her.

"Chris."

"Shh," he whispered. "Kiss me."

She tilted her head away. "Please don't. It's been such a nice day."

He took a step back. "Isn't that the point?"

She grabbed the leftovers and handed them to him. "This is where things change. We agreed on that."

Without protest, he walked to the refrigerator and deposited the plate on a shelf. "I guess I thought you'd change your mind."

She turned around and leaned against the counter. "I guess I should have told you, but I didn't know how to say it. Sawyer's moving in when he gets back."

He dipped his head as he closed the refrigerator door. "Yeah?"

"I'm sorry."

He returned and stood close, fixing his eyes on her. "I'll respect your decision, but at the risk of sounding like Peter Pathetic, I want you to know I'm here if you change your mind."

She put her hands on the side of his face. "Thank you for saving me. And thank you for letting me go. You did the right thing. Now I can do the right thing, too."

His voice caught as he tried to speak. He cleared his throat. "It'll never be right until we're back together. But you do what you need to do. I have to believe you'll be back. No one could ever love you like I do." He wrapped his arms around her waist and drew her to him.

She closed her eyes and inhaled his scent, remembering the musky aroma she had so often attributed to his ability to make her lose her head. At last, she pulled away. "Do you mind getting Jordan and putting her in the car?"

When he left the kitchen, she made a final pass, rinsing off their plates and the few utensils they had used. The sound of two sets of footsteps entering the room caught her attention. She turned around to find Jordan rubbing her eyes and yawning. "Can I go see my super bedroom now?"

"Of course you can, sweetheart." She dried her hands on a dish towel, then tossed it on the counter before grabbing her purse. "Let's say goodbye to Uncle Chris."

Chris knelt down and took Jordan into his arms. "You be good for your mum, okay?"

She nodded sleepily. "Will you come over and see me tomorrow?"

"I'll be there whenever you need me, Jordan. That's a promise."

"Uncle Chris?"

"Yes, my love?"

"It's Jade."

"Ah, yes. So it is." He stood and petted her hair. "Now let's get you all buckled in Mum's car."

Farin touched his arm as he passed. "Hold on a minute."

He stopped and gave her a quizzical look.

She reached into her purse and pulled out a velvet box. When she looked up at him, she could tell he recognized it.

"Don't." He stepped back.

"You need to take this."

"I gave it to you."

She shook her head. "I don't have any right to keep it. We both know that. Please, let's start clean like we agreed." She handed it to him. "Take it."

He hesitated, then raised a hand to accept it. Standing taller, he inhaled deeply. "I'll keep it for you. Like I said, it's not over. It can't be."

She gave his fingers a squeeze. "Thank you."

He nodded, then smirked to lighten the moment. "Stop acting like we're not going to see each other. In case you didn't hear, I have a date with my niece tomorrow. And I'm going to guilt you into listening to a couple of tracks I've been working on for my next album."

Jordan nodded off on the way home but awoke to the sounds of shouting reporters and never-ending camera flashes as they pulled up outside their house. Farin glanced over at her as she activated the gate. "You okay?"

She scowled out the side window. "These people need to go home and go to bed."

"I couldn't have said it better myself, honey." A thrill of excitement filled her as she helped Jordan out of her seat and led her through the back door into the house.

The child's eyes widened in disbelief as she visually scanned the large open space, bright colored furniture, oversized wall hangings, and plush rugs throughout the house. Her voice pitched an octave higher as she squealed, "This is *my* house?"

Farin smiled and suppressed a laugh. "It is."

"With you too?"

"That's right."

She bounced up and down with delight. "Can I see my super bedroom now, Momma?"

"Say the magic word and I'll take you right there."

Jordan wiggled uncontrollably. "Please!"

Farin stuck out her hand. Jordan grasped it and followed along upstairs and down the hall. "Your room's right next to mine so you know I'm close by anytime you need me, okay?"

She wriggled as she trotted. "Okay!"

When they entered the room, Jordan leapt up and down, clapping her hands. "It's my forest!"

Farin hit a switch on the door, filling the room with green and blue twinkle lights strung along the painted trees and the river. Jordan drew in a sharp breath.

"Do you like it, Jade?" Farin asked, forcing herself to concede her daughter's preferred name.

The girl turned and hugged her legs. Farin sat down beside her and held her close.

"Momma?"

"Yes, baby?"

"I think I want to be Jordan now."

Tears filled Farin's eyes as she peered down at her. "You sure?"

She nodded. "Thank you for my super bedroom, Momma."

Farin rested her head against Jordan's. "You're welcome."

"It's like my happy ending!"

"It is a happy ending, Jordan. For both of us."

THE END

About the Author

Heather O'Brien lives in California. She enjoys music, documentaries, travel, research, and amateur video production.

To learn more about the series and to read free excerpts, please visit: www.tiesthatbindsaga.com.

CPSIA information can be obtained
at www.ICGtesting.com
Printed in the USA
BVHW060125041122
650954BV00004B/140/J

9 781948 225519